The
Astonished Earth

A Novel

Christopher Beck

Amelia Press

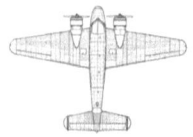

Amelia Press

ISBN 978-0-692-87411-0

Book layout by e-book-design.com.

Printed in the United States

List of Figures

Note to the Reader

One man is emblematic of the Great War, one hundred years later. Perhaps his memory is the echo of a clever epithet or maybe he is the archetype for the modern superhero. Possibly, we needed something human amidst the horror that mankind inflicted on itself in that second decade of the last century and our collective psyche found him.

The simple and extraordinary life of the Red Baron, Manfred Richthofen, needs no embellishment. Richthofen is emblematic that, despite our human lust for conflict, we are each individuals on our own journeys and that every victim of the Great War was a person, brave and unique and substantial. Richthofen is legend.

The Astonished Earth is the story of his journey and of other legendary men that surrounded him, defined him and created him. Richthofen lived among icons, spoke with them, learned from them, flew with them and killed them. His story would be incomplete without telling their stories as well.

He was human: frail, at times broken, at other times desperate or valiant, but not in a way that created great outcomes. He is not the sum of his victories. Rather, he emerged as heroic, but not a conqueror. He was an individual, in gladiatorial combat, amid the first true mechanized, industrial scale horror. His life marked the end of an age, and the beginning of a new one.

What follows is the product of twenty years of unraveling the fables and facts of World War I. Despite a hundred years of research by untold authors, we know surprisingly little about Richthofen, the man. Several periods of his life are recorded in a single sentence in a single journal. While this novel is as factually accurate as I found possible, some literary license was needed. Most often, I found it necessary to draw upon experiences of other individuals with more complete records of shared times and places. In some cases, I drew upon first person accounts of individuals that were with Richthofen, or perhaps a few hundred yards away at the same moment in time.

While the sequence of historical events is correct, in some cases the timeline is compressed. Each of the major events depicted, occurred. Also, a great many details are accurate and true to the time, people and places from curiously specific records: exotic pets, unusual affectations, the direction of the wind, the smell in the air, and the phase of the moon.

The personalities of these great people are my interpretations of them based on their actions. For flow, a few minor figures were merged into single characters; for example, the character of Boelcke's batman, Fischer, is a composite of several of Boelcke's aides through his short career. Nevertheless, this chronicle of the flying legends of the Great War is true to the original first-hand accounts and is my attempt to be authentic to the experiences, events and people of his time.

This happened. Thus, legends are born.

Foreword

I. Flight

Human flight has inhabited man's imagination throughout recorded history. The ancient Greek legend of Daedalus and his son Icarus—who flew too high on wings of wax—is echoed in the Hindu myth of Jatayu, the Chinese myth of Kua Fu, the Babylonian legend of Etana, and many others. Over the centuries, these dreams of flight inspired many creative minds. Leonardo da Vinci drew conceptual flying machines in the 1400s that were remarkable not just for their technological boldness but for their artistic sensibility and grace. The early balloons were ornate, colorful works of art, as beautiful on the ground as when airborne.

In the 19th Century, the invention of groundwork technologies and concepts, including gasoline engines and aerodynamics, made powered human flight a practical possibility. At the end of that century, a generation of European and American inventors foresaw the prospect of human flight and raced to achieve it.

In Ohio, two bicycle builders were among those who took an interest in flying machines. Borrowing from the efforts of generations past and from theoretical work dating back to da Vinci, these brothers began flying manned gliders. Heartened by this success, the Wright brothers fashioned their own powered airplane.

On December 14, 1903, Wilbur and Orville Wright tossed a coin in the air to determine who would be the first person in the world to pilot a powered airplane. Wilbur won and succeeded in flying their craft for a total of three seconds. By December 17, after several further attempts, Orville succeeded in flying 120 feet in twelve seconds, shattering his brother's record.

The Wright brothers sent a telegram to their father in Dayton, Ohio, requesting that he inform the press of their success. The *Dayton Journal* refused to print the story, stating that the distances and times were so short as to render the events unimportant.

More flights followed with varying degrees of success, as each brought gradual increases in time and distance aloft. The American press grudgingly began to acknowledge that the Wright brothers were succeeding. Nevertheless, even as the Wright brothers improved their performance, across the Atlantic, their claims to have accomplished controlled powered flight were met first with skepticism and then open derision. The French press referred to the Wright brothers as the Wright *bluffeurs*, or liars.

Then, on a warm, bright Parisian afternoon in October 1906, Alberto Santos-Dumont became the first Frenchman to fly an airplane. Flying down the length of a soccer field, he crashed before he could reach the other end. His audience, many of whom had either never heard of the Wright brothers or believed the brothers to be hoaxers, were convinced they had witnessed the first powered flight. They carried Alberto away on their shoulders, hailing the miracle. Santos-Dumont had reached an altitude of three meters during the flight, winning the Deutsch-Archdeacon prize for the first European powered flight, which led to him becoming a national hero. The cat was suddenly out of the bag, and the world realized that *men were flying*.

Watching Santos' flight with great interest was an Englishman named Alfred Charles William Harmsworth, the Lord Northcliffe. Inspired to encourage the development of flight in England, Lord Northcliffe offered a prize of £10,000 for the first successful flight between London and Manchester—a distance of 163 miles—through his newspaper, the *Daily Mail*. Not to be outdone, the *London Star* responded to Northcliffe's offer by offering its own prize of £10,000,000 (roughly $14 billion in 2014 dollars) to the first flyer to manage five miles in any direction from London and return safely. The *London Star* believed their money was safe. After all, in Europe, no manmade flying machine had demonstrated a capacity for such distance, nor did it seem feasible to attain the altitudes such a flight would require.

During this period, the German Count Ferdinand von Zeppelin was developing rigid airships of enormous size. His airships were more than twice as long as Santos-Dumont's entire first flight in 1906. Germany caught Zeppelin fever, creating a national fervor for the huge airships. The ego of the German Kaiser stoked this national passion. Indeed, Kaiser Wilhelm imagined an aerial fleet that would eclipse even the battleships of the English Royal Navy.

With international tensions already running high in Europe, the Zeppelin menace became a subject of national concern in England. H.G. Wells responded to the Zeppelin scare by publishing a frightening and peculiar vision of war, entitled *The War in the Air*, in 1908. At the same time, England began to see cases of a kind of Zeppelin neuroses, a condition in which sufferers believed that Zeppelins secretly threatened them personally. During a period of barely four months in 1909, hundreds, if not thousands, of illusory sightings of enormous, flying, cigar-shaped objects were reported around the British Empire and even as far away as New Zealand. Eventually, this condition would be overshadowed by the more general "aviation insanity," a diagnosis that required institutional treatment and manifested as a fear of all aircraft.

As a panicked vision of the British Isles under aerial siege hovered over the English psyche, Wilbur Wright, a lean, stoic figure, arrived at Le Mans, France. He came to Europe to address the European dismissal of the brothers' claims to the first powered, controlled flight. At Le Mans, he assembled the most recent model of the Wright Flyer. His flight there on August 8, 1908 made believers out of a continent of skeptics. For one minute and forty-three seconds, the brothers' aircraft was able to bank, maneuver, and perform aerial acrobatics that stunned even the assembled French flyers. Shortly thereafter, the *London Star* quietly retracted their £10,000,000 prize.

However, an inspired Lord Northcliffe encouraged the Wright Brothers to compete for the *Daily Mail's* prize. Doubting their ability to make the flight from London to Manchester, the Wright brothers demurred. Lord Northcliffe modified the challenge, allowing for a much shorter flight across the English Channel with a purse of £1000. He again approached the Wright brothers. They declined once more, stating that pursuing prizes was "not the work of honest inventors". Privately, they were also concerned about the reliability of their engines.

There were others, though, that would take up the challenge. With this advent of competitive heavier-than-air flight, a new type of adventurer emerged: the sportsman aviator. These flyers, usually hailing from backgrounds of wealth and privilege, and gripped by a desire for adventure, became the subjects of public adulation.

Henri Farman, who would later found the Farman Aviation Works in France, already wealthy from sales of another invention, the automobile, overtook Santos-Dumant's reputation as the preeminent French flyer when he successfully flew twenty-seven kilometers in twenty minutes.

Another Frenchman, Hubert Latham, a wealthy playboy from three generations of Le Havre shipbuilding—bored by big-game hunting in Africa, speedboats, automobile racing, and ballooning—entered the arena of flight, pursuing the *Daily Mail* prize. Dapper in his tailored English suits, he made an elegant subject for an admiring press and became the next aerial celebrity to take the public stage. Latham, when asked what his vocation was prior to becoming an aviator, informed the French President that he was *un homme de monde*, 'a man of the world.'

Flying from Calais, France, Latham attempted to cross the Channel in poor weather on July 12, 1909, but crashed when his engine failed. Rescuers found him on the floating wreckage of his airplane in heavy seas, calmly smoking a cigarette. This marked Latham as the first pilot to 'ditch' an airplane in water. He returned to a hero's welcome in France.

Before Latham was ready to attempt the flight again, a Frenchman named Louis Blériot set up camp on the Calais coast. Blériot was dark: black eyes, hair, and moustache framed an equally joyless and intense perspective on flight. As dispassionate and determined as only an engineer could be, Blériot was most famous at that point in his life for the frequency of his crashes. Blériot had watched Latham fly away on his ill-fated attempt while standing on crutches, his legs badly burned from his most recent mishap. Now Blériot sensed an opportunity. Before Latham could build an airplane for another attempt, Blériot flew.

When heavy clouds over the Channel broke up into a hazy sky with a westerly wind at dawn on July 25th, Blériot took off, flying across the water to Dover. Latham watched Blériot launch with tears in his eyes, sensing his own fame slipping away into the haze. Flying blind through thick fog near England, Blériot maintained his heading by pure tenacity and arrived over the English coast several miles north of his intended landfall. He turned south, followed the coast, and arrived at the meadow above the cliffs of Dover to win the *Daily Mail* prize.

Then he crashed.

Blériot, unhurt by the accident, calmly returned to France that afternoon on a French warship, but was encouraged to immediately return to England at the behest of Lord Northcliffe to receive his reward. Fêted at the Savoy Hotel, Blériot sat next to Lord Shackleton, the conqueror of the South Pole. Guglielmo Marconi, the inventor of radio, sent his congratulations to Blériot from a ship in the middle of the Atlantic via wireless signal, itself a remarkable event, in what may have been a vain attempt by Marconi to hold onto his own elusive celebrity.

Upon Blériot's return to France, well-wishers lined the railroad tracks from Calais to Paris, a distance of 180 miles, calling out to Blériot in adulation. Arriving in Paris, a crowd of 100,000 Parisians greeted him at the train station, Gare du Nord. Vendors hawked copies of his portrait and singers bawled out songs composed in his honor.

So began the golden age of heroic aviators that lasted between the years 1909 to 1914.

Aviation enthralled the world. Few countries were as passionate about early aviation as France. Given their numerous fliers and early achievements in the field, it is perhaps little surprise that the French held the First International Aviation Competition at Rheims in August 1909, and the first Paris Air Show in September that same year. On the last day of the inaugural Rheims airshow, 250,000 people attended.

The aviation obsession left everyone racing to experience it. At a planned airshow north of Paris in 1910, an estimated 200,000 people packed onto trains in order to attend, completely shutting down the Paris transportation network. When the disappointed people arrived too late to witness the air show, rioting ensued and continued in rail stations throughout Paris the next day.

Nevertheless, across Europe, airshows became events of monumental popularity attended by hundreds of thousands and hosted by royalty and the wealthy. On the airshow circuit, aviators become larger-than-life figures, national heroes of superhuman skill.

Always mindful of war, the leaders of the various European militaries, though doubtful that aircraft could make any real contribution to their armies, still quietly hedged their bets by forming small air forces with the available, privately developed aircraft types. Following the assassination of Austrian Archduke Ferdinand in Sarajevo on June 28, 1914, the nations of Europe begin to mobilize for war to honor their national treaty commitments. When the war broke out, the military leadership of the time possessed a poor sense of what aircraft could and could not do. Because of their ad hoc approach to aviation in war, the experience of the first fighting flyers was highly idiosyncratic. Ill-defined missions, non-standard equipment, and little or no training characterized their struggles.

And thus, on August 1, 1914, at the beginning of the Great War, the romantic golden age of showmen flyers ended with a bang, and the infancy of military aviation began.

II. The Men

Of the German-led Central Powers:

Anton "Anthony" Herman Gerard Fokker, a young Dutch aviator, born in the Dutch East Indies. From an early age, he showed a natural tendency to tinker with the dangerous and volatile. As a boy, he once tapped his neighbors' gas line and, on another occasion, electrified his bedroom door to keep the nanny at bay. He was the son of a wealthy Dutch coffee plantation owner but had no interest in the family business, preferring to study the new science of aviation instead. Wiry of build with sharp, angular features framing a perpetual buck-toothed grin, Fokker was the figure of an awkward youth grown to an inelegant young man. Despite his enduring smile, Fokker could be just as volatile as his experiences. He was frequency abrasive and was difficult to like, but nonetheless, was surrounded by a small cohort of committed and tolerant friends.

Passionate about flight, with a real love for aircraft, Fokker committed himself to this new industry over the objections of his family. Prior to the war, he was most famous for having made the first flight over Haarlem, Holland in August 1911 to an audience of 250,000 Dutch on their monarch's birthday.

Beginning in 1910, Fokker attempted to sell aircraft of his own design and construction. He eventually settled in Germany after failing to sell his aircraft to the French, English, Dutch, and Russians. There, he opened a meager aircraft factory, which subsisted on small contracts for sport airplanes from military and civilian customers. His customers included the Crown Princes of Germany. His father and uncles funded his factory through personal loans that, when the war broke out, Fokker was desperate to repay.

Indebted to his father and uncles for the financing for his factory, and inspired by his father's contempt for aviation, Fokker struggled on. Driven by a thirst for business success, his imagination and creativity guided him.

As Europe moved toward war, Fokker's factory started producing a small order of airplanes for the German military. At the beginning of the war, Fokker had just returned to Germany from an airshow tour where he was performing loops: the latest innovation of the world's flying community. He was twenty-four years old.

Manfred Albrecht Freiherr von Richthofen was born a minor nobleman in the province of Silesia in western Prussia on the fringe of the German empire. Due to his birthright, he attended the Imperial cadet school at Wahlstatt. By the time he joined the military he had become an accomplished gymnast and competitive equestrian. Despite his aristocratic upbringing, he wore his uniform a touch askew, his cap tilted, and often bore an impish smile on a face with fine, chiseled features. He was an adequate but unexceptional student.

At Wahlstatt, he fought his fear of heights by scaling the school's cathedral and tying his handkerchief as a flag of victory from the spire.

After graduation, he was assigned to an elite cavalry unit, the *First Regiment Uhlans; Kaiser Alexander III* and was stationed at a remote and insignificant cavalry outpost on the frontier with Russian occupied Poland. Oddly, his cavalry unit was named for a Russian Czar, a commemoration of the complex relationships between the ruling royalties of Europe at the time. His cavalry unit were Uhlans, lancers famed since the time of Napoleon a hundred years earlier as swift and fierce light cavalry, armed with wickedly sharp long spears.

Manfred Richthofen's great-uncle and his namesake was a General and commanded a German cavalry corps on the German western frontier with France. Manfred Richthofen, the younger, carried the weight of the expectations of his family and his class with him.

The young officer Richthofen possessed a gymnast's physique and agility, an equestrian's finesse, and a Prussian's devotion to duty. He was classically handsome, with fine cheekbones and a sensitive mouth, of average height, with golden blond hair and gray eyes. He was often quiet and solitary, albeit friendly. Richthofen shared a belief common to many people of the era: that all aviators were shameless frauds, akin to circus performers, charlatans, and hucksters.

He had hoped to compete in the 1916 Olympics in equestrian events, but the outbreak of war prevented that. He was twenty-two at the start of the war.

Oswald Boelcke was the fourth child in a family of six children, the son of a schoolmaster. Stricken with whooping cough as a youth, the illness left him physically small and asthmatic. He fought the effects of the disease by becoming an active athlete. An exceptional swimmer and diver, he often snuck away from school and competed under assumed names, as he wasn't allowed to compete by his parents.

At age thirteen, he had the temerity to write a personal letter to the Kaiser requesting appointment to a cadet school. The Kaiser granted his request, but Boelcke's parents did not allow him to attend.

In school, he excelled in mathematics and physics, with little interest in history or the arts. With purloined telephone wire, he strung the first phone line in his neighborhood between his bedroom and his best friend's house across the street.

In his late teens, his father introduced Boelcke to mountain climbing, taking him on weekend train trips into the German Alps where he climbed with his father and brothers. Boelcke often ran ahead downhill and would find a patch of flowers or grass where he could stand on his head and wait for his family to catch up to him.

After graduating high school, he joined the army and received a commission as a Leutnant in a telegraph battalion.

Boelcke was charming, broad shouldered, with a slim body and dark steel blue eyes. Perpetually cheerful, he enjoyed the company of others and they enjoyed him. Everyone he knew remembered Boelcke as their best friend.

In May 1914, seeking adventure and prior to the aeroplane having shown any military potential, he requested and received a transfer to the fledgling German air force, the Fliegertruppe. Boelcke was twenty-three when the war began.

Of the Allies:

Eugène Adrien Roland Georges Garros was born on Reunion Island in the Indian Ocean and raised in Saigon in French Indochina. A daydreamer, the man was deeply sensitive and moved by everything he imagined beautiful and great. So it's little surprise what happened when he watched Santos-Dumant's 1906 flight and later attended the 1909 Rheims airshow. He was so inspired by flight that he gave up his dreams of becoming a concert pianist to learn to fly. A self-taught flyer, he made the decision to commit himself to the art after only three hours of solo experimenting. Flight brought him to tears of joy.

Garros was also an avid, but not a particularly good, tennis player.

Short and bandy legged, he was ideally suited for flying Alberto Santos-Dumont's diminutive Demoiselle airplane. Garros flew on the airshow circuit prior to the war and entered the 1911 Paris to Madrid air race and the Circuit of Europe (Paris-London-Paris), where he came in second place.

He set an altitude record of 18,410 feet in September 1911, without bottled oxygen. In 1913, he made the first flight across the Mediterranean when he flew from France to Tunisia in a Morane-Saulnier aircraft.

In July 1914, the German army arrested Garros at an airshow in Berlin when it became obvious that war would break out. Two weeks later, in pre-dawn twilight, Garros slipped from the hotel where he was being held and made his way to the local airfield. Loading extra gasoline into his Morane airplane, Garros then escaped by flying out of Germany. Arriving in France, Garros joined the French army. By the standards of the day, he was old for an aviator at twenty-six years of age in 1914.

Lanoe George Hawker was born in Longparish, Hampshire in 1890. Struck by pneumonia as an infant, he slowly recovered and then, oddly, learned to speak at the age of six months. As a toddler he dismantled each mechanical device around the house, and when left unattended, would quietly put them back in working order.

When Hawker's father left to fight in the Boer war, Lanoe Hawker and his brother were shipped off to boarding school in Geneva. Upon his return to England, he was enrolled into Stubbington House, a school where boys were groomed for entry into the Royal Navy. Unable to keep his attention on classes, though he attended the Royal Navy College, he never graduated due to poor grades. Intelligent, creative, and restless, Hawker transferred to the Royal Military Academy, but, again, left without graduating. Hawker then joined the Royal Engineers as an officer cadet.

After watching a film about the American Wright Flyer in 1910, Hawker and his brother visited the Bournemouth International Aviation meeting where he became obsessed with flying. Avoiding the limelight of most sportsmen aviators, he bought his own airplane, and then attended flight school at his own expense.

Tall and thin, with a classic hawk-like nose and the English's wry wit, Hawker would claim that he had to be properly folded to fit into a cockpit.

In 1913, he fell in love with his best friend's sister, Beatrice Bayly, "a beautiful girl, spiritually and physically." She was the "perfect model for a Rosetti painting." With war looming, Hawker proposed marriage, but

Beatrice turned him down. He wrote to her most days, waiting for the day she changes her mind. Despite his love for her, she remained formal and aloof, and declined even to refer to Hawker by his Christian name.

With the outbreak of the war on August 1, 1914, he transferred to the Royal Flying Corps and awaited deployment to the continent. He was also twenty-four at the beginning of the war.

Book One

Lances

'Tis better to be vile than vile esteemed,
When not to be receives reproach of being;
And the just pleasure lost, which is so deemed
Not by our feeling, but by others' seeing:
For why should others' false adulterate eyes
Give salutation to my sportive blood?
Or on my frailties why are frailer spies,
Which in their wills count bad what I think good?
No, I am that I am, and they that level
At my abuses reckon up their own:
I may be straight though they themselves be bevel;
By their rank thoughts, my deeds must not be shown;
Unless this general evil they maintain,
All men are bad and in their badness reign.

—William Shakespeare
Sonnet 121

Chapter One

Schwerin, Germany
July 14, 1914

The sky blushed rose in the twilight. The coolness of a northern German day hardened into the coldness of the night. The airfield, a motley collection of shabby wooden buildings cast around edges of a grassy meadow, had gone quiet. Beyond the structures, trees began to collect the darkness.

A spindly man, comfortable in the twilight and silence, stole across the field, past a ragged row of delicate wood and canvas aeroplanes. Behind him trotted a dog, misnamed a Dachshund as he was more ears than legs. The man paused and glanced up at an emerging star, sighed wistfully, and then opened a hangar door and stepped inside. Striking a match, he lit a kerosene lantern, then used it to light his way. Calmness settled over him as he focused on his decision and how he would tell de Waal. He walked to the back of the building where rows of workbenches stood. At the bench, he pushed a pile of tools away and set his lamp down. He peered into the darkness of the building around him and listened closely. The man half-expected to hear footfalls, but none came.

They should be all gone now, no one here, he reassured himself.

From a leather blueprint case tucked under his arm, he extracted a map, which he then unfolded, smoothed and flattened. He opened a protractor and quickly checked distances. Calculations ran through his mind: double-checking, kilometers, average wind speed, time aloft, and fuel consumption. Somewhere beyond the light, a rat scurried and the dog circled and tensed, staring into the darkness, mostly afraid.

Bare frames of unfinished aeroplanes floated on the edge of the light like empty cages. The sweet elemental smell of welding hung in the air and he drew it in deeply. Sharp, chemical and metallic, it always brought him a visceral exhilaration, evoking something supernatural, otherworldly.

He smiled.

His family called him Ton, an endearment. The Germans called him Herr Fokker or "The Dutchman." The English and the French and the Russians called him Fokker. The English and Americans sometimes smirked when they said it, but not always. Some would swear when they said it. For many it would be the last word they spoke, but that would come later, along with other names. No one yet called him Antony, Anthony, or Tony, but they would.

Fokker laid his protractor against a ruler in the pool of light on the map and went over the distances one more time. Calculations flew swiftly in his head. From Schwerin to the Dutch border was nearly 500 kilometers: too far for a single tank of fuel. He would have to land to refuel in order to complete the trip. If they didn't fly for the border, they would have to drive almost ten hours and even then only reach the border in late morning.

Questions rumbled through his mind: *If we don't have enough fuel, then we would need to stay, wouldn't we? Would anyone even notice if I left? Would they raise an alarm? Are the borders even still open?*

Then: *But really, does any of it matter? The danger, the distance and fuel are hardly the only reasons not to go.*

Satisfied, he let the decision linger in his mind and began to wrap words around it, framing an argument.

In the shadows, a door creaked, and he heard steps on floorboards. Fokker folded the map quickly, picked up a welder's chipping hammer and the lantern, and took two quick steps toward a bare frame. He bent as though he were inspecting it.

A voice boomed from the darkness, followed by the wild chattering of an indignant monkey, a sound so perpetually out of place that Fokker always jumped when he heard it.

"Really? Fokker, could you act more suspiciously?"

Bernhard de Waal stepped into the light of the lantern. He set down a leather bag. On his shoulder sat a tiny monkey, his Cuckoo. The animal bared its teeth and babbled again, making a nervous jungle sound that rang against the walls of the building. De Waal removed his prized ascot cap and brushed off imagined dust. He reached up and stroked Cuckoo's back, soothing them both. The monkey glanced at Fokker's dog, flashed sharp teeth and then glared at Fokker.

Fokker scowled at the monkey, turned to the workbench and spread the map out again. De Waal stepped closer and looked down. Cuckoo retreated to the shoulder furthest from Fokker and peered around de Waal's head.

De Waal said, "So, I'm packed. When do we leave?"

Fokker bent close to the map and drew invisible lines with his finger, acting. He glanced up but didn't speak, his face set. He feigned being deep in thought, but was just pondering how to break the bad news to de Waal.

"We even have enough fuel, I've set some aside," said de Waal impatiently.

Fokker glanced at Cuckoo. The creature unnerved him. The monkey seemed to smile an evil smile and Fokker backed up a little and leaned against the bench. Fokker folded his arms and flashed an embarrassed grin for being afraid of the animal. He took a deep breath and finished composing his speech in his mind.

"Let's stay, Bernhard, just a little longer," he said. "We can always make a run for the Dutch border later."

De Waal stood up straight and grimaced. He stroked his hand over his face, pressing his moustache flat against his lip. "I thought you'd made up your mind."

Fokker stared off into the darkness of the hangar and at the dimly lit row of aeroplanes in various stages of assembly.

I've come so far, thought Fokker, *so far. What's one more gamble?*

He began. "Bernhard, we're Dutch. The Germans will try to maintain good relations. They won't want a neutral nation turning against them unnecessarily."

De Waal tried to read Fokker's expression. "That's good, Fokker, keep trying. Convince me," interrupted de Waal. "Tell me what you really think. Honestly, I think I know why you've come to your decision; I just want to hear you say it."

Flustered and derailed, Fokker improvised: "Well, Bernhard, there is so much of other people's money tied up here ... I can't abandon it," said Fokker. "It wouldn't be right ..."

"Dammit. Fokker, you'll be the death of us." De Waal sighed, walked over to his bag and picked it up. "I'll keep my bag packed, Fokker. You should, too, and I'd keep an aeroplane fueled and ready to fly. If we need to leave, it'll be in a hurry." He retreated into the darkness and stopped and turned back. "Fokker, it's not about the money, is it? Not really. You think you can see something in the future ... and, that we can finally be in the right place at the right time."

Fokker seemed as if he might speak, and de Waal paused.

De Waal pressed him, "What you don't understand is that, once things begin to happen, they can get out of control. This is war, not flying. Momentum will build and ... you won't be able to talk your way past the chaos. We'll just be innocents caught up in the flood."

Silence reigned for a moment.

"There were no innocents in the Flood, Bernhard," said Fokker. A serious expression crossed his face and de Waal frowned at him. Fokker smiled, nervously.

De Waal, turned, and walked away, shaking his head, disappointed. Cuckoo, sensing his mood, tugged at de Waal's collar.

Fokker called out after de Waal, his voice too loud. "No, Bernhard, it's not the money, and you know that."

De Waal turned again, raising his voice, almost shouting. "It's the risk, isn't it? The gamble? You just want to gamble! You think you know the cards, and you want to play your hand. Fokker, is that it?"

"Yes, Bernhard, I suppose that's it." The thin smile melted from Fokker's face. He cast his eyes down and repeated, "Yes, I suppose that's it. Bernhard, I can sometimes see things in the future. I don't always see everything, usually don't. It's just ... it's just that I can see where it's going, but not how we'll get there. And, I want to be here, in the middle of it. If we run for Holland, we'll be spectators, reading about it, instead of living it. Do you see?"

"Where are you headed, then, Fokker?" asked de Waal.

Fokker glanced back, perplexed.

"I suppose I'll drive to Johannisthal for the flight in the morning," said Fokker.

"You know what I mean," said de Waal, exasperated. "Traitor, villain, hero, opportunist? Which is it? Which are you?"

"I don't know, de Waal, I don't really know."

De Waal took a step closer to Fokker. "Think about how you want to be thought of, Fokker, will you? Careful with those cards. Don't overplay them. You could lose more than your father's money." Then de Waal turned and walked away into the darkness. When he was out of Fokker's sight, the monkey chattered, the eerie sound echoing in the gloom.

A shiver ran up Fokker's spine. A door closed and quiet settled into the building again. He glanced at the map once more.

I feel it, de Waal, don't you? Opportunity. It just needs to be grasped.

~~~

Fokker drove in the dark, south toward Berlin. Around him, an early morning twilight was the gray of a forgotten thought. The city was a faint glimmer of electric lamps ahead through the trees.

If someone had seen him, if a man were to fly and peer down, the weak headlamps of his little Peugeot roadster would appear to be a tiny blob of yellow light, moving across a colorless ocean.

He drove swiftly, barely touching the brakes, letting the car roll fast through corners, scattering pebbles that clattered against the side panels of the car.

Beside him lay Zeiten, his dachshund, curled up, asleep. For the first fifty kilometers south of Schwerin, the dog had stood on the seat, his front legs on the dashboard, his ears flying in the breeze. Fokker imagined that the dog leaned into corners, adjusting for speed. Eventually though, the dog had lost interest and slept from boredom. Fokker reached over and laid a hand on the dog and stroked him, feeling the warmth of the animal's fur under his fingertips

For Fokker, this was his time, a few moments when he could free his mind and think problems through.

He thought of himself as a businessman, and from that, he imagined his single goal was to acquire wealth. He didn't see himself as a daredevil or an aerobat, or even a pilot really, not any more. Nor did he think of himself as just an inventor, either. He despised the label 'engineer' for it seemed to drain the imagination out of what he did. The word implied calculation, a shared conclusion, logic without creativity. No, Fokker believed he applied virtuosity to a creation, making something unique, something that no one else could.

Perhaps I'm a romantic, and little more, thought Fokker, in a flash of doubt, then, *No, I am more than that; I'm a creator.*

Fokker thought then of Schwerin, land of fables, of ghosts. His city of exile. Schwerin was his home now, a city amidst lakes in the German countryside, dotted by islands. His factory at Schwerin was an acknowledged secret, where the German army wanted him to build their aeroplanes. As a Dutchman, not a German, Fokker half believed that the need for secrecy mattered. Often he pondered if the secret wasn't that the German Army had hired a young Dutchman to do their work for them.

Perhaps I am the secret, thought Fokker.

He imagined himself the ghost of the Schwerin castle, the Petermännchen, a remnant of a pagan religion, left behind to play noisy pranks in the night, the keeper of the keys, unlocking doors, speaking the truth when others didn't want to hear it. He smiled to himself.

As the little car rolled off the dirt farm roads and onto the cobbled streets of the city, the ride grew rough. The Berlin streets were a leaden, solid landscape, filled with sharp corners and shadows, dimly lit by light from windows and flickering electric lamps. He drove along the Ring Bahn, the circular road that enclosed Berlin, and then through the city, over the canals, skirting the Tiergarten, to the Brandenberg gate. He slowed the car and glanced up at the Quadriga, the horse-drawn winged chariot. Over the chariot, the Prussian Cross stood tall, illuminated from below by gaslights. He thought it vaguely ridiculous. *Such seriousness, the Germans, still chasing the glory of a dead empire.*

This morning, for the first time that he could remember, there were soldiers stationed around the gate. The sight of them left him at first curious, and then ill at ease. It was a visible sign lending truth to all the rumors of war.

He drove past the gate and back into streets of the city, and then drove hard again, pushing the car enough to make the tires squeal and his heart thump. Fokker couldn't help but smile at the noisy rattle of the little engine filling the space between buildings. On a whim, he called out into the darkness and waved a hand in the air as he drove, "Hello! It's the Petermännchen, come to call!" He glanced back over his shoulder, watching house lights flicker on behind him and laughed.

South of Berlin he chose the eastern-most highway and drove past the Berlin garrison. German army tents stood along the road, stretching off in vast rows. An oil torch marked each tent, as though a match burned in a hall of mirrors and reflected away into a shrinking infinity. It was obvious that the German Army was pulling together, gathering itself in hard knots of manpower and equipment, and Fokker's unease deepened. That same German army had asked Fokker to move to Schwerin to make room at Johannisthal for the German aeroplane builders. He scowled, *my banishment.*

Leaving the city behind, he drove toward the airfield at Johannisthal, to the old farm lots that were now the flying field south of the town. Johannisthal was where flying happened, where people came to be thrilled and amazed. The airfield was an aerial circus of skill, daring, and danger: the center of all German flying.

He thought it should be a good turnout today, for two days ago an aeroplane had cartwheeled across the field. Both occupants had died rather pulpy deaths, and the crowds would grow thicker in anticipation of another tragedy. The Berlin papers printed a photograph of the mess, thankfully muted in black and white. The place the aviators struck was convenient for the crowd, virtually the dead center of the field.

Fokker knew that accidents were inevitable, but hoped it wasn't going to be another one of those days with dying in it. The thought made his belly squirm.

He thought: *Showmanship, a spectacle, gladiators, death. The same since the Romans. Self-imagined Christians now, but still pagans, heathens, all. The crowds always gather for blood, don't they?*

For Fokker, it seemed that though the people came to be entertained, they possessed an air of superiority. *They laugh too soon and too long,* he thought. *They watch silently, smug, like parents watching someone else's children play with dangerous toys.* It was as though the spectators thought these aeroplanes were just impulsive creations, with no substance: like an unplanned valve in a gas pipe or an electric train set with too much current.

Do they expect the aviators will just lose interest and move onto something important?

During the airshows, the throngs moved too close and their shouts of encouragement were cheerful, but condescending. After an accident, the crowds surged around the wreck. They showed no respect and, consequently, little solemnity; displaying quiet, curious smirks and steady gazes at the pieces that had once been whole. They would reach out, perhaps taking a hat, glasses, a scarf, loose pieces of aeroplane fabric, and broken pieces of the aeroplane, some souvenir to commemorate their presence at the moment of demise. They were so thorough that, once, a Rumpler aeroplane had crashed, vertically, outside the field, and when the mechanics reached the site, little was left of the machine save the engine, propeller, a clump of wires, and the partly clothed corpse of the flyer.

Perhaps, when they move on, we will have won. We will have made something that can be so dangerous—that will always be difficult—commonplace. Flying will be normal. Ordinary. That a man flies could be 'normal'? Is it possible?

For the aviators, each flight was truly an experiment, and there was nothing routine about it. Each was different from the last, each a learning experience and an opportunity to go just a little further, to go a little higher, turn tighter, climb faster, land more smoothly. Breakthroughs in flight were happening daily, only throttled by time, money, intensity, and the limits of courage. These were small victories: the first turn for aeroplanes that once merely flew straight; then the figure-8; and then, astoundingly, the loop. All these had happened with great fanfare but little import; it was always the next victory that mattered, the next *stunt*. Fokker hated the word, for it reeked of trickery instead of talent. Each act of aviation was also an occasion to know fear.

The American, Wilbur Wright, stoic to the point of asceticism, taught them by example to remain inscrutable, to appear calm, always. Only confidence could inspire confidence, and only the appearance of coolness, well-practiced, could suppress and control the terror that could seize a man up there: the lethal grip of panic that was so often the verdict that cast a man to his end.

Fokker knew that the aviators felt the accidents deeply, that each dreaded the mishaps that portended their own deaths, and so they tried to gain meaning from them. Over schnapps, warm beer, and whiskey, late at night, after the crowds had gone, the pilots gathered around the retrieved wreckage for quiet wakes in the back of the aeroplane sheds. The smell of lacquer, aeroplane dope, gasoline, and sweat hung in the air. There, the fliers didn't talk of death; they didn't dwell on the departed; and they respected only one another. Hands would bank and tilt by the gaslight, mimicking the flight of the fallen pilot. Together, they would try to discover a certainty, one that mattered to the next flight: that he had banked too steeply; the structure of the wires wasn't sound; he hadn't tested the engine properly. Gathered around their fragment of illumination in the night, numbed and loosened by drink, they would try to convert death into some objective truth. They knew they were still interlopers in a strange hostile place. Air, altitude, gravity, speed, and gasoline were an unforgiving mix.

Rarely did they mention names; names were for family, friends, lovers, and newspapers. Fliers used respectful substitutes, titles that were earned: "the pilot", "the aviator," and "the designer."

Fokker came back to the moment, to the cool moist air of the open country flowing over him. How ironic, he thought, that he was driving so far to meet someone that was most probably another of the cynics. This latest German officer, of a string of many, was sure to be one who believed that these aeroplanes could only matter to the crowds that came for the show, that it was all a circus.

He accelerated again, the Peugeot moving fast through the night, the wind whipping his face. With a sigh, Fokker imagined he was flying.

~~~

The tiny town of Johannisthal, overrun with guests, emptied in the pre-dawn light, as the people streamed onto the field. At the distant edge was a ring of automobiles and carriages and, inside this ring, were tents; within the ring of tents were people, and inside the ring of people stood the airfield, itself a ring. From the air, the landscape gave the impression of a giant oblong target, the green landing field a bullseye in the middle.

Soft billows of patchy, thin fog hung low in the still air. A wide expanse of clover and closely trimmed grass stretched over a nearly flat landscape. Even before dawn, the spectators were up and moving around the field. They knew the aviators preferred the cool, still air of the mornings, for it was the best time for flying the light fragile contraptions.

On the western edge of the field stood an oddly shaped, wooden, two-story building. Resembling a spectator box at a racetrack, but with a garden party on top, this was the Imperial Aero Club, built for the Kaiser, his family, and the royalty of Bavaria, Saxony, and Prussia. The building sported two tiers of fenced-in observation decks, which formed the roof. On the upper deck, two large arches stood, from which the club members had an unimpeded view of the field. From their perch on the building, the members of the club, attired in their club's special navy blue uniforms with distinctive Aero Club buttons and naval caps, watched the flights over the field.

The flying ground itself was grass, lozenge-shaped, several hundred meters at its greatest span, and oriented in its length along the direction the wind generally blew. A tall wooden fence, built by the Prussian military, encircled the field to keep out non-paying guests, and grandstands stood inside the fence for those who paid. Dotted around the edges of the field were hangars, each with long rolling doors. All the big German aircraft factories were here now: Rumpler, Albatros, LVG, Aviatiker Gustav Otto; their names emblazoned across the broad fronts of the hangars. But not Fokker. Not any longer.

The crowds had already grown to the tens of thousands in the pale grey light though there was little sound; everyone was oddly quiet. Soft conversations and the gentle murmurs of vendors with carts selling hot coffee, tea, and small sausage sandwiches wrapped in waxed paper wafted over the field. The fog swirled behind the visitors as they pressed in. The visitors were mostly families with some older, well-to-do couples milling about; all were dressed in their finest attires. Women wore intricate, long, beaded skirts with fashionably enormous hats. Men sported dark suits and top hats. Children in school uniforms with huge sleepy eyes gaped about, glancing at the empty sky.

Watching aeroplanes was grand theater.

Some of the long doors of the hangars were partly open, and mechanics and crews loitered around the buildings. Occasionally spectators would stroll to an open door and peer in until politely shooed away by the mechanics.

As the horizon lightened, clumps of visitors parted for a black Mercedes limousine at the north entrance of the field. The crowds squinted into the rear windows, hoping to recognize the passenger but turned away in disappointment. The car drove to the front of an unpainted hangar on the north edge of the field and stopped at a closed door. A soldier bounded out to open the rear door of the vehicle.

Hauptmann Herman Geertz stepped down from the car onto the field. He ran a gloved hand over oily black hair. He was a tightly built man, gracefully muscular, with a jaw line that worked in spasms of tension. In tall riding boots, with the crimson cuffs and the high-striped, collared uniform of the Hussars, he struck the image of a member of the German Imperial Heavy Cavalry. His aide reached into the car and extracted Geertz's Pickelhaube, the peculiar spiked helmet of the regular German army. Geertz perched it on his head, drew off his gloves, folded them, and held them stiffly at his side.

He turned to his aide and spoke, "Is this the one ... ?"

The aide cast his eyes about the front of the building. At the end of the rolling doors, a smaller door held a sign. It read 'Building 6'. The aide turned to Geertz, "Yes, this is it."

Geertz gestured to the door. "Well, see that we're introduced."

He strode to the smaller door and knocked. After a moment with no answer, he turned to Geertz, and tipped his head to the side.

Geertz waved his gloves at the door, "Knock, again."

The aide lifted his hand to the door and rapped, louder this time.

Geertz shifted his weight from one foot to the other, impatient. He glanced about at the groups of visitors wondering about the wide field. The nearest stared back at him in curiosity. *This place looks like a zoo, with people peering into cages,* Geertz thought. It seemed pointless to him, senseless; the crowds propelled here by a need for shallow excitement, for entertainment.

Geertz held the gaze of a tall fellow who stared back with cold eyes. The man's back was ramrod straight and unwavering, unflinching. They'll not see my discomfort, Geertz thought to himself. It occurred to him that they knew why he was here, and he felt the military man's mistrust at the thought of civilian eyes peering into places they shouldn't. He formed a jowly frown.

Turning back to his unsuccessful aide, he gestured to the door. "Well, try it," he said.

The aide turned the doorknob and pushed on the entrance: stuck. He hesitated a moment and then pushed his shoulder into the poorly hung door, forcing it open. He glanced back at Geertz and stepped into the darkness of the building.

A few quiet moments passed, and one of the rolling doors slid open, propelled from inside the building. A tall, young man with peculiar silver hair, dressed in grease-streaked coveralls, peered out. He greeted Geertz in crisp Silesian German and, gesturing, said, "Come! Please, come in!" The man pushed the door wider, letting light into the building. Turning, he braced himself against the hangar door, shouldering it along the rollers to expose the interior.

Geertz strode into the dark hangar as the doors rolled back. The silver-haired man stepped up, extending a hand in greeting. Geertz took it while his eyes moved over the man, carefully measuring.

"Herr Fokker, I presume?" Geertz released the hand, removed his awkward spiked helmet, and tucked it under an arm.

The man's expression changed and bemusement crossed his face. "No, not I. Martin Kreutzer. Herr Fokker will be along shortly. I'm ... a designer."

Would you like a cup of coffee?" He gestured to a side table, draped in a tablecloth, with a coffee service set out. The smell of coffee competed with the smell of gasoline in the stale air of the building.

"Yes, of course, thank you." Geertz turned to the nearest aeroplane. He'd never seen such a thing up close and he felt the need to stare.

Kreutzer nervously peered out the open door, hoping Fokker would arrive and save him this inconvenience. He stepped next to Geertz and gestured to the aeroplane. It was Herr Fokker's newest, but he was sure Fokker wouldn't mind a brief tour. "Have you seen an aeroplane before?" he asked.

"Yes, at a distance, merely while flying. On maneuvers," lied Geertz, afraid to appear amateurish. His eyes took in the fragile wings. Up close, they were translucent. He touched the canvas covering with a finger and felt it depress. Geertz's mouth went dry.

Kreutzer moved to the end of the wing and took the wingtip in his hands, grasping both front and rear edges. He twisted the wing tip and the entire wing moved and flexed. Cables, running from the edges of the wings up through pulleys, moved in response. The wooden spars in the wings creaked as the wing moved. In the open cockpit, the stick moved back and forth in response to Kreutzer moving the wing.

Geertz was dumbstruck; the wing seemed so fragile, delicate even. Confusion played over his face. He took a half-step back.

He was a horseman of farmer stock, not born to be an officer. He was there by good fortune and painful hard work; at twenty-five he was considered old for a Hauptmann. Mechanism mattered little to him, only flesh and blood was tangible and real. Science and mathematics were abstractions, calculations were something for pedantic math instructors. The thought of such a fragile thing holding a person in the air seemed reckless, foolhardy. He thought this even more so as he watched the wing move up and down in Kreutzer's hands.

Kreutzer released the wing, and it returned to its normal shape, the cables relaxing and shifting, and the stick in the cockpit moving back to its central position. "Don't be alarmed. It's normal and how the aeroplane is steered," he said.

Geertz eyed Kreutzer, sizing the man up. Am I being toyed with? He forced his expression to appear blank now, but merely succeeded in looking bewildered.

Kreutzer opened his arms in a gesture of encouragement. "Hauptmann, please, let me show you around the aeroplane."

At the back of the hangar, two of Fokker's mechanics stood by, chatting in a language that was strange to Geertz's ear. Geertz was startled by their voices. He turned to Kreutzer and lowered his voice. "Herr Kreutzer, may I speak frankly?"

"Yes, of course." Kreutzer stepped closer to Geertz, surprised at the candor from a military man.

Geertz gestured to the mechanics. "In confidence."

Kreutzer took in the request. "Yes, of course." He waved the mechanics from the hangar. Geertz dismissed his own aide with a wave of his hand.

Geertz cleared his throat, abruptly, and sipped his coffee. "Herr Kreutzer, as a fellow countryman, you must understand my unease. Military matters bring me here. Having these ... Russians ... in attendance is a matter of some concern."

Kreutzer nodded, acknowledging the comment. "Oh, the mechanics? Estonians. They are Estonians. Yes, of course, I understand."

"These are issues for fellow Germans to discuss." Geertz sipped his coffee again.

Kreutzer waited for Geertz to continue. Meanwhile, his eyes traced over the aeroplane, taking in cables, clevises, connections; examining it. He could never be too watchful for a flaw, an error. He felt the need to do something useful.

"Herr Kreutzer, tell me about Anton Fokker."

Kreutzer winced at Geertz's tone. He nodded once, pausing to gather his words. Then he began. "He's quite young, you know." He paused, gazed Geertz in the eye, and added, "and Dutch."

All color drained from Geertz's face.

~~~

Fokker saw the flags first as he approached Johannisthal. At the north end of the field stood two tall sharp towers. Each had tiny platforms on top for spotters to follow the aeroplanes with field glasses and shout down instructions, information, and warnings. At the tip of each was a flag to show the wind's direction and strength. Enormous cloth pennants, embroidered with the names of factories, hung from the height of each tower.

He thought the towers useless save as obstacles, impediments that made a difficult thing dangerous. Adorned with their banners, the towers reminded Fokker of turrets on a feudal castle.

Fokker drove his little Peugeot to the edge of the crowd, outside the field, and gradually wound his way through the mass of people. Fokker noticed that military police, draped with the triangular metal chest plate of the Feldgendarmerie, had replaced the usual civilian guards at the perimeter. A young soldier halted Fokker at the entrance until a German mechanic recognized him and convinced the guard to let Fokker pass.

On a good day, a fair portion of the population of Berlin turned out. It appeared to be a good day. The unpaid visitors were furthest out, camping in cars and tents around farmers' fields. Meanwhile the paying visitors, outside the ring of buildings, pressed against barriers that prevented them from wandering onto the field. Even so, royalty, military, stray guests, and crews still roamed the field itself. The crowds were surging inward, anxious for the show to begin.

As Fokker drove across the field, he glanced again at the flags on the towers. They barely stirred in the breeze.

Good! At least the Leutnant won't have to worry about the wind. One less thing ...

He arrived at his borrowed hangar and parked behind it, putting the Peugeot out of the way. Like errant schoolboys, he found Leutnants Muhlig-Hoffman and Reinicker eating their breakfast behind the building. They greeted Fokker and shook his hand, their cavalry uniforms unbuttoned at the collar and their gloves tucked into their belts.

"Perhaps you should put yourselves in order; the observer has arrived." Fokker gestured towards the parked staff car.

"Jawohl, Herr Fokker. Good idea." Reinicker was the quicker to acknowledge the slight. He tossed the paper from his sandwich onto the ground, rubbed his hands together, and buttoned his collar. He drew his gloves onto his hands and straightened his cap.

"Are you ready, Leutnant?" Fokker studied Reinicker, trying to stare him in the eye: the best way to gauge a man's mind. Reinicker looked away across the field, avoiding Fokker's gaze.

"I do hope they clear the guests soon," Reinicker said.

"Certainly; just a few minutes until the engines begin to start," added Muhlig.

Fokker glanced at Muhlig-Hoffman. Muhlig subtly shook his head from side to side.

"Leutnant Muhlig, perhaps you could give Reinicker and me a moment."

Muhlig turned to the hangar. "Of course. I'll be inside."

Fokker addressed Reinicker quietly and quickly. "Are you prepared?" Then, "You don't have to fly if you're not ready for this."

Reinicker braced his hands at his sides. "Herr Fokker, I mean no disrespect, but I have made my decision and am ready for the next step."

Fokker nodded in understanding, but felt saddened. He wasn't sure for what, or for whom. Fokker pondered whether to try to stop the process, but Reinicker was a customer, of sorts, and so the Dutchman drew a breath and acquiesced.

"Very well, let's join your colleagues and begin," said Fokker.

As they entered the hangar, the sun broke over the horizon and bands of light cast across the field, punctuated by the line of hangars along the eastern edge. The light set the entire field into relief. In the distance, an engine started and the Feldgendarmerie began clearing the visitors from the field. Soon the fog disappeared as though it had never been there.

Fokker introduced himself to Hauptmann Geertz, ignoring the man's obvious surprise at Fokker's boyish face and unruly mop of dark hair.

"Herr Fokker, I'm pleased to meet you. We will be working closely together in the coming months, I'm sure," said Geertz.

"And why is that?" asked Fokker.

"Well, surely you understand that there is a certain urgency of late. A war? I will be your liaison."

Fokker took a second glance at Geertz, assessing the man with fresh eyes. "Very well," said Fokker. "Herr Hauptmann, allow me to explain the process."

Geertz glanced at Muhlig-Hoffman and at Reinicker for acknowledgement, but both stared ahead. Geertz swallowed. "Proceed."

Fokker explained. "This is the most important step in the process of learning to fly. In the beginning, each flight was, how we term it, 'a solo.' Now we are able, with our more powerful machines, to bring each prospective pilot to flight, flying along with an experienced pilot. Then, when they are ready, they make their first flight by themselves. Leutnant Muhlig-Hoffman has already done so. Leutnant Reinicker is prepared for his flight. You will be the official witness so that he may obtain his flight certificate upon completion of his solo flight. Do you have any questions?"

Geertz flushed, surprised, a little dumbfounded. He blinked his eyes rapidly, and then collected himself. He smiled, slightly. "Then, I won't actually be ... flying, is that correct?" he said.

"Well, of course not. Perhaps if you'd like to take a flight, that could be arranged," said Fokker. Geertz's eyes widened and Fokker pretended not to notice.

Muhlig-Hoffman and Kreutzer exchanged quick smiles.

"No, no, that will be perfectly alright," Geertz promptly replied.

"Very well, let us begin. The Leutnant has stated that he is ready. I accept his statement of readiness." Fokker felt the strange sadness, again, washing over him. "Herr Kreutzer, prepare the aeroplane."

Kreutzer turned to the Estonian mechanics, Arthur and Johannes. The men were Fokker's crew brought back from a failed sales trip to St. Petersburg the year before. Fokker had a certain fondness for unusual companions; young, silver Kreutzer, de Waal and his monkey, mechanics that couldn't speak German and very little Dutch. Kreutzer nodded and waved his hand in a flourish toward the open door. Johannes and Arthur pushed the Spin, Fokker's training machine, out the door and across the field.

Leutnant Reinicker strode to the back of the hangar and removed his uniform jacket. He put on a leather jacket, wrapped a silk scarf around his neck, pulled a woolen cap onto his head, and followed the aeroplane out the door.

The Spin rolled along, the uneven ground making the wings flap a little. It lacked subtlety, grace, or pleasing lines. All about it was inelegance and lightness. Delicate wings, delicate wires. It had so little structure that, in flight, it appeared the man in it might be floating in a cage with sails. The Spin was functionality incarnate.

As there was no wind, they pushed the Spin to the usual launching area in front of the Imperial Aero Club. Fokker, the two Leutnants, and Geertz trailed behind. Kreutzer carried a ladder to allow Reinicker to mount the aeroplane. Geertz found it all a little frightening.

"Have you seen an aeroplane fly before?" Fokker asked.

Geertz turned to Fokker, judging his own reply. He was unsure how to respond to the informality of Fokker. He decided that, as a foreigner, Fokker shouldn't be taken too seriously.

"No, I have not," Geertz responded.

Kreutzer glanced at Muhlig, cocking an eyebrow.

Fokker cleared his throat and drew himself up.

"My dear Hauptmann," Fokker began, never losing a chance to sell to someone, "you will be amazed. This is the future. We have entered a new age, a new time, and we will forever be changed by our ability to fly. The possibilities are endless; your profession will be eternally changed, and, God willing, humanity will be forever reaping the benefits of the aeroplane."

Ahead of them, backs to them, Kreutzer, Muhlig, and Reinicker all grinned.

They arrived at the staging area and joined a group of men clustered around two other aeroplanes. Crews from other factories pushed another half-dozen aeroplanes across the field.

Fokker gazed curiously, across the arena, at the strange array of flying machines, always seeking something new. Other crews were pushing two Wright machines across the field. They were the original aeroplanes, American imports, little changed from the first aeroplane to fly ten years before. With open wings, the pilot sitting between them now rather than lying on one's belly on the lower wing, and a new engine, they were otherwise the archetype for every machine that came after them.

There was also a Rumpler Taube: a design clearly inspired by birds, perhaps an homage to da Vinci and his flying machines. It was an abstract artist's rendition of a bird though, drawn crudely and expressed in poor materials. Styled like a dove, the Taube was complete with delicate ribs in its wings and a bird's tail. Fokker enjoyed its lines, the simplicity of it, but was amused at the conceit. "The more like a bird, the better it flies?" he had once asked, gently mocking the shape.

The newest machines were French: Blériots and Moranes, the victors of the races to fly across the English Channel and the Mediterranean. They had single wings with tapered ... what was the word ... a new French word: *fuselages*.

He thought of Louis Blériot with his ridiculous long moustache. Blériot, the first to cross the Channel. And Morane, the first aeroplane to cross the Mediterranean, with Garros flying. Beautiful, brave Garros. He would be looping for show somewhere right now, Fokker supposed.

Kreutzer and Arthur turned the Spin away from the stands, pointing it to the east as Johannes directed the tail. They prepared the engine, applying oil from a can into the open valves and rods over the cylinders, and then pumped fuel up into the gravity tank.

Reinicker saluted Geertz, Muhlig-Hoffman, and then gazed up at the deck of the Imperial Aero Club. A figure, clad in dark blue, stood under an arch, his hands clasped behind his back like a captain at sea. Reinicker saluted upward, and the man in the arch returned his salute. He mounted the aeroplane.

Fokker explained the machine to Geertz. "This is an older airplane." He deliberately used the new term, "airplane".

"Very safe. It is automatically stabilized." Fokker enjoyed the phrase and used it often. It sounded so ... safe, gentle even, but scientific. He didn't acknowledge that it also meant the Spin was horribly difficult to turn and was stable up to the edges of its performance, but then became unbalanced and impossible to recover. Otherwise, it was fine to fly. As long as there was no wind. No wind at all. "It is named for the insect, the spider. It is a Dutch word, '*Spin*,'" Fokker told Geertz.

A memory flickered in Fokker's mind. An Englishman, or was it an American? Ah yes, the ridiculous self-proclaimed cowboy—Cody, Bill

Cody, the one with the preposterous hat—had pointed out the irony of the name. Fokker knew that he wasn't the real Bill Cody, but he was happy to let people believe he was the genuine article. Cody had pointed out that the English word "spin" was what happened when an aeroplane was out of control. He had laughed when Fokker said the word meant spider. "Like hanging by a thread, you mean?" he had laughed again, an obnoxious, braying, American laugh.

Fokker continued telling the story of the Spin to Geertz, that the framework over the top of the aeroplane connected all the supporting wires together; that the wires and the fuel tank at the top reminded one of the legs of a spider. Fokker thought: *It had been Ljuba who saw that. Beautiful, young Ljuba, and an excellent flyer, no less.* She had been *his* Russian, brought to Berlin from St. Petersburg. How enchanted he had been by her. *Spin* it became. She was gone now. Ran away; gone for a month, she had flown off to Paris with her new French boyfriend. Her previous boyfriend hardly dead a fortnight before she left. Fokker: only a friend left behind. Fokker wondered if he might ever see her again.

"Herr Fokker?" said Geertz, bringing Fokker into the moment. "Please continue."

Kreutzer glanced at Fokker. Fokker nodded. Johannes grasped the tail and dug in his feet. Arthur stood at the left side of the propeller and pulled it down until the blades were horizontal. Reaching up with both hands, he grasped the blade and swiftly lifted himself off his feet as he pulled the blade down. He instantly leapt back as the blade, lethal now, blurred into a silver disk. Kreutzer joined Johannes to hold the tail as the engine bellowed, a harsh rasping jangle of noise, the sound evening out a little as it warmed. The aeroplane pulled against their weight as they adjusted its alignment, pointing the Spin at a gap between towers.

Reinicker peered back at Fokker and waved. Fokker waved him along, dreading the moment. Fokker could not say no to the Leutnant and knew that, to do so, would cast a pall over his business; to do so, would mean admitting not every person could fly, that there might be limits to how many aeroplanes could be sold. Worse yet, that a soldier, an *officer*, no less, couldn't learn to fly. But saying yes may mean dooming the man and the aeroplane.

And, to make it worse, it was one of his best Spins. He had made only a few.

Reinicker pushed the throttle, and the note of the engine rose into a deafening roar. Kreutzer and Johannes glanced at each other, then simultaneously let go of the aeroplane. The machine began to roll. It built up speed, and the spectators and crews all turned to watch.

Take-off was a common time for crashes, so the crowds in the grandstands stood, holding their collective breath. The Spin rolled faster and faster. Reinicker hunched, leaning over the stick and the controls. He hung on stiffly with both hands clenched on the controls, his eyes fixed straight ahead.

"He'll do fine," said Fokker to Geertz. Fokker's smile was a thin line across his pursed lips.

He's scared out of his mind, thought Fokker. *God help him.*

The Spin lurched headlong, its front skid digging into the ground. The Spin tipped, seeming to almost touch its propeller to the ground. Even Fokker held his breath now. Reinicker leaned back, riding the aeroplane like an errant horse over a gate. The Spin came level, and then rolled a few feet more. The machine was pregnant with lift. It lifted a bare few feet, almost floating, then settled.

At last, the wheels lifted. A loud "aahh" rolled through the crowd, and the aeroplane rose, gently upward, moving away from earth in a direction few had ever gone, but that all had dreamt of. The Spin bucked, sagged, and gradually climbed away. There was no grace there; the elegance was in the act, not the machine.

To the crowd it seemed a farce, a poor magician's trick, lacking the right explanation to bring it crashing to earth. Try as they might to find the flaw, their eyes continued to deceive them, to befuddle them; a magic act with a hidden wire, perhaps, or a sleight of hand with a hidden card, but anything other than what it really was: a man, perched on the back of a poor piece of art, flying.

Leisurely, the aeroplane rose, lifted into the air toward the sun, the nose tilting upward. Then Reinicker leaned headfirst, settling the aeroplane and leveling out. It passed over the east-most buildings. Fokker breathed again.

Geertz turned to Fokker. "All in order, then?" Blissfully free of imagination, he seemed confused at what he had seen, unimpressed, wondering if he had seen all there was to see.

Fokker nodded. "Yes, yes, of course. Just the landing now."

Kreutzer and Muhlig exchanged glances of concern.

The other mechanics and aviators went back to their machines; the crowds in the grandstands turned and watched the Spin lift and clear the field, then begin to curve to fly in a wide circle. Fokker and his crew watched the turn, knowing that Reinicker could easily over-control the airplane, tip the Spin over and slide into the ground. Nevertheless, the Spin banked and then leveled, wobbling in the air as Reinicker fumbled at the rudder. It disappeared behind a tower and then behind the stands. After a moment, it reappeared between trees to the north, and then vanished in the distance again.

"He needs to complete one orbit of the field to complete his solo," said Fokker to Geertz.

They could hear the Spin now, west of the airfield, moving from north to south. The sound reverberated over the field. It was a droning, mechanical roar, echoing off the buildings and towers. Fokker hoped to himself that Reinicker would try to land now, after just half an orbit; that he wouldn't think to complete a full orbit around the field. Fokker was relieved that, so far, Reinicker was holding his own, but for how much longer? He didn't share his concerns with Geertz.

As other aeroplane engines started, they drowned out the distant rattle of the Spin. A Wright flyer rolled across the field and lifted smoothly into the rising sun. Geertz relaxed. He turned to Fokker. "Herr Fokker, where is the restaurant?"

Fokker blanched and said, "Just a few more minutes and we'll have time for breakfast."

Just then, the Spin appeared in the east, turning toward them, lining up between the towers. Fokker felt Reinicker could do it, was beginning to have hope. He said aloud, "Almost, almost."

The Spin completed its turn, leveled its wings toward them, the rising sun behind it now, framing it.

"Almost. Almost," repeated Fokker.

Then Reinicker pointed the Spin downward, too steeply. As he neared the ground, he pulled upward, flattening out the aeroplane's flight. The machine struck the ground on its wheels and bounced back into the air.

"Cut the engine," Fokker said softly. "Cut the engine." His heart thumped in his chest.

The other crews had turned now, watching. The crowd was on its feet again, all eyes on the Spin at the middle of the field.

Reinicker pointed the nose down again, struck the ground, bounced upward. Twice more, at full power each time. At last, he realized that he was moving across the field too fast to stop in time, and he yanked back on the stick. As the Spin hopped over them, Fokker saw the letters written across the bottom of the wings in stark relief against the sky: F O K K E R. He felt his own panic rise like bile. The Spin rose and passed over the Imperial Aero Club, just clearing the arches on the top. Blue-clad club members scattered and threw themselves down onto the roof of the building. Fokker watched a chair tumble over the side and smash to pieces as it struck the ground. The Spin roared away west. Fokker buried his face into a hand, regretting his advertising.

Muhlig was white as a sheet. Kreutzer had stopped watching and was pretending to talk to a mechanic from Rumpler. Johannes and Arthur sat on the grass, feigning disinterest, while Johannes cleaned his fingernails with a penknife. Even Geertz knew something was wrong. Fokker stared off into the sky over the club, expecting the sound of a crash to roll over the building.

"I'll kill him," Fokker said, aloud.

"Pardon?" asked Geertz.

"Nothing. Nothing at all," replied Fokker.

In a few minutes, the Spin reappeared again in the east, turning back west. A Wright flyer passed under Reinicker as he turned, barely missing him, though Reinicker didn't notice. He piloted the Spin over the field, descending, sluggishly creeping downward, still under full power. Fokker knew that Reinicker had forgotten and wouldn't remember to stop the engine. Fokker hoped merely for a survivable crash now.

"Almost. Almost. Almost," Fokker chanted under his breath, trying to soothe himself.

The Spin struck the ground, bounded up, struck again, the engine racing hard. It bounced upward again. Then, once more, Reinicker pulled the aeroplane up and ascended, passing over the Aero Club building a second time.

Muhlig had left for coffee, and Kreutzer appeared as if he was going to cry. Johannes and Arthur found a deck of cards and were busy ignoring the spectacle overhead. Even the other mechanics and aviators had stopped watching, not wanting to see the inevitable crash. But they stole glances over their shoulders at the Spin as it approached the ground just in case they needed to be able to run if it came their way. The crowds cheered each time he bounced.

Geertz grumbled. "He is going to ... 'land' the aeroplane, at some point, is he not?"

Fokker's lip trembled. "Yes, he will land at some point." He knew that to be true, for, eventually he must run out of gas. *Whether his arrival is a landing, might be another matter,* thought Fokker.

Twice more Reinicker repeated the process. Muhlig was back with coffee. Kreutzer had left now, mumbling something about using the loo. Johannes and Arthur tried hard to seem bored.

As the Spin struck the ground once again, Reinicker pushed his controls forward, and, by a miracle, the aeroplane leveled and steadied, then settled. Fokker gaped at the sight. Reinicker had gotten it down, but the Spin was still careening along the ground at full speed, bearing down on the parked aeroplanes waiting to launch. Fokker ran toward the aeroplane, sensing a disaster to his reputation much greater than just a crash.

Reinicker clenched the controls and stared straight ahead at the crowd of crew and aeroplanes, unable to think through his own shock. Fokker ran in front of the Spin and Reinicker at last came to his senses, then drove the rudder hard over to the right, and the aeroplane turned back on itself, hurtling to the north across the field. With a sputter, the engine ran out of gas, and the Spin rolled, finally, to a stop.

Johannes and Arthur set down their cards and began walking toward the Spin. Arthur reached into his pocket, pulled out a coin, and handed it to Johannes. Johannes laughed as he pocketed the bet. They reached the aeroplane and helped a shaking Reinicker to the ground. As they steadied him, his knees collapsed. As Reinicker picked himself up, they turned Spin and began pushing it toward the hangar.

Kreutzer, having never made it to the loo, ran out to help Reinicker. Finding him shaken but unharmed, Kreutzer led him back across the field to the shed.

As he watched the scene unfold, Fokker mumbled, "Well, he is brave."

Geertz caught up with Fokker, standing in the middle of the field, staring at the aeroplane. "All is in order, I take it?" he asked.

Fokker glanced at him, and then looked back at the Spin. "Yes, all is in order." Fokker thought a moment and turned to Geertz, facing him. "But, I'll need another pilot." Fokker turned away and walked back toward his hangar.

Geertz stared at Fokker's back, thinking about foreigners and breakfast.

At the shed, Johannes and Arthur were turning the Spin around to back it inside when Fokker caught up with them. Reinicker sagged on a chair. It appeared to Fokker as if he might slide off onto the ground. Kreutzer and Muhlig huddled over Reinicker, and Kreutzer was offering an uncorked hip flask. Fokker turned away, feeling something like shame welling inside of him.

How could I have let him fly? He could have killed someone or crashed into the damned Aero Club! My God!

With a sigh, Fokker composed himself, and tried to feel relief that Reinicker wasn't dead.

Well, at least his didn't wreck my Spin.

He glanced at Reinicker and threw his head dismissively, a little angry at the foolish German. Fokker called Johannes and Arthur over to him. "Take care of the Spin, drain any fuel from the tanks and check the oil levels; make adjustments."

Kreutzer called for Fokker to join a conversation with their new patron, Geertz. Geertz looked at Fokker as though he needed to put Fokker in his place. Fokker scowled back.

The time had come for something he dreaded and he steeled himself.

He glanced over at Reinicker and lowered his voice; then, put his hand inside his coat and removed a long leather wallet. He turned his back to Kreutzer and Geertz and drew out a wad of currency. He split it between Johannes and Arthur, then pressed the money into their hands.

"Gentlemen, it has been good working with you. It's time for you to go home." Johannes's eyes grew wet and his hands shook. Arthur stared in disbelief at Fokker.

Fokker studied the men for just a moment, a realization dawning. He exclaimed, "No, no. It's not like that!" Fokker smiled gently. "There's something coming, perhaps even war ... I can't see the future, but I think you'd better leave Germany while you can".

The men glanced at each other, and Arthur said something to Johannes in Estonian. They glared back at Fokker, tension on their faces. Fokker reached out and shook hands with each of them. He turned to Arthur, who seemed to understand better than Johannes did.

"Run, Arthur, get to a train and head home, head east; get out of Germany. Now. Run."

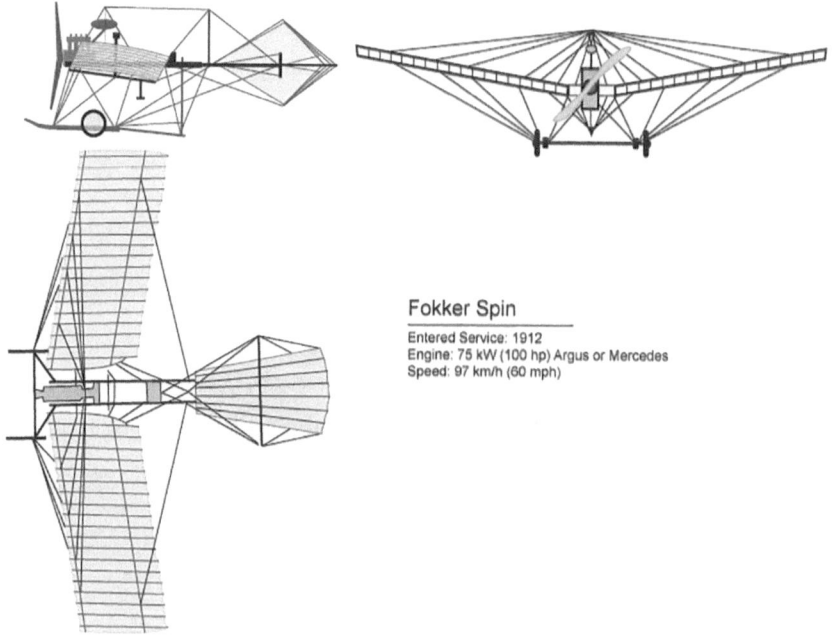

Fokker Spin

Entered Service: 1912
Engine: 75 kW (100 hp) Argus or Mercedes
Speed: 97 km/h (60 mph)

Chapter Two

Ostrowa, Western Prussia
July 31, 1914

Richthofen turned the column of horsemen back toward town. The horses always knew first when they were headed home. He smiled as they picked up their heads, and their pace quickened.

Yes, that's it. To the barn. Feed, water and off with your miserable saddles, thought Richthofen. *How do you always know?*

The cavalrymen, trying to be impassive, stirred in their saddles, straightened their backs and exchanged glances with small smiles.

Wedel rode to Richthofen and reined up alongside. "Long day, Leutnant," he said.

On horseback, Erich-Rüdiger von Wedel sat a head taller than Richthofen. Sweat rolled from under Wedel's helmet and he tugged at the strap under his chin. He was long and lean, sinewy and tall, ropey. He moved fluidly, comfortable on a horse, surprisingly since he seemed almost too big to mount a horse, let alone ride well. But, Wedel rode tight, never letting his grey mare choose her own way, the way he been taught to ride since he was a boy. It was the way his father had learned and the way his father learned from his grandfather. In his family, they said it was the way that Louis IV taught the knights Wedel in 1320. Wedel examined his hands and adjusted his gloves, letting the blood flow back into his fingers, having grown numb from the tight grip.

Richthofen glanced at Wedel and down at his hands.

"Oh, dear God, Wedel. Let her have her head. She's nearly home!" He grinned at Wedel and Wedel cast back a crooked smile.

Tradition, thought Wedel. *Must everything have a tradition?*

Wedel looked back at the column behind them, German and Polish boys, and mostly farmer's kids, comfortable on horses the way a city boy is comfortable wearing shoes. Their backs moved with their saddles, their long sharp metal lances held effortlessly upright. *Natural riders, all.*

Richthofen spoke. "You know Wedel, that's why she won't jump for you. You've got to give her head just before she reaches the jump, or she won't trust her own balance ... you know that, right?"

"You keep telling me that," said Wedel. "But I'll never learn."

Wedel peered down at Richthofen, realizing he sounded overly blunt, then made his gaze respectful. "Yes, sir. Some day."

Richthofen smiled back with grey eyes, reflecting the sky. For the moment, they dazzled blue. They sparkled in pleasure, Richthofen was truly happy, for a long day of riding was his greatest joy in life. "Some day, Wedel. I'll teach you to ride," he said, teasing.

He turned his chestnut, Santuzza, and rode back along the column of cavalry. The young riders—straight in their saddles, tired and dusty—dressed their lines of horses and tightened their column by reflex as their commander rode past. Richthofen spoke in low tones, addressing the men as he rode.

"There, tighten your straps ... Don't slouch ... Lances straight. Shake out your pennants ... We'll be in soon ... Act like Lancers ... Uhlans."

The young cavalrymen rode from the country roads to their barracks in the late afternoon, aching with tiredness and coated in the dust of the Prussian countryside. After a quick splash of water to clean their faces, they shuffled inside, then gathered in their dining room. A mess attendant dragged a half-barrel of ice into the room, covered in fresh oysters on the half-shell. The men gathered at the barrel, took oysters and began slurping the plump meat into their mouths, washing it down with warm beer. The beer lifted their spirits and the fatigue at last seeped out of reflexing muscles. Soon all was laughter, their energy returning.

Since it was a mixed unit of Germans and Poles, the celebratory atmosphere opened doors normally closed between the men. One of the German troopers invited two of the Polish boys to play Skat. Initially, the Poles protested, not knowing the game. He convinced them with a friendly jibe and dealt the cards.

The young commander of the cavalry squadron, Richthofen, leaned against the wall of the casino, a flute of champagne in one hand, his legs crossed casually. He stood within reach of the barrel of oysters and ate them methodically as he watched his men relax. A layer of yellow dust hid atop his blond hair, but stood out on his sunburned face and gray-green uniform. Streaks from sweat drew lines down the dust on his brow.

Leutnant Richthofen rubbed his left shoulder, expecting soreness to radiate. When it didn't, he smiled. He was on the mend. His adjutant, Wedel, stood at his side, watching his commander survey the troops. Wedel sipped a stein of beer and bit into a piece of white Polish bread slathered in butter.

A boy, younger than even the teenage troopers, appeared in the doorway, holding a telegram, searching the room with near-panic in his eyes. His face was brown from life in the open, and he had the dark Slavic eyes of the Silesian country folk. He was slight and thought himself invisible among the Uhlans; he often wished he were.

Richthofen spotted the small boy, his aide, his batman, and called to him across the room, "Menzke, over here!"

His black eyes darted back and forth, trying to pick a way through the men before he made a dash. He spotted Richthofen across the room and straightened himself, lifting his chin. The Leutnant requested him, had called to him. He felt enormous pride. He glanced at the paper in his hands, examined the lines and swirls, unintelligible to his eye, but of such importance to the commander.

Wedel turned to Richthofen and whispered, "I think you scare him to death, Leutnant."

Richthofen smiled and half shrugged. "He's a good boy, does what he's told; I like him."

Menzke slipped through the throng of men milling about the room, working once more at being invisible. Steins of beer and champagne flutes swung wildly from outstretched arms as Menzke ducked and dodged his way across the room. He tottered to a stop in front of Richthofen, drew himself up to attention, and saluted.

"Sorry you couldn't ride today, Menzke," said Richthofen, waving a return salute at the boy.

"Yes, sir," said Menzke, noncommittally. He kept his eyes moving, watching the men mill around him.

"They won't bite." Richthofen smiled. Wedel grinned and clapped a hand on Menzke's shoulder.

"They might bite a little, Menzke." Wedel laughed. He leaned over and spoke in a low tone. "But you can ride the britches off most of them."

Menzke smiled soft and slow, and a light glinted in his dark eyes.

"Did you send the telegram?" asked Richthofen.

"Yes, sir. Here's the reply." Menzke reached out and handed the sheet of paper to Richthofen. Richthofen read it quickly.

"Thank you, Menzke. Dismissed. You may join the party."

Menzke retreated across the room, ducking his way through the men. A trooper, a slim German with a reedy mustache, took Menzke by the arm and led him to a table loaded with drinks. He teased Menzke into taking one.

Wedel leaned over to Richthofen now, his voice still low. "Did you tell them to stay or go home?"

"I told them to get out of there and head home." Richthofen thought of the panic welling in his mother, and of his little brother, Bolko, nonplussed, as always. His father would be the one who knew what it meant. Being told to leave the Baltic coast in the middle of their vacation would be something he would treat seriously. He would know it meant war.

Wedel frowned and shook his head at the implication, but stood in agreement. "I understand. Are they ... ?"

"Yes, father is packing them, getting them moving. They're better off at home."

In the middle of the room, a circle of men gathered around one of the troopers. The young man at the center of the circle bent his knees and sprung into the air. He tried to land a back flip, but crashed hard onto his spine and laid himself flat out. He lay still, either winded, humiliated or both. The men roared in laughter.

"Oh, no. You know what this means," said Wedel to Richthofen, grinning.

"Yes, I'm afraid I do."

Another man tried it. He leapt practically straight up, his hands striking the ceiling before he could rotate, causing him to land on his butt where he laughed at himself. Someone handed him his beer, and he sat drinking and making excuses until another trooper helped him up.

The men looked over at Richthofen, talking amongst themselves, knowing that he would not be able to resist much longer.

"Well, how long will you keep them waiting?" asked Wedel. He took Richthofen's champagne glass and swished the contents around. "Perhaps you need another one?," he teased before nudging Richthofen. "Go on."

Richthofen frowned at Wedel, it occurred to him that this party would be one of their squadron's last together, so he would need to make the most of it.

Soon, they'll all be bound for glory.

"So, what's the worst you could do? Break your collarbone again?" Wedel grinned.

"Oh, alright then."

Richthofen took a step as Wedel pushed him in the middle of his back. The men parted to let him through.

"Let me show you how this is done," said Richthofen. He unbuttoned his sleeves, rolled his cuffs up, and entered the middle of the circle. He bent at the knees and swung his arms at his sides, a little behind him, bouncing on his legs. Sweat matted his gold blond hair against his head. When he drew himself in, he became a gymnast.

The other cavalrymen chanted his name, and he began to laugh and then lurched on his feet.

Wedel joined the group and counted down as Richthofen took his position again, swung his arms and dipped his knees. The men joined the count, and Richthofen found that he couldn't stop laughing.

He stood straight and raised a hand, "Okay, quiet now! I can't do it while I'm laughing."

A Polish boy handed Richthofen a half-full stein of beer. Richthofen laughed again and tilted it up for a long swallow. "Alright then. Just one. Quiet though."

The room grew silent except for the old record player winding down in the corner. Richthofen bent his knees, squatted, swung his arms swiftly, and then sprung into the air. Tucking his knees up, he tipped his head back as he flew. He rotated and then extended his legs: a perfect back flip.

"Hurrah!" The room erupted.

Wedel shouted over the other men, "I told you, I told you all! No one can beat Richthofen at the backflip!," as he jabbed a finger around the room, pointing at each man. Richthofen laughed and another stein of beer appeared. He took a long belt.

Outside their barracks, a black lacquer Imperial carriage rolled to the front of the building, pulled by two fat plow horses. The coach was weatherworn and past its prime, the tin siding had begun to loosen, and a piece or two was missing. It was a relic of another time, a carriage for the fringe of another century's empire. Still, it had been a gift from the Kaiser and was a source of pride for its owner.

Count August von Kospoth opened the door as soon as it came to a stop. He swung himself down and placed a frayed top hat on his head, though he was only walking to the door. He straightened himself, adjusted his coat, reached into the carriage and took up his walking stick. Though he tried to affect the same proud bearing and gait that he had learned in youth, he had grown fat. The best he could manage today was a waddle, though an imperious one. He flattened his vest, sucked his belly in, and refastened the brass buttons that held in his gut.

Kospoth could hear the raucous party inside; shouts and laughter. Uniformed young men moved past the windows, blind to the darkness outside. He could hear a young woman's laughter somewhere in the building. Kospoth reached the door and saw it was untended. There was no one there to greet him. Removing his hat, he hesitated before reaching out and letting himself in, though the indignity made his face turn hot. He moved to the dining room door and took the handle in his hand, paused, and composed himself, mashing his hair down in an effort to manage a wiry gray shock that was sticking out. He swung the door wide and stepped inside.

Wedel saw the Count first, standing in the open door, upright, hat tucked under his arm, stiff, and red-faced. Wedel turned to the room and announced,

"Count Kospoth." It came out flat, disappointment evident in his voice.

The cavalrymen turned to the door, snapped their heels together, and tucked their elbows to their sides. They still held steins of beer, oysters, and champagne flutes. The gramophone began to play *The Uhlans March* for the tenth time that evening.

Richthofen looked over to Menzke, running the gramophone. Richthofen slashed a finger across his neck. The boy picked the needle up and the room fell silent. Somewhere in the building, a glass smashed and a feminine laugh echoed again.

Richthofen stepped forward. He was broad through the shoulders and neck, thin through the arms. Riding had left his legs a touch bowed, giving the false impression that he was shorter than average. He bore an impish grin that he was trying, and failing, to suppress. Giving up, he instead flashed a broad smile. He reached out a hand to the Count in greeting.

"Count. Welcome. Come in. Join us."

Richthofen waved his arm to a table loaded with dark bread, ice, and oysters. The Count shook Richthofen's hand, not returning the smile.

"Freiherr Richthofen. Leutnant," said the Count stiffly. Kospoth was panting, needing to catch his breath.

The room stayed quiet. Kospoth glanced around. "May I speak with you?"

"Oh, certainly. Of course," replied Richthofen.

With a flourish of his arm, Richthofen mock-ordered his men, "Resume party!" The men returned to their conversations and drinks.

Richthofen swayed from the exertion and beer. He leaned in close to Kospoth, conspiratorially. "Yes, tell me. What may I do for you?" He clipped his sentences, a little drunk.

Kospoth sighed, and then drew himself upright. "Is it true, Leutnant; is it true what I've heard? Are the borders closed, bridges barricaded?"

Richthofen tipped his head quizzically as he pondered an answer. "Well," he paused. "Count. Let me assure you ..." Richthofen placed a hand on the older man's shoulder. "No, let me re-assure you. The border is normal, perfectly fine. Nothing unusual."

Kospoth leaned in, his round pale face flushing darker red. He loomed over Richthofen, his best attempt at menace. "Tell me the truth,

Herr Leutnant."

Richthofen smiled, unbowed. "My dear Count Kospoth, in your position as the Imperial Administrator for the region of Ols, should I have any knowledge of war, I would certainly find it in order to tell you. Moreover, I would have done so. You may rest assured. We are not at war," he lied, confident that the business of soldiers was not the business of politicians.

Kospoth straightened and exhaled, his belly straining against his vest.

"Now then, dear Count, please join us. The champagne and beer are warm, but the oysters are cold. You are welcome to partake." He swept his hand toward the table again, knowing now that his bluff was leading him close to impertinence.

Kospoth would not be easily turned aside. "But the papers, the stories, are all of war!" he hissed, his frustration showing.

"Stories of war, and war, are entirely two different things. Worry and handwringing mean nothing. Worry and reality are two greatly different things, as different as, say, glory and bloodshed." Richthofen laughed aloud now, having crossed the line of insolence, but tiring of the charade.

Kospoth, an instinctive man, knew now. He felt it, and now he knew it. A wave of relief washed over him. The knowledge he could deal with. It was the uncertainty that had left him so anxious. He sighed, the color draining from his face, leaving it its normal ashen pink once more.

"Certainly. I understand." Kospoth glanced at the table and considered it. "Perhaps one oyster and a glass of champagne then."

They stepped to the table, Richthofen, the gracious host. "A drink for my dear friend and mentor, his Excellency Count August von Kospoth, Imperial Administrator!"

A cavalryman snorted and Richthofen stared him down. The man held his laugh before it could escape.

Kospoth and Richthofen raised their glasses. "Zum Wohl! Dear Leutnant."

"Prost, dear Count," Richthofen replied, staring straight into Kospoth's eyes in the German tradition.

The Count leaned in, holding his gaze. "How soon?"

Richthofen's mask of mirth broke. Confusion flashed across his face, then he lifted his chin, looking stolidly at the Count. He released a deep breath like a man emerging from underwater. He touched the Count's elbow and turned to him.

"As soon as tomorrow," he whispered.

~~~

Erich Wedel opened his eyes gently and braced himself for the special kind of pain that followed too many oysters and too much champagne.

It was still dark and starlight filtered through the bare window. He was, however, pleased to be up before dawn and happy that he might be awake earlier than Richthofen. It was good to be ahead of the commander from time to time.

He sat up. His head responded with a hammer blow, and he belched. It tasted like a liquor-soaked cigar. After several valiant attempts to climb out of bed, he relented and dressed himself without standing. Finally, he staggered to his feet, pushed the window open, and stuck his head out to take in fresh air. His head cleared in weakening throbs of pain. At last he stood upright and tried to think.

It was warm enough that he didn't need his jacket. He dragged on his tall riding boots and put on his fatigue cap. He was out of uniform, but in these early hours, he supposed that no one would notice.

Stopping in the kitchen, he picked up a chunk of dark bread and some jam, and walked out to the barn to check on the grooms tending the horses. The boys minded a fire near the barn and were stirring corn and grain into a hot mash to feed the animals.

Wedel stopped and peered into the pot. "Good job; they'll need it today."

A Polish boy looked up at Wedel and smiled, an uncomprehending expression on his face.

"Well, anyway." Wedel patted the boy on the back. Wedel supposed he didn't speak any German. Many of the Poles didn't.

In the barn, other boys were ladling out the mash into troughs. The horses were already moving, pawing the ground as they ate, the grain warming them and filling them with energy.

Wedel watched and chewed on his hunk of black bread. He lifted it up and inspected it to confirm the jam was still there, though he couldn't taste it. He bent his back and pressed his hands into his spine, flexing his muscles, trying to drive out a dull soreness. A memory crept back into his mind: a failed back flip. He'd rotated just far enough to land flat, but high enough to slam his head into the ceiling of the mess hall. Quite a feat in its own right. It had been a wild night.

Wedel tore another hunk from his breakfast and walked into the barn. The ugly smell of horse urine and manure struck him a blow in the doorway, but was strangely calming. Wedel took a German boy by the arm and said, "Be sure Antithesis is turned out and brushed. Comb him and trim his mane and tail."

"Yes, sir," replied the teenager, barely younger than Wedel. He had the eyes and the demeanor of one easily intimidated.

"Do it well, and Leutnant Richthofen will be pleased," said Wedel, bringing a smile to the boy's face.

Wedel pulled down a bridle from the barn wall and walked along the line of feeding horses. Antithesis was easy to spot, black and a head taller than the other horses. The horse recoiled as Wedel stepped in front of him, then lifted his head and rolled his lip; then pulled his ears back and cocked his head.

Wedel reached out and lightly stroked the warhorse's nose. He spoke in soothing tones, "Calm there. Quiet, boy. Gentle." Antithesis bobbed his head, shaking Wedel's hand away, but not backing away from his grain. Wedel pulled back and spoke to the horse in soft tones. "Perhaps you're not ready, perhaps another war. But no race for you today." He turned away from Antithesis and looked around for Santuzza, Richthofen's mare. His eyes rode down the line of horses and couldn't find the chestnut bay. He turned to a Polish teenager and shouted, "Boy, where is Santuzza, the chestnut?"

"Leutnant Richthofen has her; they've gone for a ride." The boy turned back to ladling mash into the troughs.

"Shit," said Wedel.

In the morning twilight, behind the open barn doors, Wedel saw a figure riding, cantering around the arena in loops.

"Oh, I see him."

Wedel strode to the fence surrounding the arena and put his arms on the top rail. He rested his chin, watching the rider and horse turn circles in the dark. He recognized Richthofen's profile, the chestnut horse a nondescript shadow.

Richthofen moved fluidly with the horse. He held his back straight; his chin dipped, his focus on the movement, as though the two were one. He didn't lift his eyes when Wedel jumped the fence and walked over, but instead stopped the horse and spoke to him. "Good morning, Wedel. How did you sleep?"

Wedel swallowed to clear the taste of old champagne and young oysters. "Excellently, Leutnant Richthofen; excellently."

"Glad to hear that, Wedel; you'll need your rest."

"Will it be Santuzza, then?"

"Yes, I think so. Antithesis is stronger but a little unpredictable in the dark. Best to take a known horse."

"Have you examined his teeth, yet?" Wedel tried to remember an old joke, and failed.

"I'm sure my mother did, and I needn't."

Richthofen rode to the wooden rail bounding the arena, pulled Santuzza up and stopped. He dismounted and, after tying the reins to the top rail, yelled for one of the hands to tend to the horse. He felt a stir of displeasure at being interrupted in his morning ride, but couldn't hold it against Wedel. From his coat pocket, he pulled out a carrot, and Santuzza slurped it from his hand and crunched down on it. Then Richthofen leaned close to the horse's ear and whispered something that Wedel couldn't hear. He felt a special affection for the horse, a gift from his mother. A solid jumper, fast and calm, a rare combination. A war horse with heart. Santuzza pressed her neck to Richthofen's head as she bounced her head up and down, noisily chewing the carrot.

Richthofen picked up a brush from the top rail and ran it up through the cropped mane, and then down the sides of Santuzza's neck. After a few moments, a barn hand appeared at Richthofen's side and took the reins to lead the horse to the edge of the arena. Richthofen followed behind.

Wedel watched the curious spectacle of the boy holding the horse while Richthofen unfastened his own saddle and lay it over the rail. Richthofen continued brushing the horse in the half-light, running his hands over Santuzza as he did so, feeling her legs, smoothing the horse's coat, and testing for tenderness or sore spots.

"How is she this morning?"

"Fine, she's in fine shape, recovered from the crash better than I, I'm sure." Richthofen rubbed his mending collar bone, the memory awakening the ache. "Collar bones never seem to heal well; slow and sore."

"Well, Richthofen, if you'd just break it once and leave it be, it would be one thing. Perhaps you should break something else, next time: your skull or your neck or, perhaps, both legs ... ?" Wedel felt loose, comfortable with Richthofen in the dark, away from the men. He grinned at Richthofen and Richthofen glanced back, his mouth in a tight smile, the effort making him appear younger than he was.

"We'll see who breaks what, Wedel. I've seen you jump, remember?" he chided.

"Well, a jump without a horse is one thing now. With a horse, I'm infinitely graceful, aren't I?"

Richthofen rose to the bait. "Perhaps infinitely *grateful* that you don't land on your head with your horse behind you." He grinned again, running his hands over Santuzza's legs. He turned to the groom. "Walk her out, boy, and then cool her, then feed her again. Understand?"

The groom nodded, grunted a Polish word. Richthofen repeated himself and the boy mustered a "Jawohl."

Richthofen sighed, always perplexed by the Poles, so docile and yet so full of energy. They confused him.

"Let's check on the armory, dear Wedel."

Richthofen and Wedel walked back to the brick barracks building, a converted school for boys. Now, it belonged to the Uhlans: German cavalry. It was a Polish word, Uhlans, dating to the Napoleonic wars, the term for Polish light cavalry armed with sabers and fine lances. Richthofen knew this from military school. He didn't bother to mention it to his German troopers; he knew that the Polish troopers knew the truth and were secretly proud.

The men had cleared the library of books, taken the shelves away and gutted the room. A cook filled his empty hours making racks that fit their weapons. Now, along one wall, stood a rack of lances, laid out horizontally. Against the opposite wall stood a rack of carbines. The first sunlight broke through its window.

The lances were medieval in form and function: long, smooth, and sinister. Richthofen pulled a lance from the rack and laid it across a table in the middle of the room. The lance was three meters long, rolled polished steel, hollow, and strangely light. Sharp on both ends and meant for one thing: to run a man through. Richthofen bent and examined the tip. The tip was a sharp point, but the edges were dull and showed bits of rust. He glared up at the young soldat on duty, pointed at the edges and said, "Sharpen this."

The young man had just started in on the carbines, pulling one apart and then reassembling it by gaslight. He set the gun aside and stepped to Richthofen's side, but saying nothing.

Richthofen stood straight and glared at the young man. "Did you hear me, soldat?"

The soldier snapped to attention, his hands at his side. "Jaaah. Jawohl, yes, sir."

"I want each of these sharpened, then polished. Like a razor. I'll send another man to help. I'll be back at the end of the day inspect them, do you understand?"

The boy almost shouted, "Yes sir, but the carbines ..." He gestured to the rack of short rifles. He had barely started on the first one.

"Damn the carbines. We'll be slicing Cossacks by tomorrow morning; there won't be anything left to shoot." Richthofen bent to the lance head and slid a finger along the double-edged blade. "And, I want this sharp enough that they don't feel any pain." He smiled, toothy now.

Wedel winced, the look on Richthofen's face brutish, unsure if Richthofen was acting.

"Wedel, turn out the men and assemble them outside." Richthofen straightened himself and fixed his jacket and cap. "And take care of your uniform."

Wedel glanced down at himself, silently embarrassed.

The men assembled in the courtyard of the school. Wedel called them into line. Behind the troopers was a second line: orderlies, batmen, cooks, and the armorer. Richthofen cleared his throat and addressed them.

"Men of the Third Squadron, First Uhlans, we have orders. We will cross the Prosna this evening and pass over into Russian territory." The reality of what he said washed over the cavalrymen. Some faces grew white; other men tensed their jaws; and a Polish trooper tipped his head, seemingly perplexed.

"Yes, I know what that means. We're no long riding the border, no longer playing at Indians and cowboys." Richthofen paused and gazed out at the young men, at their expressions, ranging from awe to feigned indifference. A Polish boy, Bilik, a stocky blond boy with dark eyes, looked nervously around himself, as if he just realized where he was.

"We're going to close with the Russians, the Cossacks. Remember, this isn't a war against the Poles but a move to free them from the tyranny of the Russians. They will be under the protection of the German empire. We will fight the Russians if they resist and I expect them to do so. Do you have any questions?" He paused, watching their faces. The men stood silently, the reality of the war dawning on them.

"No questions, then?" He paused a brief second more: Nothing. "Very well, here are our orders. Come forward."

They gathered around the table. There were fifteen cavalrymen, Richthofen, and Wedel. Seventeen Uhlans in total.

Richthofen pointed at a map. It was printed on heavy paper, of good quality, but the figures were simple, almost crude, with rivers marked in artless blue lines, and forests in clumps of green circles. What mattered to cavalry was there, though, obstacles, cover, open space. It was a map for men who needed to be in motion and cover to stay alive. "We will depart Ostrowa at midnight and will cross here, on the road bridge, if it is open."

"If the Russians are defending the bridge, we will move to the rail bridge and cross. Should we not be able to cross there, then we move to the south ford, here, and cross the river, wet. Skirting Kalisch we move east, here, at Opatówek, Cienia, and Tłokinia. There we will establish vedettes to screen the city and detect any Russian reinforcement that may be approaching Kalisch from Lodz. If they come, we warn the infantry behind us. The Fifteenth Infantry Regiment under Major Pruesker will occupy Kalisch tomorrow morning. We defeat any Cossack riders that try to interfere. Questions?"

The perplexed Polish trooper, Bilik, cocked his head again. "Herr Leutnant, are we going to invade?" He had heard the lecture so many times about defending against the Russians that he seemed to have never thought about actually crossing the border in the other direction.

Richthofen blanched and gathered his thoughts. "No, we are not going to invade, but yes, we are going to cross the border. We will remove the Russian occupiers from our territory." He was careful to use 'we' to refer to the mixed squadron of Silesian Germans and Poles. "This is as it should be."

Bilik hesitated, more confused. He started to speak, and then stopped himself. He smiled.

"You are amused?" Richthofen asked.

"Why, yes. I've always wanted to invade Kalisch." He beamed.

Richthofen wasn't sure if the boy knew that to take the city meant war with Russia, but then he wasn't even sure if the boy knew the meaning of the word invade. But Bilik rode hard and tended his lance, so Richthofen chose to ignore his ignorance of strategy or, at best, his limited command of German.

He smiled and said, "Very well. We ride tonight. Rest today. See to your horses and equipment." The cavalry men backed away from the map and began to think thoughts of war.

"Expect five days on hard rations. A short pack train with ammunition and equipment will follow. Horses are being fed hot, so let them rest. We'll be riding hard at night. Dismissed."

The men spread out in the courtyard, low conversations starting, as they cast their eyes, nervously, east.

Chapter Three

West of Kalisch, Prussian Frontier
August 1, 1914

The Cossacks blew up the old road bridge at midnight. At that moment, an orange glow appeared on the thin low clouds in the sky east of Ostrowa. Like a flash of lightning from below, it blazed and then faded. From the darkness that returned, a deep, booming thump rolled across the hills and over the Polish villages. Burning pieces of the bridge rained into the river and sizzled as steam rose. On the east bank of the river Prosna, a group of Cossacks mounted their horses, gave their eerie high whooping cheer, and rode off into the gloomy tree line. All grew quiet again in the Polish woods.

So the war began.

The German army sentries on the west bank gathered in the roadway, their lamps extinguished for the first time that any of them remembered. They brushed dust and embers off themselves. A half-moon peered from behind clouds over their heads.

"What shall we do?" a bespectacled Polish conscript asked his sergeant in rough German. It appeared he might cry.

The old infantry Feldwebel stared off across the river, waiting for his night vision to come back and for his ears to stop ringing. His heart was racing, though he'd done nothing more than throw himself behind his guard shack as the Cossacks flung their dynamite, fuses already burning. "Impressive," he mumbled to himself, staring out at the open water, where the bridge had been a couple of moments ago. "I didn't think they could tell time ... let alone do something like that." He scowled as he surveyed the destruction. "Well, boy. Are you a Papist? A bead rattler?"

The Pole flinched, confused. He studied the sergeant and searched his mind for a response, hesitated, not knowing how his German would come out. "I ... Well ... Yes, sir. I am a Catholic."

"Very well, boy, you can pray while you run back to Ostrowa and tell the Uhlan Leutnant that the bridge is blown. Tell him that. Tell him that we are moving to the railroad bridge and we'll try to defend it. Wait for a reply. Then run to the rail bridge and join us. Repeat it back."

"Sir, yes. Tell the Leutnant that the road bridge is gone. Tell him that the guards are on the rail bridge. Wait for instructions. Run back."

"And pray, boy, pray. Now run with you. Go."

The Pole turned and ran, his heavy rifle in one hand and the other holding his felt hat down. His thick canvas pants made him waddle comically in contrast with the moment.

The Feldwebel waved the other guards toward the rail bridge. "Move. Run. Cross it."

Without a word, the border guards turned and ran off down the river path at a trot.

He peered back at the river where the bridge had stood a few minutes ago. "I'd pray, too, if I thought someone other than my mother was listening. I'd pray long and hard." He turned and jogged off behind his men toward the dim silhouette of the rail bridge.

Behind him, the last pieces of the road bridge lurched and collapsed into the dark river.

~~~

The air had finally cooled from the heat of the day, and Richthofen was enjoying the night.

The Uhlans were awaiting orders. A few of the officers had gathered around the flagpoles in the courtyard of the barracks. Hubert Loen, the Leutnant commanding the Second Squadron, had ridden over to visit with Richthofen. When he rode up, the other officers were passing the last of the champagne around. Each man took a deep swallow and then handed it on.

Loen stared into the dark sky and listened to the rumble of the explosion fade away into the trees. Richthofen stood at Loen's side and drank from a champagne bottle, swallowing a big mouthful of the warm, sweet liquid. He'd expected bubbles, but found it flat. He held the bottle up and swirled it. Disappointed, he handed it to Loen. "Here, Loen, finish that. We need to celebrate."

Loen took the bottle, swallowed and then screwed his face into a scowl. "Celebrate what, Herr Richthofen?"

"Our opportunity, of course. Here it is."

"Glory then, Richthofen?"

"Make my uncle proud, and my father. Our adventure, Loen; they had theirs."

"Let's hope that it's not too big of an adventure," said Loen. "How long do you think?"

"A few weeks; maybe a few months."

The sergeant-at-arms, the Uhlans' unteroffizer, approached Richthofen and saluted. He held his sword tight on his hip as he awaited acknowledgement. Richthofen turned to him and returned the salute. "What is it?" he asked.

"Your orders, sir?" The unteroffizer was expectant, knowing the flash meant something big, but he was not a man to act without orders. Richthofen turned and searched the dark eastern horizon with his eyes. He expected more flashes, more lights. He had hoped it would be more dramatic than that. He took a mouthful of champagne and tried to rinse out his mouth. He could still taste dust.

Richthofen thought, *One flash. One explosion. And that's it? So easy.*

Despite the unteroffizer being twice his age, Richthofen didn't hesitate to command him. "Turn the squadron out. Issue arms. Issue rations. Tack the horses. Stand by."

"Jawohl!"

With that, the unteroffizer gave a stiff salute, turned and ran to the barracks. He yelled for the alarm. The young cadet on barracks' watch rang an old fire-alarm bell. In the barracks, the troopers turned their lamps up. Richthofen watched the lamps light the windows in a checkerboard, window by window. Men began to shout short, sharp commands.

Spilling from the barracks, they surged into formations, standing in the light cast from the windows. The sergeant called out the roll of men and then gave them their orders. "Standard load, five days' rations. Ready to ride in fifteen minutes, boys. Move!"

Loen slipped on his white gloves, testing the leather as he pulled them tight over his hands. "Well, Manfred. Have a splendid war. I'm off to my boys." He snapped a salute and extended his hand. Richthofen shook it.

"And you, too, Loen, see you on the other side," he said, as he motioned with his arm in a grand sweep toward the border.

~~~

The cavalry column snaked down the forest path. Horses picked their way, barely managed by their riders. As they passed under branches, each rider would tip his lance; they dipped, seemingly in a wave from one rider, one branch, to the next. Scarlet pennants hung from the shaft of each lance, the cloth triangles black in the night.

For Richthofen, the border became an idea rather than a thing. He imagined he could put his hand up, palm outward and press into the space where it would be, into the place beyond, feel the rough texture of its surface. He knew that behind the border lay uncertainty, smoke, fire, and perhaps blood. At the very least, he felt a sense of strangeness, unfamiliarity; enough to make it feel like an attraction, a place that he was drawn to satisfy his curiosity. He thought, *My opportunity; my brothers and I; here we have our chance to prove ourselves, to bring honor to the family name. We just have to cross.*

On their training rides, he had been able to guide them by the line on the map; he could trace the imagined separation with a finger. Now, though, the space on the other side was anywhere and everywhere. Perhaps they had crossed it; perhaps they were already over the line, the invisible barrier, and now in the other place.

Fear crept into Richthofen's mind. The nighttime was a yawning void, ghostly and uncertain, a vacuum that could close around them and draw them in, never releasing them. He shivered, not cold, tightening the muscles in his belly and trying to think of anything, something that would calm him. He thought, *If I were a boy again, I could hide here, in the dark, safe.* In the column, surrounded by his men, he felt exposed, concerned for their vulnerability and the tender legs and flanks of the horses. The men stood out like mounted targets. The darkness amplified sound, their fears, and the reality of what they were doing.

Richthofen called for a halt, quietly, the whispered order flowing down the column. The Uhlans stopped in place. Wedel rode to Richthofen. Richthofen peered into the murky woods ahead of them, the waxing moon casting shadows under trees. He imagined each shape a man, a lance, a rifle. Richthofen turned to Wedel. "Ride on, it's nothing."

They pressed ahead, generally east, without the hot certainty of the sun in the sky to give them direction. Richthofen drew himself up in the shadows and tightened his grip on his lance. He wanted to feel it, wanted to feel the hard conviction, to feel that they were powerful, but the feeling wouldn't come; he just felt isolated and exposed.

The path gave way to a rutted dusty road. The column spread out, single-file. The horses, without branches to worry them, lifted their heads. German boys led the column, then Wedel and Richthofen, with the five Poles bringing up the rear. The Polish boys were small for their age, farm boys, but more comfortable than most with horses. Their mounts were a mixed lot, varying breeds and coats, greys, mostly; the only thing the horses had in common was their long legs. Regardless of the horse or the man's pedigree, all of Richthofen's men could jump a horse over a fence while holding a sword, lance or carbine, with one hand on the reins.

Richthofen rode along the flank of the column to the lead. As they moved away from the frontier, the risk of ambush decreased. Deciding the extra speed was worth the risk of the noise, he brought the line up to a canter. The hollow sound of the horses' hooves in the dust became a steady bass drum beat. They followed the roadway that led along the southern edge of Kalisch and pressed on. In half an hour, not even an hour since they had crossed the frontier; they crested a rise in the road and peered down on the border city.

Gas lamps lit the streets of the Polish town with a pale yellow light, deepening the shadows between and around the buildings of the town.

It was all so simple, riding into, no, invading, enemy territory, Russian land. Little more than a grand trespass, a bit of mischief, then we ride back, eat oysters, and drink champagne. Well, maybe not this time, perhaps not ever.

Richthofen rode down below the crest of the hill to avoid being silhouetted along it. He surveyed the town. To the south, near the rail yards, something burned, casting long flickering shadows across the buildings there. Nothing else moved save shadows and flames.

The men followed as Richthofen led them off the road into the adjacent fields.

He thought, *If the Cossacks ambush us, I don't want to be on the road where they'll expect us.*

The dry grain crackled around the horses' legs as they rode, the barley already brown from the summer heat. A fine dust rose, bringing with it the smell of dry earth. An occasional stand of trees forced their column to adjust their course and then circle back to parallel the road again. Wedel and Richthofen kept their eyes on the roadbed through the trees, watching for Cossacks or a Russian roadblock.

They passed a crossroad that led south from the Kalisch road. Through the trees, a mansion loomed, a darker void behind a stand of larch, recognizable from the glint of moonlight on its windows. They rode on, the trees thickened and they could smell water, and then hear it; a creek flowed nearby, hidden in the gloom.

Where the woods were thickest, the tree trunks glowed green; forest spirits, the Poles called them. The Poles murmured amongst themselves, upset by the omen. Richthofen turned, rode to the Poles and calmed them, "Quiet now, it's just moss, glowing on the tree trunks. It's nature, boys." The Poles hushed and tried not to look. Richthofen thought of the other name for the moss, Goblin's Gold, but didn't say it.

Superstitious. Like my grandmother. Seeing ghosts and spirits in everyday things. There's plenty to be afraid of without fearing a little plant.

They reached the fringe of the woods south of the city; Richthofen drew them up, halting the column in the last of the forest shadows. To their front, the railroad approached the town from the south and led to the rail station on the edge of the town. At the station, a row of railcars stood burning, the cars already gutted, charred timbers standing starkly upright in the flames. Sparks blew upward and floated over the town.

No one fought the fires.

When he saw the flames clawing though the railcars, unchecked, he knew his own omen in the flickering light. Here was destruction for its own sake, left to run unbridled.

Richthofen rode to Wedel.

"Ride in, past the tracks; I don't want us all in the light at once," whispered Richthofen.

Wedel nodded at Richthofen, his expression masked by the darkness. Then he rode east, angled away from the town, crossed the tracks, and passed south of the railcars. For a few seconds, the flames hurled yellow light against him, throwing the shadow of a giant horse and rider on the distant trees. Wedel disappeared into the far darkness.

Richthofen watched after him, felt heat in his belly, like he might throw up. He pulled out his canteen and rinsed out his mouth.

Wedel, don't meet a Cossack out there; don't be murdered, killed ... which is it? We're at war ... it's not murder ... is it?

In a few minutes, a figure emerged from beyond the burning cars, and then rode into the light of the flames: Wedel. He trotted toward the Uhlans, not seeing them, orienting off the woods and the angle of the railroad tracks. As he came closer, Richthofen rode out, signaling to him.

"No one there, Leutnant," Wedel said, his voice just above a whisper.

"Very well. Let's move, shall we?" Richthofen turned in the saddle, gave two short whistles. The column moved from the forest, materializing from the darkness under the trees, in line abreast, with their lances tipped down. Flames reflected off the polished steel, making them seem to twinkle. Quietly, they maneuvered into a column of twos and rode toward Wedel and Richthofen.

Behind them and on the road, Loen's column of cavalry appeared. Loen rode into the light from the flames and waved to Richthofen; then he led his men into the town toward the tall spire of a church.

Richthofen motioned his men along, and his column passed the burning rail cars at a walk. All eyes were on the darkness to the south, instinctively knowing that was where trouble might emerge, where their nightmares of Cossacks and sabers could turn rapidly real. Like boys at a game, they whispered taunts at one another to hide their fear.

Wedel rode close to Richthofen and whispered. "You do suppose we came to the right war, right? Aren't there supposed to be Russians? Bloodthirsty Cossacks?"

Richthofen frowned at Wedel in the dark.

"Dunderhead."

Wedel reined over and grinned, then rode to the back of the column.

The column moved along the outskirts of Kalisch, and onto the forest road east of the city. They rode quickly, galloping, needing to make up time and be in their places before first light.

They were the first German pawns moved on the chessboard of the Great War.

At a junction in the road, Richthofen split his squadron into three. He sent a troop to the south toward Szałe and another troop along the northern route to Tłokinia. He led the third troop east.

"Close up, boys," he whispered. "No straggling. I don't want you out here by yourselves."

Richthofen reformed his remaining seven troopers into columns of twos. He led at the head of one column, Wedel in the rear, and they rode east. Through the trees, in the moonlight, the dim rectangles of buildings materialized.

Richthofen halted the column and rode ahead. At the town of Opatówek he stopped and nudged Santuzza to a fence along the road. He stopped and listened. It was the early hours of the morning, too early even for farmers. Silence cloaked the town.

Somewhere a horse nickered and then a dog barked. Then the dog barked violently. Richthofen waited for a few more minutes for the dog to quiet, dismounted, and led Santuzza, hugging the darkness under the trees, moving from shadow to shadow into the village. Nothing stirred. Beyond a line of rough wooden buildings rose a church steeple. Satisfied, he rode back to the troop.

"Forward, on me. Dismount," he ordered. The troop gathered around him, with Wedel at the rear of the group. Richthofen said, "Follow me into the village. Once we're in, lead the horses to the church in small groups and gather there. If we're challenged, walk away until you can mount. If we're fired on, lead your horse to cover, then rally here." He tried to read the shadowed faces; some men nodded, and others stared down the road into the darkness.

The troop mounted behind Richthofen and they rode to a barn on the fringe of the town. Once out of sight, they dismounted. Then Richthofen pointed at the church and sent them off at intervals, each man leading his horse. The first three disappeared into the darkness.

Suddenly, vicious barking spilled over the town, the deep, angry baying of a guard dog. Richthofen grimaced and held the other riders back, bunched up in the shadows.

The barking ended with a howl, followed by sudden silence. Richthofen couldn't hear the troopers' horses and motioned the others to stay in place. He leaned to Wedel and whispered, "Hold them here. If you hear anything unusual, take them to the rally point and I'll join you."

Richthofen dismounted and led Santuzza into the streets. He guided the horse through the shadows until he reached a trooper mounted in the middle of the road. The trooper gazed intently toward the church.

"What's happened here?" asked Richthofen.

"Herr Leutnant, I don't know. Just barking and then nothing."

"Check behind and around you," Richthofen scolded him in a hiss. "Dismount and stay behind me ten paces, but keep me in sight. If I stop, find some cover and wait."

Richthofen moved again, and, in a few meters found another trooper, hiding in an alley, watching the church. Richthofen led the two troopers forward. In the middle of the road, he could see the dim outline of a horse and a man. A formless shape lay on the ground. Richthofen halted, and the troopers behind him led their horses into the shadows.

A hoarse whisper came from the figure in the road. "Leutnant?"

Richthofen moved toward the man, his eyes moving constantly into the gloom around the buildings. Even at this hour, the village was unnaturally quiet as though abandoned or ... waiting to ambush. The thought made Richthofen tense; he worked his jaw against itself. The town ached with silence. He stopped at the trooper and looked down at the shape.

The body of a dog lay there: a big hound, square head, with a wide jaw gaped open. The trooper's lance ran through the dog's mouth and erupted out the back of the animal. The dog's blood was a black pool around the carcass, creeping through the cracks of the cobblestones.

Sharp, thought Richthofen.

Richthofen whispered, "Good work. Retrieve your lance; take the body out of the village and dump it. Don't bother hiding it. Hack its throat out; it may appear it was a wolf attack. Tell Wedel to send the rest of the men one at a time." Richthofen looked to the church, a bare hundred meters further.

Almost there, he thought.

The trooper knelt and pulled his lance free with a sickening butcher sound. He threw a short lead around the animal's feet and drug it away.

Richthofen led his few troopers on foot, each man leading his horse behind him. The clash of hooves on cobblestones rang through the town, putting the troop on edge. Richthofen moved to the church gate and tried it; it opened outward and creaked loudly. He tied it open and listened. After a few moments, he handed the reins of Santuzza and his lance to a trooper and then walked into the shadows of the inner courtyard of the church. He moved along the inner wall, brushing against thick ivy, to the door of the rectory. He listened again. Someone was snoring through an open window.

Richthofen tried the door and it swung open into an inky interior. He drew his curved saber, and pushed the door wide. He followed the sound of snoring to an inner door. By the faint light of the half-moon through an open window, he could see a big man, mouth agape, snoring, his dark beard spread over the bed sheets drawn under his chin. He stirred in his sleep as Richthofen slipped to the side of the bed. He lifted his saber up to his shoulder and, at the last moment, flipped it around, and slammed the butt end into the forehead of the sleeping priest.

The man clutched his hands to his head and groaned. He sat up and stared around, blood streaming down his face. Richthofen clamped a hand over the man's mouth.

"Shhh." Richthofen put a finger to his lips.

The priest dropped his hands to the bedclothes and gaped at the specter holding a glinting saber over his face. He instinctively nodded and bit down on his lip to silence himself.

Richthofen motioned him up with the saber, threw the man's dressing gown over and waited for him to put it on. He prodded him out into the courtyard. Three troopers had gathered and watched, silent, appraising the cleric. One of them mumbled derisively, "A pope".

Richthofen stationed a trooper in the thick ivy next to the gate, his back against the ancient brick wall, the plants drawn around him. "Guard here. Send the other troopers in."

The men gathered in the courtyard and tied their horses off against a rail. Richthofen joined his men.

"The priest and one trooper into the bell tower, first watch. One sentry on the courtyard gate; on the inside, hidden from the street but where you can see it. The rest of you, listen closely. We need a hole in the wall." He pointed to the wall near the rectory, away from the street, out of sight of the gate. "Right there. Big enough for a horse to pass. Make it silently; scratch it out if you have to." Beyond the far wall was a field, a road, and a small house with a barn. "That's our way out. Otherwise, we're rats in a trap here."

Richthofen led the priest and his biggest trooper to the bell tower. Wedel trailed behind, curious. Richthofen pointed at the priest, and then to the ladder. The priest stared back at him, dumbfounded. He mouthed a protest and then glanced down at a drawn saber. He cast his eyes up the ladder and, sullenly, began to climb.

Richthofen handed a bucket to the soldier. Then, a length of rope and a leather pouch of water. "There's a rock in the bucket. Don't shout. Drop the rock from the tower onto the woodbin if you see anything, and we'll hear it. We'll bring the ladder back in eight hours. Tie the pope up. If he shouts, kill him. Understand?"

The trooper took the bucket and water and began to climb one-handed. Behind him, Richthofen smiled. "Good man," he said to the darkness.

Wedel grinned. "So, Richthofen, cops and robbers, now?" Richthofen pulled the ladder away and laid it on the ground.

"No, Wedel. Cavalry and Indians. And we might well be ..." he searched for the name. "Custer."

Wedel thought the analogy over for a moment, then joined the troopers at the back wall, scraping out the ancient mortar between the stones. "Dig faster, you louses," he whispered. As each stone came loose, they pulled it away and added it to the pile in the shadows under the wall of the bell tower. "Good. Stay quiet, boys."

Richthofen re-entered the rectory and walked the quiet halls once more, peering into each room. Confident the building was empty; he entered the priest's bedroom and pulled the covers up over the bed. Outside, a toppled lance clanged to the ground. Whispered curses reached through the window. He listened, waiting for the silence to return. Soon the sole sound was the scraping of the troopers, digging at the courtyard wall. He kept his boots and saber on as he lay down on the bed, folded his hands over his chest, and fell into a deep, dreamless sleep.

Chapter Four

Schwerin, Germany
August 2, 1914

The morning sun was high in the sky when Fokker slid down the stairs, holding his robe closed with one hand, barely awake. Frau Grabitz turned the corner at the bottom step and yelled, "Herr Fokker, I'm leaving. You can find your own breakfast!" She looked up and was startled to see Fokker paused above her. She frowned disapprovingly. "Oh, sorry, Anton, I'm just off to church, and the morning is getting late." She tried to sound contrite, but it came out as impatience.

"Thank you, Frau Grabitz. I'll find my breakfast," said Fokker. He resumed sliding down the stairs, his feet slipping from one step to the next. Zeiten, Fokker's dachshund, jumped down, staying just behind. He peeped up at Fokker expectantly as his master paused on each step.

Finally finishing his descent, Fokker lurched into the kitchen and poured himself a cup of coffee. He turned around and, with a start, noticed de Waal sitting at the table with just his fingers visible on the edges of a newspaper. Cuckoo sat on a cupboard next to his shoulder.

"May I borrow some paper, Bernhard?" asked Fokker.

De Waal peered around the newspaper at Fokker and scowled. "Is that really necessary?" he asked.

"Absolutely, Zeiten gets sad and confused if he doesn't get his daily spanking." Fokker glanced down at his dog, who wagged his tail in happy anticipation.

"If you must, Anton," said de Waal. He pushed a section of newspaper across the table.

Fokker rolled the paper up as the dog gazed up at him. Fokker whacked Zieten across the rump, and he tipped his head to the side and wagged his tail harder. Fokker slid the newspaper back across the table, took a sip of his coffee, and scratched Zeiten behind the ears.

Strange dog, thought Fokker.

"Any news?" asked Fokker.

"Other than there being a war on?" asked de Waal. He retrieved the paper once more, peering at Fokker before propping it up like a shield.

"Well, yes, other than that," said Fokker.

"No, not really. Russians invading in the east; French invading France, or something like that. Germans might cross into Luxembourg and Belgium, violating their neutrality. Nothing noteworthy," said de Waal. "Tell me, again, why are we here?"

"Always the optimist then, Bernhard," said Fokker.

De Waal set down his paper and picked up a piece of toast. He tore off a corner and handed it to his monkey. "Here you go, Cuckoo," he said.

Cuckoo reached out with one hand, took the toast, and took a bite. He chewed on it thoughtfully while curiously examining Fokker.

"Your monkey gives me the creeps, Bernhard," said Fokker. "You do know that Cuckoo means 'stupid person,' don't you? I have two problems with that name ... he's not a person ... and, I don't think he's stupid." Fokker studied the monkey and Cuckoo stared back, unblinking. "Frankly, he worries me."

"Oh, Fokker, you fret," said Bernhard. He reached out as though to pet the monkey and Cuckoo pushed his fingers away without looking. "You're the one with the masochistic dog; does Zeiten know any other tricks, huh?"

"Just the trick where he protects me from your monkey. Have you seen that one?" said Fokker.

"No, Fokker, I haven't. I'd have to see it to believe it," said de Waal. "Here, this came for you." De Waal slid a telegram envelope across the table. "Might be important."

"Oh lord. Do you mind?" Fokker snatched up the telegram. "It 'might be important'?"

"Oh no, I don't mind at all," said de Waal with a smile. He picked up his paper and kept reading. "Fokker, are you sure you can't start drinking? Maybe you should. You're somewhat hard to get along with in the morning. And you come down the stairs like a little kid who doesn't want to go to school."

Fokker scowled at de Waal, tore the envelope open, and laid the telegram out on the table. He took a sip of coffee as he read. He made a choking sound and sprayed coffee across the room. De Waal picked up a napkin and wiped his face, then handed it to Cuckoo, who did the same.

"Fokker, you're an ass," de Waal grumbled.

Fokker leapt to his feet and wiped his face with the sleeve of his robe. "What time is it?" he yelled.

"I don't know, nine or so, I guess," answered de Waal. "It's a Sunday, for God's sake, what's the matter with you?"

"Geertz is coming to see me about the factory. At nine, this morning, dumbass!" shouted Fokker.

"Oh," came the reply. De Waal resumed reading, disinterested.

"I'm not going there alone, Bernhard. Get yourself moving!"

De Waal peered around the paper.

"Oh, alright." De Waal laid his paper down and handed Cuckoo the rest of his toast. The monkey spread his lips wide, baring his teeth, and hissed at Fokker. Resigned to Fokker's demands, de Waal slowly scratched Cuckoo's ears and then stood up and walked from the room. Fokker and Zeiten trailed behind him, Fokker slightly smug in his little victory.

Like a grumpy old man, Cuckoo sat and watched them go, eating his breakfast.

~~~

Fokker and de Waal walked to Fokker's offices; Fokker's typically ungainly gait was brisk, excited at the meeting, de Waal trailed, anxious to get the errand over with. Zeiten waddled behind. Fokker put the key in the door and turned it, but found it unlocked. Fokker glanced at de Waal with an expression bordering on panic. "Good lord," he whined. De Waal shrugged.

They stepped into the long hallway. The building was dark and still, everyone off for the day. Fokker turned on lights and opened windows, letting morning air enter the stuffy building. Then they walked down the short hallway to Fokker's office and opened the outer door. Fokker gave out a yelp, and Zeiten barked once, then hid behind Fokker. A man sat waiting in a chair, facing Fokker's desk, his back to the door, in the dark. Fokker cautiously walked around the desk, watching the figure.

"Good Morning, Herr Fokker."

It was Geertz.

"Geertz, you scared the devil out of me," said Fokker.

De Waal stood in the doorway, leaning against the door jam, with his arms crossed. He smiled at Fokker and gave a sound like a laugh, then stopped himself, covering his mouth with his hand.

"I didn't know you had a key," said Fokker.

"There's a war on," Geertz said simply.

"What?" Fokker wasn't sure what to think. For a quick moment, he thought of every soldier in Germany being issued keys at the first sign of war. "What does that have to do with my door?"

"Sit down, Herr Fokker. And, come in and sit down would you, Herr de Waal? Don't just stand there behind me. We Germans do not appreciate discourtesy."

De Waal drew up a chair next to Fokker's desk and sat, facing Geertz. "Good morning, Herr Geertz."

"That's better," said Geertz as he sized up de Waal. "How old are you, de Waal?"

"Twenty-three."

Geertz considered his answer before turning away from de Waal. "Fokker, is it a requirement that no one at your factory be older than thirty? It's hard enough explaining you. You look like you're fifteen."

Fokker cocked his head and opened a drawer. He rolled out a drawing of an aeroplane wing out on the desk and picked up a pencil. "So, we're meeting on a Sunday morning to discuss my age?" asked Fokker. He examined the drawing and began making notes on one edge.

"Fokker, I have some news for you." Geertz's voice was low and direct, all humor gone from it.

Fokker recognized the tone. He set his pencil down. "Herr Geertz, you have my attention."

"I'm glad you're sitting down," said Geertz. He paused. With an exaggerated motion, he took out his monocle and a handkerchief and polished the glass. "As of this moment, your factory is under the control of the Reich Armaments Ministry."

Fokker was a stone, though he wondered absently if all German officers learned to polish monocles in officer school. "I see," he said.

It was de Waal who jumped up. "You can't do that!" he shouted. He glared at Fokker. "He can't do that!" He stabbed a finger at Geertz.

"Sit down, Bernhard," Fokker said with seemingly infinite calm.

De Waal remained standing, his eyes darting back and forth between the two men.

Fokker motioned de Waal to sit. Finally, de Waal did, his mouth still moving, but with no sound coming out.

"May I continue?" asked Geertz.

"Yes, please do," said Fokker.

"Your factory's production will now be determined by the Armaments Ministry. All goods are subject to disposition as the Ministry sees fit. I need, immediately, a list of all aircraft and aircraft engines that you can deliver in the next twenty-four hours. In two days, you will attend a conference in Berlin to receive further instructions."

Geertz put his monocle back in his eye and screwed it into place. "Any questions, Herr Fokker?"

De Waal twisted his head around and stared at Geertz. His mouth hung open.

A range of emotions crossed Fokker's face; anger, confusion, irritation, an expression of awareness and finally, a calm complacence.

He spoke. "Just one question: do you actually need that monocle, or do you wear it for fashion?"

Geertz was astounded, then his mouth dropped open, and he began to stammer. "I ... I ... you ..."

De Waal cast an incredulous look at Fokker. Down the hall, a door slammed and the clomping of heavy boots thumped through the building.

The three men all turned as an enormous man, clad in the black uniform of the navy, gold braid over one shoulder, appeared in the doorframe. He turned sideways to enter and marched on Geertz. Geertz leapt to attention.

"Kapitän-zur-See Huffman," the man barked. "I am here to see ..." he pulled a piece of paper out of his pocket, unfolded it, read it, refolded it, and slipped it back into his pocket. "Anton Fokker." Huffman glanced at Geertz. "As you were, Hauptmann," he said.

Huffman glanced back down the empty hallway, then back at Fokker. He pursed his lips in confusion. "Please inform Herr Fokker that I am here," he said.

Fokker glanced at his drawing and picked his pencil up again. "I am Anton Fokker."

"Your father, then," said Huffman.

"My father, unfortunately, is in Holland at the moment, perhaps you can give me a message and I'll pass it along," said Fokker. He smiled.

Huffman wasn't dissuaded. "Please inform Herr Fokker that the Kriegsmarine requires immediate access to all Fokker aircraft."

"Oh, you wish to discuss the Fokker factory! Then, you wish to speak with ... me," said Fokker, feigning surprise. He stood and extended his hand. Huffman, without thinking, reached out and shook it.

"Bernhard, please get the Kapitän a chair, would you?" said Fokker. De Waal, still speechless, stood and pulled over a chair, then sat back down and folded his arms.

"Oh, excuse me. Let me introduce my colleagues. Bernhard de Waal is our head of flight training." Fokker swept his hand toward de Waal in a grand motion. "And, Hauptmann Geertz is the Fokker factory's army liaison."

Huffman peered at the other men, confusion frozen on his face. Geertz took his monocle out of his eye and put it into his pocket.

"We seem to suddenly have much to discuss," Fokker said.

Geertz scowled at Fokker. Fokker merely smiled back and said, "Oh! Well. Perhaps we should leave the two of you alone. Come, Bernhard."

De Waal stood automatically, far beyond thinking for himself.

"Yes, Fokker, that sounds fine," said Geertz, through clenched teeth.

Fokker motioned de Waal out the door and followed close behind.

As the two men walked, de Waal took Fokker by the arm and led him down the hallway. "What on earth! They can't do that, can they?"

"Yes, I think they can. Well, mostly, they can," said Fokker.

"Mostly?" said de Waal.

"Well, generally speaking," said Fokker.

"What?"

Through the office door, they could hear Geertz's and Huffman's voices rising.

"Just a moment, will you?" said Fokker. He walked back to his office door, knocked and then gently swung the door open. Geertz and Huffman immediately became silent and glared at him.

"We're going to step out for a coffee and pastry while you're ... talking," said Fokker. "Would you like anything?"

Geertz rolled his eyes to Huffman, who said, "No, Herr Fokker, thank you".

Fokker nodded his head to Geertz in a silent, insolent question. Geertz, with murder in his eyes, silently shook his head 'no'.

"Okay, then. I'll be right back," said Fokker pleasantly. He pulled the door closed. He turned and walked back down the hall, Zeiten trailing behind. Fokker began humming to himself. De Waal stared at Fokker's back in astonishment, and then rushed to catch up.

"Fokker!" He grabbed Fokker's shoulder, turning him. "Anton. What is the meaning of this?"

A look of calculation passed over Fokker's face, then, "The meaning? Aaah, the meaning. Well, it means we're going to have to hire a lot of people. Yes, quite a few I would think. Yes, many. And we'll need new engines. And welders. Lots of welders." Then Fokker smiled.

"What?" De Waal was exasperated. "I mean, what is the meaning of ... of that!" He pointed at the closed door. From behind it, they could hear Geertz and Huffman shouting at each other.

"Oh, that. That means I'm going to be rich."

Chapter Five

Opatówek, Western Prussia
August 4, 1914

Each day, just at first light, Richthofen would choose one trooper, and that trooper would ride west to carry a report to the Uhlans' regimental commander. Richthofen walked down the line, pretending to ponder the decision. He would make up a way of choosing each day. Who's the youngest? Who's the oldest? Even: who's the worst rider? Each time, one trooper raised his hand. Their original seven had become four.

This had gone on for three days, and Richthofen's Uhlans stayed inside the church. They watched the roads and fields from the bell tower, expecting Russian infantry or Cossacks to appear from the east at any time. They kept one horse saddled and the rest fed and watered, ready to move. Before dawn and at twilight each day, they would take their horses through the hole in the wall, into the field, and walk them in circles to stretch their legs.

The village remained quiet. It seemed the inhabitants had chosen to hide themselves as well, appearing in the mornings to hastily go to the baker, tend livestock, or gossip. By noon each day, the streets were deserted, and the Uhlans were left to watch the wind blow, and the occasional stray dog wander by.

On the morning of the fourth day, smoke appeared in the direction of Kalisch. A gray plume rose, a vertical column in the still late summer air; it thickened and flattened out in the sky before cutting across with the easterly breeze. The troopers could merely watch, curious.

Richthofen watched the smoke thicken and billow.

Strange. The city is on fire. How could that be?

The men soundlessly gathered in the gloomy courtyard for their morning ritual. Richthofen drew Menzke aside.

"Do you know what the smoke means, Menzke?" asked Richthofen.

"No, sir, I don't," said Menzke. He turned and looked over the church wall at the plume hovering over the horizon, the morning sun beginning to turn it to a pale rose. He turned back with confusion on his face.

"I'll tell you a secret ... neither do I. I'm going to keep Bilik here; I need someone who speaks Polish. You'll be leaving. Understand?" Menzke nodded his head.

"Don't be afraid, Menzke, just keep moving; you'll be riding out today." Richthofen patted the boy's shoulder. "Get off the roads if you have to and don't ride through town ... just in case."

"But, sir, what could it be?"

"It could be Russians; probably is, but you're better off riding than sitting here with the rest of us."

"Yes, sir, I'll ride fast."

Menzke retrieved his saddle and threw it on his horse as the remaining troopers gazed on in disappointment.

Richthofen turned back to his men. "Don't worry, you'll get your turn to ride out of here," he said. *One way or another.*

"Dismissed. Get out of the sun."

Menzke and Richthofen led his horse through the gap in the stone. In the open field beyond, Menzke mounted his horse. Richthofen handed Menzke the daily report and he tucked it into his coat. With an exchange of salutes, Menzke rode west through the field. At the far edge, he stopped and glanced back once, then waved and disappeared into the trees.

Richthofen looked to the smoke. *That certainly isn't good for anyone.*

The morning wore on, and the gray plume from Kalisch wrung the blue from the sky. The heat grew and drained the energy of Richthofen and his last three men. They huddled, idle in the hot acrid shade around the church.

In the early afternoon, Richthofen, Wedel, and Bilik were dozing, when a thrown rock hit the woodbin with a hollow knock. Richthofen pushed his cap off his eyes and peered up at the bell tower. The sentry peered over the side and waved frantically at Richthofen. When the trooper saw that Richthofen had stirred, he disappeared back behind the ledge.

Wedel and Richthofen placed the ladder and climbed the tower. At the top, Richthofen glanced down at the bound priest. He lay on one side, seeming to doze in the heat. He stirred and glared up through bloodshot eyes at Richthofen.

Richthofen joined the sentry and crouched below the rim of the bell tower window. "What is it?" he asked.

"There, in the trees to the west, there are people coming. Walking." The man pointed.

Richthofen nervously scanned the haze, east across the fields, down the road toward the Russian stronghold at Lodz. Nothing moved except shimmers of heat. He stood in the shadow of the bell, then looked west and watched them come. It was rabble, civilians, apparently. A few hundred, perhaps a thousand, walking, no horses. A few pushcarts and wagons, pulled by men, carried children and the elderly. Shutters opened as the villagers stepped out and began mixing with the new arrivals.

Somewhere, a long, mournful wail went up, loud enough to quiet the crowd. Then low conversations began again, a soft sad murmuring.

The villagers moved about with loaves of bread, bottles of milk, cheese in great wheels, and sausages, pressing them into the hands of the shocked throng. The refugees gathered in clumps around the village wells, filled what containers they had, and then kept moving. All the while, the villagers waved their arms, pointing east, toward the spire from where Richthofen peered down.

Richthofen watched them point at the church, at *him*. *Well,* he thought, *I guess they know we're here.* He felt foolish and exposed.

The surge of humanity moved through the town, scattering through side streets and alleys. As they reached the walls of the church, they grew quiet, shushing one another, softly trudging past the buildings as though someone were sleeping within. An occasional chattering child or the sobs of a woman broke the silence. Richthofen could hear their quiet conversations resume as they moved past. Soon they began to pass through the village and then beyond onto the road toward Lodz.

Richthofen looked west at the tower of smoke again. The air was still and Kalisch was eight kilometers away, but the fumes gradually spread and filled the sky in every direction. He could smell it now: wood, tar, and the sharp note of burned flesh. Richthofen was mystified by the smoke behind them, to the west, not where the Russians should be.

Has a battle been fought and we didn't know it? Or worse, did the Russians get past us and attack Kalisch? Have we failed? Richthofen slumped against the wall of the tower and waved Wedel over to him. Wedel sat, still groggy from the hot mid-afternoon nap.

"What is happening, Richthofen?" asked Wedel.

Richthofen shrugged, tried to appear disinterested. He nodded his head, as though thinking.

"Climb down and get Bilik, will you? Send him up." It was a request rather than an order.

Richthofen eyed the priest and then gestured to the trooper standing watch in the shadow of the column, his attention focused west. "Untie him, kavallerist."

The cavalryman cocked his head, confused.

"You heard me," said Richthofen.

After a few moments, trooper Bilik appeared at the top of the ladder. Richthofen waved the boy over, inviting him to sit on the floor of the upper tower. Bilik sat in the shadow of the bell across from the priest. The priest studied them and rubbed at the bites of the ropes around his wrists.

Richthofen handed the priest the leather bag of water. "Drink," he said. This was an order.

The Polish trooper scanned back and forth between Richthofen and the priest. From the street rose the crunching of rolling wagons and shuffling. He had heard the people streaming by but had remained hidden.

Richthofen turned to Bilik. "The pope here is going to do us a service. He's to go down into the crowd below and find out what's going on. He's to do that and return. If he does not, there will be grave consequences. Understand?"

Bilik nodded. He swallowed hard. He turned to the priest and bowed his head as he spoke in Polish. The tone of his voice sounded sympathetic. The priest watched Richthofen as Bilik repeated the instructions. After Bilik had finished, the priest took another long drink, stroked his beard, and splashed some water over his face. His actions were slow and methodical, almost ritual-like. Richthofen thought of baptism.

The priest spoke a word or two to Bilik, his eyes remaining fixed on Richthofen. The trooper turned to Richthofen. "He says that he will do it."

Richthofen nodded. "You go down first, then. And gather a carbine."

Bilik climbed down, and Richthofen pointed the priest to the ladder. He spoke to the trooper on watch. "Be sure to watch the east, too, now and again, would you?" The trooper's face flushed at the jibe, insulted. Richthofen climbed down.

Bilik and the priest stood at the bottom of the ladder. Bilik had a carbine in one hand and gripped the priest's arm with the other. Richthofen took the carbine, opened the action, and chambered a round. Pointing up at the tower, he then raised the carbine to sight down its length. He glanced at the priest, and the priest looked back, impassively, then nodded. The meaning was clear: *we will shoot you.*

"Tell him that he has one minute. No more," said Richthofen

Bilik spoke to the priest, who nodded again.

Richthofen sent Bilik up the tower with the carbine. He led the priest to the outer door of the rectory and held him. Richthofen showed the priest his pocket watch, then held up one finger. Then he opened the door and pushed the man out, closing the door behind him.

Richthofen examined the watch and pulled the curtain aside. Outside, the priest spoke to a man in the crowd. He put a paternal hand on the refugee's arm as they spoke. After a moment, the priest glanced back at the window in the rectory and then turned back to the man. Together, they knelt and prayed together. The minute passed. The man remained on his knees, and the priest remained bowed, speaking gently. Behind them, the crowd of people continued to flow by.

At last, the priest motioned the man to his feet and waved towards the east. The man rose, turned, and continued on his way. The priest turned to the rectory door and stepped inside. At the foot of the ladder, they met

Bilik coming down. The priest spoke in a gush of words, more words than he had spoken in the entire time they had been there. Bilik stood, his face flushed, muttering in Polish.

At last the priest stopped, waiting. He blinked at Bilik and then at Richthofen.

"Well?" asked Richthofen impatiently. He took the carbine from the trooper's hands and cleared the round from the chamber.

Bilik sighed deeply. "He says that Kalisch is burning."

"I know that. Ask him why it is burning."

The trooper turned to the priest and spoke a single Polish word: "Czemu?"

The priest raised his head and gazed, with wide bloodshot eyes, at Richthofen. He blinked, his eyes piercing. He raised one hand and pointed a dirty finger at him, saying nothing.

~~~

After another day passed, Richthofen sent the last German trooper west with the daily report. Now, everything simmered under a gray smoky sky. Clouds merged with the smoke from Kalisch at dusk, trapping the heat and moisture over the countryside, making the air thick and oppressive. The day turned to a night that was sweltering and sticky, and filled with the raw hot smell of burning wood.

Richthofen dreamt of insects, strange human-like insects, kept in cages. People would come and taunt them, sometimes fawn over them. The people-insects would be let out to scuttle about only to be put back in their cages shortly after. Their keepers fed the people-insects scraps of metal and shiny fabric. Richthofen woke with a sense of dread, feeling queasy and a little sick. He drifted back into a poorer, restless sleep.

He dreamt then, of the mass of civilians streaming through the town, dreamt that they walked through the church, through the halls of the rectory, that they stared down at him with black, inhuman eyes.

Richthofen woke abruptly, knowing something was wrong, but not knowing why; he lay frozen in place on the bed waiting for his mind to arrive where his instincts already were. Listening, he held still, trying to discern what had changed around him. The smell of smoke was gone.

Outside the window, he could hear a gentle murmuring, and it took a moment for him to recognize the sound: rain. It had been a long time since he'd heard it. Beyond the drizzle, there was some other sound, like the murmur of the refugees, a distant muttering.

Then Richthofen heard a hoarse shout in a strange language: it wasn't German or Russian or Polish. Startled, he rolled off the bed and fell onto the floor, knocking his wind out with a bright flash of pain. A dark figure appeared in the doorway.

"Richthofen?" It was Wedel.

"Yes?" Richthofen gasped from the floor.

"We have company."

Richthofen pulled himself back onto the bed, and tugged on his boots. "Where?" he asked.

"Close. Very close. In the village," replied Wedel.

Now, just Richthofen, Wedel, and Bilik remained. Richthofen examined Wedel, faintly lit from the window. Wedel had dressed, his traditional tall cavalry cap, his *czapka* tucked under his arm. Richthofen smiled and thought, *Wedel would be ready.*

Dressing by feel in the dark, Richthofen stood and pulled his suspenders up. He put on his gray-green double-breasted coat, his kurta, and worked the buttons hastily. The heavy canvas felt dull and rough under his fingers, and smelled stale as though mold had crept in. He pressed the stiff material flat, and then buttoned the thick canvas of his plastron over his coat, covering his chest.

It was a different feeling, a finality that settled on him, dressing in the dark. He sensed a crackling in the air, an electric tension. His motions were deliberate, unconsciously intended to be perfect and efficient.

Battle? Are they here? Combat.

He knew what the sensation was, it was of leaving. He knew their time was done and they needed to be in motion. Bugs swept into the light. Everything mattered, every thought crystalized into motion. A single mistake could be the end of him, them, of everything. His mind cleared and all was simple and deliberate, but quick.

A hard spasm hit his stomach and he thought he might wretch.

Bending over quickly, he willed the pain away. When he sat up again he glanced at Wedel, and was thankful the darkness hid his expression. A taste like salt and copper filled his mouth.

Standing, he pulled his black cloak over his shoulders and took up his *czapka*, the distinctive round, hard helmet of the Uhlans, adorned shiny black leather and gold trim, merely suitable for a parade ground now. The army had mandated that they cover the shine of their *czapkas* with grey fabric, giving the once-distinctive head gear the appearance of a lump of cloth.

Richthofen and Wedel moved to the rectory door that led to the street and barred it with furniture. Then, they noiselessly moved to the inner courtyard. They could hear murmuring and the clopping of horses in the street, just beyond the walls.

Bilik was saddling the horses in the blackness. Wedel and Richthofen joined him and, together, they finished the job without speaking.

Richthofen whispered to Bilik, "What did you see?"

"Cossacks. Twenty or so. They are riding through town. They seem to be searching."

Richthofen nodded and smiled, needing Bilik's loyalty more than ever now. "Very good. Let's get you out of here, shall we?"

They slowly led the horses to the breach in the wall into the field beyond. The rain was light, alternately fading and then condensing back into a steady downpour. The heat from the ground made the moisture rise in a haze, shrouding the village in mist. Richthofen glanced back at their temporary home and, after a few meters of walking, the church disappeared in the fog and darkness. Richthofen felt an odd feeling of safety in the open, with only dark haze all directions. The shadows felt like a cloak, a blankness into which they could disappear.

He turned to Wedel. "Wait here. I'll go see after our visitors. If I'm not back ... well, the usual."

"I understand, Richthofen. Ride like hell." Wedel sounded as if he might laugh. "Cops and robbers, *now?*"

Richthofen could see the bright grin on Wedel's face, despite the gloom, and smiled back. He handed Santuzza's reins to him.

"Take care of her, too. She wouldn't like a Cossack on her back."

Stroking the side of Santuzza's head, he murmured to the horse and then pressed his head against hers. Santuzza seemed to calm, planting her feet, and leaning into him. Richthofen patted her flank and then moved away into the murk.

Richthofen headed back in the direction of the church until he could see the black space: the breach in the wall. Obscuring himself in the darkness, he stopped, and crouched. Listening, he heard only the soft sound of the rain now.

Then, through the rain, more shouts, in that strange language. There was a foreign word, repeated between the Cossacks. He heard replies repeated throughout the town. Richthofen sensed them, echo and movement in the fog and the dark, the sound of hoof beats rising and falling; all through the village.

He waited, huddled into himself, pulled his riding cloak tight, and listened. The shouts died out, and he heard low voices and horses pacing on cobblestones, stirring, and the occasional metallic sound of equipment rattling.

He crept toward the church and stood at the outside wall, watching through the breach. The voices were louder, but seemed to be coming from the street. Richthofen snuck to the inside wall of the courtyard and backed up into the ivy. The darkness was inky and deep inside the courtyard. Through the bars of the courtyard gate, he could see riders in the street.

Cossacks.

Richthofen edged to the gate, still hiding in the ivy. He stopped and peered out, down the length of the street. Voices rose, and the strange word was repeated over and over. He imagined the word was some command, or perhaps just the word for church. *What is that language ... ? Ukrainian, perhaps?*

The collection of men and horses grew as the Cossacks gathered. They were noisier now and lit oil lamps, insolent and bold. They stayed mounted on their tall horses: thoroughbreds or Brandenburgers, but hot, and anxious despite their breed. The audacity of the Cossacks surprised Richthofen. He had never been so close to one before and had seen them from across the river Prosna only once. Back then, he had stared at one, waved at the man on the opposite bank. The Cossack had stared back with hard, black eyes, and then turned and rode off into the trees. Richthofen had felt the man's anger, or hatred, or both, even from a distance.

The Cossacks in the street were brightly dressed, their clothing an assortment of baggy, bloused trousers made from colored cloth, vests over long shirts, a variety of sabers and swords tucked in belts or hung from leather straps over the saddles of their horses. All wore soldiers' tunics over their clothing, as though an afterthought. He could tell by the sound on the cobblestones that some horses were shod, others bare. *A motley collection of ... well, can you call them soldiers?* wondered Richthofen.

After a moment watching, he realized he could smell them; they had an odor like wet sheep and old meat.

In the road stood the priest and a villager. Richthofen had allowed the cleric to leave the church earlier in the day when it had become clear that there was no point in holding him any longer. Now, there he stood, among the Cossacks. Both civilians were dressed in long nightshirts, the priest's beard unmistakable even from a distance. Through the swirl of horses, Richthofen caught brief glimpses of the men. Two of the Cossacks were speaking to them from horseback. A Cossack dismounted and pressed close to the priest. It appeared as though the Cossack would strike him; then the horses moved and Richthofen could no longer see them.

Surely, the pope will give us away, thought Richthofen. Anger at himself washed over him in a hot wave. *We should have never let the man loose.*

He braced himself to run, pressing one hand against the stone of the wall. He watched, trying to read the gestures of the priest. The priest at first shook his head from side to side and then nodded in agreement. He seemed to be barely speaking. The villager did most of the talking.

Richthofen had seen enough. He moved back around the courtyard inner wall, sliding away toward the breach. Once clear, he raced across the field, hoping that Wedel hadn't needed to move. If he had, there would be no way to find him and Richthofen would be on foot. Richthofen groped forward in the fog, examining the ground for tracks, a sign that he could follow. He was tempted to shout, knew that would be foolish, perhaps fatal. He felt cold now, inside and out. The fog swirled around him and he stood still and turned in place.

Damn. Damn. Have I lost them? Did they move? His belly went hollow and he felt his bowels loosen as fear settled into him. Strangely, his face was hot. *Is this what you feel before dying from being a fool? Embarrassment?*

He stood still, listened and heard only the sound of the gathered Cossacks beyond the church.

Think, Richthofen. Think. Or die a fool in the mud of this field.

He began to walk in deliberate circles, each circle wider than the last, silently searching.

He whispered, in a hiss, "Wedel? Bilik?"

From the fog, dark shapes formed, men on horseback. Richthofen fought the urge to run, and stopped, frozen in place. He stared at the shapes for a moment, then edged closer.

Wedel and Bilik were where Richthofen had left them, waiting with their cloaks pulled up over their shoulders, wrapped tight. Rain dripped off their helmets. Richthofen moved closer, certain now, then strode to them, stifling the remnants of his fear, to not let Wedel or Bilik see his anxiety.

At least the helmets are good for something, thought Richthofen.

"There you are," said Wedel.

Richthofen took Santuzza's reins and swung up into the saddle. "Cossacks. A lot of them. Stay very close. If we separate, ride west; stay in the trees. We'll meet at the mansion where we saw the Goblin's Gold."

It was a crude order, but the best that he could do. There were no landmarks to orient off, the church wasn't safe, and the town overrun. It was a poor rally point, and Richthofen worried it was a mistake. He unexpectedly felt hunted, and he felt the heaviness in his bowels again.

He agonized that the Cossacks were a vanguard and that the Russians were moving, so he led the two men south, away from the village, and then turned east.

They navigated by guess and hope as they entered the woods southeast of the village. Breaking a trail through the woods, in the wet blackness, they stopped often to regroup, even though there were just three of them. Before long, their cloaks were soaked through from breaking a trail through wet foliage; it took almost no time for the capes to become little more than thick sponges filled with water and weighting them down in their saddles. The rain reached through everything, even their thick plastrons, and down to their skin.

At last Richthofen stopped. He gathered Wedel and Bilik to him and spoke. "We're turning north. We'll find the Lodz road and wait for morning."

Their tiny column turned, Richthofen prayed silently that he has his bearings in the thick trees and the pitch black of the Polish forest. They rode on, wavering, beginning to tire. Bilik hadn't slept and Wedel and Richthofen had managed a scant few hours before their flight. Richthofen began to yawn and shiver. Shadows swam in liquid pools around them.

At last, though, the rain stopped, and the mist thinned, but the night remained as pitch, the clouds covering the moon. They could smell smoke, and then saw a campfire throwing sparks. They slowed and rode forward. Richthofen issued no orders. His hand, at last, went up and he stopped Santuzza. They gathered, holding the horses in place. Steam rose off the horses' flanks.

Through the woods, they could see a camp. Someone moved about, tending a fire. A cart sat in the glow of the blaze, and a small family sheltered under it. Behind the family, the road glistened, wet from the rain.

Camp followers. He pushed the thought away. *A medieval thing, but perhaps the Russians brought their families.* His eye was drawn to the motions of a father, adjusting blankets, bending low to ask after the warmth of a child. *No, something else ... a whole family ... a father, children.* Not a throng of women as he imagined camp followers to be. These were refugees from Kalisch.

He whispered one word, "Follow."

They turned east and rode parallel to the road for a hundred meters as it bent to the north. North of the road was an open field. The fields were open two hundred meters east, twice that to the west. Dismounting, Richthofen had Bilik lead their horses south, out of sight in the woods.

Now what? Now, we just wait? Richthofen considered asking Wedel for his opinion, then decided it didn't matter, they had little choice now but ride back or stay. They cut boughs and then shook them out to dry them before arranging them into a rough mattress, three men wide. With their carbines and lances beside them, they waited for the dawn.

He had felt hunted before. Stalked and ready to be taken if the Cossacks had circled the church, or ridden into the field. The memory made him shudder. Confident he had lost them, confident they were isolated in the woods, he gathered his thoughts and settled himself down.

Now, I hunt.

This was a familiar place: a hunter's stand with a long field of view. Richthofen felt at peace.

He smiled in the darkness. *I'm not some prize for a Cossack.*

He whispered. "Wedel. Take the first watch. Wake me at daylight." Richthofen put his field glasses on the boughs next to his head, rolled over, pulled his cloak over himself, and dozed. Bilik was already snoring softly.

In what seemed a moment to Richthofen, Wedel shook his shoulder.

"Leutnant. Leutnant," he whispered.

Richthofen rolled over and started to sit up. Wedel pushed him flat.

"There." Wedel pointed west. Down the road, a young boy ran, pulling his trousers up, his bareness white in the morning twilight.

"What?" asked Richthofen, startled.

"He got close. I didn't want to wake you and attract his attention. He seemed too busy to notice us." Wedel frowned.

Richthofen said, "Cops and robbers are over. We're given away." He scowled at Wedel, a feeling of anger coming for the second time in a few hours, an unnatural feeling. He reached out, grabbed Bilik's cloak, and shook him. The Pole rolled over and looked up.

They were east of Opatówek now, west of Lodz. The Cossacks were between them and Kalisch. Wedel didn't like being seen by the boy, but he wasn't frightened.

"Do we leave?" Wedel asked. It sounded like he was asking permission.

"No," answered Richthofen. "We wait."

The three of them watched as the boy reached his camp, and pointed towards them. He gestured, waving his arms, while the father studied the Germans' position from a distance. The father gathered the boy to himself and sat him down.

Good, thought Richthofen. *Calm him down. Settle him down. No need for a fuss. You probably tiptoed past me yesterday; you can do it again. Don't get involved.*

The father tended the fire as his family rose and moved about. A young wife, a young daughter, the boy. They appeared to be drying clothes. Occasionally, the father would stand, stare down the road, and then turn back to his family. He seemed to be contemplating what to do. They didn't move from their camp.

The sun rose and failed to burn the mist away, leaving the sky a pale grey. The light gathered enough that Richthofen could use his field glasses to scrutinize the family. Wedel kept watch to the south, into the woods, toward their horses.

Richthofen then looked east, expecting Russian infantry, a column.

"Surely they couldn't have passed, not without us seeing them or having left signs," Richthofen thought aloud.

He knew a marching army on a narrow road, in the rain, at night, would spread out, forage for shelter, and leave stragglers. He examined the road. There was nothing. They couldn't have passed.

"Perhaps they're moving at first light. If so, they will be coming soon."

He fixed his glasses on the furthest point of the Lodz road that he could see, held them there. His spine tingled, anticipating a column of skirmishers to materialize in the mist, imagining that they would need to run to the horses.

Wedel shook Richthofen, saying nothing. Richthofen turned as Wedel pointed. A Cossack patrol rode in from the west and reined in next to the refugee family. The father was pointing toward Richthofen and his men. The blood drained from Richthofen's face, and he glanced at Wedel, who had turned equally pale. Bilik, still lying on the boughs, looked up at them both.

I would do the same, thought Richthofen. *Better to be the friend of the Cossacks and distract them from my wife and daughter than let them be ambushed and risk the Cossacks coming back and asking how that happened.*

Richthofen spoke to Bilik. "In a moment, I'm going to tell you to run. Run to your horse, but stay low. Then ride away from the road to the south and then turn west. Find Kalisch. You should be able to see smoke if the clouds clear. If not, follow the road west of Opatówek. Tell regiment that Richthofen says Cossacks scout the Lodz road. Ride hard. Don't stop for anything until you reach German soldiers. Understand?"

Bilik was pale now, even though he hadn't seen the Cossacks. He nodded his head rapidly up and down. "But, Leutnant, what about my lance? I think I've lost it."

"Damn your lance, boy. Ready?"

Bilik nodded again, still flat against the ground.

"Run!"

Bilik rolled to his knees and turned, his carbine in hand. In a crouch, he ran away from the road, doubled over, rapidly disappearing into the thick forest. Behind them, they heard the horses stir, and the cracks of brush breaking as Bilik galloped away.

"Now, Wedel. We just have to figure out how to survive," said Richthofen. "So what do you think of this, Wedel?"

"I think it feels like we have to keep moving to stay alive."

"Yes, I think you're right."

Richthofen reached for a carbine, brushed rain from it, and quietly worked the action. Wedel did the same.

"I'll take the big one; I'm a poorer shot," said Richthofen.

Wedel laughed. "Sure, anything you say."

They both aimed.

Richthofen and Wedel waited, listening for the sound of Bilik riding away to fade.

"Now!" Richthofen barked.

Two shots rang out into the Polish forest, the sound dying a wet death in the damp woods. Without waiting to see if they hit anything, Wedel and Richthofen turned and ran to their horses. They held their long steel lances in one hand, their carbines in the other, and rushed in awkward crouches into the brush. The Cossacks began shouting after them.

Reaching their horses, they jammed their carbines into their scabbards and swung into their saddles. They held their lances out as they turned their horses south and spurred away into the thick brush. Somewhere close a shot rang out; a bullet, spent, buzzed by.

Santuzza and Richthofen led, and Wedel followed. The shouts of the Cossacks faded behind them.

Richthofen and Wedel rode hard, west, with the Cossacks likely giving chase, though they didn't stop to look. Richthofen held his lance flat, driving the tip out ahead, the scarlet pennant fluttering in the breeze. Santuzza's strides were long and open, the horse excited to move. They were crossing through the fields, staying off the Kalisch road.

As they approached a farmer's stone fence, Richthofen let Santuzza run. Meeting the fence, Santuzza coiled and sprang, launching herself and her rider into the air. Richthofen let his lance waver only slightly, as it led the line of Santuzza's body through the air. She flew flat over the fence, stretched out, neck long, then landing, tucking her legs and galloping into the field beyond. For the first time in days Richthofen laughed, feeling the joy of riding free.

They rode through the trees, orienting off the roadway, and as they drew nearer to Kalisch, they chanced staying closer to the road and then slowed the horses to a walk.

The sun had won its battle with the clouds and early morning sunlight filtered down, casting long cool shadows. Puddles covered the road, and their horses splashed through them, enjoying the feeling of water over their legs. Richthofen turned in his saddle and looked back behind them: Nothing. He reined Santuzza up and listened. Wedel stopped. There was no sound from the east. No hoof beats, no shouts.

"That was fun," said Wedel, drily. Then, "Do you think we'll ever have a chance to go to the Olympics?"

Richthofen turned to him with a look of confusion. The Olympics had been the furthest thing from his mind. "Sure, Wedel, we'll still get a chance to try out; don't worry about it."

Wedel grew silent, with deliberation on his face, before he asked, "We both missed, didn't we?" He seemed to imply the answer he wanted to hear.

"Yes, I think so, but they hit the ground like we shot them," said Richthofen, with a tight smile. Richthofen turned Santuzza, and brought her again to a walk with a squeeze of his legs.

They rode on and began to pass refugees heading east from Kalisch. The smell of smoke was gone now, leaving behind the clean smell of the rain and the forest. Finally, they rounded a bend and ahead saw a barricade of felled trees across the road. Heads in spiked helmets bobbed about behind the barrier.

Together they rode, holding their lances upright. They opened their cloaks to expose their plastrons, marking them as Uhlans. Richthofen shook the pennant loose from the end of his lance and brought Santuzza to a canter. Wedel trailed half a length back to Richthofen's left. They approached the obstacle, and a bored German voice shouted out, "Stand and be recognized!"

"Commander, Third Squadron, 1st Uhlans," shouted Richthofen in response. He stopped Santuzza and lowered his lance as though he might charge. "Leutnant Manfred von Richthofen."

The voice replied, "Approach."

They rode to the barricade. "What unit are you?" asked Richthofen.

"Fourth company, Second Battalion, 155th Infantry."

Von Pruesker's infantry.

"How is your war?" asked Richthofen, almost mockingly. He felt exhilarated at their escape, still felt his heart thudding, just now starting to calm. He put his reins in his right hand, patted Santuzza's flank, and held the lance upright. The scarlet pennant fluttered.

"My war is going well, Herr Richthofen," came the reply. Now they could see the man: an infantry Leutnant.

"And what of Kalisch, then?" asked Richthofen, nodding down the road and behind the barricade.

"Minor problems. *Franc-Tireurs,* you know. Had to teach them to behave."

Franc-Tireurs, the venal civilians with guns that caused so much ... consternation ... during the Franco-Prussian war. Richthofen nodded, understanding. A French word; perhaps they have another word out here in Poland.

"Did you stomp them out?" asked Richthofen. He tried to sound hearty, encouraging.

"Not I. But, they're working on it. You may pass." The Leutnant waved a gloved hand. "Move along then."

To the side of the barricade a narrow path led into the woods around the obstacle. Richthofen looked at the Leutnant, who nodded. Richthofen and Wedel turned and rode around the barricade and back onto the road toward Kalisch.

An ugly, oily scent filled the forest as they neared the city. The smell was sickeningly sweet, with a harsh ugly bite that clung to the air.

Wedel turned to Richthofen. "Do you smell that?"

"Yes, I smell it."

They rode further and the smell thickened as though they could taste it. Richthofen spoke uneasily, reflecting. "When I was a boy, we had an old neighbor, and my mother would make dinner for him on Fridays. I would carry it over to his house, knock on the door, and then leave it on his table with a candle lit. One Friday, I knocked and then let myself in. The house was dark and smelled foul so I lit a candle. The dinner from the week before was still on the table, molded over."

Richthofen paused and glanced at Wedel.

"I'm listening, Richthofen," said Wedel.

"He had died and no one had collected him. I ran home, retching. The house smelled of this smell. This stink clung to my clothes so that mother had to burn them."

Wedel was silent, pondering. Then he spoke, "Well, you're a cheery one, Richthofen."

As they grew closer to the city, they rode through more refugees, forcing the refugees out of their way. The civilians weren't in large groups anymore, and they carried fewer possessions. Most of these had merely a suitcase or two, and families held fast to each other's hands. They silently trudged along, keeping their eyes carefully fixed downward as Richthofen and Wedel rode past. *Perhaps the ones that left sooner had planned better,* thought Richthofen.

Richthofen felt a strange sense of superiority, of having a purpose. He commanded Uhlans, and the Uhlans had made men tremble for hundreds of years. The feeling confused him, left him a little sick, a little numbed by the streams of civilians. *It is all so ... messy,* thought Richthofen, naively.

They approached Kalisch on the southeast road. Richthofen turned to ride through town. Wedel trailed behind, wanting to avoid the city, but obliged to stay with his commander.

Kalisch was quiet. No one stirred in the streets; the refugees were gone. Richthofen and Wedel rode west to an intersection. On the corner, a single building had burned into a hollow black shell. An old man was dead on the sidewalk, his arms straight out at his sides, staring upward with gray, empty eyes. Richthofen and Wedel stopped and stared down at the corpse and then glanced at each other.

"Don't see a mark on him," said Wedel.

"Nor I," said Richthofen. He turned Santuzza and rode west another block. They came to an open park where a church with a tall steeple stood on the east side. The church had been Loen's assigned lookout point, but no Uhlans stirred around the building. Beyond the church, a block of buildings were left burnt-out husks, black and oily from the rain.

Scattered around the park were piles of dead, though they had the appearance of bundles of rags from a distance. On the wall of a building, dark brown splashes of blood marked where they had faced German firing squads. Dark drag trails completed the story.

In the window of a house, Richthofen saw a curtain move, then close, a hand disappearing. On a sidewalk next to a bench lay a heap covered in billowing white fabric. They rode toward it.

Wedel pointed. "Is that a foot?"

A bare foot stuck out from under the fabric as the wind shifted it. The bundle was a young woman, wrapped in a dress. It was her shroud now. Her dark hair covered her face. Bright blood stained the front of her dress, still wet. Wedel shuddered.

Richthofen tried to be impassive, but he'd seen enough. He held his mouth tight, trying to still his jaw from trembling. "Let's leave," he murmured to Wedel. He turned Santuzza and, together, they rode south to the rail yard. Wedel glanced back and hoped the woman would rise up, as though it were all a prank.

A small German barricade was set up in the rail yard, a pile of bricks and railroad ties, facing south along the rail tracks. *What do they expect to stop coming from that direction? A train?* thought Richthofen. He rode to the soldiers.

"Men, do you know the location of the headquarters of 1st Uhlans?"

The soldiers glanced at each other. One of them saluted and spoke, "One moment, Leutnant." He ran off to a rail car with an open door and peered inside, speaking to someone. An old Feldwebel appeared, jumped down from the car. He drew himself up and saluted.

"Herr Leutnant. Regimental headquarters is adjacent to 155th Infantry headquarters, about four kilometers due west. They are just south of the main road; follow it and you'll find them." He smiled an old yellow smile. He seemed to be enjoying himself.

"Sergeant, where are the infantry and the other Uhlans?"

"They have been withdrawn temporarily, pending further action."

The word *action* rang oddly to Richthofen in the circumstances. "I see. Thank you, Sergeant," he said.

With that, Richthofen nodded, the proper substitute for a salute while holding a lance in one's hand. He turned Santuzza and began to ride west across the railroad tracks. Wedel hesitated, then turned, and followed Richthofen.

Somewhere in the city, a single shot rang out, echoing against the brick buildings. Wedel tensed in reflex. Richthofen rode, his eyes always ahead, away from the town.

In a few minutes of riding, they had crossed the Prosna rail-bridge, not far from the site of their original crossing. To the south of the road, the forest opened into a field where the Uhlans' horses stood roped among a stand of trees, the Uhlans' tents pitched, and wagons pulled up in a line. Cooking fires were burning. Richthofen and Wedel rode to the largest of the tents. A row of lances leaned against wooden rails in front.

Menzke ran out to greet them and took their reins, his face a broad smile.

"Sir, glad to see you, sir," said Menzke. Panic crossed his face as he realized he'd forgotten to salute. He drew himself up and saluted stiffly.

"How was your ride back, Menzke?" asked Richthofen.

"Sir, I didn't see any Russians." Menzke beamed. "But, I was afraid you weren't coming back."

One of the Third squadron troopers emerged from the tent and gave a shout, and then the rest of the Uhlans spilled out. Shouts of "Urrah! Urrah!" echoed across the camp.

As Richthofen and Wedel dismounted, a pair of young soldiers came to lead their horses away. Both men walked stiffly after days without riding followed by hours in the saddle.

Loen emerged from the command tent and smiled broadly. "Richthofen! Good man. I heard you were dead!"

Richthofen scowled and looked for his men. "Wedel, form them up; let's get a head count."

"No, really, Richthofen, the dispatch has already gone out. Trapped by Cossacks near Kalisch, you and Wedel both. Dead." Loen grinned and stroked his chin. "You don't seem very dead."

"Oh, good lord, man. The rumors of my death are greatly exaggerated." Richthofen grinned back at Loen. He flashed his eyes around the troops, caught Bilik's eye, and mouthed, "We'll speak, later."

~~~

Menzke drew a bath while Richthofen stripped off his week-old uniform. He climbed into the tub and began to soak. Menzke laid out a new uniform while Richthofen watched a line of artillery moving along the road, through the open tent flaps. Infantry walked in escort. Once he was clean, dry, and dressed, he walked to the mess area to meet Loen.

"What's the artillery for, Loen?" he asked as he sat.

"I haven't a clue, Manfred. Just in case, I suppose."

A dull boom immediately followed by a sharper *crack* rolled over the camp. Loud and close. Richthofen joined his troopers, already looking east.

Loen stepped to his side. "The artillery."

"Wedel, you're in charge of the men. I'll take one trooper and ride out. Await orders. Would you like to ride with us, Loen?" Richthofen asked.

Loen nodded, and called for his horse. In a few minutes, they rode east together, guiding by a cloud of smoke rising from the hills to the south of Kalisch. They crossed the rail bridge, angled south through the woods, and arrived on a road leading up into the hills.

As they rode upward, they could see Kalisch through the trees to the north, shrouded in dust. They reached the crest of the hill where the battery of artillery lay, four guns lined up. The cannons pointed at the city, their barrels depressed. The big guns were so close to their targets that the gunners sighted through the barrels at the city. An explosion in the city below followed each blast.

Richthofen could see the city clearly now, the rail yard below them, and a line of houses on the first block. Two of the houses were already blown apart, bricks and rubble scattered over the streets around their foundations. A cannon fired, the sound harsh and sharp, the muzzle blast washing over them. Their horses jerked and pranced, frightened.

Richthofen and Wedel stopped, and then turned to look down on the city. A shell struck as soon as the cannon fired; ripping through a building, and the exploded in the street beyond. The second cannon fired at the same building, and the structure tottered in on itself as the roof erupted into the sky, raining debris into the street. A third cannon fired, and the building collapsed in gray dust, more debris erupting upward and cascading down.

East of town, the road was filled with a fresh surge of Polish refugees, all seeking to escape the doomed city. They seemed to emerge from nowhere and shuffled east. Richthofen watched, speechless, as the guns trained on the next house and began to fire.

Chapter Six

Ostrowa, Western Prussia
August 9, 1914

Richthofen took a swallow of cold coffee, rinsed out his mouth, and spat it on the ground. He surveyed the stars with his eyes and then turned to Wedel. "Turn everyone out. Let's get them moving."

"So early, Leutnant?"

"We have a busy day ahead of us."

An ancient fire bell hung on a wagon. Wedel rang it, waking the men. It clanged with a high tinny note. The troopers quickly emerged with the night sentries moving from tent to tent to awaken the heavier sleepers. In the dark, they formed up in lines: horsemen in the front rank; armorers, orderlies, grooms, and the medical staff lined up in back.

Richthofen called the roll himself, going over each name by the light of a candle held by Menzke. He could barely make out faces, but he moved from man to man, acknowledging each as he called out their name. Then, he explained their orders, his voice low and steady.

"We're moving back to Ostrowa and embarking on trains for redeployment elsewhere. That's all I know," said Richthofen.

The men whispered amongst themselves, trying to see past the orders.

"Fall them out, Wedel."

Wedel dismissed the men and the group scattered. Someone lit a lamp on a wagon, then another. The tents were brought down, blankets were rolled, and tack was set out. In a few minutes, the wagons were loaded, with each man placing his own war trunk onto a wagon, making sure he could account for himself. They saddled their horses, and the squadron split, one troop in front and one in back, as they formed up on the road.

Wedel reported to Richthofen. "Ready, Herr Leutnant."

"Let's move."

The sun had just begun to light the sky as the Uhlans moved west, back across the Prussian frontier to Ostrowa. The column moved steadily, their pace set by the wagons. After two hours riding, they entered the town in full daylight.

Ostrowa was another old town, and to Richthofen the resemblance to Kalisch was remarkable, except that artillery hadn't blown chunks of Ostrowa into dust. The town was just waking. The windows of the houses stood open, farmers were driving carts to market, and sheets and blankets hung in the warm morning air. Richthofen and his column of men moved through the town and into the central square.

First children noticed them, then adults. They gathered along the sidewalks, shouting out: "Welcome! Hurrah for the Uhlans!"

Wedel grinned at Richthofen, but Richthofen just glanced back, embarrassed at the attention, anxious to keep the men moving. As they passed the road to their old barracks, the Polish boys chattered amongst themselves.

"Wedel, ride back there and reassure them. Tell them we're under orders and not to worry." Despite what he said, Richthofen did fear for the Poles now, and wondered how they would react to being sent to the west away from their homeland.

The column moved through the town and emerged on the other side, then turned north. They stopped at the railroad tracks, lined up their wagons, and tied out their horses. The cooks began making breakfast; hot cauldrons of mush, served with cold sausage, curd cheese, bread and butter. Behind them, the First and Second Squadrons rode in followed by the regimental headquarters.

The men began to mill about and talk amongst themselves, guessing aloud at their destination.

"We'll take the train to France to guard Paris, we will," said a trooper. There rose an appreciative shout.

"No, we're going to ride the train across Poland and chase the Russians to Siberia." Laughter.

Just before noon, a train rolled in, backing in from a spur. The squadrons organized into formations: three rough squares of men, and the fourth for the headquarters staff. The train stopped, and Oberstleutnant von Koss, the regimental commander, mounted a car and addressed the men. Von Koss wore his czapka uncovered, the black lacquer and gold gleaming.

"Men of the 1st Uhlans, congratulations on your successes in subduing Kalisch. You are to be commended. In fact, the 1st Uhlans have been mentioned in the first war communiqué to the Kaiser." He spoke formally, stiffly, as though the war made his words matter more.

The Germans beamed at one another and put up a hearty cheer. Richthofen noted that the Polish troopers cheered less loudly than the rest.

The Oberst waved his hands to quiet them, settling them down. "You will have many more successes ahead of you, and I wish you a pleasant journey. We're headed west. That is all I can say, but I will give you further orders upon our arrival. You will be remembered as the victors of Kalisch."

Wedel turned to Richthofen. "Victors—I like that. Kalisch seemed to be a bit of ..." He searched for the word.

"An adventure? A ride in the country?" Richthofen waved Wedel to silence. He frowned. *What was the word he'd heard Pruesker, the infantry commander, use?*

"Ah yes, it was a bit of *schrecklichkeit.*" Frightfulness.

Wedel nodded. "Richthofen, permission to gather provisions?" He jerked one thumb toward Ostrowa.

"Very well, Wedel. Go on."

Wedel mounted his horse, called for a wagon, and signaled to a trooper to join him. They rode into town.

As the regiment loaded horses into rail cars, Loen joined Richthofen.

"Loen, have you ever met Biffy?" asked Richthofen. Richthofen reached out and patted a fat flea-bitten grey mare walking by. "Looks good for sixteen, doesn't she?" Richthofen grinned.

"Sixteen?" said Loen, "A bit old for the cavalry."

"Yes, she's an old riding horse from Wahlstatt; one of my teachers owned her. I rode her quite a bit. Seems von Koss bought her." Richthofen leaned close to Loen and whispered, "The Oberst thinks she's eight."

"She's quite the miracle horse, then, isn't she? Aging backwards."

The two exchanged grins.

~~~

Wedel, Loen, Richthofen, and Loen's adjutant made themselves at home in a train compartment. They threw their saddle packs and bedrolls into the bins above them. Their lances were stowed in the baggage car, but each man kept his saber and carbine close. Loen leaned back and stretched his long legs across the compartment, crowding Wedel. Loen's aide, a young teenager barely out of cadet school, curled his legs up on the seat and dozed. The window and door were both wide open. As the train began to move, hot air blew through the window like the breath of a furnace.

"Bilik and the other Poles seem troubled, Richthofen," said Wedel.

"I wouldn't worry about it. The Poles may be a little upset, but they'll come around. You needn't worry," Richthofen said.

"They aren't mixing up with the men as they normally would. They seem to have ideas about the Kalisch business," Wedel responded.

"No matter, Wedel. If you feel the need to, take them a bottle or two." Richthofen indicated a crate of Champagne bottles sitting on the seat between them.

"I think I will."

"Go ahead, Wedel, take them. It's simply a few days for them to get over it, I'm sure," insisted Richthofen.

Wedel picked a couple of bottles and rose to leave the compartment. "Back in a few minutes, boys. Don't get away without me," said Wedel, smiling.

"You know, I think I'll follow you, Wedel." Richthofen said, lifting himself to his feet. "I need to stretch my legs anyway."

They walked down the corridor of the passenger car, bumping past restless men milling around in the passage.

"Do you know how long we'll be on the train, Richthofen?" asked Wedel.

"No, I don't. The Oberst couldn't say."

"I even asked the conductor. He seemed baffled. Don't think I've ever seen that before, a conductor not knowing where his train was headed."

"Well, surely someone must."

Wedel ducked his head into each compartment until he found the Polish cavalrymen. He put on a broad smile and let the bottles lead his way.

"Thought I'd cheer you boys up," he said.

The Polish Uhlans looked up at him, their quiet conversation fading away. Wedel reached out with a bottle in each hand. Bilik glanced around at the other Poles and shrugged, then smiled and took a bottle.

Wedel sat next to one of the Poles and twisted the cork from the other Champagne bottle. He took a long drink and then handed it to the man next to him. Wedel grinned at Richthofen. He would handle things with them.

Richthofen turned and walked the length of the car and crossed to the next, then passed beyond to a baggage car. The Uhlans' lances lay out across the floor under a layer of boards, then another layer of lances. They had rusted in the wet of the Polish forest. He paced the car and imagined how the baggage might be arranged, paced the car again, and headed back to his compartment.

Richthofen gathered his saddlebag, and grabbed a full bottle of champagne from the case before slipping back out. "Tell Wedel not to worry. I'll be in the first baggage car if you need me."

He walked down the corridor and crossed to the baggage car. In a few minutes, he had organized a space on the floor, gathered hay from one of the horses' cars, and a tent from a wagon. Spreading the hay, he lay the tent over it to make a mattress. That done, he opened the door of the car to let the breeze in. He lay down, opened the champagne, and stretched out, happy to have some long-needed solitude.

Soon Richthofen slept, dreaming in the hot summer air as the car rolled west. Occasionally the sounds of cheering crowds at the stations disturbed him. The train would slow and roll through each station where the odd flower or two would sail through the open door of his baggage car. As their train left each town, the flowers would go back out the windows, leaving a fragrant floral bedding along the tracks.

The crowds cheered for the Uhlans—the new heroes of the Second Reich.

~~~

After two days in the bright sun of the open plains of Eastern Germany, their train slipped into a tunnel in the mountainous west of the country.

The brilliant sunlight made the sudden change to the darkness of the tunnel impenetrable and inky. The men roused themselves, perhaps expecting to see another town, more crowds, and more women. All they could see, however, was darkness as the train thundered through the mountain.

"Where are we, Wedel?" asked Loen.

"I really don't know," replied Wedel. He had noted the name of each town, but without a map, the best he could do was guess a province. "Saxony, I suppose. Perhaps the French frontier or Luxembourg."

"Luxembourg? Don't be ridiculous, man." Loen frowned.

Loen and Wedel contented themselves with watching the darkness pass them by. The train slowed to a walking pace, and finally halted. In the black, there was no sign or sound of life. The engine cooled with a hollow hiss somewhere further down the tunnel. Men grew uneasy and murmured among themselves. The air grew charged with a primeval fear of the dark. Voices rose, first whispers, then shouts.

From somewhere, Wedel heard: "Franc-Tireur!"

Suddenly a bang and a flash: a firearm, going off. The muzzle flash lit the tunnel; the sharp bang echoed against the walls of the tunnel and stung their ears. Another shout: "Stupid shit! Be careful!"

Another bang erupted. Wedel dove to the floor as bedlam ensued. More shouting welled up from along the train: "Franc Tireurs! Franc Tireurs!"

Shots exploded from the train, as though a single volley. Soldiers fired their carbines out the windows, a continuous chain of ear-splitting noise. More shouts. Somewhere a scream. The men who weren't firing dropped to the floor, covering their ears against the cacophony. Glass shattered as ricochets glanced off the tunnel walls and drove the bullets back into the sides of the cars. Somewhere a man screamed in pain, but the firing continued in waves, the men somehow remembering at least part of their training and cycling the actions of their carbines in unison.

At last, Loen heard a sound of a spring releasing and the soft clatter of a magazine follower hitting the floor of the car. Then another, another, as the men struggled in the dark to reload their weapons. Men fumbled for clips of bullets, the dark defeating them. Wedel heard the officers shouting now. "Cease fire! Cease fire!"

One more shot rang out, followed by a man yelling and a heavy, meaty thud. Broken glass fell from the window frame and shattered on the floor of Wedel's compartment.

Then, quiet arrived, followed by some swearing. The men on the floor of the cars raised their heads and uncovered their ears. Wedel felt his way across the floor, cutting his palms on the broken glass that littered their compartment. He tried to brush shards from his seat, and then sat down. Blood ran off his fingers.

Wedel's face went hot, embarrassed for them all. *Nothing ... ,* he thought, *shooting at nothing ... a pack of damned children scared of the dark!* At that moment, the train began to move, lurching once, and then jerking painfully through the black tunnel. Wedel knew that the hot anger of the Oberst was sure to follow, but for now, he could only hope that no one was dead or wounded.

The train rolled out into the sun and stopped again. The men squinted as their eyes adjusted to the harsh light.

The windows of the train were nearly all broken; bullet holes ranged all over the sides of the car, and dents covered both the walls and ceilings.

Loen stood and, after glancing around the compartment, said, "Stay here." He stepped into the corridor and over the few men who were still lying on the floor beyond their compartment door.

"Into your compartments; get seated!" he ordered, yelling. "Sit down!"

He moved through the car, asking about any wounded at each open door. Finding none in their car, he returned to their compartment as the Oberst's aide arrived. They spoke briefly and Loen assured him that no one in their car was injured. The aide related the same. They both relaxed a little.

"Is he angry?" asked Loen.

"Furious," came the reply.

Loen nodded, his jaw clenching. "Dumb shits."

Wedel stepped from their compartment, looking to Loen. "Richthofen?"

Loen shook his head. "I don't know."

Both men turned and ran down the corridor, across to the next car and then the next, to Richthofen's place in the back of the baggage car. A dark wet smear streaked the tent canvas of Richthofen's makeshift bed, but Richthofen wasn't there. The door stood open, and streaks of sunlight filtered through the bullet holes that stippled the sides of the car.

"I'll look forward and in the tunnel, you search back in the train," said Loen, his voice tinged by fear.

Loen turned and ran ahead to find von Koss. Wedel ran back to the horse cars.

Beyond a broken pane, Loen saw the Oberst standing next to the train. His staff gathered around him, along with the engineer and conductor, all talking rapidly. Loen jumped down and ran toward them.

"Oberst." Loen pulled himself to attention and saluted stiffly.

The Oberst held up his riding crop at the engineer, silencing him. The man paused and began to speak again. The Oberst glared back, his expression commanding silence. He turned to Loen.

"What is it, Loen?" asked von Koss.

"Sir, Leutnant Richthofen ..." he began.

Wedel opened the door of one of the livestock cars and jumped to the ground. He yelled, "Come here! Bring a doctor!"

Loen's eyes darted from the Oberst to Wedel. The Oberst ordered his aide to get the doctor, and, together, he and Loen trotted along the tracks towards Wedel. Wedel leaned into the open door of the livestock car.

They ran to the car and peered inside, taking a moment for their eyes to adjust to the darkness. There sat Richthofen, huddled over the neck of a horse. His shirt was off and he pressed it over a wound on Biffy's neck. It was balled up and soaked through with blood. Richthofen stared back at them, his eyes empty and wet.

Biffy lay dying, her tongue already hanging from her mouth, her legs twitching and growing still. The other horses had huddled at one end of the car, away from the body on the floor. They smelled blood and sensed death.

Chapter Seven

Bouzonville, German Alsace-Lorraine
August 13, 1914

Richthofen stood in the open door of the baggage car, enjoying feeling the hot summer air blow over him. The train rounded a turn into the wide plains of Palatinate, approaching the contested lands on the French border. Stands of chestnut trees and alders stood like green islands in a brown sea of harvested fields. A neatly painted sign reading "Busendorf" stood along the tracks. Richthofen knew it was the German name, that the town had been called it Bouzonville by the French, but he also knew that it belonged to Germany now and that it would damn well have a German name. He realized where they were abruptly, the map games and studies in military school having drummed it in. This was the Frontier.

The train began to brake, the drive wheels on the engine halting and sliding, then rolling for a few meters, then stopping again. The tracks turned from the southwest to the northwest and the train slowed until it moved at a walking pace. Men jumped down and walked alongside, eager to stretch their legs.

Ahead, Richthofen could see lines of rail cars and a switching station. Troop trains stood alongside one another, men and horses moving between. The air stank of coal smoke, human waste, and dust. Their train hit a switch and swung to the left, then stopped with a squeal as the engineer clamped the brakes. Richthofen saw the regimental staff immediately jump down and gather next to the engine. Shouts swept the length of the train, "Detrain. Out. Get everything. Move!"

Men threw bags from the train, then clambered down with carbines and packs and clothing. They formed up in rows and columns. Heat radiated up from the rocky rail beds, and the air was still, trapped between the cars. The smell and heat made Richthofen's belly churn.

The word was passed to the men: "We form up; prepare to move north."

Richthofen gathered his things, leaving the tent canvas for an orderly. He left his shirt, soaked in Biffy's blood, behind, only keeping a small pack, his saber, and carbine.

Wedel took the roll of their squadron, grateful to be doing something productive. He turned to Richthofen. "All present, sir. And happy to be off that damned train."

"Collect the equipment; be ready to move in fifteen minutes, Wedel."

"North is it, Richthofen? Belgium?"

"No, Wedel. Look at a map, man. Luxembourg."

Energized to be out of the train and moving again, the men of the squadron quickly set wooden ramps in place next to the rail cars and led the horses down them slowly, one at a time, then through the confusion of the rail yard. They put the horses on leads and strung them together nose to tail in two long columns. A rail car was unhitched, and the engine pulled forward several car-lengths, creating a gap for wooden ramps to be set up allowing the wagons to be unloaded.

Richthofen moved among his men, excited at the knowledge of where they were, and what they must be doing. He called out orders, bellowing cheerfully at the throngs of soldiers. At the north side of the tracks, next to the station, the Uhlans tried to gather with their units, in the midst of a dozen other units trying to do the same thing. The great crowds of men surged north across the tracks and between trains and into the streets of the town.

The Uhlans moved through the town; the horses tied together in their strings, with the wagons pushed by hand, trying to find space gather themselves. The town was no better than the station: thousands of men were moving in a crushing sea of humanity, waving arms and rifles and an occasional saber to clear the way. Excitement gave way to annoyance and tempers began to flare. Men shouted and then fists swung, the fights swallowed up by the moving throngs. In the growing press of an army, soldiers hung on to the sides of wagons to keep from being swept under in the press of bodies.

The air was still and sour; its heat drained their breath and sweat turned their uniforms from gray to black.

Richthofen stopped the string holding Santuzza and Antithesis. He untied the lead rope and held onto Santuzza with Antithesis tied behind and following. Menzke walked alongside Antithesis, patting the horse's flank to keep the horse calm in the crowds and noise. Fortunately, the soldiers were nervous enough to give way as the horses passed, allowing them to make slow progress through the streets. Richthofen watched ahead, at the back of a wagon that belonged to their regiment. His stomach was in knots as he recognized his own men swirling through the mob, mixed up and confused.

At the north edge of town, the army spread out into side roads and fields. Richthofen held his gaze on the Uhlans' wagon and plodded along, a little sick, angry and full of energy. The wagon stopped in a field and Richthofen found his way ahead. He tied Santuzza to a wheel on the wagon and then turned to the wagon driver.

"Hobble your lead horse, then get back to the main road and point any Uhlans to this wagon. We'll form here," he barked, strain in his voice.

The army was pulling itself back together. The chaos of humanity began forming into units in the fields. Turbulent groups of men stretched for hundreds of meters in every direction, and a steady flow of soldiers was continuously moving north from the train station. East of town, whistles blew, signaling the arrival of new trains, and even more fighters.

The squadrons of the Uhlans' regiment gathered, muscling for space in a trampled beet field, using their horses like a living barrier to keep men from other units out. Each squadron assembled, lining up their wagons, and tying their horses on rope lines. The horses were dry and hot, stiff from their long confinement on the train. They stood still, barely stirring to move to small patches of shade.

Richthofen directed the arriving men. "Damn it, don't let them just stand there! Water the horses; get into the wagons; use whatever you can find. Get water where you find it."

The Uhlans spread out, tending the horses and organizing themselves as the sunset. In twilight, the grooms walked the horses in circles to keep their legs warm while they waited for orders. The German infantry gathered in the roads and marched past through the night. Here and there, the Uhlans spread blankets and slept in the open under a star-swept sky.

~~~

In the pre-dawn light, Richthofen rode with von Koss and the other squadron commanders to the division headquarters. Rested, Richthofen was intent and excited again, anxious to hear their orders. He listened raptly to the division commander and then chatted with von Koss briefly to confirm his squadron's role, then rode back to their makeshift camp.

He pulled Santuzza up to a stop in the dusty air. A sentry took the reins, and Richthofen slid to the ground.

"Wedel! Up!" he shouted.

Wedel emerged around the corner of a tent as the sun broke hot over the horizon. The tramping Germans had beaten the ground, and dust was already thick from units marching throughout the night. Wedel wore a bandanna over his mouth. "Orders, Richthofen?"

"Form the squadron up; we move north." He grinned. "Belgium. We're going into Belgium."

"Sir?" replied Wedel.

"Yes, north into Luxembourg, we'll gather there. We ride north in columns of twos, the regiment together, Second Squadron leading. Come, Wedel, I'll show you!"

Richthofen picked up a stick and then smoothed a patch of dirt with the bottom of his boot. "We're attached to the Ninth Infantry Division, Fifth Corps, and Fifth Army. Our armies are in line from Holland to Switzerland. First Army in the north, opposite Belgium; then the Second, Third, Fourth to the Seventh, all the way to Switzerland. It's a thing of beauty Wedel." Richthofen grinned, scratching out shapes and arrows in the dirt.

Wedel puzzled over the makeshift map. *We actually numbered the armies in order, from north to south? If that wasn't so pedantic, it would be absurd.* He fought to keep his face a mask of seriousness.

"From there, we form up here on the Luxembourg border, push north into Luxembourg, and then turn east to pass the French fortress at Verdun. All the armies north of us will swing like a door through Belgium to the French northern border. We're the axle that they rotate around. The French will have to pull their armies from their eastern border and redeploy them, and we'll drive through the porous French northern border, capture Paris, and end this. It should take no more than three, perhaps four months. Just like they taught at school." He stood up, beamed at Wedel and tossed the stick aside and brushed dust from his hands dismissively.

"So, we have to move twice as far as the French, through defended country, over days, and the French won't be able to turn to meet us? And what of the English?" Wedel's voice was low, respectful, but he couldn't mask trepidation.

"Not to worry, Wedel. The English don't have the will to join a continental war, and their army is too small to matter. And, the best: the French have already attacked to the south of us into Alsace and been repelled. It's 1870 all over again!"

"I see," said Wedel with a frown. He squinted at the sun breaking through the trees. "We should get moving, I assume we have to push out ahead of the infantry."

The men were mounting, holding their lances upright; sun glinted down their length like mirrors. The flashes of the light on lances played across the field. Dust swirled thick, the beet field well-trampled. Gear was being thrown into wagons, coffee and soup poured onto the ground. In a few minutes, the wagons were fully loaded and the squadron lined up in two ranks. As they moved onto the road, the Second squadron led, and other squadrons and the headquarters fell in behind them.

The column rode through the dry afternoon, passing between alternating patches of shade and sun. Their pace was slow, almost leisurely, letting the horses stretch their legs after the long train ride. Richthofen rode ahead on Santuzza, running back and forth as though waiting for playmates to catch up.

~~~

In the late afternoon, over the trees, Richthofen heard a sound like an angry hive of bees. He looked up to see an aeroplane flying from the east. He recognized it for what it was, though he'd never seen one before. From below it appeared a spindly contraption of tubes, wires, and translucent canvas, and even to his untrained eye it seemed delicate.

Noisy fools, thought Richthofen, *doing their ridiculous act out here where a war is to be fought.* As it grew closer, a man waved from the top of the thing. Richthofen gawked at the sight and reflexively waved back.

Somewhere, at the rear of the column, a carbine popped. Men scrambled for rifles, dropping their lances in the dust. The cracks of the rifles grew until the whole column of lancers had their carbines out, aimed upward, banging away at the machine over their heads. The pilot turned the aeroplane and seemed to pick up speed as he descended, then disappeared, over the trees west of the column.

Wedel rode over to Richthofen. "That was an aeroplane," he said.

Richthofen nodded. "Yes. It was. Strange to see it out here."

"Did you see the crosses on its wings?" asked Wedel.

"No, I can't say that I did."

"German, I suppose," said Wedel. "Probably shouldn't have shot at it."

Richthofen frowned. "No matter. He has no business here. Let's get the men moving again."

He thought flyers frauds, as low as circus performers or players, and a distraction from real soldiering.

"Damn useless snake oil, wasting our ammunition and scaring the horses."

Wedel shouted to the men, they dismounted and gathered their lances and then formed back into columns. Soon after, the Uhlans crossed into neutral Luxembourg.

Chapter Eight

Portsmouth, England
August 14, 1914

The ground far below him was a patchwork quilt of jade, olive, and emerald fields, bounded by hedges, and dotted with tiny farmers' cottages with thatch roofs. Louis Strange flew the tiny Avro under the clouds toward where rain fell in colorless walls. He rose up in his seat to try to see past the lower wings of the aeroplane and judge his height, but he soon gave up trying, for he could only see just beyond them and straight ahead.

The Avro was a simple machine with two huge wings over and under a long, box-shaped fuselage. A seven-cylinder French rotary powered the aeroplane, and constantly pulled the aeroplane to the right as the mass of the engine spun. Today the Avro rode through the air like a boat in deep swells, rising and falling, tipping over on its nose, then tilting until Strange looked almost vertically up. He suspected that the aeroplane, while normally mild mannered, might yet find a way to surprise him in a horrible, final way.

On his third flight of the day, he was reaching his limits; the Avro was draining him like a circuit gone to ground. With no instructor or student weighing down the other set of controls, Strange's own were light and unbalanced. Every motion Strange made was amplified in the motion of the aeroplane and each seemed to make the machine feel as though it might tumble. The vibration of the rotary engine and the rushing cold air routinely left his hands and arms burning, but eventually they went numb. It was the tingling of that numbness that now moved through his shoulders until he felt his teeth chatter.

So this is exhaustion, he thought, placidly.

Strange painfully skirted around a cloudburst and then flew to the northwest toward the town of Upavon. Despite his efforts to avoid the rain, he was soaked, and his jacket and trousers were wringing-wet. The wetness sapped the last of the energy from his body, leaving him shaking, and his fingers blue and stiff. With aching hands, his fingers tightened until they felt like stiff claws, like hooks.

I can't. I can't do this.

Exhaustion gave way to frustration which gelled and congealed into quiet desperation.

As he flew under the clouds, Strange watched the farmers' houses pass by ahead of his lower wings. He began to bank back and forth so he could see the ground. Warm columns of smoke rose from farmers' homes. Occasionally, the orange glow of a daytime fire played through the windows, the light a friendly beacon. He dodged a downpour and turned to the northwest, but the edge of the deluge still clipped the Avro and left him drenched anew in a sudden gust of wind and rain.

Enough. Enough.

He could think only of the heat of the fires below and the promise of a cup of tea. Near the town of Over Wallop, he angled downward, and then circled, moving north as he went from field to field. The few people who were about heard his aeroplane and gaped upward, awestruck at the strange contraption. Some ran and hid. Eventually, he found a field that looked level and smooth. He flew toward the adjacent farmer's cottage and circled it low, once, then twice.

Strange had no throttle to lower the power on the rotary, instead, he 'blipped' the engine with a button, shutting it off briefly, then letting it restart. Looking down, he blipped the engine again and turned a circle over the field. He released the switch and the engine started with a loud pop as it spat orange flames below and behind the Avro.

Damn, thought Strange, *too long on the switch, mustn't scare them down there.*

Smoke rose from a cottage below, and the windows waved with a welcoming light. He watched the smoke, saw it blowing from a north wind, and then turned in over the field from the south, blipping the engine once more. The Avro wallowed and surged, each gust of air trying to overturn the delicate little aeroplane. Strange settled the Avro over a hedge and lifted its nose as it fell until it touched the ground and began to roll. He held the aeroplane straight as it angled toward the cottage, and then he pressed the rudder bar to turn at the last moment. The Avro turned sideways, skidded and stopped. Strange flipped the magneto switch, killing the engine.

Well, this should be interesting, thought Strange.

Golden reflections painted the cottage windows, but no one stirred. Strange worked his hands against his legs, pushing his fingers apart, forcing them to move. He realized he was panting from desperation and he willed himself to breathe slowly. Every joint creaked as he pried his hands open. Painfully, he pulled his cap from his head, smoothed his wet hair with a hand like a claw, and dragged his goggles from around his neck. He swung one leg, then the other, slowly over the side of the aeroplane, before sliding down the edge of the cockpit on his belly. His legs were dead under him so he bent at the waist, waiting for the feeling to return enough for them to hold his weight.

Taking short, stiff steps, Strange staggered to the cottage door and knocked. His hand felt as though it might shatter. He drew it back and held it against his chest and moaned a little from the pain. There was no sound, so Strange pressed his ear against the door. Oddly, he thought he heard sobbing, and then silence. After a trice, he heard a chair slide on the floor and soft footsteps. The door opened silently, and a short woman peered around the edge, her eyes bloodshot and ringed.

She was strong and lean, a dirt farmer and tough as the soil, but the grief on her weathered face seemed unnatural, an invader that she couldn't fight off.

"Yes, yes, what do you want?"

Louis pulled himself upright and painfully pushed his shoulders back, trying to make himself presentable. He was a short man, wide through the chest, with a cleft chin that made him appear somehow elegant, despite a meager tiny moustache adorning his upper lip. He held his leather flying cap in his hands, massaging them against the leather in a vain attempt to warm them.

"Forgive me, ma'am, I was just flying to Upavon, to the Flying School, and I've grown so cold. Well, I've landed in your field, and thought that I ... perhaps ... might trouble you for a cup of tea?"

The woman leaned further around the door and looked out at Strange's aeroplane. Her eyes grew wide as she examined it, making them appear even redder. But then they narrowed and she pushed the door open. She was holding an old shotgun behind it.

"Flying? You'll not be a German spy, will you?"

Strange lifted his hands and noticed they were blue. "No, ma'am. I'm just a lost Englishman, an aviator, a flyer." He waved toward his aeroplane with a hook-like hand.

She set the shotgun on the butt end and leaned on it. Her hand went to her mouth. Her eyes examined him, as though he were a man that had just fallen from the sky. Then she looked past him.

"I've grown quite cold, you see. And a bit of warmth and a cup of tea would do wonders." He smiled a thin, wan smile.

She ignored him again and hoisted the shotgun up. Instinctively, Strange backed up out of her way, keeping his hands up. He continued backing as she advanced toward him, approaching the Avro. She kept the barrel of the shotgun pointed past him at the aeroplane as though it might pounce at any moment.

"It's a machine," said Strange. "Just a machine. Come, I'll show you." He stepped to the aeroplane and laid a hand on it. "See, merely canvas and wires."

She moved closer and peered around Strange, content to keep him between her and the aeroplane. She studied him carefully. He felt like livestock, under the cautious eye of a farmer, a farmer not knowing what she was buying.

She tipped her head slightly and stared at him with one eye wide. Strange took a half step back. "That thing will be staying there; do you hear me? I'll have none of that ... conjuring ... any closer to my home. Do you hear me?"

"Yes, ma'am." Strange bobbed his head up and down like a schoolboy.

She backed up and held the door open. Strange followed her inside. She kept an eye on the aeroplane as she shut the door.

Once inside, she gestured to a chair by the fire and Strange sat. He pulled the chair closer until the heat made his clothes steam. She prepared tea, poured Strange a cup and then set the teapot on the side table.

"Thank you; you're very kind," he said.

Without reply, she put another log into the fireplace and then pulled her own chair closer to it. She sat staring at the blaze, occasionally glancing at Strange as though she didn't quite believe he was there. After a few moments of silence, her eyes lost their focus and she seemed to stare far away. She dabbed at one eye with a handkerchief, then sat back and began to rock, silent.

"We're going to France, you see," said Strange, trying to skirt the awkwardness of the situation. He sipped his tea and held his hands tight around the cup to soak up the warmth.

The woman looked at him as though he were mad, and then turned away. "I'm afraid you're going the wrong direction then, young man. Upavon is west."

Strange smiled, peering into the fire. "No, I'm returning an aeroplane to the Flying School. There I'll pick up another, then off to the coast, you see."

"Oh," she replied. She bent her head and dabbed her eyes again.

"Strange, ma'am, Lieutenant, Royal Flying Corps."

She looked at him, her eyes clearing. "I'm sure you're quite normal, young man. Although the idea of men flying is peculiar."

"No, ma'am, it's my name. Louis Strange," he said.

"Oh," she said blankly.

"If I may, ma'am, is there something the matter?" asked Strange.

Her eyes glistened. She bent her head again as tears welled. Strange put one hand on her knee to comfort her and patted her lightly.

She sat up after a minute and leaned back in her chair. "My son, I've just received the post; he's off to the war."

"There, there, ma'am, he should be fine. The war shouldn't last but a few weeks, then he'll be home to you," said Strange.

"No, you don't understand, I know he'll never be back. It's the last I'll ever see of him," she said calmly, but with a fragile sadness that belied her wind-toughened face. She looked at the fire, but didn't seem to see it. She tried to find words, couldn't, and shook her head.

Strange sat with her into the afternoon, telling stories of flying and of the weather, and listening to her speak of her son. By the late afternoon, the sun appeared, and Strange coaxed the woman outside to help him start the aeroplane's engine. He took off, rolling across her field; then climbed into the air, just clearing the hedge. Turning, he circled over her cottage, waving down at her.

Watching upward as Strange turned back toward Upavon, she said to herself, "Just men, I suppose."

~~~

Strange flew in on the west wind, landed smoothly on the grassy plain and let the Avro roll down to a stop. One Avro with a missing wing and a single forlorn Farman stood on the field next to Strange's weather-battered Avro. The field was still and quiet; he heard only the sound of the wind gusting past the empty sheds. So empty. *Two hours ago a mad house, now, a wasteland, abandoned.*

He wandered around the now desolate field at Upavon, following the sound of tool clanking, peering into each hangar in turn. At last, he found two mechanics loading tools into a purloined commercial lorry. It had all happened so quickly, that they hadn't really thought about what would happen if they were called up. Called to war. So they, the pilots and crews, had scoured the countryside with letters bearing the Royal seal and the signature of their colonel, trading promissory notes for trucks, trailers, tools, and fuel. A day later they were loaded and headed for the coast, and an hour after that the aeroplanes were flying, fading over the hills to the east like gnats.

Strange watched the mechanics throw the last of the tools into an old steamer trunk.

"Is the Farman ready?"

"Aye, as ready as she'll get. And good luck to you. You're to leave the Avros for the junk pile."

Strange looked back down the field, between the buildings, at the last of their misfit aeroplanes. He eyed the Farman like it was a dog that might bite. The English flyers called the Farmans by the onomatopoeia 'Rumpety', and the nickname helped Strange hate the airplane less. He thought of the Farman as outdated, although it was barely a month old. It was rickety and dangerous on its best day. He walked to the Farman.

You were past your prime when they built you, Rumpety.

The last lorry, loaded now, drove past the aeroplanes, and one of the mechanics leaned from its window and waved to Strange. Painted on the truck were the words, "McVitie and Price's Digestive Biscuits." Strange frowned at the reminder that they were a vagrant air force of borrowed and stolen equipment.

Strange shouted to him, "And where's my mechanic? I can't fly this thing without a man in front, dammit!"

"They're bringing him along!" came the reply.

Strange pondered what the devil that might mean.

From the far corner of a shed, two military policemen emerged, leading a man by the arms. They were nearly carrying him, his feet moving in a half-attempted drunken shuffle. One of the policemen carried the drunk's kit and the other his rifle. They propped the blotto mess of a man upright and held him that way.

"And where have you been, Gaskell?" asked Strange, annoyed.

Gaskell stood, wobbling. He smelled of beer and horse manure, and staggered as though he might fall off his feet. "Beggin' your pardon, sir, I'm not a flyer, never been, and never shall be. I'm a driver, nothin' more."

Strange's voice rose. "Well, you're about to become more. The mechanics had to drive your lorry, you sot. Now I need a man to balance the Rumpety. Everyone else has left, and, if you'd been here then, we wouldn't be having this conversation."

"Well, then, I'll be making the most of it, I reckon," said Gaskell.

"Gather your kit and let's get you loaded," said Strange, holding back his frustration. He turned to an army policeman. "Bring him; I need him for ballast."

The MPs glanced at one another, then at Gaskell, and led him across the field.

The Rumpety had the peculiar appearance of a pulpit with wings: the engine in the rear of a giant nacelle, the pilot and observer stuck out in front. They called it a "pusher" because the engine *pushed* from the rear. The wings, nacelle, and tail all seemed to be baled together by wire. Wires everywhere, flying wires, landing wires, and wires for wires.

A Lewis machine gun was clamped to the edge of the observer's cockpit, poking upwards into the sky at a sharp angle.

Gaskell wobbled and stared, his gaze floating around like ice cubes in a glass.

Strange wiggled through the maze of wires until he stood on a tire, then climbed up into the cockpit and motioned to the policemen. They picked Gaskell up, arms and legs swinging, and put him into the Farman. Gaskell slumped into the cockpit and helplessly mumbled something about needing another minute.

Strange held Gaskell's shoulders and threw the leather straps over them, then cinched the straps. An MP tossed Gaskell's bag up to Strange, who stuffed it down into the cockpit alongside the drunk's rifle.

Looking up at the wind flags, Strange could see that the wind had changed direction and said a quick silent prayer for a sudden storm to keep them grounded. He examined the uncooperative clouds, thin and puffy overhead, and blowing along with the breeze.

Damn, thought Strange, *the one day I could do with really poor flying weather.*

Gaskell was resting his head on the stock of the Lewis gun and falling asleep. A policeman looked up at Strange and shrugged.

Strange grasped the controls, two metal loops, side-by-side on a stick. 'Spectacles' they called them. He worked the spectacles back and forth, and then did the same with the rudder bar. He watched the wings and tail move, then, satisfied, he called out to the policemen to spin his propeller.

The engine caught and roared. Strange let it run wide open. The police stepped back, holding their helmets to their heads. Strange motioned to them to pull the wheel chocks. The Rumpety began to roll and to bellow out its name.

RRRUUUUMPETY ... RRRUUUMPETY ...

As the wings gripped the air, the tail came up and the aeroplane pitched level before lifting. Gaskell tipped over, face down in his cockpit and didn't stir.

Taking off, they flew into the stiff wind, crawling over the ground, the engine straining to give them any airspeed at all. Strange turned from the west to the east, putting the wind behind them. They flew downwind for the coast.

After half an hour in the air, Gaskell raised his head and looked around, his eyes huge and staring. He stared back at Strange in horror, seeming to have at last realized where he was. His head swiveled around, and he held onto the sides of the cockpit with white knuckles.

Strange pointed to Gaskell's goggles hanging around his neck, and then pointed to Gaskell's eyes. Gaskell, not understanding, pulled the goggles away from his neck and stared at them. Strange pointed again at the goggles, and then at Gaskell. With an air of revelation, Gaskell put them over his eyes and grinned. Then he pitched forward and vomited over his lap.

At Shoreham, they landed to refuel, and Gaskell climbed down, trying to brush puke off himself; and staggered away. In a few minutes, he was back, holding his coat closed with his hands in his pockets. The man's shoulders sagged down as though he regretted grabbing a bottle today, but he climbed back into the cockpit.

From Shoreham, they flew east, following the shoreline. South of them, they could see the French coast on the far side of the English Channel.

Gaskell opened his coat and produced a bottle of whisky, then grinned back at Strange, the sort of mirthless smile you saw on a monkey in a cage. He uncorked the bottle and waved it at Strange. Strange gaped at Gaskell's gesture. Gaskell repeatedly tipped the bottle up, took a long gulp, and then turned back to Strange, waving the bottle each time. Gradually his movements became more uncoordinated until, as he turned, the bottle left his hand and flew backward and down. Strange clenched his teeth and hunched his shoulders, expecting the collision of the bottle and propeller, and the resulting spray of propeller and glass shards. When it didn't happen, he sighed in amazement and relief.

Gaskell tipped over and didn't move again.

Strange briefly considered turning the aeroplane over and letting Gaskell out, then thought better of it.

They followed the coast east past the Dover Castle until he could see, ahead, a group of landed aeroplanes scattered along the top of the white cliffs. In the distance, the French shoreline was in clear view, crisp and sharp. Strange could see the shapes of the houses of Calais along the distant French coast.

Civilians from the town stood round the edges of the field, staring up at him. Scarlet flags dotted the field, marking ditches and obstacles. He circled once over the Channel and landed into the wind, dodging between flags. As the Farman settled onto the ground, still rolling, the aeroplane struck a grass-hidden dip in the ground. The clumsy machine pitched up on its nose and, with a loud cracking sound, lifting as though it would fall over upside down. Then, the craft hung, balanced, for a brief second, before slumping back onto its wheels.

The crowd politely applauded.

Gaskell was draped over the front of the fuselage, wedged under the Lewis gun. Strange stood up in his cockpit and grabbed him by the cuffs of his pants, lifted his legs and pushed him out onto the ground. The drunk hit the grass on one shoulder, flopped onto his back, and then lay still. He mumbled something about his mother.

Strange turned stiffly to a crewman, too exhausted to be exasperated with Gaskell. "Call the guard and have that man arrested." He pointed at his one-time co-pilot.

~~~

Lanoe Hawker stood with Beatrice Bayly in an open tent, watching the aeroplanes come in and land at Dover. His men had set up a row of shelters along the side of the field, and Lanoe and Beatrice stood in the lee of one, trying to find a little protection from the wind. As the aeroplanes landed, crewmen would run out and stake each aeroplane down where it had stopped, pounding tent pegs and stringing ropes. Aeroplanes were scattered everywhere, pulling at their restraints.

Beatrice was dressed in black. She wore a dark bonnet and mourning veil, pulled back from around her face. She looked out with equally dark eyes at the field, wide at the chaos of the aeroplanes landing and the commotion of men running back and forth between them. The expression on her face was soft, unlined, but her gaze was intelligent and aware, watching the flow of men and machines across the grassy plain.

"I'm sure he'll be here any minute," said Hawker. He took one of her hands in both of his. She let her hand lie.

"Miss Bayly, I'm sure it will be quite alright. Gordon's an excellent pilot, and flights over land can be quite uneventful. You see, there are so many places to come down."

Beatrice looked at him with quiet alarm. Hawker blanched and held her hand tighter. "No ... so many places to land safely, not ..." Hawker floundered.

Beatrice smiled to hide her worry and turned back to the aeroplanes. Hawker watched as a Farman came in, the observer hanging out of the nacelle. The aeroplane struck the ground too fast, rolled, and hit a hole. It stood up on its nose, and then fell back on its wheels. The observer fell out. Two guards appeared and carried the limp man into one of Hawker's tents. A ground crewman, efficiently and belatedly, planted a flag in the hole where the Rumpety had stuck.

"Oh, my," Beatrice said. Hawker heard the soft notes of her South African accent. He warmed. The sound was charming.

"Strange, I think," said Hawker.

"Yes, quite," said Beatrice.

He looked at her askance. "Louis ... Never mind."

Behind the Farman, an Avro landed and rolled to a stop. Hawker pointed, "That may be Gordon there, landing just now".

"Oh, excellent; I haven't missed him then," said Beatrice. She smiled a broad smile and the edges of her eyes crinkled.

"Miss Bayly, may I have a few moments to speak with you? While we wait?"

Beatrice nodded. Hawker led her to one of the tents, and pinned the tent flaps open.

"Mr. Hawker, what is it?" asked Beatrice.

Hawker took off his cap, and laid it on the table. "Miss Bayly, I would like to ask something of you, if I may."

"Please ask, Mr. Hawker. You've been very kind to us since my father's passing; if I may return a kindness, please, ask." She untied her bonnet, uncovering her dark hair, and then she reached out and took Hawker's hand again, holding it between hers.

Hawker reached into his pants pocket and pulled out a ring. Beatrice shook her head and mouthed the word 'no.'

"Oh, no. Please understand. It's not that." Hawker smiled uncertainly.

"I'm sorry, Mr. Hawker, but I've declined your proposal once ... please understand." Beatrice's face grew soft, and her voice faded.

"No ... no ... It's not that, at all," said Hawker. He lifted the ring, held it up. "We'll be leaving for France soon. Could you, please, provide safekeeping for this, for me? Keep it safe, only. And know that my offer is always yours to reconsider."

"Mr. Hawker ... I ..." She reached out and closed her hand over the ring.

The tent flap opened and Gordon Bayly strode in. "Is that my sister?" He came up behind her as he pulled his flying cap off his head. She turned.

"Oh, Gordon," she said, throwing her arms around him. They embraced, tears welling in her eyes. "Oh, Gordon, it's so good to see you."

Gordon released Beatrice and put out a hand, and Hawker took it.

"Been taking care of my baby sister, have you, Hawker?" said Gordon, his eyes bright. "You're a good man, Hawker; a true gentleman."

"Yes, he certainly is. He's been most kind. How good it is to see you, Gordon! How long do we have?" said Beatrice.

"An hour, or two. The squadron needs to fly together over the Channel, touchy thing that ... need to get there while there's plenty of daylight left," said Gordon. "If you'll excuse us, Lanoe?"

"And yes, Mr. Hawker, I will honor your request," said Beatrice, smiling. She slipped the ring into her pocket.

~~~

Strange's squadron flew across in the afternoon, leaving him and his broken Rumpety behind. He watched them fly, their motley assemblage of aeroplanes, Farmans and Avros and Sopwiths, all in a sinuous cloud of noise. He turned away, disappointed, and patted his Farman.

It's alright, we'll be over there soon.

In a Rolls-Royce staff car borrowed from one of Hawker's officers, Strange drove all afternoon and into the night to find parts for his aeroplane. At two in the morning, he arrived back at the temporary field at Dover. He found his Rumpety tucked into a tent for the night.

Strange roused some of No. 6 Squadron's mechanics and lit lanterns around his aeroplane.

Wake up, girl, time to fix you up. You'll get us over the channel won't you?

Unboxing tools, he climbed inside the nacelle and began pulling broken parts out and throwing them over the side.

As he worked, Hawker appeared at the open flap of the hangar tent. "What is it, then?"

Strange glanced up, "Longeron. Just one, fortunately."

Hawker stepped up and pulled the flap closed behind him. He stuck out a hand and Strange took it. "Lanoe Hawker," said Hawker.

"Louis Strange," said Strange.

"Yes, I've heard of you, the man with a Lewis gun on his Rumpety." Hawker climbed on the ladder and reached out to inspect the Lewis gun. "Strange, is this regulation?" he asked.

"No, not by a far cry," answered Strange. "Mounted it myself. Squadron commander hasn't said a thing, as yet."

"Well, Strange, this may be the lone aeroplane in the entire Royal Flying Corps that's armed," said Hawker.

"Maybe. Give a man a hand, will you?"

"You have cause to be proud," said Hawker, his face a mask of seriousness.

"Really? And why would that be, Hawker?"

"Well, you crashed right at the spot where Bleriot crashed. Within a few feet, I should think." He grinned.

Strange grinned back. "Is that right, then?"

Hawker pulled off his jacket and climbed into the rear cockpit, then lowered himself until he was inside. A lantern lit the interior of the nacelle.

"How may I help?" asked Hawker.

Strange pulled at the shattered wooden end of a brace.

"Can you take instructions?" asked Strange.

Hawker beamed. "It's your aeroplane, you're in charge."

Through the early hours of the morning, the two men dismantled the aeroplane, pulled rigging from the wings, and canvas from the fuselage. Just before sunrise, Strange re-rigged everything, pulling cables tight and aligning the wings with the fuselage. Hawker stood by, taking orders from the junior officer as Strange gave them.

At last, the wires were restrung and the canvas stitched back down.

"You haven't got a sparrow, have you, Hawker?" asked Strange.

"What? No, I'm afraid I don't."

"Bloody shame. We won't be able to tell when we're done without one."

"Really?" replied Hawker, playing along.

"Well, you put a sparrow in the wings, and if it can't get out, you've got all the wires back correctly."

"Sorry, Strange, perhaps a seagull ... would that do for you?" asked Hawker, keeping a straight face.

"Might not do the trick ... probably too big. I guess we'll just have to fly without one then," said Strange, grinning.

Hawker grinned back. Sleeplessness circled his eyes in dark rings.

An infantry corporal opened the tent flap and stepped inside. "Message for Lieutenant Strange," he said.

"That would be me," said Strange.

"Well, sir, a bit of bad news. Gaskell's escaped, sir," said the corporal.

"Find the nearest bar then," said Strange. "I'll fly when you find him."

Hawker wrinkled his brow, not sure he'd heard the exchange correctly.

"Does that happen often, Strange?"

"Well, all the time that Gaskell flies ... which would be yesterday and today ... if they find him."

"I see. In that case. Join me for tea and breakfast, Strange?" said Hawker, holding the tent flap open and letting morning light in.

"Yes, thank you. I could do with that."

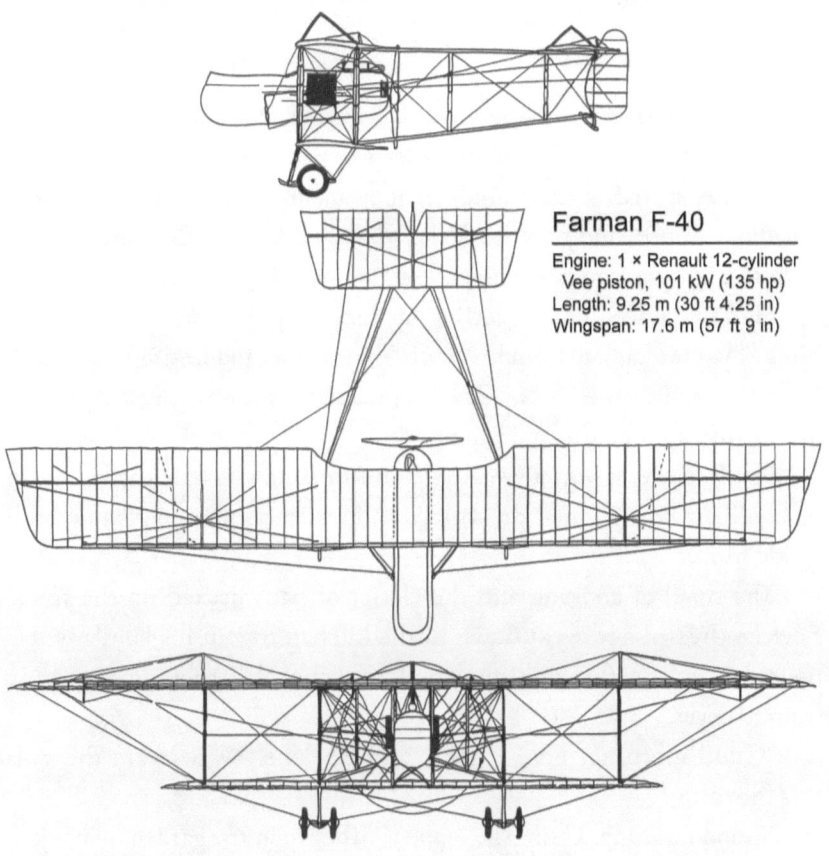

Farman F-40

Engine: 1 × Renault 12-cylinder
    Vee piston, 101 kW (135 hp)
Length: 9.25 m (30 ft 4.25 in)
Wingspan: 17.6 m (57 ft 9 in)

Chapter Nine

Döberitz, Germany
August 15, 1914

The thick stone walls of the chateau held the cool night long into the morning, leaving Oswald Boelcke asleep in bed well after the family had woken. He stirred at the sounds of movement from the kitchen below, rolled out of bed, and drew back the window curtains. The sun streamed in from high over the trees and bathed the room in warm golden light.

He took a deep breath, feeling his lungs expand, tensed for the first hints of pain to radiate from his chest. None came, and he drew the breath in deeper, and then let it out. The cool release of air was refreshing, like a long drink of water after a drought.

For Boelcke, it was a sweet pleasure to simply exhale easily. When he couldn't, he imagined drowning, and a silent and lonely panic built inside him.

The smell of cooking and the clatter of pans drifted up the stairs. Boelcke dressed and went down to the kitchen to join his landlady. He poured a cup of coffee for himself and sat at the table, rubbing sleep away from his eyes.

"Good morning, Frau Kunz," said Boelcke. "Where are the girls this morning?"

"Good morning, Ossi," she replied. "They're in the garden, playing at knights and dragons, I suppose."

"I'll see to them before I leave," said Boelcke.

"Please do; they'll miss you so."

Frau Kunz's two girls threw the kitchen door open with a bang and flew inside in a cloud of giggles. They circled the table, snatched up pastries, and then hovered around Boelcke. Each lay a hand on one of his shoulders or arms as they ate, as though they needed to touch him to keep him real. They both glowed in silence, staring alternately between their mother and the young man.

"Is it true, do you have to leave?" Mieze, the older of the girls, asked at last.

"Yes, young lady, it is true," replied Boelcke. "Today I report to Trier and await my orders."

Mieze took a bite of her pastry, then looked out the window at the pecan tree in the garden. "Will you climb it with us, once more?" she asked.

"Now, Mieze, leave our guest alone. Let him have some breakfast," said Frau Kunz.

Sadness darkened Mieze's face. "Yes, Mother. Come on, Isolde, you can be the prince this time." She turned and ran out the door and disappeared into the garden, her sister trailing behind.

"We've enjoyed having you stay here. They've never known a soldier before, let alone an aviator," said Frau Kunz. "Forgive them, but they think of you as a brother."

"They're wonderful children, Frau Kunz. Thank you for having me here."

A stiff silence settled over the kitchen. Frau Kunz turned back to her stove. She began frying sausage while tending a pan of rolls in the oven. Boelcke sipped his coffee.

"Where will you go, Ossi?" asked Frau Kunz.

"I don't know," he replied. "I'd like to join my brother, but my orders haven't come."

"Will it be long, the war?" she asked.

"I don't know. Really. No way to know. I need to get to the front, though, before they don't need me anymore." He smiled.

"It's good for your asthma, you know," said Frau Kunz. She pointed at the coffee, and Boelcke lifted the cup. She refilled it.

"I also bought your cigarettes. The pharmacist prepared them for you. Just in case." She set the box of cigarettes on the table, patted his arm. "Datura and Belladonna, with Virginia tobacco. One a day, he says, no more. He says you shouldn't smoke them before you fly. But, how would he know?"

Boelcke smiled. "Thank you, Frau Kunz. You're very kind. I hope I won't need them."

"How on earth did you ever climb mountains with your condition, Ossi?" she asked.

"I needed to, I suppose. It let me rise above it, and the air is cleaner up there." He thought of the drowning sensation again, and then shuddered to shake the idea away.

Boelcke thought then of the slurs from his aunt: *an asthmatic's wheeze is from the mind; it's just a child crying for his mother.* An absurd, ridiculous woman. How it stung to hear these things, how they drove him; how he needed to be away, above, with nothing but clean, cold, dry air in his lungs.

He drew another deep breath, a testing breath, waited for the ache, and sighed when it didn't come. He sipped his coffee and looked out at the garden; he could smell the dust and the pollen. He flinched as he thought of breathing it in.

"You know, I can tell when you're trying to breathe. You think people can't see it, but you seemed so serious for a few seconds; I know you're thinking about your lungs."

"Yes, I suppose it's obvious," replied Boelcke. He sifted through his thoughts, seeking a new subject; this one had become stale, unpleasant.

"Will you be taking in more boarders after I've left?"

"Perhaps, yes ... probably. I don't think we'll charge for soldiers though. Our contribution to the war effort," she replied. "Ossi, you're always welcome here,"

"Thank you. You're very kind."

Boelcke smiled, stood, finished his coffee, set the cup down, and stepped to the back door. He drew a deep breath, and then let it flow out of him. "If you'll excuse me then." He strode outside, eager to join the hunt for the dragon. Perhaps it was up the pecan tree.

~~~

Fischer, Boelcke's orderly, stood in the entrance of the hangar, waiting for his eyes to grow accustomed to the dark interior. He spotted Boelcke and walked over. "The deputy commander wishes to see you," he said.

"And, what about, Fischer?" said Boelcke.

Boelcke had grown restless at Trier, the depot aerodrome, where pilots waited for a real assignment. In the distance, he could hear another train whistle. The steady flow of them moving west made him feel isolated, left behind. Stranded there, he'd become short-tempered and frustrated from waiting. In fact, all the airmen were near-idle while awaiting orders, always expecting a great mission that never materialized.

"Another ferry flight to Sedan," said Fischer.

"I see," said Boelcke. He glanced out at the bright afternoon. "How long have we been waiting, Fischer?"

"Waiting here? Four days, sir."

"That seems a long time. And what time is it?"

Fischer drew out his pocket watch. "Three-thirty, nearly, sir."

"That will do. Pack me a bag, will you?"

"Yes, sir, of course," said Fischer.

"Meet me outside the operations building. Pack the bag heavy; everything you can fit into it."

"Is there something I need to know, Leutnant?" asked Fischer.

"Not at the moment, no," said Boelcke.

At the operations building, he felt his palms grow sweaty, and his lungs tightening.

Not now. Not now, he told himself. The deputy gave him his orders. The base at Sedan had called for another delivery flight. Boelcke was to deliver an aeroplane and return on the morning train.

Boelcke nodded, saluted, and stepped outside into the warm afternoon. In the west was a clear blue sky. He smiled to himself. *Perhaps today is the day then,* he thought.

Fischer stood waiting, a canvas duffel slung over one shoulder. He had stuffed the bag so full that it bulged and sagged in the middle like a fat sausage.

"Come along, Fischer," said Boelcke.

Outside the hangars, the mechanics prepared a Taube for the flight. It was a civilian aeroplane, just commandeered. To christen its new role, a mechanic was painting German crosses on its wings in black.

The sunlight through the Taube's translucent wings cast a strange skeletal shadow as though from the bones of an ancient bird.

Boelcke moved about the aeroplane leisurely, pushing at the wings, the tail, pointing out minor flaws in the machine to the mechanics. They trailed behind him, listening to his concerns. Then they would run between the aeroplane and the hangar for tools, an oil can, whatever they needed to fix the problems that Boelcke saw. Boelcke circled the aeroplane and left the mechanics scattered in his wake, working intently to get the craft ready.

Gradually, the mechanics finished their tasks: adjusting, tightening, and then they stood back to await his inspection and approval. Once again, Boelcke moved around the aeroplane, crawled underneath it, prodded and pointed, leaving the mechanics with an assortment of chores. Again, they finished and waited.

Boelcke climbed into the cockpit, and moved the controls around, watching the wings move and twist under his hand. He shouted for the maintenance chief, asked for more adjustments on the controls, then sat and waited. The mechanics worked again. The chief mechanic climbed the ladder and bent over Boelcke.

"Herr Leutnant, perhaps you don't wish to fly today?" he asked quietly.

Boelcke smiled. "Oh, of course I wish to fly. It's just a matter of when," he replied.

The chief nodded. "I see. It is getting a little late in the afternoon. Is there a specific time that the Leutnant wishes to fly?"

Boelcke leaned close and whispered, "I believe six is ideal."

The chief nodded again, his face expressionless. "Very well. Another hour, then."

The crew chief raised his voice, speaking too loudly, "I'm sure that we need to remove the magneto and replace it. I recommend that. But it will take an hour."

"Yes, that would be fine, chief. Please do so," said Boelcke.

Boelcke called from the cockpit to Fischer for his bag, and stuffed it behind the pilot's seat. A few moments later, the sergeant assigned to fly with him arrived, carrying his own bag. He stood at the base of the ladder, looked up, and saluted.

"They'll need to change the magneto. That will take an hour. Come back then," said Boelcke. He climbed down and took Fischer by the arm, leaving the sergeant dumbfounded. "Let's take a walk, shall we?"

Boelcke walked around the base, Fischer tailing behind. They talked of mountain climbing and swimming, of flying. Of the war. At last, they circled back and arrived at the Taube.

The mechanics stood by, the sergeant already in the rear cockpit. Boelcke reached out and took Fischer's watch from his pocket and checked it. "Six. Excellent. I'll be in touch, Fischer. Wish me luck." With that, Boelcke climbed into the pilot's cockpit, turned, and greeted the sergeant.

"May I have the map, please?" he said.

The sergeant handed the map to Boelcke, who sat down in his cockpit and clipped the map to his wheel. Boelcke called to a mechanic to spin the prop before the sergeant could protest. The engine fired, roared, ran up, and then back to an idle. Boelcke waved to Fischer and then saluted the chief and his mechanics.

Boelcke pulled the throttle all the way out, the engine roared, sputtered and then smoothed out, running wide open. The Taube started to roll, the wings of the aeroplane waving up and down with the rough ground. When it lifted, it did so abruptly, pulling itself upward in a lunge. Boelcke turned the wheel and pressed on the rudder bar, turning the Taube west.

They flew for an hour into the setting sun, until the clear sky darkened to steel, when Boelcke saw the tents of the German field at La Ferté. Circling, he lined up to land from the southeast. He landed the Taube in the center of the field and then let it roll to the hangars.

The ground crew set up a ladder next to the aeroplane. Boelcke stood in the cockpit and turned to the sergeant. "Too dark to fly further, don't you think?" he asked.

The sergeant just nodded agreement. "Obviously, far too dark to fly, Leutnant."

Boelcke handed his bag to a crewman, climbed down, and turned to their crew chief. "Is Wilhelm Boelcke about? Could you tell him that his brother has arrived?"

~~~

In the cool morning light, after the first patrols had gone out, Oswald and Wilhelm Boelcke met with the commander of the squadron. Hauptmann Streccius sat behind his desk. Streccius made a point of not rising to greet the Boelcke brothers when they entered his office. The argument had begun immediately.

"Send him back, leave the aeroplane, send this Boelcke back," said Streccius, talking to Wilhelm and pointing at Oswald.

The brothers stood at his desk, caps in hand, bound together by family and separated by appearance. Wilhelm the elder, was tall, broad shouldered, dark haired with a serious temperament. He wore a short beard and long moustache in the style of Czar Nicholas of Russia, barely skirting German military regulations. Oswald was shorter, with wheat colored hair and sparkling eyes over high cheek bones. He had to force himself not to smile.

"But we need pilots," insisted Wilhelm.

Streccius stroked his beard, seeming to relish being the decision maker. "Yes, we do, and observers. But why should I keep your brother here?"

Oswald stood patiently, watching the conversation, trusting his brother.

"Leutnant Maertens is exhausted. Clearly. So, I cannot fly without a pilot," explained Wilhelm. "Also, the relationship between pilot and observer is a marriage of sorts. Both parties must commit to the relationship if it is to work. We are brothers, and close brothers. We already trust one another implicitly. There will be no need to start two new men together; we can already work together."

Streccius turned to Oswald. "And you, are you prepared to enter combat immediately?" he asked.

"Yes, Herr Hauptmann, I am. I've been waiting assignment for two weeks at Trier. I'm eager to fly," said Oswald.

"Very well. But just until Maertens is healthy. I'll contact Sedan and let them know that their aircraft is here and that you are safe. I'll contact Trier, also. Wilhelm has current orders."

The Boelcke brothers saluted and left the tent smiling, arms locked together. Streccius followed them with his eyes and stroked his beard, suddenly feeling manipulated.

"Well, Oswald, shall we begin?" asked Wilhelm. He led Oswald toward the hangars where mechanics prepared an Albatros two-seater for flight. A cold wind blew across the field from the west. On the western horizon sat a fat storm, billowing into the sky.

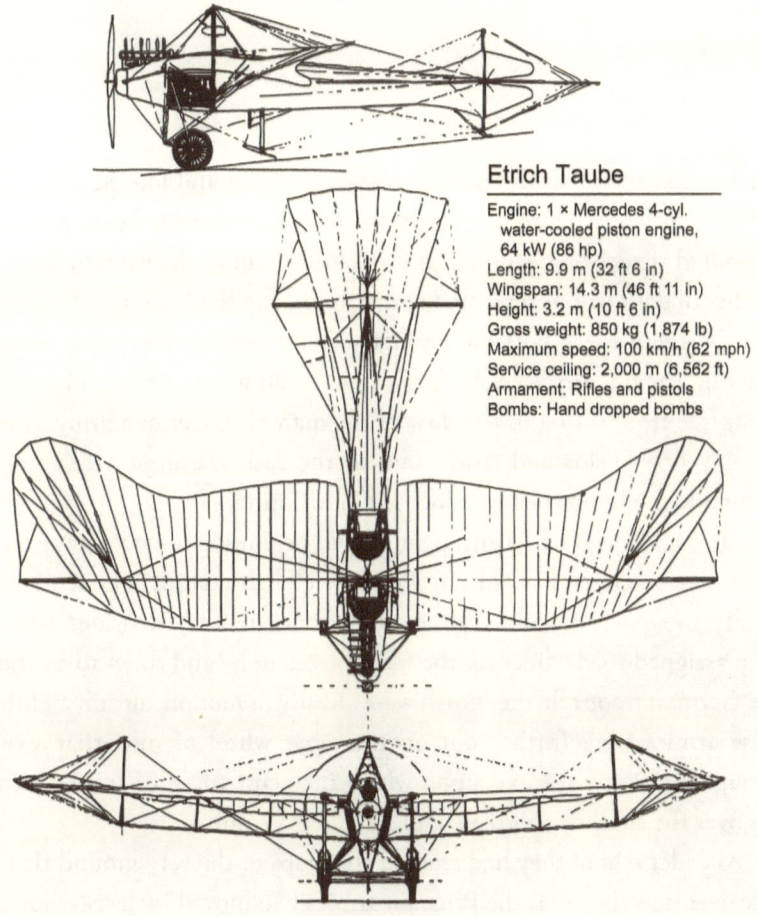

Etrich Taube

Engine: 1 × Mercedes 4-cyl.
  water-cooled piston engine,
  64 kW (86 hp)
Length: 9.9 m (32 ft 6 in)
Wingspan: 14.3 m (46 ft 11 in)
Height: 3.2 m (10 ft 6 in)
Gross weight: 850 kg (1,874 lb)
Maximum speed: 100 km/h (62 mph)
Service ceiling: 2,000 m (6,562 ft)
Armament: Rifles and pistols
Bombs: Hand dropped bombs

Chapter Ten

Arlon, Belgium
August 20, 1914

Richthofen rode Antithesis to a crest in the road and looked down into Belgium. A warm azure sky, cloudless, stretched over his head. Fields, in a hundred shades of greens and browns, rolled out to the western horizon. Patches of dark woods separated them, promising shade from the morning sun. On the western horizon, a solitary church steeple pointed at heaven, breaking the line between sky and earth. It felt good to him to be out in front, free from riding in the dust of the marching German army. Ahead lay only open fields and roads, but, to the east, the inexorable force of Germanic might on the move loomed in his mind.

He could feel it, the army, pent up and beginning to flow onward, like a river that had burst its banks. It arrayed itself behind him in Luxembourg; cavalry in squadrons and regiments in front, infantry divisions behind. Each assigned roads, lines on the map, places to be and times to be there. The German troops further north were already in motion, already fighting; those armies were further out on the great wheel of men that swung through Belgium. The axis upon which the giant wheel of armies turned was over the southern horizon, a place called Verdun.

At cadet school they had studied the maps of the very ground that he rode over now. In 1871, the Prussian armies had moved in decisive lunges, like a fierce fencer—turning, parrying, and encircling. They carved out great gaps in the French armies, consuming French soldiers in massive bites, all marked by colored arrows, neat and tidy, all advancing to Paris. He had always known what those arrows meant. They had never been an abstraction to him; they were the ruthlessness of an intention that wouldn't be denied. The arrows were an army, his army, and he was, right now, right here, at the forward point, with all following behind him.

He was the tip of the Fatherland's spear.

They had been victorious.

He waved to Wedel, who rode up beside him.

"Excellent view, Richthofen."

"In front, at last, with space to ride out and do our duty," said Richthofen.

"Yes, Leutnant." Wedel rose in his stirrups, as though he might glimpse the French army in the trees or on the distant horizon, if he were just a little taller. "Do you think we'll see their men today?"

"Perhaps their cavalry. I don't think they would advance this far. Too exposed, too easy to find a flank and pin a unit down. They'll be further south in the dense forests." Richthofen was thinking back to military school, to one of the lessons he had absorbed.

He straightened in his saddle, stiffened his spine and drew a deep breath.

"Wolfram is dead," Richthofen announced abruptly.

Wedel turned, cocking his head. "Did you say Wolfram is dead? Your cousin Wolfram?"

"Yes, I heard it from a runner from his regiment last night." In the open, away from strangers, Richthofen felt the need to give words to his emotions. A hot tightness gripped his chest. He thought of himself and Wolfram, of playing together as boys; throwing rocks at his grandmother's geese; stealing his sister Ilse's dolls and hiding them in the trees; riding the old horse bareback. Now the boy was gone. Just memories remained. It all seemed mere moments ago.

"What happened? How?"

"Franc-Tireurs," Richthofen said flatly. "Shot as he emerged from a house where he'd been sleeping. Shot down and left to bleed to death in the street. No one saw the assassin." The horror of his cousin's pointless death made his mouth go dry, and his throat to tighten, like a parched man.

Wedel shuddered. All throughout cadet school the instructors had warned them about the Franc-Tireurs. How a man could step so far outside of his place and take up arms against the men of the Reich with no nation or uniform to support them could be nothing short of madness. But there they were: godless highwaymen that killed honorable soldiers and murdered without right or cause. Wedel had hoped that they were just a fable, a boogeyman used to keep the sentries alert at night. *Could they actually be real, dangerous in a shifty, savage way?*

"Where?" asked Wedel.

Richthofen pointed to the horizon. "That steeple is Belgium—Arlon, I believe. North of Arlon somewhere." He waved his arm northward.

"Wolfram's men burned most of the village afterwards. The runner said they stood where he fell and burned every house they could see from the spot." Richthofen tried to find justice, satisfaction in the knowledge, but he felt nothing, just a ragged, vacant hole, and that feeling of thirst, a desire to be cooled and refreshed.

Wedel grew quiet, bit his lip. *A whole village, burned? What if the murder had really been an accident or a single crazy Belgian?* Wedel shook again, but held his tongue.

"There is worse news, Wedel." Richthofen looked behind him, at his squadron of troopers, in the road below the crest, then off to the eastern horizon where no marching troops had emerged yet. They had time.

"Wedel, the Kurassiers met with disaster. In the north, over a single bridge at Haelen, fighting dismounted Belgian cavalry. Very bad." His voice trailed off, staring off to the west, trying to pick out details, movement in the countryside. The dryness in his throat was fear, real fear, something he had never felt before. It was a feeling that your body might burst, and flow away.

"How bad?" Wedel asked.

"Most of a division lost. Six hundred in an afternoon. The battlefield was left covered with armor, dotted with the Kurassiers' polished helmets. Horrible. They charged against rifles. A waste of men and horses. German cavalry dying that way; such a senseless loss."

Wedel nodded, stared west. "I see." The ugly images turned over in his mind. Horses in line; the charge; lances and men and armor tumbling; then stillness. He felt a headache starting to throb in the back of his head.

"Return to the men. Send a scout to ride with me. Into Belgium."

"Very well, Richthofen," said Wedel. "I'm sorry about Wolfram. I liked him ... he was ... a good boy."

Richthofen pursed his lips. "Yes, Wedel, he was."

Wedel turned, rode to the men.

Richthofen looked down from the crest at a guard shack marking the border. No one stirred; no horses. It was abandoned. He felt the breeze die out and the air grow still. Heat radiated up from the road in shimmers. He took a swallow from his canteen and rinsed his mouth out. Then he gulped the cool liquid down. It calmed him.

A trooper joined him, and they rode down the hot road. At the border shack, the door was closed. Through the window, they could see papers laid out neatly on a table, a full cup of coffee sitting next to them as though someone might return for them at any moment.

Neutral Belgium is gone. Run away, like a coward border guard. Not that it ever was neutral ... a British puppet hiding behind international law. It was a foolish calculation, a false neutrality, thought Richthofen.

He waved to his men to come ahead, and they joined into a single column, and then rode west. At Arlon, they halted.

"Put the men in those trees, Wedel." Richthofen pointed.

"And where will you be?"

"I'll be in town. I'll not lead you men in without knowing what may wait ahead. Horses in streets will not fare well ... the damned Franc-Tireurs."

"Very well, Richthofen. But hurry, we have to stay ahead of the infantry." Wedel glanced east, watching for German infantry columns in the heat haze.

Richthofen pointed at a farmhouse and smiled at Wedel. A bicycle stood against the wall.

"I'll be on wheels," he said.

"Any last words, then?" Wedel grinned.

"Wedel, you worry too much. See the steeple? I'll climb it and look around. If all is well, I'll wave my handkerchief. Then I'll ride back. If I have trouble, I'll start shooting. Simple." He unholstered his pistol and waved it down the street.

Richthofen climbed on the bike and rode, wobbling on the unfamiliar machine, pushing hard on the pedals to keep it moving against the rough cobblestones. The town was still alive, moving with civilians whose heads turned to watch him ride by, curious. A group of boys watched him pass, their dark sullen eyes seeming to bore through him. He glanced at them over his shoulder, keeping them at the edge of his vision as he rode by.

At the church, he leaned the stolen bike against a low wall and entered the bell tower. He unholstered his pistol again and brandished it ahead of him as though it might scare away things that he couldn't see. The tower was silent. He waited and listened, blind while his eyes adjusted to the darkness. The sudden darkness made his head throb.

The stone stairs led upward, worn smooth from hundreds of years of feet—bell ringers, watchmen, and priests. He climbed the stairs by twos, moving quickly in the gloom of the tower. He felt his heart pounding and pressed harder, enjoying the sensation of his pumping legs. He reached the top of the tower and moved through the shadows, keeping his silhouette from any eyes below. Then he surveyed the town, picking it apart street by street, covering all that he could see of the town. He searched, in turn, for riders, a column of men, a man in uniform, or a glint of metal. He saw nothing interesting, just civilians, carts, and a solitary motor car parked at the town hall.

He looked west into Belgium, down the road to Virton. It was there that he saw movement. Silver helmets and black helmet plumes slipped through the heat-haze. He couldn't be sure, but it appeared to be a column of riders, silver armor on their chests. Then, nothing.

Damn this. It's not a game. Damn Kalisch and those bloody cannon. Damn the woman in the white dress.

He stared, trying to part the heat shimmers on the road and to find the phantom army again. Rubbing his eyes, he glanced down to clear his vision. Again, he scanned the countryside hastily, then looked back to the road. Nothing. Just dust in the still air. No color, no movement. No civilians on the road. He felt his testicles tighten to his body.

What was that? Anything? A mirage? Cuirassiers? French cavalry?

Turning back, he put his eyes on the horizon, expecting—though not hoping—to see German infantry on the march. He pulled his handkerchief and leaned out of a window, waving the handkerchief at the end of his arm in wide sweeps. He counted to thirty and then drew back, settling into the shadows. At the eastern side of the town, he saw movement in the trees, then a man emerged—Wedel waved his handkerchief in response.

Richthofen took one more look around the town and then at the countryside ahead. Still, emptiness.

He climbed down hastily, almost running. At the bottom, he paused at the tower door, hearing voices outside. He pulled his pistol again, tucked it to his side and gently pushed the door open. Across the street, leaning against a building in the shade, the group of boys had gathered and stared back at the church door, as it swung open. They continued to chatter among themselves. One of them laughed aloud.

Richthofen strode from the church. The bicycle he had stolen was gone. Feeling foolish, Richthofen started to search for it, as though he'd misplaced it, and then looked up at the Belgian boys. His throat became hot and dry again.

The boys grew quiet. They eyed him, silent and hostile. Richthofen brought his pistol around from behind his back and turned, his eyes not straying away from the boys against the wall. He spoke in German, "Another time, perhaps, and I will put you against a wall. Just once." He unhurriedly, deliberately, holstered the pistol.

He turned east and began walking. As he reached a corner at the end of the street, he quickened his pace, staying against the walls, glancing back to see if the boys followed. He inspected each window as he passed, expecting a gun barrel to protrude, pointed at him. He felt fear rising, a shallow pool of panic around him beginning to deepen, to submerge him. He thought of Wolfram, bleeding to death alone in the Belgian street. He shuddered and felt bile rise in his throat, hot acid in his mouth.

Richthofen stopped, stepped into a doorway, and calmed himself, breathing deeply and letting his heart slow, all the while watching the windows. Minutes passed, and the blood that had been rushing in his ears quieted. He stepped back into the street and turned back the way he had come. Nothing.

At a trot, the heavy foot falls of his boots sounded like explosions echoing against the walls of Arlon's buildings. Every few steps, he stopped to find a tight corner to hide in and then looked back. Curtains drew closed in the windows around him, but the Belgian boys didn't reappear. When he felt momentarily safe, panting, he moved on in short bursts of energy followed by more hiding and watching. Panic crept up on him in short rushes, a few footsteps behind. The faster he moved, the closer it drew. Eventually he ran, panting. At the edge of town he forced himself to halt and threw himself into a dark doorway, gathering his wits, letting the panic pass him by. After a minute of composure, he walked down the middle of the road past the farm to the copse of trees where his Uhlans waited, forcing himself to stay calm.

"Well, Richthofen?" asked Wedel. He studied his commander, but his face was unreadable.

"Nothing." Then, not wanting to feel the fool for telling the truth, he added, "The bicycle broke, so I had to walk."

"I see," said Wedel. "Shall we, then?"

"Yes, Wedel, let's continue our ride."

The squadron of Uhlans, in two columns, spaced out as they rode through Arlon at a walk. Their hoof beats, sharp and metallic, echoed off the stone buildings. The gang of youths was still absent, but civilians peered from windows now and then.

Richthofen knew the plan, the route, and the timing; his job was to feel their way, to feel toward the enemy, and then back away, stealthily. To be the eyes of the army but not to leave it blind by risking getting caught.

They rode through Arlon and to the western edge of the town and examined the hard-packed dirt road. He couldn't see any tracks.

Did I really see French cavalry? Richthofen asked himself.

He thought of mentioning it to Wedel and then thought better of it. It might give the impression that he was seeing ghosts.

They rode out from Arlon and headed west, deeper into Belgium.

The day grew hotter, the sun so bright that it drove silver spikes of pain into their skulls. They ate as they rode: hard black bread washed down with water. They crossed a stream and rode the horses out along the bank to let them drink while still mounted.

Cool shade swathed the side of the road against a stand of trees, and the cavalry column remained in the gray-green shadows. They didn't speak as they rode. Instead, each rider alternated his attention between his mount and the next dark tree line. In short pulls of the reins or in the gentle nudge of a leg against a flank, they guided their horses, lances up and pennants lying flat in the still, hot air.

As the sun began its descent, they rode into the cool of a wood and dismounted. Each rider soothed and quieted his horse while Richthofen laid his maps out on the ground; his finger traced the lines of roads on the paper.

At last Richthofen spoke. "Wedel, stay here. I'm going to ride on a little way further. There should be a hill to the front of us and a deep wood—a fine place for the French to find cover."

He mounted Antithesis and rode off, disappearing into the trees. For a few minutes he was alone in the cool woods and he imagined himself on a peaceful ride on his family's estate. Richthofen rode gradually up a small rise in the road so he could see up over the hill without exposing himself to anyone that might be lurking on the other side.

Beyond, there was a wide forest. It spread out to the north and south and to the west as far as he could see. The road continued down into the woods.

Peering over the top of the rise, Richthofen put his field glasses to his eyes and studied the dark tree line beyond. He watched for movement in the foliage or a flash of color, something to expose a sentry or cavalryman watching the road.

That's where the French would be, in the cover of the trees. They must be out there somewhere. Surely, they wouldn't let us get behind their eastern fortresses so easily, he thought.

He scanned the shadowy trees, moving the glasses and settling on a new section of woods, watching for a few seconds, then moving over. One section at a time. Slowly, patiently. An error now would be costly. Perhaps ultimately so.

Having seen nothing, he turned and rode back to his Uhlans. The men, dismounted, held the reins of their horses in a shaded meadow, letting them crop grass. They were quiet, each staring off into a different part of the woods around them. The only sounds were of shifting equipment and the horses moving about.

His fear had left his throat now, and settled in his belly, a hollowness, like hunger. His uncle had said it was something inside you, a Polish word, *nadnerczyna*. Like a drug the body gives you.

"Wedel, we ride on. Single file spread out twenty meters apart. One scout. There's an open field to the front of us and beyond that a thick tree line. Good for an ambush. I don't like it."

Wedel pressed his lips tight from sudden tension. "Very well, Leutnant. I'll take the lead."

"No, Wedel, you'll be with me in back. If we need to form the squadron up to repel an ambush, they can fall back on us. Understand?"

"Yes, Leutnant."

"Form them up and give the order."

Wedel waved the men up and lined them into a single file. Richthofen rode ahead to his vantage point in the road and watched the trees. Nothing stirred.

Wedel started the first man moving. After the first had gone fifty meters, he started the next, waited again, and then started another. The lead caught up to Richthofen and passed him, cresting the rise in the road.

As the rider passed, Richthofen said, "When you get into the trees move in about fifty meters and stop. If you see anything, turn and ride back to me. Understand?" Richthofen's throat went dry and his voice croaked.

The trooper nodded, and then prodded his horse towards the woods below. Richthofen took his field glasses out again and watched. He followed the back of his trooper as he moved into the trees. The next trooper passed by, crested the hill and moved toward the trees. The column passed by, one man at a time. Then Wedel rode up next to Richthofen.

"Anything?" He asked.

"Nothing. Quiet. Let's go."

Richthofen prodded Antithesis at a walk, and, as they crossed over the rise, brought Antithesis to a canter. Richthofen's eyes swept the edge of the trees, north and south and back again, expecting something, anything.

They entered the woods and joined their men gathered in the roadway.

A rider had gone ahead, stopped and watched through the thick trees. He turned and whistled, waving an arm. Richthofen and Wedel rode to join him.

The rider pointed with his lance. Richthofen followed the line of the lance and saw an old cottage. The windowpanes were broken. A curtain blew in an open second story window. Richthofen studied the windows for signs of movement. Seeing none, he joined his men.

"Column of twos, scouts ahead. On the road. Form up and move on my order. Quietly," he ordered.

The men arranged themselves; two riders rode out close to the cottage, the rest of the squadron arrayed along the woods.

"Forward!"

The column began to move, the scouts disappearing down the road. As the column moved past the cottage, each trooper glanced cautiously over at the building.

As the last riders passed the cottage, a hollow explosion rang out, the sound echoing and rolling away through the trees. Richthofen turned Antithesis in the road and raced back into the clearing. An Uhlan was sitting on the ground, holding an arm; troopers gathered around him. Blood dripped from the trooper's arm and from the belly of the man's horse.

"What happened?" shouted Richthofen. His fear began anger.

The trooper pointed at the cottage. "It came from there. A shot!"

Richthofen jumped from Antithesis and drew his pistol. Menzke rode to Richthofen's side and slid to the ground, taking Antithesis' reins in his hand.

Richthofen shook with rage and quiet dread.

Never let the men know you're afraid, he told himself. Wedel was just behind. Richthofen heard voices in the cottage and pushed the door open with his foot. Inside, a boy stood up from a crouch against the wall, his wide eyes fixed on Richthofen, full of panic. Richthofen leveled his pistol at him. The pistol wavered in his hand, his tension becoming fear as he struggled to see in the sudden darkness inside the shack.

"Did you shoot my man?" shouted Richthofen in poor French.

The boy raised his hands, his arms at full length over his head. He spoke rapidly, shaking his head from side to side.

Wedel pushed past Richthofen and kicked the inner door open. In the next room, he shouted a sharp command before he emerged with four more boys herded ahead of him. Dirty faces stared back at Richthofen, the boys appearing as though they had been living in the shack for days.

Richthofen's hand was unsteady as he pointed the pistol alternately at one then another, trying to pick out the leader.

"I should shoot you all. Little bastards. Tireurs, be damned; you're just vermin."

"Richthofen, look at this." Wedel held out a firearm. He was smiling.

Richthofen took the thing and could smell that it had been fired recently. Holstering his pistol, he stared at Wedel's find, dumbfounded. It was a musket, a relic from a different age. He had seen one in a museum once: A blunderbuss.

The Belgians bolted for the door, colliding with one another in the doorway and stumbling out the back door of the cottage towards the trees. Richthofen dropped the musket and fumbled at his holster. He worked the pistol free as the boys disappeared into the thick undergrowth. Richthofen fired once, without aiming. The rest of the troopers ran from around both sides of the cottage, raising their carbines to their shoulders, but the boys were gone.

Richthofen thought a moment and then shook his head. "Let them go. Search the cottage." He walked to the horses, shaking with rage and frustration. He bent to examine the wound on the belly of the horse while the men entered and angrily ransacked the cottage, throwing furniture through windows, breaking pottery and dishes.

After a few minutes Wedel emerged, "Nothing. Some bread and cheese, a bottle of wine."

Richthofen glanced up. "Burn it, then."

Wedel protested. "But, Leutnant, the smoke ..." Wedel stammered.

Richthofen glared back at Wedel, his face masked by tension and fury.

"Yes, sir," said Wedel. "Burn it."

The troopers gathered dry branches and piled them up in the doorway. In a minute, a trooper put a match to the kindling. Richthofen stood watching the fire take hold, smoke billowing into the still air. The voices of the men died out, until no one was speaking as they watched the building burn.

"Leutnant ..." A trooper spoke in a low whisper, distracting Richthofen from the flames. "Leutnant?"

Annoyed at his man, Richthofen turned and a glint of metal caught his eye. His men faced toward the road now and gawked, wide-eyed, at two mounted horsemen. Each wore silver French armor, cuirasses, across their torsos. The metal was polished and gleamed as though on parade. From their tall silvered helmets stood even taller black plumage, giving them the air of peacocks. They held their drawn sabers upright at their sides and glared down at the Uhlans scattered around the burning cottage.

For the moment, all was still, the solitary sound the crackling of the growing fire.

Someone shouted. Richthofen grabbed his pistol as the men scattered, running for their horses. The men at the fire moved for their carbines strewn across the ground. The two Cuirassiers elegantly turned, as one, in the road and galloped away.

"Mount up! To your saddles!" Richthofen barked the orders, waving his pistol down the road.

Wedel leapt up onto his gray and turned to give chase.

Richthofen shouted, "Follow them! We'll be right behind." His face flushed scarlet, knowing the Cuirassiers had heard the gunfire and seen the column of smoke. Shame beat through him. *I've told everyone for miles that we're here. Those little Belgian bastards with their ancient gun; they did their job.* "DAMN!" he shouted aloud.

Hoof beats faded into the trees as the Cuirassiers, followed by Wedel, galloped off west. The Uhlans mounted in an awkward rush and gave chase only barely seconds behind.

Riding hard, the squadron spread out, charging single file through the narrow space cut through the trees, razor sharp lances held straight out in front. Richthofen looked around the clearing, his eyes stinging from smoke and humiliation, then mounted Antithesis and rode behind them.

When Richthofen caught up, the column had stopped in the road, and Wedel had circled back. Two Uhlans faced down the road, menacingly, holding their horses still with lances pointed to the west. The rest of the horses, hot now, pranced in the roadway.

Wedel pointed at a path branching from the narrow road. "Richthofen, they've gone this way."

Richthofen saw hoof prints on the path leading from the road into the woods. "Are you sure?" Richthofen looked back to the roadway, hard and dry. There were no tracks there.

"I can't be sure; I believe so."

The obliqueness of the answer disturbed him. *Sureness would be a comfort here,* he thought.

"Very well. Stay here."

Richthofen dismounted and again handed his reins to Menzke. He pulled his pistol and walked into the woods a short distance. It was a narrow path, but recently crossed by horses. The woods beckoned, dark and cool, simultaneously inviting and sinister. He took a deep breath. He walked to the road and remounted Antithesis.

"We'll take the path. Two scouts ahead; then myself, Wedel, and then the rest of you. Single file unless the trail widens." Richthofen turned to Menzke and smiled, reassuring him. "Bring up the rear. I don't want any stragglers." As Menzke rode to the back of the line, Richthofen signaled the squadron to move on.

Richthofen's Uhlans rode on across a shallow stream cut and then up the opposite bank. The cool quiet of the forest settled around them, only the huffing of the horses breaking the stillness. They covered a kilometer, then another.

Though his thoughts were clearing as the mortification of having the French cavalry ride up on them subsided, his face still stung red. He shuddered, intuitively feeling he had made a wrong move, but not knowing when or how. It was more than being surprised; he felt he was outguessed, anticipated, a move behind on the chess board.

Wedel was right. I shouldn't have burned the shack. I'm being a fool. Richthofen chastised himself. *And the shots, the firing ... Damn! This feels wrong, but we must press forward.*

He thought of his uncle, who, in 1871, had heroically led a charge over open ground into the flank of exposed infantry, crippling a French battalion in a single, devastating maneuver. Then he thought of his reality: sneaking poorly and blindly through a wood toward an unseen enemy. He scowled at the absurdity.

His bowels rumbled from tension, a fear that stirred deep in his belly. Possibilities flew through his mind, but no decision came. His humiliation had given way to a quiet unsettled wariness. He saw Wedel riding ahead and wondered what he was thinking; wondering if Wedel understood the position they were in. Close terrain, rifles, mounted; an image of a battlefield, scattered with dead riders and horses crossed his mind. The Kurassiers' silver helmets strewn over a battlefield, thickly sown with the souls of dead German cavalry. *What harvest would the planting bring?* His jaw tightened, teeth clenched.

From the middle of the column, he could see the lead rider sporadically as the trail wound through the trees. When the opportunity presented itself, Richthofen stood in his stirrups, craning his head, trying to see the trail ahead of the lead. Rarely could he see anything more, as the track would disappear around a bend through the trees or into a ripple in the terrain. He could feel the momentum of his decision to ride onward, but felt that he lacked anything other than his anger to justify it.

Two kilometers into the woods, the lead rider called a halt by holding his lance overhead, pointed ahead and then swung his arm down to his side. With a quick wave of his hand from the wrist, he motioned for Richthofen to come up.

In a moment, Richthofen was at the man's side.

"Report, Sergeant."

"Leutnant, to the left, a break in the tree line. I think I see fieldworks."

Richthofen nudged Antithesis a half-length into a clearing and stood in his stirrups.

"Yes, fresh dirt, I believe. No sign of troops though," he said. His instincts quieted now; he tried to think, to rationalize, but the feeling of being unsettled and out of place lingered.

Richthofen nodded into the clearing. Then, after a moment, "Proceed."

"Sir, I believe we'll be exposed to fire from those positions," replied the sergeant. He pointed with his lance.

"Two riders then. I'll follow."

The scouts broke their mounts into a canter and covered the few meters across the clearing in seconds. They crossed a small bridge and, on the other side, they reined up.

Richthofen rode into the meadow in the sunlight and began to cross. The glare of the sunshine nearly blinded Richthofen. He squinted and looked toward his leading scouts. Ahead, on the other side of the bridge, he could dimly see the barricade that had halted the scouts and left them unsure of what to do.

Mounds of light, earthen fieldworks extended along the woods to their front and then to the west; a shallow stream rolled right to left; behind it was a line of barbed wire. To their east was a rocky cliff, five meters tall, an insurmountable obstacle. From hedges beyond the stream and the wire, rifles protruded, with a helmet or two to mark a French or Belgian soldier.

Richthofen grew cold, and his vision narrowed into a tunnel. He braced for the crash of rifles or the vicious bark of a machine gun. Nothing happened. His mind quieted. *Perhaps they aren't on guard; or it's a dummy position; or they've chosen not to fire?* Richthofen allowed himself to breathe again.

Behind him, still in the trees, the rest of the squadron gathered. They bunched together, a tight group of men, a single fat target, but still sheltered and in the cover of the woods. Their saddles touched, boots in stirrups brushed, unfriendly mounts nipped each other. The twelve mounted men swirled in the track as the horses reacted to being so confined.

"Sergeant! We return!" Richthofen shouted to the scouts.

"Yes, Herr Leutnant," came the anxious reply.

The scouts turned to ride back, digging their heels deep into the sides of their horses. Then a rifle cracked, and a single puff of smoke drifted over the top of the fieldworks. Richthofen raised his hand, signaling for the rest of the troop to stay where they were.

Misunderstanding the sign, anxious, and startled by the gunfire, the troopers, as one, charged out into the meadow. A violent crash of rifles erupted around them as Richthofen's heart landed in his stomach.

The realization bored home within Richthofen. Doom. A disaster. A mistake turned to tragedy.

As the first trooper passed Richthofen, the back of his head erupted into ruby fragments. His face fell slack and his mouth moved silently, already dead. His horse, still at a gallop, collapsed; legs stiff, their momentum carrying them into a ball as they fell and then rolled together in a heap of dust and sod. The horse and rider lay still.

Time froze for Richthofen as his squadron died in a storm of bullets.

Half the troop went down from the first volley. Lances fell to the ground and bullets raked the field, tearing into his Uhlans. One trooper's lance stuck into the ground when he left the saddle. He vaulted over the remains of his horse like a macabre gymnast. His spear remained planted upright.

Bilik rode to Richthofen's side, as if to rescue him, or to ask for orders. He looked at Richthofen quizzically. A single bullet bored into Bilik's face, he fell from his horse and thrashed on the ground in his death throes. Richthofen watched Bilik die. It was the last thing his mind could handle.

After that moment, all was motion and flurry and noise. Rifles crashed again, bullets thudded wetly into horses and men. A geyser of blood erupted from the neck of a mounted trooper struggling to unsling his carbine. Another trooper stood and calmly patted dust out of his clothing. He smiled at Richthofen. Then a volley of rifle fire tore great rents in the man's chest and arms. The trooper sat heavily, looking at the holes in his body spouting blood. Then he closed his eyes with a grimace of pain and toppled over, dead. Yet another rocked back and forth wailing as he tried to hold his helmet down with the remains of a shattered hand. Soon the faces, the blood, and the chaos swirled and collapsed into a noisy morass of shrieking men and crying horses. Richthofen lost all bearing and could hardly focus enough to even run. Finally, he looked to his scouts, began to shout an order, but they had spurred their horses toward the barricade and, at a gallop, both jumped over the obstacle into the dark woods beyond, into a void.

Richthofen turned Antithesis' head, and dug his spurs into the horse savagely. Menzke's horse collapsed, rolling on its side, pinning Menzke's leg underneath. Driven on by Richthofen, Antithesis gathered himself and quickened, jumping over the downed horse and rider. As Richthofen looked down, Menzke struggled to get free. He looked up at Richthofen with pleading eyes, but, if he spoke, Richthofen could no longer hear it.

Richthofen looked across the field, through the dust. Blood formed a mist in the air, casting the field in a pink light. He rode hard and made it to the woods, alone. Somewhere Wedel shouted. Richthofen and Antithesis plunged back down the trail and deeper into the shelter of the welcoming dark. Fear gave way to panic as he rode, still spurring Antithesis, who frothed and spat. Behind him, he could hear another rider, perhaps two. He did not slow until the woods grew darker and cool; then he reined the horse off the trail and pulled his pistol, pointing it back up the track. Moments ticked by like hours before he leaned over and vomited yellow bile into the foliage without lowering his gun.

Wedel, still mounted on his gray, emerged from the green.

"No!" shouted Wedel. "It's me!"

Richthofen lowered his pistol. Tears started, but he wiped them away with a sleeve. Another trooper rode up behind Wedel.

"Spread out, weapons up," ordered Richthofen.

The three riders spread out across the trail, raised their firearms, and pointed them back the way they had come.

"Have you seen Menzke?' asked Richthofen, his voice shrill.

"He was down," replied Wedel.

In the distance, the firing slowed, and then stopped. A man screamed an unintelligible curse, over and over. The occasional *pop* of a rifle echoed through the woods. They could smell gun smoke now.

No more riders appeared.

Richthofen drew a heavy breath and bit his own lip, his pistol up and trembling. He thought of raising the barrel to his own head.

No. Not like that. With my men.

He lifted the reins and tightened his legs to spur Antithesis back to the ambush. Wedel saved him, deftly reaching out and grabbing Antithesis' reins, pulling Richthofen to a stop.

"No!" Wedel snapped through clenched teeth. "It's too late. They'll kill you, and laugh while they're doing it. Don't!"

Richthofen ran the back of a sleeve over his eyes, wiping away sweat and tears. He swallowed hard, then again. His stomach retched and he felt like gagging.

Yes. Fight another day. Thank you, Wedel. Make the bastards pay.

Then, he motioned Wedel and the trooper to the trail, away from the ambush.

Lingering, he pointed his pistol down the trail, and he prayed for a Cuirassier to appear. Just one. Please.

He vomited again, rage and fear in equal measures making his belly wrench, but it cleared his mind by another notch, his shame slipping away in increments. There was an emptiness in him, as if he had vomited out his anger. He felt hollow and intensely alone.

My whole squadron down. In a matter of seconds. Gone.

It felt like a nightmare, and one that had just begun. He was trapped, but something in him insisted that he could reason his way out of it; that he could make himself wake from it.

Is this really what I've spent my life training for?

Chapter Eleven

Bois de Bon Lieu, Belgium
August 22, 1914

The moon rose late, after midnight. It was a new moon, a black orb in a black sky, leaving a dark, starless hole. A fog had thickened the night air, and the trees outside the tent seemed to drift in and out of focus as it shifted around them. Richthofen couldn't sleep. The idea of closing his eyes and being alone with his thoughts left him weak with dread. Though they had returned hours ago, Richthofen hadn't bothered to clean himself up. However, wishing the blood away, he finally rose from his blankets and moved to the wash basin. By the light of a candle, he rinsed off his face in a bowl of tepid water, turning the water a grim shade of pink.

Richthofen's limbs were heavy, all his energy bled away. He moved slowly in the fog, feeling it bear down on him. His thoughts raced from vivid, brilliantly-colored memories, visions of the day that had passed, and then lapsed into the grays, blacks, and whites around him. He felt quieter, safer, and more whole in the blackness; the lurid day had been more than he could bear.

Antithesis stirred outside the tent, tied and pawing the ground. The black horse was a void in the fog. Like its rider, the animal couldn't rest, instead nickering into the trees, calling out for the other horses of the squadron. Then, standing, head lifted, ears cocked, holding his breath, Antithesis would listen to the silence. It was the saddest thing Richthofen had ever seen. Richthofen went to him, and, holding the candle, ran a hand over the animal, feeling for injuries. He found raw cuts from his spurs. Surprisingly, he found no other wounds, no bullet holes, and, for the third time, he felt wonderment.

The cavalry regiment stirred around him. The First and Second Squadrons had come in, gathering all the Uhlans in one place. Near the smoking remains of the forester's house, the surviving troopers of his Third squadron camped, the shack now a smoldering pyre. The troopers moved in the murkiness, brushing out horses, tending to tack, and dressing injuries.

Richthofen felt relief, relieved that he wasn't out in front, all alone, anymore. The adventure had become a nightmare.

In the late evening, the infantry division had come up. Thousands of men on the march entered the forest and then ranged themselves among the trees. Quiet stories of the losses of Richthofen's cavalry spread out through the untried infantry, and the men moved past the Uhlans leaving a murmur of awed whispers in their wake. When they had joined with the Uhlans, the infantry had moved to the western edge of the Bois de Bon Lieu, where they put pickets out into the open fields, then spread out into a front and lay in the crooks of trees, on patches of grass and moss, and slept.

The fog deepened with the night, and the shadows in the trees merged with the starlight, leaving the forest cloaked and small.

As most of the men attempted to sleep, two Uhlans rode down the road alone and watched distant French campfires burn. The fires stretched as far south and west as they could see, across a long valley. Then the fog thickened, and the campfires winked out, leaving a wall of gray, hiding the French army.

The orders came down from the army, to the corps, to the division, and to the regiment 1st Uhlans; the regiment *Kaiser Alexander*. They were to advance to where the woods ended and the road spilled out into the fields, to where the campfires burned, where the French soldiers were.

The survivors of the Third squadron; Richthofen, Wedel, and the last Polish boy, mounted. Richthofen couldn't remember the boy's name—couldn't pronounce it—but didn't care anymore. The three of them joined the other Uhlans of the regiment in the road, Richthofen and Wedel ahead with the boy riding behind them. Richthofen looked back at the solitary figure, now alone where fifteen troopers had ridden just hours before. In the darkness, Richthofen let tears roll down his face, swallowing a sob. Wedel stared ahead, west down the road, silent. If he noticed, he said nothing.

The once-elegant Uhlans were now soldiers. Excess equipment was gone, lances were missing, and soft caps had replaced czapkas on many of the men. The plastrons, the ceremonial chest armor of the lancers, had all but disappeared, thrown away in realization of how pathetic they were against rifle fire.

Equipment rattled beyond them: the sound of restless horses held in place. Then a hand signal flowed from row to row down the column, and the horses and men began to move. Richthofen squeezed Antithesis with his legs, and they moved at a walk. The men rode without speaking. The jangle of equipment and the metronome of hoof falls were the only sounds to drift out into the fog.

Richthofen ached with fatigue and docilely trailed behind the line of riders as it plodded along the track. Exhaustion settled into the men. Though they sat upright in their saddles, the men still managed to doze, leaving their horses to carry them onward.

Richthofen dreamt that he slept.

The column left the shelter of the woods into the foggy darkness of an open field. There, the men stirred awake and the regiment of cavalry spread outward, filling in a broad front, immense and powerful.

They lowered their lances, shook out their pennants, and, in the billows of fog, the Uhlans advanced—horses walking, a single row, shoulder to shoulder—almost sixty horses wide. Richthofen tried to conjure the imagined power of such a formation, but couldn't feel it. He had, for his entire life, heard the stories and dreamt of the great strength of massed cavalry. But, here, now, it suddenly seemed ridiculous and foolhardy, even if it was incredibly brave. He looked down the row of horses and riders and saw the horses disappear into the far darkness, wanting to believe that the row went on forever.

It's as though I'm looking into the future, and seeing them cease to exist.

Richthofen felt ill, as if he were watching an old friend grow weak on his deathbed, as if he were watching precious tradition turn to past and memory. The Uhlans moved into a softness, their power absorbed by the atmosphere of the early morning. He thought of the French knights at Agincourt, doomed, noble, and infinitely unaware as they stepped on the field that it would be the last day. He sensed it now: the *Uhlanen*—trapped in the traditions of the battlefields of Europe, unchanged for three hundred years—had come to this field to die.

Wedel turned in his saddle. "It's beautiful and sad, isn't it, Richthofen?"

Richthofen swallowed hard, feeling a knot in his throat that would not budge. "Yes, Wedel. It is."

Somewhere to their front, a French voice challenged the Uhlans. The Germans insolently rode forward, ignoring it.

Richthofen glanced impassively into the mist. "We need daylight and an enemy to charge. And we get darkness and fog. Perhaps it's best ..." his voice trailed off. "Where are we, Wedel?"

Wedel laughed, then fell into a nervous chatter. "I saw the map at regiment. To our front is a farm—Belle-Vue. Can you believe it? I can't see ten meters and we're on a field named Belle-Vue. War is an irony. The woods we just came from ... Bois de Bon Lieu. 'A good place in the woods.' The Belgians are clever with the names, aren't they? But, never more aptly named than at this moment, don't you think?" He laughed again.

From the dark came another shout. French. Wedel stopped speaking. The hot snap of a bullet whipped between Wedel and Richthofen, sizzling as it flew past, then came the bark of a rifle, muffled by the fog, the muzzle flash invisible. Several rifles popped from their front. They heard sizzling sounds again, followed by the horrible wet thumps of bullets striking flesh.

If we live through this, I wish to never hear that sound again, thought Richthofen.

At Wedel's side, a horse dropped to its knees, rump in the air. Its rider rolled out of his saddle and landed on his feet, still holding the reins of his charger. The horse hung its head. Dark blood, almost black, gushed from its mouth and nostrils. The trooper stroked the horse's head, behind its ears, speaking gently to the dying animal. Mercifully, the fog closed around them as the line of cavalry moved ahead, leaving them to their fate.

Richthofen patted Antithesis' neck and spoke in soft tones, afraid for the animal.

"Richthofen, we should do something. We can't just keep walking along," said Wedel at last.

Richthofen looked at him and began to speak. An order rang out from the darkness to their north, "Canter! Close ranks!" It was the order that preceded a charge. Richthofen wrapped his reins around his wrist and tightened his hand around his lance. The line grew tighter as the riders worked to match the pace of their mounts with those around them. They rode quickly into the fog and darkness, blind.

A long row of rifles erupted to their front, the flashes closer than before. More wet thuds, more horses falling; kicking, and screaming. Figures rolled on the ground, men and animals, shrouded in gray mist. A man screamed, high and sharp, then abruptly stopped. Richthofen was suddenly glad that he could not see.

"They're not impressed," said Wedel, flatly.

"Halt!" came another order.

The row of horses stopped. The French rifles fired again, reaping another savage harvest of Uhlans.

"What do we do, Wedel? Do we charge without seeing anything?" asked Richthofen, rhetorically, his voice was flat too, calm. Shock was overwhelming him, making his mind listless, and dampening his emotions, his mind revolting against what his body was experiencing.

"I suggest that we don't do what we did yesterday," said Wedel humorlessly.

A shouted order passed.

"Withdraw two hundred meters at a walk and reform."

The Uhlans turned about, each turning right, then closing together. The fog and darkness hid their losses. They rode away, east. Behind them, the rifles fired again, bullets striking men in the back, horses in rumps and legs, driving them down in sharp agony. Richthofen flinched as each new volley snapped out.

The French firing slowed, and then stopped, as they moved away. Finally, their formation halted, turned to the west, and reformed. To the south, a cheer went up from the invisible French infantry in the mist.

The Uhlans had not fired, not a lance had been driven home, they had merely walked out and been shot. Richthofen shook, his face drained of color, his jaw clenched hard. Disbelief gave way to anger, the quiet rage.

German infantry emerged from the woods. Like wraiths, they

crept from the fog-shrouded tree line. Unaimed bullets sizzled by. An infantryman clutched at his chest, threw out his arms, silently toppled over onto his back and lay still.

The German infantry formed skirmish lines, one line after the other, each soldier spaced a few paces from the next man. Infantry sergeants shouted out hoarse orders, and then each line ran forward at a crouch, bent to the ground like heavily laden badgers. One line would pass the next, each throwing themselves flat, as the line behind overtook them and passed by.

At the road, a machine gun erupted in flaming gusts like an enormous bed sheet in the sky ripped through. The glare of its muzzle flashes illuminated the fog in a flickering glow. The sound echoed through the woods as the gun fired in measured bursts—firing, tearing the sky, halting, and reloading.

Wedel turned to Richthofen. "I don't think we belong here."

Richthofen turned from counting the line of mounted troopers, now visible in the gathering light.

"A quarter of our men. We lost a quarter of our strength, just walking toward rifles in the dark. God help us, Wedel," Richthofen's voice cracked as he struggled to comprehend.

In the fog, the German infantry started to sing, the men's voices resonating against the trees and commingling with the machine guns and volleys of rifle fire. The infantry was leapfrogging, entrenching tools in hand, and digging themselves into the ground in successive waves. The singing let them know where other German soldiers were in the fog.

The horsemen, meanwhile, stood out like targets on a shooting range as the fog thinned.

The order came to turn the cavalry formation north and scout in the open toward Robelmont. The line swung, like a door, around the far end of the formation until it was facing north. German infantry had moved into the fields toward Belle-Vue, screening the cavalry as they turned. The Uhlans rode north, crossing behind the line of infantry in the fields, toward the little town.

They followed the edge of the woods in the fog, angling to the northwest where the maps said the village would be. They could only hope that it was right, for as the fog thinned behind them, it held tight to the village. After a few minutes ride, the square shapes of buildings solidified in the whiteness. The town was a smattering of two-story brick buildings across the slope of a low rise in the ground. A single church spire rose above the fog, marking its center.

The Uhlans stopped and surveyed the town, still mounted. Behind them, south toward Belle-Vue, rifles and machine guns still barked, but from where they stood, the sounds were softer and less angry. The fog shone with the morning twilight, and time slowed as the men held to their saddles, grasping their lances.

Richthofen whispered to Wedel, trying to cheer him, "I find myself wishing that Napoleon was out there. I'm not so sure about these hairy Frenchmen, these Poilu, though ... eh, Wedel?"

"Richthofen, I didn't know you were a dreamer," replied Wedel, smiling, his teeth bright in the fog.

"Dismount, horses to the rear," whispered from rider to rider. The men swung out of their saddles, their legs stiff. They pulled carbines free, each fifth man taking the leads of five horses and walking them back into the fog. The dismounted Uhlans spread out. With an officer's wave, they moved, closing with the dark houses, moving into the shadows.

Richthofen and Wedel stayed close as they crept into the village. They stopped and listened, expecting harsh flashes to erupt at any moment, and the angry reports to bring death again. They could sense the ground sloping now, feel that the village sat on the face of a hill. Instinctively, they stayed low, moving from house to house, skirting each, trying to stay in line. Richthofen fought the urge to drop to his belly and curl on the ground. Nothing stirred in the village—no dogs barked; no lights in the early morning; no one moved. It was as though the village had died and left behind squat stone bones. The sounds of firing became muffled, and finally faded away in the fog.

Wedel took Richthofen by the sleeve as they crouched behind a building. "No one's here, Leutnant. It's all quiet."

Richthofen spoke as he peered around a building and across a dirt road. "No, the French would post someone, at the least, sentries. They're here."

The men moved again, facing north, sneaking through the village a few meters at a time. To Richthofen's right, a man yelled; then several more shouts followed. Then unintelligible voices came out from the fog, a mixture of French and German. Richthofen threw himself to the ground.

A rapid crack of rifles came from the right front and an answering volley from straight ahead. The shouts became a cacophony and then the sound of running feet came as dark shapes took shape all around them. Disoriented, Richthofen pulled Wedel to the ground and swung his carbine back and forth at the shadows in the fog, trying to decide what might be a target and what might be a friend. In a few seconds, the shapes were gone. As Richthofen's ears adjusted to the sinking noise, he heard a groan begin to rise, building into a wail somewhere in the fog to the north.

"Stay here, Wedel."

Richthofen moved, crouching as he'd seen the infantry do, into the fog. He slipped in behind a building, and then flitted out behind the line of Uhlans, easily marked by the shapes of their distinctive helmets. The group of cavalrymen had gathered around something and were looking down. He approached the men and saw a boy, curled up on his side, holding his stomach. The boy's wailing was softer now, though he would groan along with waves of agony.

Richthofen pushed his way to the boy. "What's happened here?"

"This boy crossed in front of us. We saw French soldiers—sentries— and fired on them. The boy took a bullet ... shouldn't have been out here to begin with," an Uhlan said.

"Clear that building. Light a lamp. You and you, carry the boy," Richthofen ordered, pointing.

The men moved into a brick house, and light spread out from a window into the street.

The Uhlans picked up the boy, carrying him by his arms and legs across the road. Inside the house, a farmer and family huddled together at one end of the kitchen, still in nightshirts. An Uhlan awkwardly held them at lance point.

The farmer's wife pushed the lance aside when she saw the boy, "Sylvain!" She ran over to him as Uhlans laid him on the floor by the light.

As Richthofen knelt to check over the boy's injuries, the farmer's wife pushed him away. She murmured something that sounded like French, but wasn't quite. The boy groaned. The woman then pulled his arms away as she stripped off his shirt. There was a long ragged tear in the flesh of his belly.

"Who can talk to these people?" asked Richthofen.

An Uhlan stepped forward. "I can. They speak a country dialect, local."

"Ask where the French soldiers are."

The trooper turned to the farmer, speaking deliberately in a language that sounded to Richthofen like horribly mangled French. The farmer replied with seemingly equally horrible French. "He says they were here last night, to the north, between Robelmont and the woods. Perhaps they've left."

The woman spoke next, her eyes calm and her glance firm. The Uhlan listened carefully and translated. "She says it's a cut, not deep. She wants us to leave; he'll be fine. She says '*merci*,' and that the boy is always looking at stars in the night. Perhaps he'll stop now."

Richthofen looked to the woman; spoke to her in his meager French. "There are no stars in the sky this morning." The woman looked back, perplexed. "Bonjour, Madame."

The boy spoke to his mother.

"He says he wants to be an astronomer; he didn't know of a battle ... he told his mother that he's sorry," said the Uhlan.

"It's lucky that we found him then. Maybe next time he'll be more cautious," said Richthofen.

Richthofen waved the Uhlans from the house and into the street, gathered them in a knot, and waited for orders.

Wedel walked up, a silhouette in the fog. "Doing a good deed, I hear," he called. "We're to return to the horses. Our infantry is coming up to hold the village. We're done here."

"And where are the French?" asked Richthofen.

"They left at the noise of the shooting." He stepped closer to Richthofen, whispering. "I think they ran right past us in the fog." Richthofen looked away and scowled.

The Uhlans left the village and mounted their horses. Richthofen was glad for the gloom, glad that he could feel ridiculous without being seen, happy to feel invisible for the moment.

They turned and rode to the mouth of the road from Belle-Vue and into the trees. In the light of the early morning, among their horses, the men took count of their losses, writing down the names of the missing. They lay down and slept as the sun rose and burned away the fog. To the south, a deep, thunderous sound of artillery blossomed, followed by a series of dull booms. The sleeping Uhlans didn't hear.

~~~

"Leutnant ... Leutnant ..."

Someone was whispering and shaking Richthofen's shoulder.

He squinted up at the sunlight filtering through the trees and at a figure outlined in light. "Menzke?"

Menzke sat down as Richthofen sat up, gawking at the boy. The boy smiled. A dark brown stain cut across Menzke's uniform and he wore just one boot, the other foot bare. His face was dirty, smudged brown and black. He tottered a little, looking as though he might fall over.

Richthofen reached out and hugged him. "Menzke! How are you, boy? I thought the Belgians had you. Wedel, over here. Menzke is here!" He turned Menzke loose and Menzke slid to the ground, too exhausted to keep his own feet.

Wedel ran over and laughed. "You stink, Menzke. Tell us what happened."

"I climbed and then I ran and ran some more. And, I couldn't find you and I ran to the road and I lost my boot." Menzke looked at his bare foot, cut and swollen. He looked up, embarrassed.

Richthofen put up a hand to stop Menzke from speaking. Wedel squatted next to him and slipped a canteen into his hands. The boy drank long and deep. To the south, cannons rumbled. Pouring water over his face, Menzke wiped away dirt and dried blood. As they spoke, a couple of troopers from Loen's squadron joined them.

"Now, go on, slower. Tell us what happened," said Richthofen.

Menzke looked at Richthofen. His eyes wandered and he tried to focus. "We were on the edge of the meadow where the trail led in. We could see you, sir, and the scouts on the far side of the meadow. The horses strained to move, scared, and we knew you were alone. We thought you ordered us to advance." He stopped, drank again, and splashed his face. Ruddy water dripped from his chin. "I didn't think it was a charge, I waited for another signal, but I couldn't stay there by myself."

For the first time, he looked around at the faces of the Uhlans listening. More men from the other squadrons had gathered, downcast and silent. They gathered around him as though in prayer or taking in a sermon. Menzke blanched, looked away, embarrassed at the attention.

Richthofen knelt next to Menzke and put a hand on his shoulder. "Go on, we need to know; you need to tell us. We won't make you tell it again." He took his hand away.

Menzke looked up at Richthofen, his eyes fixing. "Yes, sir. We charged. Well, not really a charge; we weren't in line; our lances weren't flat, but we rode hard." He sounded a little proud and he glanced at Richthofen again. "I'm sorry, sir."

"Go on, Menzke."

"The rifles fired; their firing was just one sound. The horses began to fall. My horse was hit, the chestnut, Ambergris, he went down so hard and rolled over my leg and just ... died ... just that fast. He didn't thrash for more than a second. But bullets kept hitting him and my leg was pinned."

"There, there, Menzke. How did you get away?" asked Wedel.

Menzke wobbled as if he might fall asleep. He spoke again, his voice slower now, a little deeper, older. A note of grief crept in. "I lay there and acted dead. God knows I had enough blood on me. They came and stripped the men of their gear. They laughed. They finished the horses that weren't dead and drug off a couple of our wounded men. They took the lances and they ... they took the czepkas, gathered them up in a bag. Like trophies. It grew hot and I tugged my leg free; I couldn't lay there forever. I could hear them talking. So I jumped up, ran, and climbed the rocks. I was halfway up before they noticed me. They couldn't follow because they would have to climb, too, I suppose."

He took a long drink and spoke hurriedly, anxious to finish. "I hid in the bushes until dark. I tried to sleep, but I couldn't. This morning, I ran again. I got to the trail and then ran to the road and followed it to the burned shack. An infantryman told me the Uhlans were ahead, so I ran down the road. Then I heard Antithesis calling and I found you."

Richthofen gulped to swallow the sadness and put an arm around Menzke's shoulders. "Trophies, you say? They took trophies?"

"Yes, sir, why would they need our helmets? Trophies, I can only imagine."

Richthofen looked away, his face clouded, and then he stood and paced.

"You did well, Menzke. We'll get you cleaned up. What time is it, Wedel?"

"Almost noon. The regiment is ordered to form up to pursue the French. They are retiring."

"I see," said Richthofen. "And you intended to invite me along, didn't you?"

"Leutnant, you seemed so tired. It seemed best."

"Nonsense! Up with us. Find Menzke a horse. You can ride, can't you, Menzke?"

"Yes, sir, I'm sure I can." Menzke smiled a tiny, weak smile. Richthofen noticed lines on his face that he had never seen before, making Menzke look newly old.

Menzke stood and tried to brush dust off his bloody uniform, keeping his weight on the foot that was still clad in a boot. He smiled weakly again and looked at the crowd of men sheepishly, once more a boy.

~~~

The regiment was beginning to move, the horses still saddled from the night before. The remaining men were throwing water in their faces or eating hard biscuits from the mess wagon. They moved together into troops, and then gathered into squadrons. The regiment was half-strength from when it crossed into Belgium two days before.

Richthofen found Santuzza with the horse string. The farrier was working through the horses, tending their hooves. Richthofen handed the reins of Antithesis over to a groom and moved his saddle, bridles, and packs to Santuzza.

He patted Antithesis on the side, dust rising in a cloud from the horse's coat. "Good man. You've done well." He turned to the farrier. "Take care of him; he's charmed, I think."

Just then, Loen rode up and extended a hand. "Richthofen, ride with me."

Richthofen fumbled with his lance to shake Loen's hand.

Loen grinned. "Glad to see you, my friend. I didn't know who we may have lost. Heard you had it rough yesterday."

"Was it yesterday; just yesterday? Seems a month ago; last summer, perhaps. Yes, lost my squadron save three troopers. All captured or dead."

Loen's smile vanished. "Sorry to hear that. Wedel?"

"He's fine, he's here."

"That's good. Glad to hear it. Lost one to a Franc-Tireur south of Arlon. Then two troopers in the fog at Belle-Vue. That could have been lot worse. Thank god we didn't charge." Loen's voice trailed off. "Well, you're to ride with me, the Third and Second formed into a single squadron. Can you do that, Richthofen?"

"Of course, old friend. Proud to ride with you."

The regiment formed two squadrons, in two columns of twos, with their headquarters at the lead. They rode south to Belle-Vue, past the bodies of horses and men scattered around the field.

The bodies of the French soldiers still wore crimson trousers and blue jackets of peacetime, the colors standing out starkly in the midday sun. Loen's squadron rode ahead, moving fast, hoping to maintain contact with the retreating French army and to break up units before they could reform. Artillery fire still fell sporadically in the fields, filthy gouts of dirt and dirty smoke sprouting upward. Richthofen rode Santuzza hard, trying to clear his head. He felt strange, outside himself, detached. It was all so unreal, so obscene and alien. A landscape from a nightmare. Cresting a ridge, they rode toward a gray barricade across the roadway. Loen slowed the column.

Wedel saw it first. "Is that what I think it is?" he asked.

Richthofen turned impatient. "And what do you think it is?" he asked, quieting Wedel.

Richthofen looked at Menzke. His face was white and had stayed white all day. *Perhaps he is accustomed to horror already,* thought Richthofen.

The column turned off the road into a field, riding out to the edge of the barricade. A French shell hurtled overhead, rumbling past. Behind it, an eerie sound followed—a low whistle as the shell split the air. Somewhere behind them, it struck the ground with a bang, blasting smoke into the sky.

The column stopped at the gray mound, a hundred meters wide or more. It was no barricade. It was a pile of bodies—hundreds of German soldiers stacked upon themselves.

Loen waved to them to advance, and the cavalry column rounded the end of the pile. The men had died by ranks; one row then the next surging along and dying on top of the first. Those at the front were blown flat, their bodies raw and bloody. Behind them, another row propped against the first, more upright. At the feet of the front row, fresh earth was churned, craters opened wide, smoke still smoldering from the holes. The ranks of men were arrayed geometrically, as though some terrible demon had engineered the whole, awful maneuver with this outcome in mind.

"A buttress," said Wedel. "That's what it looks like."

"Yes, I suppose," said Richthofen. He closed his eyes, shock finding him again, imagining the front rank walking into a salvo of shells; then the next walking around their bodies; another salvo, another rank of men. On and on until a battalion was pulverized; the final rank couldn't even fall to the ground. Their bodies stood, arms hanging at their sides.

"Imagine the discipline to keep advancing into that fire. Remarkable," said Richthofen, trying to sound sincere.

"Yes, imagine ..." Wedel stared at the side of Richthofen's head.

A crow landed on a dead soldier, then cawed loudly into the hot air.

They rode on to the south. In the field ahead, they saw a group of blue-clad French infantry walking the same direction, helping their own wounded along. Loen halted the column and called one of his sergeants up. Richthofen watched from the rear of the column, and Wedel rode to Richthofen.

"French stragglers, we should drive them in," said Richthofen.

"Yes, of course," Wedel agreed.

In the field, a French soldier saw the Uhlans and called out a warning. The French ran in panic.

Six of Loen's troopers left the column and drew into a line; they lowered their lances and rode at a walk toward the French. Then they charged. The six troopers thundered across the field onto the French. An Uhlan assailed the nearest French soldier, who looked back with wild eyes. The French soldier turned to the rider and threw his hands over his head, pleading for his life. The Uhlan, riding hard, ran his lance through the Frenchman's cries. Blood sprayed into the air as the man screamed, the lance piercing him. The soldier began to fall and the lance macabrely held him upright where it protruded from his back.

The remaining Uhlans rode the other Frenchmen down in turn, slaughtering them to a man. In moments, it was over, and the Uhlans dismounted, retrieved their lances, and rejoined the line. One rode past Richthofen and Wedel, his spear wet and dark. Something black hung off the end. The man panted as he rode past, a look of quiet desperation in his eyes, his training overcoming his own humanity.

"The Uhlans. This is what we're for, isn't it?" said Wedel.

Richthofen turned and looked at Wedel. "Wedel, yes, this is what we do. We keep them from regrouping; drive them as far as they'll go. Don't let them turn."

"Yes, Richthofen, I know. I know why we're here." Wedel looked away. "You sound like a textbook."

The column formed up and moved again, holding to the roads. Groups of French stragglers ran into the trees as the Uhlans passed, though Loen sent no more riders to harry them.

Finally, Loen signaled a halt and put his map into the last sliver of daylight filtering through the trees. Wedel and Richthofen joined him, drawing their horses together. The column moved up into the shadows of the trees to give them some sense of cover.

"Well, backward or forward?" asked Wedel.

Richthofen grimaced. Something in Wedel irritated him today.

"Now, isn't that just the thing? A soldier that gets to make his own decisions; what more could you want?" said Richthofen.

Loen laughed; Wedel stared off down the road.

Loen spoke. "I intend to send two riders back, report on the French units being broken up and moving south. We can find someplace nearby;

perhaps here." He pointed at a crossroads on his map. "Spend the night, move again in the morning. Richthofen?"

"I agree. We should rest and let the French try to figure out where they're going; otherwise we're just counting their stragglers, and we can't do that forever."

They rode. At the crossroads stood an abbey and, behind it, a long low building. The arriving Uhlans could see the monk's heavy plow horses moving about in corrals behind the buildings.

"A monastery," declared Loen wryly. "Perfect for weary travelers!"

The column moved into the abbey's courtyard. Richthofen and Loen dismounted and let themselves into the building. The Uhlans circled, still mounted, their lances upright.

Loen reappeared at the door after a moment and yelled out to his men. "Horses to the stables; clean them up and feed them; then join us!" He slammed the door as though it were his own.

Wedel and Menzke led Santuzza through the courtyard, around the building, and to the stables. A Belgian groom was feeding the horses there. He looked up at them blankly, not saying anything. Wedel raised a finger to his lips and, with a smile on his face, shushed Menzke. Menzke grinned back and dismounted, leading the horses into the stable. Wedel hushed each of Loen's troopers as they came in, all of whom nodded agreement and moved about the stable in silence. They lit lanterns and unsaddled their horses, then they began brushing, feeding, and watering them.

The Belgian moved about, wordlessly offering tools and implements to the men. At last, the boy stepped to the door of the stable, and waved his hand to say goodnight, then slipped away into the darkness. Wedel looked at Menzke and laughed, a deep, long laugh, harder than he'd laughed in days.

"He didn't have any idea who we are, did he?" laughed Wedel.

"No, sir, he didn't," said Menzke, grinning.

The troopers joined in, laughing aloud. The groom looked back at the stable and shrugged his shoulders, heading home to his dinner.

Wedel posted two sentries by the road and led the rest of the men to the monastery door. Wedel reached up to knock, but thought better of it. Instead, he pushed the door open. The ancient, heavy, beam door swung open silently, much to Wedel's surprise. Candles in medieval iron holders lit the corridor. He thought of Templars on a crusade, smiled, and led the men inside.

At the end of the corridor, a door stood open, light spilling into the hall. He could hear Loen talking, then Richthofen's light laugh, and spoken French murmuring from inside the room. Wedel stepped to the doorway as the troopers crowded around behind him.

A long low table nearly filled the space, the communal dining table used by the monks. Rough-hewn chairs stood empty, propped around it. The table was heavy with bowls of blushed buttery yellow Boskoop apples, pale green pears, mounds of gooseberries and currants. Large round loaves of bread, brown and dusted with flour, stood on the table, heavy bread knives standing upright in them. Cheeses and butter, a heavy fork and a broad, dull knife lay at each table setting. An early-season fire burned in the fireplace at the end of the room. Two monks moved about, putting food on the table.

Richthofen beamed, then waved one of the robed monks toward the troopers. Loen leaned back and took a long drink of something from a wooden cup.

"So, our guest of honor has arrived!" shouted Richthofen as he beamed at Wedel. "The war is won. We'll ride after the French in the morning, and then run off to Paris to seduce their women, and, you, dear Wedel, will ride home to tell our valiant tale. Drink up!"

A monk moved up, took Wedel by the arm, and led him to the head of the table as Loen and Richthofen laughed.

The troopers joined in and spread out around the table, helping themselves to fruit and bread. A monk served them bowls of soup. The troopers passed wine, ate and drank, while Loen, Richthofen, and Wedel exchanged jokes.

Richthofen was the first to retire. He led a toast to the monks, and then was escorted to a bedroom by one of the order. He called for Menzke, and Loen followed along behind, staggering from the wine.

The monk led Richthofen to a rough bedchamber with a straw mattress on a plank bed and a small open cabinet with a bowl for washing. He threw open a window and had Menzke pull off his boots. Tipping over backward onto the bed, he fell asleep immediately with his arms straight out at his sides, snoring.

Richthofen dreamt of French soldiers staggering, dragging their guns, and of a gunshot; of Loen yelling something, and then the sounds of laughing.

~~~

It was daylight when Richthofen awoke. Through the open window, he heard horses moving in the courtyard and low voices speaking in German. His head ached from the monks' wine. He rose, pulled his boots on, and peered outside. The Uhlans had gathered in the courtyard.

Richthofen walked the corridor of the monastery, past the dining hall. A monk approached him and pressed a bit of round bread, thick with currants, into his hand. Richthofen thanked him and stepped outside. Taking a bite of the bread, he pressed his way through the silent Uhlans. He looked to where they were looking.

Two dead French soldiers lay on the cobblestones, their arms stretched over their heads. The brilliant crimson and blue of their uniforms made them look like murdered clowns. Blood had pooled around them and one stared upwards, his eyes not aligned: one straight, the other askew. Richthofen winced.

Loen looked up at Richthofen. "We had guests last night. Didn't want to wake you."

Richthofen took another bite of bread. "I guess we had better get moving, hadn't we?"

"Perhaps. They've been passing by all night. These two got nosy, wandered into the courtyard, and the sentries had to shoot them," said Loen. "Just as well. We should get moving, contact our army, then we can play 'chase the Frenchmen' some more."

Menzke led his horse and Santuzza into the courtyard; he'd cleaned himself up a bit, but his uniform still bore the dark brown smear across the front.

Richthofen looked over his aide. "Glad to see you've pulled yourself together, Menzke." He smiled at Richthofen, nodded, proud. He didn't look at the bodies of the French soldiers.

Loen and Richthofen lingered as Wedel led the men from the courtyard and north toward their own lines, and then followed behind. They left the road as soon as they were out of sight of the monastery, rode cross country for a kilometer, then turned north again, staying off the roads, and riding tight against the edges of woods where they could. At noon they passed the wall of dead German soldiers again.

As they rode into the valley of Virton, they could see groups of men moving about the field, collecting wounded and bodies. Loen led the column over to a large tent where wounded were being tended. As the column drew up to a halt, Loen looked into the open sides of the tent and spoke in German.

"Where is Ninth Division headquarters?" he said.

Faces turned toward him and no one spoke, then they turned back to tending wounded.

Loen asked again. "Will no one speak with me?"

A nurse approached him, her clothing streaked in gore, and her eyes lined and bloodshot from lack of sleep. She spoke gently, in French, wary. "This is a French field hospital, but we will treat your wounded."

Loen looked startled. Just then, Richthofen rode alongside Loen and said, "I think we should be going, Loen. They're French." He turned in his saddle and pointed across the field. Men with crimson trousers moved all around them, amid medical men and women with white aprons and white cotton hats. The nurses wore crosses on their sleeves, like German nurses.

Loen looked across the field; his face drained of color and his hands shook. "Yes, of course."

They rode north, past the French soldiers and medical people in the fields. South of the town of Virton, bodies lay in rows, faces covered by odds and ends of fabric, a shirt, a pack, a piece of canvas—anything that had been at hand to dress their wounds. One row, the longer one, was of men dressed in bright colors. The other was of men in the gray-green of the German army. All of them had their hands carefully crossed over the chests. Richthofen chose not to guess at the number of bodies and didn't count them.

Something burned in Virton. In the center of town, a tall column of smoke stood up in the afternoon heat.

Loen led the column, angled around Virton, across the fields west, toward the town of Robelmont where they had last seen German infantry. The French soldiers hardly noticed the Uhlans. Their faces turned up to watch them go by briefly, then they returned to their work.

Robelmont sat on the north side of a hill, bounded on the north and east by woods. At the top of the hill, the single church spire stood over the town.

The town itself was quiet; a few solitary civilians moved about. Miraculously, it was unmarred by the battle, save for a barn that seemed to have been target practice for French artillery. Richthofen and Wedel rode together, recognizing the house they had hidden behind; then the boy's house. Loen rode up on a civilian, blocking the man's way with his horse.

"Where are the German soldiers?" He asked in broken French, forgetting the strangeness of the local dialect.

The man looked up, quizzically, seeming not to understand.

Loen repeated the word, *"Allemand?"*

The man smiled with a look of joy and pointed to the woods to the north. *"Disparu!"* he said.

Loen gritted his teeth.

"Perhaps we didn't win the battle, Loen," said Richthofen.

"Perhaps," replied Loen. "Or, perhaps we let them have the field while we regroup. To the woods, then."

The column rode to the north edge of Robelmont and passed a large barn. Loen drew the column to a halt, and turned them in line. Richthofen rode up from the rear, his gaze following Loen's. Behind the barn, a large group of French soldiers had gathered, almost a hundred, all with rifles in hand. The French soldiers stood in a line, each taking a turn at placing their rifles against a cornerstone, and then driving their foot into the weapon, bending it, making it useless.

A German soldier walked away from the group of Frenchman and approached Loen. He saluted. Sheepishly he whispered, "Leutnant, there are only six of us, could you help us with all of these prisoners?"

Loen waved his troopers to advance. The Uhlans surrounded the Frenchmen while they broke their rifles, one by one.

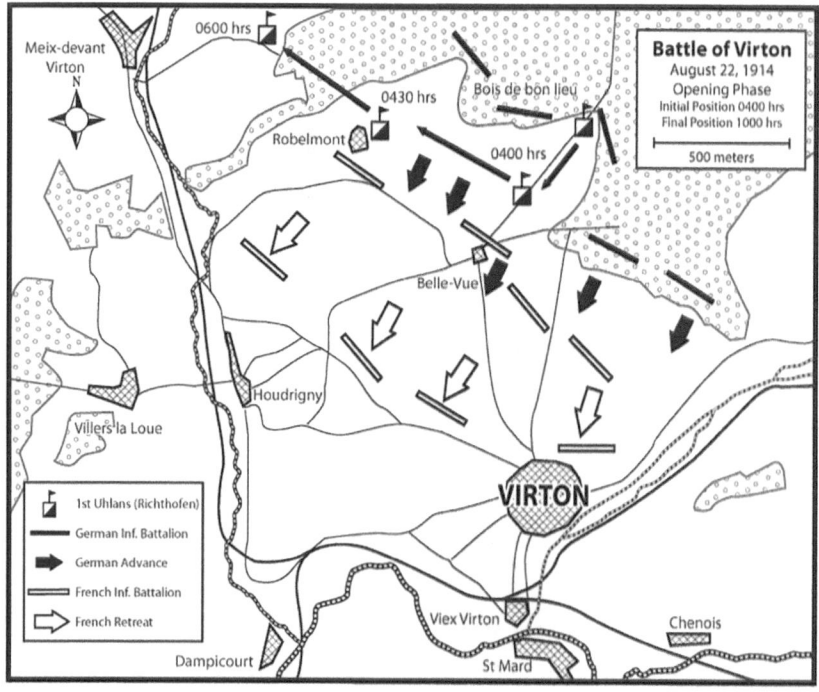

The Battle of Virton: Opening Stages

Chapter Twelve

London, England
August 25, 1914

London no longer slept. Across the city, at all hours, men in army khaki and navy blue surged and flowed. They stood on every corner, loitered in train stations, and milled about on station platforms, all on heedless errands for God and Country. Binges and assignments intermixed into a tableau of semi-productive chaos.

As Hawker drove into the city, a line of lorries blocked the road, leaving for a port and the trip across the Channel. Hawker waited until they had passed then drove his hired car to the gate of the Bayly's home.

He paused to gather his thoughts and looked toward the quiet house.

Black ribbons hung from the fence, and a black bow hung forlornly from the gate. The windows were shuttered and dark. A knot of black crepe bound the doorknocker.

This won't be easy. My God, worse than that, this is impossible. He bowed his head and cupped his hands for a quick prayer. *Please Lord, give me strength, help me to do Thy bidding.*

Hawker stood from the car, straightened his uniform and knocked on the door. From inside came the sound of quiet footsteps, and then the door opened slowly.

Beatrice stood in the entry, her fine features drawn taut from grief. The house was dark and hollow; no air moved. She stood back from the door, letting Hawker in. He stepped inside and set his bag down. The silence of the house gathered around them. Hawker felt heat rising in his throat, threatening to choke his voice.

His own grief rippled across his face in a succession of expressions, all variations of sadness.

Beatrice looked up at him and began to shake, seeming to absorb his emotion. She read his face, could see the odd set of his jaw, the look of a distracted man that had no choice to be in the moment. Intuitive, she felt his sentiment before she understood that she did.

My father, he already knows my father has died. Why is he so upset?

"It's Gordon, isn't it?" she said, her voice raw.

She reeled on her feet, as though invisible waves crashed against her, as though the next wave, larger than the last, would drag her off. She pulled her arms around herself, found a chair and seemed to melt into it.

Hawker froze, confused, nonplussed.

Does she read minds?

He was expecting tears and was unsure how to react. Now this. There weren't words he could find. Pushing the door closed he sat across from her and held both her hands in his. Beatrice stared at the floor and seemed to steady herself against the arms of her chair.

Hawker rose, drew a glass of water at the sink and set it on the table within her reach. He sat, then reflexively took the glass and took a sip.

"Oh, I'm sorry," he said, "This is for you. Let me get you another."

He flushed and stood to get another glass.

Beatrice smiled a little, then took his hand.

"No need for that."

Dear absent-minded Hawker.

"I'm sorry. Here, drink a little; it will cool your throat," he said. He sat again.

"Thank you," Beatrice said. She took a sip.

"Please, answer me, Mr. Hawker. Is it Gordon?" she asked, looking up. Her eyes, steady and dark, contemplated him. He felt outmatched, out of his depth.

"Where is your mother, Miss Bayly?" asked Hawker.

"She's sleeping. The doctor came round and gave her something; she hasn't been able to sleep," said Beatrice.

"Miss Bayly ... Gordon's aeroplane is missing," said Hawker.

"His aeroplane is missing?"

"Yes, Miss Bayly."

"Say it, Mr. Hawker. Please."

"Gordon is missing," Hawker managed at last.

Beatrice stiffened in her chair. She lifted her chin. No tears came. Her eyes moved to the stairs and then back to Hawker.

"He's missing," she said in a whisper, a statement of fact.

Hawker looked at her quizzically, as though she might explain the world to him.

She paused a moment, then asked, "How long?"

Hawker pondered an answer, then formed words.

"Three days. He was on a flight over ... behind ... German lines. Belgian civilians found his aeroplane. Gordon and Lieutenant Waterfall, Gordon's observer, are both missing," said Hawker.

"First Father and now Gordon?" said Beatrice aloud but to herself. "Mother ... she ... my God ... This may kill her."

"It must be the Lord's will, dear Miss Bayly. One can only hope there is some consolation in that," said Hawker. His voice broke as he spoke the words. "Perhaps prayer ... May I call your vicar?"

Beatrice's eyes were unexpectedly hot. "Mr. Hawker, no!" She lowered her voice, "I'm afraid this is not the time; it is too ... soon."

Hawker blinked and looked away, confused, unsure of how to continue.

What else is there to do? What else is there for such impossible loss but the knowledge that the Lord has a plan?

"I do think you should reconsider ... there is no need to suffer alone," he said softly.

Another wave of grief rose in Beatrice. Dryness tightened her throat and tears began to well. She leaned forward and sipped her water, then pressed a handkerchief to her eyes, blotting at tears. Watching Hawker's face, she felt shame, embarrassed that she had shouted.

She spoke quickly. "I apologize. Not now, Mr. Hawker, is all. It's just that there is much to do with our moving to the coast. I'll speak with Mother. We'll find time to consult the reverend. Thank you."

Hawker felt his own shame. He thought he should be consoling

Beatrice, but instead, found her apologizing to him.

I've bollixed this up. She must think me a fool.

He rose and paced the room to clear his mind.

"Yes, of course, all things in their time. Certainly," he said.

Beatrice rose from her chair, feeling the need to move as well. A wave of physical pain washed through her, a deep spasm in her belly, the realization of Gordon's loss becoming real. Hawker saw her pause, her eyes shut tightly, and he took her arm.

Hawker led her to the sitting room, where he helped her lie back on a sofa. He arranged a pillow behind her. "Please, lie down a little. I'll get your water."

My connection. Hawker. Gordon's dear friend. You may be my only link to Gordon.

She smiled. "May I call you Lanoe?" asked Beatrice.

Hawker handed her the glass. "Please, do, call me Lanoe. Please." He felt dull soreness through his entire body, as though his own grief sapped his strength. He studied her, not understanding his own feelings. She was an enigma, a mystery to him.

Why now? he thought. *Why wish to call me by my given name, now?*

"Have you hired a car? Will you be able to take us away?" asked Beatrice.

"Yes, yes, of course. It's all arranged, we may have to contend with troops moving to the docks, but we should be able to have you there by dinner," said Hawker. "You will be able to stay with your aunt, then?"

"Yes, she says we can stay as long as we wish," said Beatrice. "It will be good for Mother to get away ... good to see her sister."

"Miss Bayly?" Hawker began.

"Please ... Beatrice. Call me Beatrice."

Hawker paused, taken aback. He didn't know where her sudden openness came from, didn't understand that grief had bonded them.

"Yes, of course, Beatrice. Gordon was a good friend and a good man. I'm sorry. We can hope for the best. Perhaps the Germans have him."

Beatrice flinched.

He continued, quickly. "They have been surprisingly good about ensuring that our soldiers' letters get out."

"That's very kind. Very reassuring. Thank you."

"You shouldn't give up hope, Beatrice." Hawker sighed, and pondered asking her why she hadn't accepted his proposal. As the thought crossed his mind, he realized the selfishness of the question.

"Lanoe ..." She looked at him with eyes that seem to read past his expression to his thoughts.

He started. "Yes, Beatrice?"

"You need to survive. Survive first. Then think about the rest of your life."

"I don't know what you mean."

"Yes, I think you do. Please, think about it; you'll understand. Gordon lived his life well, and he may not have ... any ... time."

"Yes, Beatrice, I'll try."

From the top of the stairs, Mrs. Bayly called down. "Is that Mr. Hawker? Is it time to leave?"

"Yes, Mother, it is. We're just discussing the arrangements."

Beatrice stood and hugged Hawker gently. She kissed his cheek.

"You are a romantic, Lanoe. Try not to become a hero ... or something dreadfully memorable ... then, ask me again."

She looked up with her dark eyes, and Hawker imagined he would kiss her. He felt silly again, a ridiculous lout. She pulled away and climbed the stairs.

Hawker looked after her, without longing, just a sense of wonder.

Yes, I shall. I'll ask you again.

Chapter Thirteen

Paris, France
September 3, 1914

The German armies streamed south from Belgium, wriggling in long columns like a thousand gray serpents. They drove the French and English armies before them, drawing nearer to the French capital and to the German vision of a captured city and victory. The French and English field units withdrew to the south and east of the city, leaving Paris to coil into itself in an agony of waiting. Panic was an undercurrent, sweeping people away from the city in quiet acts of desperation. Those citizens of Paris with the means fled, taking what they could carry in suitcases thrown into overcrowded railcars. Those who couldn't leave outright moved into the center of the city, imagining that the old fortresses around Paris might offer protection, that the soldiers there were a barrier rather than gilding. The heads of the French government had already boarded trains, during the night, to Bordeaux.

General Joseph Galliéni, the commander of the defenses of Paris, prepared to fight to the last cartridge. Galliéni had retired in April, already ill with the cancer that would eventually kill him. In July, with war looming, he was recalled to service, and now he held the greatest responsibility of his career: nothing short of saving the French capital from annihilation, using only colonial soldiers and the scraps of decimated French army units.

Grandfatherly in appearance, with a thin face and gray beard, and a pair of Pince-nez glasses perpetually teetering on his nose, Galliéni took ruthless control of Paris. Under his orders, his troops flattened buildings to clear fields of fire and wired the Seine bridges and even the Eiffel tower with explosives.

In the Lycée Victor Duruy, an abandoned girls' school, Galliéni made his headquarters. The building stood south of the bend of the Seine, four blocks from the empty National Assembly building. Among a stand of hazelnut trees, it became the center of Fortress Paris. Where young girls had dreamt of fashion and flying and romance, an old man, desperate and dying, tried to find a way to avoid destroying the city that he loved.

Within the school, an empty classroom became Galliéni's center for intelligence, the Deuxième Bureau. The French and English aviators of the Paris garrison entered the room with reports on the movement of the German army and left with new orders, directing them where to look next.

In a corner of the classroom sat a sofa, plush with crimson velvet, and upon this lay an injured infantry colonel, Pierre Girodon, his wounded leg propped on pillows.

Girodon was aggravated and grew more so as he studied an enormous map of northern France pinned to the opposite wall. He doubted the intellect of the pilots, thought they were entertainers, boys playing at soldier.

Flying instead of carrying arms. Damn them.

A flyer slipped into the room and placed a pin on the map, marking a sighting of a German column.

"What is the meaning of this?" shouted Girodon, finally pushed to the edge. "Can you not follow orders?"

The aviator stood, confused and embarrassed, cupping a handful of pins in his hand as if he might offer them to Girodon in contrition.

Girodon bellowed, "Get me up. Get me over there!" A nearby corporal rushed to Girodon and helped him hobble to the map. Girodon perched himself on a crutch. "What is your name, flyer?" he roared.

"Watteau, sir, Lieutenant Watteau ... like the painter."

"Like the damned painter? Like the goddamn painter? Are you a soldier or not? What the hell are you on about? Was he a blind painter? I don't give a damn about painters if you can't see!" Girodon's face turned crimson and his hands balled into fists.

From the next room, General Clergerie, Galliéni's chief of staff, emerged. A step behind Clergerie stood Galliéni, pensive and thoughtful. He wrinkled his brow at Girodon. At Clergerie's side was a flyer, goggles in one hand, a man with big brown doe eyes and an enormous dark moustache.

"What's the shouting about, Girodon?" Clergerie asked.

"The damn map, General. These pilots! They can't follow orders. Don't seem to understand simple directions. This is a waste of our time," Girodon fumed, but tried to calm himself before the general.

Galliéni stepped up and examined the map, his arms braced behind his back, his shoulders so thin that he appeared to be melting under his uniform. "Perhaps the instructions aren't clear," offered the dark-eyed man with Clergerie.

Girodon's eyes went wild. He rounded on the man. "And just who in the hell are you?" he demanded.

"Roland Garros," said the young man. "Perhaps the instructions aren't clear; perhaps I can help."

"The damned tennis player? What do they call you, 'ace?' Are you going to fly me a loop? Or fly to Africa? Perhaps you should. What the hell do you know about war?" Girodon was quivering now, in danger of falling.

"Girodon, calm down. Speak civilly. What do you mean?" said Galliéni.

Clergerie turned to Garros. "My apologies, Garros."

Girodon's eyes flew back and forth between the two as though they had gone mad. He hissed, "Who is he, royalty? What on earth are you apologizing to him for?"

Clergerie looked at Girodon, his face dark. "Colonel, you will speak in a courteous tone."

Girodon sighed and braced himself against the wall. He pointed at the map with a crutch, aiming it like a rifle. "Can't you see? Right there! They're not looking," he said. "All these damn pins, all over the map. Germans here, Germans there." He looked at Watteau. "And, you can't follow orders and look here ... how can I believe anything you tell us, if you can't follow orders?"

Garros turned to Watteau. "We are flying there, aren't we?"

"Yes, of course we are," said Watteau. "I can't help it if we don't see anything."

"Is it foggy or cloudy; are there many trees?" asked Garros.

"No, just roads. Empty roads," said Watteau.

Clergerie stood back, looking at the map. An English pilot entered the room and made his way across the room. He stopped and drew himself to attention at the sight of Galliéni. Clergerie waved him to the map. "Carry on, young man," he said.

At the far right corner of a string of pins on the map, northeast of Paris, he placed another row of pins. Turning, he excused himself.

The room grew silent while Clergerie and Girodon examined the map. Clergerie took a step, placed a finger on the map and traced the Aisne River with a finger.

He turned to Garros. "These are open fields, here and here, aren't they? No forests."

"Yes. Quite clear," said Garros.

"And here, there are German columns," he asked Watteau.

"Yes, the Germans move fast and stay to the roads, but they deploy equally quickly."

"Sir, they are looking. There appears that there is simply nothing to see," said Garros.

Clergerie went white, his face a mask of astonishment, which then broke into a wide smile.

Girodon hobbled back and looked at the pattern of pins on the map. He tottered, and Garros caught him before he fell and then helped him to the sofa, where Girodon sat down heavily.

Girodon was panting now. "Can you see it? Can you see it?" he stammered breathlessly.

"Yes!" said Clergerie, too softly, not wanting to lose the thought, afraid he might wish it away.

Girodon, emotional, and wrung out, couldn't contain himself. "I see it! They've turned. They think Paris is empty; that we're beaten." His voice was steady, unforced. He let each word linger as though enjoying the taste of them.

Garros turned to Girodon, "I don't understand."

Girodon took Garros' hand and held it, tears welling in his eyes. "It means that Paris may be saved. The Germans have shown us their flank.

We can hit them in the flank!"

Galliéni turned to face them. Energy seemed to gather inside of him as his brow unfurrowed and his shoulders lifted. He didn't smile, but a look of delicious realization played over his face.

Garros looked at the map, at the arrays of pins, the markers reaching far to the north of Paris, and then away to the west, another group of pins pointing away from the city to the southeast of Paris like an arrow. The two masses of pins didn't touch. *My God! They've turned! The Germans have turned away from the city!*

Chapter Fourteen

Northeast of Verdun, France
September 16, 1914

Outside, explosions from French artillery stomped closer, then further away, pounding the ground like a petulant giant. Near midnight, the men had grown uncomfortable, expecting a shell to crash down on the house where they slept, so they had moved into the basement. They dragged their straw mattresses, packs, and weapons into the clammy cellar. There they tried to sleep, tossing in fitful dreams, and pretending that they could ignore the shellfire.

In the morning, Wedel lit a lamp, casting a wan light around the space. Richthofen and Menzke stirred, feigning that they were waking.

"It should be light soon," said Wedel.

Menzke lifted up on his elbows. "What are they doing, shooting like this?" he asked, his voice raw and tight.

"Just harassment, I suppose. If they were serious, they'd concentrate their fire," replied Wedel. He tried to sound reassuring.

Richthofen stood and stretched, feeling absurd in his nightshirt. He started to change, stripping to his underwear. He poured water from a tin canteen into one hand, wiped dust off his face and neck, and then ran a wet hand through his hair. He began his dressing ritual: uniform undershirt, jodhpurs, shirt, boots, plastron, jacket, and helmet last.

Again, the artillery fire drew closer and louder, the sounds growing sharper, more distinct, until their ears rang and dust jumped off the beams of the cellar and rained from the walls. Then the shellfire marched away, growing fainter, toward the north, into the open countryside; the French using random chance as a weapon, fate raining down from the sky.

"I hope the horses are alright," said Menzke.

"We can hope," said Richthofen. "They should be safe in the trees. The French are firing at a town on a map, no one is adjusting their aim. They don't know where we are."

Richthofen began to climb the stairs up from the cellar, but the artillery fire came back into town from the north, moving south. He paused to listen and imagined the French artillerymen adjusting their weapons, one small notch at a time, moving their aiming point across the town a few meters, then another, and another. The explosions would grow nearer and louder, reach a crescendo of noise and then move away like an angry passage at the end of a sonata. Richthofen thought better of stepping outside and instead stepped behind the stairs to urinate. The shellfire reached its crest and moved away.

"I suppose they're hitting buildings," he said.

Wedel nodded in acknowledgement. He tried not to think about a shell dropping through the building over their heads, crashing into the cellar. It was an ugly thought. A messy thought.

Richthofen offered more platitudes, distractions from the moment. "Small stuff. It sounds like 75s. They're just being annoying."

The men sat around the lantern. Wedel brought out a deck of cards, shuffled it, shuffled it again. He didn't want to ask to play, knowing he needed to let Richthofen decide. It was one of the few decisions left to Richthofen – his squadron dead, the survivors pinned into cellars, waiting.

A last shell, full of spite, its whistling distinct in the gathering silence, sailed overhead and burst in the village. Then silence settled over the town. Their ears rang from the explosions.

"Suppose I'll have a look," said Richthofen.

He climbed the stairs, one at a time, not cautious, just aware of each step. He pushed the cellar door open and looked around the interior of the house. The owners had gone, refugees to the south into France or north into the quiet parts of Belgium, he supposed. Dreary light filtered through the windows; another overcast day. Through a fresh hole blown in one wall, he saw German soldiers moving about. He heard urgent shouts. At the edge of a window, he saw the top of a wagon pass by, pushed by soldiers.

A runner came to the hole, leaned over to peer in and asked for the Leutnant. Richthofen took the order—instructions to report to headquarters—and sent the runner away.

He shouted to Wedel, "Off to regiment. Wait here."

Richthofen straightened his uniform, brushed off dust and walked out into the ruins of the village, in awe at the landscape around him. Where the night before trees stood, still thick with summer leaves, now solitary, wintery bare sticks remained. Across the village, a carpet of green leaves covered the ground, pockmarked by brown shell holes, a few craters still smoldering. The scene struck Richthofen as strangely beautiful and surreal.

Several houses had collapsed, turned in on themselves, and smoke filtered up from the rubble in delicate tendrils. Knots of soldiers moved from house to house, shouting into the wreckage, and then dug through boards by hand when someone, trapped, shouted back.

Richthofen walked toward the south end of town, to the brick building that served as their headquarters. He swept his feet over the mat of leaves, resisting an urge to kick his way through them like a boy through new snow. He passed by groups of rescuers, and then wondered after Loen and his troopers.

Regimental headquarters stirred, up and moving, men rushing to and from the building. It had once been a store; empty shelves sat piled up on one end of the room. Another set of shelves, tipped over with a door laying over them, served as a table. Oberst von Koss looked at a map. Loen glanced up, sipped coffee, and raised the cup to Richthofen as he entered.

Von Koss was saying "... we need to find a hole in their lines, perhaps here or here." He stabbed a finger at the map. "They keep digging and stringing wire, like mean little French gophers." He smiled at his own joke. Loen winced.

Richthofen took up a coffee cup and poured from a china service. The coffee was hot and dark. He took a large swallow in his mouth, enjoying the heat on his tongue.

Loen looked up. "Ride with me today, old friend?"

"Always at your disposal," replied Richthofen. It seemed to him that his consolation for having no squadron was riding with other officers. It would have to do.

"To the south and west again, feeling for an edge in the French formations." Loen pointed, vaguely, past Verdun into the French countryside.

Von Koss turned to Richthofen. "How'd you weather the artillery, Leutnant?"

"Disturbed our sleep, so we moved to the cellar. The French must have nothing better to shoot at than empty buildings. How did we do?"

"Perhaps they had extra shells just lying about and didn't know what to do with them. Casualties are light; 18th Brigade infantry mostly. A couple of troopers in Second Squadron buried in a house; they're digging them out. Loen has your orders, Richthofen. Have a good ride."

Loen and Richthofen saluted and swallowed their coffee. Richthofen gathered three slabs of dark bread from the table, began to eat one, and walked outside.

"I'll see you at the paddock, Richthofen. I'll just gather my boys." Loen walked away to the east, stopping at houses as he went, shouting for his squadron.

Richthofen walked back to his house, giving in to the urge to kick through the carpet of leaves, then gathered Wedel and Menzke. He handed them their bread.

"Off for a ride, again, boys. Should be a pleasant day for it." Richthofen examined the thinning clouds, the sun trying to burn through. In the distance, he heard the buzzing of an aeroplane, the sound echoing off the clouds, made louder by flying under them. He moved his eyes over the sky but couldn't determine the direction of the sound, as though the aeroplane was everywhere at once.

They walked north on the road, and until they met the trail that led to the paddock. They carried their lances, carbines, and packs. Loen's men followed behind them on the trail, laughing.

One of Loen's horse guards met them on the trail. He saluted Richthofen.

"How are they this morning?" Richthofen asked.

"The artillery fire stirred them up, but they have settled now. They've grazed down the forage, and the ground is getting muddy. We should move them this afternoon. Bad for the hooves, you know."

"Anything close?"

"No, seemed to be aiming at the village; a couple of rounds hit the trees, nothing more." He smiled, as though he'd just played a trick on someone.

Scattered over a meadow, the horses ate from feed brought in that morning. A single rope, strung through the trees, converted the small space into a paddock.

Antithesis was snorting, huffing, still anxious, never having calmed after combat. Richthofen knew now that some horses never did. He called Menzke over.

"Menzke, take care of Antithesis for me today, would you? Ride him out to the north, gently, let him stretch his legs and then bring him back and brush him."

"But sir, shouldn't I ride with you?" he asked.

Richthofen put a hand on Menzke's shoulder. "Just for today. There's nothing to see; we're just looking at trees."

"Very well, sir," Menzke looked over to Antithesis, took up a halter and began saddling the horse.

Richthofen walked over to Santuzza. She recognized him and lowered her head, rubbing her face on Richthofen's arm. He scratched inside one of her ears, patted Santuzza's coat, and spoke to the horse in a low, soothing voice.

The Uhlans pulled saddles and bridles from a wagon, anxious to get moving while the morning was still cool. They pulled horses aside, troopers taking turns helping each other, holding bridles for one as the other gave their horse a quick brush over the back. They smoothly checked each hoof, scraping out the thick mud. Occasionally a laugh rolled through the meadow, the Uhlans happy and eager to get out in the open, riding. In a few minutes, they had the horses saddled and ready.

Over the village, another aeroplane engine droned, the sound echoing through the forest. A few rifles popped, and then a machine gun screeched, startling the horses. The Uhlans looked east and saw the aeroplane over the trees, turning toward them to escape the fire. The craft was descending, accelerating. Two goggled men looked down at the men and horses, and then passed over the paddock.

The ruby and blue circles on the wings marked the aeroplane as French.

"Examining their handiwork in the village, I suppose," said Richthofen.

Loen nodded, "I suppose. Damn eyes. Makes me feel naked when they do that."

"Let's just enjoy our ride, shall we?" asked Richthofen.

Loen smiled, "Of course, of course."

The column formed, single file, to pass through woods and moved south, then west. They clung to the tree lines, stopping to scan for French fortifications. They had learned that the rolls of barbed wire stood out in the sunlight from a kilometer or more away. The Uhlans moved in bounds, racing through open fields, then slowly and in single file through woods, to the next tree line. All the while, the drone of an aeroplane passed over every few minutes, and each time they drew up and clung to the shadows under trees, pressing into the darkness.

They moved field-by-field, wood-by-wood, always keeping the French fortifications just in sight to the south. Eventually, they turned west and repeated the process. Loen marked his map with penciled Xs, marking the line of the French and German armies, where they drew close and felt each other. Each hour, Loen took a trooper aside, wrote a note, and sent the man back to the regiment, conveying what they saw.

In the early afternoon, Loen looked south, across a broad, deep field, still thick with untrammeled grain. He turned to Richthofen and handed him the field glasses. "Take a look," he said. "Anything?"

Richthofen put the glasses to his eyes and scanned the edges of the field, "No, nothing. Can't see into the far trees; but nothing – no wire, no trenches."

"An open flank? No French?" asked Richthofen.

"Perhaps. Many ways to find out. But we'll go look," said Loen.

Loen waved two scouts up and spoke with them briefly. They rode ahead a hundred meters, stopped, and waited. Loen brought the column up, riding along the woods that bounded the east side of the field of grain.

The scouts rode quickly toward the southern edge of the field and closed to within two hundred meters of the dark trees. Then they drew their horses into the shadows and stopped. Their lances stood straight up, the butt ends against their stirrups. *A good sign,* thought Richthofen.

Loen checked along the trees to the front of the scouts with his field glasses once more, and then waved the column to advance.

"Wait," said Richthofen.

Loen looked at him, and Richthofen pointed toward the scouts.

One of the scouts had raised his lance over his head, holding the lance level, pointed side to side. Richthofen shuddered. It was the signal for 'enemy in sight.' Then the scout pumped his arm up and down, the lance waving as he did so. The other scout turned his horse, looking to the column behind him. Richthofen could see a silent plea on the man's face.

Across the field to the west, a German infantryman appeared, shouting at the Uhlans, waving his hands.

Too late, a French machine gun fired, a harsh roaring, then another; two guns converging on the scouts. Both turned, spurring their horses wildly when the first rounds struck them, blasting them off their mounts, and flattening their horses as though hit by an invisible avalanche. The scouts and their horses lay still, not even thrashing as they died. The awful pink mist hung in the air. The firing stopped.

Gun smoke wafted across the meadow. The German soldier that tried to warn them was already gone. Mere seconds had passed. Loen stared, his mouth open.

Richthofen dismounted. "I'll crawl up, see if they're alive,"

Loen looked at his scouts and horses, blown flat in the grain, where nothing stirred. The stink of cordite drifted over the field in a gray haze. Loen shook his head. "No, Richthofen, not today."

Loen silently turned his horses and led the column back the way they had come.

The line of cavalry headed north in short bursts of speed, moving through the edges of the trees. Richthofen tensed each time a trooper moved out into the open, expecting the awful machine guns to fire again. No one dared relax until they gathered at the place where Loen had originally sent the scouts out.

Loen put a sentry on the verge of the trees with a set of field glasses, laid his map on the back of a fallen log and studied it. After a moment, he said, "This is as far as we go. We can move east, join this road, then north and east down these roads to the paddock. No need to cross the fields, we know where the French are." He pointed with a thumb to the south.

Richthofen nodded consent, saying nothing; a hard knot in his throat choked his words. He patted Santuzza, letting the dust puff up off the horse around him.

Once again, they mounted, rode along the trees, and then turned east to a road, then north. They passed German infantry in columns, moving south to fill out the front lines opposite the French. They passed an engineer's wagon, full of shovels. Infantry men had queued up. Each man took a shovel and moved on.

Wedel looked at Richthofen quizzically. Before he could speak, Richthofen guessed the answer to Wedel's question: "We all dig now."

They rode to a crossroads, a stable and a monastery to their left.

Wedel smiled and spoke. "It's our old haunt, Richthofen. The friendly monks with the apples." He turned to the trooper next to him, who laughed and smiled. The column quickened its pace.

Wedel looked over at the stables where they had rested their horses. The corrals stood open, gates standing wide, the monks' horses gone.

They rode to the gates of the abbey. The smell of death filled the road. German infantry passed in dense columns, skirting around the gates to avoid the stench. The column of Uhlans turned into the courtyard. The reek of decay was thick and cloying.

～～～

Loen noticed them first, and then reined in. All the eyes of the Uhlans turned up to the row of windows across the front of the building. From each window hung a cleric, in an evenly spaced row of ten bodies, hanging level, executed with precision. Their necks, fractured, appeared to be stretched rubber, growing longer and more fleshy as their bodies dangled. Their hands were tied behind them, their faces purple and black. Foul liquids dripped into fouler pools underneath them. The bodies swung in the quiet air.

Richthofen looked down at the monastery door, standing open. He dismounted and started breathing in short, shallow breaths to avoid taking in the stench. He led Santuzza toward the door and smoothed out a piece of paper tacked there. He read it and then rejoined the Uhlans. Loen looked at him, a question in his eyes.

"They spread sedition. It seems they printed some fliers that weren't flattering," said Richthofen. "Serves them right, I think."

Loen nodded, running one hand over his face.

"Then, perhaps they received justice," Loen offered weakly, unconvinced. He smiled tightly, his face pale in the sunlight.

Richthofen felt he might gag and he spat out a mouthful of bile. It splattered over the cobblestones. He mounted Santuzza and rode away from the courtyard. Santuzza flipped her head, looking back at the hanging monks, the smell making her skittish. Richthofen stopped in the road and patted Santuzza's neck, trying to calm her.

Loen turned his horse without saying anything and led the column into the road behind Richthofen, and then east away from the abbey. Richthofen joined them as they rode silently, double file, back toward their paddock.

The horses, at first tired, sensed that they were returning and quickened their pace. They seemed to know that the day needed to end.

At a junction, they turned south and met their original trail from the morning. They turned into the woods, following the trail into the paddock. A sentry dropped the rope.

The man spoke to Loen in a stuttering ramble. "Sir, the aeroplane came back again."

Loen looked at the man blankly, exhaustion deepening the lines on his face.

"The aeroplanes come, then the shells. Sir, a shell landed right there!" The sentry pointed at the north edge of the muddy paddock.

Loen looked, seeing nothing, the mud having swallowed the crater. He glanced at the sentry and shrugged his shoulders. Richthofen rode past Loen and turned Santuzza among the dismounting troopers.

Menzke greeted Richthofen from the far end of the pasture. "Leutnant, welcome back!" He waved and began to lead Antithesis through the mud.

A rough whistling fell from the sky; broadened, deepened, then became a sound like a train plummeting into the meadow.

A colossal explosion shattered the trees on the fringe of the paddock. Almost immediately, another ugly eruption came, in line, leading from the trees into the field. Another followed – a salvo of artillery was plunging down on them. The shells drove deep into the soil, and then burst upward in flaming muddy geysers. The men and horses froze; the explosions so loud and close that shock held them in place. To freeze was an instinctive and horrible mistake. The shells stomped across the paddock, crashing among the rigid men and horses.

Richthofen dropped his lance in the mud and swung his right leg over Santuzza onto the ground.

"No! No!" he shouted, holding up one hand in an effort to warn Menzke away.

Menzke dropped Antithesis's rein and tried to run, but the mud clung to his boots and slowed him as though he were in a nightmare. He waved his arms and clawed at the air, trying to swim through it. His scream was long and unbroken as he pulled against his muddy prison.

With a flash, an explosion consumed Santuzza in a gust of mud and flames. The impact hurdled Richthofen backward and down into the filth, with the shreds of one stirrup wrapped around his foot. He rose, astonished, covered in mire and fragments of horse. Menzke ran toward him, his mouth working, and his eyes full of panic.

"Leutnant, Leutnant, are you alright?" cried Menzke.

Richthofen stared back, watching Menzke's mouth move. Deafened by the explosion, he heard nothing. He reflexively wiped bloody gore from his face with a muddy sleeve. He reached out to Menzke for balance as the boy threw his arms around his Leutnant.

It is so quiet.

He sank to the ground as his world went dark.

Book Two

Dicta Boelcke

So it was that war in the air began.
Men rode upon the whirlwind and slew and fell like archangels.
The sky rained heroes upon the astonished earth.

—H.G. Wells, 1908

Chapter Fifteen

November 2, 1914
Béchamps, France

Richthofen awoke in their basement to the smell of unwashed bodies, smoke, and something small and dead. He stirred from his blankets and greeted the morning air, watching Menzke feed wood from the splintered building into the stove. Two candles cast a timid light into the space, leaving the corners of the basement deep in flickering shadow. Wedel listlessly dug at one wall with a large spoon, extending the space in their refuge inch by inch.

Sitting up on the mound of boards and blankets that made his bed, Richthofen put his head in his hands. His ears rang with the sound of a distant bell. He rubbed his temples, as though to pull up a thought from the back of his mind, as though there were something important he had forgotten and couldn't remember. When he closed his eyes, he could still see geysers of filth erupting upward, consuming horses and men as the shells plodded toward him. It was like watching a silent film, absent the garnish notes of a bad piano player. He could recall only one sound: the same high-pitched buzzing that always accompanied him now.

At last, the headaches were diminishing, and he felt grateful for that. He cupped his hands over his ears, heard the sound change pitch, and then listened to the outside, beyond their hole.

No artillery; it's stopped, he thought. He looked at Wedel, watching him dig.

"Do you ever stop digging, Wedel?"

"No, Leutnant, I will dig forever. Or, until I dig us out of here." He smiled at Richthofen, showing a gap where a shell fragment had knocked out a tooth.

Richthofen pulled his riding boots on.

"Time to go, boys. I'm off; anyone to join me?" asked Richthofen.

"Not today, thank you," said Wedel.

Menzke stared into the fire.

Richthofen shook his head, again trying to shake away the constant humming.

"How are they today?" asked Wedel. "The ears."

"They still ring. Perhaps they will forever. Did you bring me more eggs?"

"In the bag outside the door," said Wedel. "Be careful this time."

"Ready, Menzke?" asked Richthofen.

Menzke nodded silently.

They climbed the dirt stairs at the end of the shelter, pulled back the blanket that covered the entrance, and looked out onto the moonlit landscape.

The town was burned out and blown flat now. No sign of buildings remained except heaps of broken boards arrayed in rows and the occasional brick chimney. A succession of bombardments had steadily blow each building flat until all that stood upright were brick shells and the trunks of ruined trees. Footpaths wound through the haphazard piles of debris. The air over the town stunk of smoldering rubble and cordite. From a basement nearby, a candle's pale glow found its way out onto the ground, marking another band of survivors.

At Richthofen's feet sat a bulging burlap sack. By habit, Menzke picked it up.

"Off with us, Menzke," said Richthofen. He led Menzke onto a dirt path, through the rubble and south into the darkness. Ahead, a flare went up, low on the horizon, and then drifted down, burning, before disappearing behind skeletal trees.

A German sentry on the edge of the town moved to challenge them, and then stepped aside when he recognized Richthofen. "Good morning, Leutnant," he said as he waved them past.

They trotted along the path in the dark, occasionally breaking into a run where it leveled. Their running caused the bag over Menzke's shoulder to rattle. When they reached the edge of the woods, the sky had lightened and they stopped, overwhelmed by a field of emptiness and craters.

Richthofen looked south through the stumps of trees toward the French. The familiar trail through gave way here to the open ground, its features pounded flat by the beating of artillery. All was gray around them, the sky and the ground both; the trees were blasted, bare, and scorched. Gnawed stumps and craters lay before them as far as he could see: a landscape from a circle of hell. Yet the craters were forever changing; taking new shapes, the soil constantly moved under the impact from French shells. Each morning they ended their familiar journey to the frontlines at a new and unfamiliar space.

Richthofen glanced over at Menzke as he completed his morning ritual: Menzke peed against a tree, steam rising.

He couldn't make out the French lines in the distance; normally marked by French wire and wooden beams propped up like crosses. On the clearest days, they could see a kilometer or more south before the shattered woods began again on the French side. Today, a clinging haze obscured the lines. The expanse of dead ground stretched off into the fog and faded into gloom. The sight cheered Richthofen: he could imagine the French weren't there.

"It should be a good morning, Menzke. Their snipers won't be able to see us. Or shouldn't." Richthofen pointed into the distance. "Let's try that way, to the first trench, then across to the next from the west; belly crawl from there, shall we?"

Menzke nodded his head up and down, silent, his face expressionless. He crouched, half behind a tree.

"Okay. Go!" Richthofen hissed.

They moved swiftly at an angle to the front line, to force any French snipers to lead them. They dropped into a crater, then crossed the bottom, rolled over the other lip into another crater, then ran at a trot and fell into a trench with dusty thuds.

The German corporal at sentry in the pit glanced up sleepily. "Good morning," he said. He nodded them onward down the length of the trench. Richthofen and Menzke ran to the far end, where another sentry held up a hand and stopped them. Richthofen nodded a greeting, and then popped his head up above the edge of the trench. "Go ahead," he said to Menzke, jerking his head back down.

Richthofen and Menzke climbed a ladder to ground level, and then Richthofen, moving first, dropped onto his belly. He squirmed across the ground, rolled into a crater and looked back. Menzke was crawling in a rush, smoothly, a small, low target in the dirt. The remnants of his uniform were the color of the soil. He dragged the bulging sack behind him.

A bullet sizzled by, nearly spent by the sound of it. Richthofen didn't hear the report of the rifle that had fired it. He looked south across the craters and stumps but still couldn't see the French lines.

"Unaimed," he thought aloud to himself.

Menzke joined him in the crater, saying nothing. They moved across the floor and then rolled over the lip and dropped into another trench behind a log bunker.

"Good morning, Richthofen."

An infantry Leutnant was standing in the entrance, sipping at something in a steaming mug, his legs crossed casually. He leaned against the wooden frame. "We were expecting you. Come in." The position, a company command post, was quiet in the early morning. The pre-dawn runners from the platoons were already back at their posts.

"Good morning, Leutnant." Richthofen threw out a salute. "Where's the company commander?"

"I'm the company commander now, he's out there." The Leutnant threw a thumb up toward the south. "Rommel. I took over last night."

"Richthofen. Uhlans. I'm the courier for the regiment."

"Come in. Please." Rommel swept his hand toward the opening of the bunker.

Richthofen and Menzke stood upright, brushed off some of the dirt they had collected, and stepped into the darkness of the bunker. The dugout sat at the apex of several trenches, each running away to the front line positions. Beyond the bunker was a machine gun nest, the gun shrouded by chunks of stone and concrete.

"What do you have for us this morning?" asked Rommel. "Let's see."

Menzke lifted the bag up onto the pile of logs that served as a table. He grabbed the bag by its bottom and tipped it up, emptying it. A liquor bottle, a metal bottle of milk, a packet of tea, and two hand grenades spilled out.

The infantry Leutnant picked up the liquor. "Glad you didn't break that." He picked up a grenade and then set it down. "Is my *Pour le Mérite* in there?"

Richthofen laughed. "Yeah, that's how they deliver them. Ludendorff got his in a sack after he crushed the Belgians."

"So, all I have to do is capture France to get mine, then," said Rommel. "What about these, Richthofen?" He picked up a grenade.

"They keep the frogs busy while I cross the front. Besides, the bangs make them jump," said Richthofen.

"They make our boys jump, too. Remember that when you start trouble. Bribery so you can throw grenades? How bored are you, Richthofen?"

"If it's alright with you," said Richthofen, smiling. He picked up a grenade and stuffed it into his jacket. "What do you have for me?"

Rommel shrugged and then handed over a flattened sheet of paper folded in thirds. Richthofen stuffed the paper into a jacket pocket.

"The usual report: sent out a patrol last night; one casualty from a bullet. Hit him in the eye. He lasted a while, but died about an hour ago. Company commander is missing. Sad. Other than that, not much." Rommel held the bottle up to the light from the door, swirled it to check its clarity, then pulled the cork and smelled it. "Whisky, huh?"

"Okay, then, down the sap trench. They may not be expecting you," said Rommel.

The Leutnant reached out and took Richthofen's arm. "Richthofen, you and your sport ... you've got to find something to do. You're becoming a creature of habit, and habits get people killed out here. This is honest advice; you understand?"

"Thank you, Rommel. I appreciate that."

Menzke picked up the other grenade, moved to the bunker door, then looked out and around the corner as if he expected a French soldier to be standing outside. Richthofen shrugged, then saluted Rommel again and joined Menzke. Together, they silently walked from the bunker and down the angled approach trench, the sap, toward the French lines.

Reaching another sap, they turned, drawing closer yet to the front lines. Midway down the trench, they reached a German sentry huddled in a great coat. The man examined them through bleary, sleepy eyes. "Eh, you again. What is it now?"

"Whiskey. Back at the bunker. You look like you could use some," said Richthofen. "Go ahead, go on back."

The sentry stood, wobbled, his face flush with fever. He staggered, then caught himself and moved back toward the command bunker.

"Give me a minute, will you?" the sentry murmured over his shoulder.

Richthofen and Menzke watched him totter away, and then each slowly chambered a round in their carbines so as to make no sound. They crouched, even though they were deep in a trench, and then stalked to where the channel ended. They stopped there, backs against the wall.

From the French trenches, tobacco smoke wafted. Someone on the French side was speaking, but no one answered him. It sounded to Richthofen like the man was reciting a poem.

Richthofen whispered, "Five meters." He held up his hand, fingers splayed out.

Menzke nodded.

They stood their carbines against the trench wall. Each removed his grenade from his jacket and gently unscrewed the bottom cap from the handle of the bomb. They stepped into the middle of the trench, holding their grenades by the handles, poised to throw. Richthofen nodded to Menzke. Then they pulled the caps from their grenades, igniting the fuse. The fuses sputtered and then sizzled in the cold air.

In the French trench, someone heard the fuses and then swore, yelling a warning.

Richthofen and Menzke flung their grenades high and over into the French lines. The grenades tumbled end-over-end, spiraling smoke through the air. The men were already running when the grenades exploded with two sharp cracks.

At the corner of the sap, they stopped and looked back the way they had come. Dirt rained down, the echo of the blasts died away, and then all became silent. They could smell the sharp, chemical stink of the explosions in the damp air.

To Richthofen, the scent was strangely clean smelling.

Silently, a French grenade, round and rough, sailed through the air in a long arc and landed where they had just been. It rolled across the floor of the trench, and came to rest, its fuse smoldering. Menzke gasped as Richthofen shoved him against the wall of the trench around the corner from the bomb.

The French grenade exploded with a thudding *whump*, less sharp than the German. Fragments of metal and earth pattered against the walls of the trench. Richthofen peered around the corner at the puff of smoke hanging in the air, like a ghost, where the grenade had just exploded.

"Well, then." Richthofen took a step back and released Menzke, then dusted himself off and straightened his uniform. "Let's get back, shall we? I'm on phone duty this morning."

Chapter Sixteen

December 9, 1914
Douai, France

A light snow had fallen overnight, leaving the airfield deceptively smooth and glistening under the morning sun. Despite the cold, Fokker and Kreutzer had driven to the airfield the night before, towing their latest aeroplane. The tail of the aeroplane sat on the back of the truck, and the nose stuck out behind, bouncing along after the truck on the craft's spindly wheels. For the trip, they had detached its wings and laid them in a frame alongside the fuselage, leaving the aeroplane appearing like a bird mid-dive with its wings folded back. While the Boelckes and the other German flyers were up on the morning reconnaissance flight, Fokker and Kreutzer put the aeroplane together. They fueled the machine and made it ready to fly.

When the Boelcke brothers landed, Fokker's little monoplane, the Eindekker, sat before the hangars. Oswald and Wilhelm Boelcke joined the squadron commander and other pilots gathered there. Fokker's truck, old and beaten and spattered in mud, sat forlornly next to the modern looking aeroplane. On the truck was a sign that read *Fokker Werke*. The crude letters were roughly painted by hand and it showed.

Oswald Boelcke thought Fokker's truck looked like a gypsy wagon from which shysters sold mystery elixir to country people.

The Eindekker sat perched now, still a bird, but now like a fledgling with its wings spread, unsure but willing, as though it might try to spring into the air on its own. Its wings were broad and rectangular, the edges laced via cables into a column that stood upright from the fuselage just behind the engine. Brilliant gleaming black crosses adorned the wings and fuselage, painted over the pale beige of the canvas. The crosses looked out of place: a failed attempt at making the aeroplane fearsome.

The returned German flyers were walking around the new machine, cautious not to touch another man's craft uninvited.

Fokker, moving in his graceless lurches, climbed a ladder next to the Eindekker, stepped onto the wing and up into the cockpit. He wore the uniform of a German Leutnant. Then, he stood in the cockpit while Kreutzer stepped to the propeller. Fokker looked to the squadron commander, Streccius. "Gentlemen, have we all gathered? May I begin?" Fokker spoke in German, but his Dutch accent, relaxing the consonants, sounded like a lazy drawl to the assembled Germans.

Streccius, self-important, looked around at the pilots as though his permission were vital to the proceedings. "Yes, proceed, Herr Fokker," said Streccius. Then he clasped his hands behind his back.

Oswald looked over at Streccius and stifled a smile. He thought Streccius' moustache grew bigger each day, and that it made the commander look like Czar Alexander. In his imagination, Streccius' beady eyes would soon peer out from a face covered entirely in moustache. Oswald glanced at his brother, a look of pained amusement on his face. Wilhelm stared straight ahead, betraying nothing.

"This is the newest of the Fokker designs," Fokker began. "I've been working on it since the spring of last year, and I flew the aeroplane in June for the Kaiser." He paused for dramatic effect upon mention of the Kaiser. Then, "We use welded steel construction. A steel tube frame, very strong. This strength will allow you to accomplish any maneuver you may wish without fear of a structural failure. Steel also keeps the aeroplane very light."

Oswald leaned toward Wilhelm and whispered, "A sales pitch. From a Dutchman. In wartime. This is ridiculous. Do you suppose that they're actually squeezing oil from snakes in the back of his truck?"

Wilhelm quieted his brother. "Let the man speak."

"The controls use conventional warping as my factory has used in all our designs. The engine is the Oberursel rotary, producing eighty horsepower," Fokker continued.

"Rumor has it that Kreutzer is the designer, and Fokker brought the money. Shall I ask him about that?" Oswald whispered to his brother.

"Quiet, Oswald; you can jeer later," said Wilhelm.

"This is your aeroplane, and I will be leaving it in your capable hands." Fokker patted the edge of the cockpit. "But first, if I may, I would like to demonstrate the machine in flight, and then I will take your questions." The pilots applauded congenially.

"Please proceed, Herr Fokker," said Streccius, his mustache bobbing.

Fokker sat in the cockpit, pulled straps over his shoulders, pumped the fuel handle, and set the switches for the ignition. He shouted out to Kreutzer, "Switches on!" Kreutzer spun the propeller. The engine started with a rattle and then roared. Fokker pushed the magneto button, and the engine made a *brap* sound and slowed.

Fokker shouted over the roar of the engine, "You'll notice the aeroplane can be flown immediately, with no need to warm the engine prior to flight!"

He waved to Kreutzer, who motioned for two crewmembers to pull out the wheel chocks. Kreutzer waved his hands up over his shoulders, signaling that all was clear. Fokker adjusted the fuel mix, released the magneto button, and the rotary became a gray blur, the engine and propeller spinning together. Immediately, the little aeroplane began to move while Fokker worked the controls, getting a feel for the motion of the rudder, elevators, and the twisting of the wings. The aeroplane accelerated and quickly lifted, rising smoothly into the cold, thick air.

Fokker waved to the pilots and climbed steeply; then, using his rudder, turned the aeroplane around and, skidding a little, dove back down at the field. A few meters above the ground, he leveled the aeroplane out and flew low and fast past the pilots.

The pilots applauded and glanced at each other in wonder. In a few seconds of flight, they had seen the Fokker monoplane perform maneuvers that their Albatros two-seaters couldn't possibly do. Fokker waved to the pilots as he flew by, and at the end of the field, he twisted the Fokker into a climbing, spiraling turn, letting the aeroplane continue twisting as he rose over the field.

"He can fly, I'll say that," said Oswald.

Wilhelm nodded agreement and said, "Come, let's talk to Kreutzer."

Overhead, Fokker leveled out the monoplane, and flew toward the field from the south.

Kreutzer stood, watching Fokker while Wilhelm and Oswald flanked him on either side. Wilhelm introduced himself and his brother.

"Tell me about the aeroplane, if you'd be so kind," asked Wilhelm.

"What would you like to know?" Kreutzer asked without taking his eyes off Fokker.

"Is it a French aeroplane?" asked Oswald.

"No," Kreutzer said flatly, then, "Here comes the loop."

Fokker rolled the monoplane upside down, pulled back on the stick, dove the aeroplane inverted, then looped downward, a few meters over the field. Then he climbed upward in a long arc. At the top, he rolled the aeroplane upright again.

"He was the first in Germany to loop, you know," said Kreutzer, smiling. He looked at Wilhelm. "Please, continue; ask whatever questions you may have."

"Is it a French aeroplane?" asked Oswald again, impertinently.

"Why do you ask? What makes you ask that?" asked Kreutzer, his smile faded a little.

"I saw a French Morane at Johannisthal before the war. It looks like a Morane," said Oswald.

"Aaah, I see," said Kreutzer, finally glancing at Oswald, the smile gone. "It has the lines of the Morane, but, rest assured, that's the only resemblance. It is a new design."

"Are you the designer, Herr Kreutzer?" asked Oswald.

Kreutzer's tone became sharp. "We are a team, Herr Boelcke. Our factory is a team."

Oswald stepped ahead of Kreutzer, blocking him. "See here, Kreutzer, we've all heard the stories that Fokker's a sham and that you and the other designers do the work and he takes the credit. Don't you think we deserve answers? We have to fight in his damn aeroplanes." Kreutzer looked from Oswald to Wilhelm, watching their faces, gauging their seriousness.

"Very well. Walk with me." Kreutzer brushed his silver hair back from his forehead and turned, pretending to fetch something from the truck. Oswald and Wilhelm walked behind him.

"Yes, it appears as the French aeroplane. Fokker bought a wrecked Morane last year and brought it back to the factory. The French wouldn't sell him one that was intact, you see. However, we rebuilt it entirely, kept the geometry and basic wing design, the shape of the fuselage, and threw away everything else. We used new structures and controls, a new undercarriage. Changed the shape of the wing, the airfoil. It's a shame that it looks so much like the Morane, for it is very different; much better." Kreutzer finished, looked back and forth between the two brothers again. "Is that more clear?" he asked.

Oswald smiled, "Yes, thank you. I appreciate knowing," he said. "And ... the designer?" he asked.

Kreutzer stopped, sighed a long breath. "All rumors, I assure you, nothing underhanded here. I perform the calculations. Reinhold Platz and I. Herr Fokker is very creative, a little impetuous. He has many ideas. Design is a collaboration among all of us. Please don't feel that one man could do it all; it isn't true. Isn't possible."

Fokker approached the field now, blipping the engine to lower the power and to slow the aeroplane. He settled it onto the field in a smooth landing and killed the engine. He stood up in the cockpit as it rolled to a stop. The flyers gathered around and Kreutzer started a round of applause. Fokker stood, hands on hips, poised on his stage. Oswald thought Fokker might bow.

"But ..." Oswald pointed a finger over his shoulder at Fokker lecturing from his cockpit.

Fokker began answering questions, about the loop, about the handling.

"He has 'the gift of the first person,' as my mother, the writer, would say." Kreutzer shrugged.

"I see," said Oswald. "But, is he a *whore*?"

Kreutzer flushed scarlet. He considered turning away, ignoring the question.

"He is a businessman. The Dutch are neutral; he is a neutral," said

Kreutzer. He leaned close, his voice low, almost a whisper. "Be glad he's working for us."

Oswald took Kreutzer's arm, turned him. He wasn't willing to let the matter lie. His words came out in a hiss, a heat evident in his voice, rising anger. Oswald felt the familiar ugly tightness in his chest, the clamping down. "And what about the damned uniform?" Oswald threw his head toward Fokker.

Kreutzer peeled Oswald's fingers back, releasing the grip on his arm. "It's not his idea, Boelcke. Geertz put him up to it, and it's a smart idea if we want to keep him." Kreutzer stepped back, brushed his hand over his sleeve where Oswald had held him.

"Just imagine, if you will, that he were out here and he flew in civilian clothes, a Dutchman, in an aeroplane with German crosses? Now, imagine he lands on the Allied side. Then, he's a spy, in a combat aeroplane, out of uniform. They'd stand him against a wall and sell tickets to his execution ... now, wouldn't they?"

Oswald glanced over at Fokker, considering the man, absorbing Kreutzer's words.

"Now, then, imagine that he lands on our side and some bored military policeman finds him in civilian clothes, flying one of our aeroplanes. It could happen anywhere, not just out here near the front. It could happen between Schwerin and Berlin, anywhere in Germany or Belgium. What are the chances he'd be shot just on principle? By the time he was done stammering out his explanation, he'd forget how to speak German. Hell, I'd shoot him. So, just give the man the benefit of the doubt, will you? Fly his aeroplanes and see what you can do with them. Judge the aeroplane, not the man."

"Thank you, Herr Kreutzer," said Wilhelm. "You've put our minds at ease. Hasn't he, Oswald?"

Oswald still looked at Fokker, and then glanced back at Kreutzer. "Thank you. I appreciate your loyalty," he said vaguely. Oswald turned back to Fokker, and walked over to join the crowd.

Wilhelm turned to Kreutzer and put out his hand. "My apologies for my brother; he's a little bullheaded."

Kreutzer took his hand, shook it. "We're getting used to these questions." He shrugged.

Fokker continued talking with the flyers. Each would patiently raise their hand and Fokker would point and answer their questions. Oswald thought they looked like schoolchildren and the thought troubled him. The questions gradually subsided, and the men looked around at each other, satisfied.

"Any further questions?" asked Fokker. "Anything at all?"

Oswald glanced at Streccius, saw his commander turned away in a quiet conversation with his adjutant. From the back of the crowd, he raised his hand.

"Yes, Leutnant," said Fokker.

"Will you stand by your aeroplane, when we fight it?" asked Oswald.

"I don't know what you mean," said Fokker.

Oswald Boelcke glanced again at Streccius, who turned back and looked toward Oswald. Streccius' enormous moustache seemed to be moving of its own accord and the whiskers hid his expression.

"We've only flown German-designed and manufactured aeroplanes. Taubes and Albatrosses. Clearly, those companies have a stake in our success. Do you?" asked Oswald.

Fokker's face flushed, and his hands clenched. He began to stammer an answer, at a loss of words.

Streccius held up a hand, stopping Fokker before he could speak. "Herr Fokker, there is no need to answer that question. That is a matter for you and our command."

Fokker glared down at Oswald, his face set in grim anger. He took a deep breath, tried to force himself to relax.

Oswald felt his lungs tense, and he let out his breath gradually in a shallow wheeze, holding the air to muffle the sound so no one would hear.

"Very well. Thank you, Hauptmann," said Fokker, smiling to Streccius. "Now, then, who will this aeroplane be assigned to so that I may begin flight instruction? Your best pilot, I presume."

Streccius glanced at the Boelckes, contemplating his decision, then with a shrug he lifted a hand and pointed at Oswald. "That man, our

Leutnant Boelcke."

"I see," said Fokker, his hands clenching and unclenching at his side.

Oswald felt his lungs flare into pain; the tightness holding his breath in until he felt his chest would burst.

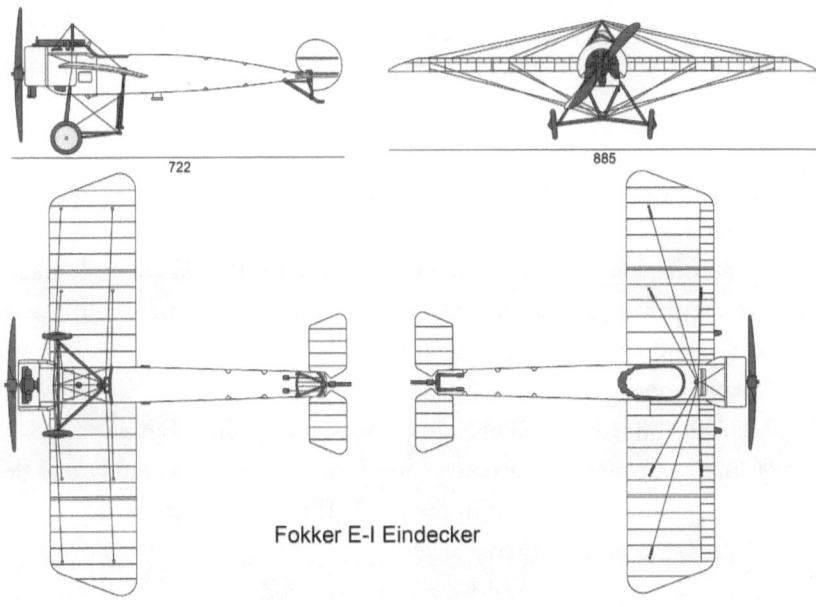

Fokker E-I Eindecker

Chapter Seventeen

January 2, 1915
Béchamps, France

"It really stinks in here, Leutnant." Menzke wrinkled his nose, pretending he had just noticed.

Richthofen looked up from where he sat against the wall of his bunker. He was sharpening a long French bayonet with a steel. The sound was a soft scraping like a rodent clawing at the wall.

"So, you do speak," he said at last.

Menzke nodded and pinched his nose, signaling his disgust.

"Can't be helped." Richthofen waved the bayonet at a muddy puddle next to the crude stairs carved in the dirt. "Throw some dirt on it."

"Will it stop soon?" asked Menzke.

"My, you are feeling positively talkative suddenly," said Richthofen. "Waiting for the rain to stop isn't healthy, is it?" Richthofen waved the bayonet in a circle in the air, pointing up beyond the ceiling to the artillery shells coming down. Menzke looked past Richthofen; his eyes seemed to focus far outside the walls of their hole in the ground. He didn't reply.

Richthofen cocked his head to the side, listening, judging the distance of the impacting French artillery by sound. He now knew the whistle of the small shells, the peculiar whirring hiss of the mediums and the rushing freight-train sound of the heavies. The shells walked toward them, crashing in threes and fours, battery fire: cannons firing together. Then the shells marched away. The walls had shaken so often and so long that they didn't spray dust from the close ones anymore. This struck Richthofen as an improvement.

"Yes, it will stop soon. Then it will start again, then it will stop," said Richthofen. "Does that help?"

Menzke stared at Richthofen, not speaking.

"I can't sleep, even without the artillery. I just dream of it, and horses. Santuzza deserved better," said Richthofen. "Shall we go for an evening ride, Menzke?"

The boy nodded silently, his expression unchanging.

There was a rustling at the top of the stairs, the outer blankets moved, and the inner blankets opened. Wedel came down the stairs, his arms heavy with bread and cheese. He held a bottle of something green in one hand.

"Good evening, gentlemen." Wedel wrinkled his nose. "Shovel the piss, would you, Menzke?" he asked.

Menzke stood and took up a shovel and tossed some dirt on the puddle by the stairs. Afterwards, he took a piece of bread from Wedel, sat, and chewed on it.

Richthofen looked over at Wedel, shifted his legs from one side to the other. "Dispatches in the morning?"

"No, the wires to the front trenches are still working. They'll just phone back. No matter. They'll come find us if they want us," said Wedel.

Richthofen sighed. "I never thought I'd miss running messages to the lines."

"I don't, actually. Miss it, I mean," said Wedel.

"Dinner?" he pushed a chunk of black bread at Richthofen, a thick slice of sausage lying across it. Richthofen took the bread but handed the sausage back.

"No, thank you." He patted his stomach.

"Yeah, it seems either you can't go or you can't stop. That may be the lone unpredictable thing here. Well, that, and if a shell lands on your head. Perhaps you weren't meant to eat meat, Richthofen." Wedel smiled, took a bite of sausage, and skewered it on the end of a knife. He pulled the cork on the bottle, took a long drink.

"Would you believe there's a building burning out there? I wouldn't have believed anything was left to burn," said Wedel around a mouthful of bread.

"I'm getting fat, Wedel," said Richthofen, ignoring him.

"We all are. It's the bread and sitting. But at least we have bread."

"Antithesis is sick; his head is drooping. His nose is wet. If I ever jump him again, I'll have to lose weight so I don't break his back," said Richthofen.

Richthofen finished with the bayonet and tested the edge with his thumb, brushing it across the sharpness. "Perhaps he needs to be ridden to open his lungs."

"Richthofen?"

"Yes, Wedel?"

Wedel chattered, "You sound like my mother when you talk about getting fat." He paused, as though shifting gears. "They're going to reassign us to Eighteenth Brigade to fill in some of their staff positions. Supply positions."

Richthofen tightened his jaw, slid the bayonet along his thumb, and watched blood ooze. "I see."

He looked over at Menzke, expecting a reaction. Menzke stared at something a hundred miles away. His vision bored through the wall, the earth, and the hills, to whatever place held his attention. Then he lifted one finger, pointing upward.

Richthofen cocked his head, began to ask Menzke what he was pointing at, heard the ringing in his ears and then heard the silence. "Oh," he said. "It stopped."

A round struck somewhere to the east, a long way away, the sound dull and hollow.

The boy nodded.

"Mind if I use your saddle, Wedel?" asked Richthofen. He didn't need to add: *Mine was blown to bits along with my horse.*

Wedel nodded his consent, still eating.

Menzke stood, throwing his bread on his blanket. He brushed off his grimy hands onto his grimy pants.

"Pick it up. Mind the rats." Wedel pointed an elbow at Menzke's bread.

Menzke tossed the chunk of bread to Wedel, who put it into a bag. Menzke picked up his carbine.

Richthofen put on the ermine coat that his mother had sent him; then he and Menzke put on their cloaks and helmets, and they walked over to the dirt stairs. They listened, waiting to be sure that the artillery fire wasn't moving back toward the village.

Richthofen waved a good bye. "See you later, Wedel."

Wedel, reclining on a pile of canvas, gave a casual wave back, stretched out his legs and took a bite of sausage.

At the top of the stairs, they paused again and looked around the village. Smoke from the burning building rose straight up in the cold air, the smell reminding Richthofen of a campfire made of houses. They walked north through the mounds of debris and craters that had once been the town of Béchamps. From the clumps of wreckage, men stirred, seeming to emerge like wraiths from the ground.

The ground was hard, almost frozen. A low layer of clouds hid the sunset, turning a diffuse white sky to pale gray as the sun retreated. It smelled of snow now, away from the town, but Richthofen said nothing, not wanting to raise Menzke's hopes.

"Leutnant Richthofen?" asked Menzke.

"Yes?"

"Will it always be like this?" Menzke looked at Richthofen with big, dark, child-like eyes.

Richthofen smiled, began to laugh, and then stopped himself. "No, Menzke, the spring will come, the trees will become green again." Richthofen looked at the gray, empty trunks standing along the road and doubted his own words.

"No, Leutnant, the war, I mean. Will we always be here, in holes?" asked Menzke. The words spilled out of him in a rush.

Richthofen listened to their feet on the road, the stiff soles of their boots clacking on the hard ground. "Of course not, we'll force a breakthrough somewhere; it's just a matter of time." He tried to sound confident and hoped that Menzke believed him.

"I heard some infantrymen talking. They said this is hell. That humanity is getting what it deserves, that we've all ... we've all been banished to the pit for our sins." A strange, distant expression crossed Menzke's face, grim, as if he might have found an important truth.

Richthofen replied, "No, Menzke. This is just dirt and bullets; it's not the real hell." His voice sounded gruffer than he intended, and he glanced at Menzke to gauge the boy's reaction.

Menzke's eyes stayed focused down the road, into the grayness of the descending evening. "If this is hell, though, there must be angels, fallen angels, isn't that right?"

"Yes, Menzke. There must be angels," agreed Richthofen, wanting the subject to change, a feeling of queasy uncertainty growing in him.

After an hour's walk, they reached the horse paddocks as the sky began to snow. Menzke's eyes grew wide as soft, sticky flakes drifted down, gathering on the shoulders of their cloaks. He fumbled and found his gloves and smiled at Richthofen. Soon the snow was falling thick, collecting on the frozen ground. Richthofen wondered to himself if they should ride, whether it was too cold for Menzke's or Antithesis' health. A cough had gone through the infantry. A few had died, and he didn't want Menzke sick.

The snow was beginning to muffle sound and make the world around the horses softer, soothing them. At the corral, Antithesis was eating, quiet, less anxious.

Without hurry, they found their saddles and bridles, letting the horses enjoy their peace in the falling snow. They put bridles on Antithesis, then Wedel's borrowed blanket and saddle. After tying off Antithesis, they pulled a gray from the string for Menzke: a big, calm mare.

Mounted, they pulled their cloaks around themselves and rode to the northeast, away from Béchamps, toward the thicker woods closer to Luxembourg. A few German soldiers passed them, in small groups, marching down the road, replacements or supply people. The soldiers greeted the sight of the two horsemen with hearty "hellos" and smiles, cheered by the vision of the men riding peacefully; a remnant of a world that seemed a long time ago.

Menzke and Richthofen found a narrow path that led north into the woods, and rode down, Richthofen leading. They rode leisurely, slowly. The snowfall and the trees soaked up the sound of their passage. As they rode, the sounds of cannon fire to the south faded, and then finally disappeared.

The sky over them turned from gray to black, the clouds parting, leaving behind a soft, white blanket on the ground.

Then a full moon rose, lighting the path through the trees.

Eventually they came to a pond ringed with ice. Hornbeam trees grew along the east and north shores, impassible on the north side. The branches of the trees strained up to the dark sky like dead fingers.

"We'll come back in the spring and let the horses swim, shall we?" Richthofen suggested. He smiled at Menzke. A tightness around Menzke's eyes suggested that he wasn't so confident that they would still be there in the spring.

Menzke raised a hand and pointed to the east shore.

Richthofen looked, and saw something stir there, dark shapes low to the ground, moving in a line around to the north shore of the water. He smiled, almost laughed.

"Let's have some sport, shall we?" he whispered.

Richthofen dismounted and handed Antithesis' reins to Menzke. He reached across Menzke's saddle and pulled his carbine from its straps, opened it, and put a bullet in the chamber.

"Wait here."

Richthofen headed west at a trot, enjoying the feeling of his legs in motion. His breath billowed in clouds around him. The sounds of his footfalls were soft in the snow, but the snow was not deep enough to slow him so he moved swiftly. He ran for a short way, and then slowed again, crossing a fallen tree onto an open field. Then he walked along the western shore of the pond and turned when he reached a tree line.

He found a stump—the tree chopped down by the owner of the fields to let the sunlight in—sat, and waited. The moon was behind him and making the field brighter for the snow. Richthofen's heart pounded in his chest, and he tried to breathe deeply to force it to quiet. A short time later, a rustling came from the bushes, and then stopped, followed by the sound of grunting pigs chattering among themselves. He drew the carbine to his shoulder, braced it there, then held the muzzle down, and waited. His breath was the only thing that moved around him.

After a moment, a line of wild pigs slipped out of the bushes, creeping out into the field. They appeared single file, and then spread out. They tipped their heads down and began nosing through the snow. Another group of pigs appeared behind them. There were six now in the field, rooting. Every few minutes one of them would offer a deeper grunt, a sign of acknowledgement, then stand in place and paw the ground, overturning a potato or a beet from the cold soil.

Richthofen trained his rifle from one to the next, eyeing them each through the sights of the carbine. He smiled to himself, enjoying the moment. His heart had quieted.

From the brush came another grunt followed by more rustling. Richthofen lowered the carbine, waiting. The sound grew louder, more distinct. A small pig appeared from the brush. Then, behind it, came another, larger animal. It was a boar, a moving blackness in the moonlight: the leader of the group. He strode out into the field with his head tilted up, looking around into the darkness and across the snow. Richthofen could see tusks on the sides of the boar's head reflecting the moon.

Richthofen steadied the carbine, settling the sights on the animal, at the shoulder blade. The boar sensed the movement and turned.

Too late.

Richthofen took a breath, slowly released it, and then gently squeezed the trigger.

The crack of the carbine shattered the stillness. The sound was followed by a long rushing sound that seemed to circle around the woods before returning to the field. The pigs, terrified, scattered, each running in a different direction.

The boar howled and tried to bite the wound. It turned once, back on itself, lifted its head upward as though staring at the sky, grew quiet and then toppled into the soft snow.

Richthofen lowered the rifle and grinned. Behind him, he heard the sound of their horses approaching and of panting in the cold air. Menzke called out, "Leutnant! Leutnant!"

Richthofen stood, and walked a few steps toward the sound. "Over here!"

Menzke rode up, leading Antithesis. "What happened? Are you shot?"

"No, no, nothing like that. We have a trophy."

Richthofen waved his arm across the field, as though making a grand presentation. Nothing stirred; the boar lay there, merely a dark mound in the moonlight. Steam rose from the animal's open mouth and wound.

"Over here. Follow me," said Richthofen.

Richthofen walked toward the boar, and Menzke rode behind him. He drew the long French bayonet from his riding boot. Kneeling, he slid the bayonet into the back of the animal's neck, then cracked its spine apart below the head. Thick steam rose from the open body as the blood spilled out onto the clean snow. Richthofen sliced downward, then rolled the animal over with his foot and sliced again, this time sawing through the animal's neck. He wiped the bayonet against the fur of the carcass and then slid the knife back into his boot.

Bending, he took the animal's head by the wiry mane and lifted it up, using two hands to support the weight. Waving the head toward Menzke, he grinned. "A prize," he said.

Menzke smiled despite himself. He hadn't seen the Leutnant so pleased since the war started and couldn't help himself.

"Here, hold it." Richthofen swung the gruesome prize up and into Menzke's lap. Blood ran down Menzke's leg and left a dark smear on the flank of the gray horse. Richthofen climbed into Wedel's saddle and Menzke handed the head over to him.

"We'll leave the meat, but, I think I'll come back, Menzke. Make a tree stand, wait for more pigs, perhaps bring them back for soup. Will you help me, Menzke?" Richthofen asked.

He smiled. "Yes, Leutnant. Certainly."

They turned and rode back down the trail, then onto the road. While they rode, they spoke of home, Christmas, and families. Dripping blood from the boar's head left a black trail in the moonlight. At the paddock, Menzke lay the trophy carefully in the snow as they took the saddles from their horses and brushed the animals.

Menzke carried the head as they walked back into the remains of the town. "What shall we do with this?" he asked Richthofen.

"I'd like to keep it. What do you think?"

"Yes, keep it," replied Menzke. "It's your first trophy since the war began," "It is that."

At the bunker, Richthofen drew the blankets back as Menzke carried the head down the steps and laid it on the floor of the basement. Wedel opened one eye, then rolled over and snored, not looking at them. Richthofen pointed at the wall of the basement and drew his bayonet from his boot. He hacked at the wall, digging with the butt of the weapon. Menzke joined Richthofen, scraping the wall with an entrenching shovel. In a few minutes, they had carved a shelf.

Richthofen and Menzke grinned at each other, proud of their handiwork. Menzke mounted the head on the shelf, a tusked dead thing.

In the morning, Wedel stirred in his blankets and looked across the bunker at Richthofen.

He saw the boar's head staring at him.

"Shit!" yelled Wedel, leaping to his feet at the sight of the leering monster.

Richthofen smiled and rolled over, pulling the blankets over his head, falling back into a dreamless sleep.

Chapter Eighteen

March 18, 1915
Saint-Pol-sur-Mer Aerodrome
20 km South of Dunkirk, France

The briny smell of the sea blew in through the open hangar door. Inside the building, tiny drops of red-hot metal flew through the air and added their molten scent to the fragrance of the ocean. Their odor was of chemical vapors and iridescence, as though their glow and smell were one.

Garros bent over the anvil and struck hot steel with a hammer. Each blow sprayed more sparks up and across the floor. Raymond Saulnier watched, shaking his head with quiet disbelief. He held a single upright index finger across his chin and over his lips. Garros paused and lifted the shield from his face, letting his eyes adjust to the daylight. He drew a heavy breath and sighed, a little frustrated at the slowness of his labors. He glanced at the drawings and then back at the metal wedge. It didn't help that Saulnier was watching. He closed his eyes, waiting for a fatherly scolding.

Saulnier's enormous moustache hid his mouth, but his eyes betrayed his frustration. An old man in his thirties, Garros' mentor, could read his emotions in the wrinkles around Garros' eyes.

"So, dear Roland, how is your project progressing?"

Garros paused, not rising to the bait. "I can complete it. It will work." He spoke simply, plainly, trying not to condescend, but not to engage either. He resisted the urge to reach out and touch the hot metal wedge.

"Sit, Roland, let us speak." Saulnier spoke formally, smoothly, in the manner of a manager bringing an errant worker to task.

Garros glanced down, considered retreating behind the welding mask and waving Saulnier away. But his respect for Saulnier was greater than the urge for insolence, and he pointed to two stools propped next to the workbench. The two men sat, and Garros pulled the welding mask off his head. He leaned heavily on the bench.

"Monsieur Saulnier, I always have time for you." Garros picked up an awl and began to clean his fingernails.

Saulnier took the awl away, setting it back on the workbench. Garros straightened, sensitive to the silent rebuke.

Saulnier spoke. "Please, Roland, if you will, let's discuss this … project."

Garros posed his hands in his lap. He imagined himself elsewhere.

"You understand how dangerous this is, don't you? These wedges are crude, too simple, and damned dangerous. You're more likely to shoot yourself down than anyone else," said Saulnier. "Why the urgency; why now? Why not just have some patience?"

Garros looked out the open door of the hangar and scowled; he shook his head then looked back at Saulnier.

"We need to do something. This situation is unacceptable."

"Go on, Roland. Explain."

"The German artillery, directed by their aeroplanes." He waved a hand at the air, as if he could wave the thought away. His voice rose, "You've got to see it to believe it! With impunity, they direct their guns onto us, walking their shells to where the most men will die. It is horrible. Aeroplanes are doing this. Aeroplanes!" Garros' voice trailed off. "It must end."

"Oui, oui, yes, I know. But this? This is near madness."

"Ah," said Garros. He glanced at the floor, then up, looking Saulnier in the eyes.

"If I can fly close, very close, from behind, or better yet, from below, I can shoot them. Without a gunner, in a fast aeroplane." He shook as he spoke, angry at Saulnier, at aeroplanes, at the Germans, and at his impotence to change the way that men were dying so easily, being stalked by aeroplanes, then blown into pieces.

Saulnier raised a hand, stopping Garros. He looked away, allowing Garros the dignity of composing himself. Saulnier walked to the furnace, bending deeply to study the metal wedge sitting on the anvil. He placed his face close, looking at the lump of metal like a precious thing, worthy of examination.

"Dear Roland," he began, drawing out the syllables, showing respect for his friend. "Dear Roland, how may I help? I've built you beautiful aeroplanes. I've given you money and food and shelter and encouragement. Now, I ask, let me give you ideas."

Garros strode to the anvil, then picked up a hot lump of metal with blacksmith's tongs. "It is simple. I saw your drawings; I know you've thought about it. I'll attach two of these wedges, and brace them on the propeller blades. I estimate every tenth bullet will strike them, and nine will not."

Garros knew that, with every few rounds, a bullet would emerge from the muzzle of the gun and strike the propeller inches in front of his face. Thoughts of the perilous ricochets crossed his mind, but he shook the idea away before he became truly scared of what he might do to himself. He knew of the one great danger: if a bullet struck exactly at the apex of the wedge and flew straight back. He didn't *know* if such a thing could happen, but thought it could, and, if it could, then it was simply a matter of time until it did.

Saulnier felt an ache in his chest; a sadness grew and he had already begun to grieve. If the obvious risk wasn't enough, Garros' purpose defied all that he felt about aeroplanes. Saulnier believed in their inherent beauty, their delicacy, their nobility, their ability to do something fantastic and graceful and death-defying. What Garros was doing was crude, violent, and, worse yet, added a level of needless danger to something that could hardly be any more daring. And yet, it was very brave.

He steeled himself. He felt a great pressure now, as though he were supporting a wall that held back a noxious flood. The thought of the flood rushing over them all, washing away all that was theirs, all they believed about themselves, forcing them into a new world where Teutons made the rules, held him in check. What might lay beyond being conquered? That, he couldn't imagine. Saulnier had never thought of himself as a naïve patriot, but he knew that at least he lived in a world he understood and could feel himself in; where he felt accustomed, it was something worth defending.

Saulnier spoke, "Garros, is it true? Is it true that man can do something so wondrous as fly, and here, now, a few short years later, we can only think to corrupt our discovery in the name of murder?"

Garros opened his mouth to speak, but Saulnier lifted a hand to silence him. "Dear lord, Roland, I'm being rhetorical."

"But ..." stammered Garros.

"No, Garros, I don't blame you. I'm merely a man who wishes to keep one last ideal. A conceit of mine."

He put a hand on Garros' shoulder. Garros flinched, having never been touched by the man. He knew that Saulnier felt Garros' mortality in the room and it frightened him.

"I'll help you. God forgive me, Roland."

~~~

He felt the thrill of flight every time he flew. When he flew across the Mediterranean to Tunis, he felt it the entire time, the excitement waxed and waned, but it never left him. When he landed, he felt drained, deeply relaxed, and at peace. Garros flew the Morane in a steep climb, feeling the engine pull against gravity; the wings were springing in soft flutters under the power of the climbing aeroplane. He knew that he had moments to complete his ascent or the opportunity would be lost, and hours, if not days, would go by before he had this chance again.

He fastened his gaze on the Aviatik below him. The German two-seater flew parallel to the front, west, then made a flat turn and flew back to the east. The observer hung over the side, recording the deadly work of their artillery, seeking new targets to eradicate. Great blooms of dirt and fire and smoke rose from artillery explosions on the ground far below them.

Garros felt the urgency grow by the second, imagining that he could stop the shells in flight, and save the men below from the next ugly eruption, and make it stop. Anger grew inside of him.

At last, Garros judged that he was high enough. The aeroplane had enough pent-up energy of altitude that he could easily, at the right moment, convert it all into a great rush onto the hated thing below. He imagined he would strike like some thunderous titan. He pushed the stick, and then ruddered to the left, letting the aeroplane roll, the nose dipping. Then he leveled the wings, keeping the nose above the Aviatik and for a few moments, he lost sight of the German aeroplane.

Now he relished the moment and the sense of cataclysm rose in his mind.

He tipped the nose of the Morane over and began to use the energy of the surging machine. He closed swiftly on the Aviatik, ignoring the sparse clouds, knowing that the surprise would be pure.

The German aviators couldn't possibly imagine what was about to happen.

Garros dove steeply behind the Aviatik, leaving the Morane in full profile from the Aviatik for a few seconds. If the observer as much as glanced away from his task, Garros would be seen.

Garros swooped the Morane below the level of the German machine and behind it, hiding beneath. To be in the open sky and visible for miles, yet so invisible to his quarry, made Garros feel he was dishonorable. He shuddered; a small chill of horror coursed through him.

His speed was much greater than the Aviatik's, drawing him closer too quickly. He pulled the nose up to shed speed, and then pushed it back down, reducing it further while holding his altitude. He imagined himself on tiptoe, sneaking along: a killer in a dark alley whose intended victim couldn't possibly know about the knife. He knew that he must be close in order to be accurate.

He drew so close that he could smell the Aviatik and feel the way the German plane roiled the air. He imagined he could touch it. He thought of lifting upward, rising up behind the German aeroplane like a whale from the sea, like an apparition in the sky. He smiled to himself.

What would I do then? he thought. *Let them try to defend themselves; let them try to run? Let them surrender? No, none of that will end this.*

Unexpectedly he felt mercy, the need to make it quick and simple. *Painful it must be, but also brief, so brief.*

He looked down the sights of the gun, off into space. He imagined the stick drawn back for just a moment, the sights rising, and then the belly of the German aeroplane ahead of him. Above him, he saw the observer's arm wave over the side of the ship.

There, he thought. *Observer first. The pilot will be confused, startled, not know what he's faced with; oblivious, but afraid. For just a few seconds. Kill them both. Don't let them suffer the horror of falling, of burning.*

It is the time to kill them: no, it is the time to end the horror below.

Garros lowered his gaze to the sights, then drew the stick back sharply, nearly halting the movement of his aeroplane. His sights rose until he centered them on the bottom of the aeroplane where he knew the observer to be. The aeroplanes jumped around, the churned air shaking the canvas of his Morane as the German's turbulence washed over him. He fought the stick to hold close to his aiming point, then pulled the trigger on the machine gun. The gun erupted in a barking snarl as bullets spewed out into the sky. White-hot ricochets off his propeller scattered around him and he instinctively ducked as they flickered past his he head. He released the trigger, losing his aim.

Pulling back on his controls, then ruddering slightly, he settled his sights back on the German aeroplane. He could see the strikes now, the bullets had torn ugly rents in the other aeroplane, and the wind was opening the tears into voids in the German plane. *Enough,* he thought, *fifteen or so, twenty perhaps. It just takes one. Just one.*

Then, he pushed the stick, and throttled up to close; to regain the distance he had lost behind the German as he had fired. He thought of the pilot, alone. Perhaps blissfully unaware. Surely, he would have heard the firing but wouldn't recognize the sound, wouldn't associate it with his own doom.

Garros thought of the observer: *Dead? Wounded, surely. Dying?*

He pulled the nose up, and fired again; long, too long. The awful clanging of stray bullets on his propeller came far too often. More holes opened up on the belly of the Aviatik. As he pushed the nose down, he saw a dark stain appear across the belly of the German aeroplane ... or did he imagine it?

The Aviatik wobbled, the left wing dipping. It tipped over with the nose down and disappeared from Garros' view. Garros banked the Morane in a shallow descending spiral and looked out of his cockpit at the tumbling aeroplane below him. Then the German aeroplane began to spin, turning slow circles on itself, then more rapidly, swirling down. It grew smaller, until it merged with an ugly explosion rising upward, meeting flame and dirt and smoke from below.

Garros consoled himself as he watched the Aviatik disappear into the chaos. *Souls gone now,* he told himself, *their earthly trials at an end.*

~~~

A week had gone by, without another opportunity and Garros waited for a call from a courier to summon him. Garros sat in the sand, watching the waves coming in off the English Channel. He thought of the name and pursed his lips. *Their navy, their channel, their name,* he thought. *Now that we have drawn first blood, perhaps, the French will name the sky.*

"Monsieur Garros." A runner from the aerodrome drew up next to Garros. The runner was already at attention when Garros noticed him. Garros was no soldier, and he tried to recall what he was supposed to do at times like this. He felt a small wave of panic rise. He stood and returned an awkward salute, and hoped the soldier didn't think too much about it.

"Oui," Garros replied. "Relax, young man. You're too serious."

"There is an order for you at the field. You are requested most urgently."

"Very well. I'll be along." Garros dismissed the runner, waving him away. He picked up his walking stick and a seashell, and strolled back down the boardwalk to the aerodrome. The runner ran ahead and disappeared behind a dune. Over the dunes, Garros could see French aeroplanes flying over the field. He stopped and watched them for a moment before walking over to the operations building.

A very young French captain was huddled over a table, his finger tracing invisible lines over a map. Another pilot, a lieutenant, stood next to the captain.

"Garros, at last!" said the captain. The young captain pointed at the map. "The English report that the Germans are moving troops into the railway station at Wervicq. You are requested ... er ... ordered to fly to Kortrijk, here, and observe the rail station and report back. The Sous-lieutenant will fly his own aeroplane along with you." The captain looked confused, like he didn't understand what he had just said.

Garros felt sympathy and smiled. "Yes, I will fly." He paused. "My aeroplane." He enjoyed the look on the young man's face. It then occurred to Garros that perhaps he was misreading the man. Perhaps he did understand what he was asking. Garros' smile sagged. "Captain, have you ever flown?" he asked.

The young man looked away. "Non, monsieur, I have not."

Garros smiled again. "Yes. Well then, I accept your orders; we'll have to go flying some time. Yes, my aeroplane can fly there. It is not a problem."

The captain's shoulders sagged. He smiled back, "Oui, Lieutenant, we should do so. Have a good ..." he struggled with the correct word, " ... flight, journey?"

Garros placed his hand on the man's shoulder, "Oui, I think I shall."

The captain beamed, as though someone holy had touched him.

"Perhaps you will, 'shoot down' a German?"

"Perhaps, *mon Capitaine*, perhaps not. They run now. Whenever they see a single seat aeroplane, they practically fall from the sky on their own." He laughed a hearty bray.

~~~

Schlendstedt relished his boredom. He leaned on his rifle and droned out the occasional order to his soldiers as they trudged their way along the railway line, on a supposed search for saboteurs, but really just giving Schlendstedt time away from their Leutnant. To the south, a buzzing sound grew louder, the sound seeming to come from the sky. They stopped and stared into the puffy clouds, searching for the source of the sound. Black shapes appeared, darting between clouds. Schlendstedt suddenly wasn't bored anymore, and it made him furious.

The German sentries often shot at birds, thinking them to be aeroplanes. They lifted their rifles and aimed at the black object flying over the trees, imagining they might actually hit it. They would bang away, shooting at a distant target until one or another of them realized it was merely a bird.

So, as the tiny black shapes approached, and they aimed their rifles, they hesitated. A corporal paused and glanced at the soldier next to him, trying to catch his eye. No one fired. He turned his head, held his rifle up and craned his neck around to look at their leader. Feldwebel-Leutnant Schlendstedt looked back at him, took a step, swung his boot, and kicked the corporal in the butt.

"Fire, fool!" said Schlendstedt. "Or I'll ship you off to the front lines."

Schlendstedt looked up at the figures, decided they really were aeroplanes, but didn't see any markings. He assumed the worst.

"Fire! All of you!" he shouted.

The rifles exploded together, in a single bang. As the soldiers fumbled to work the actions of each rifle, the firing spread out into individual cracks.

Under his breath, Schlendstedt mumbled to himself, "Reservists ... Blind, dumb, too young, too old."

Schlendstedt could see that they were two aeroplanes now. Around the furthest aeroplane, blooms of gray smoke began to appear. He was embarrassed, knowing the aeroplanes were too far away.

"Hold fire. Save your ammunition until they are closer."

His men lowered their rifles and watched the aeroplanes dance in the sky, dodging grey explosions. The youngest soldier, a teenager from Pomerania, stared, open-mouthed.

"What's the matter, never seen an aeroplane before?" Schlendstedt asked.

"Nien! Leutnant, nien," said the boy, awestruck. The other soldiers laughed and leaned on their rifles. A couple of them sat down.

Schlendstedt watched as the furthest aeroplane turned away to the south toward Menin. The other aeroplane flew on, toward Lendelede to the northeast. Behind him, to the east, he heard a train approaching the station and ordered his men away from the tracks.

Glancing to the northeast, he lost sight of the aeroplane. As he scanned the horizon, he heard an aeroplane engine growing louder, even the sound of wind over its wings becoming audible. Panicking, he darted his eyes around the sky until he spotted it, diving steeply on them. The aeroplane was swooping downward toward the train.

No, not my train! My train!

He frantically motioned his men up and ran alongside the slowing train, yelling at his men to follow. He felt powerless. He tried to imagine what terrible purpose the pilot had.

As the aeroplane swept downward, the pilot pulled its nose up, and arched up into a steep climb. Schlendstedt imagined he might be merely performing, showing off. *Perhaps a circle or, what did they call it? A loop?* Behind him, his men had stopped and raised their rifles. They banged away briskly now. Schlendstedt turned and cheered them, "Go boys! Shoot the bastard!"

The aeroplane was in a steep climb over Schlendstedt's train now. As it clawed upward, something fell from the plane. Schlendstedt stared at the object as it spiraled downward. It passed behind the train and exploded with a sharp bang! Rocks erupted upward and cascaded down on the men. Schlendstedt stood, stunned.

A bomb?

Bewildered, he ran toward the site of the explosion as the train came to a stop. Schlendstedt rushed between the cars and to the other side of the train. His men chased after him in a ragged line. Stumbling, he fell into a smoking hole in the ground, a meter deep.

"Bastard," he breathed, looking upward now, all quiet around him.

The aeroplane must be gone, I can't hear it.

He searched the sky for the aeroplane. Over the trees to the west, he watched the aeroplane glide downward, the propeller not turning, making no sound save the whistling of air on its wings.

"After him, boys!" he shouted.

The German soldiers scrambled, scattering, some running for bicycles, others running off to the main road toward Hulste. Schlendstedt rushed back the way they had come for his own bike. He reached it and began awkwardly pedaling in the direction the aeroplane had gone.

As he rode closer to where the aeroplane had gone down, he saw the pilot standing next to a crashed plane, a plume of smoke thickening around the man. The German soldiers began to shout, and the pilot turned and ran off toward the Belgian town. Two soldiers chased after him. The aeroplane began to burn fiercely, billowing clouds of black smoke from the fuselage and burning wing.

"Put it out, put it out!" yelled Schlendstedt.

The soldiers began throwing handfuls of dirt at the flames, gradually beating the flames down. Württemberger cavalrymen rode past, following after the French pilot.

From the direction of the village, someone yelled in French, "Levez les bras! Levez les bras!" Schlendstedt ran toward the shouting, his troops following. As he turned the corner of a barn, he saw a mounted cavalryman prodding the French flyer along with his sword. The French pilot was dripping wet, partly covered in mud, with clumps of grass stuck to him. His hands were planted firmly in his pockets.

Schlendstedt grabbed the man's wrist and pulled his hand from his pocket. "Name! Unit!" demanded Schlendstedt in rough French.

The Frenchman scowled back, insolently.

"Name!"

"Garros. Roland Garros. French Flying Service." Garros put his hand back into his pocket, spread his legs slightly and swayed. Water dripped from him, his blue uniform soaked through.

"Walk, Monsieur Garros. That way. You are my prisoner." Schlendstedt pointed back toward the train station and prodded Garros with the muzzle of his rifle.

Chapter Nineteen

April 18, 1915
Gontrode, Belgium

Hawker took off alone, flew northwest, and crossed the lines almost immediately, north of Armentieres. Here, the soldiers of both sides carved their trenches through the top soil and into the chalk below, leaving pale slashes across the ground. From this height, the lines were stark and appeared random, like the fierce scribbling of a playground bully gone mad.

A spattering of Archie puffed around him, too low and behind. He flew on, ignoring the explosions for what they were: fate rolling dice with his life.

He leveled off slightly, but still in a shallow climb under the low clouds, flying into a headwind. The aeroplane burst upward through the clouds into a patch of startling blue sky. The light hurt his eyes and he shielded them with a raised hand. But now, he flew in the open air, with clear sky above him.

He let himself enjoy the sensation of freedom and space and clarity.

Hawker was a man of faith, a "believer" as Beatrice called him. The word disturbed him. He couldn't imagine what it meant to be something else. *What else could there be but God?* he thought, surrounded by cloudscape and the heavens above.

That was when he felt it, the emptiness unfilled, and knew that Gordon was gone. Looking at the vastness around him, he felt God bring him a message, that the blue that held his faith was streaming it down in the sunlight. It was more than intuition, more than instinct: it was knowledge delivered from the beyond. He imagined Gordon looking down, watching him. The sudden awareness startled him, frightening him with its stark certainty. Hawker was confused.

He searched his heart for an answer and found it in his faith.

Gordon was with God, and God was telling him so.

That was enough. Hawker felt at peace, in a perfect place, alone in the clear blue.

"I'll miss you, my friend," he said aloud.

He needed to return and write to Beatrice, to let her know what he had felt. He hoped that she would understand. But first, he had to complete his errand. Rough air jolted him and brought him out of his reverie, to an empty sky over an enemy land. With a last glance upward, he flew back under the clouds to navigate by the tiny Belgian towns.

Less than an hour had passed when he flew over the Belgian town of Waregem at four thousand feet. He oriented himself and then turned a little, flying east-northeast, toward Ghent. The gray clouds hung over his head and he felt them there like a cloak. He knew that he stood out in black against them, but he could also fly up into them and disappear at a moment's notice.

He felt a dull headache starting. The headache was an annoying acquaintance, always appearing at the wrong time, always lingering too long, the last reminder of an anti-aircraft shell that had burst too close. Concussion, the doctors called it. Fortunately, nothing more serious. At least the nausea was gone. Hawker gulped cold water from a bottle, vainly trying to clear away the pain.

Damned concussion. Damned Archie.

At Ghent, he gently turned the aeroplane and flew southeast. He watched below for the distinct brown rectangle of a Zeppelin shed.

He thought of Beatrice and of Zeppelins. Here he came to slay the giant. David meets Goliath. *David riding the air on canvas; Goliath, asleep, an inflated gas bag below.*

A disquieting thought crept into his mind.

Here I am, on the word of a spy. So far behind German lines, on the word of a paid liar. But, if there were a Zeppelin housed in that shed, still full of hydrogen, an inflated bomb ready to be ignited, it would be worth it; a single man, a single aeroplane ... more than worth it.

Hawker's eyes swept the ground, across the top of the Belgian forest. He braced his map on his knee and tried to pick out landmarks. He flew over a tiny, oddly shaped village, found it on his map 'Moscou', like, 'Moscow', Russian sounding, strange. From Moscou, he angled further south. Below him was a scene of serenity in the Belgian countryside, far from the war.

Beyond a dark green patch of forest, a brown rectangle appeared, enormous against the surrounding houses of a village.

The Zeppelin hangar. Right where the spy said it would be!

To the south of the shed, a single observation balloon floated, aligned with the easterly breeze, swaying in the wind. His throat tightened and his mouth went dry. Hawker turned toward the shed, and held his altitude.

The spy was right, thought Hawker, *the liar was right!*

As he flew toward it, Hawker picked up a bomb, a grenade with fins, from the floor of his cockpit. He pulled the pin from the fuse and held the bomb away from the aeroplane with one hand. He lined up his aeroplane on the length of the building and released the bomb. He stared down, not wanting to miss the impact. About five hundred feet from the end of the shed, a gray-brown puff of dust appeared and blew away in the wind.

Damn, thought Hawker. *A clean miss.*

He mechanically clipped the safety pin from the first bomb onto the side of his cockpit, then picked up another bomb.

Hawker turned and aligned on the length of the shed from the southeast and flew toward it. As the edge of the shed passed into view under the lower wing, he released the bomb. Again, he watched it fall. The bomb dwindled away, growing tiny, until he could no longer see it, and then vanished over the shed. Nothing happened. No explosion, no great gout of flame from a burning Zeppelin. Nothing. He noticed, rather absently, gray puffs of anti-aircraft fire around him. Frustration swept over Hawker, a deep gnawing irritation, bordering on anger. His headache throbbed, suddenly worse.

He reached out to clip the bomb's pin to the wall of his cockpit and found his hand empty. *I didn't pull the pin!* He stared as his empty hand in amazement. He was angry at himself now.

Hawker turned once more and pointed the aeroplane's nose at the shed. From the net in the cockpit, he removed a grenade, no fins, no contact fuse, just a grenade. As he angled back toward the shed, he could see bursts of fire from an anti-aircraft battery on the ground and another gray trail of smoke leading away from the floating observation balloon. As he flew toward the shed, the balloon blocked the Archie and the firing stopped.

From the basket beneath the balloon, a machine gun rattled, firing at him.

Hawker, his frustration boiling over and his headache throbbing, wrenched his aeroplane's nose down and brought it into a tight spiral, directly over the balloon. He throttled his engine back as he dove so as not to rip his wings off.

His belly clenched in fear as he realized he was doing something stupid. Just as quickly, he fathomed that he had committed to the act and needed to follow it through. If he pulled out now, he'd expose himself to more ground fire with nothing gained. He had to get as low as possible to have any protection at all.

Damn it all!

He began to pull the pins on his grenades and toss them out, hoping against hope that he might drop one on the balloon. Down he spiraled, his grenades falling below him and bursting, vainly, in mid-air, over the stationary gas bag.

In seconds, he rocketed past the tethered balloon. He looked at the balloon and saw the observer in the basket point a machine gun his way. Bullets from the gun began to fly around him with a high-pitched *zip-zip-zip-zip-thud.*

He knew each thud was a strike on his aeroplane and wondered what it might sound like if one struck *him.*

The cannon on the ground began to fire, its shells flying past Hawker as he turned and charged the Zeppelin shed like a mad lancer. His prop wash left a trail of churned dust as he flew.

All of his focus was on the target now. His blood roared in his ears, his vision a narrow tunnel, with nothing but the shed at the end. He reached down, felt around the floor of the cockpit, and found his last bomb by touch. Wedging it between his knees, he pulled the pin.

Nothing mattered but hitting it, that fat, ugly sausage inside the shed. *Goliath, meet stone.*

Hawker realized he was flying too fast from his dive. Afraid the aeroplane might tear itself apart, he cut his engine. Pulling the nose up, he banked toward the shed, aiming at the broadside of the thing. With a grunt, he flung his last bomb and looked back to see it explode as it struck the ground, three yards before the building. At the last moment, the aeroplane rose, barely clearing the giant barn.

He realized he could hear the bullets again, *zip-zip-zip-CLANG-zip-zip.* The gunner in the balloon was firing down at him now. His engine sputtered and stopped, starved of fuel from the steep dive. Hawker flipped the magneto switch and held his breath for the engine to start. The prop turned, windmilling in the gale of air, then the engine snorted again and started.

Wind sung through the wires of the wings, a shrill, hissing whisper, coupled with a thrumming noise from the wires as they vibrated. Hawker flew low across the ground, and then began to climb once he was over the trees.

With the balloon and guns far behind him, he turned to the south, toward Bailleul, cursing himself as he flew, asking forgiveness from the ghost of Gordon.

<center>~~~</center>

"Sit, Hawker. Have a seat." Major Shepard pointed at a chair across from his desk.

Hawker pulled his cap from his head and clutched it like a life preserver. He looked around the office for a distraction, for a glimpse of blue sky. "Yes, sir. Of course." Hawker sat, heavily, and then pulled himself upright in the chair. He felt the need to smooth his moustache, to soothe himself, and resisted the urge. He felt foolish and stupid. He fixed his eyes on Shepard and braced himself for the dressing down he was about to receive.

If I had taken more time; if I hadn't gotten so angry; if I hadn't been thinking about God and Gordon and ... damn headache ... !

"So, Hawker, I've reviewed your report on the flight, and I have a few questions." Shepard smiled at Hawker. A gap in his front teeth let sunlight shine onto his tongue as he spoke reminding Hawker of a snake.

Do they really taste the air with their tongues?

"Yes, sir, anything at all," said Hawker.

"Your first bomb clearly missed, is that correct?" asked Shepard.

"Yes, it struck the ground. The impact was obvious," said Hawker. The headache throbbed, threatening to return in its entire splendor.

"And, the second bomb ... you didn't see it miss, is that correct?" asked Shepard.

"What? Well ... I ... yes, I didn't see it miss," said Hawker.

A double negative, he thought, *I just confirmed 'yes' to a double negative. Who, exactly, is double-talking whom?* Confusion was settling over him now, but he began to relax, feeling the odds of a dressing down slipping away.

"So, if you didn't see it miss, then it must have hit," Shepard offered.

"I wouldn't ..." Hawker fumbled the response as he tried to grasp the suggestion.

Shepard cut Hawker off with a wave of his hand. "Well, I would," said Shepard. "And, when you began to descend ..."

"Yes, sir. Against orders, sir. I apologize ..." said Hawker.

"May I continue, Lieutenant?" said Shepard. His voice was cool, even a little menacing.

Here it comes, thought Hawker.

"When you began to descend, you spiraled over the captive balloon guarding the shed, correct?" said Shepard.

"Yes, I came down on top of it. I tried to hit it with grenades. That didn't work; a waste of grenades, quite—"

Shepard held his hand up. "So, you spiraled down over the captive balloon, valiantly attacking it the entire time, cleverly using it to shield you from the anti-aircraft gun," said Shepard. He was looking down, writing as he spoke. He seemed to be smiling to himself.

"Well, I, sir, my blood was up ..." Hawker looked at the floor and began to form an apology.

"Oh, that's good! Your blood was up ... You saw the enemy ... sized him up, and didn't waste time maneuvering ... or contemplating the danger as you descended." Shepard scribbled furiously as he spoke, capturing every word.

"Sir, I suppose. I descended too fast; didn't think about it," said Hawker.

Shepard raised a hand again, halting Hawker in mid-sentence. Shepard scribbled and then stopped, and read back to himself. " ... heedless of his own safety ... excellent." He looked up from his notebook. "So, Hawker, how low would you say you were when you dropped your final bomb?" asked Shepard.

"Oh ... below two hundred feet or so ... actually, far too low ... I know," said Hawker. He let his own words trail off this time. It was clear Shepard had stopped listening.

"Sir, I almost flew into the side of the shed. So, about twelve feet." There, he'd said it.

Shepard didn't hear him.

"Blood was up ..." said Shepard to himself again. "Oh, that *is* excellent!"

Hawker was baffled now. He stared out the window over Shepard's shoulder and watched clouds drift by. He thought of England and leaned back in his chair, deflated.

"And, one last thing. You didn't see flames, did you?" said Shepard.

"Oh, no, there were no flames whatsoever," said Hawker.

"Aha!" said Shepard. "Just as I would expect. You see, hydrogen burns invisibly in daylight, blue at night. It's a little known fact, but an important bit of science, that. You couldn't have seen flames!"

"But, sir, the shed ..." said Hawker, raising his hand, limply, in protest.

"So, Hawker, you can't be sure that you didn't destroy a Zeppelin at all, could you?" said Shepard.

"Well, no, sir, but, I don't really ..." said Hawker, letting his voice fade away in resignation.

"Sir, do you have any further questions?" He glanced toward the door now, willing it to open of its own accord.

"No, Hawker, save one," said Shepard. He put his pencil on his desk and looked up, smiling a gap-toothed smile. "When can you take command of 'A' flight?"

"Sir?"

"Well, we've lost two men to an accident, including the flight commander. We need a new leader for the flight, and, of course, you'll assume the acting rank of captain effective immediately," said Shepard. His expression looked frozen, stiff, a forced poker face.

Hawker stared, his mouth open.

"And, Hawker, I'll be submitting your action report with a commendation for the Distinguished Service Order."

"Sir, yes, sir. Thank you, Sir!" stammered Hawker.

"Captain, you're dismissed," said Shepard with a salute. He picked up the report to read it again.

Hawker stood, stepped to the door; he felt that he might be staggering and forced himself upright, then he left the office and closed the door behind himself. He stood there, wavering, then, with a limp shrug, he walked away.

~~~

The back of the hangar was dark and quiet and stank of canvas dope, painfully sharp and poisonous in the still air. The more Hawker breathed, the more his throat hurt.

"So, tell me again what Shepard said at the end?" asked Strange.

Hawker ground his jaw, trying to distract himself from the damned headache. "'A' flight commander; acting Captain; commendation for Distinguished Service Order. Can you believe it?"

"Do you suppose he didn't expect you to come back, having sent you out alone like that?" asked Strange.

Hawker stared at Strange and felt the sudden desire for a stiff drink.

Strange continued, "Don't get yourself worked up. He clearly thinks you did the right thing and, perhaps he's embellishing a little. Don't let it get you down." He reached out and patted Hawker on the back.

Hawker stayed silent, watching the mechanics bend over the engine of his aeroplane.

"If he wants you to be a hero, that's his privilege," said Strange.

Hawker looked at Strange. *Are you baiting me, Strange?* Strange's expression was guileless.

The head mechanic swung a lantern close to the engine. "Sirs, you should take a look at this. We've found why your engine was running so rough." The other mechanic climbed down from his ladder, making room for Hawker. When he reached the ground, the man began rhythmically mopping his hands with a rag.

Hawker climbed the ladder and leaned toward the engine, his head pushed deep into the aeroplane.

"See, here, sir, that's a bullet, stuck in the induction pipe, letting air leak out. No wonder your engine was gasping. Funny thing. It looks like it struck the fins of this cylinder here, and spent itself, and then ricocheted into the pipe." The mechanic chuckled.

"And what, may I ask, is the funny thing?" asked Hawker. Impatient anger rose in his voice.

"Well, sir, no offense, but it's a little odd that the bullet came down from above. Somebody shooting at you from upstairs, sir? It's a small miracle that it wasn't just a little further forward. It would have struck a cylinder, might well have knocked it loose; but, a little further back, it wouldn't have struck the fins, and it would have knocked your induction clear through and you'd have lost your engine." He wiped his hands and lifted the lantern. "Funny thing that."

Hawker pulled his head free from the engine.

"So, one bullet, one inch, then?" said Strange, looking up from the ground.

"Yes. Strange, that," said Hawker, without a trace of irony in his voice.

Chapter Twenty

April 20, 1915
Döberitz, Germany

Geertz ordered Garros' aeroplane shipped by train to Döberitz.
The charred fuselage, the framework of one wing and the French machine gun lay on canvas tarps in an empty shed. Garros' propeller, with its steel wedges, stood on one end, propped against a wall. An armed soldier guarded the entrance to the shed.

Fokker and Kreutzer stood looking down at the parts as an engineer from the Pfalz factory arrived. Geertz drew them to the propeller.

"Gentlemen, this is what Garros built, and what he was able to shoot our aeroplanes down with," said Geertz. He put out his hand, and ran his thumb over the top of one of the steel wedges as though to demonstrate how sharp it was.

Fokker stepped closer, put his face close to a wedge with its brace running to the center of the hub, and then ran his own thumb over the steel. "It looks like he pounded this out on a forge with a hammer. Not even machined," he said. "Perhaps you need a blacksmith, or a farrier?" To Geertz, it didn't sound like Fokker was joking.

Geertz swallowed to maintain his composure. "Herr Fokker, yes, I agree; it is crude. But, please bear with me."

"Well, as secret weapons go, I guess there have been some that were more crude," said Fokker. "I can't personally think of any or even imagine one, but, I suppose it's possible. Maybe the poleaxe in the Middle Ages?"

Angry now, Geertz raised his voice. "If the French can kill our pilots with this, then we need to deal with it."

Fokker shrugged his shoulders, smiled, and stood back. "How can we help, Hauptmann?" asked Fokker. He raised his hands in a gesture of supplication.

Geertz sighed. "We wouldn't normally have asked ... civilians ... but, we've had our own experiments, and they didn't work," he said.

"What sort of experiments?" asked Kreutzer.

"We've fired our machine guns through this propeller, and ... well ... it would appear that our guns fire too swiftly, and our ammunition is steel jacketed so the wedges don't hold up," said Geertz.

He paused, seemingly embarrassed. "Those dents aren't hammer strikes; they're impacts of our bullets."

Fokker grinned. "Steel on steel, then. I'm sure that was ... interesting," said Fokker. "Too fast, you say?"

"Yes, interesting! Really quite fascinating. Too fast; too many strikes. A failure," Geertz said in irritation. "We ... *I* ... am asking for your help. As representatives of the factories producing Morane ... facsimiles, I've asked you and Schmitt here, from Pfalz, to determine if there is a better solution."

"I see," said Fokker. "May I?" Fokker gestured toward the French gun lying next to the aeroplane.

"Yes, go ahead. It's a Hotchkiss. Not very reliable."

Fokker bent and picked up the gun. "It's heavy, very heavy. Are you sure we want the additional weight?" He set the weapon down again, and then stepped close to the aeroplane.

"How much of a problem is this?" asked Schmitt, conveying disinterest. "Surely, it's not that serious."

"Garros shot down four of our aeroplanes in two weeks. Our flyers are disposed to turn and fly away every time they see a French single-seater. This is unacceptable. Deplorable," said Geertz.

Fokker put his hand underneath the cowl of Garros' aeroplane, reaching up inside.

"Herr Fokker, is there something I can help you with?" said Geertz.

Fokker then put his whole arm up inside the aeroplane, behind the engine. "Le Rhône, similar to the Oberursel nine-cylinder engines that we're using. That should work then," said Fokker.

"Herr Fokker, what are you talking about?" asked Geertz.

"May I have a word with you? Alone?" asked Fokker.

"Yes, certainly," said Geertz.

"This won't take a minute, Martin," said Fokker. Geertz and Fokker stepped away to the rear of the Morane, while Kreutzer and Schmitt stepped outside to smoke.

"What is it?" asked Geertz.

"I think I can provide you with a much better solution. I can't tell you about it right now, but I need to speak to Garros."

"Garros? Seriously?" asked Geertz. "Why? And what makes you think that he'll talk to you?"

"I know him quite well. We've been, were, at several air shows together prior to the war," said Fokker.

"But, what makes you think that he'll give you anything useful?" said Geertz.

"I think he already has," said Fokker.

"Fokker, you're an ass," said Geertz, stepping close. "You speak as though you already have a solution."

Fokker held his ground. "I do ... I think I do. What do you care? There is a war on, right? You just need an answer. Why so many questions?"

"Fokker, if there's some sort of intrigue between you and Garros, you'll be shot. Simple. Problem solved. We'll have Kreutzer or your welder, whatever his name is, run your factory," said Geertz. "Shot. Understand?"

Fokker, unfazed, ignored Geertz. He smiled. "I would like a medal. You can do that, right? A nice one. The Iron Cross or something like that. Something I can wear, say, right here." He placed a finger on his coat pocket.

"Damn it, Fokker," hissed Geertz. He looked like he might take a swing at Fokker. He ran the palm of his hand over his face. "Alright, Garros and a medal. I'll see what I can do. Anything else?"

"A machine gun. The faster the better. And ammunition to shoot. That's all," said Fokker. "A few minutes with Garros, a medal, and a machine gun."

"Faster! Are you sure? Okay, at least I can understand the need for a gun. I'll need to arrange things. Come back in the morning. What about that?" Geertz pointed at the propeller with the metal wedges.

"A museum, perhaps. I don't know." Fokker thought for a moment. "Take a photograph."

Garros' Propeller- 1915

~~~

Garros sat calmly at a table inside an empty shed at Döberitz. His guard had tied his ankles together and taken up a position next to him. He deliberately lay his hands flat on the table, looking calm and composed.

Fokker sat at the table opposite Garros. Geertz lingered over Fokker's shoulder. The symmetry of Garros' guard and Geertz's perch was not lost on Fokker and Fokker scowled at Geertz. Geertz took a half-step back and clasped his hands behind him.

"Bonjour, Roland," said Fokker. He offered his hand to Garros.

Garros looked at Fokker's upstretched hand and then back at Fokker. He didn't move his hands from the table. Garros nodded. Outside, an engine started and the Frenchman cocked his head to listen. Fokker furtively withdrew his hand.

"Aahh, you miss it already," said Fokker in Dutch-tinged French.

"Oui, I do. I always will," Garros knit his fingers and leaned to rest his chin on them. He looked at Fokker as if he had just noticed he was there. "So, you work for the Germans. You didn't go home?"

"No, Garros, my business is here. I'm a businessman. I must stay," said Fokker.

"Don't be ridiculous, you didn't have to stay," said Garros. "What do you want?"

"Well, we have your propeller with the wedges. I have to commend you! That's very brave, flying with a gun going off in your face and bullets scattering around your head. Very brave!" Fokker smiled as though it might make the compliment mean something to Garros.

Garros said nothing.

Fokker leaned back and rested one hand on the table, tapping it with a finger in a steady cadence.

"It can't be done, can it? Interrupting the fire of the gun, so the bullets pass?" said Fokker.

Garros remained silent.

"Would you like something, Monsieur Garros?" said Geertz. "Coffee, a glass of water?"

"Tea, please," said Garros, nodding politely

Geertz waved to the guard, "Get this man a cup of tea. I'll watch him."

"No, Fokker, it can't be done. You cannot interrupt the fire of a machine gun so that the bullets pass. And now you have my propeller." Garros shrugged, his hands clenching and unclenching on the tabletop now.

"To be clear, you can't interrupt the fire of a machine gun while it's firing and let the bullets pass," said Fokker.

"No, you Dutch ass, you can't. Saulnier tried, so just stop asking," said Garros raising his voice.

Geertz snorted, and then chuckled a little. "I call him that, too," he said. Garros smiled.

Fokker grimaced and then stood up. "I know everything I need to now," said Fokker. "Thank you, Roland. I'm glad you're still alive."

"I'm not sure I can say the same." Garros looked up at Fokker, his gaze steady. "Fokker, why are you *really* here?" he asked.

"I just wanted to know that an interrupter can't be made to work. So I didn't waste my time. That's all," said Fokker.

"It's Ljuba, isn't it? You want to know about Ljuba."

Fokker looked at Geertz, then back at Garros. He sat back down. "No, but since you're offering,"

"A man in love is a volatile thing, Fokker. Careful you don't do something rash."

Fokker rapped on the table with his knuckles.

"So, fine. I'll tell you that. She made it out of Germany and then out of France. She went back to Russia. She's flying for them," said Garros. Garros watched Fokker, awaiting a reaction. Then, "Perhaps one of your aeroplanes will kill her."

A look of horror crossed Fokker's face followed by embarrassment that he had given himself away to Garros. Fokker gulped to calm himself.

"Is that all?"

Garros nodded.

Fokker glared at Garros. "Thank you, Garros."

"You're welcome, Fokker."

"Goodbye, Garros. Enjoy prison."

"And you, yours," replied Garros.

Fokker stood, not bothering to extend his hand again. He walked outside to where Kreutzer was waiting.

"Well, did you learn anything?" asked Kreutzer.

"Yes, I learned what doesn't work. Wedges and interrupters."

After a moment, Geertz joined them and they climbed into Geertz's car for the drive to the train station. At the station, Geertz directed two soldiers to unload a trunk from his car onto the train. He pointed at the trunk as they carried it past, "Fokker, there it is. Your machine gun. *Parabellum.* Light, but fast. Two thousand rounds. Don't kill anybody playing with the thing. You do this, and I think I can get you an Iron Cross, Second Class. No more."

"Okay, Geertz. Thank you."

Geertz reached out and took Fokker by the arm. "Fokker, who's Ljuba?"

"Someone I used to know," said Fokker.

"That's not good enough. Who is she?"

Fokker bent back, Geertz still holding onto him. "It's no matter, really." He spread his hands in supplication.

Geertz released Fokker and straightened his own uniform jacket. "Go on."

"She came back with me from St. Petersburg, a year ago. A great flyer. Had the women's altitude record. She's, well, she's ... very social."

"I see. She discarded you. Have a grudge, do you?"

Fokker bristled and stepped closer to Geertz. Geertz stood his ground.

Kreutzer stepped to Fokker's side and took his arm. "It's time we leave, Herr Fokker." Kreutzer nodded to Geertz and Fokker stepped back.

"Thank you, Geertz, I'll be in touch," Fokker said crisply.

Fokker and Kreutzer boarded the train and took a private compartment. Fokker put his feet up on the seat and leaned back.

"What was that all about, Fokker? It looked like you were going to throw a punch."

Fokker shook his head, "Nothing, a trifle. Martin, what does Parabellum mean?" he asked.

"Latin. It means 'prepare for war'," said Kreutzer.

"Oh, good," said Fokker with exasperation. "Just perfect." Fokker nodded and looked past Kreutzer, his mind elsewhere.

"So, Anton, do you think you can really make this work?" asked Kreutzer.

Fokker put his feet on the floor of the compartment and leaned over. He began to gesture with his hands. "Perhaps. It may seem impossible for a machine gun to do. The blade passes the barrel thirty or forty times per second, the gun fires three times, perhaps up to seven times per second. The math doesn't seem to work, does it?"

Before Kreutzer could answer, Fokker continued. "The answer may be a semi-automatic weapon, which cycles quickly. Saulnier had the mechanism. It's still right there on Garros' aeroplane. I could feel it inside. Saulnier just might have had the wrong gun," said Fokker. "You see, it's not an interrupter you need but a synchronizer. That's what Garros confirmed. They tried to interrupt but couldn't."

Kreutzer held up his hand, stopping Fokker. "Anton, you've been thinking about this for a while, haven't you?"

"Yes, Martin, I have. A long while. Now is just the time. Patents were published for such a synchronizer four years ago. I can't help it if the whole of the German air force doesn't bother to read."

"And, you were waiting?" said Kreutzer, scowling in displeasure.

Fokker looked out the window. "Waiting, I suppose. Waiting for the need to catch up with the answer."

"Damn you, Fokker. Damn you to hell. This could change the war."

Fokker glared at Kreutzer. "I think you mean, 'change war'. So, since the first time a man threw a rock, we change war. It's what we do."

Fokker paused, gathering his thoughts. His words spilled out then, as though they had been pent up. "Technology is business, Kreutzer. Do you think they were even smart enough to ask me the right question? I am an inventor, not a hypnotist. I can't convince them of ideas that aren't in their minds! They, Geertz and the rest, have their ideas, and, until they are shaken out of their way of thinking, it doesn't matter what one Dutchman says, or one Dutch *boy* if you look at their faces."

His voice rose until he was shouting, his face red. "It finally dawned on them that they didn't understand what was needed! But even after being told, they still don't understand. Most of them don't even know how an aeroplane flies, and I'm supposed to convince them of a need that they don't even think they have?"

He stopped then, spent, and watched the landscape pass by behind the reflection in the moving train window. A look of sadness fell across his face. "I might as was well teach de Waal's damn monkey that it needs a toaster. But they're in charge. Laughable. They're in charge of trying to understand."

Kreutzer sat up, anger clouding his face; he felt condescended to, spoken to as a child, as if he couldn't understand. Before he could speak, Fokker blurted out, "They just want blood. They can get their own blood. I'll hand them a knife." Fokker rolled his eyes, leaned back, folded his arms and looked out the window. "Knife? Hell, we might as well be doing Magic."

~~~

In the back of a shed at the Schwerin field, Fokker and his engineers worked long days perfecting Fokker's imagined device. After simple trials in the building, they moved outside once the workers had gone for the day. In the evening twilight, they fired their machine gun repeatedly, changing minor details after splintering propellers or ruining engines, often diving in desperate flight from a machine gun run wild.

One afternoon, two weeks later, Fokker hitched up a monoplane—with his new synchronizer and machine gun—to the back of his Peugeot, letting the aeroplane's wheels roll on the ground behind the car, and drove to Döberitz. His dachshund, Zeiten, rode along, ears sailing in the breeze.

At Döberitz, Fokker and his crew set the tail of the Eindekker on a wooden stand so that it sat level and pointed the nose at a berm of dirt on the edge of the aerodrome. Fokker loaded the gun.

A small crowd of pilots and engineers from the army had gathered, waiting for Fokker's secret weapon to be unveiled.

"So, Fokker, are you ready?" asked Geertz.

Geertz stood close to the propeller of the little monoplane and examined it. "Where are the shields?" asked Geertz.

"There aren't any, Hauptmann. They are not needed," said Fokker. "I have developed a mechanism that fires the machine gun when the blade of the propeller is out of the way."

Geertz looked aghast. "Do not waste my time."

"Herr Geertz, please, let me demonstrate," said Fokker with a condescending wave of his hand.

"Just a moment, Fokker," said Geertz. He stepped away to the back of the Eindekker and conferred with some of his staff. Otto Parschau, Geertz's pilot and a friend of Fokker's from before the war, stood with Geertz. Parschau looked up at Fokker and nodded an iron-faced greeting.

Geertz turned back to Fokker, "We'll watch since we're here. This had better work."

Fokker climbed into the cockpit and a mechanic swung the propeller, starting the engine. He blipped the engine to keep the revolutions down. "Are you ready, Herr Geertz?" he yelled.

Geertz nodded.

Fokker engaged the synchronizer mechanism, and pressed the firing button. A quick burst of a few rounds spat from the gun through the blades, and struck the berm, raising a cloud of dust.

Geertz's eyes went wide in surprise. "Again, Fokker."

Pressing the firing button again, Fokker fired another burst that flew between the blades faster than anyone could see. Geertz looked back at his staff, who stood expressionless. One man shrugged.

"Okay, Fokker, stop the engine," said Geertz. Fokker turned down the mixture, let the engine rumble, starving for fuel, then flipped the magneto switch. The engine thumped to a stop.

Geertz stepped beside the propeller, and his staff gathered around him, all staring at the unmarked blades. Running a hand over it, Geertz seemed to try to divine the hoax from the wood. Fokker grinned down from the cockpit, looking like a child playing a trick on a parent.

"How?" Geertz glared at Fokker.

Fokker sat on the rim of the cockpit and explained.

"It's not an interrupter, it's a synchronizer. The ... *my* ... mechanism fires the weapon when the trigger is pulled and the blade is clear. It's not a machine gun so much as it's an automatic rifle." He patted the gun on the top of the Eindekker's fuselage.

Geertz's eyes grew wide and unfocused, but Fokker continued. He began to explain cams, linkages, and firing buttons. He said something about a plywood disk and how the French might have gotten a synchronizer to work if they had used a different machine gun.

Geertz waved his hands. "Stop, Fokker, stop!"

Geertz gathered his staff together again. Fokker sat and listened, then picked up Zeiten from the floor of the cockpit and scratched the dog's ears. Geertz's conversation was in quick German, and Fokker gave up trying to follow it when someone began to yell rapidly. Geertz shouted them quiet.

They gathered around Fokker again, the group of German officers looking up at him like a mob of angry villagers. Fokker thought of an old book, *Frankenstein, that's it, Frankenstein.* Fokker grinned and put Zeiten back inside the aeroplane.

"Do it again, a full belt, a hundred rounds," said Geertz.

To Geertz's surprise, Fokker looked down and shrugged. "Okay," he said. Kreutzer and two of Fokker's technicians handed up another belt, and Fokker loaded the machine gun.

After starting the engine, Fokker adjusted the mix and let the engine run up to full speed. Fokker engaged the synchronizer and sat down in the cockpit. He feigned aiming—he braced his head against a headrest installed for just that purpose—and then pressed the firing button. The belt ripped through the machine gun, the gun spraying empty shell cases over the wings and ground. Then the belt ran out, and the roar of the weapon echoed over the field, rolling off the buildings. Dust rose in a cloud atop the berm and drifted away in the wind.

Fokker killed the engine and sat on the edge of the cockpit, holding Zeiten.

"Acceptable, Geertz?" asked Fokker.

"Now fly and shoot at something," said Geertz.

"What do you want me to shoot at?" replied Fokker, nonplussed.

"We have some old wings."

Fokker climbed down, and his men lowered the aeroplane's tail onto the ground. They pointed the aeroplane down the field and loaded another long belt of ammunition.

"Put them where you want them, and I'll see to it," said Fokker. His voice was low, verging on patronizing, his impatience beginning to show.

An old pair of wings were drug out onto the graveled verge of the field. The crosses on the wings were freshly painted, and shined in the sunlight. Geertz and his men gathered around the wings.

"Are you sure you want to be that close?" asked Fokker.

Geertz just waved his hand and dismissed Fokker. Having walked away, Otto Parschau climbed the berm, carefully spread a handkerchief on the ground and sat. Fokker and his men started the monoplane's engine, then he piloted the machine down the field and took flight. After a broad sweeping turn, he looked down at the wings and the clump of gray-green uniformed men next to them. Kreutzer and his men climbed the berm, too, and sat down next to Parschau.

At four hundred meters' altitude, Fokker tipped the nose over into a steep dive. Bracing his head against his headrest, he sighted along the machine gun and aimed at the wings lying on the ground. On the periphery of the gunsight, he could see Geertz and his staff looking up at him. For just a moment, Fokker pressed the rudder and the sights of the machine gun swept over the group of men. He poised his thumbs over the firing button. Then Fokker pressed the rudder bar again and put his sights back on the wings. It was tempting, but not too tempting.

Fokker steadied the aeroplane and fired. With a roar, the gun erupted, and empty shells flew around the aeroplane. Bullets blinked through the air, into the wings, and ricocheted across the ground like lethal hail.

Geertz, intent, watched as Fokker began to fire. He turned his gaze to the wings as the bullets tore holes in a storm of dirt and canvas. Bullets zipped past Geertz. He looked around, confused. One of his aides threw him to the ground.

Fokker pulled out of his dive and buzzed over the wings, just a few meters up. Beneath him, the German officers were scattered over the ground, lying flat, not even looking up. Some were running toward the berm, others across the field.

Kreutzer calmly waved from the berm as Fokker went by.

Fokker felt cold, icy, and horror-struck. He imagined he'd somehow killed the men below him. It was a feeling he didn't entirely dislike, but a feeling that mixed with a sense of shame. Fokker turned and landed, then taxied the aeroplane toward the men as they stood up.

Geertz's aide was brushing dust off Geertz's uniform as Fokker's aeroplane stopped. Fokker unstrapped himself and stared down in mock horror at Geertz and his staff.

"Is everyone okay?" asked Fokker.

Geertz looked around and saw nodding heads. He thought of being angry, wanted to be furious, but was too perplexed to get a grip on his own ire. Two men from his staff emerged from behind the berm. "Yes, Fokker, they seem to be." Geertz walked over to inspect the tattered wings. After a moment, he said, "Well, I'm convinced."

Fokker and Kreutzer smiled at each other.

"Let's see if you can convince the General staff," said Geertz, and then, after a moment's pause, added, "*without* killing any of them."

"Parschau, here, will work with you, Fokker," said Geertz.

Parschau joined Geertz, his uniform clean and unrumpled. He looked at the broken wings and smiled: an odd sight on the young man's stiff Prussian visage.

"And ... ?" Fokker asked in mock suggestion.

Geertz's face screwed up in confusion. Fokker pointed at his left chest with one finger and grinned.

"And, yes, a medal," said Geertz, frowning.

Parschau looked at Kreutzer with a question in his eyes, and Kreutzer looked back and shrugged.

Chapter Twenty-One

May 17, 1915
London, England

St. Paul's Cathedral filled each day, all day, and into the evening for services. The clergy, exhausted, started one prayer service after another, pausing only so the pews could refill. From the countryside, more servants of the Lord had come to lend their aid to their beleaguered city brethren, leading worship in rotating shifts.

The crowds prayed for an end to the war and for salvation from the Zeppelins.

Strange watched the movement of the worshippers, filing in, then placidly filing out, their faith restored. He thought it industrial. Prayer and mechanization merged. He felt awkward and misplaced, a stranger for thinking such thoughts. The air of the cathedral was still and musty, which surprised Strange, for he knew it to be open and breezy.

Perhaps the worshippers have consumed all the air?

Bowing his head at the appropriate moments, he waited, but remained in the shadows of the aisle where only God could see him. At last, he stood, held his cap in bandaged hands and waited in the north nave for the current service to end. The service ended, tranquilly, without bells, and the people rose and flowed to the center aisle and out the west entrance past the queues of people waiting their turn.

What an odd place to meet. He thought, *I'm here to pay Hawker's respects to Beatrice, not attend worship ... Perhaps a cup of tea instead? Heavens, what have I gotten myself into?*

Strange stepped out from behind the columns and walked against the flow, between the pews, admiring the marble work overhead as he always had since he was a boy, wishing he were anywhere else.

"Mr. Strange?"

Strange turned and saw a young woman standing at the front pew. Layers of black chiffon billowed around her. An enormous, black, layer cake-shaped hat, brim as wide as her shoulders, sat atop her head. She pulled her veil up over her hat and smiled wanly. To Strange, accustomed to men in sunlight, she appeared alien and deathly pale.

"Miss Bayly?"

"Yes, of course." Beatrice extended an ungloved hand. Strange reached out with an injured and gauze-wrapped hand and shook hers gingerly, wincing slightly.

"Mr. Strange? What have you done?" she asked, holding his hand in hers and examining it.

Strange noticed her South African accent, her S's aspiring to become Z's, and he found it charming. "I ... well ... I fell out of an aeroplane," he replied, and pulled his hand gently away.

Beatrice smiled. "I trust you didn't fall too far then."

"No, not too far," replied Strange with a thin smile.

"Thank you for coming. It's very thoughtful of you."

"Lanoe sends his regards. He couldn't be away from the front, of course."

"I understand. Men and wars," replied Beatrice. A fresh crowd of worshipers begin to fill in around them, finding seats in the pews.

"Just a moment," she said. "I have one stop to make then we can find a tea shop. I believe there's one just across the way. You'll understand, I trust."

"Of course, Miss, of course."

Beatrice led Strange across the nave to the staircase that descended below the cathedral. She smiled back at him, drew the heavy rope aside at the top of the stairs and handed the end to Strange.

"No one is down here these days. Well, no one alive," she said in a low voice, almost whispering, before descending the stairs to the crypt.

Strange looked about, uncertain, a little self-conscious. The parishioners took no notice. He stepped onto the top stair and drew the rope behind them. Beatrice waited for him, looking up. They descended into the subterranean twilight below the church. The crypt, a great empty space beneath the cathedral, was absent visitors, leaving them alone in the enormous granite and marble vaults. Electric lamps in sconces cast light upward across the arched ceilings.

Most modern, thought Strange. *I expected wooden torches, oily rags burning.*

"Miss Bayly, I've been coming here my whole life, but I've never been in the crypts before."

"Yes, haven't we all," she replied.

She lifted her enormous hat straight up with both hands. Strange watched, fascinated. As she lowered the giant hat, the long veil draped onto the marble floor. She set it on a bench. She smoothed her tightly-pinned hair and craned her neck to stretch it.

"Most uncomfortable," she said. "That's much better. That thing must weight ten pounds. The latest fashion, though. All the rage."

Strange, wide-eyed and dumbfounded, nodded in agreement.

She corrected herself. "No, quite true. Entire fashion magazines are now devoted to mourning styles. Black and mourning aren't a fashion; actually, it's horribly normal. Rather vulgar. My mother insists I wear these. Of course, these days, we can't afford the best so we make do. God help me if it rains ... the colors run so. Under this dress I look rather ... dark ... from the black dye staining my skin."

Strange imagined the idea, enjoyed the image too much, and then didn't wish to. He squeezed his uniform cap with both hands as if he could wring thoughts out of it. He looked toward the stairs.

"I trust you've met Mr. Nelson," said Beatrice. She swept her hand toward the gilded sarcophagus of Nelson's tomb. "Admiral Horatio Nelson; please meet Lieutenant Louis Strange."

Strange smirked, tightlipped, and she saw his displeasure.

She put a gentle hand on Strange's arm to soothe him. "I'm sorry, Mr. Strange, I mean no disrespect. I was just trying to put you at ease. Forgive me, please." Her face brightened, and she seemed to draw color from the gilt and dark marble of the place.

"Just one stop and perhaps we can get some air."

Beatrice, abandoning her hat, walked on, seeming to glide on billows of black fabric across the floor of the crypt. She stopped before a larger-than-life-size statue of a man with one foot poised upon a cannon. The figure clumsily seemed to support his chin on his right hand, his left hand supporting his right arm. The eyes of the statue looked downward to the floor. Beatrice drew close enough to look up to meet its gaze.

"Good day, General Gordon," she said to the statue.

Strange stepped to her side. "Miss?" he asked, pondering her sanity.

"Don't think me stra ... daft, Mr. Strange. These are unusual times we live in. What was once rare is now common and what was once common is now gone."

She turned back to the statue and spoke again. "Tell me what you told him, General. Say it. Did you lead him astray?"

"Miss Bayly?" asked Strange. "Are you quite all right?"

Beatrice drew a sigh and glanced back at Strange, then turned to the statue as though listening for an answer. At last, she walked to the bench where her hat lay. She sat and perched the enormous thing in her lap, gazing back at the statue of General Gordon.

Strange joined her.

"May I?" he asked, gesturing to the bench.

"Yes, of course, Mr. Strange."

Strange sat and stared at the statue. He heard nothing.

Beatrice looked over to Strange. "I apologize, Mr. Strange. I don't hear voices. None at all. I'm afraid I was being peculiar at your expense. I'm quite rational."

"I see," said Strange. He silently considered whether the testimony of sanity from an insane person was valid. Perhaps it was, or, perhaps ... He suddenly missed the war.

"Do you know the story of General Gordon, Strange?" asked Beatrice.

"Yes, of course, every Englishman does. Lost his life at Khartoum. Most valiant. A hero of the empire. Perhaps not Nelson, but a great man. An inspiration."

"Yes. He died at Khartoum," repeated Beatrice. "He lost his head, so they say. They never found his body or his head. Vanished. Perhaps he's drawing a pint at some pub in Wales at this very moment, a very old man. And we built him a statue." She stopped and frowned. "But, of course he isn't. He needs to be dead. We need him to be dead."

She continued, "I have not lost my mind," she said again. She swept her hand, gesturing around the room. "This was one of my brother's favorite places. You see my brother is the great General's namesake. Our great-uncle, General Charles George Gordon, lent his name to my brother, Charles George Gordon Bayly. You see, I think my brother found inspiration here. Many do, I'm afraid. Sad, really."

Strange was speechless at her sacrilege, that she seemed to mocking the inspiration of the tombs. He couldn't muster a protest as he felt Beatrice's grief soak through her words.

"Too much inspiration. Disappeared on a battlefield. My brother— the first Englishman to throw his life down as a sacrifice in our latest war. And, just gone. Do you suppose that someone will build him a statue?" She stopped, seeming to have finished her thought.

Quiet settled in the catacomb. The murmurs of chanting worshippers drifted down the stairwell. "Well. Enough. I rave," she said at last.

They sat tranquilly again. Strange examined his thoughts and rolled them around in his head, trying to understand Beatrice, feeling he knew less about her now than before he had met her. Lanoe had said she was complex, but he had no idea.

Sensing Strange's discomfort, Beatrice smiled and spoke. "Enough of me and my irreverent thoughts. So, Mr. Strange. Tell me about falling out of an aeroplane and hurting your hands. I'm sure that's an interesting story." She adjusted the giant hat in her lap, making herself comfortable.

By reflex, he said, "Yes. Of course. Certainly."

Strange had imagined that they might have enjoyed a cup of tea in a quiet teashop, share inanities and then a quick good day. He hadn't ... no, couldn't have imagined the turn their conversation had taken. Strange pondered what he could say and what he couldn't, or perhaps what he didn't want to say.

He began: "I was flying with No. 6, Lanoe's squadron, a Martinsyde. A big ugly beast of a thing, near Menin." He paused and considered again how to tell the story.

"Go on, Mr. Strange. Quite fascinating." Beatrice didn't sound fascinated.

"Well, I had a Lewis gun, an automatic gun, mounted on the Martinsyde." He said the word 'automatic' as though it made the gun special.

Beatrice was unmoved.

"Well, that made the beast's climb all the worse. I could barely climb up to the Huns' altitude to meet them. And, well, I was attempting to shoot down a Hun with my machine gun." He looked at Beatrice to gauge her reaction.

Beatrice shook her head quickly and turned to face Strange, a look of quiet shock on her face. "You shoot at people in aeroplanes?" she asked.

"Yes, Miss, we do. Now, at any rate. Such as it is, it's all very crude, lots of flying alongside, hoping the Hun will fly nice and straight and steady while you shoot him up." Strange stopped, gulped and grew quiet, realizing how bloodthirsty he must have sounded.

"I see," she replied, nodding, sounding genuinely interested now. "Go on."

Strange continued, his voice lower and slower, composed. "So, you see, I emptied a drum of bullets at a Hun and ran out. In order to change the drum, one must turn the drum with both hands to unscrew it. And, I ... well ... I turned the aeroplane upside down—inadvertently, of course."

A look of confusion crossed Beatrice's face. "So you fell out ... and cut your hand?"

"No, not really. I held onto the drum ... and, I ... well, I hung by my hands."

"I see. So you fell out and hung by your hands and then ... then, what? I trust you let go and didn't fall far."

"Seven thousand feet," blurted Strange.

Beatrice was startled. "What?"

"Oh, no, no, Miss. I didn't fall far. I couldn't let go; I was *flying* at seven thousand feet. I hung on." He paused, knowing how ridiculous the truth must sound. He collected his thoughts and continued.

"Somehow I got my feet back in the cockpit, kicked the controls and fell back inside, and then I landed." He didn't add the part about sleeping for thirteen hours afterwards, nor how Hawker had come to fetch him, thinking him dead, nor how his hair had started falling out and that what was left was coming in grey. He didn't add any of that.

Beatrice smiled again. "You fell out of an upside-down aeroplane, a flying machine, hung on by your hands and then pulled yourself back inside, and you got a little cut on your hands? You jest."

"No, Miss, it's quite true."

Beatrice's face bunched up, turned pink, and then she erupted in laughter. Her laugh, too loud, echoed against the marble and around Nelson's tomb. Laughter in the tombs seemed beyond sacrilege, something so foreign as to hold charm. Strange squirmed, not seeing the humor. Beatrice continued laughing until she cried, then wiped a tear with a glove. They both realized her laughter carried into the cathedral above them.

"Oh, my! What do you suppose they think we're doing down here?" asked Beatrice.

Then Strange began to laugh, nervously.

At last, she gathered herself. "You are a remarkable man, Strange. A credit to your name. I like you, Strange."

They grew quiet. Strange was glad he had told the story and felt relief that, perhaps, she'd found it a funny story, not terrifying. He didn't add that that it was also the reason he was in London; that he was trying to recover from the shock. That his nerves were shot.

Silence settled back over them. For Beatrice, it was comfortable; for Strange, it was not. Strange shifted awkwardly.

Beatrice spoke first. "I worry for Lanoe."

"Why?" asked Strange, perplexed. "I wouldn't. I don't."

Beatrice glanced sideways at Strange. Then she looked back to General Gordon.

"Do you suppose your ... accident ... and your salvation was an act of God?" asked Beatrice.

Strange paused, not sure if the question was meant for him. "Well, perhaps. I haven't been thinking about God much lately. Perhaps I should."

Beatrice gestured toward Gordon. "The General, my great uncle, believed that God rules over man from a throne above Jerusalem, and that His throne is perched on the surface of a ball that surrounds the Earth. I suppose that means that the stars are holes in the ball, letting the light in."

"Do you believe that, Miss Bayly?"

"No, Mr. Strange, I do not. But he also believed in reincarnation. I wish to believe in that." She let the statement hang in the air.

Strange stared at Nelson's coffin.

"What do you believe in, Mr Strange?"

"Honestly? Science, I guess. At least it explains the unknown." Beatrice glanced at him with a look of amusement. He was afraid she might laugh again. Realizing he sounded naïve and afraid of what she might say, he quickly detoured the topic, "Why are you worried about Lanoe?"

Beatrice waited a moment, thinking her thoughts through. Her smile faded.

"Because he hears Gordon speak to him."

"I see," said Strange. He paused, summoning courage. "Miss Bayly, why do you come here?"

Beatrice looked around the great room. There was a new statue of Wellington, the hero of Waterloo, that dominated one wall. The effigy of the great man sat astride a stone horse inside the walls of a church. *Absurd,* she thought, *a horse in church.*

"Because it reminds me what we're afraid of. We're afraid of them." She looked towards the tombs and memorials that crowded around the crypt.

"Whatever do you mean, Miss Bayly?" asked Strange, deeply lost and puzzled now.

"Don't you see? We're just afraid of our mortality, and we imagine the wondrous and triumphant, like these dead men, as though we can find immortality or reincarnation."

"No, Miss, I don't see," said Strange.

"I understand," said Beatrice. "I do. I do not wish to."

Strange stared at the statue of Wellington and tried to remember Wellington horse's name. Then he realized: The horse had a statue.

"Miss Bayly, would you like a cup of tea? I believe the service is adjourned." He gestured above them with his bandaged hand.

"That would be lovely, Mr. Strange. You're very kind."

Beatrice stood, donned her enormous hat, and moved to the stairs. Strange took one last look around at the crypt and then helped her as she climbed.

Chapter Twenty-Two

May 21, 1915
Schweidnitz, Germany

The Baroness Richthofen dreamt of trains passing a station, barely slowing. Soldiers sat in silhouettes in the lights from the windows, staring, immobile in their seats. One train after another came through the station, never stopping, rolling past the mothers and young women. The women threw flowers that dashed upon the sides of the train.

Then, in her dream, she rode in a train with her middle son, surrounded by soldiers. Her presence quieted them, leaving her feeling that she had intruded. Her middle son, Lothar, beamed at her, smiling. He was tall and handsome with his bronze eyes. Then he was young again, and she held him while he cried and she tried to soothe him, assuring him that Aunt Friedel was wrong; that he wouldn't die young, that his eyes weren't a curse, that he would live a long and natural life. That he would grow old.

She awoke and wept softly, the house still and quiet, not even the staff awake at this hour.

The bed was cold next to her where her Albrecht had once lain with her, but no longer, even he, an old deaf man, away at war.

Her youngest son, Bolko, was gone too. So young; off to cadet school and barely twelve years old.

She listened for the train whistle in the early morning silence and fell back to sleep.

Something stirred her, woke her, and she heard breathing in the room. "Mama."

She rolled over, sluggishly waking again. A hand touched hers, warm and soft. She was startled, but not afraid. She thought she was dreaming and clung to the moment, not wanting to have it slip away.

"Manfred." She felt his presence in the room, alive, and it filled the room with his energy. She sat up, wide awake now.

"Manfred! Son! How did you get in?" Tears leapt to her eyes. She scolded him as she beamed.

He turned on the electric lamp on the bedside and grinned at her, proud of his prank. "The garden gate was locked, so I had to jump the fence, Mama. Never stopped me before."

She stood and pulled her dressing gown over her nightdress. Her heart pounded. She held him and pressed tears against her sleeve. Finally, she thrust him out in front of her by the shoulders and examined his face.

"You're still a mischievous boy, aren't you? You look well! I didn't know what to expect. You hardly look older at all." She leaned in and kissed his cheeks, then cupped his face in both hands. "Welcome home, son. Now let me get dressed and I'll be right down. We've saved some coffee for you."

She followed Manfred downstairs, turning on lights, and shouted for the cook to get up. She took Manfred by the arm, sat him at the table, and put a kettle of water on the stove.

The cook appeared, small, with her hair mussed, embarrassed at Manfred seeing her so soon out of bed. She saw him, sitting at the table, and in her joy, she covered her face with her hands. They had all feared the worst for the young master. But it wasn't her place to speak so she stayed quiet. Upon coaxing the Baroness to the table, she turned to her stove and oven. While the two reunited, the cook turned out flour, added baking powder, sugar, and milk and began to knead. She lit a fire under a pot of oil.

Outside, the sky was beginning to lighten. In the garden, the birds woke with song, flitting about the Virginia creeper in their search for berries.

"How are you, son? When did you get here? Where are your things? Where are you staying?" The Baroness began to ramble, thoughts and questions spilling out of her.

"Mama, didn't you get my telegram? Weren't you expecting me?"

"Yes, Manfred, I did, but we didn't expect you on the early train ... I'm so happy you're here."

"Yes, Mama, I'm glad to be here. I'll be staying with you, of course, if you have room." He smiled, teasing. "And Menzke is with me; he's bringing our things. He should be here shortly."

"You've grown fuller. It looks good on you; more mature. I can tell. A mother can see such things."

"Older and wiser, Mama. Older and wiser," he replied.

They spoke then of the family, of Albrecht, the Baron, unhappy to miss combat, but busy managing hospitals. Of Ilse, a nurse now, tending wounded. Of Bolko, gone to Wahlstatt, a cadet, so proud and so young. While they talked, the Baroness held one of Manfred's hands between hers, her grasp firm and steady, clinging to him as if he might slip away.

"Lothar is better. We spent time with him in hospital in Berlin. He was sick for a month, you see; sick from the Russian winter, I think. You know how the cold can make one sick."

"He's seen more adventure than me. We've been so idle in the west," said Manfred.

"But, the great victories! We've heard so many stories. The papers, dear. It sounds so heroic, our armies so valiant! I don't mean to gush, but, even with the losses, we're so proud." She glanced at the floor, pressed her feet against it, felt for balance, feeling the room shift. "Enough of that. I needn't bore you with such things."

Menzke arrived, dragging their trunks. He smiled at the Baroness, bowed awkwardly, and found a place at the cook's elbow. He turned to the stove and an opportunity to be warm.

The coffee was hot now, and it filled the kitchen with its earthy aroma. The Baroness and Manfred moved to the garden where sunlight was just beginning to slip through the trees in the cool spring air. She let Manfred lead her by the arm to a black iron table set out under the old walnut trees.

The cook brought coffee to them in their fine china and set a plate of hot donuts, sprinkled with sugar, on the table. Manfred thanked her and winked. He picked up a donut and took an enormous bite, then licked hot oil and sugar off his hands.

"So how has it been here, Mother? You grew quiet when you mentioned losses. Drink your coffee, Mother, and tell me. I need to know who has been lost, I can't be here and walk around the town not knowing, you understand." He patted her hand.

She looked at his hands, seeing lines she had never seen before, knowing that she had to tell the story and there would be no better time.

She began to speak of who had passed: those that were gone so soon, the price paid for the war. She told of the black clothing appearing, in September; how out of place it once was then; of how dreadfully normal it was now.

Friedel Leutsch, who had married young and for love, who was killed by a fragment, a single ragged piece of steel—his young wife and two fine, small children left behind. Albrecht's good friend, the Baron Loucadou, shot while on horseback; then, most tragically, Leutsch the Elder, dead of a broken heart for the loss of his son.

She spoke of the things that she couldn't write for fear she would tell of nothing else. She told of things that haunted her, that worried her, of her fear that each letter would become dark, and that hopelessness might take root. Before she let herself slip into despair, before she gave into bleakness, she cast about for a familiar, happy subject.

"I've found you a new saddle, Manfred," she said abruptly, smiling, seeking to change the subject. "I know that you've lost yours, and there are some fine saddles at the stable on Trasa road for a fair price."

"Mother." Manfred's tone was flat and soft. He placed his other hand on her arm.

She recognized the tone, his demeanor. "Yes?" She braced her feet again, hard and flat against the ground.

"Antithesis is with the artillery now. We had no more need for horses in the cavalry, we're all foot soldiers now, and so their need was greater than mine. They are taking good care of him. Santuzza was killed ... by artillery."

The Baroness nodded and let out her breath, relieved. Horses: beautiful and fragile.

"This is the price of victory, I suppose." She looked away through the trees.

Manfred leaned back, and let his hand lay with hers. He took a long swallow of his coffee; a habit from needing to drink quickly on the front, for the chance might be fleeting.

He said, "I don't believe we will win this war."

"I don't believe that I heard you correctly," said the Baroness. She sipped her coffee. Her hands shook.

"You have no idea how strong our enemy is," said Manfred.

"But we keep on winning!" replied the Baroness.

"Have you never heard anything about our retreat on the Marne?" he asked.

She shook her head, took another sip of her coffee, and set down her cup.

He told her about his namesake, the General Manfred von Richthofen, of his cavalry division routed northeast of Paris; of the gap in the German armies exploited by the French and English; and of the German armies regrouped on the river Aisne, dug in like animals in long trenches north of the river. He spoke of the dugouts, stretching in bounds until they ran from Switzerland across France and Belgium, to the English Channel.

"At best, it will end in a stalemate," he concluded.

The Baroness began to argue, referring to the newspapers, to the pronouncements from the Kaiser, from the German royalty, all on the inevitability of victory. She let the words trail off and die in the cool air, feeling foolish.

"Mama, we will fight heroically and valiantly, but the war has become static in the west, just hard body blows that use up men but gain nothing. It may be futile." He stopped, considering whether he had gone too far. "This is not treason, Mother, it's the military situation. There is little opportunity for us to break the stalemate, and little opportunity for our enemies; it becomes a war of numbers. Sadly, the cavalry is idle, ill-used, and useless."

"And what of you, Manfred? What will you do? Wait your turn?" she asked. She felt heat in the back of her throat, and she resisted tears.

A brilliant smile crossed his face, a glimmer of a grand secret.

She grasped his forearm, excited for him and by the expression on his face.

"I am going to join the fliers," he said.

The color drained from her, her mouth grew slack, and her eyes tried to find somewhere to focus.

His face bore a mask of joy written in a broad smile. He extracted a hand from hers and picked up his coffee, tipped the cup and drained it. He plucked another donut and took a huge bite.

"But, I thought you were enjoying the infantry, that you'd been reassigned and were content?" she asked. She felt a shudder of fear and tightened her jaw so that it wouldn't show.

He looked down, an expression somewhere between dread and shame crossing his face. "I'd been reassigned as supply officer, Mama."

"I see." She could have taken joy in that, but did not let on, knowing how he would have reacted. Her expression sagged and she felt a sensation like wilting. She knew that he couldn't ... wouldn't be idle. She was dejected that he had to commit himself absolutely to action, and sad at the knowledge that that was how she had raised him. The thought made her more afraid. A dull ember of fear burned near her heart.

He smiled then, and he told her of the aeroplanes overhead. He spoke of the freedom and how he saw in them the liberty to cross the lines, to look down upon men, machines, and their plans; of his desire to be a part of something new and strange and free from the life rooted in little holes in the ground.

"But, Manfred, do remember that you had such an awful time on that American thing, the Ferris wheel at the Berlin carnival?" the Baroness said.

Manfred grew quiet. "One must overcome their own limitations."

He thought back to a memory he had tried to bury. His father put him and Wolfram, who was gone now, on the thing. They had gone up so high, so high that, at first he was thrilled and excited by the view. Then, it stopped turning, leaving them up there for how long? He couldn't remember. He could only remember the sound of someone wailing and hot tears. He remembered the shame when he realized it was he who screamed, and of how people had laughed. His gaze settled on the crook of a distant tree and lost focus. He pushed the memory back.

Was it me? Was that really me? Or someone else; a story someone had told me about someone else? Some other boy? A rumor of shame?

The Baroness sat up, watching his face contort with recollection.

His speech had bothered her; it had seemed so committed to memory that it made her unsure for him. She smiled, thinking of another time, of a boy. She choked down her fear, knowing her feelings were little unchanged from the kind of terror she had felt when the war first began, just a different flavor now, but the same fear, and the same dread.

Another memory came to her, and she smiled.

"Do you remember how you would swing from branch to branch at your grandmother's house like a monkey, picking apples? You made me want to cover my face and run away."

The light returned to his face as the painful memory drained away. He was relieved that she had left him room to believe that he could do this.

"I know you will succeed, Manfred, always. I know that you've made up your mind, and that is well."

She stood, took him by the arm, and led him to the house. "Come, let's get you settled. You must be tired after your journey."

Chapter Twenty-Three

May 30, 1915
Cologne, Germany

Richthofen sat upright, his shoulders square, his spine straight, as the instructors at Wahlstatt had, so painfully, taught him to do. His knees pressed against the bottom of the little desk. He glanced down at the old desktop and ran his thumb over a name scratched in the wood, for someone loved Hilda enough to give her some measure of immortality. Through the windows came the sound of aeroplane engines; some growing louder, some fading, others abruptly coming to life, and still others whirring to a stop.

"They reek," said Richthofen.

"What?" replied a young Leutnant at the next desk.

Richthofen waved a finger at the open window, at the sound of an engine running up. The Leutnant nodded and turned back toward the front of the room.

He looked at the other men around him, youthful men with the eyes of old men. Their uniforms were a mix of units and services, but mostly cavalry—Hussars and Uhlans. All young and obsolete. They sat at timeworn school desks arrayed around the floor of an accountants' room in an old cotton warehouse. Squeezed into the tiny desks, they looked like a joke that wasn't funny.

He felt it again, that deep pit of hollowness in his stomach, the twitchy uncertainty. There was no way to be sure until he'd done the thing, no way for the void to fill until it had been overcome. Fear was a familiar feeling now.

Can I do it? Can I go up so high and be composed, remain dignified, the way an officer should? He squirmed in his seat, thinking of the awful Ferris wheel. His mouth went dry and he tried to swallow spit to remedy it.

The instructor arrived, dressed in civilian clothes, an appearance that was disquieting for its lack of militarism. The man introduced himself, and, in a too-casual way, invited the men's introductions. He appeared to be no more than twenty, and looked to Richthofen to be younger than most, if not all, of his students.

Have I made a mistake? Is this a joke? A backwater?

The teacher picked up a piece of yellow chalk and drew diagrams on the board. First, he drew a simple picture of an aeroplane, with arrows showing forces acting on it, up and down, front and back.

Richthofen watched the man's hands as he drew on the board; they were rough and stained, but steady. *Good hands; perhaps, hands that might have been those of a rider once.*

He drew another diagram, a map, it seemed, but with simple shapes, the form of roads, rivers, and buildings. He described how to orient around them, how to judge distance, how to return to north, and how to pick a line on a map and follow the course from the air with landmarks. At last, he set the chalk down and brushed his hands together.

"How many of you have been up in an aeroplane before?" He asked.

No one raised his hand. All of the officers looked at one another, their faces deliberately expressionless; they looked back to the instructor. One of the students shrugged his shoulders.

"Not all of you will succeed here. This is as it should be. We will begin with flights tomorrow morning at seven. Each of you will fly and attempt to guide your pilot around Cologne and then back to the airfield. It is simple, but it will provide you with a knowledge of yourselves that you don't, at this moment, possess. I will judge your success after the flight. Then, I will ask many of you to leave the school to make room for others. And, many of you will ask to leave on your own." His voice was flat, factual, but tense, stressing the importance his words held.

Richthofen pondered the seriousness of the man, looked him up and down, saw someone that he wouldn't look at twice on the street: a noncombatant, a nobody.

So, that's a flyer, he thought.

Richthofen was uncomfortable at dinner that evening; he squirmed in his seat, trying to be patient as he watched the other students show off their knowledge of aeroplanes and flying, watched them trying to overcome their anxieties with bombast. He excused himself early, his own excitement and fear only feeding that deep pit in his stomach, helping it swallow his appetite.

The aeroplane engines faded at dusk, and the quiet of the countryside settled over the field. Richthofen watched the lights appear in the hangars, revealing men working on the fragile aeroplanes. He couldn't fathom what needs these machines had that they required attention through the night. He supposed them to be so frail that they needed to be touched, massaged, and nursed into flight.

What have I done? My God. Ridiculous toys; delicate scraps of fabric; kites with which to kill oneself.

He lay down, still wearing his dress uniform. He ran his hands over the sheets in bed, relishing the sensation of the smooth fabric, so far from the rough blankets and straw beds in a bunker. He lay awake, startling himself to alertness with the sound of phantom artillery in the distance. He thought of flying, trying to imagine the sensation, but couldn't. His mind was not able to conjure up an answer to something so strange.

In the early morning, he surrendered, his insomnia the victor. After hours of tossing, he finally stood and pulled the curtains open to see the barest hint of light in the east. He changed from his dress uniform to riding clothes—tall boots and jodhpurs. He walked to the mess hall where hot coffee waited. As the sun rose, he sat and sipped, watching the sky give way from black to gray. He strode to the field in the twilight, the first student to arrive.

An instructor was waiting by an aeroplane. A pilot sat in the machine, doing something mysterious with the controls. Two ground crew stood by, hands folded behind their backs, one at the engine and another at the tail.

"Good, good morning. Von Richthofen, isn't it?" the instructor asked, a different man than the young man in the classroom, a little older, armed with a clipboard. He spoke in a Bavarian accent, consonants disappearing before they left his lips. The man checked Richthofen's name from a list.

"It was wise coming early, the air should be most calm and, well, the sun low on the horizon puts everything into shadows and brightness ... you'll see." He smiled, warm, almost like a colleague.

Under the man's open jacket, Richthofen could see a uniform. He was relieved and felt a sense of some familiarity, some connection. The instructor led Richthofen to a table and explained the exercise. On the table lay a thick leather jacket, a leather helmet, goggles, and a scarf.

"These aren't yours, of course, but you can use them for today. After today's flight, we'll know if you'll need to buy your own. It'll be a warm day down here, but up there ..." He pointed a single finger straight up and wagged it from side to side. "Up there, it will be cold; the higher, the colder. Very cold."

Richthofen put on the jacket, leaving it open at the throat, where he tied the scarf loosely. He picked up the helmet and goggles, not bothering to try them on.

"Let me show you the aeroplane, and then you can begin."

They walked around the thing, the instructor reaching out to touch certain parts. "It's an excellent design, the newest Albatros from Johannisthal. It has nice lines and is sturdy if a little underpowered. But it has good manners in flight."

It sounded to Richthofen that he was describing a horse and he smiled. The propeller was a smooth varnished laminate like a piece of fine furniture. He reached out, ran a hand over the top of the fuselage, and felt the cool pliant fabric.

"Are you ready to fly, Leutnant?" he asked.

Richthofen nodded and stepped to the boarding ladder. The instructor helped him into the observer's seat ahead of the pilot. Richthofen tried to look ahead around the engine, but could see nothing to the front of the plane. Down over the sides he saw only wing. Backward and along the fuselage, he could see only the ground. He glanced at the instructor quizzically.

The instructor handed Richthofen a clipboard with papers attached and a pencil clipped at the top. Richthofen flipped through them. On top was a folded map of Cologne, and under it, several loose sheets of paper.

The instructor ran his finger over the map.

"Here is where we are. You'll be taking off to the north, direct the pilot to fly north to this point, turn east, past the edge of the city, then south, then west and back here. It should take twenty minutes or so to make the flight. Understand?"

"Yes, Herr Instructor, I understand."

Richthofen put the leather helmet over his head, loosely fastening the straps under his chin. He pulled the goggles down over his eyes and settled into the seat, holding the clipboard in his lap. He looked back at the pilot, who simply nodded. Richthofen returned the nod with a wave.

The crewman in front spun the propeller and the engine caught, rising in speed to a harsh snarl. Richthofen looked over at the instructor with doubt in his eyes. The instructor smiled and waved a goodbye. Then the pilot opened the throttle further, and the blast of wind from the propeller hit Richthofen in a small storm of hot air and engine fumes. Richthofen's helmet twisted and inflated then pulled at his throat. His coat filled like a balloon. Richthofen blanched and clung to the rim of his cockpit, suddenly starkly afraid.

The roar of the engine grew, the sound rising from a rumble to a cacophony. It became a driving thunder accompanied by a tremendous blast of wind from the propeller. The sound and the gust both drove directly into Richthofen, who was perched right behind the engine, little more than a meter behind the propeller.

Richthofen felt bile rising. The clipboard lifted and tried to fly out of his lap, the papers flapping and tearing away. Richthofen grabbed it, and wedged it between his knees. He tugged the leather helmet down and pulled the straps tight under his chin; then he pushed his jacket together and did the top buttons. He looked over at the instructor, fighting panic. The instructor stepped back and gave him another wave of his hand and another smile.

My God. I haven't left the ground yet.

Richthofen felt he'd lost all control, that the sound and air would drive him out and away, carried on that foul wind. He looked back at the instructor with pleading eyes. He thought he might throw himself over the side to the ground. He gripped the sides of the cockpit with his bare hands so tight that his knuckles turned white.

Oh, Lord, please don't let me scream; don't let me make a fool of myself.

He realized they were moving, and the aeroplane was bounding across the ground, accelerating. He was trapped now: the blast of the air, the sound, and the movement all acting together to hold him in place. Even well-fastened, his helmet and jacket still billowed.

Settling deeper into his seat, he choked down hot bile and remnants of coffee. He couldn't seem to push himself down deep enough.

With a soft bounding, the aeroplane began to lift. Richthofen was surprised at the lightness, at the sensation of being afloat.

It's like a well-mannered horse, almost gentle, he reassured himself.

Then the aeroplane left the ground, and the rolling, bounding sensation became a buoyancy in his belly, a sense of falling and then of being carried in turn. He tilted his head back and looked down at the ground behind the wing. The earth fell away. His view of the grass became the sight of the tops of trees, a rougher green carpet stretched out below him.

He had left the world he knew, as if he'd gone somewhere outside of himself, where all was strange and everything new. His hands relaxed on the sides of the cockpit, and he shifted his weight so that he could lean over the edge. Finding that he could see best looking out over the lower wing, he leaned far out to one side and watched the vast panorama below.

The pilot banked to the left, and the still air gave up its lift. The aeroplane dropped briefly, and then regained its climb, as though regaining its footing. Richthofen's stomach floated as the aeroplane fell. It was unexpectedly pleasant and exciting. Then they banked right and leveled out.

Richthofen needed to watch the ground, to absorb every sight and sensation. He glanced down at the map, pressed it flat on the clipboard, and then put his finger on the symbol for the aerodrome. He glanced over the side and then to the map and, with a start, realized that he couldn't match the two together. The aeroplane banked and he leant out. As it tilted in the opposite direction, so did he, struggling to pick out the familiar made unfamiliar by the view from above. The ground became a jumble of objects: tiny men; houses from a toy box; tiny horses; tiny carts.

A sinking sensation, not of falling, but of failing, gathered in him. He sat back, stared at the map again, tried to pick out a feature that existed on both the paper and the world below. He tried to find a point of reference, couldn't, and looked back at the pilot. The pilot appeared engrossed in his own thoughts and avoided his gaze.

Richthofen rolled the map over the top of the clipboard, and pressed a blank piece of paper flat. He began to write a note, "Where are we?" and then crossed it out. He wrote again, "Can you show me the aerodrome?" then he tore the bottom of the page from the clipboard and leaned back to hand it to the pilot.

A rush of air grabbed it from his hand and blew it away. Richthofen looked, expecting to see it flutter away, but it was already gone, as though it had never existed.

He knew that he was alone now. Accompanied, but alone. Communication wouldn't be easy, and, at best, would be trivial. He realized he didn't care where they were. Instead, he felt exhilaration, energy filling him like a solid thing. He settled himself into his seat and enjoyed the newness around him.

So what if I fail? I'm flying!

He tightened his helmet and his jacket and wedged the clipboard a little more firmly between his legs, a smile frozen to his face.

In the distance, below the right wing, a tall shape appeared, the sunlight striking it from behind, casting long pointed shadows in their direction.

"Ah," he said, aloud, to himself.

It was the Kölner Dom, the great cathedral of Cologne, the grandest in the world, appearing ornate, tiny and delicate far below the aeroplane. He absorbed the sight, admiring the intricacy of the building, shapes like a fine filigree from so high above. He thought it beautiful, opulent, and inspired. He grinned and looked back at the pilot, pointing. The pilot turned his head to look to the east, then turned back, and nodded his agreement, the expression on his face indiscernible behind his goggles and scarf.

With a sliding lurch, the aeroplane began a long turn to the left, the low sun casting moving shadows across the wings from the struts and wires. Surprised at the pilot's reaction, Richthofen thought that he needed to be sure he pointed out that he had seen the landmark. Richthofen watched, fascinated, as the shadows swept by. The pilot leveled the plane out, the sun to their left now; they were heading south now, back the way they had come.

Richthofen realized their flight would soon be over and felt disappointment sweep over him. He sat upright, higher in the cockpit, and relaxed his hands with an effort, releasing the sides of the cockpit. He massaged them together trying to force some feeling back into them. They were tight, cold, and wind-blown.

Despite his disappointment, Richthofen continued gawking, fascinated by the sights below him, and he worked to commit each to memory. He felt dismay, tension and frustration, knowing this might be the last time he saw the world from this place, and that this experience might be fleeting, that it might be gone too soon.

The engine slowed, the torrent from the propeller relaxing, and then, with a cough, the engine accelerated again. Richthofen's concern deepened, anxious for the engine to continue pulling them along. He clutched the rim of the cockpit once more for comfort. Leaning out, he looked ahead past the fuselage. Far to their front, he recognized the aerodrome, and, on the far side, the old cotton warehouse.

The engine coughed again, slowed further. The aeroplane descended at a steady rate, the objects below growing larger by the moment. Richthofen watched the ground draw closer to them, mesmerized by the process of coming down. Sunlight covered the field now, the grass a more brilliant green than he'd ever seen before. As they neared the ground, the aeroplane rocked in the air rising from the warming ground.

They passed over the tops of the trees, and then they were over the field. The pilot guided them below the level of the trees. The engine slowed further, almost stopping. With a gentle nudge upward, the nose rose, and the aeroplane sank onto the grass.

Richthofen sat upright, and turned a grand smile to the pilot behind him. The pilot ruddered the aeroplane to their starting point, and cut the engine.

The sudden silence left Richthofen's ears ringing even more loudly than normal, but he couldn't stop grinning. He pulled the helmet and goggles off and looked around for the instructor.

The ground crew trotted out to the aeroplane and propped up a ladder, allowing the pilot to climb down. Richthofen almost scolded them for allowing the lower-ranking officer to descend before him, but thought better of it, sensing that he was in a new order here. They moved the ladder to allow him to climb down while the instructor and the pilot spoke. Richthofen could see the pilot gesturing toward him, his hands sweeping out broadly to his sides. The pilot turned and looked at Richthofen, then nodded and strode away.

The instructor walked over to Richthofen.

Richthofen steadied himself on his feet, a fleeting sense of being in motion passed over him and then drifted away. He began to approach the instructor and lift his arms, and then stopped himself as he realized that he might hug the man. Instead, Richthofen pulled himself up straight at attention and saluted, the smile stuck on his face.

The instructor returned the salute.

The ground crew began to push the aeroplane away. In its wake, the air smelled of oil, gas, and burning. Richthofen thought of the smell of horses, how a horse barn could smell so welcoming and relaxing. He wondered if that smell of burning might be that way one day.

"How do you believe you did, Richthofen?" the instructor asked.

Richthofen thought a moment, and then began trying to apologize, to explain himself. "I didn't recognize landmarks, and I had a difficult time becoming oriented to the map. I'm certain that I can do better with more experience." He thought again of asking forgiveness, and then let the idea fade.

"No, not that, Richthofen. How did it feel? How do you feel now?" asked the instructor.

The smile swept over Richthofen's face again, uncontrolled, a boyish grin. "It was most pleasant, Herr Instructor. It was a ... a ... joy." Richthofen hesitated, feeling the word was wrong, that it was too soft and feminine. He let it be, the thought complete.

"No sickness, no nausea, no queasiness now?" asked the instructor.

Richthofen looked surprised at the question, then thought back again to the damned Ferris wheel. "None of that. Perfectly fine."

"Very well, you may stay."

A wave of relief washed over him.

"Very good, Herr Instructor. Thank you." He saluted again, standing stiffly in the open field as engines stirred and came to life around him.

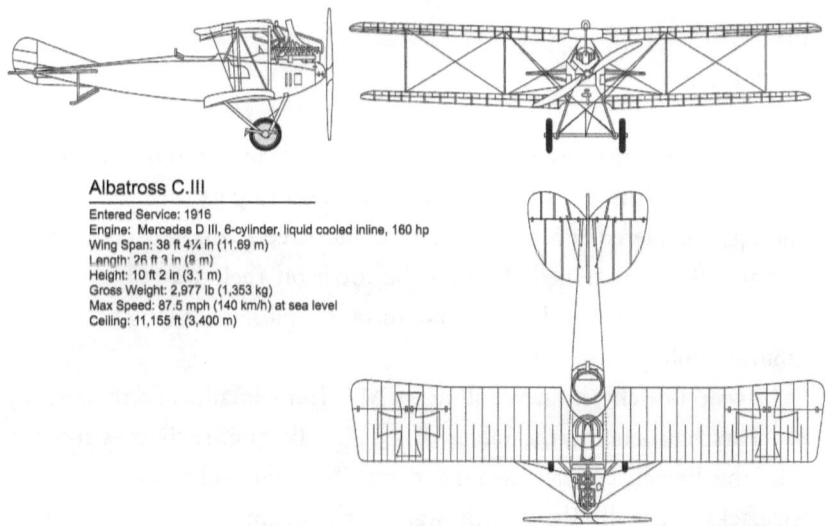

Albatross C.III

Entered Service: 1916
Engine: Mercedes D III, 6-cylinder, liquid cooled inline, 160 hp
Wing Span: 38 ft 4¼ in (11.69 m)
Length: 26 ft 3 in (8 m)
Height: 10 ft 2 in (3.1 m)
Gross Weight: 2,977 lb (1,353 kg)
Max Speed: 87.5 mph (140 km/h) at sea level
Ceiling: 11,155 ft (3,400 m)

Chapter Twenty-Four

June 3, 1915
Douai, France

Soft tendrils of mist rose from the town's central canal and stood in silent spectral pillars. The city of Douai lay quietly, waiting its turn for war. No buildings smoldered, no rubble clogged the streets. Endless columns of German soldiers marched through the town on their way to the front. From the west came the dull sound of distant explosions, a long bass drum of thunder rolling across the city.

Oswald Boelcke, his new colleague, Max Immelmann, and their guest, Otto Parschau, circled the tables of a sidewalk café, their eyes moving across the French civilians around them. They sat and faced the street, their backs to a wall. The French, wary of the German uniform, began to leave their tables and move away from them. A waiter brought them coffee and the German pilots huddled in conversation.

Sergeant Immelmann lifted his coffee cup, held the cup at his lips too long, and sipped it too loudly. He held one pinkie extended. Two pieces of white cake sat on a plate in front of him. At his feet lay his Boarhound, Tyras, sleepily scratching at his ears. Immelmann reached down and gave the dog a pat. Immelmann was deeply insecure, a non-commissioned officer among officers, a slight dandy man with impeccable manners and the tastes of a boy afraid of meat. To Boelcke, Immelmann was an enigma, an excellent flyer that seemed to desire to be known for his mastery of etiquette and style, rather than for something that truly mattered. Was he a phony or was he just a child?

Boelcke looked down the street past the shops and stores, still open, and watched the civilians move about in a forced calmness, as though they were working to appear normal. A group of schoolchildren carried a giant paper mâché puppet past them. He shook his head in amazement. "Just a week ago, they were planning a welcome for the French army. Now they look like the party was cancelled."

Parschau looked up from his coffee and glanced down the street. "I hardly notice them."

"And coffee. Back home, they're drinking whatever will darken water and then call it tea. Here, coffee." Boelcke took a long hot sip and felt the warmth radiate through his chest.

"I understand that you're having fun chasing English aeroplanes in your observation plane," said Parschau to Boelcke, attempting to steer the conversation away from the French and toward something more interesting.

Boelcke glanced at Immelmann, conscious of the difference in rank between the two officers and the foppish sergeant, and thought a moment. "Yes, I'm having fun. I'm tiring out observers, but the new one is a good hand with a machine gun, so we get by."

"That's a fine thing, Boelcke. Keep trying. You'll shoot something down eventually," offered Immelmann. Boelcke flashed a glance at him. Immelmann looked away.

"Well, we have little to show for it," said Parschau. He waved his hand at his uniform, at his pilot's badge.

"Come now, Parschau, you don't think about earning medals, do you?" Boelcke was incredulous. "There's no time for that."

Parschau smiled and pointed at Boelcke's Iron Cross. "Perhaps not, but they do look nice on one's uniform."

Boelcke pulled the Iron Cross off his chest, handed it to Parschau. "Here, I'll trade you for your secret weapon."

"You should be proud of it, not hand it away," said Immelmann. He sat straight-backed, stiff. He sipped his coffee once more, his pinky finger arrow straight.

"I am, Immelmann, quite proud. But, I don't know that it measures a man's worth. Do you?" A look of contempt flickered over Boelcke's face. Parschau caught Boelcke's eye, then turned to Immelmann.

"Here, Immelmann, try it on." Parschau handed him Boelcke's Iron Cross. Immelmann pinned it on his chest and gave it a happy pat.

"I think it looks fantastic," said Immelmann.

"It does. But it looks better on me," said Boelcke. Boelcke reached out his hand, empty palm up.

Immelmann handed the medal over and Boelcke put it back on his uniform.

"How was your stay with department thirteen?" asked Parschau.

Boelcke bent to his coffee, thought about his answer, thought about how much to share.

"It was very productive. But, all things must end," answered Boelcke. Boelcke was embarrassed, but wasn't about to show it, and he was surprised that Parschau would know about being sent away to recover from his asthma.

Parschau nodded. "I heard. Streccius can be an ass. I heard he also sent your brother away." He sipped his coffee.

Boelcke noticed how clean Parschau's sleeves were. He glanced at Parschau's boots, glossed to a high shine, nearly new. "We are all brothers, Streccius included," he said.

"Very correct. Very political, Boelcke. Not the answer I expected," Parschau conceded.

Parschau and Boelcke laughed together as a look of confusion crossed Immelmann's face. Immelmann squirmed, feeling out of place with the two officers, uncomfortable. He pulled at his collar.

"And after he sent your brother away, you needed treatment for your asthma, I understand," said Parschau. Immelmann blanched at the personal question and looked away from Parschau. He reached down to scratch Tyra's ears.

Boelcke snorted, shifted, and tightened his shoulders.

"Yes. I was sent away. Seemed that I had war nerves or some such thing. Streccius didn't like my cough, I suppose. I had a pleasant time at the sanatorium—lots of singing."

Parschau looked at Boelcke with confusion and pondered whether Boelcke had just mocked him.

"No, quite seriously," said Boelcke. "We sang; I made new friends. My lungs have never been better. Besides, the men were restless in Streccius' squadron. We couldn't fly for weeks. It made for strained nerves. The only thing worse than flying every day is not flying every day. It was better to move on," said Boelcke. "But, the rest was good for me."

Boelcke cast distrustful eyes along the street, his muscles in his jaw flexing, sharpening the angles of his face. His lips were full, almost pouting. The combination of features made Boelcke look simultaneously dangerous and feminine. He thought about how the doctors had treated him. Did I lose two days ... or was it more? One of the nurses said it was the Belladonna and that he shouldn't be embarrassed.

"And you, Immelmann? How has your time here been?" asked Parschau.

"I'm enjoying it here. We fly more. And there's more experience to draw on." Immelmann tipped his cup toward Boelcke. Boelcke didn't know whether to feel complimented or condescended to. He let it lie.

"I hear that your talent is crashing during landings," Parschau teased.

Parschau laughed and reached out and patted Immelmann on the arm. Immelmann looked like he might draw his arm back. He managed a short chuckle.

"Have you heard the expression, 'Flying is Landing', Immelmann?" asked Parschau.

"Yes, yes, of course." He gave a thin smile.

"So, Parschau, what are you doing here with Fokker? Why aren't you flying the new bombers?" asked Boelcke.

"I've been flying a Fokker monoplane since before the war. I have my own. Fokker has put a more powerful engine in my aeroplane, the green one. And I prefer flying alone," he answered.

"But what of Fokker?" asked Boelcke.

"I guess I'm his escort. I'm meant to ensure that his actions are always in our best interest, I suppose. His minder, when Geertz isn't doing it," said Parschau. "And, we have something new to show you."

"So, that's it, then, this secret weapon?" said Boelcke.

"We've brought two monoplanes, more are on the way. You, Boelcke, are one of our more experienced flyers of monoplanes. Moreover, I understand that you, Immelmann, are one of our more natural pilots."

Parschau sipped his coffee. He waved to the waiter, and then motioned to his cup for a refill.

Immelmann frowned, silently shaking his head from side to side. He didn't know what Parschau was talking about.

"What of it, Parschau?" asked Boelcke.

Parschau held his cup out for the waiter to fill it, and then waited for the man to walk away. "Have you heard of Garros?" he asked.

"Yes, of course, excellent flyer. I saw him loop once," said Immelmann.

"Wasn't he shot down?" asked Boelcke. "And didn't he shoot down several of ours?"

"Yes. What isn't widely known is that we captured his aeroplane. And Fokker has done *it*," said Parschau. He emphasized the last word with exaggerated mystery.

"That's why I'm here, to teach you how to fly the Fokker with a machine gun," said Parschau. "It fires through the propeller."

Boelcke sat upright, drawing back from Parschau. "I want nothing to do with wedges and plates and deflectors. I've heard of all that. I'm not a coward, but we'll do fine with our guns in the back seat."

"No, no, it's nothing like that, Boelcke. It fires between the blades. While the propeller is turning," said Parschau.

Boelcke thought about this. "Ridiculous!" he said. He stared down the street, his mind racing.

"What?" protested Immelmann.

"You're an engineer, aren't you, Immelmann?" asked Parschau.

"Yes," said Immelmann.

"Deflection," said Parschau. "If you shoot straight ahead, it eliminates the need to adjust your sights for the movement of your aeroplane."

"Very well," said Immelmann, dimly. "Yes, I suppose. I hadn't thought about it."

"I understand," said Boelcke. "We can close the distance while shooting. That's all I need to know. All this chasing and turning to shoot then dropping behind accomplishes nothing. Now we can attack."

Immelmann took a large bite of cake and watched a French girl walk by. She stared at Tyras as she passed, careful of the enormous dog.

"So, we can attack, head on. In a single-seater," said Boelcke.

Parschau nodded.

"Has anyone done this?" asked Boelcke.

Parschau frowned, "Well, no. Just Garros."

Immelmann dabbed at the corners of his mouth with exaggerated grace.

Priss, thought Boelcke.

"And we would do this while flying other missions?" asked Immelmann, his voice was hesitant, trying not to ask a stupid question.

"Yes, of course, Immelmann. Of course," said Parschau.

"We can stop their spotters," said Boelcke. "That's reason enough."

Immelmann gave a half-shrug, seeming to dismiss the idea.

Boelcke turned to Immelmann. "You don't take that seriously, Immelmann, do you?"

"No, not particularly," said Immelmann.

Boelcke raised his voice. "Let me tell you a story, then. Near Verdun, the French spotted a mess kitchen from the air, and they watched it, timed the meals until the men lined up. Then smashed it with artillery. Two companies of men, gone in a two-minute barrage." He snapped his fingers.

Immelmann pursed his lips, in an odd gesture that looked like he was forming a kiss.

"These things happen," said Immelmann.

Boelcke leaned toward him, his face flushing scarlet. "No, Immelmann, these things, they don't just happen. They're not accidents; they're the work of men. It's not evil, it's not the devil, and I don't believe it's coincidental. It's just men ruthlessly finding advantage for their own ends." He sat back.

Immelman looked away, embarrassed and then spoke in a tone that was nearly a whisper. "Perhaps that is the essence of evil."

Boelcke reappraised Immelmann, felt a sudden flash of affection. He realized he might like this Immelmann fellow, after all. Parschau waited for Boelcke to relax, for the passion fade.

"What happened then, Boelcke?" asked Parschau, calmly.

Boelcke forced his shoulders down and let his lungs empty in a quiet wheeze. He was strangely pleased that Parschau sensed the story wasn't over.

"My brother and I flew out and spotted the battery that did the shooting. It could only be one battery, and we spotted it, had it dead to rights." Boelcke folded his hands in his lap, stretched his shoulders back. "And, our artillery fired and didn't have the range. Two hundred meters short. Once they realized we couldn't hit them, they stood and watched our shells fall. Their artillerymen waved. Bastards. Next day the battery was gone. Moved before we could bring our artillery closer."

Immelmann looked at Boelcke with vacant eyes, not understanding.

"Hell, Immelmann, if they'd never had their eyes on our men; they'd never have had the chance. That's why I chase their aeroplanes around; so they never get the chance." Boelcke sat back, visibly deflating. "You see, one mechanism, one invention, and we can save lives. Perhaps, this changes things. Now we can fight."

Boelcke sipped his coffee, looking past Immelmann.

"Tomorrow, we'll fly the new Fokker, the Eindekker. Then you'll see, Immelmann. Then you'll see," said Parschau.

Immelmann began to eat his second slice of cake.

Boelcke reached up to his jacket pocket and felt the Belladonna cigarettes there, like a man adrift in a boat might, if he were checking for his life preserver. He felt a sense of motion, that something had shifted, wondered if the drug was still in him, and his mouth went dry. Slowly he reached out and wrapped his hand around his coffee cup, comforted by the solidness of the thing, clinging to its reality. He smelled something distant and dark in the air.

Chapter Twenty-Five

July 2, 1915
Douai, France

Fokker waved to Boelcke from the cockpit of Eindekker. Lined up alongside him, Boelcke waved back from the cockpit of his machine. Fokker listened to the notes of his engine, for an imperfect rumble, the rattle of a loose rod or bolt. He heard none, only the rhythmic beating under the sound of the roaring engine. Satisfied, he moved his hand in a chopping motion, then reached down and opened the throttle. Boelcke watched Fokker's monoplane begin to pull ahead, then began his own take-off roll. The monoplanes accelerated and sprang into the warm air side by side.

Fokker thought: *Perhaps this will be the time, just once, let's get this over with. Stop this charade.*

The air was rough, hot: the sky itself was spiraling upward under the aeroplanes. Fokker climbed straight to avoid the risk of losing lift while turning at low altitude. After a short climb, he turned the nose of his aeroplane to the east. Boelcke flew alongside, matching Fokker's movement. They flew over the town of Douai, and then clawed upward into the open air east of the city, deliberately flying away from the frontlines.

At a safe distance away from the front, they leveled out. Fokker made a quick check of his instruments and then signaled Boelcke to engage his synchronizer by holding up one finger, making a motion like pulling a trigger. Fokker pulled on his mechanism to engage it. The device was tight and chattered as he pushed it into place, and then quieted, engaging.

Boelcke put both hands on the steering yoke again, his fingers on the firing button. He felt his old anxiousness, the sense of trepidation that it wouldn't work, wouldn't fire.

Please. Please.

It had grown tiresome, doing this same thing day after day, tuning, firing, landing, and adjusting.

Damn it all, flying like this, we could be at this forever, proving nothing.

Fokker glanced over at Boelcke and waited. Boelcke's head was down, hunched over his steering yoke and firing button. Fokker expected, hoped for, the harsh pounding of Boelcke's machine gun firing. Nothing. No sound erupted from Boelcke's machine. Boelcke looked over at Fokker, and shook his head from side to side.

"Dammit!" Fokker shouted into the wind.

Boelcke bent over his controls again, his hands moving around inside the cockpit. Fokker braced himself, waited, and watched. Again, nothing. Boelcke shrugged in surrender. Fokker nodded his head up and down in understanding, and faced forward.

Fokker put both thumbs on the firing button and glanced at Boelcke to make sure he was watching, and pressed the firing button. The machine gun barked, hammering bullets through the spinning disk of the propeller and into the sky. Gray smoke flew back over Fokker's face, and he tasted the chemical ashes of gunpowder. Fokker released the firing button. He looked up at the propeller. The engine ran smooth and untroubled.

Perfect. Perfect.

Fokker smiled to himself, and shot a toothy grin at Boelcke. Boelcke smiled and waved back. Fokker pressed the firing button in a long burst. The gun hammered, cycled through cleanly, most of a belt of ammunition pulling up and through the butt of the gun.

Now, if Boelcke's would work, he thought. Fokker watched as Boelcke turned and bent over his controls once more, trying his firing button again. Boelcke mouthed an exaggerated "No." Boelcke pointed down, motioning that he was going back to land. Resigned and frustrated and just needing to fly, Fokker nodded and pointed east, indicating he was going to keep flying.

Boelcke waved, banked, turned away, and dove back to the west. Then Fokker pressed the firing button again, let a few rounds fire, and turned south, flying parallel to the frontlines.

Damn, he thought. *Damn it. One more time, over and over, again. Is there no way to prove to these fools that this can work?*

Fokker began to think about the air now, heated and spinning up in drafts. He wondered if the air over the frontlines was hotter, if the air there was more violent from the brutality below. Curious, he turned, ruddering around, skidding sideways, and flew due west. To the northwest, he could see the steeples and towers of Douai's old town.

An aeroplane flew below him, flying northeast. Fokker saw the brilliant red, white and blue markings on its wings stark and sharp against the pale ground. It was a French Farman. Fokker's eyes grew wide in disbelief. He had never seen an enemy aeroplane in flight.

An enemy. No, not my enemy. Theirs. If Boelcke were here. If only one of them were here with working guns!

Fokker impulsively banked the monoplane, tipped the nose down in a steep dive, and lined up behind the Farman. He effortlessly closed the distance between them.

So easy, he thought. *He'd never know what had happened. He'd disappear behind the lines and his squadron mates would peer out to the east and ponder another unknown.*

His gun sight was on the Farman now, the French aeroplane centered in the metal ring. Fokker closed one eye, and peered at the Farman over the barrel of the gun. He throttled back to close gradually, to allow more time to aim. His thumbs hovered over the firing button as the French aeroplane flickered through his gun sight. The French pilot flew straight, oblivious, even the observer looking down. They didn't notice him.

Why would he bother to notice me, what worry was there? Just another aeroplane, just another flyer.

Then: *He's helpless, an ignorant rabbit.*

Fokker imagined his bullets striking the Farman, erupting through canvas, tin, and flesh.

Perhaps a lucky hit on a control wire or a spar might send a wing sailing off into the blue.

To hell with this.

Fokker took his thumbs off the trigger and looked up at the Farman.

He lifted a hand and waved, but the Frenchmen didn't wave back; they still hadn't seen him. He banked left, made a show of flashing past the Frenchman, deliberately surprising them. Fokker leveled the monoplane and flew northwest, back toward the field at Douai. He throttled down and began blipping the magneto button to descend.

As he landed, Parschau, Boelcke and their new commander, Kastner, were waiting, impatient. Boelcke's machine stood with the engine cover off, two mechanics on ladders were adjusting the mechanism again. Boelcke stood close to the mechanics, pointing at something, resisting the urge to reach in and help them. Another mechanic was pulling the propeller off, a disk of plywood lying ready to be mounted so they could adjust the synchronizer again.

"Boelcke's machine gun wouldn't fire," said Parschau.

Fokker looked at the ground, then back up. He pulled his goggles and flying helmet off. Gun smoke stained his face, the goggles having left white rings around his eyes. He felt ridiculous and lost in the German uniform.

"I'm finished here," said Fokker. "I'll be taking the train in the morning. You can keep these three." He gestured at the monoplanes; Parschau's green one, the new one, and at Boelcke's.

Kastner's mouth worked and no words came out. He stepped close to Fokker, lifted his finger into Fokker's face, and shook it. Still, no words came out.

"You ... you ... will stay here until this works," he stammered.

Fokker took a step back and braced his hands on his hips. "No. No, I won't."

Kastner faced Parschau. "He's your problem." He threw up his hands, dismissing Fokker.

"It works now," said Fokker, blandly. "Well enough."

Kastner turned back to Fokker, his hands balled up into fists. He stepped toward the Dutchman. Parschau stepped between them.

"Herr Kastner, I mean no disrespect," said Fokker. He raised both hands in a gesture of surrender. Fokker's voice lowered, his charming tone returning. "I've flown for the air command, for the Crown Prince, for you ..."

"It's good enough. Parschau's gun fired. And ... and ... I could have shot down a Frenchman."

"So you say, Fokker, so you say," said Kastner.

"No, I could have," said Fokker. "I flew up on a Farman; he never saw me. I was so close he filled the sight. I wouldn't have missed."

Kastner and Parschau stared at him in disbelief.

Parschau stepped close now, his anger flaring, boxing Fokker in. "We never asked you to do that. We don't hire mercenaries!" He yelled at Fokker.

"I won't kill for you. I didn't kill for you. You can do that for yourself!" Fokker shouted back. He stepped away from Kastner.

Kastner and Parschau grew quiet, glanced at each other. Boelcke joined them. Parschau turned to Boelcke. "Did you hear this?" He pointed at Fokker as if he were pointing at a rat.

"Yes," said Boelcke. "I heard enough. I saw a Farman. It could have happened. Fokker was behind me, and the Farman passed behind me as well." Boelcke turned to Kastner. "Sir, if I may?"

Kastner sighed, "Go ahead, Boelcke, please."

"He can leave; we can handle this. The gun doesn't work all the time, between the synchronizer failing and the guns jamming, we'll continue to have problems. But, the flying and the shooting, we can handle that. And we can fix the machines without him." Boelcke gestured to the mechanics working on his aeroplane.

Kastner looked at Boelcke and watched his face, trying to judge Boelcke's words. Kastner sighed again, "Parschau, do you agree with Boelcke?" he asked.

Parschau waited, let his own anger clear from his mind. "Yes, I agree with Boelcke," he said.

"Very well, gentlemen, don't make a fool out of me," Kastner threatened.

"You may go, Fokker." Kastner looked up, but saw Fokker's back. Fokker was already walking away across the field, his scarf and cap hanging in one hand. A pink sun shone through the haze over the battlefield.

At his quarters, Fokker packed, angrily throwing his clothing at his open bag. He poured water into his washbasin and washed the gunfire soot off his face. The water grew gray and foggy.

Outside the window, the sky became the color of flames and the dome of the sky darkened.

A knock came at the door. Fokker looked back at himself in the mirror over the basin and wiped away the last smudges of smoke. "Come in."

Parschau stepped in. "Good evening, Herr Fokker."

"Good evening, Herr Parschau," replied Fokker. "What can I do for you?" Fokker was trying on a friendly tone.

"A telegram from Kurt Wintgens came in," said Parschau.

Fokker's mind raced.

Bad news? God, did the synchronizer fail and cause a crash?

Fokker sat heavily and glanced at Parschau. "What is it?" he said, his voice weak, almost gone.

"He claims a victory in your monoplane," said Parschau. "He approached a French aeroplane without alarming them. The synchronizer worked perfectly. Unfortunately, his quarry fell behind French lines, so, it won't be an official victory. But, he's a credible man. His report will be considered accurate."

The color returned to Fokker's face. "Thank you, Parschau."

Parschau waited, looked back at Fokker, and tried to gauge his reaction. "This is good news, Herr Fokker."

"Yes, yes, of course it is," said Fokker. He looked back at the sunset as it deepened to crimson. "Thank you."

"Very well, Herr Fokker. Very well. Will you be joining us for Kastner's birthday party?" said Parschau.

"Yes, I'll be along shortly. I just need to finish packing," said Fokker.

I was right, I was right. I knew it.

"Very good," said Parschau, pulling the door closed.

Fokker looked at the closed door and then out at the sunset, at the sky the color of blood. He sat on the edge of the bed and pounded a fist into the palm of his hand. Then he stood and opened the window, staring out. Somewhere artillery rumbled. The realization struck him. It hadn't been easy, but because it was difficult, did it make it worthwhile, the right thing to do? Did I do it for money? Was that it?

My God. What have I done?

Chapter Twenty-Six

July 15, 1915
Rava-Ruska, Ukraine

Acrid wood smoke from a far-off forest fire drifted out through the trees. In the distance, Richthofen heard the heartbeat of a modern war, the familiar dull boom of artillery fire.

A column of Ukrainian refugees, trudging to the west, was passing a column of German infantry headed east. The German infantry were singing, their voices carrying across the field. Richthofen stepped down from the back of a wagon as Menzke pulled their trunks to the ground.

"Well, this seems familiar, but at least we're not living in holes in the ground and most everything is still standing," said Richthofen with a smile.

"Yes, Herr Leutnant, at least we don't live in holes," replied Menzke.

With rats. At least we don't live in holes, with rats, thought Richthofen.

Ten Albatros two-seaters lined the edge of a trampled wheat field. The headquarters was just beyond in an old tent with the flaps pinned open in the hot Ukraine summer. An Imperial German flag hung limply on a flagstaff made from a tree limb. Flight crews moved in and out in small groups.

Over the trees to the east, an Albatros roared toward the field, the pilot throttling the engine down as the aeroplane approached. Another Albatros pilot ran his engine up to full throttle and began rolling to take off in the other direction.

Richthofen pointed Menzke to where their trunks should be stacked and watched the aeroplanes land and take off. He felt his heart pound, excitement rising, the energy feeling more real than since the first day he'd flown at Cologne. He adjusted his uniform, smoothed his collar, and strode to the headquarters, exchanging salutes as he walked past the men leaving the tent. Inside, an Unterofffizier stood to attention from behind a desk. Richthofen snapped off a smart salute.

"Good afternoon, Unterofffizier. Leutnant Richthofen, reporting. Assigned from Grossenhaim observer's school."

"This way, Leutnant."

The Unterofffizier led him though the dark stuffy tent around clerks huddled over desks. He raised a flap on the back of the tent and escorted Richthofen out into the woods. A well-worn trail led down a slight hill behind the tent, and then into thick brush. Richthofen glanced at his young escort and scowled, feeling he was being trifled with, or pranked.

The corporal smiled sheepishly at Richthofen. "This way, Leutnant. The woods are ... more cool." The Unterofffizier strode down the path.

Richthofen hesitated a moment, then followed.

The trail led through the dry brush along a tiny trickle of a stream, then crossed a larger stream and led up to a cleft in the rocks alongside a small waterfall. In the break of the rocks sat a desk. Behind the desk sat the group Kapitan huddled over a swath of papers. He was in deep conversation with a pale, thin pilot.

They hauled this desk in here for this man? Unbelievable, but I can see why. A lovely spot!

Richthofen came to attention as the Unterofffizier announced him. The Kapitan shook his hand and offered Richthofen a seat.

"Kapitan Frietag. Commanding. Come into my office, join us," said the Kapitan without a trace of amusement. "Georg Zeumer, meet Manfred Richthofen."

The gaunt man twisted uncomfortably in his seat, not rising. Zeumer offered Richthofen a weak hand as he met Richthofen's gaze with clear, vacant eyes. His face was gray, his eyes bordered by shadows, and his lips tinged in blue. Zeumer coughed into a crimson-stained handkerchief and dabbed at the corners of his mouth. Richthofen withdrew his hand, startled, and repulsed.

Zeumer didn't seem to notice and smiled. "Good to meet you, Richthofen. Horseman, I understand. Like to fly. Can read a map. All good."

Richthofen sat. He felt a little pleased to be recognized.

A bird settled on a branch over Frietag's head and stared back and forth at them, then took wing and flew away. Zeumer drew himself upright in a series of stiff movements. Richthofen looked around at the landscape and shifted his chair to a more stable perch on the rocks above the stream.

"Glad to have you here, Richthofen. Forgive the unusual surroundings, but the heat is insufferable. The tents drive me mad."

Richthofen thought there might be humor in Frietag's remark, but Frietag sat ramrod straight with a shadow of a grimace on his face.

Zeumer shifted, uncomfortable in the way a man that was all bones might be.

"Zeumer here needs an observer. If you like to fly, you can fly all you want, several times a day if you can keep your wits. Some grow tired, but not our Zeumer here! No, he always brings his machine back. Don't you, Zeumer?"

Nodding, Zeumer gazed at Richthofen, his eyes sunken and glassy inside their black rings. "We can fly this afternoon if you're up for it, Richthofen."

Richthofen turned to Frietag, his mouth moved but no words came out.

"Zeumer is our most experienced pilot. Trust me, I don't want to lose you till we've gotten something out of you."

Richthofen looked back at Zeumer, whose eyes hadn't moved from his face. Zeumer didn't seem to blink—like a dead man.

"We should look at the maps. I need good eyes on them so I can mind the flying," said Zeumer. "You can settle into one of the tents by the river. It's most cool at night, but there are mosquitos to contend with."

Frietag stood and then Zeumer, and Richthofen followed their lead. Zeumer began to walk away, his movements tight and stiff. Zeumer wasted nothing with excess motion; his arms held to his sides with shoulders squared. It was like watching a machine walk.

The Unteroffizier returned and laid paperwork on Frietag's desk. Richthofen stood, unsure of what to do. He glanced down at the stream, and felt the cool air on his face.

"Yes, Richthofen? Questions?"

Richthofen looked after Zeumer, turned back to Frietag. "No, Kapitan, no questions."

Richthofen saluted and jogged to catch up with the pale, stiff, little man. Zeumer emerged from the trees onto the edge of the field and walked towards the row of planes. He looked over his shoulder at Richthofen, and cocked his head like a bird.

"I thought you might not be coming," said Zeumer.

"I thought so, too, for a moment," Richthofen answered.

Zeumer laughed, a rattling cackle. His laugh gave way to another spasm of coughing, and his handkerchief returned to his mouth.

They stopped next to an Albatros two-seater, a B.III, one of the newest. Zeumer reached into the rear cockpit and extracted a map. He spread it out on a wing and pointed out landmarks on the map to Richthofen: navigation points. He drew jagged lines with an old pencil indicating where the Russians were believed to be.

"So, our job is simple. We find the Russians, draw it on the map, and come back here. They run the maps over to Corps headquarters, and we get a fresh map and start over. Sometimes they tell us where to look, sometimes they don't."

"And how do we know they're Russian and not German when we see them?" asked Richthofen.

"They'll shoot at us. Sometimes the German troops will shoot at us, just out of habit. We try to fly low enough so they can see our crosses, and then the German troops won't shoot. But the Russians, they shoot at everything, all the time. That is, when they're not running from us because they think we're a dragon or some-such damned thing. Superstitious people. Frankly, I think they believe the noise will kill us. They don't seem to aim. It's good flying; just listen for gunfire and read the map. Quite simple."

Richthofen fixed his eyes on the Albatros as Zeumer spoke. He pointed. "And what, Zeumer, is the meaning of that?"

A black cat was painted on the side of the aeroplane. The cat's painted feet were in green grass, its back arched and its tail standing straight up. Its mouth was open in a silent hiss.

Zeumer laughed his strange coughing laugh. A fresh handkerchief appeared this time, the bloody product of Zeumer's cough even starker against the clean linen. Richthofen saw that Zeumer's hand was white and bony, the veins blue under the skin.

"It's for me: my lucky aeroplane. The Black Cat. Someone started calling me that. I'm not sure how it was intended; bad luck, or nine lives, or something of the sort. I like it though. Drew the cat myself. What do you think?"

"Let's just say it's nine lives, shall we?" Richthofen said. Richthofen looked at the handkerchief in Zeumer's hand and at the bright, glistening streak on it. "Consumption?"

"Yes, if it's not obvious. Will kill me eventually, I suppose. Couldn't march in the infantry, but they let me fly. Don't tell anyone that there's nothing to breathe up there, will you? It'll be our secret." He winked. "But don't worry, I'll get you back safely, Richthofen. Shall we fly, my friend?"

Richthofen looked back into the trees, thought of the Kapitan's desk in the shade.

"He's not quite mad, you know. It's a lot cooler out there in the trees. The tents are stifling, especially at night. I sleep under the wing, personally." Zeumer pointed at a narrow patch of shade below the aeroplane. "The air is always fresh. And no one wants to be in a tent with me anyway."

"Very well, Mister Cat. When do we fly?"

"Now, Richthofen. Right now."

~~~

In the summer heat, Zeumer, Richthofen and the other crews flew scouting missions, constantly retracing the shifting lines, feeling out the positions of the Russians, and just as often, seeking out the positions of German units.

Eventually, pushing the squadron forward toward the retreating Russian lines, Kapitan Frietag ordered them onto a train. While the aeroplanes of the squadron circled ahead and occasionally landed in open fields to save fuel, the train carrying the ground crews and mechanics lurched ahead. At an open broad field with a rail spur nearby, Frietag ordered the engineer to stop the train. He jumped down and walked into the field and stomped a foot to test the soil. An Albatros circled them overhead and Frietag waved up to the crew, then he gave the pilot a thumbs-up gesture, indicating the ground was good. The Albatros pilot turned west waggling his wings to lead the other pilots to their new landing strip.

Like a circus setting up for a show, the crews unloaded the train, while the showmen, the aeroplanes, flew in. The Albatros lined up in the air, one at a time, and landed. Once on the ground, all the men of the squadron turned out to create an aerodrome, tending aeroplanes or setting up tents. Officers took their jackets off, stripping to their shirtsleeves in the heat of the Slavic summer. A squad of infantry strung ropes through the trees and built a barricade on a nearby road to give them some security from Russian infantry, stragglers, or partisans.

The crews stood the aeroplanes up in a neat row along the edge of the field.

Richthofen looked up from pounding in a stake while Menzke held it. Menzke let go of the stake, stood up, and shook his hands to get the blood flowing back in to them. Richthofen sat down the long hammer and watched a German officer appear in the heat haze, strolling along the tracks toward them. In one hand, the man carried a valise and tucked under his arm was a little black dog. Despite the dust, he wore tall, expertly polished riding boots.

Richthofen smiled and prodded Menzke to look at the strange vision, then called over to Zeumer and pointed out the man walking toward them. Zeumer grinned a wide bony grin. The man approached them and set the dog down.

"Count Erich von Holck," he introduced himself, saluting and extending a hand in greeting in one smooth way of his arm.

Richthofen shook the extended hand and then introduced Menzke and Zeumer.

"We heard you were coming to join the fun, Holck. But, I would have expected some fanfare." Richthofen gestured at the empty tracks behind him.

"My train broke down fifty kilometers or so back. Early this morning, in the dark. It wouldn't have taken so long, but Engel here needed to walk and tend to his business, that sort of thing."

The dog circled Richthofen's ankles, sniffing. Menzke bent over and stroked the dog's back. Richthofen stifled a laugh so he wouldn't offend the man.

Zeumer, however, laughed with a long, dreadful rattle. Holck scowled and Zeumer quieted. After a moment he asked, "Did you say fifty kilometers? You carried this pooch for fifty kilometers?"

"Yes," said Holck. The expression of a dazed child crossed his face. "Do you have any water?"

Zeumer laughed again and this time Richthofen joined him, convinced of the truth of the story.

Menzke shook his head, and glanced at Engel. "Officers," he mumbled to the tiny dog.

~~~

Richthofen peered down from the Albatros at the ground below. Along the eastern horizon grey columns soared up into the sky, each marking a village burned by the retreating Russian army. Thin smoke obscured the ground below, making roads and streams difficult to pick out. Russian infantry pouring east on the roads were thick shapeless clumps in the haze. Richthofen watched, finding the scene below strangely mesmerizing, beautiful—like a scene from Dante's Inferno. The Seventh Circle of Hell seemed to swirl around them, the fate of those that commit crimes against Nature.

He bent over the map in his lap, holding it away from the prop wash. With a finger, Richthofen traced rail lines and roads, and then looked below them again. He tried to find a recognizable crossroads to orient from but couldn't. In frustration, he reached out and tapped Holck on the shoulder, then pointed down. Holck nodded and adjusted the throttle, letting the aeroplane descend. At fifteen hundred meters' altitude, Richthofen discerned a road in the haze, running through thick woods toward a town with an enormous cloud of smoke rising over it. He tapped Holck on the shoulder, then pointed at the road, and then pointed toward the burning town. "THAT WAY!" Richthofen shouted.

Holck turned the aeroplane to the southwest to line up with the road.

As they flew south of the town, an odd three-way intersection caught Richthofen's eye. He held the map up again, and placed a pencil dot on the intersection, then traced a line to the circle where their new airfield should be, straight ahead, on the far side of the column of smoke. The smoke rose in a thick black wall, at least a kilometer wide. Richthofen put a hand on Holck's shoulder and pointed, holding the map up so that Holck could see it.

Holck nodded. They needed to fly around the pillar of hot soot. Holck swiveled in his seat and looked back at Richthofen, all while holding the plane level.

Not bothering to shout over the sound of the engine, he mouthed the words, "Are you sure?"

Richthofen nodded and mouthed the word "Sure". Then he pointed a finger to the left and in a sweeping motion, pantomimed a sweeping turn around the smoke.

Holck looked at Richthofen and shrugged. He grinned and turned them toward the thick column. Sparks flickered through the smoke now, tossed up through the billows by the inferno below. Holck glanced back at Richthofen, grinned at him again, and adjusted his goggles with exaggerated glee. He leveled the aeroplane and steered the Albatros directly at the billows.

Richthofen froze in shock at Holck's recklessness as he drove their aeroplane into the wall of smoke and ash.

The aeroplane plunged in. His eyes and lungs burned and he gasped for air. In a stomach-twisting lurch, the aeroplane rolled and tipped nose down, tossed about in updrafts of superheated air, rising invisibly in the sky.

Then they began to fall. Dropping, then rotating, then corkscrewing.

Richthofen cried out and dug his fingers into the sides of the plane. He grabbed one of the wing braces, using it to leverage himself downward, deeper into the cockpit, as the aeroplane spun violently. An orange lake of fire materialized below them through the smoke and soot. Richthofen squeezed his burning eyes shut and said a quick prayer.

Holck crouched over the controls, working desperately to recover the spin. The aeroplane whirled from the smoke and into daylight. Holck knew that he had a brief moment to regain control, and he centered the controls. The aeroplane stopped rotating nose down in a steep dive. Holck brought the nose up, and leveled the aeroplane.

The moment of terror had passed. Richthofen relaxed his grip on the sides of the cockpit and the strut. He looked back at the column of smoke behind them now. Then he looked over the side and clearly saw Russian infantry in the roads below. With a horrible shock, he realized that he could make out their individual faces.

The Russians raised their rifles and banged away at the German plane. A machine gun joined in with staccato popping. Then a metallic rattle rang out as bullets hit the engine.

Richthofen had enough. He pounded Holck on the shoulder, and then pointed back the way they had come, toward their old landing field. Holck nodded and banked the aeroplane hard to the right, turning it around and flew them south out of smoke. The aeroplane faltered, seeming to sag as the engine ran raggedly.

Trying to spot a place to land, Richthofen hung out of the aeroplane. 500 meters, no more, he thought, gauging the distance to the ground. They flew past the burning town, then turned and ran parallel to a road running to the southwest. The engine popped again, then sputtered and went silent. The propeller windmilled, and then stopped. Suddenly quiet, the only sound now was the rush of the wind over the wings. Engel began to bark from the floor under Holck's legs.

Holck looked back at Richthofen. The grin was gone from his face, replaced by a strange vacant gaze and he, too, began to look for a clear spot to put the aeroplane down. Richthofen pointed past a line of trees at a large clearing dotted with circular dugouts and mounds of earth. Holck nodded.

In a glide, the aeroplane soared over the trees. Holck let the aeroplane sink, and brought the nose up. Without power, he had to commit to the descent before he was ready, so he lifted the nose, and let the aeroplane slow.

Then they fell onto the crest of one of the earthen mounds.

Richthofen gritted his teeth together, tucked his head down and closed his eyes. The aeroplane struck in a grinding roar that ripped its landing gear away. The ruined machine skidded along the ground and tipped up onto its nose, as though trying to bury itself in the dirt. Richthofen's face slammed into the cockpit rim and he tasted blood. The propeller shattered, sending splinters of varnished wood flying around the two men. Abruptly, their craft stopped, and crunched back onto its belly in a cloud of dust. Gravel and bits of aeroplane rained down. Silence and stillness followed.

Richthofen sat dazed. He looked around them at the open field, dotted with empty entrenchments, and abandoned artillery pits. Quickly getting his wits, he pulled himself from the cockpit and climbed to the ground. Holck reached into his cockpit, picked up Engel, and handed the whimpering dog to Richthofen. Then Holck climbed out, leaned heavily against the aeroplane, and vomited.

Grabbing Holck by the arm, Richthofen scooped Engel tighter against his chest and led them away, to the southwest, toward another tree line.

"Dumbass!" shouted Richthofen as he helped Holck away from the smoldering wreck. "You had to fly through the damn smoke? Come on, move! We can't stand around and wait for Russians!"

Holck stumbled and fell. Richthofen turned to help him as Holck staggered to his feet. Together, they crossed the gun pits, picking their way through discarded Russian equipment and mounds of soil.

They reached the edge of the field and slid into the forest. There they collapsed onto their bellies in a breathless heap. Richthofen handed Engel off to Holck and put his field glasses to his eyes. He examined the open field and the wreckage of their Albatros, the place where he expected Russian troops would gather.

"You better hope the Russians capture us. Because, otherwise, Frietag is going to kill us," snipped Richthofen.

"No, I don't think so, Russians cut the noses off flyers and I like my nose too much. I'd rather deal with Frietag," said Holck. He grinned at Richthofen as though it were all part of an adventure, the man having clearly recovered from his earlier shock.

"Holck, you are crazy. I'd rather keep flying with Zeumer; at least he knows he can die."

After a few moments, a single soldier in a soft cap ran to the Albatros and peered into both cockpits, then began searching around the entrenchments adjacent to the wreck.

"Holck, we've got company." Richthofen pointed across the field. "There. In a cap; not a helmet. He's a Russian."

Richthofen dug into his pockets, laid his pistol out on the ground and handed the field glasses to Holck. He pulled the magazine from the pistol and counted the shells.

"Six. Six bullets. Do you have anything?" asked Richthofen.

Holck just shook his head and stroked Engel's ears. He didn't even look up.

Richthofen watched with growing dread as the soldier in the field began following their tracks through the dust, heading across the field. He stopped, stared at the trees and yelled something. Richthofen froze.

Holck jumped up and waved. In response, the soldier pulled a pistol and began stalking toward them in a half-crouch.

Richthofen was aghast. "What the hell is wrong with you?" He jumped to his feet, raised his pistol and thumbed the hammer back.

Holck pushed Richthofen's hand away. "He's German, my deaf friend."

Richthofen lowered his gun and slumped to the ground. "Ah. Good," he managed.

The soldier advanced: a German grenadier in a Russian cap.

"Gentlemen! Wait with your aeroplane, please. Less likely to be shot than if you jump out from behind trees," he said. "German infantry is right behind me."

From the trees at the edge of the field, German soldiers began to trickle into the open, moving in short leaps across the field, sprinting from cover to cover. A German officer made his way to Holck and Richthofen and offered them water.

"Do you have any horses?" asked Richthofen.

"Yes, I think we can find a couple of them," replied the officer. "You would appear to be done flying for the day." The officer sent a runner back into the trees.

Soon an orderly appeared leading two nags tacked with artillery saddles. Richthofen mounted, laid his map in his lap and turned his old horse to the road. Holck frowned, and mounted his horse. Richthofen handed Engel to Holck. Together they rode into the trees and along the roads to the west, following Richthofen's map.

At dusk, they arrived back at their field. Frietag's orderly approached them and saluted.

"The Kapitan requests your report." The man clicked his heels, formally, as though they had just ridden in from a parade. Richthofen climbed down, stiff from riding, and thought briefly of punching the man.

Frietag's new office was a small rise situated in a grove of pecan trees. He had a view across their long green field from his desk. He stood as they approached, and saluted briskly, and then sat, leaving them standing.

"Gentlemen. Report."

Richthofen told of the smoke, seeking the advanced field, and of descending to see roads more clearly, then of approaching the column of smoke over the village of Wisznice, and of needing to pass it to get to the airfield.

Frietag stood. He was shaking in anger now and braced his hands against his desk.

Holck cleared his throat and interrupted Richthofen. "I chose to fly through the smoke; Richthofen pointed around it."

Richthofen nodded, but continued. He told how they emerged over the Russian troops, of their engine being shot up and damaged, then crashing.

"The aeroplane, is it salvageable?" asked Frietag.

"Parts, Kapitan. Just for parts. Local troops were to remain with it until we could salvage anything useful." Richthofen added, "The aeroplane will not fly again."

Frietag's face was scarlet with anger now and his hands were claws hooked to his desk.

"You are both out of my squadron. Now. I'm transferring you out of this unit immediately. You'll not fly for me again." He waved them both away.

"Sir!" said Holck, beginning to protest.

"Not another word, or you'll never fly for anyone," said Frietag.

Richthofen and Holck saluted, turned, and walked away. Richthofen's jaw worked, anxiety straining the muscles in his face. Holck smiled as though he'd put something over on the headmaster. Then Holck stopped and looked around at his feet.

"Engel. Where is Engel?" Holck asked suddenly. Distress passed over his face. He began to call out and trotted off through the pecan trees. "Engel! Engel!"

Richthofen looked after him, astounded, and watched him go.

Grounded! thought Richthofen. *Grounded and a forced transfer? All because of him?*

Richthofen was too shocked to even be angry.

Chapter Twenty-Seven

August 1, 1915
Douai, France

The sun hadn't yet risen when Fischer rapped on Boelcke's bedroom door. Fischer rubbed sleep out of his eyes. Behind the door, he heard a girl's giggle and he rapped again. The bedroom went quiet except for whispering.

"What is it?" asked Boelcke from behind the door.

"Sir, you told me to wake you. There's an Englishman about," said Fischer.

The door opened, and Boelcke stepped into the doorway dressed only in his nightshirt. "This early?" said Boelcke.

"Yes, sir, and it's quite foggy," said Fischer.

Fischer heard bed sheets rustling and tried to look past Boelcke. Boelcke stepped into the hallway and closed the door. "Foggy? Have you been outside? Any stars?"

"Yes, sir. It's pretty thick, no stars," Fischer answered.

"Just a minute."

Boelcke stepped back into the bedroom and closed the door. A minute later, he came out, having added trousers and boots to his nightshirt. Behind him, a pretty, dark-haired girl stood in the doorway.

"Fischer, this is Ninette. See that she gets back to her quarters, will you?" Boelcke bent and gave her a hug followed by a quick kiss, and then he bolted off down the stairs.

"Yes, sir," said Fischer.

Outside, Boelcke saw gray skies in the east, no starlight, no moon. *Damned awful flying weather,* he thought.

He started his motorcycle with a kick and rode through the empty streets of Douai, over the canal, and to the airfield. He parked the motorcycle behind a shed and entered it. Two mechanics were working by lantern light on one of the Eindekkers. Boelcke took his flying jacket from a hook, put it on over his nightshirt and tucked the nightshirt into his trousers. Immelmann was already there, pacing in front of the shed. Boelcke joined him while ground crew opened the shed doors and pushed two Eindekkers out.

"I think he's gone," said Immelmann, looking up. They listened and heard distant popping: gunfire from the front. Echoing in the fog, the gunfire seemed strangely close.

"Are you ready to fly that thing?" said Boelcke. He pointed to the Eindekker.

"I soloed yesterday," said Immelmann, drily, feigning offense.

Pompous little ... thought Boelcke.

"Orders from the commander. We're not allowed to give rides anymore," said Immelmann. He frowned. "Seems your nurse is enjoying your fame too much. Ninette, is that her name?"

"Shhh," said Boelcke.

Being shushed like a child brought Immelmann to anger.

"So you brought one French aeroplane down in your two-seater and I would have thought they'd give you a crown," said Immelmann. "You're famous, even with the French. Rescuing a French boy from a canal? The Frogs want to give you a medal. My God."

"Shut up, Immelmann," said Boelcke. Immelmann glared at him.

Boelcke cocked his ear to the sky but heard nothing. Then he turned to the east and watched the sun spread light under a layer of clouds. "It wasn't my victory, it belongs to my observer, von Wuhlisch. He shot well. I just want one from a monoplane, and then I think it will count for something," said Boelcke.

Immelmann nodded. "Fine. Yes, it will count for something. You're a hero."

He calmed his tone, not wanting Boelcke to be angry with him. "I heard the observer in your French aeroplane crashed on his own land."

Boelcke paused, listening. Still nothing.

"Yes, he did. Ugly coincidence, that. Didn't have far to carry him to bury him at home. Sad, really," Boelcke said. He scanned the skies one more time. "I'm headed back to bed. False alarm." As he walked away, he turned and shouted back at Immelmann, "Go back to bed, Max."

Boelcke reached his motorcycle and rode back to the house in Douai, puttering between the early morning farmer's carts and German troops beginning to move in the morning twilight.

~~~

The morning warmed, and the sun had burned through the fog when Fischer woke Boelcke again.

"Sir, they're back," said Fischer, "over the field."

Boelcke rose from his bed, still dressed in nightshirt and trousers. Blinking at Fischer to clear his mind, he then quickly left and pounded down the stairs to his motorcycle.

The Eindekkers were rolled out of their sheds and waiting when he arrived.

"No Immelmann?" he asked the chief mechanic. The man replied, "No, sir."

"Just as well; he can't be ready to fight in that thing."

Four English aeroplanes flew low over the field. They dropped a string of small bombs, each hitting the ground with a sharp crack followed by the dying echo of each explosion rippling the trees. German troopers in the trees banged away with their rifles at the English, hitting nothing.

"Shit," said Boelcke, matter-of-factly.

A bomb struck an Aviatik sitting on the field, blowing it into pieces. Scraps of the aeroplane fluttered down as the wreckage burned. The English aeroplanes turned away to the west.

Boelcke climbed into his Eindekker and a mechanic spun the engine. The bombs had stopped by the time his aeroplane was rolling down the field. He took off, climbed to their level and opened his throttle, using all the power the Eindekker had to chase the English. Still, Boelcke couldn't catch them. He returned to the field, a dark headache starting behind his eyes.

As he neared his landing ground, a flight of five more English aeroplanes lined up on it and dropped another trail of bombs. Startled, Boelcke watched in horror as another Aviatik blew apart. Determined, Boelcke curved his plane in behind them, and with a grinding rattle, he engaged the synchronizer. He test-fired his machine gun.

Finally. At last, the perfect chance.

The English pilots turned their aeroplanes in a long slow wheeling bank to make another run over the field. They were oblivious, or uncaring, that Boelcke's monoplane was behind them.

Resolute, Boelcke closed on the last English aeroplane in the line. He throttled down to match speed with the Englishman and followed it through its turn, aiming down his machine gun. He drew a breath and slowly released it, then pressed the firing button on the control yoke.

Nothing.

Boelcke bellowed and pounded a fist on the butt of the gun. Furiously, he reset the synchronizer and worked the bolt on the gun, lined up his shot, and pressed the firing button again. Nothing.

The pilot of the English two-seater reached back into his observer's cockpit and retrieved another bomb. The man glanced at Boelcke quizzically. He leisurely leaned out of his craft and released the projectile. Boelcke watched it drop and explode in a puff of gray. Again, he yelled out his frustration and furiously worked the bolt on his machine gun.

The thing was jammed, and Boelcke could see the mangled shell wedged ahead of the bolt.

Boelcke wrenched the control yoke around and lined the monoplane up on the field. As he did, he saw Immelmann's Eindekker rolling across the field to take off. A bomb exploded harmlessly behind him.

Immelmann climbed past, as Boelcke landed in the opposite direction. Boelcke blipped his engine, using the magneto to stop the engine from firing, too impatient to use the throttle and mixture to lessen the power of the engine. He let the Eindekker roll to the sheds, flipped the magneto off to finally kill the engine and jumped down.

Boelcke yelled for a mechanic and saw no one. All the men had taken shelter from the bombs.

He yelled again. A single brave man came running from the trees toward Boelcke, saluting as he ran. "Yes, Leutnant?"

"Help me clear the gun! Get a ladder, a hammer, and a screwdriver!" Boelcke ordered.

Boelcke watched Immelmann turn in a low circle around the field, following the English aeroplanes as they began another pass. It appeared Immelmann had over-controlled the Eindekker as one wing dipped, but he leveled the wings and turned with his rudder. He began to close on an English aeroplane, drawing so near it appeared he might collide with it.

The mechanic was back and already in the cockpit of the Eindekker when Boelcke turned around. The man forced the screwdriver into the open breech and pried the bolt back, then pulled the jammed shell out with his finger. He tossed it to Boelcke, who looked at it and then threw it onto the ground. Another line of English bombs began to explode across the field in a series of sharp bangs. Boelcke, furious, ignored the explosions.

From overhead, he heard the hammering of Immelmann's machine gun, firing in a single long burst. The English aeroplanes, unloaded of bombs, began to turn away, and Immelmann followed, firing his weapon in a near continuous torrent.

Boelcke and the mechanic lifted the tail of the Eindekker and swung the aeroplane around to point it down the field. Boelcke climbed into the cockpit and yelled for the mechanic to spin the prop. The engine barked and started.

The formation of English aeroplanes, followed by Immelmann, disappeared over the top of the trees to the west as Boelcke began to roll down the field.

~ ~ ~

William Reid was confused. Behind him, a German monoplane was giving chase, little more than fifty yards away. He could hear gunfire from the German plane, but when he looked back, he could see just the nose of the German plane. There was simply no way that this German should have been able to shoot at him.

With a sound like gravel thrown against a tin roof, a burst of fire hit his aeroplane, tearing holes across one wing. Reid gawked at the wing in amazement. In a growing panic, he pulled out his pistol and turned his aeroplane so that he could get a clear shot at the pursuing German.

As his aeroplane came around in its turn, Reid raised the pistol and aimed. It was then that he saw the flickering of a machine gun firing magically, it seemed, from the front of the German monoplane. A savage spray of bullets struck his arm, shattering it into a useless pulp. His own blood washed over him. His pistol fell over the side of the aeroplane.

Reid looked down at his devastated arm in stunned surprise. Shock struck him and his head reeled. He stared numbly at sharp shards of his own bare white bones. More bullets struck his fuel tank, splashing cold gasoline all over him, over his clothes, and in his mouth. Terror seized him and he shook violently with shock as he tried to keep his aeroplane under control.

William began yanking at his aeroplane with his healthy arm, trying to find some way to escape the German guns. He looked for a field to land in, then released the yoke to throttle the aeroplane down, but it was too late. Wide-eyed with horror as the awful sound of the machine gun reached him again, he looked back as the stream of bullets overwhelmed him.

~~~

Boelcke flew west, watching Immelmann from behind, both flying as fast as their Eindekkers would fly. Boelcke could hear Immelmann's machine gun firing, the gun smoke behind Immelmann's aeroplane a trail of gray puffs. Suddenly, Immelmann and an English aeroplane were descending and then they disappeared below the height of the trees.

Boelcke thought they had crashed, and he throttled back and dove to descend to where they had disappeared. Below him, he saw the two aeroplanes in a field, landed together.

The English aeroplane, in its green livery, was sitting next to the pale beige of the Eindekker.

Both pilots were standing on the ground. Immelmann pointed a pistol at the English pilot.

Boelcke couldn't believe his eyes, and he stared in amazement at the scene below him. German troops were running from all directions. Boelcke turned his aeroplane, throttled back further, and circled over them. He watched Immelmann help the English flyer sit down. The Englishman was holding one arm with the other.

"You little pompous son of a bitch," Boelcke whispered to himself. "You did it. You damn well did it. Lucky little bastard!" As Boelcke looked down, he could see the German troops gathering in a crowd, some lifting their arms over their heads in celebration.

Boelcke imagined he could hear them cheering.

Chapter Twenty-Eight

September 22, 1915
London, England

Louis Strange led Lanoe Hawker and Beatrice Bayly to an empty table in the sitting room of the National Liberal Club, sat them down and offered them each a cup of tea.

Hawker looked around the club, and drew in the scent of expensive cigars and old wood, trying to relax. He watched as a stream of visitors passed through the sitting room from the large drawing room in the back, exiting into the cool gray air of Trafalgar Square. His dress uniform rode up on his neck and the wool felt stiff and unfamiliar. He hooked a finger in his collar and tugged at it. Gas lamps on the walls lit the room in a flickering yellow light, giving Hawker the impression that each of them were themselves flickering back and forth. The sensation gave him vertigo.

"I knew that you wouldn't want a formal meeting so, I've arranged for us to speak here," said Strange.

Hawker nodded and sipped his tea. He sat poised, his feet pointed toward the door, as if he might bolt at any moment. "I appreciate that, Louis. But, this is unusual."

"Everyone in London is talking about you, and he's one reason why. His novels are, frankly, unnerving. He seems to have predicted all of this. It's most uncanny," said Strange.

"A coincidence, Louis, or a deduction. Are you becoming a Spiritualist now, as well?" Hawker's words grew shorter, clipped by his impatience.

Hawker glanced at Beatrice, who had flushed. "My apologies, my dear. I mean no disrespect for the dead." He smiled at her, and she patted his arm.

"I understand; of course, Lanoe, all this attention must be most trying," said Beatrice. She put her hand on his to console him.

"Thank you, Hawker, I appreciate your patience, I do hope this won't be a waste of time. Can we join the reading, now?" said Strange. He nodded toward the open drawing room door.

Hawker sipped his tea once more and set the cup down. "Yes, of course, my friend," he said.

They rose and moved into the drawing room. At a podium in the front of the room, a man with a thick mop of dark beard was reading something aloud to an audience seated at tables around the room. Strange offered Beatrice a chair and they sat at a table in the back.

"Is that the man?" asked Hawker, gesturing toward the speaker.

Strange looked around the room for his friend.

"No, that's him," Strange whispered, nodding toward a man at a nearby table. "Mr. Wells."

The presenter spoke, his voice high and scratchy, raw to the ear, as though it were fixed in perpetual puberty.

He said, "Then there was war in heaven. But, it was not angels. It seemed as if the cosmic order were gone; as if there had come a new order, a new heaven above us; and, as if the world, in anger, were trying to revoke it. So it is the end – our world is gone, and we are like dust in the air."

The audience clapped, and a woman at the next table from Hawker wiped a tear from her cheek. He watched her in disbelief. The crowd began to rise as the reading concluded.

Hawker leaned over to Strange and asked, "What is he talking about?"

"The Zeppelin raids on London, I believe. He seems to think it prefigures the end of the world, I suppose. Not a member of my club. Ah, here's our man, now," Strange said.

Strange's friend approached them, a plump graying man in a bowler hat with a sardonic expression permanently affixed to his face. "Strange! Good man, still falling out of aeroplanes?" said the man. Hawker, Strange and Beatrice stood to greet him. The man bowed to Beatrice, then took her hand and kissed it, startling Hawker.

"Wells. Herbert Wells. My pleasure, Miss."

"This is Miss Bayly, Wells, and may I introduce Lanoe Hawker, recipient of the Victoria Cross." Strange smiled as he spoke, his unmasked pride plain to see.

Wells put out a hand and Hawker hesitated, then reached out and shook it.

"Silly American thing, adopted habit from the Yanks, but a most personal greeting, nonetheless. Please, call me 'H.G.'," said Wells. "Only my wives and mother call me Herbert! It is my pleasure to meet you, the first English aviator to become the 'Ace', if I'm not mistaken."

"Yes, Mr. Wells. That I seem to be." Hawker pulled again at his collar, even more uncomfortable.

"Aaah! Mr. Wells, so good to see you. Thank you for coming." The bearded man, the reader from the podium, joined them. A buxom young woman in a silver gown held his arm, her round face framed in an unfashionable bonnet, light brown curls peeking from beneath it.

The bearded man and Wells shook hands warmly and for far too long by Hawker's estimation.

Strange stood and turned to the newcomer. "Oh, my manners. Allow me to make introductions. Beatrice Bayly, this is Mr. Herbert Wells, and this is our club guest this evening, the novelist, Mr. David Lawrence. I'm afraid, though, I don't know your companion's name, Mr. Lawrence. Would you be so kind?"

"Please, call me David," said Lawrence. He turned to the woman at his side, her face made beautiful by a wide smile. "May I introduce my dear friend, Miss Frieda Richthofen."

Beatrice gasped and covered her mouth with her hand. The men looked toward her.

"I ... well ... I've heard of you," stammered Beatrice.

Lawrence paled and then smiled. "That's quite alright. We will survive the notoriety."

Frieda studied Beatrice, seeming to assess her.

Beatrice started, and took a step backward.

"Good evening, all, most pleasant to meet you. Come, dear," said Lawrence. He turned and took Frieda by the hand, leading her away.

Hawker and company stared after them, casting glances at Beatrice, who was still recovering from an as of yet unknown shock.

"Well then," said Strange, "shall we speak?" He gestured toward their table.

"My pleasure," said Wells, drawing a chair for Beatrice.

Hawker sat stiffly, awkwardly upright. He stole glances at Beatrice when he thought she wasn't looking.

"Tea, everyone? It's a little early for cocktails," said Strange.

"I'll have a brandy. Small," said Beatrice.

"At your service. I'll leave you two to speak." Strange walked into the sitting room to gather drinks.

"What, dear, was that about?" asked Hawker.

"Haven't you heard of her? Frieda von Richthofen? She's some sort of German royalty. Married an Englishman and then ran off with this Lawrence, left three small children behind. Scandalous. More than scandal. Debauchery. They are unmarried," said Beatrice.

Wells looked away. He seemed to be gathering his thoughts. "A matter of some indiscretion. Perhaps just fodder for his novels, one might guess. Perhaps he loves her. *Titillating* writing, I've heard." Wells let the word 'titillating' drag on past the point of being appropriate.

Beatrice fidgeted, out of her element.

"I say. What are we here to discuss?" Hawker asked, bringing both Beatrice and Wells back to the moment.

Wells sighed deeply, set his hat on the back of his chair and turned to Hawker. "I believe that Louis believes I can help you with the problem at hand."

"And what problem would that be, Wells?" said Hawker, curtly.

"The war, of course," said Wells.

The phrase hung there, leaving an awkward silence over them.

Strange returned and set down their drinks.

Beatrice took up her brandy and drew a long sip. Her nostrils flared wide, and she felt the warmth flush through her skin.

"The war in the air," said Wells. "It is what you're fighting, isn't it?"

"Yes. It is. But, you're an author, correct? You write books. Forgive me,

I mean no disrespect, but what do you know about aeroplanes or war?" Hawker struggled to keep his tone flat and pleasant to avoid condescending to Wells.

Wells pondered his reply. He turned to Hawker. "Louis has asked that we meet. I'm a defender of the Crown as much as you are. We must win this war to survive as a culture. If you wish to discuss these things, I'll do so, but I won't pretend to tell you anything. I can relate an opinion, strongly held. Respectfully."

Hawker nodded. "Then, out of respect for your time, and for Louis' opinion on the matter, please proceed."

Wells began. "May I relate what I believe is happening?"

"Of course, Wells, certainly." Hawker waving a hand as though to hurry the conversation.

"I believe that we are in a scientific war, for the first time in history. The high ground is not some bloody beaten ridge outside of Verdun or some piddling hill on the north bank of the Somme. The high ground is aloft." Wells pointed at the table with a finger, drew a line across the surface with a fingertip. "And, the high ground is being fought for by airmen, such as yourself, and the bloody generals don't realize it; won't realize it. Can't realize it. Their minds cannot question their own assumptions."

Hawker drew himself up stiffly, then leaned forward.

"Yes, Mr. Wells ... 'H.G.', I understand and can appreciate your point," said Hawker.

"There is more if I may be impertinent."

"Yes, go on."

"I believe that the reason for the trenches is the aeroplane. These huge armies, and I mean theirs and ours, can't move fast enough to avoid having some nineteen-year-old aviator with ten hours flying experience see exactly what is going on. The mobility of men on foot isn't enough to allow for anything other than straight-ahead attacks; logistical, attritional warfare." Wells paused, took Beatrice's brandy and a hard swallow. "Because the aeroplanes can see you."

Hawker frowned.

Wells took another sip and returned his glass to the table.

"May I continue?" asked Wells.

"Yes, please do so," replied Hawker.

"The great maneuver battles that were supposed to end the war, like the Battle of the Marne, were ended by aeroplanes because we could see this huge damn gap in the German armies. This brilliant German, Ludendorff, credited Tannenberg, the great German victory in the east, to the aeroplane for telling him where the Russians were; better than the Russian generals knew! The generals will bleed your men dry because they can't see this. They're not fighting the last war. They're fighting the only war that they can imagine, and that's far, far worse. They don't understand." Wells stopped and looked around at them.

He took a breath, expecting to be silenced mid-sentence. When he wasn't, he continued. It was clear to Hawker the man had ideas that needed to be let out.

"You and you." Wells gestured to Hawker and Strange. "You are men of imagination, or so I'm told. You can see the sum of the pieces and the pieces themselves, how they can all be rearranged, made into a different whole. Surely, you understand. This has never, ever, happened before in history."

Hawker screwed his face up, as if to protest, but Wells held up a hand.

Hawker and Strange exchanged glances; Strange's gaze was that of someone engrossed, Hawker's was that of a skeptic. They both looked back to Wells.

"Oh, don't look at me that way. Not like this, it hasn't. The longbow and the crossbow, each ruled for hundreds of years. These aeroplanes ... I watch them fly. They're changing every damn day. Every day matters; every *hour* matters. The Fokker monoplanes ... they'll reach their end in a few months; and then one of ours will rule the sky; then one of theirs; on and on. You just have to get ahead far enough, long enough, to end this thing, or it will drag on forever, and millions will die because they'll fight to the last man. The last German, the last Englishman, the last Frenchman."

Wells spoke in a hoarse whisper now. "My apologies. This is not sedition. I see it, and it eats at me."

Hawker held up a hand. Wells stopped, straightened up in his chair sheepishly and looked at Hawker.

Beatrice took up her glass and tipped it up, emptying it of whatever Wells had left behind.

"Brandy for all of us, Strange, if you would, please," said Hawker. "I like you, Wells. You're a rare man of intelligence, imagination, and conviction. That much is clear." He paused. "Do you know why I really received the Victoria Cross?"

Wells looked perplexed.

"No, Hawker, I'm sure I don't know. I've read the papers, of course, something about three Hun aeroplanes shot down in one day, quite an accomplishment ..." Wells trailed off.

Hawker glanced at Beatrice, who gave him an encouraging smile. "Go ahead, dear."

"Well, Wells, here's what happened. I was going up for a flight, when I realized I'd forgotten my map. So, I left the engine running in my aeroplane, a Bristol it was, and ran over to the squadron office. And, lo, no one was there and the phone was ringing. Naturally, I felt obliged to answer it."

Strange returned and placed brandies on the table. Wells swirled his and took a long sip.

"Oh, this story again, is it?" asked Strange.

Hawker beamed, and continued.

"So, who's on the phone, but General Gott, and he's complaining that his luncheon has been disrupted by a German artillery battery, and would someone please go quiet the thing. So I, naturally, put the phone down and ran out to my aeroplane."

"Naturally," said Wells.

"Off I flew, and, flying low, I spotted the German battery firing, one that I'd marked down before. So, about I turned, landed, and ran to the office to call for counter-battery fire ... and, there lies the phone, with Gott still droning on about the artillery breaking his crockery and leaving his tea table covered in dust, that sort of thing. I picked up the phone and told him precisely where the German battery was and, well, there you are. He awarded me the V.C." Hawker waved his hands, illustrating his story as he spoke.

Wells stared at Hawker, dumbfounded, then glanced at Strange, who broke into a broad grin. Wells looked like a man who had boarded the wrong train.

"I say, you've put me on!" Wells shouted. Hawker and Strange erupted with laughter. Beatrice smiled indulgingly and sipped her drink. Hawker raised his glass to Wells, who raised his and tapped it against Hawker's.

Hawker had tried to change the mood with his anecdote, but even so, he couldn't shake what Wells had told them. A mask of seriousness slipped over Hawker's face as he stared into his glass. He looked back at Wells. Strange and Beatrice, sensing Hawker's change of mood, grew quiet.

"There is another possibility," said Hawker. They sipped their brandy.

"Go on, please, Hawker. You've indulged me," Wells offered.

"Well, maybe your friend Mr. Lawrence is right." He swirled the drink in his glass. "Perhaps hell *has* reached earth from below. And our aeroplanes are the creation of the devil, meant to drive men down into its fires."

Chapter Twenty-Nine

October 1, 1915
Douai, France

Richthofen ran his hands over the linen on the tabletop. He picked up a crystal glass and felt the hard facets on the surface under his fingers. It felt comforting and familiar. Fine crystal, once more, gilt-edged flatware, clean linens: the proper place for a man of status. It reminded him of home.

He looked around the empty dining car: dusty, dark, ornate woodwork curled over the walls and hung from the ceiling, while round tables with tablecloths dotted the space within. In another time, it would have been a traveling car for the wealthy. Now Germany's officers claimed it. A meek-looking mess attendant stood in the corner with a white coat on over his gray uniform, a towel draped over an arm. Three young flyers huddled around a single table at the far end of the car. They laughed about something.

The aroma of ersatz coffee filled the air—the smell of acorns and beechnuts first charred and then boiled. Richthofen inhaled deeply, hoping the scent, however unpleasant, would drive out the lingering stink of castor oil and gasoline from his nose.

Zeumer had given him a book to read, which he held stiffly, and then set down as if he could gather all he needed by staring at the thing unopened. He had not had the time or the inclination to read a book since school, but obliged Zeumer nonetheless by taking it. Now, carrying the thing made him feel pompous.

As Richthofen considered a cup of coffee of his own, another young officer entered the back of the car. The pilots turned and shouted greetings.

"Boelcke! Join us!"

Oswald Boelcke waved to them, and walked over to their table, acknowledging Richthofen with a quick smile and a nod as he passed by. Richthofen stared at the living legend, appraising him. Boelcke greeted each of the other men by name and shook their hands warmly, enveloping theirs in both of his. He declined their invitation to join them, holding up a sheaf of papers and shrugging helplessly. Boelcke took a table near Richthofen and laid his documents out.

Boelcke. A hunter of men and aeroplanes. The hero. A new legend, thought Richthofen.

"Good morning, Leutnant," Boelcke said to Richthofen.

"Good morning, Leutnant Boelcke."

Richthofen glanced away, self-conscious for having greeted Boelcke by name. He rubbed his bookmark, a single folded sheet of paper, between his thumb and forefinger. Richthofen pulled the sheet from the book, pressed it flat along its deep creases, and then tilted the book to hide the sheet within it. Boelcke's name was affixed to the top.

Richthofen glanced up as the waiter approached and offered him the fake coffee. He laid his hand across the page and held out his coffee cup while the waiter filled it, then spread the sheet back out again. He began to read what the great man had written:

AIRCRAFT DEFENSES AGAINST TROUBLESOME QUESTIONERS

PLEASE DO NOT ASK ME ANYTHING ABOUT FLYING!

You will find the usual questions answered below.
1. Sometimes it is dangerous; sometimes it is not.
2. Yes, the higher we fly, the colder it is.
3. Yes, we notice it's colder because we freeze.
4. We fly at 2,000-2,500 meters.
5. Yes, we can see things at that height, although not as well as at 100 meters.
6. We cannot see well through the telescope because it waggles.
7. Yes, we have dropped bombs.
8. Yes, an old woman was supposed to have been injured and we put the wind up some transport columns.

9. The observer sits in the front and can see a little bit.
10. We cannot talk to each other because the engine is too loud.
11. We don't have a telephone in the machine but we have electric lights.
12. No, we do not live in caves.

Richthofen was puzzled. *Was this a joke?* Was it meant to keep people like him away, or for all flyers to ward off annoying people?

He looked over at Boelcke, hoping he might find the answer by studying the man's posture long enough. Zeumer said that Boelcke had written the thing, had it copied, and had posted it in his quarters. Richthofen didn't know how to interpret the document and Zeumer didn't explain. He had just laughed.

He looked again at Boelcke, and tried to read the man's face. If it were a joke, then no matter; if not, then to approach him might bring on an embarrassment in front of the other officers.

Boelcke's eyes were down, reading. He turned over each sheet one at a time, working his way through the stack. The corners of his mouth tilted into a small grimace, his lips pursed tight. He seemed to be holding something in. His shoulders sagged a little under an invisible weight.

Richthofen folded the paper and put it away, then opened Zeumer's book. It had been written by a Czech and was describing something very like Richthofen's dream of insects. It left him uneasy, as though the author knew something secret that he couldn't quite make out. Yet again, it felt like a joke was being made at his expense. Richthofen finished half of a chapter before setting it down, feeling melancholy.

Soon the rumble of the train was lulling him towards sleep. Richthofen thought about Menzke, probably curled up in some corner of a second-class car, or in the luggage carriage, sleeping the ride away. As his mind drifted, he soon fell asleep.

~~~

Richthofen woke with a start and looked about the carriage. The waiter was offering sandwiches from a giant silver tray, thick black bread and coarse mustard, smoky slices of ham. The three pilots had spread out around the car, put their feet up, one having removed his boots. The others dozed. Boelcke sat, sipping the fake coffee, staring out the window, his stack of papers now all faced down.

Boelcke looked over, noticed Richthofen was awake, and seemed eager for company. He smiled and nodded.

"How was your nap, Leutnant?" he asked, his grin broadening.

Richthofen sat up straight, pulled his jacket tight over his shoulders, and ran his hand over his collar, self-consciously. He smiled back tightly.

"Very pleasant," replied Richthofen. "Thank you."

"I take it that your book wasn't very entertaining." Boelcke pointed to the beaten volume on the table.

Richthofen picked it up and handed it over to Boelcke. "You're welcome to give it a try. I can't recommend it, but my pilot seemed to think it was worthwhile."

Boelcke took the book, held it up, and read the cover. He lay it on the table and flipped through it. When he reached the folded paper Richthofen had been using as a bookmark, he unfolded it and laughed aloud: a rich, warm laugh. The other officers glanced over, and then settled back to their dozing.

Richthofen smiled, but he couldn't help feeling, once more, that the joke was on him.

"Have you found it useful?" Boelcke held up the paper, showing it to Richthofen.

Richthofen stiffened. "It seems a vain joke," he said in chopped syllables.

Boelcke laughed harder before recovering himself. "You may find it useful when we get to Germany, people will see your badges and want to ask the most annoying questions." He grinned again.

Richthofen relaxed, his shoulders settled, and his color returned. *That question is answered,* he thought. *A joke.* Suddenly, he began to feel at ease with the man. Boelcke's mood was infectious.

"Please join me," said Boelcke. He gestured to the other chair at his table. As Richthofen sat, he pointed to Richthofen's observer badge. "And who is your pilot?" Beolcke asked.

Richthofen folded his hands on the tabletop as the waiter moved to his side and poured fresh coffee for him. Once the waiter moved on, Richthofen said, "Georg Zeumer."

"Ah, The Black Cat. I've not seen him in some time. Still unlucky, is he?"

Richthofen laughed again. "Well, he says it's because he has nine lives, but I've heard the story both ways."

Boelcke reached out a hand, and Richthofen shook it. Boelcke's grip was firm and strong. "Oswald Boelcke. Very good to meet you."

"Richthofen. Manfred von Richthofen."

"Go on then, Richthofen, tell me about Zeumer. Tell me if he lives up to his legend."

"Where can I begin? So many stories. The man is either a miracle or an accident incarnate."

Boelcke laughed and snorted a sip of coffee. "Anywhere, then."

"Well, he doesn't ride anymore; he broke his thigh in a fall. And he rarely rides in an automobile, as he had an automobile accident. I'd never heard of such a thing. Nevertheless, he keeps picking himself up. You must respect that in a man."

"Perhaps it's both then," said Boelcke. "Perhaps he needs nine lives because he's unlucky." They laughed together.

Richthofen was glad that Boelcke seemed to *like* Zeumer.

"Perhaps he is blessed, though. He survives. But not always those around him, I'm afraid. We purchased dogs together, brindle hounds, Moritz and Max. Moritz is with my orderly in the baggage car. Max, sadly, was struck by an automobile and killed. Zeumer was quite grieved."

Richthofen relaxed, took a bit of a sandwich, and relished the sharp bite of the mustard on his tongue, its pungency rising in the back of his nose. He glanced out the window for the moment, feeling he was on a journey with a friend.

Richthofen continued. "And then, there was the episode at Ostend, at the Palace Hotel. Have you heard?"

"No, I'm quite sure I haven't," replied Boelcke.

"We'd been flying over the channel, maritime patrols, in twin-engine crates. Flying barges, really. Takes miles of sky to turn around. Well, we were on leave and staying at the Palace Hotel. One morning, we were relaxing on the terrace, enjoying breakfast in our bathrobes. A British fleet appeared and began to fire on the shore. We scattered; took cover. A terrific racket, enormous shells, bigger than anything we saw in the forests around Verdun. A salvo struck the building, shattering it. Zeumer sat and watched, finished his coffee. Amazing. The man has a death wish or a guardian angel, I'm not sure which."

Boelcke's eyes sparkled as he sipped his coffee, listening; then he snorted and held his hand to his nose. He looked like he might choke and swallowed hard. He held up a hand.

Richthofen stopped, perplexed.

"Did you say bathrobes?" Boelcke asked, his face growing red. "*Bathrobes?*"

Richthofen nodded.

Boelcke tipped his head back again, his laugh deeper, his hand over his mouth.

"So you and Zeumer were dining in the Palace Hotel, while it was being blown up, in your bathrobes?"

Richthofen grinned and nodded.

"Well, the joke is that the Palace is an English-owned hotel. Well, at least it was," he added.

Boelcke laughed again, almost braying, his voice growing rough from laughter. Boelcke stretched out a hand, took Richthofen's in both of his, shaking his hand again. "I am happy we've met Richthofen. I'm always happy to meet a flyer."

Richthofen blushed slightly, and looked around at the waiter and the pilots.

"Oh, no, I'm not a flyer, I'm an observer," he corrected Boelcke.

Boelcke leaned toward Richthofen, and spoke, lowering his voice.

"Leutnant Richthofen, any man that flies with Zeumer *must* be a flyer," he said and smiled.

Boelcke began asking questions of Richthofen, of his experiences, of his flying. Richthofen described his cavalry missions and of joining the air service when the cavalry could no longer survive in the west. He told of flying with Zeumer and Holck in the east, following Mackensen's army, of the Russian columns shooting them down, and of being transferred to the west after the crash with Holck. Then, of rejoining Zeumer, who was already there, and of the long flights over water.

Boelcke pointed at Richthofen's bandaged hand.

"And how did that happen?" he asked.

"Do you know the Riesenäppelkahn, the Apple Barge? The AEG?" asked Richthofen.

Boelcke nodded, "Oh, yes, I know it."

"Zeumer and I were dropping bombs, and I was pointing at the target, an English boat. Well, the propellers are each on either side of the observer's seat, and I stupidly put my finger in the propeller. It took off the tip. My war wound." He smiled.

"Lucky it didn't take off a hand," said Boelcke.

Richthofen sat up, startled, and then nodded agreement.

"I guess I hadn't thought of it like that," said Richthofen.

"Are you a lucky man, Richthofen?" asked Boelcke.

"At the beginning of the war, I lost my whole cavalry squadron. Or nearly so. All shot down in an ambush before the Battle of Virton. Damned awful. Lucky to be alive, now, when I think about it. I never thought of it as lucky though. Quite the opposite," he concluded. He waved the waiter over for fresh coffee, pointing at his cup.

Boelcke nodded, but said nothing. He smiled to himself.

"Leutnant Boelcke. May I ask a question?" said Richthofen.

"Of course! For a flyer, of course," said Boelcke.

"Zeumer and I have met other aeroplanes, English aeroplanes, over the Channel. I've shot at them, and we've been shot at. I've had no luck bringing one down. Your reputation precedes you. How many have you shot down?" asked Richthofen.

"Four." Boelcke laughed again. "Not counting myself of course."

Richthofen cocked his head to the side. "I'm sorry?"

"Once, my synchronizer ... well ... didn't. I lined up on an Englishman, flew right up his ass, and then blew my propeller right off when I fired.

Engine ran wild. Vibration made it jump out of its mounts. The English, well, they waved and smiled as I fell away. Lucky to glide down." As he spoke, Richthofen listened and looked on, his mouth ajar, aghast. "Why do you ask?"

"It's like this, Boelcke. Zeumer tries to fly well, and I try to shoot well, but we've had no luck. We've counted dozens of bullet holes in the Apple Barge though." He shook his head, frowning in frustration. "How do you do it? Shoot down other aeroplanes; not yourself, I mean."

Boelcke grew serious. "Richthofen, here's the thing. I fly right up to them." He motioned with his hands, one behind the other, fingers pointed the same direction. Richthofen sat rapt, staring at Boelcke's hands.

"Like this. I get right behind them."

He moved the hands closer, one gaining on the other, slightly lower. "And I pull the trigger." The lower hand began to vibrate. "Tat-tat-tat-tat." The hand on top tipped over and spun, spiraling toward the floor of the train. Boelcke laughed and put his hands back on the table. "And they fall down."

Richthofen scowled, feeling as though Boelcke was putting him on. His face flashed red.

Boelcke leaned back and folded his arms, then set them at his sides, leaning on the arms of his chair. He stopped laughing and a mask of solemnity crossed his face.

"Forgive me, Leutnant Boelcke. It's just that many of us want to know," said Richthofen.

"Is it Zeumer or me? My shooting? What can be done?" asked Richthofen. His voice rose in pitch, growing higher as he pressed the question.

"You are married, Richthofen; do you know that?" said Boelcke.

Richthofen started to speak, but then froze, his voice stopping in mid-sentence. "What?"

"You are married, Franz and Emil, pilot and observer. Do not blame Zeumer and do not blame yourself. You need each other to survive, and, if that marriage is broken, you have one more thing to overcome when you fly. Understand?"

Richthofen grew quiet. He didn't care for being told how to manage his fellow officers. For a moment, he thought of seniority, began to calculate dates of rank, began to think of the impertinence of Boelcke speaking to him this way. He took a deep breath and leaned back in his own chair. "Yes, I understand," he said at last. He fixed his eyes on Boelcke's. For once, there was no mirth behind them.

The feeling evaporated almost immediately when Boelcke suddenly said, "I like you Richthofen! You're lucky and not so proud that you're deaf. So where are you headed?"

"Metz. Brieftauben-Abteilung-Metz, BAM, the bomber squadron at Metz," Richthofen answered.

"So am I, Richthofen, to Metz that is. May I be candid?"

"Yes, of course, Leutnant Boelcke; I'm an avid student," lied Richthofen.

"The French are attacking in the Champagne region, and they are massing small, light aeroplanes with machine guns. The fighting will be difficult. You must cooperate with Zeumer, or whomever you fly with. Don't let your marriage fail or the French will kill you." Boelcke placed one hand on the stack of papers, palm down. Richthofen looked at the papers, suddenly realizing what information they contained.

Boelcke's face was impassive now, his mouth locked in a frown, his eyes boring through Richthofen. Richthofen felt as though this was a new man before him; that they had just met and their conversation had just begun.

"It is very difficult to shoot down an enemy aeroplane as the observer, harder than a pilot in an Eindekker. This is because of speed through the air, angles, deflection." He paused, a look of concentration on his face. "Oh, another time for that," he waved off the thought. "Just try to defend your pilot and aeroplane and you will do fine. You will survive and perform your mission, and that's what is important. What you are doing for the soldiers on the ground is most important."

"May I be candid, now, as well, Boelcke?" asked Richthofen. His hands clenched together in a single fist, his elbows on the table.

"Of course. We are becoming friends, aren't we, Richthofen?" said Boelcke, not smiling.

"Yes," said Richthofen.

"You must tell me. How is it done? Shooting down aeroplanes, that is. No more riddles." Boelcke was clearly a complicated person, and Richthofen was convinced that Boelcke held a secret. It was a secret Richthofen craved, but he wasn't just asking for the secret. He was asking how a man became a legend.

Boelcke studied Richthofen, then sighed and leaned forward with his hands in his lap. When he began to speak, his voice low and dark.

"First, you must learn to fly a fighting machine. A fighter. You must tend the aeroplane like an untrainable, ill-mannered thoroughbred, and care for the machine gun as if it is your life. Then you must do what you can to get close, very close, to get so close that your bullets become holes in his aeroplane. So close you can see the holes. So close you can see blood. How you do that is up to you." He paused. "Can you do that?"

Boelcke leaned back. "So, you see, I was being quite precise a moment ago ..." he trailed off.

Richthofen realized they were whispering as though conspiring, and that the pilots at the other end of the car were watching them, wondering what confidence Boelcke was imparting to him. He glanced out the window at the countryside passing by and thought for a moment. He thought of the boar in France, stepping into the moonlight, of the gun at his shoulder, of the hard snap of the carbine in his ear. He thought of the blood and steam that poured into the morning as he sawed off the animal's head and of mounting it in their dug-out as a reminder of the hunt.

"Yes, Herr Boelcke, I can do that."

Chapter Thirty

October 3, 1915
Metz, German Occupied France

The sun was low in the west. Zeumer flew them north, following the banks of the Moselle, using the river to guide them to the aerodrome south of the city of Metz. A thin mist held to the banks of the river, and above it, toward the sun, the sky was a pale, clear blue.

Richthofen looked down from the Albatros at the ground flowing by. Below them the countryside was an abstract painting of orange, rust, and green. His attention faded, unfocused and he felt a sense of guilt for allowing himself the luxury sightseeing.

Looking back toward the sun, the hard knot of fear in his belly congealed and he heard his blood rush in his ears. His sense of exposure became real fear now, for only a hunter can truly understand when one is hunted. They were moving slow, slowing down, heading straight toward their aerodrome on a well-beaten path. They were tired at the end of a flight, hands weakened and nearly numb from vibration and cold.

This is a game trail. We're the weak member of the herd, exposed and alone. And you, the sun, are the hunter's blind in the sky.

Richthofen instinctively quartered the blue, studying one section, seeing nothing, and then moving his eyes to the next. He knew the real risk was an attacker flying from the sun itself, and knew there wasn't a thing he could do about it. Scanning north to south, high, then low, then he turned to check the sky behind them. Elsewhere, over the front to the west, this would mean something. But, here, now, it was little more than a distraction from the real danger.

But, perhaps he would see a speck, away from the sun. A rookie to the front, not knowing their vulnerability. This clockwork search had become second nature for him. He had learned not to worry about the things that moved against the background. Rather, he worried about the ones that were harder to see, the ones that seemed to hang in the air, like a speck on one's eye. He thought it a cruel trick of nature that the tiny dot that stood still was the most dangerous. Those that didn't seem to move were deadly, and worse yet, harder to see. The ones that were flying to intercept you, didn't seem to move ... they grew larger as they approached, until they grew wings, landing gear, and the flicker of a machine gun.

The black dots that didn't seem to move killed.

He looked north toward the aerodrome; almost home, safe again and allowed himself a breath of relief. Ahead of them lay the silvery length of an enormous Zeppelin docked to the ground. The airship, moored to a pylon, slowly swung around with the wind. As they drew closer, Richthofen could see tiny aircrew moving along the top of the airship and around it on the ground, tending to the massive vessel.

Zeumer lined up the Albatros along the length of the Zeppelin, using it like a windsock, and throttled the engine back. The aeroplane descended until it was over the southern trees, and then over the field. As they flew past the Zeppelin, Richthofen raised a gloved hand and waved to the men on top of the thing. A single man waved back as Zeumer gently landed the aeroplane.

Their Albatros rolled to a stop and four men ran to the aeroplane: two on the wings, one at the tail, and the fourth man running alongside with a stepladder. That last man placed the ladder next to Richthofen's cockpit to let him, as the senior officer, climb down first. Zeumer followed and they headed towards the operations tent together.

Richthofen shook his hands to get feeling back into them. His fear faded quickly and become a rare thoughtful moment for him. Feeling pleased and relaxed to be back on the ground, he wanted to talk. Clenching and unclenching his hands twice to get the feeling back, he turned to Zeumer. "Zeumer, teach me to fly."

Zeumer looked away across the field, averting his eyes from Richthofen.

"Why, Richthofen?" he asked.

"I wish to fight. It's a simple thing," he answered.

Zeumer looked away again. "Is that enough of a reason? You'll have to get Siegert's permission and that won't be easy. It'll also take up a lot of our time and occupy an aeroplane."

Richthofen took Zeumer by the arm and turned him. Behind them, an Eindekker sputtered to life, and ran its engine up.

Richthofen yelled over the sound of the engine, "I want this. Very much. I have a passion for this. Please, my friend, I wish for this to ... stay sane."

The engine of the Eindekker roared, drowning their words in noise. Then it rolled away, taking to the air, its engine sound fading. It left the smell of burning castor oil, light and sweet, hanging in the air. Together, they watched the Eindekker climb away.

Richthofen turned and continued back to the tents on the far edge of field. Zeumer turned with him, a half-step behind.

Finally, Zeumer said, "You'll have to get permission from the commander. That's up to you. But why now, Richthofen; what's got the wind in your sails? The war could be over soon and we need every man for what we're doing now."

Richthofen stopped and looked back over his shoulder, then matched his pace with Zeumer. "I wish to hunt." He smiled.

Zeumer cocked his head but didn't reply. Richthofen took the cue to continue.

"Being a passenger is, well ... tedious. I wish to control the aeroplane, to feel the sensation of having the aeroplane respond. And, hunting ... it is something that I have an instinct for ..." The last words trailed away. Richthofen knew how empty they sounded. The heat of a memory, like a hand over a candle prompted him to try again. "When I was very small, my mother would wake me up in the morning by leaning close to my bed and whispering 'hunt' over my head. No matter the time, it would wake me."

Zeumer looked at Richthofen as if he were a child, or possibly mad.

"You think I believe that? You're making it up." Zeumer grinned. When he smiled Richthofen saw the face of a skeleton in Zeumer's gaunt face.

"It's true!" he protested. "Well, I was usually awake anyway because I could hear her come in the room. But, no matter, she thought she was waking me up."

"She also made you believe in ghosts by rolling rocks across your bedroom floor in the middle of the night, isn't that so? So, who have you been talking to?" asked Zeumer.

"Boelcke," replied Richthofen.

"Not Immelmann? Or Parschau?"

"Boelcke," said Richthofen again.

"Does he think you lucky, Richthofen?"

Richthofen turned and began to walk away.

"Well, Richthofen, does he?"

"Yes, I believe so," Richthofen yelled over his shoulder.

"Does he or doesn't he?" shouted Zeumer, louder.

"He does!"

Zeumer watched another Eindekker turning to land. "Get permission from the commander, and get the time scheduled, if he'll allow it. Then I'll do it." Zeumer took out a handkerchief and coughed into it. Raising his voice made his lungs burn.

Richthofen stopped and turned back to Zeumer. Richthofen's smile broadened, his eyes mere slits.

"You know, Boelcke thinks you're unlucky, Zeumer, but I don't," Richthofen shouted to Zeumer.

"I know, Richthofen. That's why I will help you!"

~~~

On a cool October evening, after dinner, Richthofen cornered Kaptain Siegert. With some convincing, Siegert agreed that Zeumer could take Richthofen flying, off to the east where the French single-seaters didn't fly, and to let Richthofen have the controls of an Albatros. When he heard the news, Menzke found an old chalkboard and some chalk and set up a classroom for Zeumer and Richthofen in the back of a hangar. Zeumer and Richthofen worked there together in the evening hours, after their day of flying was done. As Zeumer conducted his informal class, the mechanics would come and go, sometimes standing and watching as Zeumer explained one thing or another. Then they would wander away, back to the aeroplanes that had to be ready to fly the next morning.

After a few days of this, with Zeumer drawing crude pictures of aeroplanes on the chalkboard and illustrating certain theories, he looked over to Richthofen, who was staring off into space, his eyes glazed over. Then he glanced over at Menzke, who watched Zeumer from a perch on a tall stool, dangling his legs, listening avidly.

"Dammit, Richthofen. You talked me into this! This is important. Pay attention! If you don't know what you're seeing when we fly, you won't learn from it." Zeumer's frustration was growing.

"Very well, Zeumer," Richthofen said, half aloud, "but I'm afraid, that I won't retain half of what you're telling me. I have to see it ... you understand."

Zeumer set his chalk down and leaned against the back of a chair. Richthofen's eyes were moving over an Eindekker in the shadows of the hangar. Zeumer followed Richthofen's stare and saw where he was looking.

"Richthofen, shall we talk about the Eindekker?"

Richthofen grinned, stood up, and pulled his jacket tight. "Definitely!"

"Very well. If it holds your attention, and I don't feel like I'm wasting my time." Zeumer walked to the machine and Richthofen followed close behind. "This is a Fokker E.II, 100 horsepower, with a bigger wing. A new Fokker, but not the newest."

Zeumer picked up a kerosene lantern for light and stood at the end of one wing. The light created long shadows on the wall of the tent and the wing cables seemed to move back and forth across the wing as the lantern swayed. He handed the lantern to Richthofen and then gripped the wing. He twisted it so that the control cables shifted ever so slightly.

"That's all it takes, all the movement that is needed to control the Fokker. You have to pay attention because you won't even feel the control wheel move, but, when you fly a Fokker, the wings will be moving constantly, turning the aeroplane."

Richthofen reached and ran his hand along the smooth wing, stroking it. Zeumer let out a wheeze and began again.

"It's vital that you inspect the aeroplane before flight, just as with the Albatros. And, never trust someone else to tell you that the aeroplane is ready without going over it yourself. Let's review the most important parts. The turnbuckles and pulleys on the Fokker are most vital. If one fails, you can't control the aeroplane, and then it will kill you."

Richthofen ran his hands along a control cable to a wing pulley, and then ran his hand over the turnbuckle on the wing. He grasped the turnbuckle and attempted to tighten it.

Zeumer watched Richthofen explore the machine. He was sharper now, more focused.

"Go ahead; touch it if you need to. This is an ill-mannered, untrainable machine with no heart and no brain. And, it will kill you," said Zeumer.

Richthofen looked at Zeumer, his blue eyes wide and dark in the dim light.

"You cannot tame this thing. Listen! When I tell you that, for the first time in history, man has a machine that must be able to kill you in order to function. It is not a weapon. It is not magic or merely a trick. If it is exposed for what it is—a crude machine of canvas and wire—then you will pay the price. To do what it was designed to do, it can, and probably will, kill you. Do you understand, Richthofen?"

Richthofen nodded.

"Let's try again. You may have fine hands for a thoroughbred, but this is not an animal that will protect itself. It has no instinct to survive. You cannot make a mistake. This machine will kill itself and you without an animal's sense of self preservation. Simple; right, Richthofen?"

Richthofen looked back at Zeumer, trying to decide if the man was patronizing him.

"I understand, Zeumer. It is a machine," he replied.

"A machine that holds your life in the balance, Richthofen. That's the adventure, isn't it?" Zeumer smiled, feeling like he was finally connecting with Richthofen. "Now, let's talk about some of its more *pleasant* traits, and then we'll come back to all the ways it may murder you." Zeumer reached out to a workbench, and picked up a can of oil.

"Castor bean oil. Made from just the castor bean, no husks, which is just as well, because the husk makes for a wonderful poison that will kill you even quicker than the aeroplane. Did you ever take it as medicine as a child, Richthofen?"

Richthofen nodded.

"Then you understand that, when you're flying an Eindekker, you'll be exposed to enough of this to not ever have to worry about being constipated. It will soak into your skin; you will breathe it; and you will taste it in the smoke from the exhaust. You will clench to keep from soiling yourself. But you will learn to love the smell of burning castor oil as you love the smell of horse shit today."

Richthofen was listening raptly.

"It is also good for inducing labor in pregnant women and easing the flow of a mother's milk."

Confusion spread over Richthofen's face.

"Good. You are paying attention." Zeumer stepped to the front of the aeroplane and waved Richthofen to join him. Zeumer placed two hands on a blade of the propeller and pressed downward. The propeller and the entire engine rotated together.

"I see," said Richthofen.

"Do you?" asked Zeumer. "Do you see what this means?"

"Yes, of course. The engine rotates together with the propeller, a rotary. Of course," replied Richthofen. He waved a hand, dismissing the question.

"Do you see, Richthofen, do you see how it can kill you?" said Zeumer.

Richthofen took a step back, "Zeumer, it isn't necessary to tell me everything will kill me. I understand this is dangerous."

Zeumer waved a fist at Richthofen and jabbed a finger in his face.

"It is necessary, Richthofen! You must understand how each thing can kill you so that you know what to do about it!" His whole body shook, the anger filling him. "So, tell me, Richthofen, tell me the ways that this engine will kill you! Tell me three ways."

Richthofen hesitated, and then raised a hand, his own fist clenched. "One. It stops working; fails. And, I can't make it to a safe landing place." He lifted a finger. "Two. It flies apart and parts injure me so that I can't fly or just die outright." He showed two fingers now. "Three ..." He hesitated, staring hard at Zeumer.

"Three?" asked Zeumer.

Richthofen's shoulders sank. He had no idea.

"Three. This turning engine will make your Eindekker wish to pull right. It will turn right when you're not paying attention. All the time. It will turn right when you don't want it to. It will turn right harder than you want it to. It will pull against the controls because it wants to turn to the right. And when you want to turn right, it will turn right and want to continue turning until it's on its back and falling to the ground. And as it falls, it will keep turning right. And then you will be dead. Understand?"

"Yes, Herr Zeumer, it will try to kill me by turning right," answered Richthofen.

"Very good, Richthofen. Perhaps you understand now."

Zeumer walked to the rear of the aeroplane and picked up a folding ladder, then set it up against the machine.

"Climb in, Richthofen."

Richthofen handed the lantern to Zeumer, climbed the ladder, and settled onto the hard wooden bench that served as a seat. Zeumer climbed the ladder behind him and peered over his shoulder.

"Feel this, Richthofen." Zeumer reached into the cockpit and put his hand around an exposed frame inside the fuselage.

Richthofen reached out and touched it, then ran a finger over a rough weld.

"Steel, steel tubing, makes the Fokker much stronger than the French aeroplane that this is copied from. It can take a bullet strike and not break. I've seen it; it will make you thank the Dutch for something. Fokker hires women to weld these frames. Can you believe it? Women!"

Zeumer began to point out controls and instruments. A single gauge for fuel pressure marked the instrument panel. Above it was a curved bubble gauge, taken from a carpenter's toolbox, which served as an indicator if the wings were level. A crude barometric altimeter hung from a bracket on the right rim of the cockpit. Zeumer pointed down at the wing on the starboard side.

"There is the compass. The designers seemed to have been concerned that the steel frame would interfere with the pointing of the thing." He shook his head in mild disbelief.

He pointed out the steering column with the double handgrip. "Just like the Albatros." Below the column was the rudder bar with boxes for footrests below it.

He pointed inside the cockpit, at the sides, just next to the pilot's knees. "And there, you can open those doors to see the ground or just be able to look below you. And there, behind your feet, more doors to let you see underneath the aeroplane."

Then he began to point at objects in the cockpit, as though running through a memorized list, his voice growing louder.

"Fuel gauge, there. Run out of fuel, you will crash and die. Control column and rudder with which you will fight this thing in flight. It will porpoise, nosing up and down and try to turn right no matter what else is going on. If you roll on your back at low altitude because you're not paying attention, you will die. Air intake, that round tube, there. Don't let it suck up your maps; it will clog and the engine will die and, then, so will you. Manual fuel pump; keep the gravity tank full. There, the indicator for oil flow. If it runs dry of oil, the engine will seize."

"And, I will die?" Richthofen couldn't help but smirk.

"Yes, you will." Zeumer's face betrayed no hint of humor. "Any questions, Richthofen?"

Richthofen reached up and put his hand on the butt of the machine gun, and ran his palm over the cold metal. "Tell me about this."

Zeumer reached into the cockpit and under the machine gun. He put two fingers on a lever, and pulled it toward Richthofen. "This engages the synchronizer. When this is pulled, the gun can fire. Pull this to chamber the first round and release it." He reached down and depressed a button on the control wheel. "And this fires the weapon." He depressed it, and the weapon gave a hollow click.

Richthofen stood in the cockpit and reached out across the length of the machine gun, running his hand along the sights, then over the cocking handle, feeling the metal under his palm. He sat back down, braced his head against the headrest, and sighted along the weapon. With a determined focus, he put his thumbs on the firing button on the control yoke. "I see," he said

Zeumer picked up the lantern and held it in Richthofen's face. "Not everything."

Richthofen shifted so that he pressed himself against the aeroplane. He felt comfortable now that he had a sense for the weapon, the aeroplane. He longed to begin to master it.

Zeumer brought him back. "Look, Richthofen. You have a long way to go before you can begin to even try to fly this type. Learn the Albatros, and then your day will come when you can fly this."

He reached out and put a hand on Richthofen's shoulder. Richthofen looked down, surprised that Zeumer, who never touched anyone, would place a hand on him.

"Flying the Fokker will be challenging even with experience. The controls are very stiff, they will seem like they've not moved at all, but the aeroplane will begin to maneuver. You will need two hands at all times. Try it. Take the yoke and move the wings. Go ahead."

Richthofen turned in his seat and grasped the control yoke in two hands, rotated it as if he were turning the Albatros. The yoke barely moved, and as he looked out at the wing, he could see no movement. In the Albatros, the yoke would easily move halfway around. He scowled, surprised.

"Not all aeroplanes are the same, Richthofen. The Fokker will seem like it's trying to buck you out in level flight, and you will need to constantly work to control its tendency to pitch up and down. The rudder will blow around in the wind, and you'll feel the rudder bar move in response. The tail will yaw back and forth on its own. You will need to learn to smoothly control the rudder, or you will over control and make the yaw worse."

Richthofen braced his feet on the rudder bar and pressed down on the right side. He craned his head around and watched the rudder swing back and forth. Where the wings didn't seem to move at all, the rudder seemed to flail about in comparison.

"Take your feet off the foot rests, and lock your heels on that cord there, the elastic for the landing gear, then brace them in tight against the cord and the rudder bar. Now try the rudder, lightly."

Richthofen did as he was told, and he watched the rudder swing; a soft, shallow swaying back and forth. He felt the smoothness from the subtlety of the change and he smiled up at Zeumer.

"You must learn not to be afraid of the Eindekker, for, when you fly it, it will seem like it wants to tumble. You have to control it precisely, but not over control it; it won't like that and will kill you. If the Albatros is a plow horse, then this is a steeplechaser. Climb out, Richthofen."

Richthofen stood up again in the cockpit, putting one hand on the pylon where the control cables ran from the wings into the fuselage.

"Oh," said Zeumer, "that reminds me. If you ever flip over in the Fokker on the ground, lean forward so you don't get your neck broken, the pylon will protect you."

Siegert's orderly entered the tent and passed a note to Zeumer. He read it, frowned, and shook his head. "It seems, Richthofen, that you have the commander's permission to attempt your first solo flight."

Richthofen felt a cold rush his body, like ice water dumped over him. He ran a hand across his scalp. "How soon?" he asked.

"As soon as we're ready. Tomorrow, Richthofen, first light? Is that soon enough?" said Zeumer.

~~~

Just before dawn, Richthofen rolled out of bed. His neck was sore and stiff and his head was foggy from lying awake in bed most of the night, drifting in and out of sleep, never truly resting.

He saw the first gray light in the east, and he needed to move, to get up, and get his head clear. Menzke had laid out a clean uniform, polished his boots, and rolled a single cigarette, leaving them all in a neat stack by the door in the middle of the night. Richthofen was surprised when he turned on the electric light to see them sitting there. *I must have slept a little,* thought Richthofen dully.

He dressed and stepped outside into the cool winter air. Richthofen felt his own deep coldness, the hardness in the pit of his stomach. It was a familiar, but unwelcome sensation: the pangs of fear. At the far end of the field, the Zeppelin hangar was open and empty, all the lights still lit inside, while men stirred around. Some of the men peered up into the sky to the west. He lit the cigarette and walked to the mess and collected a cup of coffee. He swallowed the hot coffee in gulps and stepped back outside, taking a moment to watch the stars fading in the morning twilight, before finishing Menzke's cigarette.

Across the field, an AEG was starting its engines, the first aeroplane up for the day. It would fly reconnaissance over the French positions near the Mort Homme to determine if the French army had moved in the night. Next to the AEG, an Albatros two-seater rolled out, a half-dozen ground crew going over the aeroplane. Two figures stood by in the dark and watched the ground crew at work on the Albatros.

The AEG rolled away down the field, the sounds of its engines briefly synchronizing and rattling the entire field, making the walls of the mess hall thump before the aeroplane lifted and then began to climb away to the south.

Richthofen crushed the cigarette under his boot heel and set his empty coffee cup down on a rail outside the mess. He walked over to the Albatros. Zeumer and Siegert's adjutant stood in the cold, their breath a thin gray fog. Zeumer's was punctuated by an occasional dry cough. He sounded particularly bad this morning.

"Good morning, gentlemen," said Richthofen, saluting.

Zeumer and the adjutant returned his salute and then returned to their conversation. The adjutant was remarking that a Zeppelin was overdue from an overnight mission, and the crew was lingering, watching for it. He looked toward the Zeppelin shed mournfully.

The ground crew around the Albatros picked up the aeroplane's tail and walked it further out in the field. Zeumer, Richthofen, and the adjutant trailed behind. In the pale light, Richthofen could see a crowd of men gathering outside the mess hall to watch his flight.

He frowned to himself, feeling the coldness inside again. He wanted to blurt out that he was afraid, but he swallowed hard and bit the inside of his lip to suppress the impulse.

"Are you ready, Richthofen?" asked Zeumer.

"No," said Richthofen. "But I am prepared." He smiled broadly at Zeumer. Zeumer's eyes were lost in shadows, blending with the perpetual dark rings around them.

Siegert's adjutant looked back at Richthofen with something like disinterest on his face.

Richthofen saluted the adjutant, then Zeumer, and walked to the Albatros. He stood at the right wing tip and nodded to Zeumer. Richthofen began inspecting the aeroplane, running his hand over the wings, the struts, cables, and then the propeller.

He enjoyed the sensation of the smooth, cool wood under his hands; it relaxed him. He felt the iciness inside subsiding, the knot in his stomach releasing. He moved down the left side of the aeroplane, repeated the inspection process and then stood next to the stepladder.

"Permission to proceed, sir?" he asked the adjutant.

"Yes, proceed." The adjutant saluted, and then stepped back. Zeumer gave him a nod.

"Good luck, Richthofen. Just a single circle out and then land; turn where I showed you." He saluted, and Richthofen returned it. He climbed into the front cockpit, moved the switch that closed the circuit for the engine magneto and then called out, "Contact!" to a crewman at the front of the plane.

The ground crewman put his hands on the prop and pulled down hard enough that he pulled himself off the ground. The Benz engine sputtered, coughed, and then roared, the propeller blurring into a shimmering disk.

Richthofen glanced over at Zeumer, who waved him on. Richthofen opened the throttle, letting the engine warm and settle into a steady din. Then he pulled the throttle out further, and the engine accelerated; the prop wash blew hard and cold on his face.

The sensation of cold in his belly was gone, now replaced by the sudden heat of adrenaline and the beating of his own heart. He pulled the throttle the rest of the way out, the power making the aeroplane begin to roll. He glanced over at the mess hall, where the men had gathered. They waved their hats as Richthofen started down the field. Richthofen was tempted to wave but lacked the confidence, so he kept his hands firmly on the control yoke.

The Albatros rolled down the field as the sun was just beginning to emerge through the trees, painting yellow stripes of sunlight across the brown grass of the field. The aeroplane lifted its tail, flew level, and then lifted away from the ground, soaring upward.

At once, Richthofen could feel it want to buck, the nose settling lower than he'd ever experienced with Zeumer. His stomach felt queasy, the adrenalin and coffee making it burn. His gut told him to pull back on the stick, causing the nose to rise, and then he pushed the stick to correct the motion. The aeroplane began pitching up and trying to nose over repeatedly.

He calmed himself by gulping air and taking deeper breathes, then relaxed his hands on the yoke, letting the aeroplane settle. It dipped down and pitched nose low again.

Is it too low? What's wrong?

He stopped his climb and flew to the south; he throttled down. The sun shone brightly on the aeroplane as it moved over the trees. Ahead of him, he saw the open field with the single tree: the turning point he had agreed on with Zeumer.

As he approached the tree, he banked right, the sensation of movement was unsettling with the nose of the aeroplane so low. He felt awkward, like he might tip over and go straight into the ground. He shook the thought out of his head and banked back to the left.

The sun crossed into his vision as he turned and blinded him momentarily, but he used it now, orienting its reflection off his starboard wing, and lined up to fly north. He leveled out and pushed the rudder bar to put the nose of the aeroplane to the right of the giant Zeppelin sheds.

The aeroplane seemed to crawl through the air, each slight sensation of motion seeming to slow time further, dragging Richthofen's fate along on a string. After a flight that seemed longer than he had ever experienced, at last he was lined up for his landing.

Once he had cleared the trees on the edge of the field, he pushed the throttle in, then a little more. The aeroplane slowed and settled downward, the wheels nearing the ground. Then he pushed the throttle all the way in.

The aeroplane sank, tipping forward unexpectedly. Richthofen pulled the stick back, lifting the nose as the wheels struck the ground a glancing blow. He continued to slow, but bounced the aeroplane again, the thing rising as though it were refusing to rejoin the earth. Richthofen felt his body tighten, and he took in a deep lungful of air and held it. The nose rose, and he reflexively pushed on the stick too quickly.

With a bang and a rhythmic thumping sound, the spinning propeller ripped into the ground, and then shattered as it dug further into the soil of the field. Richthofen's head cracked against the rim of his cockpit. He felt a brilliant flash of pain. Shards of wood burst around the aeroplane before the nose buried itself into the dirt.

The aeroplane tipped forward until it stood vertically, its tail straight up. It hung there, and all was silent. Then the aeroplane fell back on its wheels while the nose remained pinned to the ground.

From the end of the field, men were already running: the crowd from the mess hall, the ground crew, and Zeumer.

Richthofen sat, stunned, huddled in his cockpit. Astonished, he threw a leg from the aeroplane and rolled out, his legs over his head as he fell to the ground. He stood up and put his hand to his forehead, expecting to find blood but found none. He smelled gasoline and castor fumes.

Zeumer reached him first, put an arm around his shoulder, and began walking him away. The ground crew came up, barely glancing at Richthofen, and examined the wreck. The crowd of men from the mess hall gathered and stood back at a few meters' distance. They murmured, and then one man laughed, followed by another.

Siegert's adjutant walked up, and casually shot them a look, silencing them. He glanced at the ruin and at Richthofen, made a note on his clipboard, then turned his back and walked away back down the field.

Richthofen shook off Zeumer and put his hand against his forehead again, still surprised that he wasn't bleeding.

The ground crew took his Albatros by the tail, and pulled it down with a creaking sound. Something inside cracked with a sound like splintering wood.

"Richthofen, I have something to tell you," said Zeumer.

"What is it, Zeumer?" Richthofen's voice was too loud, nearly shouting.

"I forgot to tell you it will be heavy in the nose without me in the back seat."

Chapter Thirty-One

November 15, 1915
Döberitz, Germany

The enormous Zeppelin-winged bomber wallowed through a turn, both pilots working the controls together, using all their strength to restrain the beast. Inside the hollow empty cavern of its fuselage, Richthofen sat holding onto the sides of a canvas chair, nailed to the floor. It stank of smoke, oil, sweat, and fear. Other passengers, all deafened by the engines, and horrified, but numbed, by the sensations of the turbulent air, looked back at him with unease in their eyes. He heard the engines change their note, descending from a steady thunder to a deafening rumble. He felt he was flying inside of a barn blown away in a storm.

The aeroplane lurched, dangling in the air a moment, only to sink downward. It struck the ground and bounced, then settled to earth and rolled. The walls of the fuselage shook like the skin of a drum, rattling the teeth of the men inside before the engines began to quiet, and the aeroplane came to a stop. The man next to Richthofen looked at him and said something, his mouth moving, but Richthofen couldn't hear a word the man said. For the moment, the flight had taken what hearing he had left. He stood and staggered down the inside of the fuselage and found the door, then threw back the handle and pushed the door wide, letting fresh air inside and engine fumes out.

Richthofen tottered in the open doorway and looked down at the ground far below. The blast of air from the engines slammed into him, and he slapped his hand onto his head to keep his cap from blowing away.

He looked across the airfield, past a jumble of aeroplanes at a distant row of buildings, and, behind them, the abandoned village of Döberitz, his new home. The townsfolk, displaced by the airfield, had sold to the government and left behind a tidy little village that had become a town of flyers. And to the east, Richthofen could see the tallest buildings of Berlin lined up along the horizon.

Ground crew propped a long ladder up, waving it around until it fell against the aeroplane. Richthofen swung his canvas bag over his shoulder and climbed down.

"Where's the operations building?" he shouted over the roar of the engines.

A man pointed across the field, past a mixed jumble of aeroplanes.

Richthofen walked out across the field, turned and looked back at the giant aeroplane. He marveled at the size of the thing and hated it a little. Men walked around underneath it, their heads not even touching its belly. It stood like a flying battleship, as long as a soccer field, and as tall as a four-story building. Its angles were sharp and ugly, its engines exposed between the wings, ungainly, and unfinished-looking. Men in their own tiny cockpits along the engines worked on them as the engines still ran.

Richthofen turned away, relieved to be on the ground, done with bombers after a single flight, and now looking for fighters.

Better to die alone and fighting than die in a crate along with the other cargo, he thought.

A line of Eindekkers stood on the field, on display from oldest to newest. At the far end of the row, where the newest would be, a group of men had gathered, Richthofen joined them.

A tall Leutnant stood at the back of the group, peering over their heads. He, too, held a canvas travel bag in his hand.

"Good afternoon," said Richthofen. "What is there to see?"

The man turned to Richthofen and looked down with deep-set eyes. An incongruously delicate moustache decorated the man's mouth.

"It's Immelmann's newest Eindekker, with three guns. It's going through trials. Fokker just flew it in from Schwerin," he said. The man pursed his lips with an expression of impatience.

He looked at the bag in Richthofen's hand.

"Just arriving?" he asked.

"Yes, flew in on the giant," Richthofen shouted, his voice too loud. He pointed with a thumb over his shoulder at the Zeppelin bomber.

"I see. I'm here for flight school. Bodo von Lyncker." He put out a hand.

"Manfred von Richthofen." They shook.

"I thought you'd be much older and a general and commanding a cavalry corps." Lyncker grinned broadly.

Richthofen looked up, trying to decide if he liked Lyncker. "My uncle. My namesake. And we needn't mention that again."

"Very well, Richthofen, agreed."

Lyncker and Richthofen stood for moment and listened to Fokker speak from the pulpit of the Eindekker's cockpit. He was explaining the three-gun mount.

"So, that's Fokker," said Richthofen. "He seems ... inelegant."

"Yes, our Dutchman. Strange bird. Some say genius; some say carnival barker; some say spy," replied Lyncker.

Richthofen replied, "Perhaps all of those."

"So, giants, then?' asked Lyncker, gesturing toward the parked bomber.

"No, I think not. It was just a ride here. Fighters for me. At least that way you can see the ground before you crash on it," answered Richthofen.

"Me, too. Fighters, eventually. Have you piloted before, Richthofen?" asked Lyncker.

Richthofen rolled the sad facts around in his head and opted for candor. "Crashed on my first solo, failed my first exam; now I'm starting over."

Lyncker laughed, failing to hold his mouth in a frown. "Well, stick to it, Richthofen. I'm right where you are. Well, except that I haven't crashed or failed an exam and I'm not starting over. Except for that. Perhaps you can teach me something, since you know how to crash." Lyncker laughed and put an arm over Richthofen's shoulders, turning them both toward the operations center.

~~~

Richthofen pushed open the shutters to let in the morning light. Dust flew through the air in the sunlight and officers moved in the streets, heading from the town downhill toward the airfield. In the silence of the room, he could hear his ears ring, an audible scar of his distant calamity. He thought of Santuzza and missed the warm smell of horse. Mornings reminded him of horses, of the eagerness and the expectation to ride. He tried to find the feeling this morning, about aeroplanes, but just felt sorrow for the horses that were gone. He recalled Antithesis, how he had let Menzke take the stallion to the artillery depot, handing the charger over to pull cannons. *Such a waste!* Sadness burned at the back of his throat. He wondered about Wedel, left behind, running fool's errands to the front lines, still living in a hole in the ground.

Menzke had made tea and left hard biscuits out on the table. Now, he stirred about in the kitchen, masking his own nervousness with activity.

Richthofen turned to the dining room and stood stiffly, not wanting to sit, feeling that living in the commandeered house was intruding on someone else's small tragedy. When the air force had expanded Döberitz, the last of the villagers had moved away, into Berlin, he supposed. It had happened quickly though. The shelves of the abandoned home still held their possessions, curios, and ceramics. A picture of the Kaiser adorned the fireplace mantle and a family portrait hung on the wall of the dining room. The now-missing family's stern faces seemed to glare at Richthofen, captured for posterity.

If all went well, he would see his family today. If Christmas was happy. He thought of his sister, tending wounded; of his younger brothers, off playing at war.

All gone, scattered. Would their family ever return to itself? Was their home as hollow as this one? *Perhaps today is the last day we'll all be together.*

Lyncker pounded down the stairs, smoothing his hair with one hand and buttoning his jacket with another. He ducked through the arch into the dining room and grinned at Richthofen.

"Happy Christmas," he said.

"My friend. Good morning." Richthofen's mood lifted, smiling back. "Well, Lyncker, time to fly, then?"

"Yes, let's see if you can do this without crashing."

Lyncker picked up a biscuit and gnawed a bite from the thing, then shrugged his shoulders, accepting the staleness.

"Not hungry, Richthofen?" he asked.

Richthofen replied, "No. Perhaps later."

Richthofen pulled on his overcoat and stepped to the front door and outside. He nodded good morning to two fellow flying students passing by. Lyncker joined him and they walked down to the flying field.

"Now remember, Richthofen, if you crash, be sure to kill us, and not just scar me. I couldn't stand living without my beautiful face." He grinned again at Richthofen who frowned, shaking his head in feigned contempt.

"Lyncker, some scars would do you good; they're quite fashionable these days. Everyone is wearing them."

At the field, a new Albatros two-seater had been made ready, the ground crew standing by. Richthofen's trainer stood near the aeroplane, his crimson cap vivid amongst the drab gray uniforms and overcoats of the other men. Richthofen looked at the cold, colorless sky as he donned his goggles, helmet, and scarf. A smattering of thin gray clouds looked as though they might congeal into something worrisome. He looked across the field at the flags that served as wind markers. The flags hung limply in the cold air.

"Ready for your flight, Richthofen?" asked the trainer.

"Yes, I'm ready. Today, my present to myself will be my pilot's badge."

"Yes, Leutnant, if you succeed. Check in at Schwerin when you arrive and have them telephone to confirm your success. Any questions?"

"No. None. I'll have them call." He saluted and began walking around the Albatros, touching and prodding the aeroplane.

Pre-flight inspections were now his new ritual. He followed a pattern that was strict, crisp, and formal, always carried out precisely. Each step was as vital to his confidence as the next, and the physical sequence quieted him, gave him focus and assuredness. He started at the left wing, his right hand on the aeroplane. He moved it along the surfaces, over the struts and wires, his hand always touching. He moved around the craft, stroking, pulling, softly talking to himself; his hand sometimes flat, other times, only his fingers examining, fondling, and growing closer to the machine.

He paused, called a mechanic over, asked after the engine, when it was serviced, how many hours it had been run, when it had flown. Satisfied, he knelt, reached out and examined a wheel, the structure of the landing gear, the bottom of the aeroplane. Then he moved back to the right side and climbed the short ladder, conferred with the mechanic in the back seat, and then swung a leg over into the front cockpit. Lastly, he called the mechanic over to the aeroplane and began moving the controls, pushing them out to the extents of their motion, running the rudder to its stops, and the ailerons to the limits of their travel while the mechanic watched.

Richthofen looked to the trainer and to Lyncker, and then gave a wave into the air. The trainer waved back to him, his hand bent in a shooing motion. Lyncker climbed into the rear cockpit, adjusted himself, and strapped in.

"Well, Richthofen, does your steed meet with your approval?" he asked as he cuffed Richthofen on the shoulder.

"Yes, Bodo, we'll do fine," said Richthofen. He pulled his goggles over his eyes, tightened his scarf at his throat, before tucking the ends under his jacket.

The engine started cleanly. The propeller bit into the air with a hard chop, and the blades accelerated into a shimmery disk. Richthofen smiled to himself and felt the warmth of excitement in his belly as the engine also warmed up for the flight. He adjusted his goggles, pulled his scarf a little tighter, and then signaled for the ground crew to pull the wheel chocks.

As the Albatros began to roll down the field, a light spatter of raindrops wetted the windscreen, making it useless. Richthofen, undeterred, leaned out around the windscreen and pulled the throttle out further, making the engine work a little harder. The wings began to flex, and then the lightness came, that first delicate sensation of lifting and beginning to rise. The ground fell away in a rush as the Albatros slid up into the air. They climbed quickly.

Richthofen could see all of the city of Berlin far to the east. The roads, the river, and bridges crisp and gray in the soft light, all converging toward the heart of the Second Reich. Richthofen pushed the throttle in gradually and leveled the aeroplane, flying just below a layer of clouds. Then, with a gentle turn, he steered northwest to Schwerin. He felt thrilled and intense:

alive. Each motion of the aeroplane was his motion; the machine was an extension of his hands, of his will.

The rain stopped and the clouds grew thinner, hazy. Richthofen sensed the open sky above the clouds and longed to go up. He glanced back at Lyncker and pointed upward. Lyncker kissed his fingertips and tossed his fingers and thumb into the air. Richthofen pulled the throttle out to the stops again, swooped downward, and then pulled up, rocketing up through the clouds.

The aeroplane shuddered, dropped a little, and then popped upwards; it rocked and lurched as it climbed through the clouds. Finally, they emerged above the layer of billows and into brilliant sunlight.

I am the master of weather and sky, thought Richthofen, remembering an old poem. *Some day, we'll master the night and day, and nothing will be left to conquer.*

Richthofen's excitement became elation, the beauty of the moment making him laugh behind his silk scarf, his heart pounding. Nevertheless, his movements were quiet and restrained. He worked the controls with gentle motions effortlessly coordinated between hands and feet. He turned again and looked at Lyncker and saw a smile in the man's eyes. Lyncker nodded his head vigorously in approval.

Richthofen descended a few meters, allowing the wheels to brush along the cloud tops. He felt he was guiding a ship on an ocean of white, with a tiller in his hands and sweet fresh air over the deck. He pushed the craft lower, slicing into the tops of the clouds with the Albatros' lower wings, sending wisps off into the blue.

Richthofen felt a tap on his shoulder and Lyncker leaned forward and pointed to the compass. Richthofen nodded and glanced down, then adjusted their bearing to the west, reckoning on the path to Schwerin. He pulled up his map and reviewed the landmarks he had selected for himself, and imagined how he would reorient them below the clouds.

As they turned, Richthofen noticed that the soft white surface of the clouds gave way in the distance to a towering mass of gray and black, dark and foreboding. It was a massive thunderhead, swirled with wind and lightning. Richthofen felt his testicles draw hard against his body and his breath became shallow. He looked again at the map and at the compass and confirmed their path was correct. The storm blocked their way to Schwerin.

Do I turn back or fly through this? Can I fly under it? thought Richthofen.

In his mind, alone, he debated the decision: to turn back now and perhaps not get another chance and be labeled a coward? Or plunge into the mass of darkness marking the edge of the storm?

He thought of Holck and the column of black smoke over the burning town, with the firestorm raging below. *What a fool Holck had been! But this is different, Holck needed to get the aeroplane back. Here, I need to succeed or perhaps I might never get the chance again.*

An acceptable risk.

Press on.

He throttled back, pushed the stick to descend, and dropped below the clouds. A soft rain fell there, streaming around the tiny windshield on the Albatros. He rechecked the compass, adjusted their heading, and then peered from the cockpit at the ground below.

Nothing was familiar. No road, no waterway, no town was recognizable. He felt tightness in his throat, a sense of claustrophobia replacing the sense of freedom he had felt above the clouds. He looked again at the map and vainly tried to find a feature. Rain coated his goggles, leaving them useless. He tried to wipe them clear with the end of his scarf, but it too was wet now and was no help. Irritated, Richthofen pulled the goggles down over his neck. *Better off without them.*

The rain became a barrier that turned the skies charcoal gray. He descended as gradually as he could, and tried again to find a landmark. He checked his compass and held his heading midway between west and north, and pushed the throttle in slightly. He scanned back and forth across the horizon, looking for a single spire, a familiar crossroad, or a town square.

He descended lower, his eyes carefully dividing his surroundings. Finally, a shape emerged from the rain: a steeple pointing into the heavens, almost beckoning. Richthofen aimed the Albatros to the right of the point, hoping it could offer some clue as to where he was. As he passed it, Richthofen pulled the aeroplane around in a tight left bank, looking down at the steeple and the church below it. The church's gray roof was an unusual wedged shape.

Pritzwalk!

He'd passed it before, having noted the strange church on a training flight, and hoped that it was as unique as he believed. The recognition restored his confidence. He knew now that they were off track by a couple of kilometers at most. They had just another seventy kilometers to go; they were more than half way to Schwerin. He steadied them out back on their original heading and broke from the banking turn into the black wall of rain.

Quickly he glanced back at Lyncker, little more than ballast now, and nodded at him. Lyncker's hands were tight on the rim of his cockpit, his fingers blue from the cold. He didn't react but kept his eyes fixed on the storm. The thundercloud rose up impossibly over them, and Richthofen felt the first icy clutch of fear.

He took a deep breath and lowered the nose of the aeroplane. He stole another glance at the map, and then stuffed it under the seat. The ink on the sopping wet paper was already smeared and useless.

Suddenly, they were in the storm, the aeroplane slowing as the headwinds took hold of them. The rain surrounded them like a shroud, while, below them, the tops of trees and low hills flashed by in a dark blur. The storm, in its violence, threw them up and down in desperate long surges. Richthofen felt panic rise, hot bile in his throat. His vision narrowed and he clutched the controls with both hands, holding tight with the grip of a corpse.

The storm tossed them effortlessly, leaving Richthofen the feeling he was being shaken into discipline by a harsh schoolmaster.

Here, learn, or die.

He, they, the aeroplane were insignificant in the face of the power gathered in the sky ahead. Richthofen leaned over to one side in the cockpit trying to see around the rain-fogged windscreen. The storm shoved them lower in lunges until he had to steer for gaps in trees and around buildings. Richthofen felt the thrill of a great steeplechase in the sky.

The aeroplane rose and he allowed it its head, like one might with a trusted horse, letting it wallow with the wind, not fighting it, controlling it as needed to keep it upright. In lurches, they surged onward, then upward, then downward again. Richthofen adjusted their heading from one gap in the obstacles to the next, looking as far ahead as he could as the rain alternately obscured and exposed the ground below them.

In his mind, he imagined the map and recalled the terrain. Somewhere there had to be a railway line that he could follow to Schwerin. He knew it was a few kilometers further, just a few more minutes of flight. He couldn't be sure of the exact timing or the distance because of the disorientation from the headwind and the constant banking and turning of the aeroplane.

Ahead, the rain thinned, and a gray gap appeared in the dark black wall. He steered toward it, seeking any relief from the punishment. As they flew, the storm relented somewhat and, where the gap had been, he saw merely trees, and then a wooded hillside rose. It loomed up from the mist, filling his field of vision.

A cold shock passed through Richthofen as he realized they were aimed into a hill. He desperately pulled back on the stick and opened the throttle. The Albatros shuddered, the nose rising too fast, the power too low, causing the propeller to claw at the air. The aeroplane angled upward as Richthofen watched the treetops grow closer.

They grew closer still, more vivid; their details, each trunk and branch, becoming clearer and sharper.

Please, God, give me a few seconds, a few feet. Just a little.

Fate, or God, was with them. With a roar and a scrape, the wheels tore through the tops of the trees, sending a shower of leaves and branches into the air, and then they were free, up and over the hill and still fighting their way to climb into the air. Richthofen took a deep breath, then pushed the aeroplane's nose down and leveled it out.

Ahead lay a gray line of steel track, running across the fields to the northwest: The railway.

Richthofen turned to fly along the tracks, using them to guide them on to Schwerin. Lyncker delivered a hard tap on Richthofen's shoulder, and when Richthofen looked back, Lyncker was shaking his head hard from side to side. Richthofen shrugged back at him as if he were apologizing. Then, he pulled his scarf down and mouthed the words, "Trust me."

They flew above the railroad, the storm buffeting them still. Below them, the ground grew level and open.

Richthofen descended to fly just above the railroad. When he lost sight of it, he would bank and take the plane a little lower. After a few minutes, the railroad met a junction and then split, one track moving to the northeast. Richthofen turned and followed the northeast tracks, staying low.

The winds calmed, but the rain behind the thunderstorm grew in intensity. For the first time, Richthofen noticed the cracks of thunder around them. The sky and earth disappeared behind thick curtains of water. They flew on, Richthofen following the tracks at a few meters' altitude, until buildings appeared alongside the tracks.

Then he saw the great lake of Schwerin, the Schweriner See, to their left, and in it, built on a manmade island, was the city's palace, the Schweriner Schloss, a modern castle, barely fifty years old. Richthofen oriented off the castle and made a turn to the west, flying over the See. Just beyond the castle, in a gap in the rain, he could see the opening in the trees that marked Fokker's airfield.

He lined up his approach, climbed briefly, and began to throttle back. As they descended, he saw that where the field should be lay a surface of water, for the field had flooded. Panic and doubt welled up again.

How can I possibly land in that? How deep can it be? Richthofen looked around at the city as he passed over it and saw no open spaces. He wiped his eyes with his fingertips and prayed to himself that the water was only a thin layer on the surface of the field.

With no other choice, Richthofen committed to the landing, and leveled out over the field. He cut the throttle back and lifted the nose. The aeroplane settled and touched down. An enormous deluge rose around them, blinding Richthofen. The aeroplane bounced once and then a second time, before sticking to the unseen ground and rolling. Sheets of water flew back from the propeller wash and the wheels, as from the bow of a ship.

The landing gear struck a deeper section and threatened to cartwheel the aeroplane, the tail popped up into the air as the aeroplane pitched.

Richthofen, desperate now, pulled hard on the stick and tried to force the tail down. With a splash, the tail thumped to the ground before the propeller and nose could strike the ground. Under the drag of the water, the aeroplane came to a stop, leaving a wake in the field of puddles.

Richthofen began to breathe again. He punched the throttle in and flipped the magneto switch, killing the engine.

The rain thickened into torrents.

Without thinking, he took his goggles in his left hand and began mopping them with his soaking scarf.

Then, people, shouting at one another and at them, surrounded them. Lyncker stood up in his cockpit and nearly tumbled out. Hands reached up to help them to the ground. Richthofen felt saved. He pulled his scarf down and looked at Lyncker.

"Sorry, my friend," he said.

Lyncker grinned. "Are you kidding, Richthofen? That was spectacular!" Lyncker reached up and pulled Richthofen over the side of the aeroplane as hands reached to catch him and set him on the ground. His knees nearly buckled when he tried to stand.

Lyncker seized his hand and pumped furiously. "Fantastic! My God, man. That was amazing!"

"You're an unusual man, Bodo," said Richthofen, breathless and rattled.

Umbrellas appeared and men walked Richthofen and Lyncker to a wooden building on the edge of the field.

In the building, a stove was burning. A boy stoked the flames up. Two young women brought in dry blankets and mechanics' overalls, piling them by the stove. Without shame or hesitation, they both stripped out of their soaked clothes and put on the dry overalls.

Richthofen and Lyncker stood by the fireplace, shivering, waiting for the coffee to finish boiling on the stove. Richthofen held his hands to the heat and worked them open and closed, trying to feel his fingers and get his knuckles to flex again. His fingers were hooks and Richthofen looked in amazement at them, stunned that he'd been able to do anything with them at all, let alone fly. Gradually, his hands began to work again, painfully, as he pushed the blood back into his fingers.

The people of the airfield came and went to look in disbelief at them. Some offered congratulations, others just stared, bewildered, and shook their heads, then walked back out into the storm.

Richthofen's teeth chattered, making it hard to speak, but he smiled and tipped his coffee mug to each. As the crews began to slip away, an Oberleutnant came in, shook his umbrella, and saluted the two men. They each reached out from under blankets, Richthofen's hand bent in a comma, to return the salute.

"Who is the pilot?" the Oberleutnant asked.

Richthofen raised his hand from under his blanket.

"Very well," he said. He pushed a clipboard at Richthofen.

"Sign here, and here." He pointed with the end of a pencil, and then held the pencil out.

Richthofen reached out and took the pencil, and then he dropped the blanket and wrapped both hands together to hold it while he signed the form. He finally spoke, a single sentence: "Please telephone to Döberitz to let them know that we made it."

"Of course, Leutnant," said the Oberleutnant. He saluted, clicked his heels, and left again.

Richthofen looked at Lyncker, and tried to gauge his mood, still feeling apologetic. Lyncker glanced back, a twinkle in his eye. Then, he tipped his head back and laughed, a long chuckle, his entire body shaking. He laughed until he sneezed, then coughed, and spilled his coffee. Then he laughed again and dropped his cup on the floor.

"Oh, sorry," he said.

Richthofen finally joined him, laughing, but not nearly as hard.

A thin mechanic came in, wearing grimy coveralls and drenched from the rain. He poured himself a cup of coffee and drew up a chair next to them. His hair was dark and a little greasy. He smelled of aeroplane: grease, gasoline, canvas dope, and oil.

"I just had to come see you two. I can't believe you did that. But, welcome to Schwerin," he said, and offered a hand to Lyncker. Lyncker snaked a hand from underneath the blankets and shook it.

"Anton Fokker," said the man. "Good to meet you."

"Von Lyncker. Bodo von Lyncker. And this is Manfred von Richthofen."

Fokker tipped his head, looked at Lyncker and smiled. "The same von Lyncker that crashed in a snowstorm while ferrying a comrade back from a weekend pass?" he asked.

Lyncker looked appalled that *that* story had traveled so far. "The same," said Lyncker, a little sheepish.

Fokker grinned and looked to Richthofen, "and you wouldn't be the friend he was retrieving, would you?"

Richthofen nodded, still staring at the fire, his teeth chattering in bursts.

"Which one flew today?" Fokker asked.

Lyncker tipped his thumb over and pointed it at Richthofen. Fokker stuck his hand out toward Richthofen, and Richthofen shook it.

"Nice piece of flying. A little ... mad, but a nice piece of flying. I believe that makes you both equally insane," said Fokker.

"Well, I wouldn't do it again ... unless I was ordered, I suppose," said Richthofen, his voice quivering from the cold. "We'll be flying on to Schweidnitz to join my family for Christmas if the weather clears."

Fokker's smile left his face. "Truly mad," he said, "and aren't we all." Then, "If you're hungry, you can join me for a Christmas dinner. We're working, of course, but we can take a break."

Richthofen clenched his jaw so his teeth would stop chattering and cocked his head to the side. "Yes, I'm happy to and so is my friend here." Richthofen nodded to Lyncker.

"Excellent!" said Fokker brightly. He sipped his coffee. "And we can share flying stories, now that it's official that you're a pilot, I suppose. Von Lyncker. Any relation to the Baron von Lyncker, aide to the Kaiser?" He used the English word, *Baron*, not the German *Freiherr*.

"Yes, of course. My father," said Lyncker.

Fokker stood and moved his chair next to Lyncker and sat back down.

"Tell me, does your father understand the importance of the aeroplane?" asked Fokker.

Lyncker leaned toward Fokker. "Yes, I believe so," he said.

Fokker began to describe his new fighters to Lyncker, and the two men fell into discussion, but Richthofen was hardly listening.

Instead he wondered: *How many times must a man need to almost die before he succeeds?* His shivering thawed away and he smiled to himself. He replayed the flight in his head and thought about what Fokker had said. He liked the sound of that. The word Fokker had used: a pilot.

At last.

Book Three

Red

So stand by your glasses steady,
this world is a world of lies,
then here's to the dead already,
and hurrah for the next man who dies.

—English Flying Song, 1915

Chapter Thirty-Two

January 12, 1916
Douai, France

"Seven," said Immelmann.

"Yes, seven," answered Boelcke.

"It doesn't seem like many, does it?"

"No ... I suppose not."

"Perhaps today ... eight. What do you think?"

Boelcke looked down at his plate and stabbed a bite of sausage. He waved it in the air for a moment, seeming to taunt Immelmann, before putting it in his mouth. Immelmann drew back, a look of revulsion crossing his face.

"Max, how can you be so squeamish?" asked Boelcke. "It's just meat."

"I've never found it ... appealing," replied Immelmann. He cleared his throat. "So, perhaps I'll get my eighth today, Boelcke."

"Yes, I heard you the first time you said it," replied Boelcke. "And perhaps I'll get mine, then."

As they ate their breakfast, an infantry captain approached their table. He rolled his cap around in his hands, and looked nervously at the two flyers, his eyes examining the medals and badges on their uniforms. Speaking without introducing himself, he said, "Thank you, gentlemen, for what you are doing to keep the English aeroplanes away. You are saving lives, thank you."

"Yes, yes, of course. Our pleasure," said Immelmann with a broad grin. He took an enormous bite of pastry on his fork and put it in his mouth.

Boelcke looked at Immelmann, trying to determine if he was being sincere. He frowned and looked down. "Yes, you're welcome, I'm sure." He picked at his eggs.

Sensing Boelcke's mood, the captain bowed slightly toward Boelcke. "Herr Boelcke, I've just returned from Berlin. Surely you understand the importance of what you're doing."

"Yes, yes, I ... *we* do," said Boelcke, looking up at the man.

"You're in all the papers. In fact, the papers in Berlin are arguing which of you will have the next victory. Oberleutnant Immelmann was on the front page of the American *New York Times*," added the captain.

"That's quite enough, thank you," said Boelcke, raising his voice. It resounded in the crowded mess hall. The room quieted and heads turned to look at him.

"I don't mean to offend, Herr Boelcke."

"No offense taken."

The captain turned to Immelmann. "I look forward to reading your book with great expectation."

Boelcke scowled and sat straight up in his chair; he then leaned forward as he hissed at Immelmann.

"Your book?" Boelcke lowered his voice. "Did you get permission to write a book? Are you mad? Who do you think you are?"

Immelmann cringed. Boelcke's voice seemed full of menace. He glanced up at the infantry captain as if to apologize. The captain backed up from the table, retreating.

"Yes. I ... Yes, I was asked. And I've agreed to write a short book on the fighting," said Immelmann.

"*The* fighting? Or *your* fighting?" Boelcke snarled. "You know I was approached to do such a thing ... such vanity ... to write a book about myself? I turned the offer down. Do you understand?"

"Boelcke ... Oswald. This is not for me. It is for the people. The German people are inspired, and this should be encouraged." Immelmann lowered his voice, almost a whisper. "This is not for me."

Boelcke thought Immelmann's voice sounded like he was pleading. He sat back in his chair, braced his arms against his legs and shook his head.

"We're soldiers. We're doing our duty," said Boelcke. "We've shot down, between us, fourteen planes. No more. We haven't changed the war."

Immelmann paused for a moment, sipped his herb tea, his pinky extended.

Boelcke waited, letting his silence communicate his displeasure.

"We *have* changed the war. The English and French turn around when they so much as see an Eindekker. They are scared. They are scared of *us*. There are a thousand aeroplanes flying on any day, and they're scared of us." Immelmann was sure that he had made his point.

"Max," Boelcke began.

It was Immelmann's turn to frown. Boelcke had never called him Max before.

"Max, we're soldiers, and we fly. No more. Mortals. I have asthma and you wear your damn silly magical pants when you fly."

"Perhaps," said Immelmann. "Perhaps it's that simple. Perhaps not."

"Perhaps? Perhaps, what, Max?"

"Perhaps, we're ... heroes."

"What does that mean, Max? We're heroes? A medal, two? There are millions of men living in the dirt out there, in the mud and the rain and the filth. The earth will push up dead bodies when the spring rains start. And our men live in that. And we're the heroes?"

"But Boelcke ... Oswald ... we have skills, talents; unique talents." Immelmann lowered his voice again, insistent, needing Boelcke to understand.

Boelcke suddenly felt restrained, as though he'd gone too far, as though he was on the verge of humiliating the man. "Okay. Yes. We do. You're a fine pilot. Perhaps the best I've ever seen. I've never seen a man take to a rotary engine aeroplane and do it without nearly killing himself. And you can land the thing." He smiled, teasing. "But, that doesn't make us gods. And hardly heroes."

Immelmann's mind raced, he thought of the book, what he might write, whether it was of any importance at all, whether he was being vain as Boelcke suggested.

"Oswald, do you ever think about who's watching you when you fly?"

Boelcke looked at Immelmann with an expression of curiosity. "No, I don't, well, I check my back."

Immelmann saw the opening. "Millions. Those millions of men that you referred to? They are watching. Forget the civilians, if you can. But those millions of men, since they won't let us cross the lines with a synchronizer, those men are all our men. Imagine all those eyes on us. There has never been such a thing before. We are heroes because we're seen, because what we do is remarkable."

Boelcke sighed, pulled out his pocket watch, and checked the time. "Go on, Max."

"Those millions of men watch us when we fly. When we shoot down an aeroplane, they watch, and they cheer, they are ... inspired," said Immelmann. "We live in their imaginations. Isn't it wonderful?"

Boelcke's face went slack and he pushed his plate away. He took a gulp of coffee and stared back at Immelmann in disbelief.

"Really, Immelmann, we're heroes not because we have impact on the war, but because we have talents and millions can see us? Not because we change a thing, but because we're seen? And, now, you think we're immortal?" his voice came out in a hiss again, contempt returning. "We're not eternal. Far from it. Look close at a bullet hole in one of those pilots you shoot down. That's all it takes, one hole in you. One bullet. We're just as damned mortal as that."

"I didn't say we're immortal, Oswald. But, we're famous and we rouse our men, our people." He lowered his voice; spoke in a whisper, almost to himself, "Perhaps that's all we can have."

"Be careful of hubris, my friend. It's unbecoming," said Boelcke. What Immelmann meant suddenly dawned on him. "So, that's it. You think because we're famous we're important?"

Immelmann flushed, hot. He took up his cup of tea, wrapped his hand around it, felt the warmth in his hand. He didn't speak. He knew that he had said too much.

"Tell me, Max. Why do you like fighters? Why do you fly them? Hundreds of our airmen fly, but few really enjoy the fight. I think most would rather avoid other aeroplanes altogether, go about their jobs. But, you have a passion for it ... and it's not about *fame*." Boelcke spat out the word.

"I'd rather not talk about that, Oswald," said Immelmann, his voice wavering. He was struggling to hold himself under control.

"Think about it, Max. We're both going out this morning. Looking for trouble. They're scared of us and they hate us. Fame makes us targets, the best kind. The fabled giant elk in the woods, a creature of folklore. Men out there want to kill you. Not just any German pilot: you. A trophy. Surely you know that."

Immelmann pondered Boelcke's words, thought about them, and composed himself. He let out a breath, as though he had been holding it for several minutes.

Boelcke watched Immelmann, envied men that could breathe so easily and took pleasure in watching Immelmann relax into the inevitable.

"Tell no one, Oswald. Not my brother. No one," said Immelmann. "But ... I was shot down."

Boelcke smiled, almost laughed. He forced his mouth to relax, let the urge to smile fade. "Max. That's nothing to be ashamed of."

Immelmann pondered a reply, but felt a sudden urge to connect, thought that maybe Boelcke would understand. "Perhaps. But his bullets hit my petrol tank. Splashed me with gas, I was soaked. I could see sparks when his bullets hit my engine. I dove away, turned east and had to land. I was so terrified I couldn't move, couldn't talk. I couldn't get out of the plane. I felt I had lost my mind, but I tried to just sit still and let it pass, let the feeling subside. I acted as though I was tending to the aeroplane, sat in the cockpit. I could feel the cold gas all over me. I vomited on myself." Immelmann stopped, looked at Boelcke.

Boelcke nodded, newly sympathetic to Immelmann and feeling the need to let him finish. "Go on." His voice was still low, but the menace was gone.

"So, I've turned that shame into anger, but I'm still afraid," said Immelmann. "There."

Boelcke let a silent moment go by.

"Immelmann ... Max ... we're all afraid of dying."

"I'm not afraid of just dying. I'm afraid of roasting. God, help me. Just don't let me roast," said Immelmann. "And, the day I didn't burn, I was wearing those pants. Those pants didn't burn." He smiled a childlike smile.

Boelcke suddenly thought he looked like a boy with a moustache glued on his face, trying desperately to be an adult. "Max, you're a good man," he said. "Let's drink a toast, shall we?"

Boelcke raised his coffee cup and Immelmann hoisted his teacup.

"A toast?" asked Immelmann.

"Yes. To fame. And to number eight: may he be quick in coming."

~~~

It was a brilliant clear day, with a steady wind from the west. Boelcke imagined he could smell the sea on the breeze and his lungs, for once, felt strong and clean. The lines were quiet, just a few aeroplanes up, and no artillery fire. The sky was a roof of clear blue, puffs of clouds rolling by. It was a good day to fly, and to fight.

Boelcke tossed Immelmann a salute from his cockpit as his little aeroplane began to roll to take off. Immelmann saluted stiffly back, watching Boelcke begin to fly. In the manner of lone hunters, Boelcke flew north, Immelmann flew south. As his aeroplane lifted off, Boelcke patted the stone in his pocket and smiled.

Over the shattered French city of Lille, Boelcke turned west, toward the frontlines, up high where the Eindekker's engine ran rough from lack of air, where he was only a speck from the ground below. He craned his head around quickly, checking for German planes nearby, knowing he could be court martialed for what he was about to do.

Seeing no German aeroplanes near, he continued west, against orders, and crossed over the lines. He was carrying the precious synchronizer into English controlled territory, where the risk of having the device captured could bring the Allies back into the aerial fight. He thought of Hermann Kastner, his new squadron commander. One of Kastner's few orders was to not to cross the lines.

But Kastner's not here, is he?

Flying until he saw the sea, staying up high, and then, seeing no aeroplanes; he turned around and flew downwind, back toward Lille. He pitched nose down and over into a steady dive, ruddered slightly to the south. The Fokker sank through the air with the wind shrieking over its wires. Boelcke, intimate with the aeroplane, knew by the sound how far he could push the little craft, how fast he could plunge downward before the wings might rip away. He held his speed, steady and swift, needing every bit of momentum to get away with what he was about to do.

At last, he saw his goal, straight rows of British aeroplanes, beyond a thick patch of trees. As he neared the edge of a farmer's field, he lifted the nose, checking his descent, the wind behind him now. The tiny Eindekker thundered across the forest, skimming the treetops.

Then he emerged from over the trees, to where the English airfield at Hesdigneul-les-Bethune lay ahead. He turned slightly to align with the English runway, and plummeted down, until he roared over the ground and below the tops of the trees. Low and fast were the only things that could keep him safe, now. Ahead, English aeroplanes sat in two neat rows, the roundels on their wings like bullseyes. Two of the English aeroplanes were moving along the ground, facing west into the wind toward him, beginning a take-off roll. Boelcke scanned the field, saw the flagpole and steered toward it, then leveled his wings and pulled the throttle wide open. As he passed the English Union Jack, he looked down at a knot of Englishmen looking up at him with open mouths, shock written across their faces. Boelcke waved and tossed his stone over the side and watched it arc down toward the men. He waved before he disappeared over the eastern trees, running downwind, back toward the lines, as fast as the Eindekker could fly.

~~~

An English officer picked up the rock and unwrapped the paper from around it. He smoothed it out against the flagpole and read aloud to the men crowded around him, "Just a line to say that Somervill and I are alright. We had a scrap with a Fokker. Willy got a graze on the side of his head & I got one through the shoulder halfway through. We had most of our controls shot through & had to land & crashed very badly. I am in Hospital now & Willy is in Germany. Will you let my people know please, yours G Formilli. PS. It was Boelcke who brought us down."

The officer shielded his eyes and looked east, where the Fokker had gone. "Do you suppose *that* was Boelcke?" he said to no one in particular.

~ ~ ~

Boelcke recrossed the lines, low, nearly brushing the rolls of barbed wire that marked the front, then began to climb toward Lille. At last, he regained altitude, and leveled the aeroplane, then looked around. He felt the curious, sneaky, sensation of hoping that no German had seen him, but wished for a moment that an Englishman had, perhaps to find a fight that might purge the pang of guilt he felt at defying orders. He turned south, flying parallel to the lines. West of Lille, over the German artillery positions, he saw two English two-seaters, both flying east.

He thought of Immelmann's words, conscious of the audience below him. Boelcke looked behind him, back toward the English aerodrome and saw nothing in the air. Checking his synchronizer and his gun, he fired a spattering of bullets and turned toward the English aeroplanes.

He dove on the rear one.

He suddenly felt naked, aware of the millions of eyes that might be looking up. He wondered if they really were watching, if they really cared, or if they could even tell who might be the victor, and who the vanquished.

Perhaps they just enjoy seeing someone die in a new and different way, death as novelty; perhaps they don't really care which aeroplane is which. Are we their entertainment? He shook his head, trying to clear the dark, bloody thought away.

When Boelcke had closed to four hundred meters, the English pilots turned their machines west, back toward their lines, flying upwind. Boelcke overtook the slower aeroplane, and watched the observer aim at him, but Boelcke held his fire. The English pilot flew straight and level, to give his observer good aim. When he was a hundred meters away, the English observer began shooting, rapidly emptying the magazine on his Lewis gun. Boelcke flew straight, closing the distance gradually, and then dipped the Eindekker below the tail of the English aeroplane to throw off the Englishman's aim.

When he was close, so close that he could see the fear in the observer's eyes, and after the man had reloaded twice, Boelcke rose, steadied his sights and began to shoot. He held the firing button down in a long burst.

Bullets struck all over the English machine and the men who flew her. When it began to fall, he followed it, and he watched it spiral lower, its nose tipped down. As it neared the ground, it began to spin and then crashed into a tree. Its wings folded forward, wrapped around the fuselage in a shroud. No one moved.

Eight.

Boelcke turned east, flew to the German field at Lille and landed. While he was waiting for a car to take him to the English crash, he called the field at Douai to tell them the news.

Kastner's adjutant spoke to him on the phone. "Herr Boelcke, that is wonderful news! The Inspector General, Major Thomsen, is here and I'll tell him immediately. And, Herr Boelcke? Herr Immelmann has also achieved his eighth victory."

Boelcke laughed.

~~~

Major Hermann von der Leith-Thomsen, Chief of the Field Air Forces, and Hauptmann Kastner, Staffel Commander sat at the head table at dinner. Boelcke sat at the place of honor to Thomsen's right. The pilots of the squadron sat at tables placed in rows, each table adorned with its own giant china soup tureen as a centerpiece. The flyers and their commanders politely ate their haricot bean and ham soup as the last of the flyers returned for the day.

Thomsen tipped his enormous egg-like head toward Kastner to confer quietly while Boelcke squirmed. Boelcke looked up each time the door slammed, expecting the little martinet, Immelmann, to appear at any moment. Each time he bent his head back to his soup, hiding his disappointment.

Thomsen turned to Boelcke and ran a fingertip along the row of medals adorning Boelcke's uniform. "You're nearly out of space there, can't add another one. Perhaps a new row." He smiled a grin equally full of teeth and gaps.

Boelcke stared back at Thomsen blankly. "Yes, sir," he replied.

Thomsen cleared his throat and his smile melted away. "So, eight victories, then. A magic number, perhaps?" Thomsen asked.

"I can't imagine what might be magic about it. I saw ... I mean ... I hear that there are sixteen fresh English aeroplanes lined up at Hesdigneul-les-Bethune each morning, no matter how many we shoot down."

Kastner looked at Boelcke curiously, trying to decipher what Boelcke might have been trying to say.

Thomsen laughed, his bushy white eye brows jostling up and down. He clapped Boelcke on the back and bellowed, "Don't you worry, that's just more for you to shoot!"

Boelcke slumped his shoulders and bent to his soup. "Yes, of course. Then it's a magic number, I'm sure," he replied. Thomsen guffawed again and Boelcke stared at Thomsen, trying to divine the joke.

Kastner's aide approached and glanced at Boelcke as he spoke, "Sirs, Major Thomsen's aide is on the phone." Thomsen dabbed at the corners of his mouth with a napkin and pushed himself back from the table. "The call isn't for you, sir. It is for Leutnant Boelcke."

Thomsen made a pout from his fleshy lips and nodded to Boelcke. "Well, take it then!" he said.

Boelcke wrinkled his brow at Thomsen, mystified. Kastner nodded his approval to Boelcke and Boelcke stood. "Very well, then, I guess I should."

Boelcke followed Kastner's aide to the operations building, a half-step behind, confused. At the watch officer's desk, a phone lay off its cradle. Boelcke picked it up. "Yes? This is Boelcke."

"Leutnant Boelcke, I have received a telegram," said Thomsen's adjutant. Boelcke braced himself, a little afraid. He thought: *Immelmann, no, not Immelmann. Don't let him be dead.*

"It is from the Kaiser, and it is for you," the adjutant said.

He was more confused now, stunned, and felt he was being deceived. "Go on," said Boelcke.

"Boelcke, I suggest you sit down." Boelcke looked, saw a chair on the other side of the desk and decided he'd rather stand. "Yes, of course, please proceed."

"Very well. Leutnant Boelcke, the Kaiser has awarded the *Pour le Mérite* to you and to Leutnant Immelmann on the occasion of your eighth aerial victories."

The room seemed to shift, moving sideways. Boelcke braced a hand against the desk. He stammered, "But that can't be ... can't be ... I'm a Leutnant for God's sake, not a Field Marshall!"

"I assure you, this is correct. By order of the Kaiser. Congratulations, Leutnant Boelcke!"

Boelcke turned to the desk, found the chair and sat in it heavily. *The Pour le Mérite?* The award of kings; the award of Generals and Admirals; the highest honor that the Kaiser could bestow? He found himself panting, gasping for air. *Could it be, could it really be? This is unheard of, only Generals received the Pour le Mérite, and only for winning a great battle or conquering a country!*

Thomsen's adjutant interrupted Boelcke's jumbled thoughts. "Leutnant, are you there?"

Boelcke came back to the moment, feeling ridiculous. "Surely, you're joking?" said Boelcke, at last.

"No, Leutnant, I am not. I wanted the pleasure of telling you myself, but Kastner should make the announcement. Please put him on the phone."

"Really? You're not joking?" asked Boelcke.

"No, I am not. Please put Hauptman Kastner on the phone." Boelcke's hands shook as he sat the handset down on the desk and returned to the mess hall.

"Hauptman Kastner, you are requested to the phone," he said.

He sat down without speaking, trying to focus his eyes, a look of stunned bewilderment on his face.

Thomsen leaned over. "Are you alright, Boelcke?"

In a minute, Kastner returned. He, too, sat down in stunned silence. He gulped wine, and then stood and tapped a glass with the back of a knife.

"Gentlemen, I have an announcement," he said. The room grew quiet, and all heads turned toward him.

"Gentlemen", he started. He looked down at Thomsen with an unasked question on his face.

"Please proceed, Kastner," said Thomsen.

"Gentlemen, the Kaiser has made a special award." He paused to compose himself. "The award of the *Legion Pour le Mérite.*"

Whispers went around the room. Someone said, "Boelcke."

"The Kaiser has awarded the *Order Pour le Mérite* to Leutnants Boelcke and Immelmann, effective this date." Kastner sat down, called for another glass of wine.

Quiet fell over the room and a waiter dropped a glass. Heads began to turn, looking at one another. Someone whooped like a wild Indian.

Then all the men of the mess leapt to their feet and moved toward Boelcke. Thomsen reached out, picked up Boelcke's hand from the table, and shook it. Boelcke's mouth moved but no words came out.

Cheers and shouts, 'Hurrahs!' for Boelcke and Immelmann, erupted around the room. Someone pulled Boelcke to his feet, and the men crowded forward to shake his hand or clap him on his back. An orderly ran out the door, to spread the word across the base.

The Iron Cross had made them knights, but the *Pour le Mérite* made them princes.

Chapter Thirty-Three

February 4, 1916
Hounslow Heath Aerodrome, England

Lieutenant Wilkinson didn't fear the little de Havilland fighter. He liked the big broad wings and the engine in back, so he didn't have to gag on its smoke. He especially liked the gun in front: his very own. Something he could aim and shoot with, something he could battle the damned Fokkers with. He knows they would go to France soon, and fight the Germans on their own terms, fighter against fighter.

Won't they be surprised? Little bastards.

It was his second flight of the day, and he was a little tired; his arms were growing sore and unsteady. Wilkinson longed for a ride into Hatton Cross for a pint, a game of darts, and a night of turning in early. Perhaps his sister could take the train over to meet him, she worried so. It would settle her nerves to get together, to reassure her.

He turned left, a shallow banking turn, just the way Hawker had instructed. His stiff right arm twitched, the muscles over-tight. Jerking, the DH-2 lurched sideways for a second. Wilkinson heart raced and his blood roared in his ears.

The nose of the DH-2 began to slew, then to rotate, slowly at first, then more quickly.

No! Could it be? Not now, damn this bloody thing!

It pitched down and the rate of spin increased, the ground whirling below Wilkinson now.

My God! No! Not me! Not me!

The engine made a sound like glass breaking, something shattering inside it and the propeller ground to a stop. Gas poured from the engine, siphoned through by the forces of the spin. The cold liquid, weighty with energy, hit the hot exhaust and burst and turned to fumes, then mixed with the air rushing over the wings. With a deep bellowing 'Whoosh!', the fumes burst into scarlet flame. As the aeroplane spun, more gas fed through the engine, until the back of the aeroplane was a single, brilliant furnace of flame, plummeting downward.

Wilkinson, doomed, felt reality slip away. He tried to calm himself, to think through the situation. No training came to him. No simple trick. No elaborate maneuver. He thought of jumping, but saw no point. *This can't be happening, this can't be so.*

Then, desperate and without options, panic seized him. He began to pant and cry out into the air. Maniacally, he pulled at the control stick, shoving it one way or another, desperate to turn out of the spin, away from the rotation. As the flames burned away his wings, he continued to try to work the controls, moving the stick after it no longer controlled anything, after it was useless, after his fate was already sealed.

Above the sound of the flames and the rushing air, the men of No. 24 Squadron below could hear Wilkinson scream.

The aeroplane struck the ground, still spinning, nearly vertical in its dive, a tower of black smoke rising a thousand feet above it, and disintegrated.

The flames consumed the wreckage and became a pyre.

~~~

"I understand, Andrews, really, I do understand. These engines are terrible. But, it's what we've got," said Hawker.

John Oliver Andrews stretched out his legs in front of himself. He reached up with both hands and cocked his Scottish cap, his Glengarry, to the side and then he folded his arms. He smiled at Hawker.

"Sir, 'tis a trifle. The men need some confidence, is all, reading the papers, you'd think these German flyers are supernatural, monsters or somethin'. An' the DH-2's, they've taken t' callin' them 'Spinnin' Incinerator'. It's a shame, 'tis."

Hawker listened closely to Andrews, picking his mind through Andrews' thick Scottish accent. He clearly understood the phrase, 'Spinning Incinerator', but wasn't entirely sure of the rest.

"I've heard the phrase. No matter, gallows humor is good for a man who deals with death." Hawker stood, looked out the window and instinctively checked the wind. "Sometimes, Andrews, I feel like a sailor, always looking at the wind flags." He sat back down. "I'm not convinced these Eindekkers are that good, perhaps not even as good as a Morane. The 'Fokker Scourge', the papers call it. It's exaggeration and nonsense."

"Yessir, I understan'. Entirely," said Andrews. "So wa' do we do?"

"We need to do the right thing, get back into the fight. If we press them in groups, we can knock them down, one at a time. We attack them, together, and we'll prove them mortal," said Hawker.

Andrews sat back, stretched his legs again, comfortable around Hawker. "Then we need t' make Wilkinson the last t' die like that. The men need t' know it can be done. 'Tis a show, really, a show for the men. We'll get the men there an' then we'll fight 'em. But, for now we need t' prove the bloody DeHavillands are na' the enemy."

Hawker thought for a moment, trying to be sure he understood Andrews, and decided he got the gist of it.

"Very good, Andrews, I knew we could agree on this," said Hawker. "Have the men assembled?"

"Yessir, they should be waitin'."

Andrews rose and opened the door for Hawker, then followed him out to the parade ground. The squadrons' pilots came to attention when Hawker approached, and stood until Andrews, the senior flight leader, put them at ease.

A DH-2 was on the field, with two ground crew standing by. The prow of the pugnacious little English fighter stuck up in the air like the chin of a boxer.

"Gentlemen, please come closer," said Hawker. He motioned the men toward the aeroplane.

"I won't sugar coat this. These engines are dreadful. It's simply a reality," Hawker said flatly.

The assembled pilots stood silently, listening intently as Hawker continued. "It's clear, if the engine fails over Hunland, then you must use your altitude to glide back to Allied territory. Maintain orientation, and think about the glide path back to our lines, do this instinctively. All we can do, other than recover and survive, is maintain the engines well."

A short pilot with bowlegs and a top knot of red hair drew his cap. He raised his hand. "Sir, what about the damned thing's spinning? Two DH-2s lost to spins in one month, sir." His question was open, innocent, not accusing

"Yes, Lieutenant Knight, excellent question, we'll focus there. Recovery from a spin is something you all will practice. You all will be proficient at it. It is an acquired skill, and you must have it." Hawker ran his eyes over the men. A thick-armed Welshman named Cowan looked away and coughed too loudly, exaggerating the sound.

"Cowan, did you have a question for me?"

"Sir, no, sir," growled Cowan.

Hawker bored holes in Cowan with his eyes. Cowan looked away.

"Very well. First of all, do not stall this thing, not unless you intend to. Despite reports to the contrary, the DH-2 stalls gently and will give you signs to let you know that a stall is coming. Push through it, keep the nose down, accelerate, avoid the stall, and you won't have to worry about the spin. For god's sake, do not jab the rudder bar if you need to turn at low altitude. If you do, I'll write a pleasant letter to your mother and explain how you died being an ass."

The men laughed nervously. Cowan's face was an impassive mask as he listened. Hawker climbed up the ladder and into the cockpit. He shouted back, "I'll demonstrate. Watch carefully."

One of the ground crew spun the propeller, and Hawker took off into the wind, climbing straight and steep. He continued climbing to the west, until the aeroplane dwindled to a dot in the sky. The pilots watched as Hawker turned back over the field, circled into the wind and pulled the aeroplane's nose up. Far above them, the little DH-2 tipped over on one wing and began to spin, circling downward. The men looked upward with hands shading their eyes and watched the little aeroplane gyrate overhead, collectively holding their breath.

Andrews moved to the back of the crowd of men, where no one could see him. He couldn't bear to look, dreading the sight of Hawker spinning into the ground in another flaming heap.

Hawker spun lower and lower, the spin tightening as he came down, everyone tense and watching the spiral. At a few hundred feet, the spin began to open, broadening into a wider circle, and, suddenly, the aeroplane flew out, straight and level. The pilots let out an audible sigh. Andrews took that as a sign that it was over and then turned and looked. He applauded.

Cowan spoke, "Well, you'll not do that while you're on fire, mate."

Andrews responded, "That'll be enough Cowan. Bloody bad that Wilkinson burned."

"He was my friend, too, Cowan," said Knight.

Hawker flew past the men, a few feet over the ground. He waved and then he turned and circled upward, soaring up to several thousand feet in wide arcs. The men stood and watched. Hawker flung the aeroplane's nose up and then ruddered over, starting another, even more violent spin. Andrews looked away again, and took a step backward, not able to watch, not wanting the men to watch.

Hawker spun down, lower and lower, until it appeared he would strike the ground directly in front of them. With a harsh, 'brap-brap-brap' sound, Hawker began blipping the ignition on the little rotary, lowering its power. The DH-2 popped out of the spin, with just feet to spare before slamming into the earth.

With that, the display was over and Hawker landed. He taxied the aeroplane to the men and killed the engine. The men gathered around Hawker to shake his hand and ask questions.

After a few minutes, Andrews stepped forward and dismissed the men, and then stood close to Hawker. "Sir, was that ne'cessary? Once't ha' been enough." Andrews' voice cracked with strain.

Hawker stepped back from Mitchell. He took a few steps away from the ground crew handling the aeroplane and lowered his voice.

"Andrews, what do you mean?" asked Hawker.

"The second spin, was i' needed?" said Andrews. "If you'd hi' the ground, we'd been months building any confidence in the men, if ever. An'a holder of the Victoria Cross would be dead." Andrews' voice quavered, anger or fear seeping in, though it was unclear which.

"Andrews, I respect you, I understand your concern. But, be assured, the second was more important than the first. The first could have been a fluke, the second couldn't have been. The men are confident now," said Hawker.

"Well, sir, than' God for that then." Andrews didn't sound very convinced.

Hawker sighed. "Sometimes, Andrews, one must take risks. Without risk there can be no breakthroughs, no ... moments." Hawker wanted Andrews to agree, to understand.

Andrews frowned and stiffened.

Hawker raised his voice, "I will not ask the men to take risks that I will not take."

"Sir, beggin' pardon, sir, but, that may be the death of you," said Andrews.

~~~

No. 24 Squadron's aeroplanes were scattered over the plains above the cliffs of Dover, tied down against the wind, waiting for a gale to subside so they could cross the Channel. The wind howled against the little aeroplanes, rocking them in place, threatening to lift them against their ropes and hurl them over the cliff.

Hawker watched the aeroplanes bucking in the wind, knowing that if the wind damaged them, they might never cross the Channel. Thought: *Is it always so windy here?*

He tied the tent flaps shut and sat down; Andrews and Hawker's adjutant, Mitchell, were already seated, quiet, listening, waiting for the wind to break so that they could fly.

"Gentlemen, I won't be crossing with you," said Hawker.

Andrews and Mitchell stared as Hawker as though he had just babbled.

"I said, I won't be crossing with you," he repeated louder.

Mitchell looked at Andrews, then back to Hawker. "Sir, whatever do you mean?"

Hawker suddenly understood Mitchell's reaction. "Oh no, I just won't be flying with you. I am ordered to travel by boat, I'll see you off, but I won't be flying."

Mitchell smiled. "So, you're ordered not to fly? What's that about?"

"Well, I'm also ordered not to fly once we reach the continent, at least, not to cross the lines." Hawker looked away, his face clouded and troubled. "I may as well be grounded."

"It's only reasonable sir. You're a squadron commander, and with the Victoria Cross, you've done your duty, and ... well ... you're more valuable in command." Mitchell's voice relaxed. "Sir, does command know about your spin *demonstrations* in the DH-2s?"

"I don't know, I suspect so. You wouldn't know anything about that, would you, Mitchell?" asked Hawker.

"No, sir. Andrews, would you know anything about that?" asked Mitchell.

Andrews shook his head. "Nay."

Hawker stood and walked back to the tent flaps and peered outside. "No, I don't suppose you would. Bear in mind, I won't ever ask a man to do something I won't. You understand that, don't you, Mitchell? Andrews?"

Mitchell looked at Andrews again, who nodded.

"Yes, sir, I understand," Mitchell said at last.

"And, if the men are at risk, it's my duty to reduce that risk, you understand?" asked Hawker.

"Yes, sir," said Mitchell.

"And you, Andrews, do you understand?" asked Hawker.

Andrews didn't react. When Hawker turned to face him, he agreed, silently nodding his head.

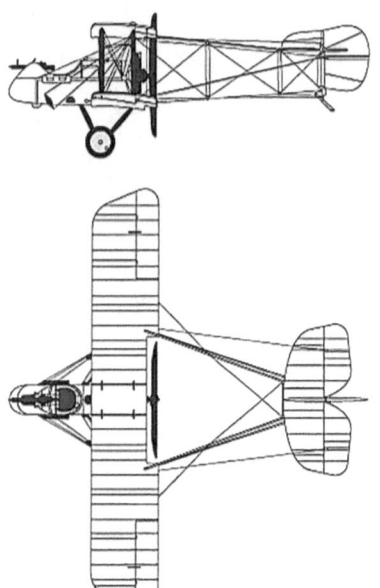

Airco DH-2

Entered Service: February 1916
Engine: Gnôme Monosoupape, 9 cylinder, air
 cooled rotary, 100 hp
Wing Span: 28 ft 3 in (8.61 m)
Length: 25 ft 2½ in (7.68 m)
Height: 9 ft 6½ in (2.91 m)
Gross Weight: 1,441 lb (653.6 kg)
Max Speed: 93 mph (150 km/h)
Ceiling: 14,000 ft (4,267 m)

Chapter Thirty-Four

April 30, 1916
Metz Aerodrome, France

The air was heavy with clouds and the sky, unable to bear the weight, released its hold on them and rain fell to the ground, in sheets. The windows of the flyers' casino rattled from the thunder and streams of water seeped around the panes. Gusts of wet, bitter wind blew past the edges of the thin doors.

The German flyers stirred anxiously inside, unable to fly.

Pilots circulated back and forth from a table at the far end of the room to a ring of old sofas and a dining table made of boards, leaving and returning to a never-ending game of Skat. Every few minutes, some would gather by the windows in twos or threes, and look out at the storm clouds, eager to be the first to announce a hole in the clouds, to spot blue sky. The weather held them in check without an outlet for the tension.

Some flyers braved the rain, running across the field to the hangar tents, spending their time during the storm seeing to their aeroplanes. They would make adjustments, modifications, tuning and re-tuning, trying to replace chance with a finely-honed nuance, a slight edge that might separate them from the dead when the moment came. For the most part, they played at it, not really sure what they were doing. The mechanics, in the meantime, hovered nearby, watching, hoping that they wouldn't have to undo the actions of the restless pilots.

Richthofen sat back in a soft leather chair in the pilot's casino, sipping hot coffee with schnapps and smoking one of Menzke's hand rolled cigarettes. Boelcke was perched on a stiff wooden chair across from him;

his arms folded across its back. Count Holck sat with them, swirling a large brandy glass that never seemed to empty. Four other flyers had gathered around them, all drinking coffee and smoking. The sound of the rain on the roof was a soft rumble overhead.

"Tell me about it again," said Boelcke.

Richthofen looked up and felt the same odd sense of pride and shame. He began to say 'no', to let the matter lie. "Is it necessary? I mean no disrespect, but the matter is sealed, let's move on." He paused and added, "This is the second time this has happened."

"So it really wasn't your *first*, then?" said Boelcke. The men around them laughed. Richthofen scowled.

"It's fine Richthofen, we know. It happens a great deal, it's the rules, we all know that, just don't let yourself get down about it. So what happened the 'real' first time?" asked Boelcke.

Richthofen straightened himself up in the chair, his left hand clenching and unclenching. He sat his coffee cup down and folded his hands across his lap. Drawing deeply on his cigarette and exhaling slowly, he let the cloud of smoke hover in the center of the assembled men. *Am I missing something, is he baiting me?*

Studying the *Pour le Mérite* hanging around Boelcke's neck, he felt a lump gather in his throat at the sight of the gold cross, painted with blue enamel, and his hand moved to his throat as though he could feel it there. He lowered his hand quickly, embarrassed at his own envy.

Boelcke stared back at Richthofen, patient. Richthofen began.

"I was flying observer with Paul Osterroht in October, before I had gone to Döberitz to go to flight school," said Richthofen. "We were flying behind the English lines and we saw a French two-seater, a Farman."

Richthofen smiled now, remembering the fight.

"I really should enjoy the fight more, shouldn't I, Boelcke?" he asked.

"Of course, Richthofen. We all should." Boelcke glanced away, at the window, at the dark afternoon. Boelcke felt the frustration inside him rising and choked the sensation down. "Go on, finish the story."

Richthofen smiled again, sat up straighter, and snuffed out his cigarette. "He wasn't paying attention at all. Perhaps he just didn't expect to see a German aeroplane so far behind his lines."

"That's a fair guess, I'd say, but that's no excuse to be lax. What happened then?"

"Osterroht did a masterful job of flying, calm and steady, we moved up alongside the Frenchman, and a little below. I don't know how the observer didn't see us, he had his head down over the side of the Farman, just didn't ever glance up. The pilot was staring straight ahead, and only occasionally would glance down into the cockpit. We flew steady, and I aimed the machine gun true, aiming at the engine, so I could adjust after I got a sense for the deflection and not waste bullets."

"Smart, and then you shot him down?" asked a young Feldwebel.

Richthofen glanced up and glared at the man, who grew quiet. "Well, I aimed fine at the engine, and then I pulled the trigger, and nothing happened. Jammed on the first round. Osterroht kept turning his head round, boring holes in me with his eyes. So, I cleared it, while watching the Farman the whole time. And, don't you know, they still didn't see us! Amazing thing really ..." He leaned forward in his chair; his elbows perched on the arms and lit another cigarette.

"That was just before we met, Boelcke," said Richthofen.

"Yes, I remember," said Boelcke. He glanced up again at the door and then at the clock standing against the wall. "Finish your story, Manfred."

"Where was I?" Richthofen sipped his coffee. "Oh, the machine gun jammed and the Farman flew on. Well, I cleared the jam, and then reloaded, and put a full belt on the gun. I aimed at the Frenchman's engine, and pulled the trigger. I had to look up to watch where the rounds hit the Farman, nearly at the observer, so I aimed further ahead of the engine, and watched the rounds jump forward until it seemed I was hitting the pilot. Then I ran out of ammunition, just like that. One hundred rounds." Richthofen snapped his fingers.

"So, it fell, then?" asked Holck.

"No, strangely, it flew on. The pilot actually looked at us, and you could see his mouth open in surprise ... like this." Richthofen threw up his arms, and hung his mouth open, his cigarette waving in the air. The men laughed. "And then, he turned, and descended, and his turn became a spin. Osterroht just kept flying. I had to knock him on the head to get him to look ... and the Frenchie hit in a crater behind the lines and dust flew up." Richthofen looked around and drew on his cigarette. "And that was my first time."

The men grew quiet, voyeuristically satisfied. They sipped their drinks, looking up at the windows to watch the rain pelt down.

"Let me tell you about my first time," said Holck, leaning forward in his chair. He twitched his long aquiline nose as he spoke. Holck was tall in his chair, wearing his perpetual clean riding clothes. Holck tipped his brandy glass up and took a patrician sip.

Boelcke turned his chair, focusing his attention on Holck.

"Richthofen's fellow vagrant from Frietag ... you speak? Fly into any firestorms lately?" Boelcke clapped a hand down on Holck's leg.

Holck mustered a tight grin, and shallow laughter moved through the little knot of men. Boelcke laughed and managed, as always, to make the sound warm and friendly; it was his gift.

"Well ... I was by myself ... and I pulled up over the top ... and she didn't seem to know what was coming ... and I shot her down." Holck waved his hands like aeroplanes, and then slapped them together. The men stared at him, confusion on their faces. "But, no matter, I married her, so all is well," Holck added.

Boelcke, nonplussed, laughed. Then the men joined him.

"So, you married your first, did you Holck? Charming thing that," said Boelcke, friendly.

"Tell me, Holck, any children?" he asked.

Holck looked down at his brandy, swirled it in the glass. He looked up and smiled back at Boelcke, a little pride crossing his face. "One, a boy, and one more on the way." He reached into his shirt pocket and drew out a photo. In it he sat, his wife standing next to him, a small boy on his knee.

Boelcke took it, held it up to the light. "Beautiful family, Holck. A fine family." He passed the photo along before glancing at the door again.

Boelcke turned to Richthofen, who had gone pale.

Richthofen stammered, his eyes boring holes in Holck. "You're married, and have children? What on earth are you doing here? All this time and you never thought to tell me?"

The room hushed, all eyes on Holck. Boelcke's eyes moved between the two men, trying to judge Richthofen's anger.

"Were you watching?" asked Boelcke. His voice changed, subtlety, lower and calmly intense. The men stared at him now.

"What?" asked Richthofen. He shook his head in disbelief. "What are you talking about?"

"The Farman, when you were doing all this aiming, and clearing your machine gun, and reloading, and shooting him up and watching him fall. Did you look around, even once? To see if someone was sneaking up on *you*?" Boelcke reached to his throat and put his thumb behind his *Pour le Mérite* and his fingers over the front, as though hiding it.

The color drained from Richthofen's face, leaving him pale. He sat back in the chair.

"Next time, you might look around, at least a little," said Boelcke. A small smile crossed his face, and then disappeared.

Someone handed the photo back to Holck.

"So, what was it yesterday, Richthofen?" asked Boelcke.

"Nieuport, single seat. He saw me," Richthofen said. He spoke in tight, cropped phrases now, his mind on a distant place, behind the French lines, watching the Farman fall out of the sky. He couldn't remember if he'd looked around, and not being able to remember made his skin crawl.

"And what happened?"

"He ran, turned his back. He was working at his machine gun and standing up; he must have been flying with his knees. I was flying the *Walfisch* with the British Lewis that I rigged on it. And I flew close behind him, very close. I fired the Lewis in short bursts."

Richthofen shook his head slightly, bringing himself back to the moment. He raised his hands, one behind the other, flat, fingers pointed the same direction, one hand following the other.

"Then, he reared up, like this." The hand in front tilted upward. "And then he fell away, and into a spin. The Allied planes seem to spin without any effort, all the time. Well, I thought he was faking, but he wasn't, unless he faked falling into the forest behind Fort Douaumont. But, I don't think he feigned that. Didn't count, though, it was behind the lines. No witnesses."

Menzke came in, shaking off the rain. He held a thin cardboard folder. He looked around, spotted Richthofen, strode over and pulled himself to attention.

Richthofen waved a salute to Menzke. "At ease, Menzke. What is it?" asked Richthofen.

Menzke beamed, his smile occupying his entire face, his pleasure evident in being in the company of Richthofen and Boelcke. "Leutnant. You are mentioned by command in Fifth Army dispatches. Well, at least your victory was." He reached out and handed the folder over to Richthofen, who opened it and read quickly. Richthofen handed the folder to Boelcke.

"Your victory belongs to the Fatherland now, Richthofen, officially," said Boelcke. He smiled and handed the folder to Menzke without reading it.

Richthofen looked at Boelcke, a question evident on his face.

"It's typical: the victory is still recorded, but, it just isn't added to your tally. Rules, again, Richthofen," said Boelcke.

The sound of the rain slackened, and stopped. Boelcke looked toward the window and saw blue in the sky over the field.

"Time to fly, gentlemen," said Boelcke, standing.

Chapter Thirty-Five

May 1, 1916
East of Verdun, France

The thick drenching sky became a dome of spotty clouds overnight. The war resumed. French artillery roiled the ground near-constantly now, crashing in waves over the German lines on the east bank of the river Meuse. To the east of the French fortress city of Verdun and south along the river, the German artillery struck back. A constant cloud of dust covered the ground on dry days, but, thanks to the rain, the artillery impacts erupted upward in muddy spouts.

Richthofen dreaded the next week; he knew that the rain would soak the rotting corpses around Verdun, and then the sun would ripen them, and the wind would blow the stench down onto Metz. On particularly bad days, he could taste the death in the air. He tried not to think of how bad it might be for the men in the midst of the corruption, in their holes in the ground.

He flew the *Walfisch* to the east of the city, over the Meuse, flying south, and three kilometers high in the sky. Richthofen and his observer, a young Hannoverian soldier named Erben, were looking for a fight. They sought the fortunate opportunity of wind, altitude and position that would let them close on a potential victim and remain safe from direct attack. Richthofen ran the ideas through his mind, seeking to know how to hunt here, in the air. High was good, but not too high or he couldn't close the distance during his diving descent. Upwind was important, or he would struggle against the headwind as he tried to close, making a fight possible on his opponent's terms, for, if he wasn't upwind, they were. The resemblance to fighting sailing ships wasn't lost on him. Richthofen was a privateer; unfettered, looking to take a prize, free to maneuver in three dimensions.

The *Walfisch*, or "Whale," had the shape of its namesake, deep through the belly, with a round and smooth fuselage of molded plywood. Attached directly to the fuselage, the upper wing left no gap to see down and forward. With the pilot perched on the top of the fuselage, behind the upper wing, practically nothing below the pilot and observer was visible without hanging far out over the side of the fuselage. Thus, from below, they were vulnerable. But the *Walfisch*, with twice the power of the Eindekkers, could be fast, particularly with the wind behind it, fast enough that the French needed to dive to catch it. So, most of the French attacks came from above, unless he was slowed by winds. Then they were in a truly lumbering whale, or perhaps a flounder, slow, with eyes only able to look up. Unfortunately, today, they were a flounder, bucking the wind from the west, fighting to climb, up where they could put the wind back behind them and have a chance to cut through the French aeroplanes that were always circling Verdun.

Below and in front of them, a patchy layer of clouds covered the city. Between the gaps in the clouds, a brilliant sun bore through in rays to the ground. The effect was spectacular and unearthly to Richthofen. As they were high enough to no longer smell the stinking mud and corpses or hear the artillery, the view was untarnished.

To the west, a French Caudron bomber lumbered, heading south. The outline of the aeroplane was distinctive, even at a distance, with its long tail booms and enormous rudders. The Caudron was big and bristled with machine guns. Two more Caudrons were above and behind it, flying downwind toward the east. From the north an Eindekker appeared, in a shallow dive, gaining speed toward the lower Caudron, closing the gap between the two craft.

Richthofen could see the aeroplanes coming together in his mind, and he knew the intersection of the Eindekker and three Caudrons was inevitable. He worked his jaw muscles in tension, watching the scene unfold. It was apparent the French weren't just hunting, they were playing chess. Chess with blood and bullets, through altitude and speed: a game played for lives.

The lower aeroplanes, the Caudron and the Eindekker, were almost close enough to fire at each other, and Richthofen knew that bullets would be flying soon. His first instinct was to think of Boelcke, so brave and capable, taking a calculated risk, knowing how much time he might have to fire and then dive away before the pair of Caudrons above could close and join the battle.

Then, he felt a shudder of fear as he watched the lower Caudron turn east, its profile changing in space, a brilliant move, allowing the higher pair of Caudrons to converge more quickly and box the Eindekker in from above. The pilot of the Eindekker continued his approach, adjusting his path only slightly to gain on the lower Caudron.

Richthofen swung his head around, scanned the sky quickly in all directions, and began a shallow dive to the west to join the fight. He flew for the lower French aeroplane, certain that this was where the fighting would begin. The west wind checked the *Walfisch's* approach, and slowed them, leaving the *Walfisch* vainly trying to close and Richthofen stuck watching in frustration. As one, the higher two French aircraft, turned and dove, boxing the Eindekker in.

The shudder of fear turned to coldness at the sight before him. The French were springing a trap on a comrade, and he was helpless to intervene. He pushed the stick forward slightly, to steepen his dive and close more quickly, and he tugged vainly at the throttle, trying to add a little more fuel to the engine, to gain a little more power, anything to increase the odds that he got there in time. The coldness turned to an ache in his chest, a sense of grieving already begun, knowing there was nothing he could do.

Richthofen sat back in his seat, resigned, for the die was cast.

Trails of grey gun smoke streamed from behind all four aircraft as they fired at one another.

The pilot of the Eindekker rolled his aeroplane, and then leveled, seeming to struggle with controlling it, and then the nose rose. The aeroplane stalled and fell away into the worst kind of spin: inverted and flat.

Smart, thought Richthofen, wishfully, deluding himself, *leaving the battle before it gets the better of you.* The aeroplane began to flutter, wobbling back and forth in the air like a leaf falling from a tree. Then he knew. The Eindekker pilot wasn't faking, wasn't feigning. *Only a dead man allowed an aeroplane to tumble like that.*

Richthofen was closing on the three French aeroplanes now, diving toward them, and still fighting the west wind. He felt anger and fear in a fresh wave now. He was spooked, and knew that to throw himself into the middle of the Caudrons would accomplish nothing. He watched as the three French aeroplanes, triumphant, joined together in a formation and continued south. Richthofen could imagine them looking up at him in glee, urging him into a fight he couldn't win.

Defeated before he could even begin, he turned the *Walfisch* back to the east, and tipped the nose down, separated quickly from the Caudrons, and flew back in the direction of Metz. Fury made his hands shake.

Richthofen landed at Metz and climbed down quickly from the cockpit. He sprinted across the field to the operations center and stood in front of the flight board. He ran his hand down the left side of the board, chalked himself back in, marking down that he had landed. In an afterthought, he remembered his observer, Erben, and logged his name, too. Then he ran his hand down further, across the other units on the base.

There: The only Eindekker airborne. His hand slid across the row to the pilot's name. *Not Boelcke, no, not Boelcke.*

Holck.

Richthofen's blood turned to ice, his vision narrowed and hot bile rose in his throat. Holck would never spin away, and not upside down, he would stay and fight. To turn his back, to use trickery, would never even occur to him.

"DAMN HIM!" Richthofen shouted into the room.

The staff looked up from their desks, and the duty officer put down his paperwork and walked over to Richthofen. He put a hand on Richthofen's shoulder. "Quiet, Leutnant. What is the problem?"

Richthofen turned, his pale blue eyes gone dark, like a stormy sky at dusk. "Holck, that bastard Holck. I just watched him die."

The operations officer took Richthofen's arm. "Get a grip on yourself, Richthofen."

"Selfish son of a bitch. He has a family, did you know that? He has a son and a new baby coming! Damn him." Richthofen wrenched his arm away, and then tugged his coat down tight with both hands, pulling down at the bottom seam. He put a thumb and a finger at the inside corners of his eyes and tipped his head down for a moment. When he looked up, his eyes were wet and blue again.

"My apologies, Oberleutnant. I wish to report that an Eindekker appears to have been shot down over Verdun."

The duty officer glared at Richthofen.

Richthofen straightened himself, drawing his shoulders up.

"I'm sure it was a fine death, Richthofen. Let me get you the proper paperwork to make the report." The officer turned and walked to his desk. He rummaged through a drawer and pulled out a form, then picked up a pencil.

"A fine death," repeated Richthofen, "Yes. A fine death." He straightened his cap and drew himself upright, his chin lifted and eyes clear.

When the duty office looked up, Richthofen was gone.

Chapter Thirty-Six

May 15, 1916
Metz Aerodrome, France

The German mechanics pulled the engine from Boelcke's Eindekker and put the tail up on blocks, leaving the aeroplane looking forlorn and broken. Boelcke stood behind the men as they took the engine apart, his hands on his hips, silently watching them. The afternoon became a cool evening, and he took off his jacket and replaced it with his bulky flying sweater. He turned and walked around the aeroplane, returned to the bench, sat, then stood and took another impatient circle.

Richthofen opened the door of the hangar, and peered inside. "Leutnant Boelcke, may I speak with you?"

Boelcke looked up and made a sound like a grunt, and waved Richthofen through the door. There were deep lines around Boelcke's eyes that gave Richthofen a sense of unease. "What is it, Richthofen?" he asked.

"Leutnant Reimann is overdue from the afternoon flight," Richthofen said.

"Another," said Boelcke, his voice flat.

Boelcke looked up and the lines around his eyes softened. "Keep at it, boys," he said to the mechanics. He turned to Richthofen, then led him to the front of the Eindekker. The bare engine mounts looked skeletal and dead to Richthofen.

"How long?" asked Boelcke.

"An hour and half," answered Richthofen.

"I see. What's he flying?"

"Our Eindekker, he's flying afternoons, I fly mornings," said Richthofen.

"We've been sharing the aeroplane. There are so few, you know."

"Your commander is aware that he is overdue?" asked Boelcke.

"Yes, of course," replied Richthofen.

"Then why are you here?" asked Boelcke.

Richthofen reached out, put his hand around the rod for the gear that led up to the machine gun. He pushed it up and down lightly, watching it move in response.

"I need to speak with you. To understand what is happening. For the past two months, it seems that nothing is changing, that we're simply throwing men out one at time into situations where we simply let them ... *vanish*. It feels as though something is shifting, that we have reached a turning point, but we're still waiting for something," said Richthofen.

Boelcke looked at Richthofen in the fading light, then turned and stepped outside into the cool spring air. Richthofen trailed after him.

"Richthofen, yes, things are changing, badly. Verdun is carnage embodied." He waved his hand to the west. The death smell was weak now, the west wind having died down; but the odor, like a nightmare, lingered in the mind long after you wished to forget it.

"The French are forming escadrilles, squadrons, formations of aircraft, all dedicated as air fighters. You may have seen them. Many men have seen them and not seen anything again. Their Nieuports are as good as or better than our Fokkers are. Faster, more nimble. And, even worse, the French are growing confident and aggressive."

Boelcke's eyes flashed in the light of the setting sun.

"We are feeding them our Eindekkers and our men, one at time. That's where our men are going," Boelcke said.

"That is ridiculous, Boelcke. What are we going to do about it, keep feeding them pilots?" said Richthofen. "We should do as they do, concentrate our planes."

"It's not that simple, Richthofen, our fighters are being outclassed. We don't see it, because the men who need to see it aren't out there," Boelcke said. Boelcke's expression was stiff and the sunlight etched lines onto his young face. "These are state secrets. Your commander still has his orders, and we all must obey our orders, you understand."

"Of course, Herr Boelcke, of course," said Richthofen.

Boelcke led Richthofen to a bench in front of the hangar and sat down. Richthofen joined him. Boelcke stretched his back and then leaned forward, resting his elbows on his knees. He felt a wheeze building and swallowed to choke it down.

"So, what must we do?" asked Richthofen.

"Better aeroplanes are coming, Richthofen. These damn Eindekkers will be the end of us. Do you know that we are losing a quarter of our victories to failures of the machine gun synchronizers? I've shot myself down twice when they failed. Twice! Immelmann has too. You've probably heard the stories, but this can't go on. You were right to put the machine gun on your *Walfisch* over the propeller, take the synchronizer problem out of the equation." Boelcke wrung his hands, and then clenched them together; he inhaled deeply to calm his breathing.

Boelcke continued, "But, it's more than that. There needs to be a fundamental change in the way we fly, a shift in thought and thinking that changes the way we do this, or we'll keep throwing pebbles at the wall. Do you know that at Verdun they're fighting over a single ridge that is no more than two hundred meters high, and two kilometers long? Hundreds of thousands of men, tens of thousands of casualties, are fighting over a ridge that one farmer could plow and plant in a week."

Richthofen leaned back, pretending to watch the sunset. He was looking across the sky for a single dot, a returning plane.

"I have to apologize, Richthofen. You shouldn't have flown, become a fighter," said Boelcke.

Richthofen looked at Boelcke with amazement, his eyes moving over Boelcke's face, trying to discern the jest.

"You must be joking, Leutnant," said Richthofen.

"No, I'm not. Now is not the time to fly fighters. Not Eindekkers. Not now, it's too late," said Boelcke.

Richthofen looked back to the west, to the direction Reimann had gone. The sky stayed empty, and the sunlight filtered from behind the trees, the heavens an eerie crimson over the battlefield of Verdun. He didn't know why they weren't blue or yellow, having heard that the bloody skies were from the trenches: someone's superstition, perhaps, the color of hell. Even Menzke had asked if it was the underworld erupting from below. *Perhaps it is,* thought Richthofen. *The gates opening up to claim the dead, casting such a grim light into the world.*

"They're just beginning to hunt us, but it will grow far worse," said Boelcke, bringing Richthofen back from his thoughts. "The English have their pushers, rear engines, their Vickers-types. You've seen pictures I'm sure. They look like bathtubs between wings, with a machine gun in front, either a gunner or the pilot shooting the thing. They're not that good, but good enough. Better than the Eindekkers. It puts pressure on us."

Richthofen felt himself sweating in the chilly air, his stomach tight.

Boelcke was lecturing now, driving the point home. "And they've followed the French, they've assembled squadrons around their fighters. They're bringing them over from England *en masse.* Fortunately, we captured one of their pushers when it landed on our side after crossing the Channel. But, they are coming, and they will kill more of us. They may take control of the sky."

"Surely, you're being dramatic, Leutnant. It won't happen like that ..." said Richthofen, his voice trailing off, uncertainty at his own words creeping in.

"It already is happening. We can't panic of course, we must act deliberately. But our own command doesn't see it yet. They're not convinced. Something dreadful must happen before they'll commit to what needs to be done. But you're safer where you're going," Boelcke said. The last of the sunlight had faded into twilight now, the crimson sky becoming pink.

Richthofen began to ask what Boelcke meant, but an orderly interrupted their conversation, throwing a salute. "Leutnant Richthofen. I understand you requested a report as soon as we received it. Infantry has reported that an Eindekker fell behind Mort Homme."

Richthofen looked up, his face gone grey in the pale light. "Very well. Thank you. Dismissed."

Boelcke sat silent for a moment, then said, "You're headed for the east again, your orders are coming in the next few days. It's probably best."

"Best? How can it be for the best?" said Richthofen, his voice rising.

"Manfred ..." Boelcke said the single name, stopping his protest.

Richthofen looked back at the sunset, and stood up. "I need to stretch my legs, I feel restless."

Boelcke rose and said, "Very well, let's walk."

Together, the two men strode across the aerodrome. "Richthofen, things will change, new aeroplanes are coming, biplanes with more power and maneuverability and synchronized machine guns," said Boelcke.

"Leutnant, I must ask, if I may..." said Richthofen.

Boelcke looked back at Richthofen, and then he increased his pace. "Come, Richthofen, we need to use some energy. Please, feel free to ask anything."

"Boelcke, I don't feel that I'm the best pilot, and this has been a difficult few months of learning to fly. Perhaps you're right, not just that I shouldn't be a fighter, but that I shouldn't be flying," said Richthofen.

"Nonsense," said Boelcke. "Look at the best pilots from before the war, the acrobats, Pégoud, Garros, Bleriot. They're all dead or grounded."

"But Boelcke, what sets a great pilot apart, if not the skill?" said Richthofen.

Boelcke ignored the question.

"I'm glad you're here, Richthofen, and not out there in your head worrying about Reimann. Or Holck. It's too late for that. I want you to know that. You need to be able to put it aside, let the grief come at a time when it doesn't cost you everything," said Boelcke.

"I try not to let it come when I fly," said Richthofen.

They grew quiet, and a cool sorrow hung in the air like a spider web, clinging and invisible. Grief was a sign of weakness, a sign that other thoughts could creep in, that their duty wasn't all-consuming. It was a crack in the façade. Both men understood this.

"For me, it comes when I'm alone," said Boelcke. "So, I'd rather not be."

The thought, the idea, settled on them now, in the grey light, and they let the moment play out.

"It was difficult, flying over Holck's funeral," said Richthofen.

"It was important to everyone, you know that," said Boelcke.

"Yes, a strange thing, that, using the aeroplanes to symbolize something

... I don't know what though ..." said Richthofen.

"Change, I suppose. That we will carry on, also ..." Boelcke thought for a moment, then, "Consistency, reflexes, *trained* reflexes, doing the right thing without thinking about it."

Richthofen was confused, and he looked over at Boelcke, and tried to fathom where the conversation had gone.

Boelcke continued, answering the question that he had ignored. "I don't know what makes a pilot *and* a fighter. But that may be the most important part of adapting. We have to figure out what works and show people, train them, or at least keep them alive long enough to let them figure it out for themselves. New aeroplanes, new tactics, new units, none of that matters if we don't know how to shape someone, how to give them a chance to stay alive and succeed. That may be the magic of the thing, Richthofen. Perhaps there is something inside a man that you can't train, can't teach, and can't even identify. Perhaps there is the hand of God at work, or perhaps luck is a real thing, or there is something deep in the mind that guides you, that shapes who you are, that you never realize is there..."

Richthofen let the words remain for a moment, and tried to form an answer, but couldn't.

"So, Richthofen who do you think you are?" asked Boelcke.

Richthofen hesitated to answer, wondering if Boelcke was going to make a fool of him. He took a deep breath and looked up at the last of the light in the west, knowing now not to look for the returning Fokker. He wondered if he was more anxious for the loss of the aeroplane than for Reimann. That such a thought crossed his mind at all left him feeling like a bit of a bastard.

"Before the war, I was a horseman, a terrible student, a ..." Richthofen hesitated. " ... hunter," he finished, looking away, not letting Boelcke catch his gaze. The admission made him feel childish, ridiculous. He knew now that fighting for your life wasn't hunting, not at all. "And you, Boelcke, who were you?"

"The son of a teacher, a wanderer, and a mountain climber," said Boelcke. The speed of the answer startled Richthofen and it made the revelation sound rehearsed. Boelcke could see Richthofen's displeasure on his face.

"I think about it a lot," said Boelcke in reply to the unasked question.

Richthofen's face flushed, and he felt anger rise. He felt toyed with, manipulated. How many men had Boelcke had this conversation with, exactly? He felt patronized. It was a strange, uncomfortable sensation, for he'd never thought that he could be angry with Boelcke.

"And now, I'm a dedicated soldier, a flyer, and a killer of men," said Boelcke. He laughed. "And you, Richthofen, are the first, have almost become the second, and wish to become the third, am I right?"

"Yes, I suppose so," said Richthofen, his anger fading.

"Then you will have to figure how to take the pieces of who you are and rearrange them into the thing that you wish to become," said Boelcke. "And not get killed doing it."

Chapter Thirty-Seven

June 2, 1916
Schwerin, Germany

The aeroplanes circling Fokker's aerodrome marked the way for Geertz. In the sky over the buildings, he saw aeroplanes flying in and out of Fokker's field. Birds, song thrushes and blackcaps, sang in the spring air, but the sound was drowned out by one aeroplane after another passing over Geertz. He didn't mind.

He strolled south from the Schwerin train station through the grey brick buildings of the city, enjoying stretching his legs. He began to hum to himself. The orbiting aeroplanes reminded Geertz of buzzards circling a carcass. The thought made him smile.

At last, Fokker brought to bay. The insolent little ... foreigner.

At the field, he let himself into the administration building, and made his way to Fokker's office.

"Hauptmann Geertz, here to see Herr Fokker," said Geertz.

Fokker's receptionist looked up in surprise and stood. "Hauptmann," she said, "we weren't expecting you."

"I understand. Please forgive the intrusion. I'll wait," said Geertz, smiling.

She looked at Geertz, amazed, never having seen Geertz so polite. "Just a moment, I believe he is out on the field, with the new aeroplane."

Geertz rose. "May I walk with you then?" he asked pleasantly.

"Yes, sir, of course," she said.

Geertz followed her as she led him out of the building and past a row of administrative buildings. They skirted the field where noisy aeroplanes with student pilots were either landing or taking off. She led him to a large hangar with the main door shut and the side door propped open to let a little air in. "He's in there, I'm sure," she said, pointing to the shed door.

"Thank you, Fraulein," said Geertz, tipping his uniform cap. "I'm sure I can find my way."

"I'll introduce you," she replied.

"No, no need, I'll see myself in."

She backed up, turned and walked quickly away, sensing a problem and not wanting to be part of it. She was sure that Geertz being polite was a bad sign.

Geertz opened the side door, let himself in, and removed his cap. In the middle of the shed, under a skylight, sat a biplane with parts and tools strewn around it. Fokker stood on the ground next to the machine, Kreutzer was in the cockpit and de Waal leaned against one wing. De Waal's little monkey perched on the end of the wing and looked toward Geertz. Geertz started as he noticed the little simian staring at him. The monkey bared its teeth, hissed and then leaned back on its haunches, tipping its head and fiercely glowering at Geertz.

Fokker was discussing something with Kreutzer. At Cuckoo's cry, they all turned and stopped their conversation.

"Good afternoon, gentlemen," said Geertz. "Forgive me for the interruption."

Fokker looked at Geertz, worry shading his face as his thoughts tumbled like a bird dying in flight. He tried to sweep away his apprehension with a broad smile. "No, Geertz, not at all, please, join us."

Fokker stepped toward Geertz and extended a hand in greeting. Geertz took it, shook it firmly and then stood close to the aeroplane, he greeted de Waal and Kreutzer.

"So, this is the newest? Excellent," said Geertz. "And a biplane, very good."

"Yes, this is it, our biplane, and we were just discussing test flights," said Fokker. He looked up at Kreutzer and Kreutzer looked away.

By instinct, Fokker began to sell. "We've adopted a standard wing from the Eindekkers, in order to optimize production. So you'll recognize the basic structure." Fokker ran a hand over the side of the aeroplane and then patted it affectionately.

"Has it flown, Herr Fokker?" asked Geertz.

"Oh, no, not yet, we're just making final plans for flights, but, soon, very soon." Fokker, still suspicious at Geertz's sudden appearance, paused. "Hauptman, surely you aren't here to see this aeroplane."

"No, Fokker, not entirely, there is a small matter that I need to discuss with you, privately," said Geertz. "It won't take but a few minutes. Nothing too painful, but something I wanted to chat about in person." Geertz smiled up at Kreutzer, as if to reassure him. "Carry on, gentlemen."

"Very well, Geertz, shall we take a walk then?" said Fokker.

"Oh yes, of course, no need to disrupt your men," said Geertz. Geertz made an awkward flourish with his hand toward Kreutzer as if to indicate he should proceed.

Fokker walked to the side of the shed and rolled open each of the doors. "We need to let some sunlight and fresh air in here anyway," said Fokker.

Fokker and Geertz strode out into bright day and walked down the edge of the field. Fokker's mind raced over and around thoughts, trying to imagine what Geertz was up to, why he could be here. *Is he here to close us down? Surely, he didn't think the Eindekkers could rule the air forever? They couldn't close us, they need us!* He took deep breaths to calm himself, and hoped that Geertz wouldn't notice his unease.

Fokker spoke, trying to get ahead of Geertz, to try to direct the conversation, to lead it where he wanted it to go. "Geertz, I've been meaning to thank you for the order for the AEG aircraft. It's a little unusual to build to another factory's design, but we'll certainly do our best. I'm afraid that it suggests that the AEGs are more important than our own designs, though. But ours are coming along nicely," said Fokker.

"Perhaps it does," said Geertz, quickly, cutting Fokker off. "Perhaps it does suggest that their designs are more important ... at this moment."

A training aeroplane passed by overhead, drowning out Geertz's words. They walked without speaking while the rumble of the aeroplane engine passed by and faded. Fokker kept his eyes up, watching; wanting to be anywhere else but here, while Geertz merely looked straight ahead.

"So, what is it you wish to discuss?" asked Fokker.

Geertz reached into his pocket, and handed a folded sheet of paper to Fokker. "I'm sure you're aware of this ..." he said.

Fokker stopped, took the paper and unfolded it. It was a personal letter, addressed to the Inspector of Idflieg, written by Boelcke. "Aaah, Boelcke's masterful memo. Condemning the E four. Yes, I'm aware of it. But, I have not read it." Fokker's temper flared and his voice shook as he spoke. "The end of my orders for twenty aircraft, yes, how could I not remember it? An unfair condemnation of my latest design. The E four is the best of the Eindekkers, more powerful, with a better rate of climb. For Herr Boelcke to condemn is beyond the pale. An injustice."

"I thought you would want to read it personally, Herr Fokker," said Geertz.

Fokker handed the paper back to Geertz, his anger getting the better of him.

"Thank you, Geertz, but the damage is done," said Fokker. Fokker scowled, then tried to force out a smile.

"Boelcke's memo was not the only basis for the cancellation. The three-gun, 160 horsepower Eindekker for Immelmann was not well received," said Geertz. He seemed to be enjoying himself. "Herr Immelmann nearly killed himself, if I understand the events correctly."

"Yes, but so did I ... nearly kill myself. At Essen," blurted out Fokker. "Doing what I was asked to do. The three-gun mount was not my idea." Fokker flushed and wished he could take back the words as he said them.

Geertz cocked his head to the side, implying a question. "Tell me, I don't think I know that part of the story," said Geertz.

"No matter, what is done is done, Geertz," said Fokker. The recollection of the accident flashed through Fokker's mind, a diminished memory, one he tried to forget. The synchronizer failing so spectacularly, all three guns out of sync. The only thing that had saved him was blowing off both blades of his propeller so quickly, before the engine could run out of balance and jump out of its mounts.

My God! The aeroplane had been a sound machine one moment, the next, a flying wreck! Three guns ... never my idea ... Immelmann's idea ... his fault ... not mine. Fokker shuddered and pushed the memory down once more.

"Is that all? You came just to show me Boelcke's memo?" said Fokker, impatient.

"Fokker, the Eindekkers are being beaten. We know this. We captured a new aeroplane, an English aeroplane, a single seat Vickers type. We have flown it and it flies better than your Eindekker. The English and French have other ... fighters ... that are better. We didn't ask for a new biplane on a whim," said Geertz. His voice grew louder but stayed even, calm. Fokker imagined he had practiced the speech.

"Oh, I see. The disloyal Dutchman," said Fokker. "I gave you the synchronizer, the Eindekker. For nearly a year the German air force has ruled the skies because of me." Fokker thumped his own finger against his chest, his voice rising. "Don't forget that. Until they have a synchronizer, they won't be a match for the Eindekkers," said Fokker, forcing his voice to sound matter-of-fact. He knew he was bluffing, but he didn't know how much Geertz knew, or believed.

"Fokker, the English pushers don't need a synchronizer. Nor do the French Nieuports, they put a machine gun on the upper wing. Surely you know this," said Geertz. "They went around the need for a synchronizer. Obviously." He reached out and patted Fokker's arm. Fokker let him.

"Herr Fokker, there have been many ... inferences ... leveled at your operations here," said Geertz. Geertz lowered his voice, and spoke softly and slowly. "You have been accused of sending profits out of the country. I came here to ask for your side of the story," said Geertz.

Fokker began walking again, slowly. He wasn't watching the aeroplanes overhead anymore, and seemed to be thinking, staring at the ground. Not knowing how what he had been told; or worse, what Geertz imagined.

Is he really going to shut the factory down? Stop Eindekker production? Or something worse ... arrest, expulsion?

After a moment, he decided to speak frankly, an uncomfortable decision. "Herr Geertz, I have Dutch investors, I've paid them off as they were entitled to their return on investment. So, yes, I've sent some money to Holland." He tried to change the subject. "But, I can build you new aeroplanes, better aeroplanes."

"Yes, I'm aware that you are doing as we requested," said Geertz, dismissing Fokker's argument. "Although, even to me, it looks your new aeroplane is just an Eindekker with another wing added ... as though you're not really trying ..." His voice trailed off, before letting Fokker continue.

Fokker let the accusation lie.

"If only we had new engines, the new Mercedes in-line engines, but we're forced to use these old rotaries ..." said Fokker, his voice on the edge of panic. "The other manufacturers take them all. They are conspiring against us," he was almost yelling now.

Geertz stared at Fokker, unmoved. "So, that's it: a conspiracy, is it?"

Fokker felt like a pensive child, grew quiet, and looked down at the ground.

"Fokker, you may become a German citizen, and swear an oath of loyalty to the German empire," said Geertz his voice suddenly tense, almost a growl. "Or, you may leave the country."

Fokker was staggered and bewildered. Not by the request, the *order*, but because he didn't see it coming. In his imagination, he saw so many things, saw their connections, anticipated each. Now, he imagined a domino, a light shining on it, lying alone, already tipped over. He shook and his vision closed, darkening.

Geertz smiled at Fokker, the smile strangely warm.

"But," said Fokker. "But ..." His thoughts flew, but no words came.

Geertz reached out and put a hand on Fokker's shoulder again. "Fokker, take a day or two and let me know."

Fokker looked up, watched an aeroplane fly over, the hard, black crosses unexpectedly ugly and fierce on its wings.

"But, what if I don't ... can't ... accept?"

"Then, we'll see that the factory remains useful," said Geertz. "These are military considerations, Herr Fokker."

He took his hand off Fokker's shoulder and replaced his cap. "Good afternoon, Herr Fokker." He tipped his cap and walked away.

Fokker stared after him, silent, realizing suddenly just how alone he was.

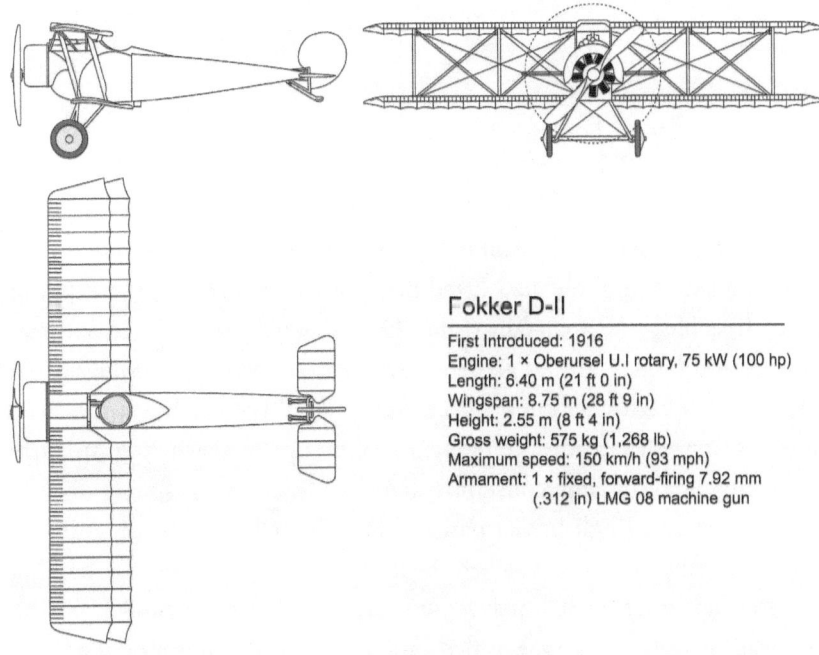

Fokker D-II

First Introduced: 1916
Engine: 1 × Oberursel U.I rotary, 75 kW (100 hp)
Length: 6.40 m (21 ft 0 in)
Wingspan: 8.75 m (28 ft 9 in)
Height: 2.55 m (8 ft 4 in)
Gross weight: 575 kg (1,268 lb)
Maximum speed: 150 km/h (93 mph)
Armament: 1 × fixed, forward-firing 7.92 mm
             (.312 in) LMG 08 machine gun

Chapter Thirty-Eight

June 18, 1916
Auchel Aerodrome, France
30km South of Lille

The day had dawned grey and damp. A layer of clouds hung close to the ground all morning, but had lifted away by noon, opening the sky into a cloudless blue like a curtain rising. On the north bank of the Somme, English and French armies gathered, waiting, congealing building for an offensive that both sides knew with certainty would come. The armies were quiet, as tranquil as armies could be: massing supplies, gathering strength, organizing, and digging, constantly digging.

The soldiers, English, German and French, looked up by the millions to a stage of heavens and watched the air battles form; above were arching contests that resolved themselves into forlorn columns of smoke, tracing arcs leading down to scraps of flesh and canvas and wood, pounded into the wreckage of men.

Sometimes the players in the sky were obvious, the markings on the wings letting each side know which aeroplane, which pilot, which country, was the victor or the loser. Yet often the battles were anonymous to the audience, the aeroplanes too high or the wreckage too charred to identify exactly what might have taken place thousands of feet overhead. Bored soldiers would place bets on 'The Hun', or 'The Little One', and the money would quickly be scraped up from the floor of a trench when an aeroplane tumbled away, erupted in smoke or both, and fell, flickering, tumbling, burning to the wastelands below.

The trails of smoke led to the pyres of men that would usually be mercifully dead. Sometimes they were not. By a quirk of fate or a trick of nature and air, some would survive the plummet, only to be left with shattered limbs and horrible burns, screaming, in the middle of no man's land, while patrols fought over the scraps of their existence with machine guns playing like footlights across the curtain call.

The first great drama of the day had played out in the afternoon, and the time for the final act before darkness drew near. Now, the sun was low on the horizon, and what was nearly the longest day of the year was ending with a darkening blue sky.

Second Lieutenant John Raymond Boscawen Savage strolled toward the line of aeroplanes on the verge of the field. He walked in a long stride, with the legs of a runner—legs that he had to fold up inside his aeroplane when he entered the cockpit.

John Savage was the youngest of a line of military men stretching back to Nelson's Battle of the Nile against Napoleon. In a cliché of the times, he had lied about his age, with the tacit approval of his parents, in order to join the Royal Flying Corps, fulfilling his destiny.

His aeroplane, already fueled and armed, sat otherwise ready with ground crew fussing over it, adjusting, prodding and double-checking.

Airman Robinson, Savage's gunner, ran to catch up and clapped Savage on the back. "Bloody hell, boy. You really read stuff like this?" Robinson slapped a book into Savage's stomach, hard enough for pain to flow through Savage. Savage didn't, *wouldn't*, show Robinson any indication of the discomfort. Savage gripped the book, tugged it away from Robinson, and tucked it under his arm protectively. Robinson reached out and stroked a finger under Savage's hairless chin.

"Boy, you should be reading about women that can entertain a man, not a blighty tight little girl ..." He grinned broadly, letting the insult linger. He gestured to the book: "'Baby Mine'? A book for women, not for men on a battlefield."

Savage glanced at Robinson quickly, not letting anger cross his face. "You may be twice my age, but, you'll do better to mind your manners, Robinson." He lowered his voice, softly speaking the last. "You'll remember that I'm your officer and I loaned you the book on my own good graces, not because I pushed it on you. But I suppose at least now, I know you *can read*."

Robinson grinned, briefly proud of his jibe, then the smile sagged and faded. He slapped Savage on the shoulder. "No offense intended, of course, Savage. We're a team, aren't we now? That's a good boy, there, you needn't worry. I'll be shooting down those bloody Fokkers before they put a bullet in your arse."

The two arrived at their aeroplane together. Savage walked around the machine in a slow clockwise circle, caressing as much as examining the aeroplane. Robinson practically leapt to his cockpit, his own hands immediately running over his machine guns to make the final adjustments.

The Fee was a pusher, the tail suspended behind the rear-set engine with an elaborate, delicate framework of booms and cables. Even to Savage, it appeared fragile, like something a child might make from a handful of toothpicks and a blob of library paste. Up close, the latticework seemed too purposeful, like every wire, cable, boom, and clevis was in just the right place. The deliberateness wasn't comforting; it left the impression that any single part was essential for the whole structure. That one wire could snap and the entire tail would cleave away into space.

In front, the fuselage resembled the open prow of a dinghy, with the gunner in front and the pilot behind and just above him. Savage thought it an especially ugly design.

Robinson saw only to his guns.

Savage, his inspection complete, climbed into the cockpit behind him. Robinson grasped each drum of Lewis ammunition out of the rack, released it from the side of the cockpit and checked the bullets within. Then he remounted them. He stood and inspected the Lewis attached on a pole to the rear, and then again checked the Lewis in front. Satisfied, he turned to Savage.

"Boy, how old are you, anyway?" he asked through a toothy grin, full of jagged and yellow teeth.

Savage ignored Robinson and adjusted himself in his seat. He turned to the mechanic waiting to spin the propeller. Savage held up a thumb, and the mechanic pulled down hard with both hands on the propeller, lifting himself off his feet. The mechanic quickly dropped to the ground and scrambled out from underneath the cage of wires and booms at the rear of the aeroplane, mindful of the horror that might come if he were to tangle himself within the arc of the propeller.

The engine spun, coughed, spat out a puff of powder grey smoke, then fired and began to run, emitting a harsh bray. Savage winced at the bark of the engine behind him, then hunched his shoulders defensively as it fired and then began to run smoothly. Relieved that the engine wasn't tearing itself apart, Savage cut its power back, blipping the ignition with the magneto switch.

Robinson stood in the gunner's position, adjusting the rearward facing Lewis gun.

Savage jabbed a finger at the seat. "Sit down!" he shouted.

Robinson frowned at Savage, turned and sat; he pulled his goggles over his eyes and tightened his scarf and jacket. Savage looked over at their flight lead, McCubbin in his Fee, and waved. McCubbin waved a hand forward in a chopping motion. The ground crew pulled the chocks from their wheels and Savage released the magneto switch, letting the engine run at full power.

The Fee rolled, lightened, and lifted. Together, the two aeroplanes climbed straight to the west, into the wind, and after a few minutes of climbing, turned north.

Savage was a steady hand at the Fee, which was to say he was only a little afraid of the aeroplane and he fought it constantly. His hands trembled as he adjusted the Fee's heading, trimmed out the roll to the right, and kept a watch on the skies around them. The Fee could scare a man, surprise him. Nevertheless, despite its odd quirks, its desire to roll and its awkward looking fuselage, the Fee gave a good view toward the front.

The crews of the Fees liked to imagine that having the engine behind gave them some protection from stern attacks. The fact was that the engine and the big plate of a radiator gave the Fee an awful blind spot to the rear that could only be overcome by the gunner standing, fully exposed and untethered, to fire to the rear over the top wing. Robinson was a skilled gunner, especially with the rearward gun, but Savage could see Robinson's knuckles whiten as he held onto the trigger when it came time to fight.

Robinson's life depended on Savage's smooth piloting lest he fall away in to the sky, unhindered. It was a delicate partnership, gunner to defend, pilot to keep the gunner alive.

For Robinson, the true advantage of the Fee's rear engine was that the hated castor oil fumes stayed out of the cockpit. No more did pilots have to breathe in the fumes and swallow the oil that coated their faces. Savage didn't remember those days, but Robinson did, recounting stories to Savage of the vomiting, painful cramps and emptying of bowels next to the plane due to the laxative effect of the oil, of awful messes to clean up in the cockpits. However, pilot-comfort didn't figure in the design. The reason the engine was behind was to allow gunnery to the front of the aircraft. Without a synchronizer, the aeroplane's design fulfilled one need: a free field of fire to the front.

Savage peered down into the ground haze, to the west, toward the setting sun. His eyes moved quickly back and forth, scanning constantly as he'd learned. Seeing the Jerry first was the key to survival, and he worked hard at it. Robinson, in front of him, looked to the right, away from the sun, looking for the Eindekkers they had met earlier in the day, the same group that had taken Rogers and Taylor.

Just a hundred meters ahead of them, McCubbins was leading them straight toward the town of Lille, skirting the German aerodrome at Douai to the west. Savage and McCubbins were out for revenge.

As they flew, Robinson occasionally glanced back at Savage. Robinson couldn't fathom Savage and Savage knew it. Savage was young and steady, and the combination made him an oddity. He refused to take a drink with the rest of the squadron and wrote his mum every day. Robinson, however, took to drink and didn't socialize with Savage, their ages being a difficult gap to fill. Robinson had a hard time trusting someone so aloof from the rest of squadron, but when it came time to stand up in the blast of the wind and fire his guns, he put his life in Savage's hands. A single quick movement, a reflex, a desire to zigzag or dodge, and Robinson knew he would tumble out, and the chance of Savage throwing him to his death by a mistake was a sobering possibility.

Robinson turned his eyes back to their left and held a free hand above them. Harshly backlit, the outline of Eindekkers, angling downward, began to form.

In the glare of the setting sun, the closing act of the day began.

~~~

A Bavarian infantry colonel had just entered the Officer's club in an old French barn, when a runner came in behind him from Douai aerodrome. With the crowd of young officers still at attention at the beginning of their meal, the runner called out for Immelmann in the dark smoky room.

Immelmann waved his dining companion, Heinemann, toward the door. Immelmann saluted smartly, but quickly, and excused himself past the senior Oberst in the mess as he ran out to the runner's duty car. For any other junior officer, the act would constitute insolence, the type of offense that would get a man posted into an attack over open ground, or a succession of night patrols until he didn't come back. For Immelmann, the disrespect had grown to a habit, a knowledge the rules didn't quite apply to him anymore. Heinemann, baffled and cautious, hesitated until the Oberst waved him along behind Immelmann. Behind them, as the door banged shut, they heard cheering. Hoarse shouts echoed out of the building, "Three cheers for the Kaiser! Three cheers for Immelmann!"

Immelmann smiled at Heinemann. "Well, now, we'll need to give them a show, won't we?"

Heinemann jumped into the front of the open duty car and Immelmann climbed into the back. The runner spoke over his shoulder. "Two English, crossing the lines, over Loos, high. Mulzer may be on them already. More may be coming."

Immelmann twisted sideways in the seat, pulling his pants off. "Do you have them?" he asked.

The runner reached down into the floorboards and lifted up an old pair of oil-stained felt trousers and handed them back to Immelmann. Heinemann, his eyes wide, and confusion on his face, watched the trousers go by. The runner then pulled an old tunic from the floorboards and handed them over to Immelmann. Immelmann clapped Heinemann on the shoulder. "I'll never burn with these on!" he said with a smile.

Immelmann, undressed in the back of the car, and pulled the old trousers on. Heinemann glanced over at the driver, who looked back and shrugged.

Only two Eindekkers waited on the flight line; Mulzer, Prehn and Osterreicher had taken three up on the evening patrol. Only two birds were lined up: Heinemann's new 160 horsepower Eindekker and an old 100 horsepower E.II machine.

Immelmann had counted eighteen bullet holes in his usual E.III from their fight earlier in the day. Consequently, the machine wasn't airworthy. Immelmann looked wistfully toward the maintenance tent where the machine rested, the bare front frame of the engine mounts protruding from the tent, the engine already pulled. He groaned and began to walk around his replacement plane, the E.II.

The E.II was one of their older birds, nearly nine months old now, far past its prime, and this particular one had already shot its own propeller off twice when its synchronizer gear had failed. It needed a fresh engine, instead of the old one that was in it. Immelmann considered taking Heinemann's machine, but let the thought escape; the youngster needing all the help he could get.

Heinemann stood by, not climbing into his aeroplane, expecting to turn his aeroplane over to Immelmann, the squadron leader, the Staffel-fuehrer.

Immelmann waved Heinemann toward the powerful E.III with a shooing motion, moving him along. He broke into a broad grin, knowing that he was giving Heinemann a gift. "Well, go on now. Go fight," he said.

Heinemann turned and began to run, then slowed and turned back, smiled broadly, and saluted. At the E.III, he climbed in. He furiously began pumping the fuel pump while he gave the startup signal to the ground crew.

Immelmann turned back to the forlorn E.II and then glanced up in the sky. Over Loos, far to the west, he could see black puffs of German anti-aircraft fire, a signal drawing him into the battle.

Heinemann's Eindekker was rolling down the field now, headed west into the sun. He'd chosen to fly straight to the fight, straight toward Loos. This would force him to climb out under the anti-aircraft fire and then up into the swirling battle now unfolding. Heinemann would be under the

English aircraft as he ascended, giving them the advantage. Immelmann could only wish him well, too late to advise him otherwise. Immelmann shook his head, watched Heinemann take flight and begin to climb, and wondered if he'd wasted a perfectly good E.III on the youngster.

Immelmann climbed up and settled in. He looked up at the anti-aircraft shells bursting in the distance, gauging it to be German by the dirty grey puffs. The machine felt wrong, uncomfortable and unfamiliar, and for a moment he considered climbing back to the ground and letting someone else fight today. Resigned, he pulled the leather straps over his shoulders, cinched them down and checked the gravity tank. With a couple of quick pumps of the fuel handle, he topped off the fuel tank in front of him from the main fuel cell behind him. He gave the signal to start the engine, and a mechanic spun the prop. The heavy radial spun, faltered and stopped. Immelmann signaled again, adjusted his goggles, and tucked the *Pour le Mérite* hanging from a ribbon around his throat down into his jacket.

This time the engine caught, barked, and fired, spinning quickly. Crewmen pulled the chocks away and Immelmann adjusted the mixture to run the old beast to full power, listening as the engine wound up. The aeroplane began to roll. He glanced out and down at the magnetic compass mounted in the starboard wing and pushed the rudder to the right as the needle spun. When the compass settled on a bearing of northwest, he pushed the rudder straight and let the Eindekker roll down the field.

Moving quickly, the aeroplane took flight. Immelmann relished that first sensation of weightlessness as the aeroplane pulled at the air and the wings began to work. He smiled to himself and imagined one day flying for the pure fun of it. Today though, he was last to the fight, the last to join his staffel. All four of his pilots were already fighting, or would be soon enough. He had more important things to think about.

Cautiously, Immelmann chose to climb away from Heinemann. Knowing that Heinemann would climb more quickly; he didn't want to be in the position of being behind Heinemann as they flew under the dogfight over Loos. If an Englishman saw Heinemann and descended, Immelmann might well fly into the Englishman's sights. Immelmann flew north toward Lille, to pass east of the fight at Loos as he climbed.

The Eindekker's engine was tired, and the aeroplane clawed for altitude, slowly winding up. The altimeter indicated 400, 500, 600 meters, as each minute dragged by. The fight appeared to moving south from Loos, toward Lens; he could see that the anti-aircraft fire there now. He briefly wished that the German flak would stop, worrying for his staffel mates, but dismissed that thought, knowing the explosions were the only thing guiding him, for he couldn't yet make out the specks of the fighters circling each other in the darkening sky.

South of Lille, he turned southwest, toward Lens and the frontline. His altitude was nearly 2,000 meters now, almost fighting altitude. Leveling out, he focused on the black puffs ahead of him, and strained to see the aircraft in the waning light. In a last rolling barrage, several anti-aircraft shells burst in soft puffs far in front of him, and then the anti-aircraft fire stopped.

What could this be? he thought.

Either the Fokkers had signaled they're at altitude and for the guns to stop firing, or the fight had moved away. The low bright sun distorted his vision to the west. He throttled ahead, level now, and in a few minutes, was over Lens. He felt isolated, alone in the battle, vulnerable. Craning his head around, he checked his stern for attackers and then stared hard into the setting sun, ensuring that he wasn't flying into an ambush.

Seeing nothing, he turned gently to the east, heading to parallel the front and passed south of Douai. If he didn't see anything, he could turn north and land back at the aerodrome before night fell. His vision cleared as the yellow glare subsided in his eyes, and then he saw bursts of anti-aircraft appear in a carpet over Henin-Lietard, southwest of the airfield. If the fight had moved here, then he was flying with the sun behind him into the battle: a perfect position for attack. In a few moments, specks of aircraft appeared, turning and circling, and then the shape of the battle came to him. Relieved, Immelmann finally knew where the fight was and where he needed to be.

Two of the English flying bathtubs, the two-seaters, their 'Fee's', circled each other at altitude, just above Immelmann and directly ahead, turning a defensive circle, covering each other's tails. Above them, the three Eindekkers of Mulzer's patrol revolved. With a diving swoop, the E.IIIs turned into the English circle and fired from the sides of the English machines, firing deflection, trying to lead the English aeroplanes and hit the most difficult of targets. Then, pulling up, the Eindekkers would trade airspeed for altitude and circle again, looking for another opening. Mulzer, the most talented pilot on the patrol, would dive, swoop and rudder turn at the top of each short climb, the way Immelmann had taught him, quickly re-entering the defensive circle of the English, snapping angry bursts of fire at the closest Englishman to keep the pressure on and force the English into a mistake.

Soft grey-black puffs of German anti-aircraft fire resumed, bursting around the circling aeroplanes. The sun was almost on the horizon now, and the lower blasts were in the twilight shadow. These showed their colors, the white explosion of each shell preceding the expanding black puff. He knew that the hard shrapnel of the shells cascaded away from each shot, an invisible fountain of hot steel, silently sinking below them. The situation was complex, more so than he'd ever seen, and he felt the pang of fear, a momentary shudder of uncertainty. He had to make the best of the fight, to see it through and the hope that the frail old Eindekker could hold itself together.

I need that damned anti-aircraft fire to stop before it shoots down an Eindekker!

Immelmann pulled a flare gun from the holster inside the cockpit, flipped it open to check it was loaded with a white shell, and fired it over the side of the cockpit, behind the aeroplane. This was the signal for the German anti-aircraft fire to stop, as the Germans and the English were at nearly the same altitude. The white-hot flare dropped away in the sunlight, barely visible in the glare of the low sun.

The English were boxed in, and Immelmann was closing from out of the setting sun. It should have been a glorious set up to finish them both.

~~~

Savage was tiring. Robinson was standing in the observer's tub, holding onto the upper machine gun, angling the gun upward at the Fokkers circling above. In brief sputters of fire, the Lewis would erupt over Savage's head as a Fokker made a firing pass. Each swoop of the Fokkers came from above and outside the circle, the Germans trying to lead them with their fire to finish them off.

Twice Robinson had changed magazines on the Lewis gun, while Savage flew smooth circles, watching McCubbins' lead aeroplane in order to stay behind him. Over Lens, McCubbins had made a break to the east, through a hole in the circling Fokkers. Savage had followed but the Fokkers overtook them, forcing McCubbins to turn tightly, and lead Savage back into a defensive circle.

Savage's shoulders ached with hot stinging needles of tension, and his forearms trembled. He held the stick with both hands now to keep the aeroplane steady so that Robinson didn't fall. It was a sorry Fee pilot that came home without his gunner, and Savage would be damned if today was the day that he bucked his.

He held his eyes on McCubbins, while adjusting his aeroplane to keep McCubbins in the same portion of his field of view, tracking in a tight circle around each other. Savage used all the strength in his arms to hold the stick steady, and very, very gradually applied small amounts of pressure to adjust their flight. His hands grew numb from his grip on the stick, and he felt sweat rolling inside of his shirt and down his back.

The Fee lurched suddenly, his hands slipped and Savage let the aeroplane slide sideways in flight. Robinson wobbled, his aim thrown off as he pulled the trigger on the Lewis gun, sending an errant burst across the tail of their Fee. Quickly Savage adjusted his grip and steadied the aeroplane, and Robinson glared down at him. Savage looked down at his numb hands to check if he still held the stick, all feeling gone from his fingers.

Savage looked to Robinson, not turning loose of the stick, and shook his head in apology. Knowing he was near his limit, and feeling panic begin to well, he yanked the Fee level, breaking the circle, relaxing the tension in his arms. He waved Robinson down into his seat, and ruddered the Fee around until the sun was to his starboard side. Savage threw a glance at McCubbins, still turning, and then gave McCubbins a brief wave of his hand as he dove to the south, back toward the English lines and safety.

He never saw Immelmann, climbing in a wide turn, just above him as he began his sharp descent.

~~~

Immelmann watched the English fighter break away from the circle. His position was now perfect to turn into the diving aircraft from astern. He glanced to his left and saw the other Fee just turning north, maintaining the circle, not having noticed that his wingman had broken away. Taking the opportunity, the German ace turned in behind the descending Englishman, letting his dive take him slightly below his target, allowing the descent to increase his airspeed to overtake fleeing aeroplane.

As Immelmann settled in behind the Fee, in a perfect stern chase, he moved the controls smoothly and gently, adjusting his firing position, lining up, centering his gun sight into the top of the Englishman's engine.

Glancing back, he saw the second Fee break his turn, hard, beginning to dive in behind him. He had only seconds to fire before the higher Englishman would have Immelmann in his sights. Behind the threatening Englishman, two of the higher E.IIIs each turned and dove. In a chain, the aeroplanes descended to the south: Savage, Immelmann, McCubbins, von Mulzer, and Prehn. As each pilot adjusted to the aeroplane in front, the procession rippled like a snake: Immelmann on Savage, McCubbins on Immelmann, von Mulzer on McCubbins, Prehn behind Mulzer, looking for an opening.

Immelmann fired.

~ ~ ~

Over the roar of the engine, and the sound of the wind as he gained speed in his dive, Savage heard the impacts on his wings: dull fabric pops, as bullets punched through. Startled, reflexively he looked over his shoulder and watched the linen puncture and tear in small rents, leaving a flap of fabric to rip away in the violent air. The pops changed to metallic clangs as the stream of bullets flew into his engine. It sounded like a handful of gravel thrown against a tin shed.

A single machine gun round flew between the engine cylinders behind Savage, bore into his back, burst from his chest and then bore into Robinson's right shoulder.

Savage's right lung burst like a balloon.

Numbness washed over him, then agony seized him. Time slowed and he tasted copper in his mouth, warm, and thick. His vision narrowed and he gasped, struggling to breath. In shock from the impact, Savage pulled the stick hard over to the right, and kicked his rudder pedals, turning steeply back towards Lens. Panting with his remaining lung, his vision slowly cleared. Desperate, Savage pushed the stick down, forward, and steepened his dive, fighting to get out of the stream of bullets.

With a cough, blood bubbled up into his throat and mouth, choking him. He spat the blood away, the air blowing it into a long streak of scarlet. As his dive steepened, he drew the stick back, and leveled the aeroplane slightly. He began sweeping his eyes over the cratered countryside, trying to find a place to land. They were flying west now and falling. Robinson had slumped over in front of him from his own injury, and Savage hoped that Robinson was able to hang on as the little Fee plummeted downward.

A farmhouse and barn near a road, just south of Lens, appeared on the darkening landscape below them. Savage checked their descent, and aimed the Fee for the tiny roadway. As the aeroplane leveled, he pushed forward again. He was in agony now. Pain, in waves of searing heat, made his muscles contract uncontrollably. Savage fought his own arms, to keep some control of the aeroplane. The Fee settled as he struggled to line it up on the roadway.

Too late, Savage pushed the stick forward, and then yanked it back to drain airspeed. It was not enough. The frail aeroplane slammed down into the roadway, bounced high and then stalled back down to the ground, spun, fell over onto a wing and tipped back onto its wheels as it slid sideways to a stop. Dust settled over the stationary wreck. Savage pulled the control knob for the ignition and the engine slowed, spun, sputtered and stopped. All was silent, except for the gurgling of blood in his throat and soft moans from Robinson.

Robinson picked himself free from his seat, and moved to help Savage. He could see blood and foam trickle out of the boy, leaking down his chest. Savage's chin was covered in scarlet, his eyes beginning to roll back into this head. Grasping his shoulder, Robinson pressed his jacket hard against Savage's wound. Savage managed a weak smile through crimson teeth as a fresh line of blood trickled down his chin. Painfully, slowly, Savage pushed

Robinson away and opened his coat, looked down at the ghastly pink bubbles frothing at the wound, then pressed his hand to the injury, trying to hold the blood and air in. He began to cry, softly.

Robinson leaned toward him, faced Savage and pressed his own hands over the wound, soothing him. "There, there, boy, you've done well. Thank you, son."

In his last moments, Savage didn't think of his uncles, his father, grandfather, or all the long generations of military men of which he was the last. He thought of his mother. At seventeen, John Savage died in a field near Lens.

~~~

McCubbins watched as Savage fell away. The Fokker that had fired turned, with wings and rudder, hard, to his right, to escape. McCubbins adjusted the arc of his turn in response, crossing behind the Fokker, angling toward his own lines, but allowing his gunner to line up on the German that had shot down Savage. Looking over his shoulder at the Fokker behind him, he watched it turn and steepen its own descent, diving out under his Fee and pursuing Savage to the ground.

Around them, a salvo of German anti-aircraft shells exploded in angry puffs once more.

Airman Walling, McCubbins' gunner, settled the sights of his front Lewis gun onto the cockpit of the Fokker, a low deflection shot, but one that he would only have a few seconds to make.

"Fire, damn you, FIRE!" shouted McCubbins over the sound of his engine.

~~~

Immelmann sensed, as much as he saw, the Fee turning behind him. He turned hard toward to Douai, and glanced back at the string of Fokkers behind the Englishman. The closest, von Mulzer, fell away like a stone, clearly pursuing the aeroplane Immelmann had just fired on. He twisted his neck and looked right back at the Fee crossing behind him, at the gunner huddled over his machine gun, only yards away. He heard the English machine gun fire. German anti-aircraft shells burst around them, in puffs of grey centered with white.

The old Eindekker bucked upward, the stick wrenching forward in Immelmann's hands and then back again. The Eindekker was fighting his control, flying of its own accord. It tipped perilously onto its left wing and then leveled, dropping 200 meters in a single, stomach-twisting stagger. Immelmann wrestled the stick and rudder, the engine chopping fiercely at the air. His mouth went dry and felt himself biting his own tongue. Again, the Fokker reared and settled, bucking like a savage ethereal horse. Hard, vicious movements slapped the stick against the seat and then forward out of Immelmann's hands.

With a grinding, tearing sound, the fuselage burst apart behind him. For a second the longerons held it together, but they failed and the tail of the aeroplane fell away. The wings and front of the fuselage leveled in flight and then the nose tipped back. Without further warning, the wings collapsed upward at the sides of the cockpit. The engine rotated, the propeller still turning, chopping into the wings and splintered them apart. They sheared away and began a slow, fluttering descent, the remains of the cockpit and engine dropping past them.

Immelmann dropped now, weightless; his engine no longer running as it ran out of fuel and stopped. He looked up at the sky, still in the cockpit, his teeth gritted tight, holding the now useless stick with both hands. It seemed to him to be forever and a moment that he fell, though he never saw the ground that claimed him.

~~~

The Bavarian infantry had watched the show, and they ran toward the pieces that rained down. Some ran toward the wings, others toward the tail. Others gathered around the engine, staring bleakly at a hand sticking out around the edge.

"It's a Frenchman," someone said from the crowd.

Officers gathered and shouted orders. Another man, walking over from the wings said, "He's a German." The crowd threw angry glares at him and shushed him into silence.

The officers, impatient, barked out orders to lift the engine, and a small group, with much effort, lifted it away. Pressed down into the mud and flattened like a stomped bug, a crumpled body appeared, smashed, but the face untouched. A Bavarian sergeant pulled open the man's jacket, reached into the pockets, and searched for papers.

With the jacket open, the *Pour le Mérite* glistened wetly at the throat of the body in the last light of day.

A cry spread out, relayed quietly through the crowd of soldiers. "The *Pour le Mérite*. Max. Blue Max."

Another soft cry rose behind it, harsh, a question: "Boelcke or Immelmann?"

The sergeant's hands slowed now, moved reverently. Pulling the coat wide, he searched further. Over the shirt pocket a monogram appeared as the jacket was drawn back, the letters "M.I." written in gold thread. Whispers moved outward then, leaving silence behind as it moved through the gathering crowd. "Saxon Max is dead." The men stood, removed their head gear and bowed their heads. The sergeant cried.

The news radiated outward through the German army and across Europe, to the Kaiser, and then around the world.

Max Immelmann, Saxon Max, the Eagle of Lille, was dead.

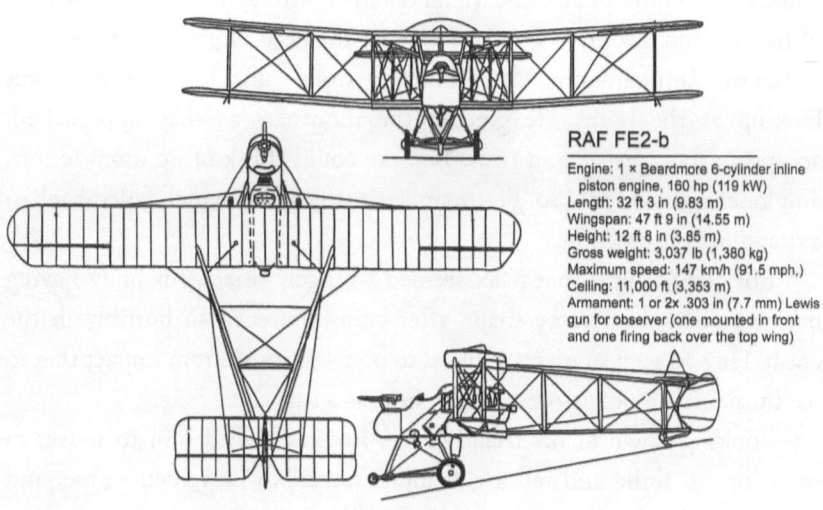

RAF FE2-b

Engine: 1 × Beardmore 6-cylinder inline
  piston engine, 160 hp (119 kW)
Length: 32 ft 3 in (9.83 m)
Wingspan: 47 ft 9 in (14.55 m)
Height: 12 ft 8 in (3.85 m)
Gross weight: 3,037 lb (1,380 kg)
Maximum speed: 147 km/h (91.5 mph,)
Ceiling: 11,000 ft (3,353 m)
Armament: 1 or 2x .303 in (7.7 mm) Lewis
  gun for observer (one mounted in front
  and one firing back over the top wing)

FE2-b (June 1916)

Chapter Thirty-Nine

June 20, 1916
Douai, France

The smell of death, high, cloying and ugly, lingered in the courtyard, competing with the scent from the flowers and torches.

Oswald Boelcke struggled not to retch.

Max's casket sat on an operating table in the square of the Douai hospital, with the lid open and Max propped up on pillows. Smoky torches cast a harsh, flickering light across Immelmann's face. His *Pour le Mérite* hung freshly polished at his throat, the cobalt blue and gold brilliant against the grey of Max's uniform and skin. Flowers barricaded the makeshift bier in thick, sickly sweet bunches, giving the appearance that the casket was afloat on a mound of blooms. Metal obelisks—the symbols of the Royalty of Bavaria and Saxony—stood on poles at the head of his display.

Franz Immelmann, Max's brother, stood next to the casket, not looking at the body. He greeted the mourners as they approached, accepting their respects in turn. Boelcke could think of no more forlorn and lonely job and said so. Franz smiled a tiny smile, which faded back to a drawn soft expression.

Boelcke thought that Max seemed strangely intact, his body having been put back into some shape after being flattened so horribly in the crash. He had seen so many reduced to boneless mush from impact that to see Immelmann nearly presentable came as a surprise.

Looking down at his friend's face, Boelcke willed him to move, to stand up, to smile and tell a ridiculous story. No movement came, and Boelcke, at last convinced that Max's stillness was forever, moved away through the crowd. A bleak emptiness filled him. Leaning heavily against a wall of the hospital, he stared out across the grim scene in the courtyard. Fischer, his aide, approached him, handed him a glass of water, and then stood quietly to his side. Boelcke breathed in long, deep lungfuls of air, forcing his lungs to remain open with a conscious effort.

Mourners moved around and through the enclosure, and swirled in small groups, their caps and helmets tucked under arms. The princes of Saxony and Bavaria were there, with their entourage of generals and obersts. Boelcke began to count generals, but became bored when he reached twenty. Aides to the royalty and generals flitted back and forth, tending to their needs. The gathering left Boelcke with a queasy feeling of quiet, useless chaos.

Leith-Thomsen, commander of the German Air Force, arrived, greeted the princes, and then stood next to the casket, his head bowed, while a photo was taken. Boelcke marveled at Thomsen's enormous egg-shaped head, bald and so shiny that Boelcke suspected him of waxing it. Thomsen said something over Immelmann's corpse. He scanned the crowd, and settled his gaze on Boelcke.

Boelcke stood, waiting. He felt his back stiffen unconsciously as Thomsen approached. Boelcke shifted on the balls of his feet, his legs tightening. The prospect of a conversation with Thomsen only deepened his unease. He felt the urge to move, to be out of this place, to do anything but linger.

The two men exchanged salutes, and Thomson spoke. "I'm sorry for your loss, Leutnant; I know he was your good friend."

Boelcke nodded, and clenched his jaw tight. He felt the urge to move away again, but knew that he couldn't show that kind of disrespect.

"Have you seen the wreck, Major?" asked Boelcke in a rasping whisper.

"No, Leutnant, I have not," replied Thomsen.

"Well, Thomsen, perhaps you should look at it," Boelcke said, his voice rising.

Thomsen stepped in front of Boelcke, and stood close. Boelcke pressed up against the wall, the comfort it had provided slipping away as the man cornered him. Boelcke stretched upright and fought the urge to laugh at

Thomsen's attempt to menace him. Up close, Thomsen's round, smooth forehead and tiny eyes reminded him of an English nursery rhyme, but he couldn't quite remember it. Something about not being able to put someone back together again.

"It's Oberstleutnant, now, Boelcke. Please address me appropriately."

"I see," said Boelcke. "Oberst." Boelcke touched the *Pour le Mérite* at his own throat as though it were a talisman to ward off senior officers.

"Would you excuse us, Fischer?" said Thomsen.

"Yes, of course." Fischer nodded to Boelcke and disappeared into the crowd.

"Boelcke, we need to speak. This is a most serious matter," said Thomsen, gesturing at Immelmann's casket.

"Yes, I believe it is. Max is dead. That seems most serious," replied Boelcke with a flicker of a tight smile.

"Let's find somewhere we can talk," said Thomsen. Boelcke turned and led Thomsen into the hospital. The halls smelled of alcohol and dried blood. Opening doors until he found a tiny office, Boelcke ushered Thomsen into a space crowded by a single desk. Thomsen closed the door behind them.

"The Kaiser is concerned. This is a tragedy for our troops, for our people," said Thomsen.

Boelcke blinked, surprised. "Well, he's dead, that I can understand. What are our losses in the war, two, three million? Why is the Kaiser so concerned?" said Boelcke.

Boelcke remembered now, *All the king's horses, and all the king's men, couldn't put Humpty Dumpty together again ...*

"Surely you understand he's a national hero, and he's considered irreplaceable," said Thomsen. "Except for you, of course."

Boelcke waited a moment. "Go on," he said. "What are you getting at, Thomsen?"

"Your loss would be more significant. After the loss of one of you, losing the other would be significantly worse," said Thomsen.

"Thomsen, surely you understand that we're on the cusp of another tragedy, far worse than the loss of my friend," Boelcke said. "We're getting beaten. Where are our new aeroplanes and the hard decisions that need to be made?"

Thomsen stepped away from Boelcke, pushed some papers aside and sat on the edge of the desk. "Boelcke, you're withdrawn from flying until notified otherwise."

Boelcke grew quiet, motionless. He felt bile rising in his throat. He bunched up both fists and swayed gently, breathing in draughts of stale air. He felt he might wheeze.

"Do you understand?" said Thomsen.

"I ... I ... yes, I understand," Boelcke's voice quivered slightly.

"Boelcke, this is an Imperial decision, the Kaiser himself has expressed this concern. You are a national figure now, a hero to the people; your ... death would bring about a loss of morale." Thomsen lowered his voice back to a stage whisper. "There are already riots, butter riots they're called, over food. Strikes ... in munitions factories ... can you imagine?"

"Yes, I can imagine," said Boelcke, blurting out the words, suddenly angry at being singled out. "I can imagine the English and French, concentrating their aeroplanes and wiping us from the air. That I can imagine. Do you really think putting me on the ground will matter if things continue the way they are? Did you see the wreck, Max's wreck? The propeller shot through. That's what killed him. The damned synchronizer."

"Now, there, Boelcke, it's not that clear, Fokker has examined the wreck and has declared it was struck by an anti-aircraft shell ... now we can't be saying that out loud, can we? That one of our greatest heroes was killed by his own artillery, can we?"

"Oh, damn Fokker. And the English say they shot him down. The fact is, we've lost Max and they're better than us. Better than us." He stabbed his finger at the desktop and demanded, "Where are our new aeroplanes? The new biplanes to replace the Eindekkers?"

Thomsen folded his arms, leaned back and stared up at the bare electric bulb in the middle of the ceiling. His huge head glowed white and glistened with sweat. He stared until the hot glow of the wire hurt his eyes.

"Boelcke. I'm not a fool. You know that I support ... no, I've been actively making the changes needed to form units that can hold their ground." Pulling a handkerchief from his pocket, Thomsen mopped the sweat from his enormous head. "We still fight on even terms, and hold the French and English at bay. But the aeroplanes aren't ready yet; perhaps August, not July." He let the news hang in the air and let Boelcke absorb it.

Boelcke's color drained away. He too leaned heavily on the desk, feeling himself deflating. His mouth moved and no words came out.

Thomsen's face softened. "You see ... it's pointless ... don't die now flying an outclassed machine ... it will do no good, but rather a great deal of harm."

"Fokker has gotten to you, hasn't he? He's sold you snake oil and you've bought it. What about Halberstadt and Albatros, where are their machines?"

"The same, perhaps later. Nothing for two months or more," said Thomsen. Boelcke watched Thomsen's body sag and he felt the inevitability of good men dying, fighting mysterious, distant, unwatched battles. Disappearing into the void, gone. Flying off into a bright blue sky that would consume them. So many gone, and no idea where they were, what happened. Not knowing made it worse. It was bad enough, but not being able to gather a body or look at a wreck, created a void in him, one he knew he would always have. At least they could bury Max.

"At least Max died where we could find him and give him a proper burial," Boelcke said aloud, his shoulders sinking. He felt very old. Then Boelcke's expression softened, he tilted his head down, and he stared at an ugly dark brown smudge on the floor. Suddenly he felt compassion for Thomsen, felt the weight of Thomsen's decisions, could feel that Thomsen felt them too.

"Yes," Thomsen said, finally. "There is that."

"So, Oberstleutnant, what then? When the new aeroplanes come? What then? Can I fly?"

"We will have to ask; again, over and over, through the chain of command. Chief of the General Staff von Falkenhayn, the Kaiser. It's not in my hands. But, I think you need a rest, need to wait, at least give yourself a chance to survive. I understand now, flying these old Eindekkers will do nothing," said Thomsen.

"I can't just wait and do nothing. I can't do that!" Boelcke felt frustration rising and his lungs contracting. He felt a space in himself shrinking around an emptiness in his chest; a hollow enclosing a void.

"Then, come to Charleville, to headquarters. Help us. We have to make plans, regroup, live to fight another day," Thomsen said. "We have a Fokker unit there, untrained, loose, you can work with them."

Boelcke looked up, baffled. He felt condescended to.

Thomsen could see the expression on Boelcke's face, read his reaction. He shook his head. "I'm sorry, Boelcke, that's the best I can do. But there's something else you need to know: below the bend in the river Somme, opposite the Second Army, the English and French armies are massing. It's inevitable that they'll attack, and soon. We have to prepare, be flexible and buy time."

"Thomsen, what if I could teach others, make men into fighters ... then, surely, you would know that I'm not some superman. I'd be a hypocrite to send men to fight in these conditions and not fight myself. I can't stay on the ground, not fight, and let others do the fighting for me!"

"Perhaps. Perhaps, Boelcke that might make a difference. Come work with us, give us time, give *me* time to a least give you a chance."

"Very well, Thomsen. I'll come to Charleville," said Boelcke. Then: "I don't have a choice, though, do I?"

"No, Leutnant, you don't. A few weeks, we'll see what happens with the new aeroplanes, react to the British and French, adapt. Then...perhaps, then, you'll be back in the fight."

"Very well, Thomsen." Boelcke donned his cap, stood to attention to be dismissed.

"One more thing, Boelcke, do you know anything about this?" Reaching into a tunic pocket, Thomsen extracted a crumpled sheet of paper. He flattened it and handed it to Boelcke.

Boelcke looked down at the sheet, torn in half across the middle. His name was scribbled across the top in pencil, addressed to him. The note was in English. Shaking his head, he handed the note back.

"I can't read this," he said.

"Perhaps you should. It is a request to attend Immelmann's funeral. Written by an Englishman, their Immelmann I understand, a man named Hawker."

"What?" stammered Boelcke.

"He wishes to cross the lines in an English aeroplane and fly over Immelmann's funeral, out of respect. He requests our permission to do so. *Your* permission. He seems ... chivalrous. He seems to think you can communicate with him. That isn't true, is it?"

Boelcke stepped back and stared away from Thomsen, at the wall, as though he saw something that wasn't there.

"I've never heard of the man," said Boelcke, half answering.

"Very well. He also thanks you for the kind notes regarding the fate of their flyers. Do you know something about that?"

Boelcke stood, silent.

"I didn't think so. Goodnight, Boelcke."

"Goodnight, Oberst."

"Boelcke. Go ahead. Tell him to come. He may attend the funeral, if only in the air."

Boelcke nodded wordlessly, feeling he might have misjudged Thomsen. He needed to be in the open air. To find fresh air. To breathe. He saluted and walked quickly out of the hospital, into the cool air of the town, away from the hospital, and away from Max.

Chapter Forty

June 24, 1916
Bertangles, France

Louis Strange squirmed in his seat, tired of the board that served as a bench, weary of the banging of the truck over every pothole, drained by the day.

Around the truck, columns of English solders filled the roads, all flowing in endless files cast from the western horizon toward the valley of the Somme River. The smell of the army on the move was like an open latrine mixed with gasoline and machine oil.

The great English army pushed forward; gathering in holes dug in the ground in dense knots of young men, piling small mountains of arms and ammunition, spreading fields of canvas.

To the west of the Somme River, where Strange had recently seen only empty fields, now stood rows of cannon, banked by shells neatly stacked in polished brass heaps. The sight struck Strange as a paradoxical testament to humanity itself. Here was the most meticulously organized endeavor man was capable of—a seamless gathering, tables of men and munitions, straight rows, carefully stacked explosives—civilization at its most systematic and scientific with the sole purpose of creating savagery and chaos.

Around the Somme, the army gathered and waited.

At first, he had stared in amazement, then in curiosity, until the sheer magnitude of the gathering of arms was itself dull, grey, and interminable, an infinity of waste and lost potential.

He looked across at his companion and tried once more to make conversation. His companion was a quiet Irishman with flaming hair and dark eyes.

"Langan-Byrne, you say?"

"Uh," said Langan-Byrne. He barely glanced up from a book of poetry.

"Irish?"

"Aye."

"And this your first squadron? No. 24?"

"'Tis."

"You don't talk much do you, Byrne?"

Langan-Byrne stroked his chin as though he needed to ponder the question. After a moment, he stared out past Strange at the crowded and forlorn landscape. "Nay," he said.

The truck hit another hole in the road, bouncing Strange briefly into the air. In a blink, the plank seat under him fell away and then rose quickly, smacking him in the behind. Strange scowled and stared out at the sea of khaki-clad men around them. He took a tighter grasp on the bench below him.

Finally, cresting a rise, the truck rolled next to the first empty field Strange had seen for miles.

"God help me. At last." Strange pointed past Langan-Byrne at a row of sheds, lined up by the remains of an old French farmhouse. The late twilight of solstice lit the buildings from behind. Light spilled onto the ground from the nearest building, a canvas-sided shed, and the sound of muffled 'whoops' rose over the engine of their clanking wreck of a truck. The truck nosed its way through columns of infantry, and then rattled to a stop, where, mysteriously, the driver managed to grind the gears once more. The driver jumped down.

"Bertangles, gentlemens," he said, dropping the back gate. He waved a weak salute at Strange and stepped back.

Strange stood, stretched his back, rubbed his sore bum briefly, then tightened and relaxed his legs. He took up his kit bag and jumped down, throwing it over his shoulder.

"Help with that, captain?" asked the driver.

"No, I'll mind it myself. Thank you."

Langan-Byrne jumped down behind Strange and trailed him. At the near building, Strange threw his bag down, pulled back the blanket that served as a door and stepped inside. A cheer went up and Strange smiled, began to wave a greeting to the room, and then realized that no one was looking his way.

Two groups of men bunched together, each at either end of the long room, facing off. In a corner, tables and chairs were heaped in a mound. Lanoe Hawker stood on a plank propped on two barrels and shouted to the men.

"Now, twenty-four, you'll mind your manners, won't you? Just enough men for the scrum ... no more!"

The group of men nearest the door shouted what sounded like agreement back at Hawker.

"And twenty-five, you know the rules, now, don't you, boys?"

"Yes! Aye!" came the reply.

Both groups of men split apart, and, from each squadron, men formed a rugby scrum.

"Now then. We'll begin."

"You, Strange, there." Hawker pointed at Strange and grinned. "Here you are." Hawker waved a bottle of whiskey toward Strange.

Langan-Byrne removed his cap and gawked at the crowd. "Aye," he said to no one.

Strange took the bottle from Hawker.

"Now, then, you know what to do." Strange smiled and stepped to the side of the scrum, between the blocks of men, where the front row of No. 25 men faced the front row of No. 24 men.

"Ready?" yelled Hawker.

"YES! READY!"

"Then, TOUCH!"

The forward lines of each group of men knelt and pressed forward, gripping the shirts of the men opposite, then the lines behind them knelt and took hold. The scrum wavered and lurched. Strange smelled sweat, beer and whiskey in equal measure.

"Are you mad, Hawker?" yelled Strange. "They're too drunk to stand!"

"Never mind that, Strange, there's honor at stake," shouted Hawker.

"HOLD!" Both packs lurched forward, pressing against the other.

Strange shook his head and held the bottle up. "And this!" he yelled.
"What do you think, Strange?" yelled Hawker. "It's our rugby ball!"
"ENGAGE!"

With a drunken roar, the two packs of men collided together, driving their feet forward, then began to push against the other. The men around the scrum began to cheer them.

"That's it, twenty-four! Send them home!"

Strange looked at Hawker, a little afraid.

"Put the bloody thing in there, Strange!" yelled Hawker.

Strange shook his head in amazement, then knelt and rolled the whiskey bottle into the middle of the scrum. The men roared in a continuous shout, driving their feet forward.

One of No. 25's men slipped in a puddle of beer, went to his knees, then their back row collapsed.

No. 24's pack drove forward and the front row of the No. 25 couldn't take the pressure. The whisky bottle spit out of the scrum behind them and someone scooped it up. The men of No. 25, off their feet, rolled backward until their backs pressed against the canvas wall of the hut. Other men of No. 25 joined in to try to pull their mates from the press of the scrum and were swept up in the melee.

With a ripping sound, the canvas gave way, and the men of No. 25 spilled out of the building into the dark outside. Langan-Byrne strode past Strange and picked up a No. 25 man by the collar of his uniform and the seat of his pants, and, with a heave, flung the man through the hole in the wall. A cheer went up from the men inside the building. In a few moments, the last of the No. 25 men were thrown out through the hole.

Someone handed Langan-Byrne a ceramic mug full of beer and clapped him on the back. Langan-Byrne smiled and waved the mug in a salute to the room, grinning silently. "Aye!" he said.

Another cheer went up, and the whiskey bottle passed from man to man. Hawker jumped down from the bar top and gave Strange a drunken hug. "Welcome, old sot. Have a drink." He waved to the barman for a drink.

"What are we celebrating, Hawker?"

"Well, Gerry Knight got his first victory, and rumor has it that

Immelmann was shot down."

He leaned close to Strange, blew beery breath into his face. "We think No. 25 did Immelmann in, but their boys didn't come back."

Outside, the men of No. 25 broke into drunken song, and the singing faded as they staggered away.

Men sat the overturned tables upright and gathered chairs. Someone began to pound away on a piano.

Hawker waved Strange to a seat.

"How have you been, old man?" said Hawker. "Take off our cap, you're among friends."

Strange put his hand on his head, and hesitated. Then, resigned, he pulled the cap from his head and folded it. He lay it on the table, and took up his glass of warm beer.

Hawker stared, then, "Well, the grey does seem to be fading. Shock to the system, is all. It'll grow back darker. Eventually."

"Yes, perhaps," said Strange. "No matter. How are things here?"

"Fine, we're doing swimmingly. Shooting down Fokkers when we find them, generally got our wind up."

"Any losses?"

"No time for that, now, Strange. Drink your beer."

Strange took a long swallow, hoping to find the mood that Hawker and his men seemed to be in.

"So, you've brought me one?" said Hawker.

"Yes, an Irishman, good pilot I understand, inclined to brawls, doesn't talk much. Langan-Byrne."

"So I see."

"How's your lovely wife, and how's my Beatrice, have you seen her?"

"My wife is quite well, happy that I'm in England quite a bit, working with the aircraft factories. She sends her regards. Beatrice is well, still living at the coast with her mum. Of course, you know that."

Hawker straightened, sighed and took a small swallow of his beer. He looked around the room, his eyes suddenly brighter and clearer. It occurred to Strange that Hawker wasn't really drunk, but seemed to be putting on that he was.

"What brings you here, Louis?"

"I was asked to speak with you," said Strange. "As a friend."

"Perhaps we should get this out of the way, then." Hawker rose and put his cap on his head. "Let's walk, so we can speak freely."

Strange took another big swallow of beer, realizing how dry he was after the horrible trip in the open truck. He stood and put his own cap on his head.

Hawker led them to the door and out into the night air. A thick band of stars glimmered in the clear sky. Voices murmured from the road as the infantry continued to stream past.

"An offensive, then?" asked Strange.

"Yes, of course, hard to hide all this from the Hun. Soon. We need to take the heat off the French at Verdun. 'Bout damn time, if you ask me."

"Did you swear, Hawker?" asked Strange, grinning.

"Sorry, my apologies, been out here too long. Uncivilized. Forgive me. So, what is it that's so important you had to come out here to tell me?"

"There's a rumor afoot, and I was asked to investigate it. Quietly."

"I see. Go on. What sort of rumor is that?"

Hawker looked away to the east, as though he might see something on the horizon.

"Hawker, the Berlin newspapers claim that an English aeroplane overflew Immelmann's funeral at Douai."

Hawker nodded. "Yes."

"Hawker, I haven't asked a question."

"Oh, yes, you have, Strange. That was me."

Strange held his mouth shut, clamping his teeth down to keep his jaw from falling open. "Really? You did?" Strange paused for a moment to let the admission settle in. "You did?"

"Yes, Strange, I did. With permission, of course."

"Permission? Permission from whom?" asked Strange.

"Well, the Germans of course. Boelcke. Their man that drops the notes."

Strange nodded, having heard of the German fighter, Immelmann's cohort, the one that flew over the lines with notes about English aviators. He was still confused. "So..." he said.

"So ... I dropped a note, and he answered."

"Hawker, you're forbidden to fly in combat, let alone cross the lines. You're a national hero. You have orders!"

Hawker glanced at Strange, then back to the eastern horizon. He didn't respond.

"Hawker. Explain yourself. Please. As a friend."

"I'm hardly of any use to the war; I haven't been in combat in a year. Besides, it seemed like the right thing to do. Immelmann was highly thought of."

"Yes, but not by us."

"No, perhaps ..." Hawker paused to gather his thoughts. "He was a man. God's creation. A person. A brave man, a brilliant pilot. He meant something to them. It seemed appropriate to pay my respects. Our respects."

"What did you do?" asked Strange.

"Crossed the lines, unarmed, at the arranged time, by agreement. I flew to Douai at the appointed hour, over the main street, the cathedral is quite obvious, you know."

"Not that. You've corresponded with the enemy."

"Yes, on a matter of humanitarian concern. Yes. I did. The regulations allow such things."

Hawker took a few steps out into the open field, into the darkness. Strange looked up at the stars, noticed they had grown much clearer and brighter overhead. Together, they stood in silence for a few minutes.

"What should I tell the commander, Trenchard? They call him 'Boom' for a reason, and I suppose I'm going to find out why."

"Tell them that I did the right thing. That Immelmann was a gentleman, and I did what one gentleman should do for another."

Strange stared at Hawker for a moment, letting the words sink in.

"Okay. Very well, I'll tell them," said Strange. He reached out and took Hawker by the sleeve, turning him. "Hawker, don't throw your life away, I say this as a friend, not as an officer. That was rather foolish."

"Strange, this will end. We'll have to have things to believe in when it's over. That's why I did it. We can destroy men, armies, ourselves, but we have to find civilization when it's over. That's all."

Strange turned Hawker's sleeve loose. Hawker placed his hand over Strange's for a moment, squeezed it, and then turned it loose.

On the eastern horizon, a series of flashes bloomed in a long ripple from the north to the south. Strange turned and stared to the east, where Hawker was already looking. "A storm? The sky is so clear ..." asked Strange.

Hawker spoke, "No, Louis, the offensive is beginning, our artillery, a week early, they've moved it up. The French are losing at Verdun, and we must hurry. The balloons will go up in the morning."

From the east, the dull echoing booms of artillery fire rolled over them, as more flashes lit the sky, gunners slamming shells home, reloading in the darkness, throwing hate in brilliant arches. Shells vaulted upward in fiery orange streaks, some fading out, others glowing through their full arc into the German lines. Some shells rose with a green tint, then faded to orange and then gold. Already, in the far distance, bright yellow explosions lit the German sky.

"It's beautiful, isn't it, Strange? Like fireworks."

"Yes, it is. I'm afraid it is. It makes one wonder if fireworks were transformed to weapons or if we melded weapons to fireworks."

"Yes, we do disguise our violence in strange beauty sometimes, don't we?"

Strange looked at Hawker. "Lanoe, I understand why you crossed the lines. Don't worry, I'll tell the story well."

"Thank you, Louis."

"Yes. Civilization," said Strange. "We will need to find it."

Chapter Forty-One

June 26, 1916
Kovel, Ukraine

Reaching from under his blankets, Erwin Böhme put his hand on his pistol, pulled it close and tried to sleep. A beast had come by and woken him near midnight, putting its nose under the edge of his tent. Afterward, he had tossed about sleeplessly. In the darkness, he pondered how he ever let young Richthofen convince him to sleep in a tent in the forest when the squadron's rail cars were right next to the field.

Böhme had heard the stories, how the wolves had taken four hundred people, *soldiers*, near Kirov, how the bodies on the battlefield brought them in at night; that the Russian and German armies in Galicia called a truce to fight the wolves together. The thoughts gave him shivers. He pulled the pistol closer, tucking it in near his head.

As the night crept by, the wind died down, bringing an army of mosquitos out of the trees. Böhme squirmed in his blankets, trying to cover his body and keep his small square of mosquito netting over his face. The buzz of the insects and the howling of wolves melded together into a sound like aeroplane engines, droning in the distance, growing near. He dreamt that he heard wolves and the wind howling in the darkness before dawn.

In the early morning hours, after the long night, he heard canvas rustling, heard the sound of men stirring in the darkness, then voices and coughing. Böhme felt a bleariness, the ache that comes from drifting into rough sleep just before waking. He fought through the sensation, that treacherous ache for sleep, then rolled onto his back and lay his pistol across his chest and folded his arms. He sighed in exasperation, already weary for the day.

A runner came down the path from the field at a trot, moving in the darkness, the first runner for the first flight. Böhme heard the heavy footsteps and saw the light of the man's lantern flicker though the trees and under the open edge of his tent. Though he longed for sleep, he was relieved that the night was at an end, and that he could get up and move around people again, safe from wolves.

He dressed quickly, opened the canvas flap of his tent, tied it back and stood up. Then he pushed his hands into his back and worked out the knots, flexing from side to side. He rubbed one shoulder, sore where he had slept on it on the hard ground.

"Good morning, old man," came from the colorless shape of a man in the darkness. In his sleepless state, Böhme felt a stir of anger rise. *I'm only 37. It's hardly old.* He decided to let it go, just one more time. Though he couldn't recognize the voice, he mustered up a weak 'good morning'. He hadn't learned their voices yet, but knew that would come in time.

Something rustled through the trees, in the darkness, and he pulled his pistol from the back of his pants and held it as his side.

Böhme knew that some of them thought he was too old, that they whispered about the 'old man' when they weren't half mocking him. He knew that the other pilots questioned his reflexes, his stamina. They were all boys, the oldest pilot twenty-four, an observer or two getting close to thirty, not one of them older than that. His new commander, Wilhelm Boelcke, Oswald's older brother, was only twenty-seven.

He walked past his tent, and down the path to where the orderly stood with his lantern. The other men had already gathered. He was the last to arrive. A round of good mornings went through the group as they followed the orderly down the path. When they reached the edge of the airfield, they split up; some walked a little further to the rail cars, looking for coffee, others moving to the hangars, seeing after their aeroplanes.

Böhme followed the group to the mess carriage, and stood outside while an attendant handed down hot cups of coffee, billowing steam into the humid air. He put his nose over the mug, drawing in the smell. *Ah, real coffee.* He sipped gently, feeling the heat against his lips, letting the sensation awaken him, not minding the burn.

Across the field, crewmen drew open the hangar tents by lantern light, and they began to roll the aeroplanes out. From his vantage, backlit as they were by the lanterns of the mechanics, the aeroplanes took on the appearance of great, emaciated birds. Somewhere down the line, an engine started. It ran for a minute, smoothed out, the hoarse rumbling becoming an even roar, then they shut the engine off, satisfied. He felt exhilaration rising, a childlike giddiness, a return to adventures that he once longed for as a youth.

A young flyer was speaking with another pilot. He asked, "And where were you when you heard the news about Immelmann?"

The man answered, "I had just turned in when Menzke rushed in, going from room to room, telling everyone, waking people. It was sad; awful. We all went down to the casino and drank toasts with schnapps until it ran out. We flew with pounding headaches the next morning."

"I was at home, with my mother, on leave before the transfer. My father cried. I think he thought it was the end of us. I hope he cries for me, if ..." He let his voice trail off, then he sipped his coffee. "No one has heard from the younger Boelcke. Not even his brother, Wilhelm. Thomsen sent Oswald Boelcke off somewhere to hide him, or some such rubbish. Rumor is that the high command doesn't know what to do with him. They can't lose him, and can't waste him."

"He must be furious, somewhere in limbo," the other pilot added.

Böhme joined them. "I knew him." In the poor light of the window from the train carriage, Böhme couldn't see their expressions, wasn't sure if they believed him.

They looked up at him, towering over them: the Old Man. Tall and aquiline, Böhme was the figure of a stately Teuton made flesh, and held himself so.

"Who?" asked the older pilot.

"I knew Immelmann and Boelcke the younger as well. We called Immelmann 'his Exalted Excellency' after he received his *Pour le Mérite*," said Böhme.

The two pilots looked down, and away, and grew quiet.

"I mean no offense. He was a great man. It was a bit of sport, you see. He enjoyed it." Böhme suddenly regretted joining the conversation. He rambled awkwardly: "The Saxons are deep in mourning, and Berlin was quiet when I passed through, black ribbons hung on his portrait in shop windows. We will miss him. It is a national tragedy."

"Yes, of course. A catastrophe for us all," said the older of the two pilots.

The sky turned from black to grey, as they spoke, extinguishing the stars. An orderly passed through, calling the flight crews to a gathering at the hangar tents. Böhme set his coffee cup on the step of the train carriage and walked to the tent on the end of the row.

Wilhelm Boelcke was gathering the crews; the men circled around him. As the crews came in, they checked in with Wilhelm's adjutant, the man sitting next to a lantern with a clipboard in front of him. Böhme checked in and found his observer, Reiser. They stood, silent, waiting for the others to finish.

Richthofen approached Böhme, his cap off. His short blond hair bristled like cut wheat. Böhme thought that Richthofen looked like a cadet, fresh from school. In the early morning twilight, Richthofen's skin was dark, burned by the sun, with light rings around his eyes from his goggles. His teeth were brilliant white against his burnt face when he smiled.

"How'd you sleep, Old Man?"

Böhme looked down at Richthofen, annoyed once more at the poke at his age. "Well, the wind blew, and the wolves howled, and something tried to get under the edge of my tent. Oh, and the mosquitos were in fine form. Except for all that, it was a good night."

"It's certainly better than the rail cars, a man could suffocate in there," said Richthofen. He pointed at the railcars with a thumb, derisively, over his shoulder. Böhme nodded in agreement. It dawned on Böhme that Richthofen had truly meant well by inviting him out to stay in the woods.

Boelcke's adjutant called for quiet, and reported that all were present. Wilhelm stepped into the light of the lantern and addressed the assembled flyers. The Russians were still on the offensive, and the rail station at Manevychi was crowded with trains and troops. Their mission was to bomb that rail station. Böhme listened closely, but noticed Richthofen whispering to his observer.

"Nothing new to hear from your commander, Richthofen?" Böhme asked as the crews broke up to tend to the aeroplanes.

"Nothing new. Third day in a row doing the same thing. If the Russians had decent anti-aircraft guns, they'd cook us," replied Richthofen. Richthofen turned to Böhme and together, they walked down the line of aeroplanes. They stopped at the tail of Richthofen's Albatros.

"Have a good flight, Richthofen," said Böhme, and turned to his own Albatros.

"Böhme, do you have a minute?" asked Richthofen. He was running his eyes over his aeroplane in the half-light. His observer helped the ground crew to load bombs. "First combat flight here, isn't it?" asked Richthofen.

Böhme sighed, braced himself. "Yes, it is."

"The 'old man' stuff doesn't matter. I spoke with Gerstenberg, said you taught him to fly at Johannisthal," said Richthofen.

Böhme nodded.

"Stick with me, Böhme. We'll deliver our eggs and be back in an hour, in time for breakfast. You'll enjoy this, I'm sure," said Richthofen.

Böhme smiled, and patted Richthofen on the shoulder. "Certainly, happy to."

As each ground crew finished loading an aeroplane, they rolled it out onto the field. The wheels and undercarriages squatted under the extra weight of bombs and fuel. There, the flight crew would start the big Mercedes engines, to let them warm up.

"Oh, Böhme, one more thing," said Richthofen as Böhme turned to go, "do you have that pistol you were waving around this morning?"

"Of course." Böhme reached into his coat pocket, and put his hand around the handle of his pistol. Before Richthofen could respond, he added, "And, I know the Russians hate flyers, they'd sooner string us up from a tree than make a prisoner of us."

Richthofen held up a hand, halting Böhme, "Or worse. They like to cut ears and noses off; they think it proves we're human. I was just going to say, save one bullet."

Böhme nodded. "I see. I'll do that." He saluted and walked to his aeroplane.

The squadron flew to the train station at Manevychi; their loads making them wallow in the air. Trains clogged the station, and tents covered the fields around the village. They lined up their aeroplanes in calm splendor, the pilots holding steady courses as they passed over the village, their observers carefully tossing one bomb after another. Then, turning, the procession of aeroplanes passed over the village again and each dropped another round of bombs.

Böhme stayed close behind Richthofen, his hand and aeroplane steady in the still morning air. Below them, in the village, smoke boiled up, and obscured the trains halted on their tracks. A train and the station had begun to burn.

Böhme and Richthofen dropped their bombs, and together, they turned away from the last pass with one bomb left and approached the Russian lines from the east. Seeing a column of horses, Richthofen waved to Böhme, then pointed at his observer and down at the rows of mounted riders. Turning, Richthofen lined up on the column from the rear and gained altitude. He led Böhme in a swooping dive, while their observers hammered away at the horses and men with their machine guns. The Russians panicked, and scattered across the fields and into the woods. Some men simply ran in circles, waving their arms. Wagons overturned and horses bucked their riders and ran off, trailing reins on the ground. Böhme, astonished at the sight, blanched and grimly turned for another pass.

Below them, broken clumps of thrashing men and horses splayed out on the ground, all semblance of military order undone by the short hail of bullets. Then, Richthofen turned again, leading them back to Kovel.

Ahead of them swayed a single Russian observation balloon, helpless as a beached whale. The two planes climbed, then Richthofen aimed at the balloon and dove. As they attacked, the balloon observer jumped and drifted away under a parachute. Men on the ground, gathered around the balloon's wench, trying to haul it down. Richthofen dropped his bomb, and scattered them. Böhme followed, adding his bomb to the confusion on the ground. The two pilots turned back for Kovel, their big bombers flying wing on wing.

~~~

In the afternoon, Böhme and Richthofen sat in the shade of an Albatros, drinking cold sweet tea in the style of the Russians.

"Did you see them scatter, Richthofen? Like children," asked Böhme.

"Yes, they're always like that. They're uneducated, poor farm kids like many of our boys, but more superstitious; I've heard they think we're dragons." Richthofen sipped his tea.

"Dragons, huh?" said Böhme, smiling at the idea.

"Out here, we fly for fun. I only worry about the machine breaking. It's like playing at war. In the west, with Immelmann dead and Oswald Boelcke in exile from the front, what's to become of us there?"

"Forgive me, Richthofen, but you sound like a fat baker in Berlin, mulling over the news with a house frau over an afternoon tea," replied Böhme. "You did have one bullet hole in your aeroplane this morning."

Richthofen drained his glass, and sat back against the Albatros' wheel to watch a pair of mechanics lift a new wing onto his aeroplane. "Do you hunt, Böhme?" asked Richthofen. "Animals, with guns, not just chasing foxes on horses, like the English."

"No," replied Böhme. "I never have."

"Shame, really, would you like to try? Out here, there are elk, lynx, deer, bear, and your wolves. Menzke is quite keen on it."

"Perhaps, Richthofen. When there is time."

Richthofen looked away from Böhme again, watching the mechanics at work. The mechanics were working at the wing with wrenches, tightening it in place. Another man was stringing the wires on the wings like a villager at her loom.

"Would you go back to the west, given a choice, Richthofen?" asked Böhme.

"I don't know ... given a choice? I don't know," replied Richthofen. "Perhaps, if there is a plan, the right leader. But, of course, we are soldiers, we do as we're told."

Chapter Forty-Two

June 27, 1916
Schwerin, Germany

Fokker, de Waal and Platz were in the factory when they heard shouts from the field, the urgent, all too familiar cries of crisis drifting through the open doors. They tried to ignore the sounds, denying for just a few more moments that they heard them.

Kreutzer had tried to turn the new Fokker biplane, too low, too soon after takeoff, and, losing lift, it slid into the ground. The aeroplane cartwheeled into fragments across a grassy verge. Strapped into the wreckage, he hurtled along the ground with the debris and now was still. He was dying.

The brief twilight of the north-German summer settled over the field.

Ground crew ran to the wreck and began gently peeling away broken strips of canvas from where Kreutzer lay trapped. With enough room to pull him clear, they lifted him under the shoulders and dragged him onto soft grass. He writhed in pain, bleeding to death from the inside. The mechanics tended to him, trying to make him comfortable until the doctor arrived from the city.

A mechanic ran into the factory.

"Herr Fokker, come quickly! Kreutzer has crashed. It's bad."

Fokker scowled at de Waal. "Damn!" he spat.

The three men ran across the field, joining the stream of mechanics and ground crew flowing toward the wreck. They ran through the woods on the west end of the field. Beyond lay the ruin of the Fokker biplane, its wings in tattered shards; the steel fuselage was nearly intact, but the tail pointed upward at an awkward angle. A haze of gas fumes lay over the wreckage like a miasma.

Kreutzer rested with his head on a folded blanket and more blankets piled over him. He was ashen and covered in sweat. His once youthful face now looked hollow, grey and gaunt. With his handsome silver hair matted and dark against his skull, it was as though the young man with silver hair had become an old man with black hair.

He shivered violently, cold from shock and blood loss. One of the female receptionists knelt by him and held his hand, speaking in gentle tones. He moaned.

Fokker ran to Kreutzer and bent over him. "What happened, Martin?" His voice was high and sharp, full of strain.

"I ... the rudder ... began to turn ... but the rudder wouldn't come back ... it rolled ... too low ..." said Kreutzer. Tears of pain ran out of the corners of his eyes and he pulled his knees up, doubling up in a sudden spasm.

Fokker stood and paced around the wreck, once, twice, his body shaking in frustration and anger.

No. NO! This can't be happening.

He stood over Kreutzer and looked down again.

"Do you know what this means? Dammit, Martin, they're trying to kill us ... everything I've built here ... and you go and do *this*?" Fokker said, his voice rising in pitch, nearly yelling, and his tone ugly and accusing.

The crowd went silent and startled faces stared at Fokker. De Waal looked at Fokker, his mouth agape. Someone whispered.

Fokker looked around at their expressions and sensed himself flush with shame. He felt caught, cornered, as he realized what he had just done. Seconds of silence went by, then a few people turned away in disgust.

Fokker looked at de Waal, "Surely, Bernhard, you understand," plead Fokker.

De Waal bent over Kreutzer and took Kreutzer's free hand. "Old friend ..." De Waal looked up at Fokker now with something like pity in his eyes. Kreutzer, past speaking, moved his mouth to speak but no words came out, the strength of his lungs failing. His lips were crimson. Blood dried in the corners of his mouth, deepening to black.

Fokker dropped his head. "I ... I'm sorry ... Martin ..."

From the back of the crowd, white-coated doctors and nurses from the city pushed their way through and bent over Kreutzer. Two nurses lay a stretcher on the ground; a doctor began to examine him.

Kreutzer moaned loudly, once, and grew quiet again.

Fokker turned and pushed back through the crowd, the faces staring at him, the men sullenly backing away to make room for the Dutchman as he passed. Beyond the crowd, Fokker began to move quickly, running. Overhead the sky was grey, the sunlight gone.

At his office, Fokker slammed open the door and sat at his desk. He stared at the desktop for a moment and then rose and went to his receptionist's desk, rummaged through it and retrieved a clear bottle of schnapps, half full. Returning to his desk, he sat a glass next to the bottle and stared at them, trying to feel something besides desperation, knowing he should.

Is this the end?

De Waal and Platz came through the door, and turned on the lights in the dim room. Platz retrieved two coffee cups and sat them on the edge of the desk. He silently poured two drinks from the bottle. He handed one to de Waal and kept the other for himself. They sat down across from Fokker and watched Fokker silently, sipping their drinks.

"Martin is gone," said Platz. "He died before they could get him onto the stretcher." He drank again. Fokker stared at his desk.

Platz waved his cup at Fokker, "Join us, Anton?" he asked.

Fokker shook his head no. "You know, I don't like to drink, but this seemed like one of those times when a man should ... but ... I don't really like to drink."

De Waal tipped his cup up, drained it. He poured himself another.

"You know, I didn't mean to say that," said Fokker.

"I know," said de Waal. "I think Martin did too."

Fokker leaned back in his chair, and arranged the papers on his desk into a neat pile, then sat them on one corner.

"What are we doing, gentlemen?" Fokker asked. De Waal and Platz exchanged glances, silent.

"Building a biplane, with cast off engines, because we're told to build a biplane. Nonsense, nonsense, and *damned* nonsense." He smacked the surface of his desk. "Shall we keep adding wings, tacking them on, until Geertz tells us to stop?"

De Waal and Platz sipped at their drinks, letting Fokker vent his shame.

"You know, when the war started, and the first big orders came in, I felt ... like ... a grown up ... an adult ... as though I had arrived," said Fokker.

A thin smirk crossed de Waal's face.

"Yes, I said it: 'like a grown up'."

Fokker picked up the bottle, swirled it around, and poured a little in his glass. He held it up to his nose and smelled it, then sat the glass down without drinking. "Now, I feel like a child."

"Anton, he was a friend, a colleague; God knows he was more of a designer than any of us," said De Waal.

Fokker looked up quickly, a harsh glint in his eye.

De Waal waved him off. "Yes, even you, Anton."

"Grieve because he was your friend."

"But the factory ... what we're doing here ... it's all damaged ..." said Fokker, his voice soft and callow.

"Oh, good lord, Fokker," said De Waal. "Are you really so ruthless?" He slammed his coffee cup on the desk and stood. "Goodnight, Anton, goodnight, Reinhold. I'll see you in the morning."

De Waal leaned over the desk, his breath acrid with booze. "And I'll attend to the notifications regarding Martin, Anton. So you won't have to." De Waal stalked out of the office, his footsteps pounding down the empty hallway.

Fokker leaned back again and looked out the window. "And you, Platz?"

"I'm here for the duration, Fokker. It beats carrying a rifle. And besides, I like aeroplanes." He sipped his drink. "People die. We can't pretend they won't."

"Reinhold, I thought I was the bastard," said Fokker, glancing at Platz sideways.

"No, Anton, I'm not a bastard. My parents are highly regarded and thoroughly married ... to each other," said Platz. "Besides, I loved Martin.

But this conversation isn't about Martin, is it?"

Fokker looked at Platz again and turned his chair. "Go on, Platz," he said, "I'm listening."

"I think it's your turn, Fokker," said Platz, "What's on your mind?"

Fokker stood, and began pacing behind his desk. He started to speak, and stopped, then stared out the window. Slowly, words came.

"Okay." He paused, and glanced back at the glass on his desk. "Perhaps I still look at this ... business ... as a business ... like a druggist. Tell me what you want ... and I'll give it to you ... what you do with my product is your business." Fokker reached down and sipped his drink, then scowled. The drink burned his throat and his eyes stung.

"How you can drink this stuff ... my God ... and my pretty little receptionist ... God knows how she drinks it..." Fokker set the glass down and pushed it away before he continued speaking. "I can't wait for them to ask, can I? I have to get ahead of the other manufacturers, otherwise, they'll just act like thugs and outmaneuver me ... holding back engines ... questioning my loyalty ..."

"Fokker, you're a businessman now, right? They're not acting like thugs; they're just acting like capitalists. They're using what they've got to beat you, and they're winning at it," Platz said. "How can you beat them, outmaneuver them? Ask yourself that. Martin might have died from any new design. He just happened to die from one that you didn't want to build, don't blame anyone for that, and just move on from that idea."

"I can't relate to them. They're stiff and dogmatic. I can hardly talk to these people, Thomsen, even Geertz, let alone the other manufacturers. The pilots may not all like me, but at least I can relate to flyers," said Fokker.

"So ... talk to the pilots ... sell to them ... don't wait for someone to tell you to build the next best aeroplane ... use your imagination. You did it with the synchronizer, didn't you? I thought you were an ass at the time, and I still do, but at least you were ahead. You're behind now." Platz took another sip.

"Okay, Platz, thanks for the encouraging words," said Fokker, sarcastic.

Platz swirled the schnapps around in his mug before finishing the last swallow. "As long as you're willing to use that big, bright imagination of yours, you've got something here, if you stop, then, you might as well hire more of those guys you got from the torpedo factory to build. They will do it the same way, every time, which is good; but if you do it the same way, every time, someone else will beat you."

Fokker sat down, putting his hands flat on the desk, as though poised to leap up.

Platz stood in the doorway, and turned to face Fokker. "You know, I hear the English are flying a triplane on the coast. I can't imagine why; all that drag, but a lot of lift, I suppose. Probably works well with a low power engine like our rotaries."

Platz turned and stepped into the hallway, and called back over his shoulder, "Martin's death wasn't your fault. You should go and say goodbye to him. Goodnight, Fokker."

"Goodnight, Platz."

Goodnight, Martin.

Fokker tried to imagine dominos, in the dark. He tried to imagine the next, but couldn't.

Chapter Forty-Three

July 20, 1916
Kovel, Ukraine

In the spring, the Russian armies attacked. Then they slowed, and were stopped, outmaneuvered in the field by smaller German armies. Now the days grew hot and the summer grass on the flying field at Kovel lay dead, for men's feet, aeroplane tires, gas and oil had conspired to kill it. But it was the sun that finally vanquished the grass, drying it until the blades were brittle and weak, left to be ground away under ceaseless traffic. The newly bare soil rose up in huge clouds of dust behind the German aeroplanes as they took flight to chase the Russians.

The afternoon flights had just come in when Oswald Boelcke arrived at Kovel by train. He wore a Turkish fez. His *Pour le Mérite* was clasped at his throat. The sun was low in the west, but still blazed, the scalding light leaving his sunburned skin aching and sore. He pulled his collar close, hiding his neck from the unforgiving rays.

Wilhelm greeted his brother with a salute and an embrace. He presented Oswald to Kastner, Wilhelm's commander, and then they walked through the aeroplanes, Wilhelm introducing the younger Boelcke to pilots and crew, proud to be parading him. Fischer followed behind them, carrying Oswald's valises.

"And this is Böhme, the mountain climber." Böhme stood up from a chess board, and extended his hand, a broad grin on his face. To Oswald he appeared to be playing the game by himself.

Böhme took Oswald's hand and shook vigorously. "Good to see you, we've met before ..." said Böhme. Oswald looked at him vacantly for just a moment, then flashing a warm smile.

"Of course. How are you? Is this your aeroplane?" asked Oswald, grinning. He stepped over to the side of an Albatros, ran his hand over an imposing image decorating the fuselage. His grin broadened.

"A dragon. Really? Remarkable."

"Yes. I like to think it scares the peasants, but I can't be sure of that," said Böhme. "I painted it myself, well, my mechanic and I."

Oswald stood back to take in the entirety of the bright yellow dragon twisting down the length of Böhme's aeroplane. He walked to the other side and back around. "Both sides, no less. I like your spirit, Böhme."

Richthofen strode from behind the rudder, von Lyncker behind him.

"And I believe you know Richthofen, and this is Lyncker, who has just joined us," said Wilhelm. Oswald shook their hands and beamed a broad smile.

"We're old friends, aren't we, Manfred?" said Oswald.

"Yes, I'm proud to say so," said Richthofen. "Where have you been? We heard you were barred from flying."

Oswald waved a hand toward the fez on his head. "This, gentlemen, is standard issue for our men in Turkey, so I'm quite in uniform." The men laughed.

"And what did you do there?" asked Richthofen.

"Raised morale. Mostly mine. The German nurses were quite friendly ... most modern and, well, lacking in shyness."

"And what brings you here?"

"I'm on a mission, an assignment, but all in good time, Richthofen."

~~~

The echoes of artillery to the east faded away, and the music of animals filled the night. The wolves were already howling while Oswald and Wilhelm talked of the war.

"Tell us about your trip, Oswald," asked Wilhelm.

"The south; Austria, Turkey, Romania. A grand tour. It was good for my lungs, dry air and all."

"That's not what I mean. Exile, were you banished?"

"Well, after Max's death, the Kaiser, the Chief of Staff, Thomsen; all were concerned that if I were to die, then there would be some great grief across the army. I suppose that's what you'd call it. A Great Grieving. As though we might lose the war because of it," Oswald said. "It seems a little absurd, doesn't it? A little odd … Isn't Teuton mythology about the fallen hero, the quest for revenge?"

"Perhaps they think of you less as a god, and more as a useful warrior," said Wilhelm. "Perhaps they don't want you dead, too. After all, the British don't let their best fly. The Englishman commander, Hawker, the one who flew over Immelmann's funeral, supposedly he isn't allowed to fly combat either. The idea, I take it, is that if you stay behind and teach others, and then you could have a greater impact than any one man in the air."

"Not you, too, Wilhelm?" said Oswald. Oswald squirmed, uncomfortable. The idea of sending men to their deaths, and not facing it himself, was something strange, foreign. *That's for generals and kings,* thought Oswald. *If I hear this again … self-serving rot, they just want me to be a face on posters … an inspiration.*

"Thomsen seemed to think that way. He had me spend two weeks with him before the tour. He had me write these." Oswald reached into a pocket and pulled out a sheet of paper. "I think he knows I won't be happy sitting behind, won't stand for it. So, he wants me to write down my ideas on paper. I humored him."

"What's this, more advice about autograph seekers?" Wilhelm took the page and folded it out flat next to the lantern. 'Dicta Boelcke' was written across the top. Wilhelm skimmed it, curious, and then leaned forward to read more carefully.

Oswald waited patiently while he listened to the howling in the distance. It's beautiful, he thought. *The sound: so ancient and pure.*

"Very interesting. That simple, eh?" said Wilhelm as he finished reading.

"Simple, but not so simple. Very difficult, really. I wonder if I didn't just write it to get them to let me be," said Oswald. "They want there to be a formula. An equation, or a recipe to make fighters. And, that will be the end of us, already grown too old, when everyone masters the machinery of the day."

"I didn't know you were a philosopher, Oswald!" Wilhelm laughed.

"Do you have anything to drink, anything strong?"

"Vodka. Made from potatoes." Wilhelm stood and reached into his desk, pulled out a bottle. He poured them each a drink.

Oswald lifted his glass, took a small sip, then another. He sat the glass down. "Max is dead. Otto Parschau is dead. Things are bleak. We're being beaten, but worse than that, so many good men, good flyers, are dying. You've heard of the Somme?"

"Yes, I've heard of the British attack there," said Wilhelm. "But, we're a long way from there."

"A long way from the truth of the matter, eh? The British and French, both attacking us on the seam between their armies. We had to halt our attacks in Verdun to build up a reserve to deal with the British. Isn't it supposed to be the other way around, we attack their weaknesses?" He took another sip of vodka, bigger this time, and felt the warmth flow through him. "Do you suppose they did it just to show us that they aren't weak when taken together?"

Wilhelm grew quiet, feeling that Oswald needed to speak. He sipped his own drink.

"They've concentrated their aeroplanes, brought out new types, British pushers, French single-seat Nieuports. They rule the sky. These are black days for us in the west. The Kaiser, I suspect, is livid. The English rules the waves, and now the Allies rule the air." He sipped again, and then smacked his lips. "But, you seem to have it good out here."

They both paused, listened to the wolves. "I suppose," said Wilhelm. Wilhelm held out the paper again, read it through once more.

Oswald reached up and pressed his fingers onto his *Pour le Mérite,* caressing it. "They've taken to calling this 'The Blue Max' now, after Immelmann. Did I tell you about meeting the Kaiser?" asked Oswald.

"No, Oswald, go on," said Wilhelm, waving is glass.

"We met over dinner, he asked a great many questions about tactics and fights. He was most interested. Not at all as lackluster as he might appear in photos. I told him about the Frenchman that I shot down, when the observer climbed out on his wing and looked at me with such terror. He laughed mightily. I laughed with him, though it wasn't meant to be a funny story. He said that he thought his grandfather must be rolling over in his grave because they give *Pour le Mérites* to Leutnants now." Wilhelm laughed.

Oswald took a sip and continued. "And I went to the opera. Schramm was singing. He changed the words, in the middle of the opera, to sing about me. And all the opera glasses aimed in my direction. I had to leave." Oswald sipped his vodka and finished it. "Max would have loved it, bless his immortal heart. He was a better celebrity than I am. I couldn't stay there like a bug under glass."

"What will you do when you go back?" asked Wilhelm.

"I don't know, perhaps I'll stay here with you. Fly dragons." Oswald shrugged. "Do you have more of that?" He pointed to his glass, and Wilhelm poured him another drink.

~~~

Wilhelm had stayed behind on the afternoon flights, and instead sat under a tree with Oswald, the brothers nursing headaches with lemonade and schnapps. The field was quiet, the aeroplanes all out, only mechanics moved about, tending to the tents and tools. Oswald wore the newest fashion: eyeglasses made of dark glass to protect the eyes from the sun.

The squadron's mascots, a stork and a jackdaw, sat on their perches next to the Boelckes. The jackdaw would fly to rest on the stork's back for a few moments, then fly back to its own perch. The stork didn't seem to mind.

As the brothers shared stories, Wilhelm's adjutant approached them and saluted. "A telegram for Oswald Boelcke from Oberstleutnant Leith-Thomsen, sir." He held out a paper. Wilhelm took it, and handed it to Oswald without looking at it.

Oswald pressed it flat on his knee, and sipped his schnapps, then his lemonade. He held the message up and read it.

"What is it?" asked Wilhelm.

Oswald handed the paper to Wilhelm, who read it quickly. "Well, that answers that question," he said.

~~~

For dinner that evening, the mechanics cleaned out a hangar tent, and rolled up the sides to let the breeze blow through. The mess orderlies brought tables from the rail cars and arranged them in neat rows, with two tables placed at one end for the guest of honor. The orderlies lit oil lamps on each table to try to keep the mosquitos at bay. Oily, sticky smoke filled the space under the canvas, and the distant familiar howling crept in from the darkness. Clear glass bottles of vodka stood next to each plate, in the Russian tradition.

In Oswald Boelcke's honor, they served venison from the forest and scavenged potatoes, baked in cream. Kastner, Wilhelm, Oswald and the other *Kampfstaffel* commanders sat at the head tables through dinner, quietly speaking amongst themselves.

After dinner, Oswald teetered to the middle of the tent, and quickly took a chair, leaving its former owner standing. "Gentlemen, I've been asked to give a few words," Oswald said as he climbed onto the chair like a boastful boy. The men grew quiet and the orderlies retreated into the darkness.

"I have excellent news to share with all of you, and with your commanders' permission I will do so, now." He waved a glass and wobbled slightly on the chair as hands went up to steady him.

"New, better aeroplanes are coming to us in the west. But, I don't think you need them here." The men laughed.

"As you may have heard, the English and French are exerting tremendous pressure on us, flying to our side of the lines. We will end this. Some of you, if not all of you, will be in the west soon, after you finish off the Russians." A cheer went up and Oswald waved his drink in the air.

Someone shouted out, "And what of you?"

"I look forward to flying with you." He stepped down from the chair.

Oswald looked over at his brother, who waved to Oswald to continue. He climbed back up on the chair.

"Well, you'll hear about it soon enough. Gentlemen, I'm headed back to the west, to form a new flying unit. We're calling it a Jagdstaffel. A hunting squadron!" The men grew quiet contemplating what that might mean, and more specifically, what it might mean to them.

Böhme stared out into the darkness, imagining something slinking through the shadows. Richthofen leaned over to Böhme and whispered in his ear. "Stop listening to the wolves and pay attention."

"Richthofen, I thought I was paying attention."

~~~

The night was at its most still. The wolves had finally stopped howling and moved away into the further recesses of the dark Russian forest.

The footfalls grew closer, and then stopped outside of his tent. Richthofen had heard them coming, the rhythmic sounds entering his mind in his sleep and waking him. Richthofen's hound, Moritz, calmed down after the wolves moved on, and curled up in the corner of the tent. Lyncker was snoring softly when lantern light shown through the flaps in the entrance. The flap drew open and Oswald Boelcke stepped into the tent.

"Richthofen?" he hissed into the darkness.

"Here," Richthofen replied, and sat up. Moritz raised his head and sat up as well. Richthofen ordered the dog back down again.

"It's Oswald Boelcke. May we speak?"

"Of course," replied Richthofen, stirring.

Richthofen stood, pulled on his pants and walked barefoot to the entrance to the tent while Boelcke waited. They stepped outside into the warm summer morning air.

"I thought you were leaving this morning," said Richthofen.

"I am. In a few minutes. I am here to make a request of you, Richthofen."

Richthofen was suddenly awake, his mind scrambled for the meaning of this visit, his head clearing. He smelled the clean cool air of the forest, trees and growth; he thought of hunting.

"Yes, of course," replied Richthofen.

Boelcke stood, tottering in the night air. His eyes were red by the lantern light.

"Will you join me? In the west, come fly for me? This is a request, not an order," said Boelcke.

Are you drunk? Mad? Then, Richthofen felt a surge of joy, a focusing of his mind, clarity of thought. Finally, he would have a chance to fight against a real enemy. He stopped himself before he hugged Boelcke, held his hands at his sides, and then raised a stiff salute in the lantern light.

"Yes. Certainly. Absolutely," said Richthofen with an earnest handshake. "But, why me?"

Boelcke wobbled slightly. His breath smelled of vodka and cigars. He sighed and lowered the lantern; letting the light cast out over the ground. "It is cooler out here, Richthofen," he said, "Not as hot and dry as up on the field."

"Yes, it's easier to sleep. Closer to the wild things, I'm afraid, though." He thought of Böhme.

Looking over at Boelcke, Richthofen watched the man reflect for a moment, patient for a well-formed answer. Briefly, he considered what a bad answer might sound like, or that perhaps there was no answer, that this was merely an impulsive move on Boelcke's part. Richthofen slapped a mosquito and stood quietly. Moritz stuck his head out of the tent, and Richthofen scratched the hound behind an ear. He waited, letting Boelcke find the words.

Boelcke gazed off into the dark, past the light of the lantern. "Because you have it ... like Parschau...not like Max. You're a technician, not an artist. I don't need finesse, I need calculated viciousness."

Richthofen absorbed the words for a minute and pondered Boelcke. Here was the man that inspired so many, friend to everyone, the man who had jumped into a canal to save a French boy. Boelcke, he of the rehearsed sermons, on the train, at Metz. His heart pounded: here was the offering to become a warrior, to not exist at the edges anymore. He must accept, to take Boelcke at face value.

Richthofen saluted Boelcke and pulled the tent flap back. He blurted out a reply, eager for the moment to be over, preserved. "Thank you, Boelcke, I understand."

Boelcke hesitated, and Richthofen stopped, casting a quizzical look at Oswald. *Is there more? An explanation I don't want to hear?*

Finally, Boelcke spoke, unguarded words. "And, I mean no offense, but killing for the sake of killing, killing so personally, is different. You've done it now, even in your two-seater. It's personal, particularly so because it's another flyer. You can see their personality in the way they fly. You can tell if they're afraid, oblivious, angry, or just stupid. You know if they're a good flyer, experienced ... all in a few seconds. Don't you?"

Richthofen nodded, and Boelcke continued. "It's personal, and you know it, and it doesn't bother you. I think you're the perfect man for a war of machines: just cold enough." The last of his words were slightly slurred and he wavered as he stood. Richthofen thought of the alcohol, wondered if it were a truth serum. He felt the genuineness of Boelcke's words, saw them in himself. He felt emptied.

"Thank you, Boelcke. I appreciate your candor. I think you'll find that you've chosen well," Richthofen said.

"Good night, Richthofen. See you in France." Boelcke turned and held the lantern out as he began walking back through the forest to the field.

Richthofen looked after him and thought of Diogenes, with his lantern, looking for an honest man.

From inside the tent, Lyncker called out. "What are you doing, Richthofen? What's going on out there?"

Richthofen stepped back into the tent and pulled the flaps closed. He found his way to his bed in the darkness by memory and sat down. Reaching out, he felt for the top of the table next to his bed and found matches. He lit one and then lit the oil lantern.

"What the hell?" said Lyncker as he squinted into the unwelcome light.

"It was Oswald Boelcke," said Richthofen.

Lyncker sat up on one arm in bed and looked at Richthofen through bleary eyes. "And what did he want?"

"He wants me to fly for him, in France. With his *Jagdstaffel*," said Richthofen.

Lyncker looked at the tent flaps as though he expected them to move.

"Well then. You accepted, didn't you?"

"Yes, I did. I told him I'd fly for him."

Lyncker ran a hand over his face and then lay back in bed. He put his back to Richthofen and spoke into his mattress. "Then don't come back without the *Pour le Mérite*, Richthofen."

What do they call it? Oh, yes, The Max. The Blue Max. "Okay, Lyncker. I won't," he said into the silence. *The Blue Max, that sounds fine.*

Chapter Forty-Four

September 15, 1916
Vélu German Aerodrome
2 km North of Bertincourt, France

Twenty kilometers southwest of the airfield lay the bends of the Somme River. Above its banks, thousands of men died each day, struggling for a few meters of ground. The British and the French attacked in waves, and the battle would surge in one direction, their men and artillery concentrating, then it would shift when the defenders inevitably pushed back.

Over the battlefield, the English fighters and the little French fighters, their scouts, were hammering the German air force, pinning them behind the lines, allowing the English artillery spotters freedom to do their devil's work. The German infantry saw only Allied aircraft over their heads, directing artillery unmolested. Boelcke's challenge was simple: Stop them.

The aerodrome was a farmer's field, ringed on one side by a stand of poplars, still bearing a few green leaves at the end of the summer. The farmer's barn was now a hangar, Boelcke's home, a headquarters. The crewmen of the staffel stood up more tents each day, scrounged from local German army units, leftovers from captured British and French canvas. The scene possessed the deportment of a circus, with roustabouts in uniforms.

Boelcke paced the field; Fischer walked alongside.

"Fischer, will they be here, soon?"

"Yes, sir, the pilots and the prisoner. They rang from the town; they are on their way."

Boelcke stopped and drew a deep breath, letting it out slowly so that he wouldn't wheeze. So many things were coming together so quickly, and his flyers were at the center of it all. It was as though he could feel the pressure from every direction. Pain radiated out from his chest and tears gathered in his eyes. He turned away from Fischer and quickly dapped his sleeve against his eyes. He put one hand over his shirt pocket and felt the box of cigarettes inside. It reassured him to know they were there. The mixture of belladonna and tobacco was his only refuge from his lungs' treachery.

The English Vickers and French Nieuports had all but finished off the last of the Eindekker pilots. Immelmann, Parschau, a dozen others, all dead. Wintgens at Jasta 1 still dared fly an Eindekker, even now, but he was among the last. The new German biplanes were arriving in a trickle, in ones and twos, not enough to put up a formation of youngsters that could hold their own.

Boelcke felt as though time was running away from him, that there was no way to gather all the parts and men, and build something that could hold back the crushing flood of allied aeroplanes. He looked across the field, and thought of what he needed to say, of the lessons he would give them today. From his coat pocket, he pulled free a single sheet of paper, all the lessons he could muster these days, his dicta. Simple, clear, direct words.

Boelcke read the sheet again. He asked himself, are they stupid? Do I talk to them like they're children? Do these words even matter? If only my pilots could divine them, take them to heart, learn them without the need to understand why each mattered. He knew it was the understanding, the clarity of the moment that was too expensive, the price in souls that paid for each line on the sheet of paper that was more than they could continue to pay.

He thought of his father, the teacher: patient, repetitious, calm. Encouraging.

Father, if there is a moment when I need to be like you, it is this one, and it is more important than any lesson you ever taught, more important than any lesson you ever scribbled in a classroom.

One of the mechanics, a deep baritone, began to sing from within one of the sheds, his voice carrying across the field. The man sang the *Hate Hymn of England.*

"French and Russian,
They matter not,
a blow for a blow and a shot for a shot!
We love them not, we hate them not ..."

No, thought Boelcke. *I don't hate any of them.*

"... We will never forego our hate,
We have all but a single hate,
We love as one, we hate as one,
We have one foe and one alone, England!"

My God, do we really hate? I don't think so, but, if perhaps we need to hate ...

The pilots' truck from Bertincourt would be rattling in at any moment. He needed to compose himself, to be ready. Play the role. He took a deep gulp of air, felt the strain in his chest again, the tightness. It was worse here on the ground than flying. Here, all his thoughts intruded, becoming interruptions and concerns. The demands of his position damaged his clarity.

He looked across the field at his three rather forlorn airplanes: his whole Jasta, the entirety of his squadron. Not power, not the ability to change, to press back the flood and gather it, just enough to hold their fingers in the dike. Two new Fokker biplanes and the Albatros D.I that Reinmann had flown over from Jasta 1 were all he had.

Three. Three God-damned airplanes.

The singing continued.

"He is known to you all,
he is known to you all,
He crouches behind the dark gray flood,
Full of envy, of rage, of craft, of gall,
Cut off by waves that are thicker than blood! ..."

There, in a shed, was the key. The one that could lay victory bare, exposed and vulnerable. *They should be ready, they've had enough time, hours. It was nearly intact when it got here; surely, the mechanics could mend it enough to tell us what we need to know.*

To the south, from the German aerodrome at Bertincourt, he heard the rumble of airplane engines. He turned and watched as a flight—five, no six—of Jasta 1's new Albatros fighters rose, climbed steeply, then turned south.

Zander's boys. Wintgens, their best, will still be flying his solo missions in an Eindekker; a lone wolf, thought Boelcke. *It will be the death of him.*

It was hypocrisy, his own hypocrisy to criticize Wintgens. Each morning that an airplane was ready and the sky was even a little clear, Boelcke flew alone. It was a rare dawn when he didn't pick out an Englishman and shoot him down. He told himself he was inspiring the men, that it wasn't foolish, that he was actually helping the effort to beat the British.

Then he thought of Wintgens' foolish commitment to his old Fokker and to flying solo and he doubted his intentions.

Is this just sport? Like Wintgens in the last Eindekker, do I fly for the sake of it? For the sake of not sleeping in a muddy hole in the ground? Perhaps what I do here will make no difference at all, and perhaps we are hanging onto a thread. And maybe, the freedom that comes from flying alone is the only thing I'm here for, having no one to worry about. The freedom to pick my own battles.

He turned from the middle of the field and walked toward the old work sheds under the trees. There had been another flying unit here, but they had gone now, as the front moved closer they retreated to the north. It was truly his field; his four little buildings, his square kilometer of grass, his three airplanes, his un-blooded pilots, his sixty-odd mechanics. All his. A house of cards.

One shell in the wrong place, one bullet, and it will fall apart, airplanes and men scattered, dead and gone and defeated.

The thought made him feel weak and brought that awful stiffness in his chest.

To the west, the sound of the artillery changed, deepened, broadened.

It wasn't the usual thumping, it rose from cacophony into a single bass note, thick and ugly and dark. Almost a hum. He hated it. He had never been under it like Richthofen, but he hated the pure randomness of it. The guns reached out, guessing. They killed people with a roll of the dice, over and over.

The mechanic reached the end of his song and other men joined in.

"We love as one,
We hate as one,
We have one foe and one alone, England!"

Then, "GOTT STRAFE ENGLAND!"

Some wag in the German infantry had coined the phrase, "God punish England, our airmen and our artillery," Boelcke had grown tired of hearing it, for he knew they deserved it, that the German airmen couldn't protect them.

Well, now is the time to change all that. Here and now. Through force of will and a few scribbles on a piece of paper. Three aeroplanes.

He looked toward a closed shed.

And that.

The truck clanked in with the pilots in the back and stopped at the far shed. Behind it, a staff car turned off the road and parked next to the truck. Boelcke took a few steps toward them and then stood with his hands behind his back. He swallowed to clear his throat and then took a lungful of air, conscious of the effort. The men, his new pilots, began jumping down and moving toward Boelcke.

Boelcke greeted the pilots. Richthofen strode over in a stiff legged gait, using an ornate thick-knobbed walking stick. Moritz trailed behind him, darting clumsily between the other pilots. Boelcke reached out and took the stick from Richthofen's hand.

"Very nice. Where did this come from?" asked Boelcke.

"My mechanic, Holzapfel, carved it for me from an old propeller. You like it?"

"Yes, fine work." Boelcke handed it back to Richthofen.

"You'll excuse me for a moment." Boelcke nodded to Richthofen. "The show is about to begin."

Boelcke stepped to the closed shed, opened the door and slid inside. He looked over their prize: the key. "Is it ready?" he asked.

"Yes, Herr Hauptmann," came the reply.

"Very good. Roll it out. We have guests," Boelcke said. Boelcke swung the doors of the shed open himself, then stood to one side, hands clasped behind his back. He watched the reaction of his men.

The mechanics lifted the tail of the English fighter, and one mechanic stood at each wing as they pushed the airplane out into the sunlight. A look of curiosity passed over their faces, then a vague dread. The German pilots looked over at the apparition, as though it was some exotic creature, as though they were looking at a tiger in a zoo. They were quiet, awed.

"And how did you do this morning, Hauptmann?" asked Richthofen, grinning, nonplussed.

"Two, both Sopwiths," said Boelcke. "It was a good morning."

A German soldier helped an English flyer out of the staff car. The bewildered young man blinked at the sunlight. His right arm was in a sling, wrapped in thick cotton cloth. Boelcke walked over and introduced himself as a young Sargent translated his words.

"Welcome to our little base," said Boelcke. "I am Hauptmann Oswald Boelcke."

The Englishman blinked again, a look of amazement on his face.

"Second Lieutenant Jack Bowring." He nodded down at his arm. "My apologies for not saluting," he said. The translator spoke Bowring's words in German.

When the translator finished, Boelcke smiled and said, "No, my apologies. I'm the man that put the bullet in you."

Bowring grew quiet, dumbstruck. "I see," he finally said.

"Please, join us." Boelcke waved his hand toward Bowring's de Havilland. "We were just admiring your aeroplane."

With the translator trailing behind, Bowring followed slowly, his eyes on the solitary Albatros fighter sitting on the field. He looked back at Boelcke and said aloud, to no one in particular, "Well, I guess there's no shame in being shot down by Boelcke."

The German translator smiled and replied. "No, there is not, I'm quite sure."

Boelcke arched his eyebrows. "What did he say?"

"He said that he's proud to have been shot down by you."

Boelcke laughed.

Leutnant Hoehn climbed into the cockpit of Bowring's fighter and Böhme took a photograph. Muller and Richthofen stood off to the side, away from the camera.

Boelcke stopped and Bowring stood next to him. "Gentlemen, I'd like you to meet the brave pilot of this fine aircraft, Leutnant Bowring."

The Jasta pilots circled him, and introduced themselves with friendly smiles. Bowring seemed pleased, and awkwardly shook hands with his good arm. The mechanics had gathered at the door of the shed to watch the spectacle. The singer with the baritone voice seemed particularly amused.

"So, Bowring, do you have any questions for us?" Boelcke smiled broadly.

Bowring looked surprised again, feeling a touch off guard. His eyes were on the Albatros. To the west, the sound of the artillery surged up, and then died down.

"Yes, one, I suppose," said Bowring.

"Please, go ahead, I'll answer if I can," said Boelcke.

"Well, Captain, where is the black one? Your black ship?" said Bowring.

Boelcke's eyes grew dark and he furrowed his brow, appearing to be in thought. Richthofen looked at Böhme quizzically. Böhme looked back and shrugged his shoulders, shook his head as if to say, 'I don't know.'

"You must understand, Bowring, that I can't show it to you. Utmost secret. But, it is in there." Boelcke pointed at the most distant shed, in the manner of a conspirator.

Bowring nodded, sagely, his face becoming serious.

"Boelcke, what's that all about?" asked Böhme.

"Which part?"

"The whole thing, I suppose, but the part about a black airplane, what was that all about?"

Boelcke laughed. "A bit of English mythos. They think I fly an all-black airplane. Like a pirate ship. The English, can you believe it?"

Richthofen bit back his laughter.

"Perhaps you'd like to see the Albatros fighter," said Boelcke to Bowring. He gestured to the Albatros fighter.

"That would be most kind," said Bowring, his face still a mask of seriousness.

"Tell me, Bowring, about your machine."

Bowring hesitated and blanched, then looked down at the ground.

"Oh, we'll fly her soon enough, Bowring. Pilot to pilot, how does she fly?" asked Boelcke.

Bowring looked up and held Boelcke's eyes for a moment. He nodded, as if answering his own question. He began to speak. "Well, she turns like a banshee, but tends to drop altitude in hard turns. Spins quickly, but recovers pretty well. Being a rotary, she turns left better than right, by a far sight." A flight of Jasta 4 Albatroses flew over from the north and Bowring looked up, mouth agape, watching them fly by.

Hoehn, the little youngster, the painter, climbed down from the cockpit and Muller, an experienced fighter with a kill of his own, took his place.

Boelcke led Bowring off to the Albatros.

My God, you're a boy, younger than even my brood, thought Boelcke. *But you've helped a great deal.*

Bowring reached out and lay his good hand gingerly on the plywood side of the Albatros, as though he were touching a myth.

"Perhaps you'll join us in our club this evening, the Sargent will see to it." Boelcke indicated the translator. Bowring drew his hand back.

"Certainly, I'd be pleased," said Bowring. His guard led him away to the staff car.

Boelcke grew serious, gathered the men. "Look closely, men," said Boelcke, gesturing at the English fighter. "This is the aeroplane type that killed Parschau, from the very squadron that killed him. They almost killed me two weeks ago, two of them attacked and I had to dive away."

The pilots grew serious now.

"They have two squadrons of these ships here. Number 24 and number 29. Number 24 has red wheel covers, and barber pole painted struts, 29 has white wheel covers. Killers, all. If you see one, shoot him down." Boelcke ran his eyes over the men, gauging their reactions.

"Gentlemen, do not turn with these ships. They will want to turn left, following their rotary. Stay above and outside their turns. Wait for them to break the turn, then turn and dive from a position of height. Understand?" The pilots nodded, murmured agreement. "Out climb them, stay above them, and use your power. Don't fight at their level if it can be avoided. It may look a little ridiculous, but it's a dangerous machine. In good hands, it's a *very* dangerous machine."

"We only have a couple of hours for training this afternoon, for, I have good news," said Boelcke.

The men all looked up, poised.

"We have new aircraft waiting for us at the railhead in Cambrai. A crew from the Albatros factory and some of our ground crew are there now. We'll ferry them over this evening. Tomorrow, we begin training."

Chapter Forty-Five

September 16, 1916
Vélu Aerodrome, France

The English shifted their artillery fire from the southwest of the field to the south, leaving the earth around Delville wood, the Devil Wood, a chewed wasteland. The forest was bare stumps now, the trunks splintered and smoldering. Rumors spread among the Germans that the French had joined the battle and were attacking south of the airfield toward Rancourt. During the night, the crewmen of the Staffel gathered and climbed ladders to the tops of the sheds to watch the flashes of artillery on the horizon in a vast show of hate and fury. They passed schnapps and toasted their good fortune that they weren't under the artillery bombardment. They would drink until they could barely climb back down the ladders, and often fell, before stumbling to their tents to sleep.

In the early morning, Boelcke and his four best pilots took the train to the city of Rethel to fly five new Albatros D.II fighters back to the field. The new fighters were sleek; where the Taubes borrowed the shape of the wing of a dove, the Albatros fighters copied the body of a shark. At the front of the fierce little aeroplanes, a rounded fairing covered the propeller hubs: a detail that gave the machines a look of motion, an air of swiftness. Their lines were uninterrupted and smooth from the nose to the tail. Each bore two machine guns in front of their cockpits, a menacing touch. Across their wings was painted camouflage, jagged blotches of rust, green and mauve—a military touch that conveyed something unique, a purpose-built machine, a true fighter.

The pilots flew them gently, learning their feel, their nuisances, by small gestures, gentle motions. Richthofen felt a sense of sureness, of pent-up power in the Albatros fighter. It climbed unlike anything he had ever flown, turned quickly in either direction; flew as if it was meant to be in the air, as though it had no other home. By the time they arrived at the field, he had the feel of the machine, and knew he could fight in it. Delicacy extended to brashness, into a series of joyful barrel rolls as they arrived over the field.

The mechanics lined the new aeroplanes up, sitting them on their tails on stands, so that their guns could fire straight and level over the ground. The chosen few pilots of the Jasta each selected one and sat in the cockpits, rehearsing the controls and instruments.

In the late afternoon, after the men had some time to learn the new aeroplanes, the mechanics began starting the engines. When the engines had warmed, they would shut each off again, then the armorers carried heavy belts of ammunition to the aeroplanes and loaded the guns. Guns loaded, the pilots and crew would start the engines again. Then the pilots would fire the guns, testing the synchronizers. The hammering of the machine guns mixed with the solid cracks of bullet strikes on the trees, deafening everyone.

As the afternoon began to cool, the field filled with exhaust, oil fumes and gun smoke. The grey fog stank of chemicals and combustion, the sharp smell pleasing the mechanics but few others.

Boelcke had bartered a case of French wine for paint from a quartermaster in Bapaume and now he had the mechanics paint the tail-planes of the Albatrosses black on one side, and white on the other. Then the mechanics rolled their precious machines back into their sheds.

By lantern light, Richthofen sat in his new cockpit, feeling the controls late into the evening. Outside, the darkness gave way to the flickering lights of the artillery on the horizon and the mechanics climbed the sheds once again to drink their schnapps and watch the show. He stayed in the cockpit long after the last truck had left for their quarters in Bertincourt.

Perhaps tomorrow. Perhaps someone will see this time, perhaps I'll get credit. We'll see, we'll see.

The controls felt smooth under his hands, flowing against their stops.

The feeling calmed him, like the feel of trained horse, predictable, not surprising. Tomorrow morning, weather allowing, they would fly. He let the lantern burn down and then out, dozing. He grew comfortable in the thin leather seat, an arm propped against the rim of the cockpit. In the hours before dawn, he slept.

~~~

It was a Sunday. The day dawned clear and warm. The air was still. The heavens were a cloudless azure blue, untinged by the grey of the artillery smoke in the west, free of the stink of death from the Somme.

Boelcke ordered the Albatros fighters brought out before the pilots arrived from town; the mechanics stirred Richthofen awake in his leather nest. He emerged from the shed and splashed water on his face, and walked to the farmer's abandoned house to try to find coffee.

Three of the new machines were gathered in a bunch, tails to the woods. Their mechanics moved about them, topping off fuel, checking oil, and loading belts of ammunition. The pilots' truck arrived from Bertincourt and the young pilots of the staffel began to gather around the aeroplanes.

Boelcke and Böhme were already flying and they came in low from the western horizon and landed. Böhme leapt from his Albatros as it rolled to a stop, and then ran to the side of Boelcke's machine. As Boelcke climbed down to the ground, Böhme hugged Boelcke, and then stepped back and saluted.

"I have a victory!" Böhme shouted, running to the other pilots. Gun smoke ringed his eyes, and his smile contrasted against the sooty mask. The pilots gathered around Böhme, congratulating him, and clapping him on the back. Even the mechanics gathered and wiped their grease away to shake Böhme's hand.

Richthofen joined Boelcke, who was examining his Albatros after the flight. He looked up and met Richthofen's smile with his own.

"A test flight today, Richthofen?" asked Boelcke.

"Of course, Hauptmann, of course! We're all keen to fly." Richthofen gestured towards the crowd gathered around Böhme.

"I see, they appear quite impatient," Boelcke said lightly. "Just the new airplanes, five only. We'll fly them together and see what they can do."

Richthofen turned, calling over the pilots and crew. Fischer passed a metal pot stacked with sandwiches made from black bread and cheese. Boelcke joined them, took one and began.

"We'll fly east gentlemen, then, turn north over Cambrai and then back to the field. We're not looking for trouble, understand, just getting used to the machines." He watched the faces of the pilots sag, and took another bite of his sandwich before pointing it towards the new aeroplanes.

"Go ahead, then, mount up!"

The pilots turned to their machines and began climbing in. One by one, the powerful Mercedes engines were started and idled, warming up.

Boelcke climbed into his machine and waved to the mechanic, who pulled at the propeller. The engine roared. With a signal from Boelcke, the five fighters throttled up and elegantly slipped skyward in a cloud of noise. They climbed steeply and then turned behind Boelcke, angling as they climbed, then settled on a course to the east.

Richthofen was elated. He pulled back on the yoke slightly, lifting the nose of the fighter, and pulled the throttle out to its limit, listening to the engine roar, full-throated. The beast pulled harder, drawing him deeper into the climb.

As they ascended, the new pilots watched Boelcke, and Boelcke watched the sky. To the northeast over Cambrai, puffs of anti-aircraft fire bloomed pale grey against the blue skies. He adjusted their course to the south slightly and let the aeroplanes climb as steeply as they could, their engines at full power. Boelcke tipped his head to the side and inspected his rough formation of aeroplanes, in echelon, staggered out and angled back, as he had taught them.

Boelcke throttled back and leveled his Albatros, then pointed a gloved hand to the left of his aeroplane's nose and down slightly. Richthofen looked and saw nothing. Boelcke pointed once more then cocked each of his Spandaus. With both guns charged, he put his hands back on the control yoke and pressed the firing button. A harsh rap of fire erupted from the guns. He looked back at his gaggle of novices and watched with amusement as the heads of the pilots began to swivel around, looking for a target. Only Richthofen's eyes were down and in front.

Richthofen cocked both his weapons. With a roar, he fired them, readying them for action. He could see the tiny moving dots now on the horizon, perhaps four or five, moving north towards Cambrai. An English squadron. The angle of flight of Boelcke's formation put them between the English and the frontline, cutting them off. Next to him, another set of guns fired, then another, as each pilot finally spotted the English airplanes.

Boelcke steered right slightly, angling a little further ahead. The speed of the new Albatros fighters was bringing them over and behind the English.

Then Richthofen saw the other formation, flying with the first group, another six. Ten English airplanes were ahead and below. He felt a chill pass over and through him and then float away. Behind the coldness, the stillness of a hunter came, a calmness, the feeling of gathering himself, quieting his thoughts. The moment became an opportunity, everything in focus. He gently rocked his wings, feeling the sense of his ship, adjusted his gloves in the palm of his hands, taking up the least slack in the leather, and then he quickly brushed a hand over his goggles. He tightened his straps, and settled himself into his seat. He remembered Boelcke's words and he scanned the sky, above and behind them, and then over at Boelcke, waiting for the signal.

~~~

Lieutenant Tom Rees stood in his cockpit, looked back over the top of the wing of his Fee and scanned the sky. He thought about the telegram that he expected anytime, his promotion to Captain, the pride of his parents, how they would welcome him when he returned home. Perhaps today, perhaps tonight. He thought about what a beautiful still day it was, the sky so clear and cloudless, a beautiful day to fly. He looked down at his pilot, Frank Morris, still a teenager but an airman nonetheless and nodded to him, as if to say, *I'm standing now, steady, boy.*

They were the last ships in the last formation, the thumb that stuck out, tender, waiting to be struck, and Rees knew it. The thought cleared his mind again, hopes of promotion fading into the future.

The sky is such a delicate shade of blue, the passing realization struck him as he resumed searching.

His eyes examined a portion of the sky, and then moved on. A glint from the west. He moved his eyes, scanning back and forth.

Then he saw them. He knew they were there before his brain registered the danger. Dark dots, hanging in space, already in a dive, their noses angling down on the formation of Fees. German fighters: growing larger, yet seeming stationary in the sky. Rees felt ice in his veins.

He watched details materialize on the descending aircraft; wings, landing gears, the dull metallic shine of their guns. Rees braced the rearward Lewis gun against his shoulder, glanced down at Morris and rocked his hand from side to side then, flattened it; *be steady* ... he glanced around the formation of Fees and saw no other observers bracing for the coming attack.

The Germans are too far away for me to hit them, he thought. *No matter, this will wake my boys up.*

He aimed the Lewis gun at the largest German airplane, still tiny, settled his sights and squeezed the trigger.

With a steady *burrrrrrr*, so quick the explosions ran together, the Lewis fired. Hot brass jangled around the cockpit, landing on Morris, and then flying back into the engine and propeller. Rees emptied the Lewis' magazine. He looked over his shoulder, at the airplanes flying in front of their formation. It had worked. The eyes of the other English observers appeared over the wings of the Fees, looking back to see what was happening. The English gunners braced themselves at their guns, barrels lifting, aiming into the German flight. Rees unclipped the Lewis's magazine and pulled a fresh one from the wall of the ship. He cocked the gun and took aim again.

As they grew larger, Rees slowly realized he had never seen this before: a German fighter biplane. The lead German aeroplane adjusted itself, angling over Rees' head, picking a leading Fee as a target. It flew over them. The biplane was streamlined and fierce, diving downward with a brutal urgency about it. It snapped past as though they were standing still in the air. *The devil's own*, thought Rees as the lead German's guns erupted with a savage ripping sound.

Rees realized he was holding his breath. Another German, to the right of the first, was still on them, the German's nose sniffing out the Fees, the outline of the German fighter held in perfect silhouette from the bow. Rees aimed at this one, swinging the Lewis into line with the German's prop. Rees could see the outline of the pilot's head, and aimed for him. Hot orange flashes erupted from the German, before he heard the horrible sound of the receiving end of twin Spandaus. Bullets rent the air around Rees.

~~~

The last English fighter in the formation turned left, in a hard bank. The Fee creaked and pushed at the air, its wings straining under the desperate turn. Richthofen followed as though pulled by a chain. Over the top of the wing, the head of the English gunner held steady, remarkably, as the airplane turned. Richthofen could see the Lewis gun firing, but couldn't hear it.

He lifted the nose of the Albatros and banked behind the Englishman, falling into a stern chase. Pressing the rudder slightly, the nose swung, aiming through the center sights of his guns, both eyes open. He fired, quickly, letting the guns roar for a second, perhaps two, then released the trigger. A dog on a hunt, Richthofen panted. He felt outside himself, his energy like a heat inside him.

He could see only the English airplane, all thoughts, all of his focus locked onto the enemy machine. The English airplane filled Richthofen's field of vision, blocking out the sky in front of him. He began to overtake the Englishman and misjudged, nearly overshooting. Richthofen pulled back on the stick, lifted the nose of the Albatros, shedding speed and swooping his aeroplane above and behind the English.

Sometimes being in a fast ship isn't good ... I can't lose position, can't give up the chase. Mustn't be a fool, don't blow past him, he'll drop me ...

The machines gyrated through the air; the English pilot wrenched his aeroplane back and forth, the gunner, hunched at his gun, gripping it with all his strength to keep from being thrown out. Richthofen flew with gentle touches now, focused on aligning his sights on the vital center of the English aeroplane, at the engine, the men.

The English ship looked enormous, the wings half again as wide as the wings of Richthofen's fighter.

I'll mount you on a wall, thought Richthofen.

With a vicious tenacity, Richthofen clung to the air behind the Englishman, holding the Albatros close, his gunsights careening back and forth across the English airplane. As the English airplane passed in front of his sights, he would fire short bursts, punching fresh holes in the aeroplane with each. Richthofen pushed the nose down, angled below the Fee and leveled off. He chased the English airplane from beneath, looking up at the bottom of the other ship now. He was so close he could see the zig-zag stitching on the fresh green canvas.

The English pilot leveled his plane, the German guns silent for a moment. Confident he'd broken away, he steadied it and fell into a shallow dive, at his full speed, to the southwest again.

Below them, Richthofen saw the town of Marcoing, and the German aerodrome to the west of the town, alive with the dust of launching German fighters.

Richthofen rose behind the English fighter, steadied his, and put the sights of his guns on the center of the Englishman's propeller. The English gunner looked at him with bloodshot eyes, filled with horror. Richthofen fired, and his guns thundered in a long steady burst. In front of him, his bullets broke into the English airplane, spraying shards of fabric, metal and wooden chips.

The propeller of the English airplane slowed and then stopping, wind milling, unpowered. The English airplane dropped, nose down, wobbling in the air. Richthofen lifted the nose of his airplane, and flew above and behind the Englishman once more. It was time to end it.

With a rush of heat up his spine, he watched the English gunner adjust his sights straight at him, undaunted. As though ducking behind a tree, Richthofen dove into the blind spot below the Englishman as the gunner's bullets ripped over his head. Anger flushed Richthofen's face, outrage, an overwhelming sense of fury and retribution.

We'll see. Gott strafe England.

Richthofen throttled back, veering away from the Englishman, gathering space for his charge. The battle raged around them. A new flight of German planes had joined the fray, but Richthofen ignored them. With unshakable focus, he lined his sights up once again on the engine of the Fee. Then, instinctively, he quickly soared up and came in for the attack. In front of him, the top of the English airplane lay exposed.

He gritted his teeth. For a long second Richthofen could look down into the English cockpit and could see the expression on the face of the English gunner, and see the man's gun aimed below him. He could make out the English pilot's hands on his controls, adjusting the airplane as he tried, in vain, to escape.

Richthofen fired and ugly tears opened across the English observer's body, tore through the pilot's back, and across the wing. He saw the ground through the rents in the canvas of the English ship.

Richthofen throttled back and watched the Englishman drift downward, almost peacefully, the pilot lining up on the German aerodrome.

Below the scene played out: the English aeroplane struck the ground level, then tipped, digging a wing tip into the earth before it settled upright onto its wheels. It rolled down the edge of the German airfield into a farm beyond and came to a stop in a spray of grain and soil. Two German fighters descended in front of Richthofen and landed on the aerodrome, their pilots immediately climbing out and running toward the downed Fee.

Richthofen tipped his nose down, momentarily uncertain, only having landed the new Albatros once before. He throttled down, determined to land next to his quarry. He struck the field too fast, was rolling too quickly, and cut the throttle too late. The Albatros hopped, not flying, not landing, and hurtled down the field. Fighting for control, Richthofen pushed the throttle in completely and held the airplane level, letting his speed bleed off. He ruddered the Albatros at the English wreck, still hidden in a cloud of dust. At last, the tail of the Albatros dropped and he rolled to a stop. Richthofen quickly cut his switches, killed the engine, and unstrapped himself. Jumping down, he too ran to the English aeroplane, still remarkably intact.

German ground crew were already pulling the wounded pilot out of the rear cockpit. Blood flowed down the sides of the fuselage. The gunner lay across the upper wing of the Fee, his arms splayed out, not moving, his eyes open and staring. While Richthofen watched, the English pilot writhed in pain, gasping for air, spitting blood and then grew still.

The German crew looked up at Richthofen. Richthofen looked down at the corpse of the Englishman, still and cooling at his feet.

"This is my first," he said. He looked down at his own hands and saw that they shook.

Wordlessly, Richthofen pulled a bayonet from his flight boot and walked to the English ship. He stabbed the bayonet into the canvas and sawed through the fabric to cut the identity numbers from the side of the English airplane. He rolled the piece of canvas up, tucked it into his jacket and turned back to his Albatros.

Silently, two German crewmen helped Richthofen turn his Albatros, and start the engine. Richthofen took off, flying east, climbing, away from the aerodrome at Vélu, away from the front, alone in the air, relaxed, and for the moment, satiated.

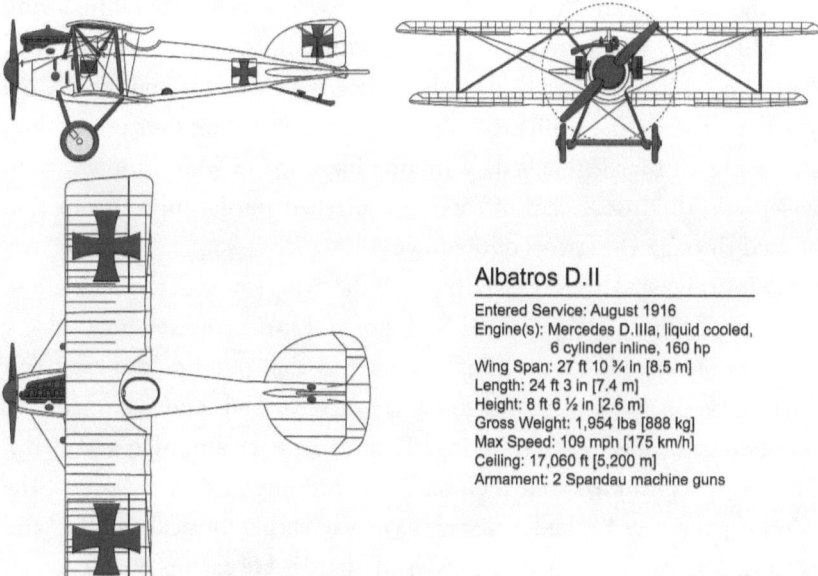

Albatros D.II

Entered Service: August 1916
Engine(s): Mercedes D.IIIa, liquid cooled,
    6 cylinder inline, 160 hp
Wing Span: 27 ft 10 ¾ in [8.5 m]
Length: 24 ft 3 in [7.4 m]
Height: 8 ft 6 ½ in [2.6 m]
Gross Weight: 1,954 lbs [888 kg]
Max Speed: 109 mph [175 km/h]
Ceiling: 17,060 ft [5,200 m]
Armament: 2 Spandau machine guns

Chapter Forty-Six

September 22, 1915
Bertincourt, France

Richthofen heard it first: the noise distant, but distinct, not threatening, but peculiar. Like the shuffling of feet in the darkness, out of place, just enough to wake him. It didn't fit into the nighttime noise of the city and left him instantly tense. It grew louder, and closer, the note changing from high to low. Suddenly, it was shrill. He knew the tone, knew it with an ugly familiarity unlike any other sound he had ever known.

He began to shout, his voice so loud and his mind so agonized that the sound seemed far away: "Artillery! Incoming! INCOMING!"

The explosion of the shell, for a split second a silent flash, lifted him, tossed his bed, and jarred the entire building. In that moment, he rolled onto the floor and covered his head. Then, with an enormous crack, the world exploded. The brilliant flash of light threw a glare over everything, shattering all that it touched. Windows blew apart. Walls erupted, split, collapsed. The initial clap of the shell softened into a duller boom that echoed through the streets of the town.

Moritz howled, the cry blending with the dying sound of the detonation.

"Shit. Shut up, dog," barked Richthofen. Moritz cowered now.

Richthofen, his ears ringing, listened as the sound of the explosion faded away in the streets. He knew a full salvo had landed, timed fire. Somewhere people began shouting. Then came a scream, high and sharp. The shouts continued, and then he heard running feet in the street. The windowpane over his bed, cracked, gave way with a musical tinkling and collapsed across his bed in a shower of shards. He sat up on his knees, shaking glass off, uncut. He listened for a moment, and then he stepped into his own outline on the ground: the only space free of broken glass.

Got the range, don't you, you bastards?

He heard shouts within the building now, the sound of men moving, and angry swearing. He reached out, thankful his clothing was close, and drew on his pants. He stood his boots on end and shook broken glass out of them.

Like pouring piss out, thought Richthofen. This war always seems to come back to piss ...

Menzke burst through the door, already dressed. Good man, thought Richthofen. Moritz ran out the open bedroom door and disappeared into the dark building. Menzke moved to stop him.

"Leave him!" Richthofen shouted as he yanked on his other boot.

"Did you hear it, Leutnant? The shell coming? I heard it." Menzke's voice was a loud whimper. "Will there be more?"

Far in the distance, Richthofen heard it again, the high hateful note beginning. He felt himself tense, the world slowed and his ears hummed. An image of muddy gore flashed through his mind. An urge to run welled up inside. "Yes, I heard it. And I hear it again. Our special curse. Let's pack our bags, shall we?"

The note dropped in pitch, growing in volume as it did. "Down!" shouted Richthofen, as he dropped to his knees in broken glass. Menzke threw himself to the floor in the hallway. The impact was near, and the entire building lurched sideways. The few remaining windows erupted. The furniture jumped up in the air, crashing back down at odd angles. For a moment, there was silence and then the tall dresser in Richthofen's room tipped over and fell as though pushed by a ghost.

Richthofen and Menzke were on their feet as soon as the blast began to fade. Menzke lit a candle. In moments, they pulled the bed sheets from the bed, pitched the broken glass onto the floor, and began throwing together a makeshift bindle with their clothes and effects. Menzke scooped it up by the corners and threw it over his back like a burglar. Together, he and Richthofen ran out the door, down the hallway to the stairs, Richthofen carrying an empty valise.

As they ran, Richthofen threw open doors and shouted out orders. Some men were still and crouched on floors. Many, never having been under artillery fire before, were shocked and frozen in place.

"Move! Get on your feet! Don't wait for the next one!" he shouted

At Richthofen's prompting, they began to move as more shells burst like lightning across the city throwing brilliant flashes throughout the building. More screams. Between explosions, Richthofen heard the unmistakable sound of a building collapsing. They ran until they reached the basement door and then kicked it in and ran down the stairs.

The din of explosions became continuous; soon there was no space to hear their echoes, only an unceasing thunder that rolled back and forth across the town.

In the basement, they huddled around a single lantern. Batmen knelt on the floor, trying to organize and pack valises. When they finished, they would run out of the basement and return moments later with their own belongings and repeat the process. They began herding the pilots' dogs into the basement, Moritz appeared on his own and trembled in a far corner.

From the empty building, they heard a voice, shouting between explosions.

It was Fischer. He threw open the basement door and ran down the stairs. He saluted, and then said, "The English have moved their guns forward, the town and airfields are in range," he shouted, as though he were deaf.

"Yes, obviously," said Richthofen, drily. The men, crowded together in the basement, laughed nervously.

Fischer looked embarrassed. "Orders from Boelcke, gentlemen, we are leaving, we are to move to the airfield to load the equipment. We will fly the airplanes at first light. Trucks will be outside in a few minutes." His voice shook as he spoke.

Richthofen reached out and put a hand on Fischer's shoulder. "There, there, man. Running through artillery fire can be stressful."

The men laughed again and Fischer smiled, panting, and drew himself up straight to try to compose himself. Fischer saluted again, turned away and ran up the stairs and into the darkness, into a night punctuated by brilliant flashes of false daylight.

In a few minutes, they heard shouts again, and Richthofen climbed the stairs and looked into the street. Shouting down the stairs, he ordered the men to move. The gathered airmen and their aides quickly ran up the stairs carrying bags and leading pets. Rubble choked the street on one end but two empty trucks stood there, their tops open. They stank of pig shit.

The men climbed in, handing the dogs and bags up, piling men on top of them, then men on top of men. As the trucks began to back out of the street, the bursts of the incoming artillery raised clouds of glowing smoke and dust over the city, filling the street with a brown fog. In the flashes of the exploding shells, they could see French civilians in their nightclothes scurrying about like wraiths.

Someone shouted, "GAS!"

"Shut up!" shouted Richthofen, sniffing the air. "It's smoke and dust. Shut the hell up, people will panic more than they already are!"

Leaving the city to the north, they looked back on Bertincourt. Hell was consuming the town, fires burning across the city, the eruptions of the cannon shells bringing buildings down in fiery spouts of debris. Bertincourt was dying.

To the southwest of the city, shells were already falling onto Jasta 1's airfield. An aeroplane emerged from the smoke of an explosion over the aerodrome, silhouetted briefly by the flash of an artillery shell, then disappeared into the darkness.

Richthofen turned to Böhme. "Did you see that?"

"Yes, but I didn't believe it," Böhme replied. "I wonder where he's going."

~ ~ ~

At their field, Boelcke was already moving about in the darkness, Fischer trailing behind him, carrying a lantern.

Boelcke shouted at groups of enlisted men, "Move the damn planes, spread them out! No, no, point it that way, down the field!"

Other men moved around the aeroplanes, readying them for flight in the pale light of their lanterns and the brilliant glare of explosions. Without orders, the pilots joined the ground crews, leaving their bags piled in the trucks.

Someone found rope and tied the dogs together in a pack, one of the batmen trying to quiet them. Two of the dogs, angry and afraid, began fighting, savagely chasing each other in circles.

The impacts of artillery fire were spreading out now, beyond the city, shells striking less frequently. The city burned. Only minutes had passed since the first shells landed.

Richthofen stood at Boelcke's side. "Where shall we go, Leutnant?"

Boelcke wavered, looked at Richthofen, and began to cough.

After a moment, he composed himself and spoke with an odd croaking sound in his voice. "I've sent men ahead to light bonfires at Lagnicourt. Have you ever landed in the dark, Richthofen?"

Richthofen frowned. "No, sir, I haven't. I haven't even flown in the dark."

At the far end of the field, a shell erupted. Boelcke flinched from the sound, and then looked up as clods of earth began to rain down. "Damn," he said. The word came out in a painful wheeze. Boelcke pressed a hand to his chest. His *Pour le Mérite* flickered with the light of reflected flames.

"Get Gerstner, have him take charge here, Richthofen," Boelcke's voice was higher, sharper.

Richthofen stared at him; Boelcke's lips were dark. *A trick of the light?* thought Richthofen.

Another shell struck, then another. The artillery fire was walking across the farm fields from the south, moving closer. An Albatros was hit, fully fueled, and erupted in a fireball, the flames casting a startlingly yellow light.

Somewhere an Englishman can see the Albatros burning. They'll adjust their fire, thought Richthofen.

Boelcke reached up, put his shaking fingers into his jacket pocket, pulling out a cigarette. He looked at Richthofen with a pleading look on his face. His lips moved, but he formed no words.

"Sir, you don't smoke, do you?" Richthofen asked.

Fischer saw the cigarette and hastily moved to help. He stepped in close to Boelcke and put an arm around him. As he did, Boelcke's knees buckled and he collapsed, but Fischer supported him as he shrank to the ground.

Having dropped it in favor of catching his commander, Fischer's lantern crashed into the grass and cracked open, spilling a pool of fire onto the field. By the light, Richthofen could see that Boelcke's lips were almost black.

Am I imagining this?

Boelcke wheezed, his breath hissing as though he were deflating.

Gerstner ran up, looked down. "Is he hit?"

Fischer sat, cradling Boelcke's head in his lap. "His asthma. He can't breathe." He began looking around frantically. "Where's the cigarette? Where did it go?" Tears ran down his face.

"Have one of mine," said Richthofen. He reached into his pocket, took out one of Menzke's cigarettes.

"No! The one the Leutnant had," said Fischer.

Boelcke's eyes were wild, unfocused, his hands clenched in fists. His mouth moved like a fish's, gulping helplessly at the air.

Richthofen looked down, saw the cigarette, and picked it up. He held it up in the light of the fires and looked at it. A shell landed in the trees behind the sheds. One of the mechanics began to swear in a continuous shout as branches and more clods of dirt and rocks began raining down.

"Light it and give it to me!" shouted Fischer.

Richthofen looked down, startled, and almost began to scold Fischer reflexively, but caught himself. It wasn't the time. He put the end of the cigarette into the flames of the broken lantern and then put it to his mouth and took a deep puff, then another, drawing the cigarette until it was fully lit. Instantly he felt a flush of heat roll through his body and his thoughts collapsed. The flames of the Albatros slewed sideways. Richthofen shook his head and handed the cigarette to Fischer.

Fischer took it, and drew a long puff, the put his mouth over Boelcke's and blew smoke into Boelcke's open mouth. Smoke flowed out of Boelcke's nose as Fischer drew his head back.

Richthofen looked down, confused and angry.

What the hell is happening to Boelcke? And why now?

He looked up as a mechanic ran past. The man looked automated, driven by motors and wires, his face grey and drawn. Richthofen looked at Gerstner and tipped his head to the side.

"Asthma, Richthofen. He has asthma."

Boelcke's wheezing stopped.

Gerstner looked down. "Belladonna, Richthofen." He knelt next to Fischer. "More, Fischer, as much as you can stand. Stay with him: his wheezing has stopped, but that could be good or bad. But just one cigarette. No more! I'll get a truck over here."

On the field, the pilots and mechanics began starting the engines of the fighters. Trucks were stopping in front of the sheds; mechanics throwing tools, gas cans, and equipment into them. As soon as one was full, it left, grinding away to north, then another would roll up, and be filled in turn.

An Albatros rolled down the field, past the still burning aeroplane, took flight and turned away to the north. Another followed, ruddering around shell holes, lit by the blazing craft, and then climbed away.

A truck stopped next to Boelcke. Richthofen, Gerstner, Böhme and Fischer lifted Boelcke into a bed of blankets in the back of the truck. Someone handed Fischer another lantern. Fischer wobbled, nearly fell and sat down heavily next to Boelcke in the truck. The truck rolled away, accelerating into the darkness, the glow of the lantern outlining Fischer in the back as it disappeared into the distance.

Richthofen barely saw them go. He was captivated by the flames as they reached up into the heavens; higher than should have been possible. His jaw went slack and his breathing slowed down. In the distance, something was moving, running across the field. Was it a horse? *Could it be? Santuzza?* Richthofen stumbled slightly, reaching out into the darkness, as though somehow, with just enough effort, he could touch the animal. Maybe it was a chance to make amends.

Suddenly, Böhme grabbed him by the shoulder. "Richthofen. Richthofen?"

"Can you fly, Richthofen?" asked Gerstner.

Richthofen lifted his hands to his mouth and touched his lips. They tingled strangely. More shells exploded in a line, salvo fire, in the trees. Richthofen looked up and saw a truck lift and turn over in the road, very slowly. It was delicate and beautiful.

"Amazing..." he mumbled.

"Can you fly?" asked Gerstner again, more urgently this time.

Richthofen blinked. His eyes were wide and his pupils black voids. "Yes, I can fly," he said finally, the words too literal.

Böhme took Richthofen by the arm and they began to run down the field, to the last two fighters. The few remaining men were lifting the fighters' tails, pointing the aeroplanes north. Richthofen and Böhme climbed into the machines, the engines already running. Together, they opened the throttles and rolled down the field into the darkness. The last truck was loaded and lumbered away into the night.

Richthofen flew over the fires, over the inferno of Bertincourt, flying on instinct, on memories of flying. Around him, colors deepened to red, until the land and the sky, the very air wept in crimson hues. The colors of flames tasted sweet in his mouth, the roar of the motor an elegant symphony. He laughed, a man aloft, skimming across the top of hell.

~~~

Richthofen, Böhme, and the other pilots of the Jasta stood in the hallway outside Boelcke's room in Cambrai. No one spoke. After a small eternity, Fischer stepped out of the room, but said nothing, taking a spot against the wall. Gerstner followed him out into the hallway.

"You may see him now," said Gerstner. He pointed at Böhme, who nodded and stepped into the room, shutting the door behind him.

The men stood silently as nurses and doctors moved back and forth. Patients went past, some walking, others rolling by on chairs or tables. Nurses had covered some entirely with sheets. Richthofen thought the place smelled like a slaughterhouse.

The pig truck from last night smelled better.

Böhme stepped out into the hallway. He motioned to Richthofen, and opened the door for him.

Inside, Richthofen stood close to the bed and studied his mentor. Boelcke's lips were pale blue, dark rings circled his eyes and he lay motionless, sleeping. A coffee-haired nurse was pulling pillows from behind Boelcke's back, laying him flat. She was buxom, in a youthful way, her face pretty and strained, the mask of a woman that had seen too much suffering. In the back of the room, a little man in a stained apron was fussing with bottles of leaves and yellow oil.

He introduced himself to the nurse. "Richthofen."

The nurse looked up. "Ninette," she said.

"I see. Boelcke's friend. French?"

"Oui. Does that bother you?"

"No, Miss, it does not."

"How is he?" asked Richthofen.

"Silly ass ..." said Boelcke, opening his eyes momentarily. "I'm not dead."

Richthofen smiled. The little man stepped to the side of the bed. He held a flat, wet cotton pouch in his hands. Something green was soaking through the thing. Richthofen looked at the nurse, a question on his face.

"A poultice, Datura with a little Belladonna. Nothing but the best for our Leutnant." Richthofen thought she meant it when she said 'our'.

Boelcke smiled, opened his eyes again, looked at Ninette, then around the room.

The little man opened Boelcke's shirt and lay the poultice on his chest, then covered it up with a rag.

"Did we get everyone out?" asked Boelcke.

"Lost one mechanic and a truck. One Albatros burned," said Richthofen. "Lucky."

"I remember everything on fire, all the men were dead, but still moving," said Boelcke.

Richthofen tried to ignore what he said, but understood what he meant. "Any orders, Hauptman?"

"No. I'll be back. Tell them I'm not dead, yet. Go fly." Boelcke closed his eyes and settled back into his bed.

Not dead yet?

Richthofen nodded, and he stepped to the door and into the hallway.

Chapter Forty-Seven

October 16, 1916
Bertangles Aerodrome, France

The English aeroplanes were oiled and adjusted and lined up in a perfect row. There were seventeen: the number of horses in a cavalry squadron. It was the one moment when civility and order reigned around them, otherwise, they were creatures of chaos and disorder, given to wandering with each invisible gust of air and the vagaries of violent men.

Andrews walked with Hawker past the line of fighters. Crews swarmed around the aeroplanes, crew chiefs barked out orders and waved salutes as Hawker and Andrews passed them by.

Hawker was happy, softly whistling, "If You Were the Only Girl in the World." Andrews held his Glengarry in one hand and mopped his sweaty hair down slick with the other.

Overhead, more English aeroplanes passed in swarms, like gnats, all flowing downwind, eastward to the German lines. The effect of so many aeroplanes all flying in one direction was like a pressure in the sky, relentless and thrumming, intending to hold the Germans on the defensive, pushing until they had to break. It was a simple strategy, and like many simple strategies, it involved piling up corpses in order to win.

Hawker glanced up, smiled, pleased. "It's working, isn't it, Andrews? We're crushing them. It's fantastic! Soon this will be over, Lord help us."

"Wi' all respec', sir." Andrews grimaced as though he were in physical pain. "Ha' you 'eard the stories, Hawker? The stories that No. 25 tells?"

"Of course. New German aeroplanes, predatory. Of course. Boogie man tales, if you ask me."

"I don't know ... they're not t' be taken lightly, they know wha' they're doing. Should know wha' they're seein'."

"My God, man, you killed their Otto Parschau. He taught Boelcke. Imagine that. You did that. Yes, perhaps they know what they're doing, but the Hun is always on the defensive now, not even crossing our lines. They're afraid." Hawker waved a hand in the air as though he were batting at something.

"Perhaps," said Andrews.

"What else could it be?" asked Hawker.

"Sir." Andrews stopped and waited for Hawker to turn. Hawker did, giving Andrews his full attention.

"Yes?"

"It seems obvious. Wi' all respec', this is like war 'ollege. The pillars of fire. Thermopylae."

"Go on." Hawker looked perplexed now.

"Wha' do you do if you ha' less numbers against an attacker?"

"Go on. Don't be rhetorical." Hawker felt his good mood melting.

"Stan' your ground, channel the invader. Defea' him piecemeal. 'ere is the thin'. They 'ave the wind, we fly t' 'em, ha' a difficult time separatin' from combat because we're flyin' against a head wind, they ha' the good ground, they can choose when t' fight, an' simply turn away when they don't wish t' continue. They wai' for the advantage of numbers an' pick the time. But we don't. We dribble through. Penny packets of men an' machines, a few at a time. My God, Langan-Byrne took on seventeen of their machines! Seventeen! He's more'n fortunate t' be alive." Andrews nervously ran a hand over his hair, and then dried his hand on his pants; sweat ran down his face despite the cool autumn air.

Hawker reached out and took Andrews by the shoulder. "You're tired, that's it. Perhaps you shouldn't fly this afternoon. Take a rest, man."

Andrews sighed and shifted his weight from foot to foot, then balanced himself and stood, poised to walk away in frustration. He held his ground.

"Sir. You haven't flown combat with us. Times ha' changed. It's not a couple of theirs an' a couple of ours. I saw a 'undred or more aeroplanes in the air at once this mornin'! At once! More aeroplanes tha' even existed four years ago! When you en'er a fight, you have t' watch constantly for another squadron of Hun t' drop in. It's beyond nerve rackin' t' fly these little patrols, i's asinine."

"I see," said Hawker.

"An', Hawker, what if it's true? What if they do ha' these new aeroplanes, these *fighters*?" Andrews voice rose, almost shrill. Two nearby mechanics turned and stared at him. "An' Boelcke. He's out there." Andrews pointed east.

Hawker glanced away, embarrassed for Andrews.

Andrews turned and saw the mechanics, who, in turn, moved away as though they hadn't heard.

Hawker's voice rose, a rare thing, impatience showing through. "I understand, Andrews. But these are our orders. Trenchard knows what he's doing, we just keep the pressure on long enough, they'll break. I assure you."

Andrews sighed, defeated. "Very well, Hawker. Than' you for hearin' me out." He carefully pulled his hat onto his head, and then cocked it to the side. "Permission t' take lunch before the afternoon patrol, sir."

"Yes, Andrews, of course."

Andrews saluted, his shoulders slumped, his energy tapped.

"Andrews, where is Langan-Byrne?"

Andrews pointed to the far end of the line, where a knot of men had gathered around the Irishman. "There."

"Very good. Enjoy your lunch, then."

Andrews nodded and turned away.

Hawker walked to the end of the row, and glancing back at Andrews, began to hum again. At the group of gathered men, Hawker hung back, standing at the rear of the crowd. Langan-Byrne smiled, answering questions, but one word at a time. His audience peppered him with inquiries, but, frustrated at his replies, began to drift away. A mechanic turned and bumped into Hawker.

"Ten-shun!" he shouted.

The men turned toward Hawker, suddenly aware he was there, and snapped to attention.

"At ease, men, and dismissed. I need to have a word or two with our hero here." Hawker gestured toward Langan-Byrne. The men relaxed and slowly drifted away.

"Good day, Byrne," said Hawker.

"Capt'n." Langan-Byrne nodded.

"How are you doing, how many is that now? Quite a tear you're on."

"Ten, now, sir."

"And one this morning?"

"Aye."

"May I speak with you about something, something private? I need ... would like your opinion." Hawker beamed a wide boyish smile. Langan-Byrne watched over Hawker's shoulder as a flight of slow, clumsy Martinsydes flew by, low, headed east.

"Aye."

Hawker reached into his uniform jacket, extracted an envelope. He drew out a letter, held it up and opened it. He handed the folded paper to Langan-Byrne.

"It's from a friend you see, a feminine friend. She sent me a poem." He pointed. "You see here ..."

Langan-Byrne looked at Hawker, expressionless. He wasn't sure if he was being put on.

"Sir?"

"You see. I'm not much for these things. What do you suppose it means? I mean, you read poetry. Perhaps you know?"

"Aye." Langan-Byrne took the paper, uncomfortable with the question. He read:

Form after form, in the streets
Waves like a ghost along,
Kindled to me;
The star above the house-top greets
Me every eve with a long
Song fierily.

All day long, the town
Glimmers with subtle ghosts
Going up and down
In a common, prison-like dress;
But their daunted looking flickers
To me, and I answer, Yes!

So I am not lonely nor sad
Although bereaved of you,
My little love.
I move among a kinsfolk clad
With words, but the dream shows through
As they move.

He read the lines again, then held the paper to his side, then read them once more. Hawker stirred, impatient. At last, Langan-Byrne handed the paper back.

"Sir," he said.

"Well, Byrne, what does it mean?"

Langan-Byrne looked at Hawker, his jaw moving, his mouth closed as though words were waiting to erupt.

"Sir," he finally blurted out. Hawker cocked his head, began to fold the letter back into its envelope. He turned as though he might walk away.

"It means what you feel that it means," said Langan-Byrne.

Hawker turned back, never having heard Byrne say so many words at once, but pleased that Byrne was speaking to him. Pleased that he had shared Beatrice's poem with someone.

"Go on," said Hawker.

"Sir. My mum, she taught me that poems are how they make you feel, not what they mean." He paused and took a deep breath. "I mean no impertinence, sir."

"No, that's quite alright, Byrne, please continue." The perplexed look on Hawker's face had hardened. The two men stood in silence.

Then, Langan-Byrne began to speak again, "Sir. Poems evoke, they aren't literal, that way. But, to me, it's about love and parting. Love, sir."

Hawker smiled, and then his smile broadened to a grin. "Love, then, you say?"

"Aye," said Langan-Byrne. "Love, sir."

"Thank you, Byrne, thank you, very much." Hawker began to turn to walk away.

A mechanic approached Langan-Byrne, "Sir, your machine is ready."

"Very good. Thank ye."

Hawker waited through the exchange, then, as the mechanic walked away, he said, "Have a good flight, Byrne, good hunting."

"Sir. I know this poem. 'The Inheritance', by David Lawrence."

Hawker beamed. "That's wonderful, wonderful. Thank you, Byrne. You're very helpful. And, between you and me, being taciturn only means you speak what matters, huh, Byrne?"

"Aye."

"Very well, then," said Hawker, he glanced down, embarrassed at his own candor. He turned away.

Langan-Byrne hesitated, then gestured toward Hawker, wanting to pull him back.

"Sir?"

"Yes?"

"Sir, I feel there's more."

Hawker paused and turned, his expression softened, a question over his face. "Go on."

"It's about separation, the feeling of parting. Sir, of parting forever."

Hawker frowned. He felt a shallow ache grow in his chest. "I see," he said quietly.

"That's only me, sir, how I feel, sir. Perhaps she just fears for you. 'Tis only a feeling."

"Yes. Yes. Of course," said Hawker. He straightened, saluted. "Good flying, Byrne."

"Sir."

~~~

The sunshine stung Boelcke's eyes now. He had learned after the bombardment of Bertincourt, and the abandonment of their aerodrome, after his humiliating attack of asthma, that he only needed a single puff of the Belladonna cigarettes before flying. Two would be too many, and bring on the rushing in his ears, the panting, and the sense of doom in small things. How a medicine could do this amazed him, just enough and he felt better, too much and he felt that death was a cloak over his shoulders. But a single puff and the smoke opened his lungs, his heartbeat would gently pound in his ears, and he could breathe long cool draughts of air. The higher he flew, the cooler and richer the air seemed to become, his mind growing calmer and quieter.

But still the sunlight jabbed at this eyes like needles.

Five German fighters, all in a new Albatros, followed him, making their way to the Somme battlefields, keeping their daily afternoon appointment with the English fighters. He led them under clouds, skipping along the bottom of soft grey billows, and then racing across a gap of blue until they were under another.

His shop was a patch of sky, bounded by Jasta 1 to the south, and the remnants of old early fighter units, the KEKs, to the north; his own portion of front in which to pick the time and manner of minding his store. Boelcke was grateful for the punctuality of the English, their aeroplanes coming in regular waves, morning and at tea time. Now that he had enough of the new aeroplanes, he could lead patrols and expect 'customers' to arrive in his shop with a near-suicidal punctuality.

Strung out behind him, just under the cloud bottoms were his best pupils; Richthofen, Böehme, and a new pilot named Immelman.

Do you eat meat, Immelman? Yes? Then you're no relation to Max, are you, now?

The line of aeroplanes wavered only slightly, oriented in a 'V' shape, with Boelcke at the apex, the eyes of the men forward and downward, looking out over their lower wings. They searched for the tiny specks of their quarry moving against the ground, the points of darkness that streaked by below them, the closing speeds of the opposing aeroplanes approaching the unimaginable speed of two hundred miles per hour.

It was the sunlight that gave them away; English fighters passed through a shaft of light beneath the clouds. Suddenly they appeared in the sky below, as though they had materialized there from some nightmarish dream. As usual, Boelcke saw the English first, low, due west, passing to the north, six of them, the Vickers types, their engines at the rear. From above, the delicate booms of the rear structure of the English fighters were invisible, giving the impression of a pair of wings, only, wings with concentric circles on them, brown-green against the ground below. Below the English aeroplanes, artillery shells burst on the ground, and all around them grey-black puffs of German anti-aircraft welcomed them.

The Germans' position was almost perfect, it would bring a clean few moments, a short predictable dance before chaos began. Boelcke cleared his guns quickly, the moment he saw the English, then just as quickly, turned and dove, in a tight graceful banking turn. He angled toward the Englishmen, his gifted students taking seconds to repeat his maneuver and close on him, in a single sweep of focused aggression; they swarmed downward, gaining speed, closing.

Boelcke felt the air now, could feel it like a liquid, flowing over him, his senses heightened. The sky streamed rich and cool over his wings, through his lungs, giving him strength, letting his mind relax into the role of a voyeur to his own violence. It was more than instinct now, it was like a memory that he could replay in his head on command; it was as though he had found no other reason for his existence, except the moment of attacking, of releasing, all that had ever frustrated him, that had ever been a barrier. It no longer seemed real, and he preferred it that way.

The English leader looked up, and Boelcke saw him. Streamers trailed the man's wings, marking him as their lead and as Boelcke's target. Boelcke coolly ruddered over to set his sights in front of the Englishman, a deflection shot, but not a difficult one, not for him. It was to set the course of his bullets like a rope in the air, which the Englishman would fly into, would be bound up by.

Boelcke sensed the shock of the English leader and smiled to himself. The man hesitated, looked back over his own shoulder. Boelcke placed his thumbs on the triggers of his machine guns. *Closer, just a little closer*, he thought.

Abruptly the wings of the English aeroplane narrowed, and then turned to knife edges in the sky as the English leader did the right thing, the smart thing.

You're not such a novice after all, are you? thought Boelcke.

The English pilot turned into Boelcke's attack, climbing, head-on toward the German leader. Boelcke took a deep breath, relishing the silky air. Puffs of smoke appeared at the nose of the English fighter, the man already firing his single machine gun upward at Boelcke.

Calmly, deliberately, Boelcke let the Englishman settle his aeroplane into his climb, knowing that the man would be aiming at the most threatening attacker, at him. Waiting would save bullets, save time; with a little luck, the Englishman would even exhaust the drum of bullets on his machine gun as they closed. Boelcke settled his eyes on the English leader, each detail brilliant and crisp, and then he saw the red and white stripes like barber poles on the struts of the man's wings.

He ruddered again, centered his sights.

He jammed down his triggers. With a sound like an awful saw in the air, bullets exploded downward at the Englishman. A few seconds of firing, only, then, abruptly Boelcke saw the familiar shuddering motion of the English fighter, the jerking slewing turn of a pilot suddenly in agony, hit and bleeding, perhaps dying. Boelcke had seen it so many times now, that it had become familiar, welcome, satisfying, calming. *How many was it? Thirty, thirty-five?* The taste in his mouth was metallic, bitter, and sharp, like blood and Belladonna, the taste of poison used as medicine.

The English fighter dropped out of its turn, sinking in the sky, already headed west, clawing for what must seem like safety. Boelcke passed under the man, looked up as the other flew by overhead, saw a peculiar saw tooth pattern on the canvas of the body of the little pusher aeroplane. Boelcke smoothly turned behind the man, throttled down, lifted his nose to shed speed and then closed slowly behind the crippled machine.

Behind and above him, his students tore into the rest of the English formation, one of the English erupting in flames and plummeting past Boelcke and his victim.

Boelcke could see the pilot hunched over, the man's shoulders drawn down and tight. Surprisingly, the man didn't look back at him. The descent of the English fighter was too steep, he would never make his own lines, and Boelcke could see this. He closed further, a few feet, looking the English fighter over. Number Twenty-four, one of the boys that killed Parschau, one of the tough ones, the dangerous ones.

The English fighter sank lower now, passed over the eastern most line of German artillery, plummeting downward now, unchecked. Boelcke lifted the nose of his Albatros, leveling his flight out, watching the Englishman descend. Between two rows of reserve trenches, the English fighter scraped the ground, then rose slightly, then dropped quickly as though all life had gone out of the thing. The crippled fighter and the dying man smacked back into the ground, the wings folding down, broken, the nose of the fighter tipped over and dug into the ground, tail in the air.

Boelcke passed over once, low, saw the pilot's arms cast over the front of his cockpit, hanging still and loose. *The moment of Death is devoid of dignity.*

He turned, east, climbing; the other aeroplanes of his flight were nowhere to be seen. The Mercedes engine pulled the Albatros upward, toward the cool dark belly of a cloud. Boelcke continued east, wanting to pass beyond the trenches, past where the artillery fire had beaten the ground, back to where roads still existed, where a church steeple might still stand, to the countryside where civilization still clung like a skin to the surface of the earth. He flew over mounds of rubble: Villers-au-Flos? Then, further east, the road to Bertincourt, a junction. He turned north, ahead an aeroplane circled. High Boelcke climbed.

Circles on its wings, roundels, the English called them. *A French word. For God's sake, call them circles,* he thought.

The English aeroplane was in flying a constant level turn, circling smoothly in the air, not losing altitude.

Strange, a spotter, a fool? Lost?

Boelcke leveled out above the English ship, one of their old types, a Martinsyde. He watched it orbit, then turned, dove, closed behind it. The English aeroplane continued on, unchecked, not reacting. Boelcke settled his sights once more, aimed at the back of the pilot, at the back of the man's head. With a gentle lurch, the Englishman's head slowly flopped from one side to the other.

The movement of an unconscious man.

Boelcke turned right, throttled up, and then flew alongside the English aeroplane. Looking over, he looked into the face of the English pilot and saw a red mask, with unseeing eyes. A dead man flew the English aeroplane. Behind the pilot, the corpse of a dead observer sat, the head tilted back and the mouth open, unseeing eyes stared upward. It was a ghost ship.

A spasm gripped Boelcke's belly, a wracking pain as though something must escape from him. Boelcke turned away, north, diving slightly. As he descended, he put his head over the side of his cockpit and wretched, yellow bile blowing away behind him. Hot tears of pain wet his face and dried instantly in the rushing air.

Boelcke wrenched his gloves free from his hands, feeling his own clothing pressing in on him. He looked down as his own hands, saw the bony, blue hands of a dying man.

~ ~ ~

Langan-Byrne's flight straggled in. Two, then one, then another. None flew streamers. Andrews stood and watched them land. Four. Two gone. He stared at the eastern sky, watched a succession of dots become airplanes, then fly away west. At last, his wishes unfulfilled, he resigned himself.

Andrews found one of the new pilots from the flight, the man still sitting on the ground next to his aeroplane. The air stank of castor oil, turpentine and gasoline.

"Langan-Byrne?" he asked.

The man answered, didn't stand. "German fighters. Sleek. Black and white tails. He went down."

"I see." Andrews looked to the operations tent, wondered after Hawker. He looked down.

"Stand up. Pull yourself t'gether, man."

The man limply stood. He pulled his shoulders up.

"Get a drink. Brandy an' milk. Get ready t' fly. I'm takin' you back."

The young pilot wavered, then, "Sir."

"Good man. I'll be back in a few minutes. Meet me here. I need a word wi' Hawker."

In the operations tent, Hawker was going over a list of something. Andrews imagined that somewhere, someone in the Royal Flying Corp made lists of lists. He saluted Hawker, stood at attention.

"Sir."

"Yes, Andrews?"

"Sir, may I ha' a moment of your time?"

"Yes. Of course." Hawker sat the list down and sat back against the edge of a desk.

"I wish t' repor' two pilots overdue. From Langan-Byrne's flight."

Hawker froze. Silent.

Andrews gathered his thoughts, composed himself. "Langan-Byrne," he said.

Hawker blinked, as though he had just emerged into sunlight. Hawker frowned. "Oh, I see." His face froze into a grimace. "Langan-Byrne. Really? Are you sure?"

"Yessir. One of the survivors confirmed it."

"Very well. Dismissed, Andrews. Put together a report this evening."

Andrews saluted, turned to the door.

To Andrews' back, Hawker said, "He was a good man."

Andrews stopped, looked back. "Yes, he was."

"He liked poetry. Did you know that?"

"No, sir. I didn't." Andrews shifted on his feet, uncomfortable, anxious to be on, having done his duty.

"Dismissed, Andrews."

"Thank you, sir." Andrews stepped outside, closed the door behind him, leaving Hawker to himself. "Thank you, sir." He said again, to no one in particular.

Chapter Forty-Eight

October 27, 1916
Lagnicourt Aerodrome, France

A deluge poured onto northern France, and the Allied offensive on the Somme slowed, then stopped, mired in the churned mud of the trenches. The grand offensive became small battles that were tapering off into futile sallies over the wet ground, trying to shape the battlefield, capture a few hundred meters, or even a single trench. The artillery continued its unceasing barrage, but it was all mechanized frustration now as it could only slam steel and explosives into the veritable swamp, erupting water, mud, and putrefied men in pointless, foul geysers. The hope of the Allies for a decisive victory sank into the filth along with the best of their young men.

Rainstorms kept the airmen from the sky. The flyers on both sides would only venture out in short flights, when the rain would let up briefly. The rain even muffled the sounds of artillery fire, a contest between the cacophony of man and nature. Mechanics scurried back and forth between the airplane sheds, holding coats over their heads, lugging tools and plane parts as Richthofen watched from the window of the Jasta's casino.

A new transfer to the Jasta, Stefan Kirmaier, sat reading in the corner of the room by the tiny stone fireplace. Kirmaier was an aberration, not a junior officer like the rest of them, for he transferred in with rank second only to Boelcke. He seemed to be watching the Jasta, absorbing it, glancing up from his book to observe the men. It was clear to all that he had come to take care of Boelcke.

Fischer walked over to the window and stared out at the rain for a moment, then turned to Richthofen.

"How's he doing, Fischer?" asked Richthofen.

"I think he's exhausted, sir," said Fischer "More exhausted than I've ever seen him. He hasn't been the same since he was released from hospital."

Fischer paused. "Sir, may I ask a question?"

"Yes, Fischer, of course."

"Yesterday, Hauptman Boelcke told me that he was almost beaten. He came back from one of his lone flights, said he met a man that almost cornered him. He only got away through luck."

"I heard. That happens. And there were two of them. He laughed about it when he told me the story." He smiled.

Fischer watched Richthofen's face, and saw how forced the smile was. He turned away, stared back out the window. "Sir, there's more. He told me a story; I don't want to believe that it's true."

"Go on, Fischer," said Richthofen.

Fischer stared out into the rain, and then shifted his focus to his own reflection in the pane of glass. He breathed in deeply and slowly let it out. He spoke in a low voice so that only Richthofen could hear.

"The Hauptman told me that he was flying back to the airfield and he saw an English airplane, and he followed it, that he began to shoot at it. Then, he saw that the crew had crumpled, heads down. So, he flew alongside and looked close. He said the men inside were shot to pieces. Dead where they sat and that their airplane was flying on its own. A dead aeroplane and crew ... flying ... like ghosts ..."

Fischer paused, gathering his thoughts. "And he said he knows now that no bullet will ever touch him; that it came to him in a dream. He shouldn't have said that. It's not right to be so superstitious." Fischer paused again, glanced at Richthofen and tried to gauge if he'd said too much.

Richthofen looked aghast at Fischer, mulling over whether Boelcke was fully himself.

A ghost ship? Wasn't it Boelcke that accused the English of mythos with their fable of the black Albatros?

Richthofen fought to maintain his composure in front of Fischer, not wanting to feed Fischer's disquiet.

"Okay, thank you," said Richthofen, attempting to dismiss Fischer. He began to turn away.

"Sir," said Fischer, "the story gets worse."

Richthofen turned back to Fischer and drew a deep breath, bracing himself, not sure how it could be worse. "Go ahead then, finish your tale."

"Sir, he said that he was with two other pilots, you and Böhme, and that you saw it too, the ghost ship. I asked Böhme, he acted like he remembered, but I'm sure he didn't. Do you remember it?" Fischer's voice sounded like he was pleading, pleading for the story to be true, and pleading for it to be a lie, knowing that each answer was horrible in its own way. His voice was brittle, as though the words might shatter.

Richthofen put a hand on Fischer's shoulder. "Fischer, he is Boelcke. He will always be Boelcke. Don't you forget that. He needs a rest, nothing more. Understand?" He felt Boelcke slipping away, the asthma attack being the confirmation of Boelcke's exhaustion and growing frailty, but Richthofen didn't want it to show. *Perhaps a man can use up his life by living it too thoroughly*, he thought.

"Sir, is it an omen? A ghost ship, of all things, a ghost airplane, how can it not be an omen?" Fischer asked.

"I honestly don't know, Fischer. I won't lie to you; perhaps there are other powers at work here. I don't know. But, Fischer, yes, I saw it too," Richthofen lied. He struggled to find a way to protect Boelcke in Fischer's eyes.

Fischer looked up, grateful and sad. "Thank you, Leutnant. Thank you." He stared out the window for a long moment. "Have I ever told you how he chose me to be his batman, Leutnant?"

Richthofen smiled, knowing that he had let down his guard. "No, Fischer, tell me."

"I was in the reserve guards at Döberitz, and Boelcke's former batman had moved on to become a mechanic. Boelcke arranged to have the guards lined up, and he walked down the line, leading his dog, Wolf, by the leash. When he got to me, he handed me the leash, and said that I was the man for him." Fischer laughed. "He said he liked my face."

"A fortunate meeting," said Richthofen.

Fischer laughed again. "Actually, I think he was referring to his dog."

Richthofen smiled, grateful that Boelcke had such a loyal companion as Fischer. "Do you know how he picked me, Fischer?"

"No, sir, I don't."

"He came to my tent in the early morning, when you both visited us at Kovel. He seemed a little drunk. He said I had 'it'. I still don't know what he meant. Sometimes I wonder if he had the wrong tent, and then he couldn't back out." Richthofen smiled, his pale blue eyes twinkling. Fischer grinned, happy to be let in on the joke.

"Thank you, Fischer," said Richthofen. "You'll excuse me, won't you?"

"Yes, of course, Leutnant. Thank you." Fischer nodded and looked back out the window. He said a prayer for rain, and thanked God for another day with rainy skies to let Boelcke rest.

Richthofen looked over at Kirmaier, an experienced and respected officer, his reputation preceding him, then pondered asking for help. Perhaps Kirmaier might know how to speak to Boelcke, how to try to approach him to ask about his visions. Richthofen walked over to where Kirmaier sat, and drew up a chair.

"Oberleutnant, excuse me, but may I speak with you?" asked Richthofen.

Kirmaier looked up, closed his book. Richthofen recognized English on the spine. An author named Wells.

"How is your book?" asked Richthofen.

"Very imaginative. Vivid. Most fortune tellers tell you what you want to hear, this fellow Wells tells you what you're afraid to hear," said Kirmaier.

"Is that a good thing, Oberleutnant?" said Richthofen.

"Not a good thing, but useful, I suppose," said Kirmaier. "What's on your mind, Richthofen?"

"It's Boelcke, he's not himself, and he seems to be getting worse every day. He's exhausted; weaker."

"I see. Perhaps, even in the little time since I've been here, he's changed, yes. Thomsen has tried to convince him that it's time to take leave ... and he won't. I don't know if anyone can convince him." Kirmaier leaned forward to Richthofen, encouraging Richthofen to speak.

"The artillery attack, the asthma, when Boelcke was in the hospital in Cambrai, well, I've seen old men who weren't as sick," said Richthofen. "He needs to rest, it would be better for all of us."

Kirmaier didn't respond.

"I assume that you're here to replace him, aren't you?" asked Richthofen.

Kirmaier looked at Richthofen, nodded. "I'm here to be available to replace him as commander when he takes leave. That's all I know. I can't replace him as a leader; these are different things."

"Have you tried to talk to him?"

"No, it's not my place, not yet. He trusts you and Böhme more than he trusts me." Kirmaier shrugged.

"It's hopeless, isn't it? Getting him to rest, I mean," said Richthofen.

"Yes, Richthofen, I'm afraid it is. Perhaps only an order from the Kaiser would be enough." said Kirmaier.

Richthofen looked out at the rain. "Perhaps it will keep raining, eh, Kirmaier?"

Kirmaier looked up and nodded. "Yes, if only." He picked up his book and continued to read.

~~~

The day passed with the pilots remaining grounded.

In the midst of a dinner of boiled ham and potatoes, the door was opened by Fischer, allowing a guest to enter behind him.

"Bodenschatz!" yelled Boelcke. He stood to greet a thin, elegant man, who stood poised in the doorway. "Come in, come in!"

"Gentlemen, Karl-Heinrich Bodenschatz, my old friend," said Boelcke to the pilots. Bodenschatz, a thin man, hobbled forward, a constant mask of pain on his face. His right leg was stiff as he held himself upright with a cane. In his left hand, he held a leather folio. The pilots stood, happy for any relief from the tedium of their day on the ground, and they crowded around the tall new comer to greet the man.

"Champagne, sir?" asked Fischer.

"Yes, certainly, please," replied Boelcke. "Pass it around."

Bodenschatz sat next to Boelcke, and lay a pad of paper in front of himself and at the top of the pad, he lay a pencil.

"Always, writing, Bodenschatz. You haven't changed."

"No, Herr Hauptmann, it's my memory, without it I couldn't find my way to my bunk."

After dinner, the pilots began to excuse themselves from the mess tables, some of them returning to the Skat table in the next room. Others gathered around the fireplace and began to stoke the flames for the evening. The mess attendants passed through, clearing plates. Böhme, Kirmaier and Richthofen lingered, sipping schnapps and coffee.

"So, Bodenschatz, what brings you here?" asked Boelcke.

"Thomsen has sent me to evaluate the needs of your Staffel. I'm to stay for several weeks. To report back if you need additional men, support, equipment, that sort of thing. As well as to provide additional operational help."

"An adjutant then?" asked Boelcke.

"Yes, I suppose. To be frank, I'm here to help you, as you may see fit."

"I see. But, we already have an operations staff. All of our billets are full."

"Any help you may need, Hauptmann," said Bodenschatz.

A fresh log was thrown on the fire, and yellow light filled the room. The light cast the men's faces into deep relief, creating depth and angles where none had existed before. Boelcke stood and led the group of men to the fireside. "Fischer, brandy if you have it."

"Yes, of course, sir."

The men settled into the leather chairs, facing the fire. Bodenschatz stretched out his legs and began to work the muscles of his thighs. "Sitting in a car for hours, it's not good for a man."

"Nor is getting shot five times. Or was it six, Bodenschatz?"

"Five. Boelcke. Just Five."

He looked at Boelcke's face, at his cheekbones, high but sharp now. The fire accentuated the sharpness, deepened the gauntness of his face, sinking cheeks and casting dark rings around his eyes. Even his normally full lips appeared thin and pursed. Fischer returned and began passing drinks.

Boelcke stared into the flames, an inferno reflecting in his eyes.

"Are you here to relieve me, Bodenschatz?" he asked.

"You're a friend Boelcke, I can't mislead you. I am here to assess the overall health of the unit, and to report back. If you appear to be in need of rest, then I'm to make a corresponding recommendation to Thomsen."

"I see. So, they sent a friend."

"Of course, I'm here to act as an officer, and as your friend. There is no conspiracy here, Oswald."

"Of course not."

"So, tell us the news." Boelcke brightened and turned to face Bodenschatz, his face once more open and warm. Bodenschatz smiled and leaned toward Boelcke.

"Well, Herr Fokker is now a citizen of greater Germany. The Fokker biplanes are officially being retired. The newest Albatros fighters are almost ready, the D.III's, they should be here in the next few weeks. But, you probably know all that."

"Yes, of course. On to more important things. What of your lovely wife, does she still make those gorgeous Bavarian puffs? Windbeutel. Filled with vanilla. Lovely. Our friend Richthofen here would enjoy them, he has quite the sweet tooth."

"I'll see that we have some delivered, Herr Hauptmann," said Bodenschatz. "My pleasure."

"Yes, do. That would be wonderful, my regards to your wife, a fine woman. You're a lucky man."

Boelcke turned back to the fire and grew uncharacteristically quiet again, his energy fading as quickly as it had come. Fischer tended the fire and lay another log on top. The firelight flickered over Boelcke's face. Böhme exchanged a glance with Richthofen, a worried look flashing for a moment.

Kirmaier spoke up, "Well, Fischer, perhaps we could see to Oberleutnant Bodenschatz's quarters, I'm sure he'd like to get settled in after his journey." Kirmaier looked at Böhme and nodded, as though he were handing over the tending of Boelcke. He stood. "Hauptmann Boelcke, if you'll excuse us."

"Yes, yes, of course," said Boelcke, absently repeating himself. "Please,

Bodenschatz, make yourself comfortable." Boelcke stood and shook Bodenschatz's hand as Kirmaier, Bodenschatz and Fischer gathered to leave for the evening.

"And, if you'll excuse me, I'm on dawn patrol, if the weather clears, as forecast," Richthofen added. He stood and saluted Boelcke, then bowed, formally. Boelcke smiled. "Yes, of course Richthofen. My baron."

Boelcke settled into the softest of the flyers' purloined leather chairs as the men cleared the room. He picked up his brandy glass. "So, I take it, you're my minder for the evening, Böhme."

"Oh, no, Hauptmann, I'm just a night owl and I enjoy your company," said Böhme.

Boelcke grinned. "Thank you for that. It sounded quite sincere."

Böhme smiled.

"When you were in East Africa, Böhme, did you ever climb Kilimanjaro?" asked Boelcke.

"Oh, yes, twice. How could one not?"

"Well said, Böhme. Well said. How could one not, indeed."

"Superb mountain. Rising out of the plains like that. A real mountain. I climbed it with my brother."

"Yes, sir. A lovely mountain. In need of being climbed."

Boelcke sipped his drink, his now-thin face cast in glare and shadows. "Did you see it, Böhme? The ghost ship. The dead men?"

Böhme shifted his long frame and long legs, trying to get comfortable and to find the right words. At last, he lied, "Yes, I saw it. I saw the ghost ship."

"Thank you, Böhme, thank you."

~~~

The day dawned clear and blustery, the winds rising and falling, shaking the sheds and buildings. The Albatros fighters sat outside, fueled, armed and heavy with energy. As the wind gusted, they would rise on their wheels, and then they would sag back down again. It appeared they were alive, as though they might leap into the air on their own. Richthofen thought they looked like gasping horses at a starting gate, anxious to run.

Whenever English planes crossed the lines, the frontline observers would call the anti-aircraft cannons, who would call the division headquarters, who would call the airfield. The pilots waited for these calls and then ran out to their airplanes and flew in the direction of the report. Most often, they saw nothing, the empty sky a mystery.

The pilots of Jasta 2 rose in the rough air, turning west, into the wind, found nothing, then returned to await the next telephone call from the front.

~~~

In the afternoon, fifty kilometers southwest of the German aerodrome of Lagnicourt, on the English airfield at Bertangles, Gerry Knight and Alfred McKay stood, being given their orders for the day. They listened to Andrews, then Hawker brief them on what to worry about, what to do if they saw the new German fighters, the Halberstadts and Aviatiks, or whatever they were. Knight and McKay were anxious, eager to fly after waiting out the rain and hardly paid attention. It didn't help that Andrews spoke of defense, while Hawker spoke of offense. The pilots left the conversation confused and a little morose.

"Northeast, Longueval. There are reports of German observation ships up there an' infantry are goin' over the top," said Andrews.

"Shoot them down," said Hawker, his eyes lit from behind.

"Yes, sir!" the assembled men barked in unison. They saluted and went to their airplanes.

Knight leaned over to McKay. "And 'shoot them down'. You heard the man."

"Oh, yes, certainly. Where are Boelcke's boys these days? Northeast?" McKay asked.

Knight looked at McKay, shrugged his shoulders. He laughed. "I heard that Hawker wants to fly."

"Fly again," said McKay. "He wants to fly again."

"Wouldn't be soon enough, if you ask me."

Their DH-2's were ready, and sat clumsy, pugnacious, rocking in the wind. Crewmen held them against the surging air. The aeroplanes faced west, their engines started; a moment later their pilots opened their throttles and they rolled across the field. The wind held them as they lifted off the ground, the underpowered DH-2's appearing to stand still in the air for a moment, and then they climbed rapidly with the wind pushing them upward like kites rising on strings.

They turned north, wobbled through the turn in the roiled air, and then settled on a course northeast, still climbing. Within moments, they were mere specks in the sky, disappearing over the trees beyond the field. With the wind on their tails, they made good speed, flashing over the fields and forests of northeastern France.

"Lots of wing," said Hawker, watching them go.

Andrews nodded. "Yes, lots of wing. Not much power, but lots of wing. God help them turnin' back int' this wind t' get home, they'll be standin' still."

"It'll be slow going, but they can make it."

"Eventually," said Andrews. "Northeast. Always Northeast. Boelcke's boys."

"Yes," said Hawker. He stared after them, yearning to be with them.

Knight and McKay crossed the lines in brilliant sunshine, flying through a smattering of German anti-aircraft fire, and then downwind, in the rough air over patches of puffy white clouds.

~~~

Boelcke sat down with Böhme to a game of chess after their sixth flight of the day. Richthofen drowsed. Three young newcomers to the Staffel were trying to teach themselves Skat. Fischer was heating milk on the top of a wood stove, stirring in sugar and chunks of chocolate for Boelcke.

The wind brought a chill to the building, subverting each crack and furrow, little gusts of air stirring through the building. With a bang, a door slammed open: an entering messenger accidentally letting the wind catch it. Richthofen scowled at the man from a chair near the fireplace, startled awake. The man, embarrassed, pressed the door shut behind him. With a stiff stride, he approached Boelcke.

"Hauptman Boelcke, two English aeroplanes have crossed the line."

"I see. Tell operations I'll be right along," said Boelcke.

Boelcke, playing white, moved a piece.

Böhme studied the board briefly and stood. "Let us take care of this. Enjoy your chocolate." His smile was weak, unconvincing. He waved a hand toward where Fischer stood at the stove. Böhme left Boelcke's single white pawn in the middle of the board.

"You have forty victories, Boelcke. It's is a good even number. Take a rest, and then go get another forty more, get eighty," said Richthofen. Richthofen grinned so broadly that Boelcke couldn't tell if he was agreeing with Böhme or mocking him.

"How many do I have this month, Richthofen?" asked Boelcke.

"Eleven," said Richthofen, quickly, the number memorized. "Twelve since we moved to the new field."

Since you were hospitalized, since the destruction of Bertincourt, thought Richthofen.

Boelcke glanced down at Böhme's hand, now resting on his, and offered a thin smile.

To Böhme he looked dry, wrung out. The dark rings under his eyes had returned, and Bohme thought that the man's lips had a touch of grey in them, but convinced himself they were only in shadow. Böhme suddenly thought that Boelcke looked like a ghost. In reflex, Böhme drew his hand back, feeling for a moment that he was touching a corpse.

"I'll rest another time, Böhme, another time," said Boelcke. He stood and took his muffler from the back of his chair, wrapped it around his neck. "We mustn't keep our customers waiting," Boelcke said, his still brilliant blue eyes flashed at Böhme. He turned toward the door and signaled to the pilots standing by, around the room. "Let's go."

They ran out to their airplanes, glancing up to gauge the rise and fall of the wind flags. Their mechanics were already waiting, ready to spin the props. Richthofen ran along behind Böhme and Boelcke, with three of their new pilots behind him. The mighty Mercedes engines started with roars, and the pilots turned into the rough west wind and launched, climbing hard to intercept the English intruders. Long red cloth streamers trailed from Boelcke's lower wings, marking him as the flight leader, after the English style.

Boelcke led them southwest, putting the wind to their right front quarter, from the west. The wind worked to roll them over, blowing steady now. The new pilots flew grimly, holding onto their yokes with white knuckles. Boelcke, Böhme, and Richthofen flew gently, their hands soft on the controls, their eyes scanning the sky for English 'customers', as Boelcke would say, come to the shop.

They were above the clouds, still climbing into the headwind, when they saw the English fighters just below them to the southwest. Boelcke looked around, checking that no other English were nearby, and then pointed. Böhme and Richthofen nodded, already seeing the English. The rookies looked where he pointed, suddenly seeing and, wide-eyed, tried to take in the abrupt reality. Boelcke pulled his muffler from his mouth and tried to impart a reassuring wave and smile. He rocked his wings, and worked his rudder, his little fighter playfully writhing in the air.

In the cold windy air, climbing hard, with an enemy ahead, Richthofen sensed Boelcke's joy.

Boelcke, together with Böhme and Richthofen, turned hard to the west, in an effort to circle behind the English fighters headed northeast. The rough formation of German Albatrosses turned with him, three below, three above. They flew in a scattered V-shape, Boelcke at the apex, Böhme to his left, and Richthofen to his right.

Boelcke motioned as though he were pushing something out and away. Böhme and Richthofen gently opened the gap between the airplanes, and the newcomers, above, copied them.

Reaching up to the charging handles, Boelcke cocked both Spandaus, and then engaged his synchronizer. He pressed the firing button and cleared his guns in a sharp roar. Each of his pilots followed his lead, firing in coughs of smoke and bullets.

Minutes passed as they closed, the English aligning themselves with the path of the Germans, Boelcke maneuvered his formation to stay above, upwind and parallel to the English.

Like opening moves in chess, thought Richthofen, *they may seem simple, draw no blood, but they dictate the whole game.*

The air, the wind, was commanding their movements, how the energy of space and time would bring the English and German fighters into conflict, and who would hold the initiative when it happened. Richthofen could see this now, trusting Boelcke to control the moment and to give them the most advantage. He flew, attentive, his eyes on the sky around them, waiting the moment.

Boelcke could have been Nelson at Trafalgar, feeling the air and sea, as the ships close. I see it, it's not in the Dicta ... He can't write it down ... it just is.

The English were below them, almost abeam of the German fighters, but passing on their left when Boelcke rocked his wings, signaling the attack. With vicious efficiency, he jammed forward on his control stick, and rolled over to the left, wrenching the Albatros into a harsh curving dive. Managing the reverse and to drop down on the English in a single maneuver, he smiled. The accelerations of the turn pushed him deeper into the cockpit, where the invisible forces felt like a comforting embrace.

A fraction of a second after, Böhme and Richthofen broke into their turns, diving behind and above Boelcke. The fledglings trailed above them as the leaders closed rapidly on the English.

~~~

Knight saw them first, level with them, crossing to their left. McKay saw them a second later, his head swiveling. Knight tracked the six airplanes flying nearly straight at them, but moving, almost gently, to their left, to the upwind side. Their graceful fish-like shapes and rounded wings were clear now: these were the new German fighters. If it were any other moment, any other place, the scene would have been weirdly beautiful.

Boelcke's boys. Always Boelcke's boys, thought Knight as sun briefly illuminated the black and white paint on the Germans' tails.

Knight imagined the next move, the Germans with the weather gauge, putting the wind behind them. He knew instantly that he was already on the defensive, out-numbered and, in seconds, unavoidably downwind. Andrews's and Hawker's words lingered in his mind.

Defensive or aggressive? Are they even different out here? Are they just moments in time?

He glanced at McKay and let the wind carry them rapidly east for a few seconds more. He braced himself; he could see the next step, and didn't like it. He felt his muscles tense and his bowels loosen. *This will be bad,* he thought. *Very bad.* He thought of the dark pit that so many had fallen into; the visions of the shadows of death, a shadow that wore black crosses on its wings. Boelcke was like a nightmare in his black airplane. It was the last thing so many Allied flyers ever saw.

Damn fables!

Knight shook the thought away and cleared his mind as the German airplanes came abeam on their left and above them. Instinctively, he sensed the Germans breaking into their attacking dives, and he broke into a left turn, yanking his controls into a hard bank, letting the nose drop. Shedding altitude, but not able to stop the fall, the DH-2's turned quickly. McKay, anticipating the break, turned with him.

As he turned, Knight kept his eyes fixed on the approaching fighters. The Germans yanked hard to their left an instant later and dove at them. The sun shone across the tops of the wings of the Albatrosses; broad irregular stripes, green and brown and rust, the elegant rounded tails, the curved wing tips. Tails black on one side, white on the other. The sunlight cast dark moving shadows across each German fighter, making them seem vibrant, each a living thing, each damned airplane like an animal. *So like sharks,* he thought, *but superb.* He looked again at each one, counting six.

As long as he lived, he never forgot the sight of Boelcke's Staffel turning and diving.

None of them are black! At least none of them are black! At least it's not Boelcke himself, thought Knight.

～～～

Boelcke focused only on the English now, his other senses clear, crisp, and his thoughts empty. He didn't feel the cold as the wind whipped around him, or the controls under his hands, or the tight pain, constant now, in his chest. His body struggled to breath, but his mind wouldn't acknowledge it, pushing out the sensation of tension and fear from his consciousness. His rasping wheezing was unheeded and unheard. He had grown so accustomed to a sense of suffocation that he could ignore it.

Boelcke watched the English airplanes turn simultaneously, almost choreographed. They broke just as he followed, pulling a grim smile across Boelcke's face. *They're not ... what do the English say? 'Rookies,'* he thought.

Boelcke acted on instinct, but held his turn longer than he had intended. He steepened his dive. Having corkscrewed through a complete revolution downward, he overtook the English and then dropped behind them.

The English weren't done though. They were flying near directly into the wind, dropping and accelerating back to the west, toward the Allied lines. *Defensive, but smart and clean, not panicked*, thought Boelcke.

Boelcke fixed the DH-2 to the left and closed with it, then lifted his nose for a moment to shed some speed so he wouldn't overshoot. He began to line up on his quarry, his eyes not on his sights yet.

Above Boelcke, Böhme targeted the same Englishman, while Richthofen went after the aeroplane on the right. The new pilots, behind them, strung out and spread to their sides, spectators. The wind buffeted all of them like currents battering ships on a rolling sea.

The English airplanes were separating now and making sharp, abrupt turns to disrupt the Germans' aim, but trying not to slow. Boelcke maneuvered gently, not overrunning his quarry, a fool's mistake, but conscious that one or the other Englishman might break into a sharper turn at any moment. He watched the right-most Englishman out of the corner of his eye as he began to aim, lining up the English aeroplane ahead in his sight. The DH-2 flickered across his field of view as he drew closer, and closer still, ready to fire.

He saw the red and white stripes now.

Number Twenty-Four Squadron, Hawker's crew. Otto Parschau's killers. Gott ... strafe ... England.

~~~

Knight flew with McKay to his left, as the Germans dropped in behind them. Glancing back, he saw two on McKay, and a single German behind him.

They're even sleeker from the front, thought Knight. *We're flying these bathtubs with wings, and they're flying in something vicious. Well, I've got plenty of wing, and I can turn like they've never seen.*

Watching the Germans close, Knight could sense them waiting to fire, to get so close they couldn't miss. He imagined thumbs over the German triggers, eyes on sights, his airplane and McKay's jinking across the sky in front of them.

Soon, very soon, not too early, they'll follow, not too late, they'll hammer holes in us ...

Knight glanced back and saw the German behind him steadying, close enough to fire.

Soon ... soon ... NOW!

～～～

Richthofen watched his target, watched as the man jolted his aeroplane back and forth, the Englishman trying to spoil his aim for a minute, then two. Richthofen closed, drew nearer, then, he, too saw the candy stripes, the red and white. These were the ones that Boelcke wanted so badly: Twenty-four.

He could feel the Englishman's skill now, devoid of panic, tight and controlled, not the wild swinging desperate moves of a beginner. The man had been here before, and he had lived to tell the tale. In precise bumps of his controls, the Englishman flew evasive jinks in the air; almost a box, up, down, right, left, each a few feet in a fraction of a second. At each stroke the Englishman seemed to disappear from Richthofen's gun sight, and then pause as Richthofen aimed anew, then again, he disappeared, each move startling, as though he might really vanish into a hard-breaking turn, a swooping climb, or a violent plummet.

He's taunting me. Waiting for me to over-anticipate, overcommit, overshoot.

The Englishman steadied, allowing Richthofen once more to rudder over in the riotous air. Richthofen put his sight on his quarry, watched it bounce around in his vision, and depressed his trigger. With a jolt, the English jerked away again, emptying the sky in front of Richthofen. He lifted his eyes from his gun sight, looking around at empty air. In the corner of his eye, the English fighter flipped up to the left, canted over on one wing, the affect like an eagle catching the air. Then suddenly he flashed past to Richthofen's left, forcing him to fly past the man, leaving only empty air.

My God! Damn!

The English pusher lifted and flipped into a hard-left turn, then dropped, wings low, toward the other English fighter. Richthofen craned his head, desperately looking back, embarrassed at being tricked. The other two Albatroses, Boelcke and Böhme, seemed to cling together for a moment. Richthofen thought it a deception of the eye, a trick of perception, then he saw fragments fly away, and Böhme passed overhead, his undercarriage hanging askew, one wheel tipped over and dangling loose under his airplane.

His face grew hot, rage and anger inside him, he wrenched his controls around, too late to follow the Englishman's turn.

Richthofen instinctively twisted his head for a moment, trying to follow his target, but his concentration was broken. His eyes found Boelcke's Albatros, losing altitude rapidly now, and dropping toward the east. Richthofen turned and followed after, quickly overtaking Boelcke, now below him. He glanced back at the English fighters, watched them descend, buffeted by the wind, all fight gone from them as they insolently disappeared into the puffy clouds to the west.

~~~

Moments before Richthofen watched them escape, Boelcke had seen the right most English aeroplane break into a violent turn at the edge of his vision, its wings outlined against the sky. Then, to his left, Boelcke sensed a shape, a darkness.

Böhme saw it too, the right-side Englishman pulling his airplane into that hard- left turn, crossing in front of them. The Englishman's wings were a sudden wall in front of them, the brilliant red, white and blue circles distinct for a moment, like eyes. Quickly, by impulse, Böhme turned hard right, up and away to avoid the reckless English pilot. The move thrust him straight into Boelcke's path.

There was a crashing, tearing sound, and that dark shadow passed over

Boelcke before disappearing behind and over the top of him.

Collision! thought Boelcke. *Who? Böhme?*

Boelcke felt his Albatros pull to the left, trying to roll over. He looked over at the left upper wing, and watched the fabric tear away, fluttering into space behind him. Panic welled up and he felt his chest tighten as though he were in the jaws of a beast. Boelcke took slow breaths, forcing his lungs to fill and empty, long and deep.

He pulled on the control yoke, fighting to level the airplane, to wrench it back level. Long lingering breaths allowed him to combat panic, fighting for each moment more of life, and finally allowed his mind to clear. He guided the airplane downward now, toward the clouds below them, with the wind behind him, heading east. The descent surrounded him in gentle, puffy, white clouds.

There was another violent clatter. The last of the fabric tore from his upper wing and blew away behind him, taking chunks of wood with it. His upper wing was a bare broken skeleton now, beyond useless. Boelcke looked out at the wing where he could see his left aileron, still covered, moving as he tried to control the airplane. Collectively, it all could only mean one thing.

His panic was gone now and a sense of peace and inevitability filled him.

Max, you knew as you went down. I know it now too. You didn't take a bullet, did you? And you didn't burn, thought Boelcke. He smiled and his lungs relaxed, the white-hot pain falling away with his wings.

Boelcke knew, he knew before the upper wing tore away, before it and his ability to fly were gone, before the Albatros tipped down into a tight spiraling nosedive. He knew as his lungs filled, calm and cool, at last, like a drink of crystal water from under a glacier with a summit just above him.

The earth grew larger below him. Then he joined it and all was dark.

~~~

The German formation was scattered. The three new pilots went after the English aeroplanes, which were quickly growing smaller in the west. But they quickly gave up as the English disappeared into clouds, too far away to overtake.

Böhme's wheels hung below his aeroplane, little more than useless wreckage now, dragging against the air. He struggled through a turn to the northwest, shedding altitude. He panted and wipes tears of rage and frustration from under his goggles. His Albatros sank rapidly as he fought to keep it upright and reach their aerodrome.

Richthofen looked down and back, turning slightly, but the air was empty were Boelcke had been. He flew east, buffeted in the turbulent air, then turned northeast, recognized the rubble of Bertincourt, and turned north. Below him, Vélu passed under his left wings. As he approached the aerodrome at Lagnicourt, he throttled down and descended. On the field, an Albatros lay wrecked, its right wings folded back, broken. The wind rocked the wreckage where men gathered around, clustered together, but did not move to touch it.

Confusion gripped him. *Boelcke? Could it be?* He began to hope.

One of the new pilots lined up to land, the others strung out behind him. Coming in behind the first pilot, Richthofen turned to land quickly. The gusting winds made him bounce as he landed and he crabbed slightly sideways. Beyond impatient, he flipped off his switches and jumped down from the cockpit before the ground crew could get to him, running in the direction of the wrecked Albatros.

Kirmaier ran toward him, crouched and fast. He held his hands up to stop Richthofen and blocked his way to the wreckage. Richthofen recognized the wrecked aeroplane now: Böhme's.

"What happened?" asked Kirmaier.

"Collision. I think. It happened so fast ..." Richthofen tried to get around him to get to the wreck.

"Richthofen. Stop!" Kirmaier shouted.

Richthofen paused and turned to Kirmaier.

"What?" he snapped.

"Richthofen," Kirmaier lowered his voice. His cap nearly blew off his head, but he caught it and pulled it away, holding it in two hands.

"He's dead," said Kirmaier. "Boelcke."

Richthofen already knew it. He had felt it, an emptiness. One of the Albatros fighters landed behind him, roared past, too fast, spun on its wheels, teetered, almost fell over. Richthofen didn't see. The heat of anger, rage, and frustration was coming, closing his mind.

"You're sure?" asked Richthofen.

"Yes, he landed ... came down ... by an artillery battery. They used a Sanke card, saw his *Pour le Mérite*. It's him." Kirmaier's eyes were empty, staring, reflecting his own shock.

Richthofen looked over at the wreck. "Where's Böhme?" he asked.

Kirmaier shook his head. "I don't know."

Richthofen ran to the wreck, clearly Böhme's Albatros. He looked around at the faces, glanced at the empty cockpit.

"Where is he?" he shouted.

A crewman pointed toward the new buildings, the officer's quarters. Richthofen turned and ran, hard, his heavy flying clothes slowing him down. He pulled his flying cap and muffler off and opened his stride as he ran. He stopped at Böhme's door, wadded his muffler up in his hand, and pushed his way inside. The wind took the door and banged it against the side of the building. Richthofen had to grasp the handle with both hands and pull it shut again. Dust swirled in the air inside.

Böhme sat on his bed, his pistol dangling in his hand. He didn't look up, only stared at the floor. Richthofen stopped on the threshold, trying to make sense of what he was seeing. He opened a hand and worked his fingers. Setting his cap and muffler on the dresser, Richthofen took a chair, and put it down in front of Böhme.

Böhme glanced up, and then looked down at the pistol in his hand. He tipped the gun sideways, inspecting it. Silence hung in the room, and the wind howled outside.

A wordless sadness settled over them both. Time passed.

"I thought I hated the wolves. But I think it was just the howling I hated," said Böhme at last. He looked down at the heavy pistol. "I kept it for the wolves, you know. That, and in case the Russians might capture me." Böhme smiled at the idea, as though he were the hero saving the last bullet for himself. A cowboy surrounded by wild Indians.

"Sorry, Böhme. Sorry that I convinced you to sleep outside," said Richthofen. His voice was low, soft. Richthofen felt light, as the though the wind might blow them away into a void, and the feeling was only growing. "Are you injured?" he asked at last.

"What, me? No, I'm fine," said Böhme.

"You smashed up."

Böhme looked up, wild-eyed, his gaze empty of understanding.

He doesn't know he crashed, thought Richthofen.

"It was a collision. I couldn't see him, you know," said Böhme.

"Yes, I know. The wind. I know," said Richthofen. He had no words, no clear ideas, but felt that he needed to keep talking. He felt choked, but couldn't, *wouldn't* cry.

Böhme waved the pistol in circles, pointed at the floor. He gripped it tightly and put his finger against the trigger.

"I kept it for the wolves. But, perhaps, I have another use for it now, a better use," he said, staring at the pistol.

Richthofen searched through his mind, searched inside, tried to find an answer, tried to get the damning feelings to move aside. He felt quiet, violent, a tightness inside, coiled.

No, it wasn't Böhme's fault, and even if it were, this will do no good.

"It was God's will, not man's," said Richthofen. "You are not to blame. Never will be."

Böhme looked up at the window, watched the trees flip back and forth, whipping against the sky in nature's rage.

"Too windy to fly, Richthofen. Perhaps nature herself is upset, some pagan god is angry." His eyes were wet.

Richthofen reached out and gently wrapped his hand around the pistol, pulling it from Böhme's hand. "The wolves are still outside, Böhme."

Böhme held fast for a moment, and then opened his hand, releasing the pistol. Richthofen looked down at Böhme's gun, felt the coldness of the metal, smelled the sweetness of gun oil, and could see that it was clean and polished: ready.

A soldier's gun. It belongs with a soldier, thought Richthofen.

He handed it back to Böhme, and Böhme slowly took it. His face wore an empty, distant mask.

"They're outside, and you'll need this when you meet them," said

Richthofen. The coil inside him tightened by a notch, an increment, wound so tight that it could only break or release, and cast time into motion.

He's gone now ... the father of all of this. My God! Even the Kaiser will grieve.

"No Böhme, it will do no good. You can't blame yourself, don't. The Englishman, the one that flipped his aeroplane in front of us, the wind ... It would have happened to anyone."

Böhme looked up with the fragment of a smile, his hand grew tight around the pistol, his finger on the trigger.

"Don't do it, Böhme. Don't. Save your anger for the fight out there. Don't waste your own redemption."

Böhme stared at the pistol, and then slowly lay it on the bed.

Perhaps we are the wolves, now, thought Richthofen.

Chapter Forty-Nine

November 21, 1916
Lagnicourt Aerodrome, France

The man with the cane, the shattered man, Karl Bodenschatz, ordered the mechanics make a table from an old door. He sat the table in the large room of a farmhouse and spread an enormous map over it. Behind the table, nailed to a wall, was an old chalkboard, taken from a school in Lille, with the pilots' names down one edge and their victories tallied.

"Only official victories," he reminded the men. "My scoreboard."

Richthofen looked at the paper landscape, and at wooden circles, painted in rings laying across the map.

"What are these?" he said, pointing.

"English air bases. The ones we know about. That's the squadron number," answered Bodenschatz, picking up a marker and showing it to Richthofen.

Kirmaier stood watching. Richthofen put his finger on the number 24. He picked up a ruler and lay it down, between the number 24 and Lagnicourt. Then he ran his finger back down the line, put it on a spot just south of Bapaume. Richthofen slid his finger along the line to the northwest, and stopped again, standing his finger up straight.

"What are you doing, Richthofen?" asked Kirmaier.

"Just thinking. This seems like a bad place to go." He stabbed his finger down again. "Boelcke fell here, that English ace from 24, Langan-Byrne, fell here. Parschau here. The devil must walk here."

"You're imagining things, Richthofen. If you put down every pilot that's died on this map, there'd be no room for anything else," said Bodenschatz.

Kirmaier spoke, "The sky rains heroes ..."

"What did you say?" asked Richthofen.

"That English fellow, the writer. The astonished earth ... 'the sky rains heroes upon the astonished earth'. Something he said. I think he's a bit of a bastard myself. Easy to be romantic when you're not the one falling out of the sky."

Bodenschatz stood upright now, painfully straightened his stiff body, looking down as the door opened.

"Yes?" asked Bodenschatz, looking up. Menzke held the door allowing a short, lean officer with enormous, innocent, doe eyes to step in. The mild young Leutnant stood at attention.

"Leutnant Voss, reporting," said the officer. Voss saluted, and held it until Bodenschatz returned the salute.

"Come in. I am Oberleutnant Bodenschatz; this is Oberleutnant Kirmaier and Leutnant Richthofen. I'm operations. Herr Kirmaier is in command."

"Acting commander; until the new operational commander arrives," said Kirmaier, correcting Bodenschatz. He shook Voss' hand. "Join us, Voss. We were just inspecting Bodenschatz' new command post."

Voss smiled a crooked, pursed-lipped smile and stepped to the edge of the map table, looking over it with the others.

Kirmaier looked down again; he stabbed a finger on the map. "So, you think if we go there, just south of Bapaume, we will find trouble, Richthofen?"

"I don't know, probably a coincidence, undoubtedly No. 24's sector of the line to patrol. But if we were looking for them, that seems like the place." Richthofen put his finger down next to Kirmaier's and looked up at Voss. "And here there be monsters."

Voss looked at the solemn faces of Kirmaier and Bodenschatz and then back at Richthofen. He was newly perplexed and worried.

"Don't fret, Voss, not for you, but soon, very soon, we'll travel to the edge of the map," said Richthofen.

"Then that's where we go. Fly them all," said Kirmaier. "How many do we have, Bodenschatz?"

"Twelve. Six new comers, and the six survivors from Boelcke's original Jasta."

"Yes, let's fly there, fly them all. See what we find," said Richthofen.

Kirmaier looked at Richthofen's face, saw the pale blue eyes reflecting the sky in the window. "Very well. We'll go looking for trouble."

Richthofen grinned. "I'm sure our friends from ..." He bent over, looked at the map, read the name of a little village. "'Bertangles' ... wouldn't want it any other way."

The skies cleared high in the afternoon, leaving bold blue over a thick grey mist that obscured the ground. Just after noon, Jasta 2 flew southwest, toward Bapaume. They were twelve Albatros fighters, hungry and fierce, six low and leading, and six high and above.

～～～

Crawford and Andrews turned southwest, back toward their airfield at Bertangles, over Beaulencourt, headed toward what they hoped was Longeuval and the front lines. The weather hid the ground with a haze that held close and thick over the battlefield and though the winter air was cold and hard on Crawford's face, it cleared his head. He delighted in the clear blue above; he watched Andrews, and watched the sky.

They'd had a quick fight near Vraucourt, and Andrews' airplane had been hit, but Andrews had waved that he was okay.

However, Andrews's engine began to fail, and he lost altitude as his engine lost power. Crawford dropped back, behind Andrews, and followed him, guarding Andrews' descent towards the English lines. Now they skimmed above the ground fog, just high enough to see each other, though they were barely able to see the earth.

As the two of them limped back home, a half dozen German fighters appeared high in the sky to the north: specks in the sky that became machines, then fighters, then dangerous. Their sleek bodies were distinctive, even at a distance. A moment later, Crawford noticed six more that appeared tangled with some British pushers, ahead and to their south. Rattled, he swept his head around, looking for help. With relief, he saw two flights of DH-2's come in from the north, higher than the six

Germans that were closing.

Crawford looked to Andrews and saw him looking up, already aware of the incoming planes. Crawford tensed, knowing the sky was newly crowded and deadly. He tightened, his body growing taut, his skin crawling on his exposed neck. He imagined bullets raking it. Crawford turned back to watch the Albatroses overhead closing, almost close enough to fire, and the DH-2's above them, diving.

Where the sharp, dark silhouettes of the wings of the German fighters had been seconds before, there were now only dark dots, framed in wings, the Germans flying nose on toward them. Crawford grimaced as he yanked his DH-2 up and into their attack. As quickly as he saw them, the Germans swept past. He heard no gunfire, saw no flashes from their guns. Amazed to be alive, Crawford watched the German fighters scatter into the haze below them.

His terror turned to joy as Crawford looked down at the German airplanes and realized he had a few seconds to attack the nearest German before they vanished into the haze. He banked to the left, and pitched the nose down. Andrews, on his right side, mirrored the movement, despite his frail engine. Together they closed on the leader of the diving Germans. The Albatros leader, trailing long black strips of cloth from its wings, was just beginning to pull up out of his dive when they caught him. Crawford settled the gun sight on the back of the pilot and held the trigger down to fire a quick, harsh bite. The Albatros flipped onto its back and fell away. Crawford and Andrews swept by.

Pulling back on his stick, Crawford leveled his DH-2 out of its dive, and instinctively jerked the airplane into a hard-right bank to clear any pursuing fighter off his tail. He looked back over his shoulder; saw streaking dots all over the sky, but nothing close. Tipping the nose back down, he pushed over into a steep dive, into the haze shrouding the ground, to finish off the Albatros. A dark column of smoke trailed down through the soft greyness below, and he followed it down. As he neared the ground, a brilliant spray of orange flames marked the end of the trail of smoke. Crawford and Andrews circled the wreckage once, twice.

Crawford felt a flush of success and grinned to himself; he glanced at

Andrews and hoped to catch a glance to share in the celebration.

Suddenly, with a bang and grinding of metal, a cylinder exploded from Crawford's engine and his propeller windmilled to a stop behind him. Crawford swept his head around, startled, confused. Drag slowed his airplane and pressed Crawford forward, the unpowered propeller digging into the air like a storm anchor. Sweat rolled down his back, terror gripping him for he knew that he must go down. Andrews surged ahead and disappeared into the clouds embracing the ground. By reflex, Crawford tipped the nose of his airplane down into a shallow dive to the southwest, suddenly desperate to reach the English lines. He looked back, behind and above him. No one followed; Andrews was gone. He let out his breath, a breath he had been holding from the moment the Germans had first appeared.

Steepening his dive, Crawford dropped deeper into the fog, hoping to hide. The airplane soared with a soft hissing sound over a line of trenches: beaten grey and pulped, pockmarked by craters. He clumsily prayed.

Jesus, our Lord who art in heaven ...

Just before he struck the ground, he lifted the nose to check his descent. Aiming for two craters, Crawford ruddered the DH-2 slightly, and settled the airplane in between. The damaged machine skidded sideways to a stop, tipped up on one wing and then shattered into wooden shards.

Crawford gasped, feeling clods of dirt spray down on him from his aeroplane's impact. Sitting in the what was left of his aeroplane, he wrapped his arms around himself and tucked his head, waiting for the debris to finish cascading down, and for the bloody awful noise of destruction to stop.

At last composing himself, he lifted his head and looked around, but saw only grey, dead ground, empty of foliage, torn apart by shell impacts. He sat, stunned, as the silence closed in again, and the grey stillness of the ground fog gripped the wreck. Dimly, and from all directions, be heard the muffled pops of gunfire. Crawford unbuckled himself and rolled out of his broken cockpit and onto the ground while pulling his pistol out of his holster. He tucked his pistol under an arm; fumbled with a coat pocket and pulled out a box of matches.

"Light the thing," he said, aloud. "Get it burning ... Dammit, burn ..."

He tried to open the matchbox, fear making his hands shake. He pulled out a match and struck it. He reached out with the flame, to hold it under a gas stain in the canvas.

"No need for that."

Crawford let out a wild sound and whirled around, brandishing the flickering match between his fingers. His pistol thumped to the ground from under his arm. He glanced down at it, then up, a feeling of hot embarrassment washing over him. Three infantrymen stood there, calmly, shrouded in the fog, watching him. The match flickered out.

"You're in our lines," said one of the soldiers. He stepped forward and carefully took the matches out of Crawford's hands and put them in his pocket. Crawford could only watch, still frozen by his own shock. He sat down heavily on the ground, with a motion like melting, the energy gone from his body. He felt his head begin to throb. An infantry major strode out of the fog, wearing a flopped-over Australian bush hat. A motley group of a half-dozen soldiers trailed behind him, each looking out into the haze, their rifles casually leveled out into the grey soft wall around them.

The major stopped and crouched down next to Crawford. "Are you injured?" he asked, with the poor relative intonation of an Australian.

Crawford shook his head and managed to speak. "No." The word came out like a croak.

"Can you stand, then?" The major was impatient with Crawford's shock.

"Yes, I suppose," Crawford looked up and considered shouting at the man, thought better of it. "I just crashed." He said matter-of-factly.

"Yes, I see that." The major tilted his head into the fog. "Shall we go take a look at it?"

"Take a look at what?" asked Crawford.

"The Jerry, about a thousand yards to the east. Came down and hit the ground in our lines, quite unusual that, they don't normally come this far west. Report came from the front trench a couple of minutes ago. Was it yours?"

Crawford leapt to his feet, suddenly flush. The shock replaced by adrenalin.

"Yes, absolutely!" he shouted. His legs shook and he wavered, then he bent and propped his hands on his knees, his head down: "Could you spare a man some water? I'm awfully dry."

A soldier passed a canteen forward, and the Aussie major handed it to Crawford. Crawford took it, suddenly grateful for everything, the air, the ground, the water, even the damned fog, for life. "Thank you. Most kind." He tilted the canteen up and swallowed deeply, feeling the coolness flow down through his body, calming him. He had never felt more alive. He handed the canteen back and wiped a sleeve across his mouth.

"Yes, show me," he said.

"Of course, this way," the major turned and led Crawford across the shattered wet ground, through the fog, towards his quarry.

In a few minutes of walking, they reached a sap—a deep trench running forward towards the enemy—and climbed down into it.

"Wait here," said the major. He motioned to Crawford to sit. Crawford leaned against the side of the trench, and then slid down onto a wobbly wooden bench. Aussie infantry began to gather around him. They were muddy, streaked and grey, the color of the fog. They stared at Crawford, as though he had just dropped in from outer space, which wasn't quite as far off as it would have been for a normal soldier. They wore the distinctive slouch hats of Aussies, the 'diggers'.

Finally, one of the men silently held out a cigarette to Crawford, who took it and nodded appreciatively. The infantryman who had taken Crawford's matches stepped forward and lit the cigarette, and slipped the matches back into his own pocket. Crawford didn't care. He took a long, languorous drag and slowly exhaled a funnel of smoke.

"You the one that shot the Jerry down, then?" someone asked.

Crawford looked back, fighting hard not to smile, "Yes, yes, I am." He tried to sound commonplace, literal, as though the question were posed every day. His voice came out in a squeak.

"He shot you down right back, did he, then?" asked the soldier with a grin.

Crawford frowned back at the soldier.

"No ... I ... my engine," stammered Crawford, and then thought better than to answer. He drew on his cigarette. "Oh, hell," he mumbled.

"Now boys, leave the man alone." The major reappeared and shooed the gathered soldiers away. "Shall we?" he gestured down into the network of trenches.

He led Crawford down the trench again, curious infantry trailing along behind them. At the end of the sap, they climbed out and began to pick their way through craters. Crawford could hear airplane engines overhead, but looking up, saw only colorless sky.

"Thank God for the fog, otherwise their artillery and snipers would be having their fun with us," said the major.

Then, out of the grey, in a clump of canvas and broken wood, the German wreck firmed into existence. Dark smoke hung close the ground, and a burning strut cast orange sparks. Crawford stood in awe for a moment. He blinked, as though he were seeing a monster, an apparition. He had never seen one of the deadly Albatroses so close. His eyes moved over it, trying to draw it in, to capture the moment.

The tails of the thing were black and white. *One of Boelcke's*, thought Crawford. A leader's streamer lay over the top of the wreck. A dozen infantry milled around it, but not too close, as though they were afraid to touch it. Crawford smelled gasoline and sulfur.

The scent of hell?

His heart thumped at being so close to a real fighter, to one of Boelcke's veterans. The thrill of victory mixed with a visceral fear of these terrible machines, the killer of so many friends.

A hand and bare arm stuck out from under the fuselage, already ghastly blue. Crawford looked back over his shoulder and said, "Help me lift this."

The major and some infantry stepped forward, grasped the side of the fuselage and rolled it over. Crawford looked down at the man. The German had a single bullet hole in the back of his head; thick crimson gore matted his hair and soaked the back of his jacket.

An Aussie medic took the dead pilot under the arms and dragged him away from the wreck, then rolled the German's body onto its back. The medic pulled one *Hundemarken*, a 'dog tag', from the corpse's neck. He straightened the man's legs and folded his arms over his chest. The medic handed the disk to Crawford.

Crawford thought the German, his eyes closed, looked at peace, despite a single angry tear in one cheek. He rolled the disk over between his fingers without looking at it.

"I'd say you've probably done that before," Crawford said to the medic.

The medic looked at him and frowned. "Unfortunately so, mate."

Crawford looked down at the identity card, and then held it up. "Kirmaier," he said, dramatically.

"*Oberleutnant* Kirmaier. God rest your soul."

~~~

"It was No. 24, again," said Böhme, "I saw their stripes and those red wheels. It was 24."

Richthofen rocked from one foot to another like a prizefighter. He clenched his jaw, working its muscles. His eyes were calm. He looked down at the map laid out on the table and imagined a cross on the ground.

Kirmaier's cross.

Bodenschatz looked at Böhme. Böhme looked back and nodded.

"You're the combat commander now, Richthofen," said Bodenschatz.

"Very well, then, what would you do about it, Richthofen?" Böhme asked.

Richthofen's voice was low, fierce without anger. "We go back tomorrow. We go find them. Make the aeroplanes ready. Now."

Chapter Fifty

November 22, 1916
Bertangles Aerodrome, France

"I don't like it. I don't think it's good form. I'll fly in his place," Hawker said.

Canvas flapped in the breeze behind Andrews, and outside an engine sputtered, failing to start. Someone swore.

Andrews looked back at Hawker, shook his head. "Trenchard will ha' my head if there's a problem."

"Just because a man is goin' on leave, doesn't mean he can'a fly," said Andrews.

Hawker smiled, sharpening his features.

"Andrews, I would do it for you, I'll damn well do it for any of our men." Hawker's voice was cool, reassuring, but intent, unwavering. "Bad luck if he's going on leave, and something were to happen to him. He should stay."

"There's no arguin' wi' you, then. I won' try. If Trenchard gets wind of 'his, there will be hell t' pay. Crawford is sittin' it out today, got in early this mornin' from his little trip t' the front. He seems t' think that was one of Boelcke's leads, or perhaps even Boelcke's replacement, that went down yesterday. A man named Kirmaier, ever hear of him?"

"No, Andrews, I haven't. We should be so lucky that he was actually Boelcke's replacement. At least Boelcke is gone; that should take the sting out of them a bit."

"Very well, fly, then, Hawker, you're the commander down here, but, up there, I'm flight lead. Understood?"

"Yes, Andrews, I'll follow your lead."

"Very good." Andrews traced a finger across a map on Hawker's. "We're flyin' an offensive patrol, here, south of Bapaume. Four ships, Saundby, Crutch, you, an' me."

Hawker beamed, exuberant at going back into combat after so long.

Andrews frowned and turned to step out of the building, shaking his head. "You'll be the death of me ..." he muttered under his breath.

Four DH-2's lifted into the sky, a thin westerly wind under their wings, into an open, empty blue expanse. They turned northeast, toward the Germans, downwind, headed for the Jastas, toward what they hoped was the remnant of Boelcke's boys.

~~~

Richthofen inspected his Albatros once more. The ground crews had lined up the machines in two rows of six, one behind the other. Böhme approached Richthofen with a child's grin plastered across his face, his hands behind his back. Voss, Hohne, Konig, and Bodenschatz trailed after him, all smiling. Richthofen turned to watch the little parade.

"What is it?" asked Richthofen. "My birthday?"

Böhme pulled his hands from his pockets and let two long streams of cloth unwind from out of his hands, long strips of knotted bed sheet, painted with black stripes. He looked at Richthofen and grinned. "You'll need these."

Richthofen smiled back, reached out, and took a streamer. "Flight lead, then?"

"Yes, Richthofen, the heir apparent, it would seem."

Voss stepped forward and clapped Richthofen on the back, already over-familiar. "Just don't fuck things up, okay?"

The Jasta flew southwest, toward Bapaume, Richthofen leading. Towards the English, towards the English squadron with the candy stripes and the red wheels, killers of Parschau, Boelcke and Kirmaier: *No. 24.*

~~~

Hawker flew to Andrews' left and behind. Docile, he followed Andrews' lead.

They crossed the line just north of the town of Albert, still climbing, scraping for all the altitude they could manage, the wind at their backs. Below them, artillery hammered away at both sides of the lines, throwing up great gusts of muck. The fog of the day before was gone. Past Albert, the German anti-aircraft began to fire, snapping around them in angry, grey-white bursts. Shards of metal clanged against their wing wires and ripped holes in canvas, but otherwise left them unchecked as they crossed over into German sky.

The ruins of Albert dropped away behind them, under Hawker's right wing. Hawker watched Andrews as he signaled a turn, leading them to the left, and pointing the noses of the four English aeroplane at Grandcourt. Hawker felt tense, keyed up, and tight. It didn't feel the same to him; it wasn't the same sky that he had last fought in more than a year before. The tension now was palpable, in the tight turns of Andrews, in the snapping of heads back and forth in cockpits, twitching eyes across the sky. Their alertness felt like fear to Hawker.

Hawker forced himself to keep his eyes moving, not to stare at Andrews, to keep scanning the sky. Above Grandcourt, Hawker saw two German two-seaters, with three English aircraft over them. All five were all running downwind to the east. Andrews steered toward them, but they moved away before his flight of four could join the fight.

Out of the corner of his eye, Hawker saw the ship piloted by Crutch fall away from them. Looking down, he saw Crutch point back at his engine. Hawker closed in slightly toward Crutch, and could hear it now: the ugly metallic shattering of the man's rotary engine as it tore itself apart. Hawker pointed down, signaling for Crutch to descend and get away, and so Crutch turned very slowly to the west, then, his turn complete, quickly disappearing behind them. Hawker looked at Andrews, watching for a signal to turn and escort the crippled English fighter back to their lines. Andrews looked coolly back at Hawker and pointed ahead. Hawker felt his belly tighten and his hands grew cold.

So this is how it is? Ruthless?

The three English fighters continued northeast toward Achiet-le-Grand. Over the town flew two German observation planes, headed west, and low. Hawker focused on them, his mind suddenly ablaze with energy. This was the fight he remembered, the fight he knew, dropping down on enemy observation ships, fighting them up close and personal. He reached up and checked the magazine on his Lewis.

Come on, Andrews, now, now ...

Hawker intently watched the German aeroplanes, his eyes fixated on them. Every detail leapt at him. He could see the German observers checking their guns, he could see their rudders twitch slightly, adjusting their course. Blood roared in his ears and his vision became a tunnel, with the German aeroplanes at the end. *Oh, hell!*

He barely glanced at Andrews as he dove his aeroplane at the enemy.

~~~

Andrews turned slightly left, leading Hawker and Saundby, and working to get in position to attack the two German airplanes. With quick, furtive glances, born of instinct and caution, he scanned the sky above the horizon, watching for the contrast of German fighters high against the pale sky. He kept them oriented above the German observation ships, but was hesitant.

He didn't buy the English myth of the perpetual German ambush; rather he believed the Germans chose to keep their fighters high to take opportunities to drop into a fight. Andrews didn't like it, felt it was too easy, and he glanced down again at the German observation aeroplanes, and then raised his eyes back to the sky to the northeast.

Without warning, Hawker tipped his DH-2 over and dove.

Andrews sensed Hawker drop away, diving, one moment there, the next, empty sky at Andrews' wing. At that moment, Andrews saw the two flights of German fighters, six airplanes each, climbing, not yet silhouetted against the pale sky, blurs against the ground, noses pointed up. He shouted out a useless, hoarse cry, an unheard shout of warning for Hawker as Hawker dropped away and below them after the German two-seaters.

Damn Hawker, damn him!

Andrews watched the new German formation climb: furiously clawing for altitude. He felt ice water had been thrown over him, and looked at the climbing fighters in disbelief, willing them away. Hawker was already committed to his descent, ahead and below Andrews and Saundby. Clearly, Hawker hadn't seen the German fighters. Andrews looked over at Saundby and shook his head in frustration. He fought the urge to turn and dive west toward home.

The three English fighters raced toward the jaws of Jasta 2.

The higher of the two groups of German fighters turned on Hawker, leaving the lower six still climbing. Andrews dove behind Hawker to protect him, with Saundby behind him. Andrews yanked his controls and aimed his airplane into the heart of the high German formation and began firing wildly, hoping to break the Germans' cohesion as they evaded the crazed Englishman. Andrews was all instinct now, the cold frozen to an icy intensity, a man governed by reflex. German fighters swirled around Andrews, filling the sky. Saundby followed close behind as they flew through the seeming cloud of Germans, fast downwind and to the east, away from the safety of the English lines, putting the German fighters behind them.

Glancing back, Andrews could see a single Albatros already behind Hawker, just beginning to fire, a stream of gun smoke rolling out from the German airplane. Andrews turned on Hawker's attacker, with Saundby following behind. He closed to within twenty yards of the German and fired his Lewis, barely aiming, desperately trying to get the Albatros to break off from Hawker.

Two more German fighters came in after Saundby. As the Germans flashed by, their tails caught the light. *Black and white!* Saundby threw his airplane into a tight spiraling right turn, forcing the Germans to overshoot. Andrews closed with Saundby to help him escape.

At that moment, a spray of bullets from an unseen attacker banged into Andrews's engine, like metallic hail pelting a tin roof. Another fusillade ripped through his wings. The sound was new; Andrews had never heard the impact of the bullets on the fabric so distinctly. He looked back at two more Albatrosses behind him; their noses erupting in orange flames.

He turned right, hard, harder than he had ever turned, the wires on his wings hummed and the turn drove him deep into his seat. Andrews' engine began sputtering and clanking. He knew that in a moment, it would spin itself apart. His intuition told him where west was, and he desperately straightened out his turn and began to dive in that direction, trading altitude for speed as he maneuvered to escape. His aeroplane accelerated down, and he pointed the nose down even further, desperate to get away.

God help me, just a few more seconds!

Another staccato rain of bullets hit his engine, throwing up hot sparks over his back. Andrews began to pray aloud, now, praying for another minute to live, another sunset: for time, just a little time. He heard a long burst of gunfire as Saundby's Lewis shot up an Albatros hounding him.

Please, God! Please!

The German turned away.

Saundby dove alongside Andrews and waved. Andrews could smell leaking gas now and could feel the liquid seeping into his boots and through his pants. The cold gas was like liquid fear over his legs. He steepened his dive.

He looked back for Hawker. Hawker was alone and still heading east, beginning to dive on a lone Albatros just below him. As he dove away toward safety, he lost sight of Hawker.

Good luck, old man. Good luck. Pray, Hawker, pray!

~~~

Richthofen was blooding his new pilots. He let the first six, his youngsters, attack the English pushers, and stayed low to let the fight come down to him. As he watched, the lead German fighters scattered the Englishmen across the sky, then they picked out their individual targets. Within moments, disoriented and confused by the melee, the young German pilots had lost their will to stay in the fight. They began to circle away to the east, as two of the English fighters dropped to the west.

With a wave of his hand, Richthofen motioned his flight of more experienced pilots into the fight. The second formation of six plunged onto the English.

A single Englishman flew over Richthofen, looking down. In reflex, Richthofen broke into a brutal climbing left turn, just as the Englishman dove on him. The English pilot fired in a quick burst, then checked his fire as Richthofen vanished beneath him.

Instantly twisting his head to look back, Richthofen could see the English pilot turn hard left, already overshooting the turn, creating an opportunity for Richthofen. In an instant, Richthofen turned and was closing from behind, nearly ready to fire. He could see the left side of the English ship, could see the red and white stripes on its struts.

Twenty-Four ... His mind cleared, and nothing else existed but that moment. Unconsciously, he cocked his machine guns. The motion was perfunctory now; automatic, clear, crisp.

Together, the hunter and hunted circled around one another, the Englishman holding his turn, clinging to his altitude. Richthofen could see the man looking back. But he was gaining, the circle as tight as he could fly, but not so tight that he began to drop. For a brief second, the Englishman filled his sights, but then he slipped away. Richthofen wanted a clean, lethal shot, biding his time.

Below him, the English pilot turned ever downward, his turn tightening, shedding lift. Richthofen looked down into the English airplane, so close he could see inside the cockpit, see hands and fingers, and see the controls move. Richthofen hesitated, let time stand still, waited.

~ ~ ~

Hawker held the spiraling descent for just a moment, knew instantly that not only had the German pilot escaped, but that he had left himself on the defensive, descending. He opened his circle, widening his turn before he dropped too far away from the German to respond. Just above him, fifty meters, no more, the German still turned, black and white streamers fluttering behind him. For an instant, Hawker felt it: the dread, the excitement, a feeling like joy.

Could it be him, back from the dead? Boelcke?

The little English fighter had one trick, one wicked trick, one nasty surprise that could turn everything around in a fight, and Hawker knew it. At that moment, he turned right, reversing his turn. The rotary engine added its inertia to the rotation, and drove the little fighter into an impossibly tight right hand turn, yet arrested the descent of the airplane.

Hawker looked up and smiled, imagining the look on the German's face.

This will get his attention ...

~~~

Richthofen could hardly blink in the time it took the little English fighter to flip into a turn and begin to spiral behind and below his Albatros. Richthofen watched, letting the Englishman make the move, and held his altitude. He chose a moment then he wrenched his controls to the right, turning with the Englishman, and bringing himself level with the English flier. He heard the Englishman begin to fire.

But some tricks weren't tricks. They were far too subtle and they crept up on a man, like a man wearing you down with his pawns. Richthofen knew this, and his confidence drove him. Subtly, he opened his turn and lifted the nose of the Albatros. In seconds, he was climbing above and outside the Englishman, using the Albatros's superior power to become an impossible target above his prey, effortlessly nullifying the Englishman's maneuver. He was in a tight turn, now, looking from his cockpit, down onto the Englishman. Richthofen had already won the battle, and he knew it, with an icy certainty.

It's all over for you, Englishman. I'm sorry for that.

~~~

Hawker looked straight out into the German's cockpit. He began to pray. The wind was steadily blowing them both east as they circled, a moving vortex, sucking them downward, like a tornado of men and aeroplanes moving across the ground. Altitude was not on his side. His gambit had failed.

Well, God, help me now, or take me into your arms ...

They descended slower now; sinking like ships at sea into a maelstrom. Hawker saw the eroded grey walls of the dead city of Bapaume, giving him a landmark to orient from. It was a matter of when, now; when he needed to break to the west, and of how he could buy time, keep the German from taking a clean shot, of buying seconds to fly west into the wind. Perhaps, then, there might be safety. It was his only hope.

~~~

Richthofen circled, watched with quiet awe as the Englishman stayed in the fight, calm, using every moment in an effort to shake him. The Englishman would have to break the turn and give up some altitude soon. He couldn't possibly follow the descending turn to the ground much further.

That break would have to come as a leftward turn as he came around to the west. That would be the best time for the Englishman to make his run. Richthofen circled, and as each orbit turned them west, just behind and above the Englishman, he would tense, ready himself for the DH-2 to break. Each time, the Englishman held fast to his turn.

Richthofen was getting closer now, no more than a hundred meters. He could see the sun glint on his opponent's goggles and imagined he could see the man's eyes.

Then, impossibly, the English pilot lifted a hand and waved.

Briefly awestruck, Richthofen raised a hand, began a salute, and then gave a quick wave.

What was that? A greeting? An acknowledgement? Surrender?

The English pilot suddenly leveled out, turned west, descending and accelerating as he did so. Richthofen turned above him and behind. Quickly, the English airplane pulled up into a desperate loop, Richthofen's eyes tracked him upward, surprised for only a second, but long enough. The English pilot began to fire as he dropped on Richthofen, his Lewis gun giving a whirring bray.

Richthofen pulled hard into a climbing left turn, rapidly shedding speed, then ruddered over at the top and dropped; the English airplane passing below and in front of him. Immelmann would be proud, he thought. He fired a long burst as the Englishman passed by, high deflection, but worth the bullets: the stream of hot metal tore holes into the Englishman's wings and rudder, but didn't slow him. Richthofen slammed the Albatros into an even tighter left turn, coming in behind the Englishman again. His Albatros dug into the air, accelerating in a long dive as Richthofen hooked in behind.

They flew west, barely two kilometers from the front, the Englishman jerking his airplane back and forth in quick, hard breaks. Richthofen flew behind him, working to get his sights on the English pilot before they both crossed the lines. He held the trigger down now, spraying bullets like a fire hose, a cloud of metal filled the air around the maneuvering Englishman.

It takes only one ... just one, thought Richthofen. The twin belts of ammunition rolled through his guns in a mechanical flow, and then, with a metallic 'clang', both guns fell silent and smoking.

Richthofen looked toward the escaping Englishman. The man was no more than a couple of hundred meters over the ground, the trench lines visible in front of them, and barely a hundred meters away. He reached up and yanked down the cocking handles to clear the jams. A brass case flew out of a gun and sailed away into the air behind him. He pressed the firing button again. His guns, cleared, spewed another torrent of bullets at his quarry.

~~~

The bullet that killed Hawker struck him in the back of his head and erupted through his temple.

He instantly pitched forward over the controls, already dead, his lifeblood spilling into his cockpit. His aeroplane, without a pilot's will, settled into a shallow glide for a few seconds and then struck the earth just behind the German lines. The machine buried itself into the side of a crater and its wings closed over Hawker like a shroud.

~~~

A squad of German grenadiers, huddled in the basement of a farmhouse, heard the roaring engines draw closer, and then the shattering impact just outside. One soldier emerged and watched the dust settle over the wreck. He called to the other soldiers and they peered out at the wreckage from the edge of a crater. Slowly, they began to pick their way across the shell-shattered ground.

After pushing aside the scraps of wood and canvas, they stared down at the English pilot. A soldier rummaged through the man's pockets, took his papers and went back to their basement, their Leutnant running off to phone in the report.

A request came for something distinctive from the wreck. The Grenadiers crept out into the darkness one evening and pried away a broken English machine gun, then had a courier trot off into the darkness to deliver the broken weapon to 'God knows where'.

Hawker lay there, exposed, for two days in the sallow autumn sun. On the third day, the Grenadiers asked their Leutnant for permission to bury him. They dug a shallow grave with shovels and helmets, and rolled him in. One of the men, a minister's son, said a few words over the mound of dirt. No one thought to write down exactly where they had buried him.

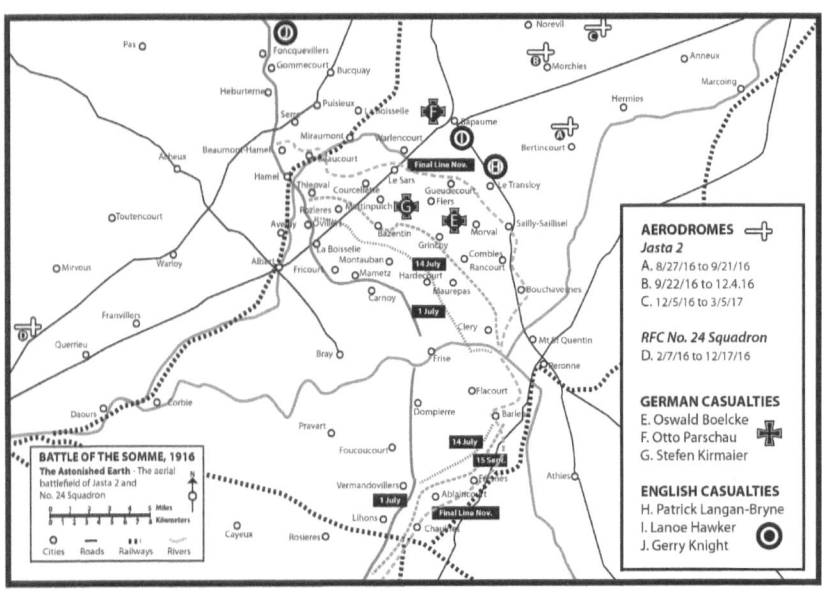

Chapter Fifty-One

December 20, 1916
Pronville Aerodrome, France

It was the wettest winter in a hundred years, and even the guns cooled. The skies had opened, and the rain streamed from low, dark clouds. The armies, exhausted and mired in mud once more, slogged into static positions, hopelessly checked. The battlefields north of the river Somme had consumed the lives of 300,000 men since July, and now the trenches were swamps of corpses. A million men were casualties, forever bearing physical scars from the Somme.

The men of Jasta 2 fell at first into idleness, waking each morning looking west at thick grey skies. When it was obvious the skies wouldn't yield, and boredom settled in, they busied themselves with work on their aeroplanes. Each machine gun was dismantled, cleaned, oiled, reassembled, and reloaded. They fired them from one of the sheds into an empty berm of earth, until gun smoke filled their shelter. When they had finished, they mounted them back on the airplanes, then went to the next. After a few days, they started over. Engines were dismounted and disassembled overnight, and then remounted by the dawn, when the aeroplanes might fly. Wires were restrung, the controls adjusted, canvas stretched, paint touched up, then reapplied, and then painted in full. A mechanic added yellow to a fighter, then the adorned engine covers, wheel covers, or fuselages, until all the aeroplanes sported some bright yellow appendage, each unique from the next.

Another mechanic took apart two old English radial engines, emptied out the pistons and cranks and strung wires through the cylinders for light bulbs. He hung the now-useful engines from the ceiling of the mess hall, creating fat, metal chandeliers.

In late October, a new commander had arrived, Franz Walz—a two-seater pilot transferred to single seaters.

~~~

The skies cleared of clouds only twice in December, and during those times, it was filled with pilots. They were anxious, bored, and eager, so the biggest air battles of the war developed: swirling, angry contests of hate and energy spread over the drenched battlefields. Walz led a single flight out in early December, but turned his men at the last moment, declined a fight and left the Jasta's appetite frustrated and unsated.

Richthofen insolently broke from Walz's formation and made a fierce single pass on a DH-2, shooting the English fighter down in flames. He flew home alone, disgusted, avoiding his commander.

~~~

On a cold still day in late December, five days before Christmas, Bodenschatz woke before dawn, moving his stiff, broken body slowly; hunched over his cane, he watched the dark western horizon, as the sun rose behind him. The western sky grew pale, blue and cloudless. A gentle wind blew from the North Sea.

Excited, Bodenschatz felt the joy of a father on Christmas morning. He hobbled his way to Richthofen's quarters and pounded on the door with his cane. He pushed the door open.

"Richthofen, up. The sky is clear." Bodenschatz bent over Richthofen's bunk, shaking his shoulder. "Walz is away at headquarters. Get up, you lead."

Richthofen grinned, instantly awake. "Hunting, then? I could kiss you Bodenschatz."

"Merry Christmas, Richthofen."

Richthofen led a patrol of five Albatros due west, climbing, over Moncy-au-Bois.

~~~

Gerry Knight walked around his new DH-2 one last time and looked to the weather. The sky remained clear. Four more DH-2's of No. 29 Squadron sat on the field with his, their pilots going over each. Knight called them over to his machine, unfolded a map onto a lower wing and smoothed it out. The other pilots gathered around, holding their flying caps in their hands. Knight smiled as he thought for a moment that they looked like they were praying.

"Gentlemen, we will fly northeast to Rollencourt, here." He pointed to the details of the city on his map. "And then turn south to Gommecourt," he said, jabbing his finger at the map. "I know this is your first time crossing the lines, so be careful and watchful. Watch me. Watch for my streamers. Stay behind me, and I'll scan the sky. If you're sure you're in formation, then watch the sky ... but, above all, stay with me."

"Sir, will we see fighters?" asked Britton, a pimply Lancaster boy, his voice cracking slightly.

Knight studied his face, so much like a schoolchild who was out after dark. Britton needn't worry about shaving yet. He smiled slowly.

"How on earth would I know that?" asked Knight. "There's always a chance I suppose."

Britton looked down at the map and bit his lip.

"We'll cross to the west of the Jasta 11 base at Brayelles. No worries there, they're a third-rate unit. Further, south, we'll be in the sector of Jasta 2, Boelcke's old unit. They may be looking for a fight, so we might see some there. We'll stay high and keep our eyes open. Any questions?" said Knight.

"Do you think with Boelcke gone that they're any good?" asked one of the new second lieutenants.

Knight looked off to the east, and said, "Of course, they're damn good. Losing Boelcke just made them cross." He thought of the fight when Boelcke went down, how Boelcke, the legend, had been human after all.

"You were there? With No. 24 when Boelcke went down, weren't you, sir."

"Yes, Britton, I was there." He spoke in a whisper, "And his airplane wasn't black, either."

There was a hush among the pilots, broken finally by Britton. "Sir?"

he asked meekly.

"Yes, what is it?" Knight replied.

"Sir, you don't have to fly, as you're going on leave ... the mechanics say it's bad luck ... I wish you no ill will, sir."

"Don't be silly, Britton, of course I'll fly," said Knight. He thought of Hawker, and his damn silly traditions, his superstitions. "Britton, thank you for wishing me well. Now, get to your aeroplanes," said Knight. The pilots scattered.

They started their engines, until all five were run up and pulling against their wheel chocks. Knight led them west in a shallow climb, two fighters on either side of him flying in a V-formation. At a thousand feet, he turned them northeast to Rollencourt, still climbing.

~ ~ ~

Richthofen flew his men into a gentle headwind crossing the fine, clear sky. They climbed gradually. Their five Albatros were all nearly new and reworked constantly for two weeks since they'd last flown, their engines in fine tune, controls balanced and adjusted, guns fresh. Their roar merged into a single steady rumble that echoed around them for miles. Below, the static German and English armies looked up from their wet trenches to watch them pass overhead. No artillery fire burst below them, no troops moved from the constant, though dwindling lines into machine gun fire. Instead, clothes were laid in the sun, and men were lying on the drying ground, catching the little precious heat the winter sun offered.

Richthofen was happy to be up, to be leading, untethered. He grinned as he looked around to his new boys, all holding tight to their leader.

At least Walz isn't hanging over my shoulder, thought Richthofen. A little freedom to fight, that's all we need.

As the German formation neared the front, English anti-aircraft fire began to erupt around them. Richthofen turned them in a long, disdainful, wheeling arc to the north, toward Rollencourt.

They leveled off and flew straight on their new course, just behind the German lines.

Richthofen saw it first: a single speck on a canvas of blue sky, hanging right in front of them, coming straight toward them. He cleared his guns in a harsh roar.

The speck divided into five distinct aircraft. At last, his students saw the English formation. Gaping looks of shock crossed their faces. Following his lead, they cleared their guns, and spread out slightly upon a signal from Richthofen, broadening their formation.

With breathtaking abruptness, the two groups met. Five German fighters to the five English. Richthofen began to fire, in a single head-on pass, aiming at the middle English fighter. He missed.

The German flight slashed through the Englishmen. Aeroplanes turned out, each in their own direction, streaks of chaos in the sky, as pilots jostled for advantage. Richthofen twisted his Albatros into a wrenching left bank, climbing slightly to separate from his own men, knowing they would be attempting to dive immediately and too soon. Richthofen knew, instinctively, that the English would lose altitude in their turns.

He was buying time, letting the combat break down into the curven-kampf, the turning fight. Looking down on the scattered English, he watched them turn roughly to the west, then scatter, running upwind toward the English lines, diving. A single enemy fighter trailed streamers: their flight leader. Richthofen turned and dove after the man.

Below them, for miles in all directions, the idle men of two armies in putrid wet trenches stopped what they were doing to look up and watch the spectacle in the sky.

Dropping, turning, Richthofen fell on the tail of the English fighter. He looked close at the thing, checking for the red stripes of No. 24 Squadron, and was disappointed. Pressing closer, he clung tightly to his quarry, feeling his own fighter bucked around by the Englishman's prop wash. The more the English fighter twisted and turned, the closer Richthofen drew.

At last, when he could see the individual wires in the tail, could hear its engine, could hear the wind singing through the English aeroplane's wings, he put his gunsight on the top of the Englishman's engine. The English pilot glanced back at him, then wrenched the DH-2 into a turn.

Richthofen followed the man through his turn, then through a shallow bank to the right, heading west. The Englishman descended, accelerating.

His flying was calm, tight. Then the man began jerking his aeroplane into short, sharp, evasive jinks through the air, not shedding speed, but throwing off Richthofen's aim. They both angled downward, Richthofen trying to anticipate the man.

This seems so familiar, I've seen this before, thought Richthofen.

The man's maneuvers were deliberate, consciously erratic, the work of a confident man, intending to convey fear, but not fearful. They were precise, quick, controlled. Richthofen knew the man in front of him. He throttled back, clung to the diving Englishman, but settled his sights high and to the left of the descending fighter. With his sights set on thin air, he waited for Gerry Knight to play his card.

~~~

Knight, convinced he'd rattled his pursuer and thrown of the German's aim, pulled back his stick and jammed his rudder bar down to the left, slewing the DeHavilland into a tight left turn, his wings pushing against the air, slowing him and arcing through the air.

He'll overshoot now, this always works, it worked when we fought Boelcke ...

~~~

Richthofen saw the move begin, then gleefully pressed down on his triggers, hosing the sky as the Englishman turned into his stream of bullets.

I know you. I know you.

Bullets ripped into the English fighter, tearing through Gerry Knight, the little red-haired Scot, killing him instantly.

The DH-2, spewing fuel, oil and blood, fell into a spin, then burst into flames, trailing a thick column of black smoke to the ground, marking its pyre.

Richthofen's blood roared in his ears, his heart racing. He flew until it settled and his mind cleared, and then turned back toward Pronville. Then he flew off, alone, into the quiet air to the east, a deep calm coming over him. The battle between Jasta 2 and No. 24 Squadron was at an end.

He grinned to himself.

Could it be? Could it really be? They'll never believe me; I killed the man who killed Boelcke ...

~~~

The next day the rain returned and lingered over the battlefields, bringing with it a thick fog that held the fliers down once more as though beneath a blanket of grey wool. Christmas slipped past without another break in the weather. On the New Year, the Staffel gathered in the early evening to celebrate in their casino, where they played Skat and poker and drank champagne when they could find it, and schnapps when they couldn't.

The survivors of the autumn gathered there: Böhme, the tall quiet old man, with chiseled cheekbones and piercing eyes; Voss, the youngster, the man that could turn an airplane inside of itself and then fly back, as though he'd flown through time; and Richthofen, the blue-eyed blonde, quiet, mechanical, obsessive. The new pilots and replacements orbited around these men, hoping to benefit from their wisdom, advice, and luck.

Drinks were poured, a first round of cards dealt, and their bids made, when a new pilot arrived, with a deep cleft chin, his moon-face framed by an oily widow's peak. Walz beamed as he greeted the man warmly, leaving Richthofen uneasy. "Gentlemen, may I introduce our newest pilot, Albert Dossenbach." Walz applauded, and the men joined in politely. Richthofen instantly knew he didn't like the man.

Dossenbach stepped forward and extended a hand, Richthofen took it. Richthofen noticed two deep slashes through Dossenbach's left cheek, cut through deep burn scars. Under Dossenbach's chins lay the *Pour le Mérite*, blue and gold, glimmering in the weak electric light.

Slowly conversations resumed, and the men turned back to their card games. Someone offered Dossenbach a drink. Richthofen, Böhme and Voss gathered around him.

"What have you flown, Dossenbach?" asked Richthofen.

"C-1's, two-seaters, mostly," said Dossenbach.

"So has Walz," blurted out Voss. He looked away before the newcomer acknowledged the derision in Voss' voice.

"Tell me, how many victories do you have?" said Richthofen, eyeing the man's *Pour le Mérite*.

Dossenbach flinched slightly, taken aback by the directness of the question.

"Eight," said Dossenbach. "Unfortunately, the last didn't go so well, that's where this came from." He ran the tips of his fingers down the scars on his cheek.

"But, I'm here to learn from you gentlemen, I know I have a great many bad habits to break. I need to learn single seaters." Dossenbach smiled and his eyes sparkled, making himself look like a fat young boy in old man's clothes.

Richthofen grew quiet, appraising Dossenbach.

Voss spoke again, his drink loosening him up. "Walz needs to unlearn some habits too, but I don't think he knows that yet. You're already ahead of him."

Böhme flashed a look at Voss. Voss grimaced under Böhme's gaze. "Werner, please," he said with the tone of a schoolteacher scolding a student.

Voss, nonplussed, turned back to Dossenbach. "And when did you receive your *Max*?" He gestured at Dossenbach's throat.

Richthofen stared across the room, where Thomsen, Walz and Bodenschatz were in a quiet conversation. He tried to imagine what they might be talking about. Richthofen was astounded, confused by the situation.

How could this man have the Blue Max and not I?

"And how many victories do you have, Richthofen?" asked Dossenbach.

Richthofen looked at Dossenbach, staring through him. "Fifteen," he said coldly.

Dossenbach blushed scarlet and smiled nervously. He had a tiny, but infectious smile that disarmed Richthofen momentarily.

I can't blame him. Hardly his fault, thought Richthofen.

Dossenbach put his hand to his throat and unclasped the medal, handed it to Voss. "Here. If you'd like, take a look. November eleventh, I think it was."

Richthofen thought for a moment, counted days in his head, the days after Boelcke died, counting Englishmen. After a moment, he reddened with anger. He reached out and set his drink down, nearly tipped it over, then managed to set it upright. His mouth opened and closed once, but he couldn't speak. He couldn't believe what he'd heard. Richthofen started toward Thomsen and Walz.

Böhme and Voss exchanged glances. "This's bad," Böhme said.

"What is it?" asked Dossenbach. Voss handed him his medal back.

"I think Richthofen has a question for Walz," said Voss.

They turned back to their drinks and looked away from Richthofen. Dossenbach looked embarrassed, but couldn't think of what he had said wrong.

"May I speak with you, gentlemen?" said Richthofen. His face was flushed and his jaw set. Walz, Thomsen and Bodenschatz grew quiet and turned toward him. Richthofen's voice was low, crisp. Bodenschatz knew the tone and took a short step backward.

"Yes, of course, Richthofen," said Thomsen. He smiled and sat back on the arm of a padded chair.

Walz turned his shoulders toward Richthofen and widened his stance defensively.

"I've been speaking with our new Leutnant, and, I wish to state that I mean no disrespect. But, I must ask ..." Richthofen began.

Thomsen looked up, a look of innocent curiosity on his face. Walz looked angry.

"Go ahead," said Thomsen. "Speak your mind."

"Sir, the Leutnant received his Blue Max ... apologies, his *Pour le Mérite* ... on the eleventh of November, nearly two months ago," said Richthofen, his voice beginning to quiver.

"Go on, Richthofen," said Thomsen.

"Sir, I had eight confirmed, official victories on the ninth of November. I remember exactly when I got to eight." Richthofen's voice was low, but hard-edged and cracking. He was fighting to keep his voice down.

Thomsen, suddenly aware and embarrassed, looked away, sipping his drink. He looked up at the engine chandeliers overhead. He smiled. "Walz, have I ever told you how clever I think those are? I must have one."

"Yes, of course, I'll see to it," said Walz. Walz looked at Bodenschatz with a question in his eyes.

"Yes, sir," said Bodenschatz to Walz. "We can get one to the Commander."

Richthofen unclenched his hands, willed his breathing to steady. "Walz, respectfully, please reply to my question." He looked at Bodenschatz, who cast back a sympathetic look and nodded.

Thomsen spoke for Walz. "Richthofen, as I'm sure you must understand, this is a decision of the Kaiser. I cannot speak for the man. It is not purely a matter of keeping score. Perhaps he considered the specific conditions of Dossenbach's eighth victory. Perhaps there are other considerations." He smiled, sipped his drink. He waved over a mess attendant carrying a tray of champagne glasses. Thomsen took one and handed it to Richthofen.

Richthofen knew he was hearing truth and lies, but didn't know which was which. He took the drink, didn't speak, and knew that he'd already asked too much.

"So, Richthofen, how many victories do you have right now?" asked Thomsen. "Remind me."

"Fifteen. Four this month, despite the weather." Richthofen took a large swallow of his wine.

"Excellent. Keep up the good work," said Thomsen. His voice was smooth now, in a rhythm. "As I've said, these are the Kaiser's decisions, not mine. I will keep General von Hoeppner and the Chief of Staff informed on the matter of our successes, naturally. So, Richthofen, what was your question, again?"

Richthofen held his breath, willed his hands to be still.

"No question, sir. I'm sure you've answered it." He gulped down his champagne. "You'll excuse me, sir?"

"Yes, of course, rejoin the party. And a happy New Year to you, Richthofen."

"And to you, too, sir," Richthofen clicked his heels together, bowed to Walz and Bodenschatz. "Gentlemen."

Dazed, Richthofen felt something slip away, a sense of faith, a military confidence in structure, regulation, formality. It suddenly became a sham, a mirage, an illusion of something greater than himself. With a nod toward Voss and Bodenschantz, he walked toward the door and slipped out into the evening air of the new year.

Chapter Fifty-Two

January 10, 1917
Pronville Aerodrome, France

Richthofen lay on his bed and listened to the night settle over the field. An Albatros fighter had come in late, trailing the noise of a failing engine over the aerodrome, leaving a final quiet behind. Outside men stirred, moving airplanes around, tucking some into tents for maintenance, then gathering in clumps to take in the clear cold sky overhead and talk about the day.

He willed himself to sleep, but peace couldn't come. Fitfully, he turned up the flame on the kerosene lantern. Upon a shelf sat a row of silver cups, each inscribed with the date of a victory.

On the walls were his prizes: pieces of canvas with a tail number, or an airplane's name. A pair of English machine guns adorned the doorway, bent back on themselves from the impact of an airplane striking the ground, grotesque in a way that only something mechanical can be, once-straight lines bent into unnatural curves. The damage to the guns made clear the fate of the men that fired them. In the center of one wall hung Hawker's Lewis gun, angled and mud caked, just like it was when the German Grenadiers had dug it out of the ground. Trophies all.

He lay back down, closed his eyes, and traced back each victory; from the first to the last, each memory still vivid. Each was a single moment of presence, of finality, and each was a placeholder in his mind, as real as his own birth.

For some, the moment of victory had been the odd tilting of a man's head on his shoulders as he lost consciousness, either dead or dying. For others, it was a stream of smoke that lingered around the engine too long, portending the brilliant blossom of flame. Sometimes it was just the way that the airplane moved, a peculiar sideways slip in the air that no man would willingly allow, just before a final spin overtook him. For others, it was a broken strut or a wing, or an aileron, a piece of the airplane that had been torn free from the impact of a bullet, or the stress of a desperate maneuver that showed that the aeroplane was no longer what it had been.

Richthofen remembered each of these moments in time, each representing the instant when his grim work was done, and he could recall them with a visceral heat. He summoned the smell, the stink of a burning airplane, of oil and gas and wood and flesh so clearly that the recollection and reality blurred together in his mind. And the men. He knew, with encyclopedic exactness, who had survived, who had died, which shot meant that an enemy, a foe, had found their ultimate release.

Richthofen dozed, calmed by his memories, with a steady drone of distant artillery lulling him to sleep.

Menzke entered and put a firm hand on Richthofen's shoulder and spoke his name.

"Richthofen."

Richthofen opened his eyes, looked up at Menzke, not moving. "Menzke," he said.

"Herr Leutnant, your presence is requested by the Kommandant." The word 'Kommandant' came out of Menzke slowly, as though he wasn't committed to its meaning.

"Very well, tell him I'll be right there."

Richthofen slowly swung his legs over the side of his bunk and placed his feet on the floor. He ran a hand over his face, and back over his hair, smoothing it. With an easy deliberateness that marked much of his actions in life, he pulled his boots on.

Menzke stood for a moment, pondering a consolation of some sort, a moment of empathy. He dismissed the notion, but pulled himself to attention and saluted sharply, drawing his heels together unnaturally. Richthofen waved a salute to Menzke without standing, then pushed himself upright, pulled his suspenders up, and donned his coat. Together they walked to the operations tent, Menzke a step behind and to Richthofen's left, the position of respect since the days of the Romans.

The operations tent was a dark, unlit shadow on the edge of the field. A maze of hanging blankets in the doorway stopped the light inside from giving the tent away. Navigating their way through by feel, they entered the inner tent, where lanterns lit the men who carried reports to the commander, then took orders and duties away in a never-ending cycle.

Walz's new orderly was at his desk. He looked up at Richthofen and pulled himself upright too slowly, insolently. He tossed a casual salute and remained standing. Walz had clearly informed the man of Richthofen's own impudence.

"Richthofen requested by Kommandant Walz. Please announce me."

The orderly nodded and disappeared behind another set of blankets, and returned a moment later, holding the inner blanket open. Richthofen stepped through the flap and pulled himself to attention. He saluted crisply, his cap under his arm.

Walz rose, saluted, and then sat back down behind his desk, leaving Richthofen standing.

"At ease," said Walz.

Richthofen remained standing, eyes ahead. He widened his stance, and stiffly clasped his hands behind his back. He tried to focus on the dark corner of the tent behind Walz's head. "Reporting as ordered," he said.

"There is no explaining or understanding higher command, Richthofen," Walz began. He lifted a telegram from his desk, held it to the light, and read it aloud. "'Leutnant Manfred von Richthofen is ordered to assume command of Jasta ... '" he paused, and then glanced up at Richthofen. His face was set, impassive. He continued: "' ... Eleven. The Leutnant will report to the aerodrome at Brayelles on January fifteenth and assume command from Oberleutnant Lang upon arrival.'"

Richthofen couldn't focus on the dark space in the back of the tent, but continued to try. He felt his breath leave him and the blood leave his head.

Command! he thought. *Finally. And no more of this imbecile.*

"Well, Richthofen, you have achieved your greatest desire. Or perhaps your second greatest desire. Dismissed." He stood and handed the telegram to Richthofen, then extended a hand. Richthofen glanced down, surprised, then reached out and shook it. He read the telegram, then folded it carefully and placed it in his jacket pocket. He saluted and stepped out into the orderly's space where Menzke stood waiting.

Menzke examined Richthofen's face, trying to judge whether this was good news or bad. Richthofen betrayed nothing. Together they stepped back out into the darkness.

"Walk with me, Menzke," said Richthofen.

"Yes, sir, of course," said Menzke.

They walked quietly for a few moments, and then Richthofen stopped and looked up at the stars. He spoke, still looking up.

"They gave me Jasta 11," he said. "Eleven! Can you believe it?"

Menzke stared at Richthofen, glad that the darkness hid the confusion on his face. "Sir?"

Richthofen looked down. "The worst Staffel in the air force. They've been flying since September and haven't shot down a damned thing. Can you imagine? An entire Staffel without a victory? How many do we ... does Jasta 2 have? Nearly a hundred? And now they've given me that bunch of bumblers." He sighed, took off his cap and ran his hand over his short hair.

"Permission to speak, Leutnant?" asked Menzke.

Richthofen looked at Menzke, trying to read his face now, in the darkness, surprised that Menzke was being so bold. "Of course, Menzke," replied Richthofen.

"Is this good news or bad, sir?" asked Menzke.

Richthofen shrugged, imperceptibly, knowing that he must try to cling to decorum, even in the darkness, even with Menzke. "It is news, Menzke, nothing more. The good or the bad will come later. It is an opportunity and a challenge, and a duty. Goodnight, Menzke." Richthofen saluted quickly and turned away for his tent.

"I'll begin packing in the morning, sir," Menzke said to Richthofen's back. Richthofen waved a hand in acknowledgement.

Menzke looked up at the stars now. "No victories. None," he said, aloud. "Amazing."

He turned for his own tent and began running. Being in motion always made him feel more at ease.

~~~

Richthofen flew his new Albatros from Pronville to the aerodrome at Brayelles, a short hop of twenty kilometers. Jagdstaffel 11 had lined up their older Halbertsadt fighter in the center of the field, on parade for their new Kommandant. The ground crews had stayed up late oiling the bare wooden fuselages of the sleek fighters, polishing them like pieces of furniture. Their wings were dull, painted in a rough brown and green camouflage. Richthofen walked past the row of aeroplanes while the pilots and crews scrambled into ranks in the open field.

Menzke walked at Richthofen's side, holding his hound, Moritz, on his lead. Richthofen paused alongside a Halberstadt and ran his hand over the gleaming fuselage, felt the oil on his fingertips, then put his hand to his nose. It smelled sweet and fresh. To Richthofen's eye, the machines were unused toys, still fresh from their wrapping paper.

A corporal approached Richthofen, pulled himself up to salute and stood at attention. Richthofen glanced at the man, wiped his hand on the rim of the cockpit and massaged the oil into the leather for a moment, then returned the salute.

"Leutnant. Corporal Wetz, Staffel administrator. The Staffel is at formation, sir." He saluted again, holding his eyes forward.

"Very well, Wetz, return to formation, I will be there shortly."

Corporal Wetz darted off to rejoin the Staffel.

"Menzke, what do you think?" Richthofen turned to Menzke, keeping his voice low.

"Sir, I. Well, I ..." he stammered, unaccustomed to such a question.

"Go on, what are your first impressions of our new home?"

"Sir, their airplanes seem very new."

"Menzke, you're a man of few words. I like that," said Richthofen. "You're only as good as your mount." He smiled, his eyes wrinkled at the corners, reflecting the blue of the sky. "Let's meet them, shall we?"

Richthofen reviewed the men on parade, pilots lined up in front of ground crew. The image of a cavalry squadron formation crossed his mind, making Richthofen smile. *All they need are horses,* thought Richthofen. The adjutant presented the unit summary, read aloud the counts and status of the men. Richthofen stepped close to the adjutant, his voice low.

"And where is the commander, Oberleutnant Lang?" Richthofen asked, quietly.

"Leutnant, he left yesterday."

Richthofen's jaw tightened, his muscles working, flexing along his jaw. *Relieved of command, turns and runs without handing his command over? What an ass.* He took a deep breath and held it. "I see. What are your current orders?" The words came out in a soft hiss.

"We are stood down, awaiting your arrival. No flights scheduled."

"Very well. Return to formation."

The adjutant saluted, and he stepped back into line.

Richthofen bent and scratched Moritz's good ear, then playfully cuffed the dog on the side of the head. He took the dog's head in both hands, and scratched behind both ears. The men stood and watched, silent. At last, he rose.

"Gentlemen, we fly. We fly to the edge of your endurance and to the ability of our crews to keep our airplanes flying. We fly, and then we fight. We all fly, together, in one hour. Crews, at my order, stand to your airplanes and make them ready, full fuel, full armament." Richthofen began to turn, but paused to add, "And stop wasting good castor oil polishing your airplanes."

He looked around at the faces in the ranks, reading their expressions. A short pilot with a narrow nose and close-set eyes broke into a grin, then tightened his jaw and reset his expression. Richthofen approached him.

"Name, Leutnant?"

"Wolff, sir, Kurt Wolff."

"Does flying make you smile, Wolff?" asked Richthofen.

"Yes, sir, it does," replied Wolff.

"Very good. Are you a fighter, Wolff?" asked Richthofen.

Wolff grinned.

"I like wolves," Richthofen stepped back. "Crews, ready your airplanes.

Pilots, with me. Dismissed!"

The formation of men dispersed as Richthofen walked to his Albatros and stood behind the right wings. The pilots watched him attentively. He leaned against the side of the aeroplane, and waved to the pilots to gather themselves around him.

One of the pilots ran a hand over the struts at the ends of the wings, and then ran a hand over the end of the lower wing. He glanced over at Richthofen, who was watching him.

"D.III, sesquiwing. The latest Albatros fighter. The chord of the lower wing is smaller than the main."

The pilot raised his hand in greeting.

"Yes."

"Shafer. Kurt Shafer. How does it fly, Leutnant?"

"It's smooth, but a little heavy. We worry for the strength of the lower wing, or, rather, half wing. It bends while diving. But it's twenty-five kilometers per hour faster than your Halberstadts, and can fly fifteen hundred meters higher. I'll have to linger to let you all catch up."

The pilots laughed. Shafer turned to the Albatros and settled a hand on it, caressing the canvas.

"Do you know how to get a new airplane, Shafer?" asked Richthofen.

Shafer stared blankly and shook his head. "No, sir." It came out tentatively. He was fearful of a trick question.

"It's easy, Shafer." Richthofen held up three fingers. "One, get shot down; two, crash; three, wear yours out. Pick one." He ticked off fingers as he spoke.

The pilots flashed grins. Low laughter moved through them. Shafer blushed.

"Oh, the answer isn't that easy. I've crashed on my own twice and been shot down twice. Got a new airplane each time." Richthofen shrugged. "It's faster than wearing one out."

The pilots' smiles disappeared.

"Your airplanes are in good shape yet, but we will soon change that." He paused, watching their faces again. "Do you know what I didn't see out there?" he pointed at the row of Halberstadts, alive, now, with ground crewmen crawling over each one.

The pilots glanced at each other quickly, hoping for some answer. No one replied.

"Bullet holes. Patched bullet holes. You can't shoot anyone down until you get close, and if ... when, you get close, then you get shot at and you get bullet holes of your own. There is no shame. You need bullet holes, must earn bullet holes. Just don't get one too many, understand?"

The pilots smiled again, nodded. Wolff laughed, awkwardly.

"Gentlemen, we start over. I don't want to discuss why you haven't had victories, I want to talk about how you will get them. We will fly together at least three times each day. We will fly east, downwind, away from the lines, where we can maneuver and rehearse. When we have grown together, we will begin flying Staffel combat patrols. Questions, objections?"

Wolff raised a hand, slowly. "One question, sir."

"Yes. Go ahead."

"How many?"

Richthofen sighed heavily and turned his eyes away up, to the west.

"Sixteen official."

"Sir?" asked Wolff.

Richthofen stared, puzzled, then, "The *Pour le Mérite*? I don't know. Perhaps the Kaiser likes a different number. That's all I have to say about it." His hand went to his throat, and he fingered the top button there.

"My apologies, sir, I mean no offense," said Wolff.

Richthofen nodded, then knelt in the grass next to the airplane, and picked up some loose twigs. "So, we begin." He started to arrange the twigs in patterns on the ground, moving them around into shapes. "First, formations."

The pilots bent over, watching, then knelt, then gradually sat, until they all sat in a rough circle. After they talked of formations, of holding speed and separation, they began exchanging flying experiences. Richthofen glanced up frequently, checking on the progress of the crewmen readying the Halberstadts.

In an hour and a quarter, the maintenance chief approached the group of pilots.

"Sir, all aircraft are ready," he said.

Richthofen scowled, and glanced at his pocket watch. "We will discuss timekeeping later. You will have to learn to work faster. Very well. Pilots, don your gear, do your checks, and mount your airplanes."

The crewmen moved to push Richthofen's Albatros into line with the Halberstadts, and then, down the row, each airplane's engine was started. Two engines coughed, died, and would not restart. On Richthofen's signal, the remaining aeroplanes began rolling in a staggered wave and then lifted into the air.

Richthofen led them east as they began their climb: a graceful curving shallow ascent. The squadron moved into a shallow V-formation, orienting off Richthofen, their eyes on him, keeping their position in reference to his machine. From above and behind, the camouflage on the upper wing of the Albatros was nearly the same as the Halberstadts', but the tail of Richthofen's Albatros still carried the distinctive markings of Jasta Boelcke: white and black.

~~~

Rain had passed over the field in the early morning, before dawn, and in the first rays of sunlight, the field lay dotted with silvery puddles. Richthofen walked down the flight line, Menzke trailing behind, perpetually leading Moritz on a length of rope. Richthofen watched the mechanics work and chatted with the pilots as he moved down the row of aeroplanes. A mud-spattered Horch staff car drove onto the edge of the field, the Kaiser's crest barely visible through the muck on a rear door. The top of the car was open and Richthofen recognized Oberstleutnant Lieth-Thomsen's egg-like head from across the field.

"Who is that, Leutnant?" asked Menzke.

"Our new Chief of Staff for the German Air Force," said Richthofen. He turned to the one of the pilots and spoke. "Wolff, spread the word that the flight is still on, hopefully this won't be long."

Richthofen turned and walked across the field, swinging his ornate carved walking stick with his stride while Menzke and Moritz trailed along. He stopped next to the car, saluted and drew himself to attention.

"Good morning, sir. We weren't expecting you," he said.

Lieth-Thomsen stepped down from the car and returned his salute. "Good Morning, Leutnant. How is your new command? Just got here?"

"Yes, yesterday." Richthofen looked around the field, and gestured with his walking stick to where the mechanics were lining up the airplanes. "My command is in excellent form. We are flying in a few minutes, but my time is yours."

"I trust they will be soon achieving victories?" asked Lieth-Thomsen.

"Yes, sir, of course. No reason why we won't. They just need a little training and the right timing."

Lieth-Thomsen nodded and said, "Walk with me, Richthofen."

Lieth-Thomsen turned, ponderously, and began a slow lumbering gait across the field, stepping around standing puddles. He pulled his overcoat close to fend off the cold. Richthofen waved for Menzke to stay behind as he followed Lieth-Thomsen away from the staff car. "Richthofen, you will be receiving a telegram this morning."

Richthofen turned white, suddenly worried for his family members.

Lieth-Thomsen read his reaction, and raised a hand in protest. "Nothing unpleasant, son." He smiled and took ahold of Richthofen's shoulder. "Leutnant, congratulations. You will be receiving the *Pour le Mérite*. The Kaiser has approved your award."

He extended a hand, and Richthofen took it. A gentle rain began to fall from the patchy clouds.

"Sir, thank you." Richthofen could barely contain his excitement, but worked to keep his face a composed mask. "This is a great honor. To follow in Boelcke's footsteps, Immelmann's; this is a great honor, thank you." His voice trailed off, his face alight, his grip on Lieth-Thomsen's hand too firm. A shadow crossed Richthofen's face, and he let go of the grasp, returned his hand to his side. Confusion settled in.

Why now? Why, at all? A count of aeroplanes? Something else?

"Forgive me, sir, but it wouldn't seem that that is worth a trip out here to the front. Telegrams are traditional."

"Very perceptive, Richthofen. As you are aware, this has been some time coming. It was, in fact, controversial."

Richthofen's expression tightened and his hand clenched at his side.

"No, son, don't misunderstand. You are not controversial. The Kaiser has raised the standard to sixteen aerial victories, and you are the first to achieve that number."

"I see," said Richthofen. "But I was at eight victories months ago."

Richthofen blanched, suddenly aware of his impertinence. "Sir." He stammered. "My apologies."

Lieth-Thomsen bored holes in Richthofen with his glassy, black eyes. He nodded.

"Apology accepted."

"Sir. May I ask a question?"

"If you mind your manners, Richthofen."

"Sir, what then, if I may ask, is contentious?"

"You don't understand, do you?"

"No, frankly I do not. What are you getting at?"

"Richthofen, you are not Boelcke. Not today. But, perhaps, someday soon, you will be as well known. Photos must be taken, newspaper articles are already being prepared, and Sanke cards will be printed. You are important, crucial even, for the morale of our nation. You are the Big Gun, the *Uber-Kanone*. You will be famous. You must be prepared."

"Oberst, what are you saying?" said Richthofen. A thought formed, a dark suspicious thought. He was beginning to understand. "Where did this number, sixteen, come from?"

A bleak curtain lifted in his mind and he imagined some clerk, with a list...*aahh*, the man would say, *sixteen, who would that be ... von Richthofen ... a fine name...a heroic name ...*

Lieth-Thomsen waved the question away. "That's not your concern, just be aware that the Kaiser and the entire high command is watching you, that the German nation is watching you. With Boelcke gone, there is only one. And you are that one."

"Thank you, sir. I understand."

No, you fat old man, I don't understand. Is this a machine, a book keeping exercise? Is this how heroes are made, by calculation?

"Very good. The Office of War Information will be in touch, please give them your full cooperation."

"Yes, sir, certainly, sir." Richthofen saluted. "May I join my men for our flight?"

"Yes, Richthofen. Of course. Congratulations again." Lieth-Thomsen saluted, and turned to begin his slow, graceless walk back to his car. He paused, turned back, and spoke over his shoulder. "And when the telegram comes, act surprised."

"Yes, sir, surprised, sir."

"And, one more thing, a Dutchman, Fokker, he wishes to see you. Should I approve his visit?"

"I know him, of course. Why does he want to come here?"

"He has a new idea for an aeroplane, three wings, something like that. He says the English have them, soon all the aeroplanes will have three instead of two."

"I see." Richthofen pondered the question a moment. "Yes, he may visit, I'll try to find time. This should be amusing."

"Very well, Richthofen. Good day. Good luck with your ... staffel."

Richthofen stood in the field, watching Lieth-Thomsen clamber into his car and then drive away without a wave. Menzke stood to Richthofen's side.

"Sir?"

"Yes, Menzke?"

"Sir. More bad news or good news?"

"Yes, more news."

Richthofen turned and strode to rejoin his men, who were finishing their pre-flight checks. He waved the chief of maintenance over to him.

"Is it fueled and loaded, engine and airframe checked?"

"Yes, sir, of course."

"It's a different airplane than you're used to; I assume you prepared it correctly?"

"The Mercedes engine is similar to the one in the Halberstadts, and one of my mechanics has worked on Albatros D.IIs. We have taken good care of her."

"Good, good." Richthofen ran one of his hands over the white tail-plane. "Jasta Boelcke. White and black."

"Yes, sir, I know."

"Do you have any paint?"

"Paint? Of course. Mostly brown and green for the camouflage, to match replacement wings."

"Anything brighter, more distinctive?"

"I have some yellow, for painting signs and insignia. And black."

He allowed his mind to drift, a harmless pastime when one's feet were on the earth. His weight shifted onto the tailplane of the Albatros. Richthofen thought of the Uhlans. Their regimental color. Then of the flying buttress of German soldiers at Virton, still spattered and sodden, and of the water after he washed his face when his cavalry squadron was slaughtered. The explosion of gore that had been Santuzza.

A memorial? Or something else? Don't be morbid, Richthofen.

"Red?" he asked at last.

"I have some red stain. We use it for the engine rigs to keep the wood from rotting, it's not very bright, but it will work. It doesn't cover very well, but it'll stick to the wood and canvas of your Albatros. Do you have an emblem in mind, or is this just for the tail?"

"That will do. When I get back, paint it." Richthofen indicated his Albatros.

"Sir?"

"Paint it. Start at the tail, work your way forward, and paint it red, the whole crate. As much as you can, until you run out of paint."

The maintenance chief looked at Richthofen as though he had gone mad. He took a half step backward, and unconsciously began wiping his hands on a rag.

"What about the insignia? The Maltese Cross?"

"Paint over it."

He began to protest, that he didn't want to be the death of the new commander. He could see Richthofen's jaw clenching, the muscles working; he choked on the words, and looked down at the ground.

"But, Leutnant, you'll stick out like a bull's eye. You'll be visible for miles. What will I tell people?"

"Tell them ... tell them that I want to be seen. Tell them that.

What else matters?"

Wolff approached the two of them, still deep in their conversation. "Leutnant Richthofen, not the best flying weather." He waved a thumb at the patchwork of clouds in the sky. He glanced from Richthofen to the chief, and saw the tense expressions on their faces. "Is everything in order?"

"Yes, Wolff, everything is completely fine. Isn't it fine?" Richthofen pointed his question back at the chief.

"Yes, sir," he answered. "Red, sir,"

Richthofen dismissed the chief and turned back to Wolff.

"What was that about?" Wolff asked.

"Just discussing our new Staffel color, Wolff. How does red sound to you?"

"I ... well ... It will be distinctive." Wolff's expression brightened. "Most memorable, sir. Most memorable."

Sic in principium

Afterword

Of the Allies:

Roland Garros. Garros is the first 'fighter' pilot, having flown missions solely for the purpose and design of shooting down opposing aeroplanes. Following his capture, he was transferred to a German prison, from which he escaped in February 1918. Garros bears the distinction of having escaped imprisonment from Germany twice, once at the onset of the war and again in the waning months of the conflict. After reaching France following his second escape, he rejoined the French air force and learned to fly the latest generation of fighters. He resumed combat flying in October 1918, and quickly achieved two victories. Sadly, three days later he was shot down and killed, a month before the end of the war.

After the war, Garros' favorite tennis center in Paris was renamed in his honor, the *Stade de Roland Garros.* This tennis center is the home of the French Open, otherwise known as *Les internationaux de France de Roland-Garros.* The fighter pilot term 'ace' is derived from the vernacular of the pre-World War one era and was used to describe an exceptional athlete.

Lanoe Hawker. At his death, he was the most famous English pilot, and was only the third pilot to receive the Victoria Cross, England's highest decoration. Unfortunately, Hawker's grave was lost in the unceasing artillery fire on the frontlines of the Somme. He is, however, memorialized at the Arras Flying Service Memorial in Arras, France and by a stained-glass window in St. Nicholas church in Longparish in his honor. His Victoria Cross was lost in France at the beginning of World War II, but a replacement is on display at the Royal Air Force Museum in Hendon.

H.G. Wells. Wells continued a controversial career until his death in 1946. When *The War in the Air* was reprinted in 1941, Wells wrote that he wished his epitaph to be, "I told you, you damn fools."

Others. Gordon Bayly, Lanoe's best friend, and Beatrice Bayly's brother, along with his pilot, Vincent Waterfall, were the first British officers to die in World War One. On August 23rd, 2014 the residents of the town of Marcq, Belgium inaugurated a monument to Bayly and Waterfall, at the site of their crash. Louis Strange, Lanoe Hawker's best friend following the death of Gordon Bayly, survived the war and rose to the rank of Wing Commander with the Royal Air Force (RAF). At the beginning of World War Two, he was stationed in France and posted to No. 24 Squadron, Hawker's old unit. He is, rather infamously, remembered for successfully flying an unarmed Hawker Hurricane fighter to England while being pursued by numerous German fighters. He was fifty years old at the time. Robert Saundby, who flew with Hawker on his last flight, also survived World War One and rose to the rank of Air Marshall in the RAF.

Of the Central Powers:

Oswald Boelcke. While Garros was the first fighter pilot, Boelcke is, arguably, the father of fighter aviation. Following Immelmann's death, Boelcke recorded ten essential rules for aerial combat, the *Boelcke Dicta*. These were simple, but revolutionary for the time, being the first systematic analysis of air fighting. Curiously, it was a violation of his rule No. 8 that led to Boelcke's death. After his death in October 1916, Jagdstaffel 2 was renamed Jagdstaffel Boelcke in his honor. Jasta Boelcke was the second most successful fighter squadron in the German air force with 336 confirmed victories and only 31 fatalities during the war. Continuing the tradition of naming units after Boelcke, the modern Luftwaffe operates a jet fighter wing named for Boelcke. In 2007, the note that Boelcke dropped, against orders, on a British airfield in early January 1916, went on auction in England. At his funeral, the Royal Flying Corps dropped a wreath which bore the inscription, "To the memory of Captain Boelcke, a brave and chivalrous foe."

Dicta Boelcke

1. Try to secure the upper hand before attacking. If possible, keep the sun behind you.

2. Always continue with an attack you have begun.

3. Open fire only at close range, and then only when the opponent is squarely in your sights.

4. You should always try to keep your eye on your opponent, and never let yourself be deceived by ruses.

5. In any type of attack, it is essential to assail your opponent from behind.

6. If your opponent dives on you, do not try to get around his attack, but fly to meet it.

7. When over the enemy's lines, always remember your own line of retreat.

8. Tip for Squadrons: In principle, it is better to attack in groups of four or six. Avoid two aircraft attacking the same opponent.

Anton Fokker. Frustrated and outmaneuvered in the marketplace by German manufacturers of airplanes, Fokker convinced the Inspector of *Fliegertruppe (IdFlieg)* in 1917 to conduct competitive trials to select new aircraft types. After watching English Sopwith Triplanes fly in combat on the Flanders coast in January, 1917, he developed the most iconic aircraft of World War I: the Fokker Triplane, which won the German triplane competition. Manfred von Richthofen painted his Fokker Triplane red, forever immortalizing the imagery of the Red Baron. At the end of the war, Fokker loaded up his remaining factory aircraft and succeeded in talking his way back into his native Holland with six train loads of airplanes and parts. There, he rebuilt his aviation company there and became wealthy from the sale of civilian aircraft. He died in New York in 1939 at age 49 from meningitis. The Fokker factory has prospered for a century and continues to make aircraft under the Fokker name today.

Max Immelmann. Max's death, which had a profound impact on German morale at the time and led to Boelcke's temporary withdrawal from flying, remains controversial to this death, with no clear cause for the mid-air break up of his aeroplane. Immelmann's trademark aerial maneuver, a climbing turn to a near stall, with a rudder turn at the apex to change direction, is, today, called the 'Immelman Turn'. This is an offensive maneuver allowing a fighter to re-engage a target following a firing pass. In modern, high performance aircraft, a similar maneuver to change direction is also called an 'Immelmann'. The *Pour le Mérite* was nicknamed 'The Blue Max', in his honor. The modern German Luftwaffe also operates a modern fighter wing named for him.

Frieda von Richthofen. In 1912, while still married to another man, Frieda convinced her father to intercede on behalf of her lover, author D.H. Lawrence, after Lawrence was arrested for spying in Germany. Following Lawrence's release, Frieda and Lawrence escaped Germany by walking south, through the Alps into Italy. Frieda von Richthofen, a second cousin of Manfred, was already notorious for leaving her husband and becoming D.H. Lawrence's companion, prior to Manfred von Richthofen's rise to fame. When Manfred became famous in England following the death of Hawker, Frieda became infamous. She remained the steady companion of D.H. Lawrence and they married in 1914. She is believed to be the inspiration for his novel, *Lady Chatterly's Lover*, as she was from the upper levels of society and Lawrence was a commoner. Following Lawrence's death, Frieda ensured that he was buried at their mountain ranch in Taos, New Mexico. She died in Taos on her birthday in 1956, and is buried alongside him.

Manfred Albrecht Freiherr von Richthofen. In January 1917, after the death of Boelcke and Hawker, Richthofen began painting each of his aircraft entirely red. No record remains as to precisely why he did this. At the front the French and English called his aeroplane *le Petite Rouge*.

The misfit unit that Richthofen took command of in January 1917, Jasta 11, became the most successful unit in the German air force. With no recorded victories prior to Richthofen's arrival in January 1917, they achieved their 100th victory only three months after he took command. Jasta 11 ended the war with 350 victory claims and 20 aces, surpassing even Jasta Boelcke.

Pilots in Jasta 11 included Manfred Richthofen, his brother Lothar, Kurt Wolff, Werner Voss, and, eventually, Richthofen's colleague from the Uhlans, Erich von Wedel. Other pilots of Jasta 11 included the second most successful German pilot of World War I, Ernst Udet, and the eventual second in command of Nazi Germany, Hermann Goering.

Jasta 11, under Richthofen's leadership, encouraged vivid personal markings on aircraft, usually incorporating the color red. When a later, larger unit, Jagdgeschwader (JG) 1, was formed from four Jastas, the tradition of wildly painted aircraft continued. JG 1 was called 'Richthofen's Flying Circus' as they moved to the section of the frontlines in trains to where the fighting was heaviest.

In April 1918, Richthofen was shot down and killed by ground fire over Allied lines, just south of the Somme river battlefields of 1916. Richthofen violated Boelcke Dicta No.7, a mistake which lead to his death. The English buried him with full military honors.

At his death, he was the most successful fighter pilot of the war with eighty confirmed victories, and probably several more for which he didn't receive official credit.

In 1927, an American writer, Floyd Gibbons, wrote a biography of him called *The Red Knight of Germany*. Gibbons freely translated 'Freiherr' as 'Baron', cementing 'The Red Baron' into the popular imagination. But, his legend, and infamy, rose from the battles over the Somme in the fall of 1916.

The Red Baron remains the most recognizable and legendary figure of the First World War a century later.

Others: Erwin Böhme, the pilot that collided with Boelcke, went on to gain twenty-four aerial victories and was awarded the Pour le Mérite. In November, 1917, he was shot down and killed in a fight with an English two-seater. He burned on the way down.

Menzke, Richthofen's trusted batman throughout his service, is lost to history.

Acknowledgments

First of all, I wish to thank my wife Alicia, for supporting me, long past the time when writing this novel was something new and different. Thanks to Amelia, who pointed out the great truth that there are worse mid-life crises than writing a book. And to Garret, who manages to convey his pride in this effort without giving in to patronizing me. To Nessie, Penny and Rigby, whose love was always soft, fluffy, unconditional and a little messy.

Also, thanks to two great history writers, David Robbins and Eric Hammel, each of whom took the time to slap me on the side of my proverbial head for harboring the idea that this novel needed to be written. Not only did they inspire me with their writing, they motivated me with that greatest of motivations, the desire to prove them wrong.

Thanks to the people that got their hands dirty helping me. James Hallman for showing me the ropes of editing and how a book can be felt as well as written and to Lauren Smith for constantly reminding me that writing IS art. To Gail Nelson for bringing the elegance of the page to life, to Don Sidle for all his patience with me and for proving that a picture really is worth a thousand words. Also, to the participants on the Aerodrome message boards, for bearing with, and occasionally surprising me with answers to all my crazy questions about Richthofen, esoteric as they were.

Lastly, to everyone that has ever written a book about the Red Baron, thank you. I think I've read them all. You each inspired me to tell this story and uniquely contributed to his legend. I hope this novel takes you there, if only for a moment.